STEERAGE AND AMOUR!

STEERAGE AND AMOUR!

Edward L. Divita

Rev. date: 05/13/2020

To order additional copies of this book, contact:
Xlibris
1-888-795-4274
www.Xlibris.com
Orders@Xlibris.com
807084

CONTENTS

ACKNOWLEDGMENTS

The real start was when Francesco Divita and Filippa La Spina, living in Valguarnera, Sicily, wanted to immigrate to America after their marriage and had gained permission from the patriarchal family, Liborio Divita and Marguerita (Vivattene) Divita. After Filippa had their firstborn son, Liborio, named after his grandfather Liborio as a common tradition in Italy, the plan was put together. By the time they had two more children, Francesco was well on his way to explore the working conditions, a confirmed reason to live in America. This happened when he immigrated in 1910.

Later, after Francesco immigrated to America and worked for two years, he returned to Valguarnera, Sicily, in 1912 to take the family to America within the next year. Francesco set their needs for the family to immigrate to America in 1913 via *steerage* on the cruise to America.

After Francesco had been in America for about two years, he was called Francesco by his Italian friends and neighbors, while his children in Sicily continued calling him Poppa. Later, when he came back to America, he was called Frank by his friends and extended families with whom he became closely associated.

At the time of their immigration, her firstborn son, Liborio, was thirteen years old. When they arrived in America with his mother Filippa and her three little children, Liborio had already learned a significant amount of knowledge from his momma Filippa about how to live a good life. Filippa had learned the teaching method from her family, who had developed a compassionate and simple way of teaching her progeny *steerage* and *amour* by making proper decisions to ensure pursuits of happiness. Filippa would tell her children to use their mind's "knowledge and experience" and, when necessary, sidetrack first mental thoughts of "will of desire" and, instead, follow thoughts to live a good life.

Benny and Josephine Divita came together years later when Liborio, now called Benny, had immigrated to America with his mother Filippa and three other children. Benny and Josephine began raising our Divita family of children starting with their marriage on November 7, 1928. They had their first son, Francisco Divita, born on September 9, 1929. His mother Josephine and dad for a time had lived with his father and mother, Francesco and Filippa, even after their marriage.

After several years, our family settled in Montgomery, West Virginia. Francisco was continually taught by his mother and grandmother *steerage* and *amour* as he grew into an adult to receive mindful voices, and later, he could recall many of the facts of living a good life and holding good memories. The same teachings were taught to their other progeny. Benny and Josephine's children continued their lives before the millennium. Their children and other progeny continued to live thereafter as they were taught by the Divita families.

During part of my mom's later years, she had started her "Journal of the Divitas," especially in our lifetimes of numerous events and actions, all involving personal behaviors and many memories. She knew us very well and was our mother of the year to all of us as each year passed.

Our dad also, as a youngster at critical times, had learned English in the local American school. He was good at least writing to Mom at times before his marriage and during his early marriage life. After his business became prosperous during those times, he mostly kept his books for reporting taxes. As we grew, we attended school with great fun and interest, and then we went to high school. Dad taught us his business accounting and recording to help with tax preparations.

There was a next group of Americans who were born to the children of Francesco and Filippa after immigration that were born in America during World War I. These progenies were trained by mindful voices with Francesco and Filippa's children that recalled their facts, memories, and hearsay from that time to the current times. The elder children who came from Sicily much later produced their children in the next American generations starting with Benny, Tony, and Joe and sister Mary. Then with their children, they produced their progeny, and their grandchildren's lives proceeded into the current generation heading toward the millennium.

Those family members of Italian heritage from 1920 to 1990, brought into modern days, were based on their collected memories, compiled notes, and even a journal of recorded information by my mother Josephine Divita, my dad, and by my eldest brother, Frank. The information gathered was also gathered by a comprehensive collection of recorded data about our Italian ancestors.

As a recognition, the newest data compilation had been extracted by Charles L. Divita Jr., the son of my dad's brother Charles, born in America, who gathered from numerous archived files in American Government Facilities and independent sources. The most recent and detailed collection of significance was investigated and prepared by Charles L. Divita Jr., published as *A Historical Treatise, A Missing Link in Divita Family History*: Rochester, NY, 2017. Charles led his review with fervor with great warmth and intensity having recently completed his historical treatise and is now concentrating on a generalized story of the Divita families.

Many thanks are extended to my elder brothers, Frank, Gene, Robert, Philip, and Richard, and sister Jane. Jane had recently written both about her life in the Benny and Josephine Divita family and with care and release of her memorable stories about her life from her memories and many conversations about our parents, extended families, and grandparents. The teachings by my sister Jane, younger than me but as an adult, helped me tremendously with writing properly formulated and timely English. Jane's review of my first draft used her known capabilities, being educated with a PhD degree in English literature.

Over time, my family siblings guided me with memory input, critique, and improvements that exposed this somewhat odd discourse to express behavior of the Italian Americans who followed the teachings of *steerage* and *amour* taken as detailed by being identified as affaire d'amour (an illicit love affair) and affaire de coeur (affair of the heart). Many of the Divita family who taught their progeny melded their Italian heritage teachings to our American-born progeny to use minds not with instinctive "will of desire" but with compassionate strength, grasp "knowledge and experience" to follow decisive ways to gain their *pursuits of happiness*.

Dedication

PATRIOTISM AFTER WORLD WAR II MEMORIAL DAY 1946(K)

By Edna S. Freer

The finest tribute we can pay
Unto our hero dead today,
Is not a rose wreath white and red.
In memory of the blood they shed
It is to stand beside each mound,
Each couch of consecrated ground,
And pledge yourselves as warriors true
Unto the work they died to do.
Into God's valley's where they lie
At rest, beneath the open sky,
Triumphant now o'er every foe,
As living tributes let us go.
No wreath of rose or immortals,
Or spoken word or tolling bells
Will today, unless we give
Our pledge that liberty shall live.
Our hearts must be the roses red
We place about our hero dead;
Today beside their graves we must
Renew allegiance to their trust,
Must bare our heads and humbly say
We hold the Flag as dear as they,
And stand, as once they stood, to die
To keep the Stars and Stripes on high.
The finest tribute we can pay
Unto our hero dead today

Is not of speech or roses red,
But living, throbbing hearts instead
That shall renew the pledge they sealed
With death upon the battlefield:
That freedom's flag shall bear no stain.
And free men wear no tyrant's chain.

END

PREFACE

For clarity, I make the following statements to reveal my mental, personal, social, environmental, and cultural behavior patterns that have evolved from within the Divita family as they lived their lives and followed worldly activities with concentration. The mind, as time passes, controls their general behavior patterns by categorizing important memories as were told many times during our lives.

As my profundity expounds, as the writer of this story, I will concentrate with the sense and depth that I have formulated. I have expanded my willingness to recover memories and actions gladly proffered or done heartily as the writer sometimes in my own words. I have received considerable detail from others in the Divita family who have told me about their incidences from their memories many times and again.

The Italian teachings in the Divita saga began in Italy and continued in America, beginning in 1910, when Francesco and his brother Paulo immigrated to America to see if they could get a good job and have a better life. Then Francesco, after working in New York for about two years, decided to return to Sicily and plan for his Divita family to immigrate to America. After making the trip and completed his plans, he decided to return to America in 1912. He was insistent that he get ready for his family to immigrate to America later in 1913.

Filippa, his wife, ventured with the children to travel with her eldest son, Liborio (soon to be known as Benny after a few years in America), the first son in Francesco's family. Filippa's other children included brothers Antonio (Tony, born in 1909) and Giuseppe (Joe, born in 1907) and sister Maria (Mary, born in 1910).

I used *steerage* as a metaphor because it related to the citing that daily ships traveling steadfastly and truthful in the seas and to ports were usually safe voyages. At unusual times, *steerage* could be devastating on the trip and might cause health to appear physically and mentally distraught at times of despair; but not when proper navigation was foremost and truthful. In this story, we use *steerage* as a method of teaching with compassionate understanding to keep one's mind full of "knowledge and experience" as guides to make the right decisions as related to *amour* (affair of the heart).

Amour is used and profoundly done with a serious belief so it may be embedded with belief in God the Creator, who is unknown to all as simply the Creator of the Universe with continuous evolution without theory, and only belief ad infinitum. The separation between the word *amour* has two different meanings—that is, affaire d'amour (an illicit love affair) and affaire de coeur (affair of the heart), and both dominate the way *Homo sapiens*, the only current form of mankind, live their lives within their own functioning minds of beliefs and pursuits that give each the abilities of making right and wrong decisions.

The thrust of my drive as the third living son of Benjamin Franklin Divita (previously known as a child named Liborio, the first grandson of his father's father) and Josephine Mary Maruca Divita was to inlay my understanding of how *steerage* and *amour* meet the personal teachings by grandparents, parents, and elder family siblings. Teaching of *steerage* and *amour* loads the mind's methods of learning with encouragement by not causing critical input into other minds' memories. The right aggressive selections of needs and wants through the mind's stored "knowledge and experience" build decisive mental selections predominantly only from within human being's minds.

This personal memoir of the Divita family saga carries my story from the 1900s to nearly the new millennium. What I followed as a youngster and with continuous efforts within my family led me to expand about matured people's experiences when they inherited *steerage* and *amour* as the family taught each to gain implied wisdom. My evolvements that happened many years later contained all that I had learned from the Divita family in my lifetime, being one of the sons of Benjamin Franklin and Josephine Marie Divita and with front-end help primarily from my grandmother Filippa (born 1879); even when my grandfather Francesco Divita (born in 1875) was sound and sober. Many children, some born in Valguarnera, Sicily, and others born in America after their immigration were taught to use sensible decisions.

Grandfather Francesco Divita was a sulfur miner in Sicily, a young man suffering daily a life at work, worse than experiencing living hell daily. This was his initial thrust to immigrate to America. In his mind daily, he was working in a place worse than hell. He felt that he could reap the freedom of life and gain a man's job that is within abilities of any human being in America.

This all happened after he became thirty-five years old and decided to immigrate to America in 1910. Grandfather Francesco left Valguarnera, Sicily, via *steerage* on the ship *S. Sicilia* from the port in Palermo, Sicily. The main pursuit that I have encamped was with this inherent feat using my mind from my primer time of knowledge to adulthood with gains from the Divita heredity.

Most Divitas followed explainable teaching methodologies that manifest true natures of their mentality and triggered proper teachings accepted from heritage of *steerage* and *amour*. With established main features are ordinary human beings who want to strive to live in the pursuit of happiness.

Many thoughts that linger in my mind with psychological pursuits use *Homo sapiens'* working minds already instilled by God's unique gift. The intent of the *Homo sapiens* evolution, as I have studied and followed, was specifically designated in my mind by God the Creator, whom all should believe, that we are unique *Homo sapiens*. Each man and woman of sound mind will be stably able to use his or her mind to make decisively desired, valued, and wise decisions as each person lives life with a complete active mind as God had also included the creation of continued evolution set in the brain's mind.

The plights of life start with Francesco and his wife, Filippa, from early lives in marriage and a joint control of how their children will be developed mentally to use their minds by God-given ways to do their best to select the proper choice of any issue. Francesco and his brother Paulo, and other Divitas that boarded the ship, all without being told they would be in *steerage*, suffered unexpectedly several days of mental and physical harm. The trip across the Atlantic Ocean was common in much better summer times and much worse in winter during in *steerage*. Both Francesco and Paulo were hell-bent to gain a new grasp on life. Several later trips included some of their related Divita Italian families who completed their immigrations and settlements in various states in America after beginning first in New York.

My maternal grandparents, Alphonso and Josephine (nee Marino—adopted as a child) Maruca were married on February 29, 1895. Then they emigrated from Calabria, Italy, to America in 1895. They were already living in West Virginia but were unknown to the Francesco Divita family at the time. Much later as they had settled, Liborio Divita, now known as Big Benny in America, the eldest son, while working with Italian friends, was popularly liked. One time, after work, his friend Al Maruca asked Benny if he would accept an invitation from his dad Alphonso to have dinner at the Maruca family's home. The answer was a friendly yes! Within a short time there, after dinner, Big Benny fell in love at first sight with Josephine Marie Maruca, with her conservative smile. And about a year later, on November 7, 1928, they were married and settled into part of Francesco's *OverHome* in Smithers, West Virginia. The *OverHome* was built by his father Francesco and sons over the past ten years after 1913.

This exposition primarily related sagas of the larger Divita family that dominated their social, environmental, and cultural living with a striving, basically inherited grasp as experienced by the elder siblings that Grandmother Filippa used her teaching methods. Filippa was excited with her new Italian-birthed siblings whose lives easily inherited mind-forming ways to accept how *steerage* and *amour* would be taught to their progeny to mind memories of "knowledge and experience." Those that followed were taught to bring good judgment to the minds of their descendant children and grandchildren born later even as first-generation Americans once the family had settled in West Virginia. It was a mental practice that the essence of what *steerage* and *amour* gained was clearly designed for a life in pursuit of happiness as prognosticated to include members of the family in modern days.

The overall story was as defined as roman-fleuve, like a long novel chronicling the history of several generations of this Italian Divita family as related to the turbulent societal and political climate, especially in Italy and other times in America during critical warring across the world.

This perspective captured Italy's First Renaissance so exposed by rodomontade—a pretentious bragging and vainglorious boasting—especially boastfulness by the Saracen king in Boiardo's *Orlando Inamorata* and Ariosto's *Orlando Furioso*, who lived during the best of the First Renaissance in 1474 to1530 period. The First Renaissance covered the years of truly evolving music, art, and technology and within latter grand technological accomplishments. The era, mostly unexpected, significantly treasured their times of extending morality, and governing involved providences and countries with recorded success.

With those born in America, a continuation from earlier immigrants from other continents brings new generations of American-born progeny. In this story, they are many times called first-generation Italian American children from the Divita family starting in the early to late 1920s; but all were born in America as citizens. All newborns cogently sparkled and constantly, as babies, were endowed with mind-stuffing wisdom, if not knowledge, that transferred via birthing inheritances, which increased the "knowledge and experience" from their parents and relatives working above average with interactions primarily by mothers, fathers, and elder siblings. The mental formulations improved under continuous verbal teachings and interactions all related to *steerage* and *amour*. All the children born in America should only be called by previous national country associations for social information only.

Flashbacks are used to related different parts of the story to relate understanding how the Divita family came to be fully disclosed and included from 1910. Their lives were based on revisited facts, memories, and enhanced stories; some maybe infused with enthusiastic legends born from sincere love or braggadocios. Memoirs become established from memories of elders for elaboration and exhibition and passed on to their progeny.

A. FOREWORD

We cannot teach people anything; we can only
help them discover it within themselves.
　　　—Galileo Galilei (from the First Renaissance)

The following of the use of *steerage* as a metaphor citing critical guidance as the same as that of daily ships traveling steadfastly on the sea and voyages ended usually safely. However, some voyages were as true in direction but were devastated; even though proper navigation was foremost and truthful. *Amour* is profoundly done with the same serious belief that it may be embedded with belief in God the Creator, who is unknown to all except by belief but, simply as the Creator of the universe, was accepted with mankind's belief without developed theory ad infinitum. Mankind has no knowledge of the beginning of the universe.

The usage of *amour* as two different metaphors is one between affaire d'amour (an illicit love affair) and affaire de coeur (affair of the heart). Both dominate the way mankind, now known only as *Homo sapiens*, lived within their own minds with beliefs and pursuits.

In this story, I uncovered what happens as time expires in minds morally and legally where the two fester many options. The use of mentally taught *steerage* and *amour* could be hard to accept, but it would be too late to dispose aftermaths and difficulty; instead, rather seek the pursuit of happiness. After one's mind is reviewed and deciphered, one's judgment must make sure directions of understanding, which forces one to make wise decisions to live a life of happiness. That is what's the story is about . . . *Steerage and Amour!—What's It All About!*

As always, a story has more than two dilemmas to be resolved on a continuous thinking basis with mind's reactions when taken as a choice. The first and most prickliness one is whether to follow the use of mankind's instinctive "will of desire" or to use the mind's functioning system as God's gift to modern-day *Homo sapiens* to make mental decisions. Proper use of the mind imparts a quick stimulus of neurons in a thought path that follows the next path with use of "knowledge and experience." Both paths evince mental judgments from minds; the former bellows to enhance individual's pursuits, while the latter uses wisdom mindfully.

On the one hand, "will of desire" rings of a hardwired instinctive first path of thought. It strikes at pompousness of sincerity; extracted by all intuitive personalities who, like blazing red roses, then later reveal themselves naturally as decaying petals suffering the ever-present instinctively inherited demands for amorous pursuits. Aftermaths usually follow the "will of desire," neglecting *steerage* and following illicit pursuits of *amour*.

The neglect or obvious disinterest in accessible *steerage* that mentally sends advisements to one's "knowledge and experience" source is easily extracted. Then in an instant, the mind does not respond to the initially instilled hardwired instinctive impulse. All human beings easily recognize *amour* because it usually ignites as a spontaneous sensual, even sexual affair unsuspectedly. Most likely an illicit one or one with intrigue for lust is determined by personal behavior and usually under clandestine conditions, with little chance of advice about the pursuit. The ingredients include the ever-present human ardor saturated in secretive actions that dominate the pursuit's choice, involuntarily because nature's pending induced guilt is waived. However, when steered by experienced pedagogy, one might adopt a continuation of the mind's next instantly registered memory response.

This epic from my mind emphasizes words that express life's behavioral actions and confrontations that have fed the dominating instinctively enhanced "will of desire" that evolved from mankind's beginnings. Words in context as related to Italian heritage and as expounded in this story explore secretive affairs, hidden within lies about loyalty, disloyalty, and infidelity. Sometimes, it is done clandestinely with little effort of privacy, even to the point of hearsay, which, to all, could be disastrous to innocent individuals. Each action and reaction may become exposed as the individual tries to avoid serious and extreme conflicts that may be alleged. In scores of many walks of life, aftermath's result can induce depression or anxiety levels and cause life-changing afflicted effects, even to a potential finality.

The minds of mankind evolved as some *Homo sapiens* may add a thrust via continuous reactions against mankind's instinctive information that mentally would allow poetic license to honor sincere pursuit of *amour*. All humanly uncomplicated natural love affairs come from where their nature is driven by understanding of the mind's use of "knowledge and experience" to sense real love known as *amour* to be an *affair of the heart*. Usage of minds performs with little effort to stop human distortions when mental persistence takes exception. The innate common sense within the mind's active memory erases driving urges just as one visualizes to quickly block the desire for illegitimate *amour* with uncountable unsuccessful times. However, there is always times when mind's functioning may lose the pursuit of an *affair of the heart*. That's when the instinctive "will of desire" wins the race. God only knows what happens thereafter with an infinite variety of aftermaths.

My story reveals and characterizes a range of behavior of the extended Divita family, including only a few disheartened personalities that stay on the same track.

Personalities can be assumed to range between honest introverts to insidiously self-imposed, self-centered extroverts, both of whom may engorge the "will of desire" extemporaneously with grand feelings. When the desire is experienced, it brings an aftermath that leaves minds of relatives, friends, and associates all predominantly unforgiving.

In the wonderland of worldly people so varied in personalities, behavior patterns and interactions cause many upsets of committed actions with human beings. There are varieties of sensuously amorous events every day. These events could extend superglorious as words artificially selected as *expialidocious* (enormous liveliness) almost as fantasies; but it could also lead to *supercalifragilistic* (extreme unhappiness) events discoursed with humor, as Julie Andrews expressed when she sang the musical lyrics in the movie *Mary Poppins*!

Humor generated extemporaneously with some character's interactions resound profoundly from outsiders as always. A few times, it's superficial, superstitious, advantageous, fastidious, daring, and sometimes auspicious, barbarous, cantankerous, clamorous behavior takes stride. At other times, the humor may be arrogant, excessive, lecherous, and not down-to-earth as expected even when amorous pursuits are made intentionally mentally but not sincerely.

Many of the *amour* events filled with lies that belittle legitimate love inferences and exposed cavalier masculine or possessive feminine behavior patterns that mock love's intentions outside of "knowledge and experience." These impulsive times cause decidedly significant changes in their lives. When enraptured parties are involved, they might affect the behavior of families, friends, and associates beyond belief.

> *Amour* as practiced with the "will of desire" involves escapades, cavorting, Casanova-esque pursuits by men. These gambols (men who cut capers and perform prankish shenanigans to gain access to desires), shams, and zingaros (as practiced by few Italian gypsies, at their best at deception) lie to cover with hurtful intentions that might compromise friendship and loving commitments.

> As Aldous Huxley wrote in "Brave New World" about exciting the reader with words that suddenly make you jump [or being pin struck or being new and excited but about life's same old story] and in response, Helmholtz responds, ". . . It's not enough for the phrases to be good; what you make with them ought to be good too." . . . I feel I could do something much more important. Yes, and more intense, more violent. But what? What is there

more important to say? And how can one be violent about the sort of things one's expected to write about? Words can be like X-rays, revealing when you use them properly . . .

[They register in memory as] they go through any human being's mind. You read, and you're pierced. . . .what on earth's the good of being pierced by an article about a Community Sing [or continuous *steerage* or the varieties of *amour* as affaire d'amour (an illicit love affair) and affaire de coeur (affair of the heart)] . . . [Can you say something about nothing or say something that happens day in day out ad infinitum since *Homo sapiens,* human beings have dominated the earth?] That's how it has finally boiled down.

A friend . . .once said . . .about language and its reflection of reality: "It's metaphors all the way down. All words are symbolic representations of ideas or things or feelings; all words, when spoken or written, manifest something otherwise invisible. The authentic metaphors we discover in fiction, nonfiction and poetry express language's nature in an artful and pleasurable way that can change how our readers feel and think, how their bodies and brains [minds] respond to the words our bodies [minds] write."

(Jeff Davis, *The Journey from the Center to the Page*, p. 79)

In a more modern sense as to what really happens when written words are delivered to the mind, it is like electromagnetic pulses (EMP) that contain packets of different wavelengths chemically coded, similar to zeros and ones in computers, and yet are embedded differently from low-energy wavelengths like sinus photons that penetrate microbionic human bioelectronic organic systems that start the heart's sinus responders to function for a healthy heartbeat primarily for a substantial ejection of blood released from heart to brain and into the body with oxygen added. In this case, these wavelengths make it through the brain to neuron transmissions in the mind complexities, causing needed responses. Responses have not been microanalyzed or tested, and the values have not been evaluated in detail. However, the brain's mind when retorting words, people are notified to respond to their impacts. The frontal lobe where memory transports a response back and each distinguishable collection is destined to memory areas where the collector hippocampus messages cause depositions to cognitive memory.

Then the stored response is exposed by the mind's reality from within the responding gray matter. The neurons are where a memory position becomes stored and accessible by simple recalled impacts as a complete thought. An immediate reaction to interactions under general mind confrontations are recorded as episodes of memories. The words are now in complete thoughts instantly within a timely process as the mind ejaculates orally at its timing to relay its responding words.

EMP waveform interactions occur unknowingly, and they could complement and further define the overall impact on total memory packets with a pending exposé as wisdom from the receiver reacts in a variety of disciplines. Even those impressed instinctively, *amour* choices made by "will of desire" or wisely evaluated by *steerage* teachings from memories of "knowledge and experience" may experience different memory extractions. The words from mind's speed are potentially unique when outplayed orally as exclaimed in complements already formed while awaiting ejaculation at oral speed.

During the Industrial Revolution, near the 1800s, many scientific and technological innovations and inventions were discovered by knowledgeable and wisely creative and experienced human beings. However, the one creative invention that came later, directly related to *amour* and the one that has had the most influence, was the automobile and its associated counterparts and new capabilities. Steam engine trains were the first developed in the early 1800s, followed by electric streetcars, and later, the automobile evolved in the late 1800s; then buses artfully evolved and unexpectedly aided by relationships and maybe even pending consequences of *amour* for either dishonest or legitimate relationships.

Some are naturally creative human beings, one being Thomas Alva Edison, who created light in an unknown electromechanical way that led to profound changes in the life of mankind universally. During that time in 1880s, little was accomplished in a biological, physiological, or psychological useful sense that directly lightened people's burdens. However, new inventions, the automobile, without expectation of added burdens, caused more complexities of people's behavior with life's embarrassing or damaging personal involvements. Also, not as an oddity, human personal pursuits do effectively use automobiles for numerous advantages under many circumstances. The automobile modified everyday and nighttime ways for many humans to gain involvements in common pursuits of all kinds of *amour* and maybe an opportunity to neglect *steerage*, not as a pun.

B. Philosophical Prologue

The happiness which we receive from ourselves is greater than that which we obtain from our surroundings . . . the most essential thing for a man is the constitution of his conscious. . . . The world in which man lives shapes itself chiefly by the way in which he looks at it. Most men [and women] never rise above viewing things as objects of desire—hence their misery; but to see things purely as objects of understanding is to rise to freedom. Therefore, it is with great truth that Aristotle says, "To be happy means to be self-sufficient."
—Footnote 107, *Wisdom of Life*, p. 27, 4–9

Since the great debate between religion and science is the main current in the stream of modern thought, it will be recorded in these pages [for now] more frankly than may seem wise to men of the world. These have long since concluded that religious beliefs fill to vitalize a function sustaining individual morality and morale, and social order and control, to justify their disturbance by public discussion. . . . but obviously it cannot release the historian from his obligation to find and describe the fundamental processes in the cultural history of modern Europe. . . . [and then eventually as the eons continue, *Homo sapiens* {and potentially even new life forms} will attempt to understand the fundamental processes of the universe].
—*The Story of Civilization: The Age of Reason Begins*, Will and Ariel Durant, Simon and Schuster Inc., Rockefeller Center, New York, NY, 1961, page vii–viii

All phenomena of earth's nature, which can be seen or apprehended by the senses such as appearances, something visible and directly observable, could fit into any similar or unknown category with minute differences. Except from after time zero, changes make things unique, and many old things remain unfounded as within the universe down to microscopic things that change by continued evolution. By God the Creator's design, all things will be created unique, and things will not be repeatable in any way, shape, form, or extent, neither under the microscopic nor viewed at macroscopic levels for both animals and plants. Therefore, changes always induce differences within the universe, never to repeat. The move to disorder is a matter of steps related to a future time unknown; but as an example, God's continued evolution could create a massive energy conversion to desolate any level of the universe via cataclysmic changes, leaving the universe with no energy phenomena to interact with existing mass.

In beliefs, as they mount, God's evolutionary creation was assumed by human beings to part of the universe with continued changes. Strong beliefs were surmised after the universe was sighted with advanced telescopes and different electromagnetic waves to uncover aspects of the universe's materialization and energy. Evolution was created by the one entity whom people eventually called God the Creator as the only way in belief. Mankind's refutations still take objection without credible scientific answers for the start. Some beginning freshmen by nature, *Homo sapiens,* with some learned wisdom as an astrophysicist, believed the universe evolved from an introduction of particles from an unknown source that multiplied every time they collided. This undefined but nearly plausible scientifically explained phenomena occurred starting with microscopes and study of nuclear interactions that created particles mentioned above with thermal neutrons that might involve evolutionary creation. It sounds probable, but other scientists of the same caliber justifiably leave it open to doubt without a start from zero and therefore, at most, a belief.

The undefined plan is wise men are yet to take on the macroscopic and microscopic processes after billions of years as the probable producer of the universe, and many believe God was the creator of all entities. The creation of all things make up the universe having everything else that evolved with animal and plant life only exist within a short past having the universe attaining ten to fifteen billion years as an estimated life with our geniuses' knowledge and experiments that will remain overwhelming to mankind's mind in the past thirteen billion years.

The eventual destruction of nonliving particles identified as elements and compounds existing as interacting molecules or mixtures, some totally decay into nonactive dust yet undefined. The unknown is where the "lost" multiplying particles might have disappeared beyond our knowledge to continue to expand the universe. Many of one particle or more than one must have had an origin even to make the beginning of the universe to occur unless it was only tended to by God. That source of beginning particles is yet unknown as to what is the nature of these beginning particles.

In theorized cases, evolutionary creation done simply by God, the Creator of the universe, with continuous changing to create natural changes in the universe, was resolved by the minds of modern mankind. *Homo sapiens* scientists now claim that universe expansion continuously changes as it expands. The Creator's plan versus the big bang theory or any version so far accounts for paradoxical explanations until a proof or a genuine theory is demonstrated. The truth may come to be realistically defined by the Creator sometime in the future only by his choice.

Changes naturally induced within the universe are outside of our potential changes living on the planet Earth. Those changes that are caused by mankind's destructive means are brought about on our planet that has continually changed for five billion years, as do all other bodies in the universe with billions of years from the past. Self-imposed destructive means within the universe happens because of actions of universal materials interacting in random concerts as stars impose ever-changing matter. Evolutionary perturbations and disastrous events that created the beginning and included their pending effects continued with a near infinity of time; however, the universe must yet be leading to an eon of time to equilibrium as God Almighty already knows.

Some changes in the universe may affect human beings' bodies, minds, and souls. Other forms of life have evolved mixed plant and animal forms in numerous places on earth and are expected to do the same in the universe. Only God the Creator, with established continued evolutionary creation, would know the answer. This deductive understanding is ever present with our earth, as did the evolution of modern mankind, likely significantly different, being in our solar system and as created on the planet Earth. Different human beings or life-forms could be different, expectedly, yet unfounded for reasons because traveling methods outside our solar system toward many light-years are not dreamed to be probable. Other solar systems might have unique human body and mind designs that exist by being on other planets and could specifically form different life-forms all with God's demands.

Simply put, the universe, composed of many materials, means the entropy theory may include the universe—that is, the behavior of mass is toward increasing disorder and inertness. The probability of further behavior tends to disorder on a real-time basis, but unknown to elimination. On the universal time scale, the dissolution is likely extremely slow as in the formation times of the past.

This leaves worldly and universal natural behavior of local things on a short time span because it is more difficult to determine the age of older things on earth and even impossible to determine the age of extremely much older things in the universe without access. No one among our human beings could ever be able to travel in light-years to distant solar systems with planets to venture to and define the nature of predicting future universal time measurements.

The extent of *amour* is a mindful humanistic behavior produced uniquely on earth by procreation with side effects at times, influences, pursuits, and outcomes both in location and under emotional sensations. Under those past times, the sensation of *amour* of *Homo sapiens* may be stained with impatience, the seductiveness of whispers of love, impending effects of minute delays, even constant worry or completely noticing the effects of sounds and sights so truly influencing their behavior during the last two world wars and those still under way.

The angel of death is a boon from God the Creator to those who died with modest consideration and expectation for their mortality but unable to hold fast to their belief in God, as a source of continuation. God has given those with belief the everlasting living spirit with a place in the *hereafter* unknown.

Wit and humor of mankind may at times have both left-handed and right-handed outlays as the written words sometimes exclaim, "The truth with the right hand and the lie with the left hand is likely poppycock!" Many right-handed persons are more likely to use smoother interpretations as criticism than to take jokes or poke fun lightly with personal amorous affairs. The only difference between truth and wit is the level of sensitivity versus understanding. At times, when truth doesn't get understood, nor does wit and humor when following the same questionable path. Women of innocence may be complacent or with a loss of affectation; but when wit and humor are displayed about family love, they could be easily attracted and trapped by a man. Certainly, it does happen when a man of means levies compliments while looking for amorous joy.

Steerage and Amour!—What It's All About! starts with the multistrained chaff of personal discontentment as one gets involved with the remnants of the dismays of life's mores, rather than with concerns of illicit *amour* events and unexpected aftermaths. Men and women claim to be powerless after commission of a first disloyalty and could continue to follow the path of false loyalty even with someone with devoted love. An enormous deposit of stress in arteries of one's heart and mind affects mind's judgments, causing people to follow a pugilistic pursuit to the finish instead of facing the life to come with mediation as a peacemaker. Disloyalty is a primrose path with infinite accesses but with only one point of exit that is the aftermath.

Amour pursuits are those of affaire d'amour (an illicit love affair) and affaire de coeur (affair of the heart), while *steerage* is taught with intended pursuit for clearly personal gain by grasping the value of "knowledge and experience" learned and memorized. The two decision actions continuously fight for the right judgment and usage. Living life does not pose clear choices at forks in the road. Instead, an individual has an infinite set of choices, and the only way to choose is to use one's mind with considered judgment. Even with backing of "knowledge and experience," one must set up for the race against disloyalty. The hare will always win when the amorous race starts with illegitimate intentions. Knowledge is there to be chosen after the instinctive time choice. However, the intent may not show' instead, it may be released when it comes to the time when one is in an amorous pursuit where choice depends on expectations of full fling or love at first sight.

Toying with words that were uncovered by my dad, Big Benny, because he used his mind to ferret gains of knowledge and with a voice of a lion's roar powered by his learning from his mother Filippa. Dad easily disciplined his brothers and Josephine's children while funning and relating other's stories. This practice by my dad casually convinced his younger brothers and sisters to listen to his teachings, and each followed his mother's daily *steerage*. And at times, when our family was with Big Mommy Filippa and my mom and dad were visiting, they were aware of their continuous teachings.

A quick example was what my dad repeated to me in my early teens one time when I was with him. He had just helped two brothers at their jewelry store. They both had returned to counters with smiles, and as I noticed Dad, I walked in and waved to my uncles and gave Dad a hug. Then as I wondered why he was with them, I said to him, "Why are Uncle Frank and Uncle Joe working so hard replacing jewelry at counters?"

Dad pulled me over to make sure I wanted to hear what he had to say. Dad said to me in words so that I tried to remember what his brothers told them— that they made a bad buy of jewelry. Then Dad said something like I heard that excuse more than one time in their jewelry store. My recall now follows my memory's release of words. I remembered hearing what he had repeated to his brothers: "I told them, 'This is what each of you should do. Don't fight over the money. Money is like gold and silver—everybody wants to earn it.' Then I said to them, 'What you bought—you now see that your buys were big mistakes.' I told my brothers they made mistakes!" Then Dad said to me, "Do you understand? There is never any getting back money spent carelessly." I agreed. Then he told me that they must make new buys at reduced prices to gain some of the money back in new sales. "Whatever you do, don't fault any of your brothers or sister. Always love each other. Don't fuss about each other. Instead, hang on to your good nature. To enjoy your lives requires happiness. Working together will allow you to compromise and minimize blame. As you have already experienced many times, sharing blaming minimizes problems, and you can quickly improve how to handle the next problem."

The thrust of pride in America has reached a crescendo of grace if not a devotion that filters into inherited mind's eyes of thinkers with vision and purpose. What I am saying generally in this story is this: all citizens of the United States of America must demonstrate allegiance to the country and be subject to all laws of the land as define in the Declaration of Independence, the United States Constitution, and the nation's laws made by both federal and state legislatures including counties down to municipalities with statutes.

The essence is instilled in words of the Constitution as this: All men are created equal, . . . endowed by their creator with unalienable rights that among these are *life* [the first proclamation for all *Homo sapiens* with their unique beginning by God the Creator of the universe], *liberty,* and the *pursuit of happiness.* That to secure these rights, governments are instituted. . . . and decree their just powers for all human beings from the consent of the governed as all people are endowed equally under the law. We the people . . . promote the general welfare.

Honor is the lady of praise who knows that giving from one's mind to others creates instilled existence of memories that stays within the heart and soul with more content factually. The opposite, however, occurs when a challenge suddenly brings a pending death toll of an instinctively instant warning of survivability. The action becomes the driver because as all of us know, dogs who have masters attack without any thought of their pending death; instead, they might fight to death for the smarter genus, their master.

The first rendezvous meeting for *amour* is full of organic exploitation of daily or weekly lovemaking between married couples. After a few years, the act of sensuous desire is nearer monthly and close to naught after seven to fifteen years, having had their children.

Philosophers' work always involved projecting thought through observation so that most human beings live on the edge of their mind's mental vision of daily life. They project in words and action, the sum of people who live within truths and acceptable mistakes. Gross negligence is the one choice that will capture your body and mind and could send it into distractions unheard of by the law.

Writers who use minds to take on "knowledge and experience" against the turmoil generated by "will of Desire" know the ever-coming aftermaths of nature's pursuit of lustful *amour*. "Knowledge and experience," as philosophers profess, feed *steerage* and *amour*—that is, affairs of the heart, to human minds with natural ingredients of love for mankind to have a happy life. As with many foods, too many people quickly neglect the good foods over those that are bad for a healthy and happy life.

C. Family Hereditary Relationships

*Art is greater than science because the latter proceeds by
laborious accumulation and cautious reasoning, while the
former reaches its goal at once by intuition and presentation.
Science can get along with talent, but art requires genius.*

(Difficulty seeing another person's point of view. Will Durant,
in *The Story of Philosophy*, paraphrased that by the use of resolute
and practical sense; it is easy to miss the spirit and zest of poetry
and art.)

—*The Story of Philosophy*, Will Durant, p. 254.

The *steerage* and *amour* pursuits in the life extracted from the family of
our great-grandparents Liborio Divita and Marguerita (Vivattene) Divita, who
birthed Francesco, their firstborn son, and later was called or referred to as Big
Poppy or Francesco by Italians in America and by Frank as American friends after
he had immigrated to American in 1910 to live the rest of his life.

Grandfather Francesco and Grandmother Filippa fathered Liborio as their
first son, and many more siblings followed. Filippa birthed and named Liborio
while living in Sicily. After Filippa and her children, four siblings, ventured to
America, their first son was renamed Benny and eventually became an American
citizen and was formally named Benjamin Franklin Divita. After Benny married
Josephine Maruca, their first child was named Francisco, after his grandfather
Francesco. Francisco born in America was called Frankie as a child and later, as a
man, was called Frank. Frank's grandfather Francesco first called his first son born
in Sicily as Liborio. As shown above, Grandfather Francesco and Grandmother
Filippa's first son, now in America, is known as Big Benny (a converted American
name), who became married to his wife, Josephine Maruca. Francis (Big Benny's
grandfather and Frank's son) is an American namesake taken from memoirs
of their primary ancestors and extended descendants to formulate and present
in this exposition of life's guidance in terms of telling its story of *Steerage and*

Amour!—What's It All About! to gain more than from memories of others whose prose was released by book attractions and discourses discussed in detail.

This story covers more than enough to reveal to others a love of music, art, poetry, and a wisdom related to other talents, innovations, and creativity that demonstratively continued from the First Renaissance that significantly influenced Italian mind-sets with advancements of new findings. We assume inherited Italians are enhanced with a striving ability to achieve high levels of creative learning along with technology and development as careers in their lives show the accomplishments, as did many others from other continents.

As Frank's brother Edward, I am the writer of this epic memoir that is clasped in the back of my mind finding a pluralism of mankind's nature. As a memoir, my mind also may wander into information that may have been passed to me as folklore at odd times and in some few cases with added details because memories sometimes wander from people's minds as time passes.

I had pursued my total career of schooling to become an engineering physicist. I listened carefully to many family members that released known memories from my progeny and to extended Divita families. In retrospect, my mind also had sensed art and writing as gifts from an early age. I believed that was what sent me into the realm of creativity of art and design even with my wondering or my wandering mind's memory and lifetime pursuits.

I was involved continuously with an attraction to art as a child practicing my creative capability even in the fourth grade. After my high school graduation, I designed art construction display pieces and sign painting for the theaters and for other's restaurant businesses and West Virginia's state locations identifying signs. Into my later age after college, even as a physicist, I studied and helped to designed nuclear reactors for Martin Marietta's Nuclear Division. Later at JPL, I evaluated earth environments and other experiments of planetary environments of space. My assignments were to evaluate spacecraft capability in various missions to selected planets that NASA began to investigate from before the early 1960s and later to meet the goal of Pres. John F. Kennedy to land Americans on the moon within the decade and thereafter beyond.

As I devotedly worked in science over my forty-year period, I did my art as a hobby. During my full-time work, I continually wrote technical reports and, on the side, personal stories about life's involvements and various activities. This mental activity of visualizing art, before I might even think of starting, led me to do sketches, paintings, and sculptures, as do many artists in my later years. I took the same approach in my engineering research and development career that involved creating designs and analytic models. With art, I visually could see sculptures that existed in a piece of uncut wood or stone. When I sketched the art idea to evolve the art piece, it was like nothing else registered within my mind. The near infinite assaults imposed as I did the sculpture using my mind's hammer's thrusts, be it cuts, digs, gouges, smoothing included and all extraneous extractions discretely, many extractions were incapable of being withdrawn. This pursuit was ardently insisted by my father Benny, who, at earlier times, had me sketch drawings from photograph covers on match packs. This type of pursuit in art makes one's sculpture a one of a kind. Up to now and from the past of my beginning, I did art as do all human beings—that is, that all entities from times of Creation were only one of a kind as related to time and work performed.

This story takes a stab at evoking a historic heritage that uniquely and unusually succeeded, but never failed to recover to some degree, leaving a finished product only as completed uniquely. These families of my heritage have procreated this family as a completed family of expounded renown but, much like many others in the world, satisfied with most of life's wonders as well as life's aftermaths even onto potential disasters, all carried out uniquely and quite differently and as unexpectedly.

This writing pursuit includes a way to primarily recognize the pursuit of happiness by using the mind's "knowledge and experience" to extracting *happiness*, through *steerage, amour,* and *humor* while enjoying using the talent, innovation, and creativity so endowed through my heritage. As a guess, my pursuits evolved like ritual hunting ventures of the past that had become more practiced and culturally directed toward a life of self-sufficiency for survivability and proper lifestyles and cultural advancements toward life.

The prey of human beings is nondescript by nature, but the prey revealed in the hunter's mind also followed the pursuit that captures conflict and interaction. The lives under assessment with these words were composed in a clearly linked way, by use of *steerage* to improve one's "knowledge and experience." The hunter's mind is always seeking memory storage, to deposit its arrow of thought with thorough reality from practice of wisdom. The contents of each human being are uniquely stored hopefully as one's life proceeds to cultural enhancement as intended by God's creation and continued evolution only in belief by *Homo sapiens.*

The path to *amour* is revealed by a maze of mental neurons that can be connected mentally to produce a truly selected path to happiness; but if the setting from practice is to be taken as a course of "will of desire," it instinctively produces a calamity of paths for a lifetime's worth of treks to more than likely destructive aftermaths. Construction with *steerage* depends on whether the mind's hand-picked mental dots are traced neuron ingredients that might lead to loyalty or deceit.

The one who establishes humorous situations, recognizing coming confrontations or even an assault, may have the best weapon. However, perpetrators may not have sufficiently mental grasp to assimilate aims of ejaculations to dominate humor. Humor should be clasped in sincerity. The thrust of words, however rare in meaning or unexpectedly preen, the mind of the action maker's train of thought intellectually controlled would be interfered, recognizing the warning in jest, as if the bell knells of death was in the cards of the coming aftermath.

In the first ten years, there was a change that, in comparison, emigrants had taken a few years of noble pursuit with divine attention on the real value of the country of the United States of America starting before 1900s. Disloyalty is a part of disorder to be quickly covered up, but it always shows as a chaos of disheartenment that led to aftermaths of various tortures of lives remaining one that started with World War I. The involvement took time for America to get into the war and then caused millions of people to be killed before it had ended.

Lust for the mind and body of women and men is a matter of degree, and the hottest degree is when a copacetic joining of pursuit reveals itself jointly through a common pursuit toward a life of *amour*. That happening under illicit *amour* with improper timing and appropriate reasons requires that one should examine further in one's mind decisions from *steerage*. Therefore, more seriously, important and demanding fidelity issues will get moral attention first. Illicit *amour* is an instant disorder because it may lead to chaos, which is among disorder that remains as part of the violation of life's needed pursuits.

My father Liborio, as he was known as a young boy, had a spark of knowing significant detail about the nature of problems, especially those he intended to solve—be it related to *steerage* and *amour*, war, peace times, and personal relationships that crop up. As my father, years after marriage and a gang of us boys and one sister in the house, Dad taught us *steerage*. He always started with "Use your mind to decide what you intend to do." He recognized the entrenched trap as it effused from both signals of relief. Dad would come out with thoughts signifying what was in his mind's memory that revealed an appropriate time to eliminate the potential problem at hand.

D. Religious
Philosophical Beliefs

Take a [moral?] bath once or twice a week for a few reasons,
and you will find that it is to the law what the water bath is to
the body. The memory within the mind although undefined and
limitless is the media of a human's personality that is within its
minutest complement containing space for wonderment, talent,
innovation, creativity and most of all vision of the times at hand.
—Oliver Wendell Holmes, Supreme Court
of the United States of America

Mother Teresa's philosophy and her work . . . we find that her faith
and her clarity of purpose gave us powerful lessons in the ways of
loving, serving and respecting our fellow human beings, especially
those who are poor and deprived. She practiced what she preached.

As far as the evaluation of Christendom, it has prospered for
two thousand years and the bulk of the people and possessions
within their grasp allowed intellect of Europe to burst out of the
shell that covered people poor, rich, powerful and royalty being
of the same surviving species of the genus Homo (mankind)
plus sapiens (wise) for as many as a million years or more.

The First Renaissance and its aftermath made inventive
progress, but overall little cultural change occurred as the
nature of man's instincts; and yet, there were enormous gains
in the arts and sciences of innovation by mankind.
—Edward L. Divita Sr.

In modern-day words, an interchange of my understanding aimed at this story is the amoral vitality that plagues our younger generations, a typical appraisal based on what I know about my generation. Over the past few decades,

I revealed within my mind a sadness because too little attention was devoted to religions. Even by conservatives, too much concern was devoted to impositions that liberal secularists, including agnostics and atheists, proclaimed their ways are within their beliefs as are religious believers.

The atheists ("believers of a nonexistence of God"), instead, are those who only follow evolution, statistically imposed random traits, which does not match the sensibility of our earth, the sun that captured the surrounding planets, and the extent of an ever-extending universe, but it extends toward infinity as only God could have created the universe. As loners, atheists with minimal support only stand in the apparent creation of increased growth of matter over billions of years, referring details to be explained as might have been caused especially by big bang theories of the astrophysicists. For those of a religious adoption in belief only in the same fashion, as all confess, as believers in a Creator who continue his time to begin and continued to ad infinitum. The outcome to evolve as it occurred daily as it was designed by God with continued evolution. We human beings are ingrained with mysteries of beliefs that they arrived in disorder as it may be part of a belief in God's plan for imposed entropy that could be at his gesture and call.

Regardless of people with religion or those with no religion, the instinctive "will of desire" is instilled hardwired in modern human beings' minds for immediacy from birth as extracted through evolution. However, with "knowledge and experience," also the mind is set to recognize the intent of the mind's use to gain proper pursuits by accessing the situation with immediate continuous use of the mind with decisive concern for response or action.

The two religions so prominently dominated by people are the Roman Catholic religion having its source from the divinely inspired birth and teachings of Jesus Christ believed by those living with the son of God. This belief continued in line with God's previously imposed sacred Judaism religion that started with the Hebrew nations of past eons from a continuation of the beginning. Religious people have beliefs from the comprised bibles containing the Old Testament and the New Testament carried into modern times as the Catholic religion.

Later in the seventh century, Islamic followers of Mohammed and their associated and extremist believers all had Allah (God's call) in their belief as their source and use of universal pray to their god as a projection of faith as a forced demand for large participants and demanded attendance under threat and fear and even death. Some Moslems, especially extremists, had demagogued the Judeo-Christian religious as infidels, and other large varieties of man-made denominations changed dogma to their intentional plan for conversion.

This demise does not linger without a concrete pursuit about Buddhists, Hindus, and their sects, though not referenced but within points of consideration since populations of these many believers were comparable to those of belief in their gods. The main pursuit was to achieve a self-satisfaction with the happiness afforded with little or no interferences of satisfaction with their counterparts.

With the promise by decree of Islamic leaders, those who are extremists, also continually directing assaults, including many who decreed death to the infidels or on a lighter scale gave notice that those human beings under pursuit must accept Islam and must convert, included believers and nonbelievers. These various denominations over years of responsiveness forced moral concepts upon parishioners who agreed to substances of changes. Now, many follow personally controlled religions of nations and those throughout earth.

Peculiar but widely suspicious of intent, people in the Islamic world, with little if any criticism, are hell-bent on dominating people of the globe rapturously, if not exultantly, driven toward converting the world's population to their man-made extracted beliefs into the founded Islamic religion. That was the intent that the desert sheik prophet Mohammed with his Arab nomads of times, near AD 632, in the seventh century. Even now, the extremists are identified as believers in Islam and Moslems, with potential threats of death to the nonbelievers.

The shift, although not clearly defined, leaves many countries wondering why religious zealots still shout their praise of founding leaders who pretended to use religious belief to ameliorate fear that might lead to a moral collapse beyond regular daily doses.

The guide for mankind was to do as he decided within man-made laws and that the government of the state was forced to contend with ways and laws. The leaders both old-fashioned and modern, as pickaxed and planted by the elected, ran people, politicians, and royalty. Unfortunately, leaders did not allow any influence by statesmen of learned stature and wisdom to make any changes.

An example, one from years past, is when mobs that created mayhem and looting were apprehended, they were subject to imprisonment or shot while in the act of looting and mayhem, causing great bodily harm to bystanders. The acts of destructive rioters were attacks on local people's businesses and homes.

A second example, taken in current modern times, such as when mobs and protest demonstrations in state capitols leaders were allowed with limited constraints to enforce their laws; but destruction and violence on the streets created a penalty because taxpayers' monies paid for damages. Achieving one's desires for demands in the broad sense legally was always a problem where freedom was the guide for individuals as well as masses of people.

The rugged individualism of mankind's past generations disappeared into the ether of marijuana smokers and opioids-crazed human beings having little fear of effects on brains shown as an effect on their minds as evidenced by captured stone appearances.

As in many cities, the people are soaked in major declines of Gotham's authority. The laws from the bottom to the top except for inconsequential demands might be imposed by "do-gooder" dominating leaders. These strands of municipal statutes and ordinances that may have become laws, followed as if inherited like DNA, were put into enforcement as civil and criminal laws.

The lack of concentrated law enforcement from the federal government to the city, top down, caused arrests of users and drug mobsters as they slyly continued black markets and deaths that induced large numbers of court cases like those that plagued tobacco industries from their beginnings to disaster of inducing concerns while doing obvious things such as raging war on unsuspecting people who smoked themselves into potential cancer victims. All these behavioral patterns primarily resulted from bad ostensibly oriented choices that predominantly were guided by hardwired instinctive recalls for "will of desire."

Mankind generally never learned from their mistakes. As time passed, the same mistakes and, more importantly, intentional guidelines were rejected with different excuses for their reason of usages. When a bag of new law ideas for the people were dreamed up by the assumed wisdom of legislative administrators with enforcement by the executive branch, a solidarity of common purposes engaged the enforcement. Otherwise, if laws were widely contented and passed, works of government disarrays could cause lack of compromise and recognition for their enforcement and unjustly lead to confrontational judgments into perpetuity.

PART 1

STEERAGE AND AMOUR!— WHAT'S IT ALL ABOUT!

In politics, as in love it does not do to give one's self wholly; one should at times give, but at no time all. Gratitude is nourished with expectation.
—Will Durant, *The Story of Philosophy*, p. 85

The reason this innovational story about the Divita family arises is to elaborate on extensions of culture and personal and moral teachings of the quote, "Steerage and Amour!—What's It All About!"

Steerage and *amour* relate to how people pursue cultural and personal, moral, social, and environmental behavior, and live daily activities and wants or needed things when one's mind chooses the right decision. Let us assume both personal and worldly social behavior events are actively ongoing based on naturally different kinds of societies established by governments who levy laws. The primary natural behavior based on beliefs in the minds of *Homo sapiens* was originally derived from moral behavior created from God in beliefs by many people from past times.

As stated above by profound philosopher Will Durant, of great reputation along with more than enough common sense that he would be broadly identified as a "street smart" philosopher, from his writings of many volumes about philosophies, he prophetically expounded during his lifetime practice about mankind, even though as many philosophers along with himself were clearly modestly brilliant.

My pursuit in exposing this story involves following practiced teachings from the Divita family's hearts and minds of my known Italian descendants and extended families who gained pertinent knowledge from our progeny to live their lives in the pursuit of happiness. The teachings herein are based on how *steerage* and *amour* aid, even with boisterous common sense, to convince novice *Home sapiens* to seek happiness while under explained conditions of making proper decisions. Of course, pursuit of happiness is not always achieved by human beings.

The pursuit usually comes from learning what is taught to the young while gaining mental usages of true teachings of *steerage* and *amour* by choosing "knowledge and experience" to select decisive answers. This type of teaching lets love ply throughout people's lives no matter how one might gain it as it comes from mindful sources. When teachers recognize needs to make kinetic modifications in personal behavior, they aim to tell progeny how to use the mind to make right decisions.

The separation in this story is between affaire d'amour (an illicit love affair) and affaire de coeur (affair of the heart), that one of which will dominate ways *Homo sapiens* live their lives. The main problem is to store understandings in the mind's memory and use it to work one's life in a self-sufficient way to primarily become self-sufficient. Living with happiness means staying away from the mentality of the mind's life's behavioral spectrum end points that identify with opposite ends of depression and anxiety that create turmoil in minds. Keeping one's mind grounded in pursuits that bring happiness to modern-day *Homo sapiens* is the expected and planned best ways to live life.

The main thrust is when people's minds receive bad positions mentally, some human beings must at least make a potential choice. As quoted, it implies that one must follow steerage guides and should at times select the proper one.

The essences of these revelations herein are put forth through a combination of my followings as taught by my parents and grandparents. I have been told to use steerage within my mind by my grandmother Filippa or directly from my father Benny and my mother Josephine. What I have gained from my eldest brother, Frank, and my other siblings throughout my life was daily teachings while living together at home until twenty-one years old. As my time of life increased, I added "knowledge and experience" and sometimes even felt I gained added wisdom that has led me in pursuit my happiness!

The *steerage* continued from the next eldest brother Eugene as he listened also to our mother and dad's teachings as did the rest of our family use *steerage* and *amour,* and it continued into new generations of Divita family progeny. The teaching techniques were relayed to other members of our related Italian families and, of course, the practice of people of Italy from where it originally came and extended to our families that immigrated to America.

My brother Frank, my father's eldest son, named after his grandfather Francesco, a young man with exposed thoughts, gathered his life's actions and observations within an earshot and eye view as he divulged his good behavior. He told us always to gain more "knowledge and experience" within his mind's memory, and it showed as he continued to teach our family during family years at home. However, much of the information was gathered as were responded to the way taught steerage led us to an easy decision. This approach of Frank's pursuit would be taken from personal sources, mostly truthful, with some equivocation or slanted distortions that could have been caused by his unique tough-minded personality as he categorized his memory storage information. As for teaching *steerage*, he always favorably practiced what he learned from *steerage* and *amour* augmented with his continuously enhanced memory that would not contaminate his purview of true heartfelt *amour*.

Frank also may have experienced some dominant effects by being continuously influenced by restraints forced by our dad's compatible paternal direction to extract our best performance. As we adapted to our family's compassionate teachings, Frank primarily supported making right mental decisions. Then he would relay to our siblings simple personal behaviors and incidences that occurred along with hardly any consequences during times in our lives. Even traits of good and beautiful can be solidly inherited especially when it was taught by our father and mother. They were instilled with an astute practice of teaching *steerage* and *amour* that easily led to the pursuit of happiness.

Then again, there were odd times when Frank was not always right. He relayed his memories of "knowledge and experience," and he failed sometimes, especially at times when he, as have we all, adulterated our "experience and knowledge" and discarded the good, the beautiful, and fell into the chasm of mentality called bad psychological judgment. As Frank aged into adulthood, he continually added to his wisdom and used his memory and mindful grasp of wisdom that was demanded. We all make mistakes by chance or behave instinctively, mindlessly, instantly without remorse or even making changes at times.

My dad Big Benny and Frank are the main protagonists and memory suppliers within this story. They either expounded from memory or that family members had stuffed our memories over years to recall what I think must have happened. I also expounded on words of conversations from Grandfather Francesco's life as expounded to his friends or as were heard or told to me by my dad and Frank. We also used our mind's memory sources to help relayed expositions afforded also told by our uncles and aunts and our brothers. We had a grand choice not to relay hearsay even from reputable uncles, close relatives, and friends of the family with whom we associated. And we gathered information continuously and somewhat qualified as credible to describe outcomes based on ensuing results taken from those teaching *steerage* and *amour* knowledge of love affairs as time passed during our lifetimes.

The story of behaviors of our first Italians emigrants is included as told from the beginning and after their settlements. The families go on with the *steerage* and *amour* teachings to beget the next generation of Americans and further generations that propagate new lives into modern-day Americans. Their interactions and confrontations revealed a historic middle-of-the-road pursuit generally toward happiness. Nevertheless, some Divitas had their human problems as do all other people.

Frank's intended usage of a collection of common sense, humanly sensible analyses as related to imposed matter, a commonly simple answer was available, even when situations were critical. He used his memory of teaching *steerage* and *amour* under natural human laws and moral situations to reveal life as it applies with the pursuit of happiness.

The main pursuit with front-end backgrounds was to cover the story in a timely path so it comes about especially with the heritage of *steerage* and *amour* highlighting staunch persons of past generations who continued delivery of true advancements to some degree of cultural improvements with their mind's usage and teachings.

This overall world step when expecting mental improvements of modern mankind *Homo sapiens* was noticeable in teachings that occurred during the initial peak of fifty years of age. It was the same way about three hundred years ago during the First Renaissance starting from the 1475. The men of the First Renaissance, as written in the book *The Man of the Renaissance*, by Ralph Roeder, signaled in words that a slow change occurred in the instinctive "will of desire" even at times of great mental change in talent, innovation, and creativity.

The main reason for such slow progress was the mind's hardwired instinctive desire insisted, first, for survivability from beginnings of mankind. *Homo sapiens* continually, but slowly, changed. No matter what is proclaimed regarding *amour* when it involves an illicit love affair, the poor, rich, powerful, and even those who have granted themselves royalty were living within their heritage from their belief in God's design, which was certainly not from God, and their overall activities lapsed continuously. This heritage also caused afflictions that were little differences for Italians. Afterward, the First Renaissance set, at its prime in 1495, was the crucial start in Italy. The Italian immigrants had experienced cited illicit *amour* throughout history but later lived with more mental and morality sense being properly maintained by popes.

The adoption of Christianity was at the front end of recognized mental growth almost two thousand years and mostly related to an enhanced belief in God the Creator. From what many believed at the time, God granted Jesus Christ as his professed son at the time of his birth, and his spirit was religiously reported by people speaking Hebrew and living at the time when Jesus said, "People's spirit would be judged after death at the end of time."

Much later in 1700s, America as a new colonized country engorged patriotism to form their own country. Great Britain prepared to take over the new country by bringing soldiers to America to start a war until they again take command. After the American won the war, they immediately gained the country, and the leader exploded with great political democratic development and began to extend exploration while accepting slaves from former marketeers being taken from European, Asian, and African continents. Then after at least eighty years, on April 14, 1863, people emigrated from countries before and during the early 1900s. Many people tendered their total allegiance to America effectively, and it showed exceedingly well during 1914 when World War I started.

Part 1 is about the coming of *Steerage and Amour!—What's It All About!* because my grandmother Filippa, with devotion, had continued her venture of teaching their children a simple loving and compassionate way of education so that their children could live under freedom in Italy and later in America. Francesco planned to bring his family to America later because critical changes of patrician government control was devastating to poor workers. After the rest of the family made it to America, hard warring times happened in 1914, and then by 1917, America was deeply involved with a new World War I. America armed a complete army of soldiers and equipment to finally go to Europe and dominated the enemy to end the war. By this time, the Divita family was settled in Smithers, West Virginia, and he was working in the mines.

As a miner full time, Francesco, the patriarch, started building a home for his family. He had settled and, with his sons, began building his commune for his families. The building continued to accommodate his family, and he called it his *OverHome*. After the war, the family settled in the new buildings, and by 1928, Benny, Tony, and Little Benny Divita were married to Josephine Maruca, Catherine Yaquinta, and Mary Divita, respectively, and their lives started new families.

Adolf Hitler, a corporal in World War I, later was imprisoned much time after the war because he was a fascist. While in prison for five years, he wrote *Mien Kampf* and began making plans for a world takeover when he was released. He started following fascism that had already been instilled as National Socialism since 1919. Within a short time, he masterly gained control as a leader and was chosen by the controlling large manufacturers as chancellor of Germany in 1933. Hitler was called der Fuhrer (the Leader).

Hitler started with his team of brownshirts, who were in Germany taking control of antisocialist, especially the Jews, that concerned all *Homo sapiens* and continued to assault them on the streets for no reason. This fighting activity then continued across German cities as his army with prime equipment was built to a supreme complement. Hitler had organized specific leaders to carry out various controls of all people in Germany with a full intent causing considerable harm and even killed Jews without concern.

As his warring began to spread into European countries and then shortly attacks on England prevailed, Americans initially joined England by sending warring support equipment via merchant ships. As small countries were overtaken, America joined England as a warring ally by December 11, 1941. All this happened at the same time as the Japanese had secretly bombed Pearl Harbor at Honolulu. America declared war on Japanese and Germany at the same time, and World War II was well under way. Widespread warring with death and massive destruction of lands and people occurred thereafter. Millions of people were being killed in various European countries.

As the warring continued, tragic cataclysmic destruction of homelands devastated parts of Europe in the early 1940s. The American people were mentally up to their necks getting ready to fight in Europe. And Americans and their allies were also ready to fight the Japanese on their Islands. All people in America were living in their homes under significant mental pressures with concerns about their families and our soldiers fighting with America in Europe.

This was an unnatural critical and worried behavior of the American people at home while soldiers were involved in two parts of World War II. The mental concerns were foremost on their minds. The warring with continued killing was the same as World War I. The continuation of warring had completely changed because people were living with fear even at home. As we all know, as time continued thereafter, different warring in other countries had begun and continued into the new millennium.

The trend has been continuously happening during daily and personal living. Warring influenced people's general behavior at home, being unaware of critical warring disasters influencing their concern about their husbands and wives and sons and daughters in miscellaneous wars. The burdens were especially heavy with soldiers, more than some with a striving for *amour* any way they might find it, including with proper thought ways *amour* was broadly defined in this memoir as affaire d'amour (an illicit love affair) and affaire de coeur (affair of the heart).

CHAPTER I

Observations of Family Steerage and Amour Impacts

Seek not to have things happen as you choose them, but rather choose
that they should happen as they do; and you shall live prosperously.
—Enchiridion and Dissertation of
Epictetus; at Rolleston, p. 81

"Music is by no means like the other arts, the copy of Ideas" or
essences of things, but it is "the copy of the will itself"; it shows
us the eternally moving, striving, wandering will, always at last
returning to itself to begin its striving anew. That is why the effect of
music is more powerful and penetrating than the other arts, for they
speak only of shadows, while it speaks of the things itself. It differs
too from the other arts because it affects our feelings directly, and
not through the medium of ideas; it speaks to something subtler than
the intellect. What symmetry is to plastic arts, rhythm is to music;
hence music and architecture are antipodal; architecture, as Goethe
said, is frozen music; and symmetry is rhythm standing still.
—Schopenhauer 129I, 333, *The Story of*
Philosophy, Will Durant, p. 254–255

If your expectations are to be satisfied, I must give my mind's continuous extractions from my memory and from others with this story about heritage and mentally striving, ever-achieving persons, as were many Italians commonly marked that came to America, to show the real nature of common people who lived through bad times. They lived in the last century before venturing to America and thereafter in the new twentieth century. Most of them were immigrants, and those that were born in America were saddled with loyalty embedded in our instinctively ingrained reactions taking place in our minds while grasping for "knowledge and experience" from our memories.

In more detail, I have concentrated on commonality of personalities whose lives began with the first Divita family Italian emigrants who entered and settled in America in 1910. From then on, many Italians were born as citizens in this great country of America. The importance of Italians was that they produced significant heritage experiences from their family's teachings of *steerage* and *amour* by their descendants and new emigrants with induced reasoning with compassion. Many Italian descendants showed their more typical behavior, but even some few were marked significantly because of poor depressed times and plagued by anxieties of pronounced proportions that caused their share of trouble.

The Italian people created more changes as *Homo sapiens* in their lives with earlier dominance of being humanity leaders more than in other countries that affected coming lives of human beings since the beginning of the Roman Empire. People from different parts of the world also immigrated regardless of nationality, race, color, or creed, and many had suffered significantly under extreme autocratic leaderships before 1900s.

These inheritable attributes of *steerage* and *amour* are critically influenced by minds "will of desire" and "knowledge and experience." Teachings were well used without concealment, defense, or deception, but with adaptation to gain new cultural, social, and environmental conditions in the minds of the young. After immigrating to America, most Italian emigrants sought personae of individuals' life control, freedom, and made pursuits of happiness.

They honored the American Declaration of Independence and predominantly followed laws from the Constitution of the United States of America and laws as legislated by the United States Congress and precedents from the branch of the nation's courts. However, there were immigrants who were already corrupt that also immigrated to America, as did many others from different countries who continued the cycle of breaking laws in America.

The people with instilled foreign mind-sets of long-term colonial settlers and indigenous residents made new immigrants feel like they needed to improve their behavior. The climate induced different perturbations and caused changes in a cyclic if not random formats with noticeable effects on earth as well as with people. By people's general behavior in response to the solar system's induced climate changes in other countries, it made little difference to their personal behavior in daily life. Extremes in all things happened within the universe, unknown and not able to be recorded; but our daily changes in earth's behavior are noticeable worldwide when earthshaking events occurred from past times when recorded.

What I had sensed, many things had changed in the world. American people were stationed on a fixed personae of living, common in capabilities, adept and few were skilled politically and who gained honorable value, by being selected and elected to properly direct the nation's republic. When elected by people into high public offices, some people were simply run-of-the-mill citizens in America and did receive high public offices. Others were even from different countries and obtained certain public offices after becoming citizens of the American Republic, but none could become president of the United States of America.

Extractions of people usually select historically extraordinary personae, not those poverty stricken or those celebrities, infamous, or those who think are aristocracy. The few specific others such as millionaires, scientists, inventors, doctors, lawyers, and military people have achieved to presidents, generals, political ambassadors, and soldiers who enlisted; we as citizens assumed they earned the call of honorable service to the country. Other grants were considered extensions of gifted honor by royalty from countries having royalty. They used an assumed granting of honorable given to members of executive, legislative, and judicial branches in our country's government at leadership levels. They had to swear to honor truths of their actions and words. At the time when past aristocracy lingered in countries, some of those first emigrants were transported either as slaves or indentured servants, poor people, from elsewhere that must serve American owners until they earned work time to become a citizen of United States of America. The slavery continued even past American independence on July 4, 1776. The ceasing of slavery in America was settled during the Civil War on April 14, 1865, by the passed Senate vote with the help of Pres. Abraham Lincoln just before his assassination.

The indigenous had their ranks as chieftains of tribal creations, although they were no different from any others among all *Homo sapiens* in their beginning times. What was needed was only the best of those with dominating gifts of wisdom, and, above all, other values knowledge was used with a dominance of honesty.

The real aristocrats that included royalty of kings and queens and their descendants who lighted as characters on life's stage revealed as uniquely common in behavior as all human beings. Aristocracy was discovered in the same bag as victims of the "will of desire," as were those that led mankind's first and dominant pursuit toward practicing instinctive human pursuits. Many of the *Homo sapiens* would take paths of *steerage*, savoring genuine *amour* to gain pursuit of happiness with "knowledge and experience" as a lynchpin for grasping at their mind's wisdom for extended use.

I think, as we all live our daily lives, *amour,* many times, is slanted with purpose such as disloyal love affairs. Those that take paths of behavior and actions of human beings and their inherent reactions to God's creation and continued evolution of species, by survival of the fittest, distinctively imaged the instinctive animal unaware of . . . *Steerage and Amour!—What's It All About!*

In extracted daily memories and recorded reports of this story, I hope to reveal to nations the teachings of *Steerage and Amour!—What's It All About!* The results will reveal that actual final decisions should be taken from the mind's "knowledge and experience."

The way world's families fit into their exposés of human behavior dominate the mentality of life itself within the span of morality with little depravity, or in more esoteric words, physical and spiritual behaviors should be guided by the mind's control over instinctive ways by using "knowledge and experience."

The inheritance be it by God's creation and continuous evolution, God disseminated live conceptions of each person's progeny through the resultant DNA (deoxyribonucleic acid) that further microscopically fits his design to add existing chromosomes and genes randomly with dominant characteristics. The characteristic modes synthesize as mind and body deliver essential unique parts to life of unique human beings. Then as one's life in the womb progresses every second to fill the mind with instincts galore, noticed movements and growth in body and brain's mind add the necessary simple grasps of "knowledge and experience." The mother of progeny predominantly functions emotionally to notice responses of stored inchoate "knowledge and experience" that grow with understanding even during immediate birthing, and it springs noticeably from progeny uniquely with a spark of common behavior as a new *Homo sapiens* without any mankind racist formations, leaving only unique origins of only *Homo sapiens* on planet Earth.

The expectation of human being's birthing experiences with coming social and environmental attributes arise from signs of enlightenment, such as crying and continuously carrying on of sounds and actions. As time passes, sounds and actions change into understandings such as smiles, aches, and, eventually, first words understood. *Homo sapiens*, with spiritually impacted minds and with infinite potential memory interactions, from the start of life's conception, presumably know differences from nature's rights and wrongs, even as weather being artificial or natural.

From a message by Diotima (Socrates states that "she was my instructress in the art of love" on page 79; and also on pages 86–87 in the book *Plato: Symposium, Procreation The Function of Love* [Penguin Books Ltd., Harmondsworth, Middlesex, England Penguin Books, 625 Madison Avenue, New York, New York 10022,USA] as expressed to Socrates), "I will put it more plainly. All men, Socrates, have a procreative impulse, both spiritual and physical, and when they come to maturity they feel a natural desire to beget children, but they can do so only in beauty and never in ugliness. There is something divine about the whole matter; in procreation and bringing to birth the mortal creature endowed with a touch of God's immortality. But the process cannot take place in disharmony, and ugliness is out of harmony with everything divine, whereas beauty is in harmony with it. . . . The object of love, Socrates, is not as you think, beauty. . . . Its object is to procreate and bring forth in beauty. . . . It is so, I assure you. . . . Because procreation is the nearest thing to perpetuity and immortality that a mortal being can attain as time progresses as already seen in past eons."

Any other behavior was disclosed by mankind's natural laws, man-made country's governing laws, and moral ways of life. With mores aside, they are subject to mankind's choices based on truths as well as beliefs of philosophers. The truth is reflected in belief in God, who continually directed and used only *Homo sapiens* to channel new disclosures from eons of times past.

Family tracks expositions of these singled-out characters' personae on which I concentrated my reviews and this story of four generations of Italians from Italy and America with referencing from time to time from mankind's first existence to mankind's current general practices of teaching *steerage* and *amour*. The learning follows an established inheritance and learning as extracted from heritage like compassionate ways families practiced living in pursuit of happiness.

The main story starts with Grandfather Francesco Divita (born 1875) and Filippa Divita (born 1879). After Francesco's birthing by his father Liborio (born 1850) and Grandmother Marguerita Vivattene (born 1856), they had raised a family in Valguarnera, Sicily. After some time, Francesco and Filippa birthed their first son, Liborio (born 1900), who was named after his grandfather Liborio as a common practice. Francesco and Filippa lived in name only with identifiers that were extracted from archival records prepared by Charles L. Divita Jr., published as *A Historical Treatise: A Missing Link in Divita Family History* (Rochester, NY, 2017).

Francesco was the living patriarch Italian whose beginning was sparse but fully achieved while a sulfur mine worker living in Valguarnera, Sicily; certainly after the family immigrated separately to America, first by Francesco in 1910 with a return home and then returned to America in 1912. Then in 1913, Filippa with her four children at the time eventually immigrated to America and settled and lived with Francesco in Smithers, West Virginia. Filippa lived in Smithers until her death in 1947. Years earlier, Francesco had lived in New York for a while with friends from Valguarnera. Other members of the first Divita family were also settled in Smithers until Francesco's death in 1963. During their lifetime, the Italian Divita family's minds had been filled with memories. They came about during real exposés of their lives of hard times in the years during World War I and World War II that led tough living times with living relatives and people; but they continued close personal Divita family contact for those years and times with coming new generations even as warring was continuously under way.

This story dominates with my memoir presentments as the writer to delve within the Divita family's true nature of their daily lives and their natural behavior patterns in daily events and incidents following family involvements that had significant influence of how they survived mentally under such warring constraints. Frustrations and incidences left many Americans seriously concerned about families whose soldiers were fighting in other countries. The effects of warring claimed many concerned discussions with saddened expectations of deaths. The reliefs of successes in both wars led to peaceful times. I have versed activities of wars, especially how well people in America were kept safely, but an enormous number of American soldiers were killed in the war in other countries.

These three new generations of Francesco Divita families led a path to promises of cultural advancements to heights beyond previous sources of heritage because they had in store with continued teachings of *steerage* and *amour* economically, socially, environmentally, and morally. However, personal mental behavior of Francesco, our Italian grandfather, was sadly inchoate because his beginnings were like millions of people with little written history prior to his marriage to Filippa in Sicily. His wife, Filippa, was a woman with a heart of gold, and she used it daily to teach her children how to follow proper paths of *steerage* and *amour*. The essences of her heart gained ways into families' siblings' minds throughout the story as it is now compiled.

Filippa, while in Sicily, taught using a poetic license with benefits to impart "knowledge and experience" from her memory. She relayed in Italian to her family while in Sicily and eventually converted to using English words of conversation to her eldest son Benny's family. Grandmother Filippa also did the same with her other sons and daughter's children using teachings of *steerage* and *amour* in English. My grandmother and my parents, Benny and Jo, were accomplished speaking in English, leaving them without learning the Italian language; but they still needed to speak with his father Francesco and mother Filippa. Eventually, Big Poppy did gain enough English language to sufficiently converse with friends.

Francesco's personal behavior was demanding in conversations and extractions intentionally when he discussed and referenced whatever was in his mind. In 1912, Francesco sailed back to Sicily after the New Year, time to plan his wife's single venture to America. He made sure he helped in her trip because she was going to take her four siblings with her.

Then Francesco sailed back to America in the summer of 1912. Francesco had set up the families' immigration to America, and their initial stay would be in New York. This memory was told by Francesco's son Liborio, known much later as Big Benny, who had helped his mother Filippa to watch and control four children during the ship's cruise to America in 1913.

After Francesco returned, he had worked diligently in New York to take advantage of daily work to earn money. He then made sure his family as well his eldest son would be able for the extreme trip. He also was anxious and happy that he met friends and relatives from Italy on his trip back to America. They told him they would help him move his family to their home in New York where they could stay while getting ready for their trip to the coal mines of West Virginia.

From an early age, my collections of saved memories may have been stretched when the story sparked my imagination as if one would create a concert of Mozart's capability, a fantastic composer of music with full expression. My expectation of their happy feelings related to going to America and adding new expectations by living in America where happiness appeared to be accepted. My memory of relayed words remained indelible in my mind continually, as was always done with music.

Indeed, my added interpretation set off with unusual twists of two ways to express lustrous luxuriate natures of *amour* . . . the true love type—that is, love in its true sense and love as demonstrated for satisfactions within the family's true love. Once as a fantasy was to delay my grandfather Francesco's ways along the path of "will of desire." The other path followed by his wife, Filippa, and son Liborio's ways along the path of "knowledge and experience" during his times was accepted with early teaching.

My dad Benny's fireside stories influenced my recollections from memory of what was said by word of mouth and an interpretation foremost in his mind. This habit revealed a continuation to show heritage and the ways a self-sufficient man turned out to be different and yet related directly educated by his mother Filippa.

Later, after Liborio was known as Benny and had married Josephine Maruca, their first son, born on September 9, 1929, was named Francisco, but in America, after being grown, later was known as Frankie. Much later, he changed his name to Francis James Divita legally, to my knowledge, but he was always called Frankie as a youngster and Frank thereafter. Then the family grew very fast with four children when we were in our home in Montgomery in early 1941. During that time, Mom and Dad had lost two of their children from diseases in the '30s, and the angst and their despair were mind changing with more added care than needed. The essences of critical remorse are covered later regarding the way life comes by at times unknown.

Frank led me from a youngster's age to gain my knowledge and teachings, because he lived as a young man with both *steerage* and *amour* desires as taught by both his parents and his grandmother Filippa. Frank knew a little bit of the Italian language, especially those action words real Italians understood, "*Cosa Tutto Italiana*" (Everything Italian). Frankie was not born to be with Italians that immigrated to America. He was born as an American, as were all of Benny and Jo's children. Also, Josephine was born in America, but her family were Italians that immigrated to America in 1895.

Josephine knew Italian fluently from her Italian parents. As a young girl, she had learned English from neighbors and in school. Those in her family even now used a method to influence members of their families mentally through a practiced *steerage* and *amour*. Many families disjoined from different countries of the world and still lived Italian lifestyles that had spread throughout America. The Italians in large cities named their areas Little Italy, as did others from different countries. It read with truth when I moved to Baltimore, Maryland, in the mid-1950s.

The Italians, for many reasons culturally, politically, environmentally, and religiously, follow similar paths. Josephine as a young beauty was reserved both with people and morally in her life of love of her family, and so did her family, who were farmers; however, her father Alphonso was also a coal miner. This acquired attraction to well-adjusted women is common for Italians even for many of second-generation, born-in-America Italians.

Liborio's father, Francesco, and men and women associated with his lineage included Liborio's grandfather in Italy, also known as Liborio Divita, who had married Marguerita Vivattene, and they lived in Valguarnera, Sicily. Later when he died at the age of fifty-two, other family members had immigrated to America. Most of them were primarily associated with older folks and were unknown to the new generations that began when the Great Depression started in 1929.

Francesco was a dominating Italian man fully exposed as an adult during the depressed and untenable living under patrician times of the late 1800s in Italy. The political turmoil was rampant to many families. For most citizens of Sicily, life was uncommonly difficult because this first young aggressive man Francesco wanted to succeed as a strong, dominating man. He developed into a headstrong, physically nonfearing Italian peasant. With that feeling, he made his way into the mines at about twenty-one years old. The way the sulfur mines were being controlled, he knew he would someday have to flee his motherland. This feeling plagued him even more so after he married Filippa La Spina for his advantage because of her heritage from a significant family in Valguarnera on the island of Sicily.

After getting married in 1899, he could take no more of extreme working conditions, so goes what my dad and grandmother Filippa told me in English much later at different times. Leaving his country remained on his mind even though he had a dominating labor job in underground sulfur mines. His brain prodded him to leave before his striving might cause him to turn crooked or some unexpected disaster might befall himself and his wife. More importantly, starting with his first son, Liborio, and three children, they had endured the family's impoverished earlier life in Valguarnera, Sicily.

Later, on the trip to America, Filippa and her children suffered both mental and physically unknown and unexpected grossly harmful experiences that transpired daily in tight steerage quarters of the ship in beds below on a crowded deck. The young, stalwart, and strong Liborio helped his mother Filippa. He protected and taught his younger brothers and sister how to be strong and take good care where possible on such a strange venture to give needed comfort to the little ones. Liborio's facial expressions set behavior patterns so that young ones complied willfully. Liborio could mentally gain common sense daily and made them smile with strength to understand that the trip on the ship will be over soon.

Their mother logically and morally followed common sense to avoid any calamity and to ease seasickness that was rampant during storms when waves tossed against the ship and decks. Her attuned comfort enabled children to grow mentally and physically with self-sufficient personalities. Steerage was used during grossly scaring and staggering traveling times when the unimaginable trip overwhelmed all their first and only time traveling to America.

Liborio, as a teenaged child possessed with only child's knowledge, helped to ease his siblings' suffering in the ship's voyage at steerage with unfathomable misery from the beginning of the trip. Frightening feelings were etched into their memories. Liborio cared for his siblings as a protector. He never complained, never mentioned the pain, and offered love and support to his mother Filippa and children.

He must have understood his mother's despair why his country's despair with life was failing Italy. Neither he nor his parents would have discerned that the turmoil was induced by poor national government leadership and was controlled by the autocratic patricians. I believe his mother's upbringing influenced him morally and taught details of how to use common sense.

From my own childhood experience with Grandmother Filippa (Big Mommy), I knew that a strong woman who instilled peace from her heart and soul was a godsend. She conveyed this comfort to Liborio, Antonio, and Giuseppe, and the poor little two-year-old Margarita along with managing her own fears and ailments carefully. Her minding of concerns of being seasick induced afflictions that were impossible to control. During their journey, Liborio gained knowledge on how to raise children, including how to use humor and wit and laughter to soothe hearts and minds of children.

After several months in America, they moved in their own time to Smithers, where he gained employment in the coal mining industry in the Morris Creek area. Liborio's adulthood expanded within that year and helped his father on his mining job. Quickly, according to the new principles of American life, he understood that in America, to gain stature in the family, he would be obligated or at least semiforced to work with his father to maintain family prosperity and a peaceable camaraderie.

Big Mommy, Liborio called her Momma, was naturally instilling his thoughts, and then he figured in his mind what needed to be done quickly. Liborio's mother's influence certainly augmented his instinctive behavior to be criticized, and he assumed inherited interactions from her on how to interact with his father Francesco.

The interest to become substantial increased after Liborio arrived in America. Although his father still had full control of his young life's time, energy, and strength. Francesco did not have his son's young life's gain of knowledge, but everyone could see him as the peacemaker of the family. This critical change came naturally by being involved daily with his siblings. The commune was built much later by Big Poppy after arriving in Smithers, West Virginia. The need to build an *OverHome* allowed the family to quickly act when incidences had to be resolved for any child that may have had a complaint or accidentally harmed themselves.

After several years with his father in mines, his new venture was to become a businessman in America as his right given in the Constitution. This friendly peaceful attitude was the impetus that instilled as he made his way to become a fully comprehensive America citizen by 1925. My dad never told us everything he did with his father, but he stressed that his devotion to working diligently with his father's demands lasted about twelve years working directly for the family's well-being. After a few years, Francesco started an Italian delicatessen store in Montgomery using his sons Big Benny and Tony's to help run the store. The family worked to keep it maintained good enough in bad times of early '30s.

Earlier in his spare time, Liborio had completed his venture in a local school for almost five years. He gained good skills in English and learned accounting easily as he was good with mathematics. As he grew older, he was renamed Benny and took any type of small jobs that came up for bid in West Virginia. He moved dirt from newly cut roads, which kept the truck busy. And within a short time and through new friends that he made daily, he was offered a clear opportunity to accept an invitation from one local Italian worker also on the road asking Benny if he would like to meet their family. With the invitation, Benny accepted and was welcomed to a good old-fashioned Italian farm meal at their father Alphonso's home. He was welcomed by the family after dinner, one and all, and to his surprise, he was enchanted the minute he saw one of the sisters named Josephine and secretly fell in love at first sight. Josephine, a young beauty among the other good-looking sisters in the family, was reserved by sight, as were the entire family.

From that first moment from what my dad told us later, Benny was a man of true *amour*. He was captured by true love simply by her presence. He was now quickly becoming a practiced conversationalist both in English and Italian when at the dinner table. After meeting Josephine several times while still working on roads and still visiting the family, Benny's thoughts were only about her personally.

When he was back home, he wrote a letter to her to express his love. As the weeks passed, Jo wrote to him. Benny knew that it would be her that he would pursue. He never said how far away it was at times. He did pray that he would be acceptable to her and that he would devote his life to her with love. He showed it with love letters found many years later. A sample of one of his letters is displayed for the true reaction to be exposed by his written words of love.

Letter from Benny to Josephine

Ireland, W VA

Oct 7 -28

Dear Sweetheart

I will drop a few [lines] to let you [know] that I receive your letter
and certainly was glad to hear from you. Jo, I hope you didn't
get mad about that little joke about baby. My Dear Darling
the reason I didn't come up Saturday because I didn't have
any way to come to Weston. But I will come up this Saturday
Sweetheart. You want to [know] I am near done where I am
working. I can't tell you anything about until we'll get alone. Jo,
I hate to hear that you have bad cold, but I hope you get better.
Josephine, I have been feeling bad all last week, but I am better
now. I must have been love-sick. Well Dear, I will close for this
time. Give Father and Mother my best regard, the same to your
brothers and sisters. I give you my best love that you know that
I love you and my dreams kisses from the one you can't forget.

Benny

Josephine Maruca was the first woman he had ever loved so dearly. Later,
my mom had told us that his excitement was from the beginning; a deep love
that smothered both into an expected marriage within the year. When they were
together, I imagined that Josephine must have been reserved and yet considerate
in her own way, kind, and talkative with a face of graciousness. She said she mostly
felt what their young lives would be like at times on their farm.

When they were apart, he wrote love letters beyond my imagination also
shown in my mother's journal, which met my understanding what true *amour*
really is. After many years, I reread the letters so I could see how they predicted
my parents' marriage for life and their model for their children to follow in their
lives. My dad's spirit revealed in his facial expression good intentions always to
his wife. I believe his instinctive ability included a purposeful intent to involve
his mind's "knowledge and experience" within his family. I think what this finely
tuned awareness gave him was an insight into behaviors of people with different
personalities that he met with interest during his lifetime.

Having encountered broad differences among men, Dad had a means of
assessing any known human beings ranging from "no-good lowlifes" to religious
extremists. All I think with specific focus and words is how one should treat men
and women. Because of his interactions with all kinds of people, he, as I would

say, meticulously taxed his mind's "knowledge and experience" to observe people with intent to minimize criticism and allot dignified attention and friendship. He gained a sense of balance of his behavior as either a juggler or a tightrope walker to maintain balance to settle temperaments of person he met.

Sometimes, he may have put himself under a mental challenge. He then would easily control his anger and disappointments to discontinue frays. The essence was that he had developed a careful attitude about expressing judgments about people and could keep his own counsel private. How some people managed to hold their interest and divulge advice or knowledge for their benefit was generally noticed by Dad. This was his mainstay that hid his sway of having lifelong friends.

From what I observed in my mind was that my dad was a steady running freight train on tracks that he took to self-education. He followed a daily schedule with personal reading, especially newspapers and variety of magazines when he was finally at his taxi business. He usually read magazine articles that convinced him that he was on the right track. He was especially interested in national, state, and city operations and politics. However, what he had been through with World War I at his young age settled in his mind decisively and was later followed in daily newspapers and radios conversations of concern thanking God for America's bravery and love of the country.

While going to different places, mentally, he made sure he noticed with a sense of interest and discussions about concerns of battles and deaths that started even in the mid-1930s. At this time, Dad's mind train raced through the newspaper and radio information that was forever nearby for him to hear about battles getting worse. He extracted from his memory people's encounters mindfully because warring times had caused more common problems with loved ones, deep within their minds, who were thinking about personal changes and happenings.

As he had told me later, as a young man, he swore to God, casting it concretely in his mind to never let his poppa Francesco's behavior extend into his mind's working thoughts and relationships with other human beings. From what I gathered when I was much older and at an odd time, I listened to my dad.

He developed a sense of humor that reflected self-confidence and a comfort especially with his father when he needed to help him to resolve his current family problems. He would smile and gesture his body to convey his friendly and loving personality around his family and friends. Dad would start at the beginning, telling his father to take it easy rather than to argue with family and especially with friends.

Francesco mostly dominated the use of his known level of wisdom that came from threat and strength. In my dad's plight, he developed a sense of humor voicing self-sufficiency when he interacted and conferred with his father. He wanted to make sure he treated friends and even someone you do not like with kindness. His facial smiles and gestures characteristically expressed his friendly personality around his family, and friends keep his father calm. With such a stalwart personality, one would think he was blessed with a special feature that allowed him to interact throughout his life with a balanced wisdom.

Francesco cooled off to the point that he would pay attention to what he says to friends. Dad's personality was stalwart, and one might think he was blessed with a special feature granted to his family's advantage. Dad interacted throughout his life with common morality teaching *steerage* and *amour*, a noticeable practice among his personal and extended family.

As old Italians called it, *benandanti*, maybe when Liborio was born, he might have been with a particularly shaped head—that is, a caul, thought to be a good omen and one that carries folklore of a portentous delivery. Sometimes, they are unspecifiable, unmeasured, or noticed without attention. In my extrapolations of my dad's personal advancements, possibility of portends leaves him with an exciting wonder or an awe omen causing one to live a marvelous life. From my knowledge, he never had any call to believe or talk of its gain such as superstition in conversation.

As an example, Dad made an unusual number of predictions about my behavior as I grew into my teens, that I remembered, many times before he would have a clue. My dad had a genius to know the essence of what might have happened before being informed about a given incident. Who can know? What God planned for hereditary probabilities within the lives of *Homo sapiens* for special abilities is unknown. The question is, what extends beyond geniuses, and yet to come, in the future of *Homo sapiens*, as new life extends to immortality with the world's new progeny being procreated?

What does heredity do to random and unique birthing, or what extends the nature that evolution of "knowledge and experience" will evolve and advance within minds beyond geniuses? The signs are continuously revealed within superstitions and differences in appraisals and suppositions made ad infinitum as a common practice by Italians. Real value is in the life of a person as revealed with growth and not with the phenomena of one's nature that comes later in a fanciful expectation of unique *Homo sapiens* after birth with no challenge.

My father Benny was a man of few equals as human beings when judged by peers and those above and below their virtual status. His specialty, which he proficiently developed, was to pursue his life desires as a self-starter, especially with things of nature, and his belief in his love of people. As noted by many, he could almost always determine his course of action necessary to solve confrontations in trying circumstances. His most natural talent was to resolve troublesome situations seemingly with little effort. He was a good mechanic, self-taught, analytical, not a seat-of-the-pants explorer; and as are so many of us, he was not easily perplexed. He had a special knack for car engines, which he gained at an early age in his twenties and continued the rest of his life. With his technical finesse, Dad could make most any car of his times start, and then he would drive a short sprint and hear the engine. And when asked how he fixed it, he would say, "I sensed where and what caused the problem and worked on it until I fixed it."

My dad's analytical talents meant that he didn't shy away from addressing personal psychological pursuits of close family members. He was known to give clear opinions and advice, helping individuals decide on a next step in their lives. For example, he had several mechanics working in the garage on his large truck that should be ready to move people to a new home. After several tries by real mechanics, Dad knew that the truck was not going to start. Dad took over with his tie hanging down over his white long-sleeved shirt as usual. He spent less than a half hour and got it running soundly and ready for the trip.

As one of the past endeavors in his life, he concentrated on teaching his eldest son, Frankie, who had a true interest in understanding detailed designs and mechanization of cars. This teaching continued with his next two elder sons, Gene and Eddie, who were parts cleaners in his garage until the garage was later sold. After that, Frank worked with mechanics, and he became a good mechanic. During their lives while in grade school, all three boys became newspaper delivery boys. Frank was ready to go to junior high school in 1941. Gene was in fourth grade delivering newspapers in town, and Ed was his helper, who had entered his second year of grade school and a few years later became a newspaper delivery boy.

Sometime later, my dad had a grievous taxi car accident in late 1943 as a passenger in the cab driven by one of his drivers named Bill. After the delivery of lunches, Bill's intent was to take Dad home to Montgomery. The wreck happened while Bill was driving in the right lane at highway speed. With little notice, he hit the back edge of a parked tractor trailer that was about two feet on the macadam road. They both were rushed to the hospital. After months of recovery for Dad, he knew he would go back into his business and behave as usual with no losses.

However, as a few years had passed, Dad had gotten a diabetic condition. After that, he still wanted to do all the things he had done before. The next few years, he had to be medicated, and he was made by his wife Jo to take his insulin daily. The care and concern that he had gotten were from his wife Jo, and she made sure he got his shot every day even with complaints. He never thought he needed a doctor.

Within the next few years, the World War II finally ended in September 1945, and his plan was to satisfy his lifelong desire to attend the Indy 500 Race in 1946. He had attended the one in 1941 and experienced a great deal with love of cars and knowing his old professional racers and a few racing friends. To Dad, it would be a more truly expected exciting time. I will cover it later in chapters 16 and 17. to relay the fun and joy of his trip of the year.

His diabetes assault deteriorated and complicated his life near the end of the '40s, and as a person who had been in great health, he was not the man he was before. His wife, Josephine, did the best job of making sure he took his insulin, and it extended his life. It may have been one of the causes that forced an attraction to alcohol even with little usage; he would become apparently inebriated. The addiction caused minor consequences to his self-reliant useful abilities much later in his life. However, his friends never abandoned him; instead, his wit continuously showed that his attractive personality was often displayed with many friends as he continued to work with his son Frank after becoming a partner in a local car dealership. He was invited to many occasions as the business grew, and he was involved with more people buying cars.

Benny was also a cogent card player. He showed no hand or face movements signifying that he might have cringed at his card set. Within his mind, he sourced and played many great card hands, usually with a slight smile afterward. My dad would be in competition with his family at any time and any place. Dad especially liked being in his son Frank's office at the Montgomery Motors dealership because he helped Frank gain the company's ownership in the late '60s. This combination of slower activity became a major factor for my dad Big Benny's general health. He had taken a semiretired pursuit, and later, he and my mother Jo were living with Frank's family. However, Frank evidently had inherited his father's stellar mechanical capability as an early devotee to detailed mechanical knowledge when his father had his automobile garage back in the 1940s.

The importance of the minutest detail from Dad was recorded by being at his side when working on a car defect; no matter what it was, it always was a complete success. And I added that Frank knew everything he had asked him even though his father's way of teaching was that as a man. Frank knew that Dad only attended grade school in Italy and for a short term through the fourth grade in America after he immigrated. What he learned was reading, writing, and arithmetic. Afterward, he was doing his own accounting and kept his own books. He made sure by reading that he covered more than thirty years of design evolution and performance, from the "Tin Lizzie" capability to the Chevrolet Corvette owned by one of his doctor friends. On reading newspapers and magazines, that is, Big Benny grasped the excitement personally of a few race car drivers and racing professional aficionados as he claimed the expectation even when the 1941 Indy 500 Race was the last race with a pending delay until 1946 because of World War II.

Three years later, Benny, with one of his friends, made the trip to Philadelphia to see Mauri Rose, the winner of the 1941 Indy Race. He talked with Mauri, and he said he would be driving in the race at the Indy 500 in 1946 with the reopening of the newly refurbished racetrack and facility. The aspects and actions of this trip will be treated fully later in the story after the story of World War II was fought and won by the American and European allies.

As it comes about, during these next five years, Dad's elder children were growing and becoming students in the local schools and growing into young adults. Also, during the war and by the end of 1949, my dad and mom Josephine had produced new progeny as a second group of three boys that had been born in a six-year period. They could see a difference in raising them. They needed much more care than the elder ones. However, they did get *steerage* and *amour* teachings, and they turned out as well as the first family of four. The good that followed was the *steerage* and *amour* teachings continued as they grew into adults. The likes of which no one could tell them apart from the elder ones as Benny and Jo's kids.

Then the two elder sons had already entered high school and finished one in 1947 and the other in 1950, respectively, as they imposed on their time to help in the home. Dad wanted then to go to college. By this time, even Eddie was a good helper and was doing well in Montgomery High School when he started in 1948. However, the two elder boys then concentrated on their studies as college preparatory students at West Virginia Institute of Technology (WVIT), and after Eddie graduated, he spent one year with Gene in WVIT College in town.

Dad wanted Frank to become a doctor, but his grades didn't support his pursuit and, after a try, the first two years in our local college at WVIT. Frank always had in his mind desires for a career in music. He wanted to be an achiever in creating and teaching music initially, and as his vocation would take root, then he could gather his talented and move in the direction of music. Frank was continually immersed with problems at this time as he had with his family's monetary growth and knowing similar deterioration in his father's business in the early 1950s.

The novelty and newly enhancement capabilities in cars attracted his common ways to store car details within his mind with complete interest in a variety of cars. This was Frank's business and his mechanical love. Big Benny knew his eldest son penciled car designs from when he was a child obtaining library documents or having car magazines ordered by his father at the taxi stand. Frank read about the details of various systems and assemblies of cars. And it sometimes included a race car or the neighborhood's rich man's car. These were the designs that significantly influenced him as it did the inventiveness of his father, who admired him with ardor.

Frank was exposed socially, and many thought he showed no more zest than ordinary men generally seeking *amour*, as most men are, by their nature regardless of their vocation, every day, attracted to women. Frankie, as he was known when younger, a handsome, better than good-looking young man, often approached one of his girlfriends with a smiling attraction. Frankie, when he was young, greeted his girlfriend likely with "Hi, Rosy! What are you going to do on the weekend? Would you like to go to a movie? It's a going to be good, one with Clark Gable and Claudette Colbert."

Rosy, in a flash, reminded him quickly, "Yes, Frankie! Let's meet at the Kayton Theater at seven o'clock!" Frankie gave her a big smile that excited her heart as she walked away in a strut. Frankie continually had girlfriends throughout high school and into college, where he met the love of his life, Betty.

As for his progeny years later, as Big Frank with their family, his first words to his girls born in the early 1950s were that they are expected to acquire the teachings of *steerage* and *amour*; and did, from Frank and Betty and their grandfather Big Benny and grandmother Jo. As the three girls Beverly, Cheryl, and Jane grew, they had a spark of life fiercely enticing to their gentile sensuousness accented with beauty and friendships galore. Then much later in high school, the girls were grandly accepted by school students, their extended families, and other friends as expected by the nature of their heritage. Their life stories are as exciting as the rest of the families. They were constantly under a demanding protection by his grandfather and Frank himself, as other Divita families, who modeled themselves with good behavior and living practices and continuously worked on maintaining a pursuit of happiness.

Frank's twin sons were born in America much later in February 1959. The first one was named as Francis but called Fran; his middle name is Charles, taken as a namesake of his great-grandfather Francesco but Americanized as Francis. The other twin, known as James Benjamin, was named after his grandfather Benny's new middle name, Benjamin.

From the mid-'50s and into 1960s, Big Benny helped his two youngest brothers, Charley and Jimmy, buy service stations and car mechanic businesses. Both brothers built the businesses in a way that outshone all others in the town with their detailed knowledge of mechanical functioning and, as a team, managing car services and repair capabilities. With their daily thinking caps running, as if ignited, creative sparks were moving smoothly, as do spark plugs of the car do continuously, starting and running the engine mechanics to produce an improvement in working time and finesse of the job's completion.

After Fran had reached adulthood, he was attracted to the opposite sex with a fevered expression for *amour* and with inherited wit as one would expect, but with only a grasp of the family's teaching of *steerage*. Fran gained some early knowledge and tried to minimize his conflicts of life. However, with the way his life progressed after his first marriage, he did not get a true accounting about his first wife's behavior from her family.

Jimmy was more conservative and took more time to get involved with the love of his life, Penny. After marriage, they had three girls, also the love of their lives. Then Jimmy decided to go into the building business, and Penny became a doctor. They all married and had children, who will be discovered when I get into their stories about some remembered and displayed incidences at critical times in their teens.

In the coming modern days, there were fewer types of attractions that excited friends but still some young girls who only saw the sunshine as the right light shone on other younger people. The newsprint glamour splashed on every face in anyone's life who made others feel an illicit greeting with a "will of desire." Even more common than sin into the '80s, all kinds of relationships existed unknowingly if not even revealed that were commonly considered amorally sustained by people's behavior. Some changes were yet to come during the '80s when men generated new behavior patterns that had categorized men as men attracted to women. The new pursuits that had become obvious operated in distorted ways when some people became a part and parcel of all humanity now so explained as lesbians, gays, bisexuals, and transgenders, now flagged by the acronym LGBTs.

Alluring things and desirous persons drove everyone to develop methods to make amorous advancements using various pursuits. Positioning to advance their pursuit by words, actions, and behavioral expressions was noticeably clear. However, by following their generation of taught *steerage* and *amour* to gain "knowledge and experience," all the while influenced by sensuous happenstance of the instinctive "will of desire," they were instinctively exposed to others who have experienced these newfangled gender behaviors and pursuits of immoral actions.

Looking back at these impacts, knowing what Frank did as the future appeared, he was always ready to relay morality as a fixture from Jesus's Christianity that had to be considered. I examined his pursuits to see how he moved to adjust to a better man, and he taught the same for the Divita family men. Frank's mind was set to carry out intentions that related to lives of siblings of the Divita family.

Frank had become the mayor of the city of Montgomery in the late 1960s and then a complete business owner of the top-notch Montgomery Motors dealership. Frank and Betty were raising his two sons and three daughters in the '60s and '70s. As they grew into adults, he trained them at his car dealership while working with his dad part time. Betty also helped with the accounting compilations continuously. Per the children, it was their choice of college and majors, and each of the children earned college degrees. The one son Jimmy became a journeyman craftsman in the building business and started a building company, while the other son Fran remained in the car dealership business, but much later moved with his second family and wife to another company in a borderline city in Erlangen, Kentucky, after they moved from their home state.

The girls worked as bookkeepers, service personnel, and car salespersons with an intent and on-the-job training in business management. While the girls all were business oriented, Janie was more interested in car sales and becoming a dealer. Janie later continued to work for other dealerships after leaving the area and getting married. Janie continued to work for a Cadillac dealer, and after her marriage to Bill, she had two children. Cheryl married Allan and had two children, Allan Jr. and Emily. Cheryl stayed in the university system and completed her doctorate in education and worked for the state of West Virginia and much later moved to the state of South Carolina where she continued her job as an educator of teachers.

Beverley had married Joe, and later, they adopted a boy nicknamed JT. Joe owned his own company as a geologist. Each of these modern-day children of Frank and Betty had selected novel educational studies that were typical of those chosen by substantial people. Frank and Betty had done the same earlier and made choices the same ways. Dad and Mom always had in mind that some might become accountants, lawyers, doctors, and teachers while interacting within the family, friends, and associates.

Big Benny and son Frank's minds were always in gear to help solve problems. This same approach was used by all extended Divita families to influence family buyers by each of their children, nephews, and nieces with proper respect and social and personal behavior. In the lives of these four senior men, Frank, his dad and his uncles Charlie and Jimmy, and all their associates and family members that worked for them, each took pride in doing things.

They believed morally, without failure, along the line of *coeur de amour* among more critical family situations and incidents. The proper use of instinctive pursuits and use of "knowledge and experience" always was mind thinking behavior. Thoughts occurred, but the right one continuously chose the right pursuit between using either the inherited instinctively fully charged "will of desire" or inherited "knowledge and experience."

Our dad's pursuit of questioning the conscious and subconscious minds goes back to earlier times with intent mostly considering what he had learned from the teachings of *steerage* and *amour* from his momma Filippa, years ago with few exceptions. Big Benny goes back to the times their children generally had a path to follow to do the right thing and would take the path from their inheritances from their father and mother's practices, morally, socially, and culturally, as was extended to their offspring as needed.

Not to be remiss with a flashback to times back in the 1940s, Dad had considered what hereditary traits were stealthy intruded into their heritage and probably caused misbehavior patterns from their grandfather Francesco's dominant traits. Those inherited in parts were the mainly concrete memory injections of his dominant instinctive functions with minor inheritance both in name and mind-set. They almost were, as if tractable neurons from their nerve system at the beginning, prewired structure as a probability that would be small. As is common for all human beings, these traits are always random and never guided to be alike but instead intentionally uniquely designed and instilled into unique mind's functions. And as for all, each instinctive extraction of desire should be combatted inherently by mind's abilities to distinguish right from wrong.

For this family, the adherence to Pareto's law is probably more than 80 percent as is typically common for the world's population pursuits with various kinds of extractions, but none are ever alike. Diverting from their great-grandfather's inheritance, an encoded, gratifying, and doubtlessly exciting path to follow is their "will of desire," so infrangibly trekked as is paths to redemption so lightly treaded in shallow areas. When following a mind's "knowledge and experience," the mind's path would lead instantly to decisive thoughts for action.

My father Big Benny was a different man altogether when he was younger and loved making decisions for his children. He only liked what really made sense to him in achievements and would be aware of unexpected consequences; but not to say he never had a failure after making the right choice with a given decision. When he faltered, he quickly would refigure his next step by changing his path of rethinking potential conclusions. He was fully aware of doctors' judgments regarding their use to help maintain human being life.

After all he had been through during his childhood and the child-rearing and rendering times, he had a mental intuition of what each of his children could do if they set their minds to doing it. Being the eldest son, Frank knew what was coming from a knowledge point of view every time he was confronted. Frank could see that his father Big Benny felt he had his finger on the responsive mind's pulse of value of his young human beings, especially when he would say his piece.

Frank's favorite words at the beat of his music physically and mentally played at home on his piano. I would listen steadily while he would make up his mind not to become a doctor. Frank's song, in my mind's eye, exclaimed often as if his timing was set to win a race by being the one so far out with the right tune in front of all other vocations. After all, Dad never dropped his insistence. All that was on his mind was if Frank achieved his dad's desired accomplishment, he would be bragging joyfully to friends, "My son's going to be a doctor!"

As Frank continued to recall from the past, with fear in his gut, he came up with, I will try to remember what to say, something like, "I'll try for one year with brave intent. Afterward, when I passed the first year, I lost interest." All he told me was "I knew I wanted to be a musician."

However, two years later, Dad did get his pride enhanced from his second son, Gene, who later planned to become a medical doctor, and he did. Gene, after quite a few years later, became a psychiatrist with a vigorous drive to help mentally afflicted people of all ages.

It is odd that as a youngster from a daydream, Gene told me later in late 1960s that Dad had recalled his birthing heritage in a dream stemming from Dad being an unimaginable imperial eagle screeching in a mating call by my father with reason to extract desired strength while entranced by his mate, my mother, whose face soars with mild beauty that a bald eagle displays to the viewer, billing and cooing with endearing responses, captivated compassionate to his sensuous call. The sensation flittered through Gene's mind's recall as his mother Josephine's hair blew in the wind, never gaining its way back to original places. This fantasy of conception at an unexpectedly odd time for me to recall from memory so much later would flicker in place when my personal strength of my life's direction was supplanted in my mind memory the knowledge of my parents' lofty intent for all of us when born.

Over the years of my observance, because my father easily spread his wings hovering over all of us, I would sense with his self-taught direction toward a pursuit of happiness. What a goal set for us. It made me wonder what he had to gain. I remembered in his own words. Years later, he ejaculated as I wondered what it was that I remembered, something like, Dad had sensed the knowledge that his first son would become a doctor and help human beings, as he proffered under my observed remembrance; but without saying that it was always in Gene's mind years after Frank's birth when he was thinking about music and becoming a musician from his early life, if not forcing it from his subconscious mind's memory.

Dad told us that he sensed Frank was in God's pocket based on his love letters to my mom after they married. His goals were set for his first son. As for me, Ed, yet to be born almost six years later, Dad's pursuit was that he expected a good choice as the other three because he sensed that he would know each in detail without telling them what to do when they grow up.

Frank had been the firstborn into the family, and it happened during the month of September just after the United States stock market disaster occurred in October. The chaos that had happened on Black Friday, October 29, 1929, became an omen to me later in my life. Then much later, when the omen appeared, among my adult memory, retroactively mentally deciphering my mind, I suspected that business was going to be Frank's forte, especially with money on his mind, and I would become one of his investors, which never happened.

When I was a kid, I was known as Eddie with more than average physical capabilities. I knew I had an average mental ability, and I worked to continually grow my mind with reading time in the library over the next ten years. The years then passed with the speed of darkness disappearing unaccounted. I struggled with a few instinctive desires, and many times, it worked to my advantage. What I did was to accommodate methods of gaining insight to people's reactions as if stopping on the pendulum that was set at about halfway from despair and anxiety and nearer happiness. This meant the mean of the achievement spectrum floating in my mind had me going in the right direction. The power and acceleration increased a little more each time in arcs as it bent toward a higher mark in my life's achievement.

At my early age, I got used to striving for the flow of happiness by accepting satisfaction of my life's pursuit. A few times, it cost me hard work by my dad. I have a psyche that sometimes becomes dismissed, and I have the mental and physical welts to show for it. It was placed on me by my dad, who was more of a righteous man by nature; but not necessarily a morally righteous man, though his nature encompassed the morality implied to *Homo sapiens* through his shallow but direct Catholic religious beliefs.

I never went through the stage of "spare the rod and spoil the child." Usually, someone could pick an incident and spread it to the right people, and my name was highlighted or "blighted" for some to decry or wither my dream and caused others to seek me out for some of the blame. Little was I influenced at my young years by "knowledge and experience" because I accepted it so easily. Usually, I followed my instincts and never tried to figure out how to combat with my mind the common instinctive occurrences of no tattling on my siblings. The new life bolstered me to proper mental concerns that made me collect my understanding of situations using my "knowledge and experience." Many times, even when I felt I made a good choice, it backfired by those who thought they knew my modus vivendi, as I had chosen a manner of living.

Striving was my main life's pursuit with my family, and being well-off mentally, I was usually accommodating in our small coal mining hub in Montgomery, West Virginia. We were not exceptions. We as a family never felt we were on the back end of the spectrum of cultural achievement, mostly because we maintained a pride of person, state, and country. This pursuit was easy for us because we emulated our parents, whose gratitude to America was surefire as the light of the morning sun coming over the Appalachians. They were morally and naturally responsible for the way the family lived daily and paid mentally and responsibly for their mistakes. They never sided with modern mankind who thought life was another gift of nature without spirit of the Creator, an added investment, to make human life unique.

Everyone my dad knew in the late '30s needed more money than they could earn. Dad was a source out of pocket to many for support. Some loans were never requested by him, and some were never paid back. Many of his supplied provisions were small, but they were more than satisfactory. He always showed mental appreciation to the needy. Sometimes, he made sure men he knew earned enough money by letting them work as helpers on some of his jobs. Friends and acquaintances were given jobs working fifty or sixty hours a week including Saturdays. The wages were agreed for the work so that they could provide for their families. From government's point of law, which was questionable at that time, wages were not specifically fixed. Anyone would work for whatever the going wage was just to keep families in food and clothing. As one would suspect to beget married life's worth, they strived with stress to earn money even when they were only doing part-time work.

New baby births in our family occurred naturally, and all the while, the money Dad accumulated in his business allowed us to live well beyond poverty. We were told we lived above the average family and never felt we didn't have enough and never complained about our lives' bequeaths even those out of thin air.

The Divita family never talked much about the World War I because most were Italian emigrants except their new children born in America. The United States finally entered the war with a gusto when needed. With the American forces fully armed with hundreds of thousands of troops and fighting equipment, it took almost two years to finish it. The gross number of killings and enormous destructions were in Europe. No warring was conducted in America; nothing happened in America except the doings of German spies. However, many of our soldiers were killed, as were so many more Europeans who were led by Kaiser Wilhelm.

The Germans suffered defeated to a level of disrespectability to have started the war from the beginning using autocratic Austria internal assaults of persons having been killed by assassination. The uncounted medical human experiments of unnatural sorts, debilitating injuries and starvation, large-scale death with property thievery, and devastating mass executions levied on human beings by meanly ardent military fighters. Even after such death and destruction was accounted, uncountable losses of life during World War I was a war referenced as a final war. After all, it was preached to be "The war that was to end all wars."

What happened about eight years later, Frank and Gene gained the knowledge of a new war that was started by an unknown sergeant named Adolf Hitler, who was imprisoned until 1933 because of his complaints and involvements with German's failures in the World War I. During his time in prison, he did minor art that was mediocre, but his good behavior caused him to be released from prison early. When he completed his documented new pursuit within his book *Mein Kampf*, within his mind, he set out to take over the world per plans in his book.

The newspapers and radios aided the people to keep memories more precisely during the next approaching critical war. I not only had memories of the Second World War but also had an advantage of reading what had happened as an advent reader of the newspaper by the time I was six years old.

With an upheaval of revival of the National Socialist German Workers' Party (Nazi) that had been founded in 1919, it was now being led by Adolf Hitler as he blasted prominent manufacturing leaders with fright and disgust because of the loss of World War I and the nature of the surrender. It was obvious to prominent and astute Englishmen in the parliament who knew the historic pursuit of the German emperor Kaiser Wilhelm II during World War I. When Adolf Hitler gathered his support from rich and strongly powerful leaders, he began secretly amassing a new team of pseudo-soldiers who fought against Jews while building a dominating Aryan race. Hitler also started to build massive military fighting equipment when he was elected chancellor by the demanding manufacturing leaders.

Within a short time, Hitler began attacking Poland, Norway, and Holland, and when occupied, everything changed, including dissolving England's old leadership to setup new leadership of Great Britain by electing Winston Churchill, a well-known and knowledgeable fighting soldier since he was a young lieutenant in India and later had advanced to parliament.

The old prevailing leaders turned their disgust and definitively intellectual distaste thinking that England would not get enwrapped in war again with Germany. They felt Hitler's war would be against little countries in Europe. However, after Churchill took office as prime minister and called President Roosevelt, the two countries again formed allies. United States started with supplying military equipment to Great Britain via merchant ships and quickly prepared our country to build troops and equipment to head to Europe, making the first station area in England.

Then the Second World War in Europe began to affect United States desperately in late 1938 because German submarines were actively attacking American merchant ships heading to England. The government and high-level enlisted military leaders quietly held the reporting as they supplied merchant ships with classified routings to make sure shipping supplies reached England.

President Roosevelt and his cabinet had moved significantly earlier to begin a strong patriotic pursuit by letting people know what was going on in Europe. Hitler's invasions of small European countries fortunately forced militia to comprehensively prepare to combat invading Germans. The United States attention peaked upon actions of Great Britain's parliamentarian change of Prime Minister Lord Neville Chamberlain to new leadership by Sir Winston Churchill, who had been critically watching growth of Adolf Hitler's military takeovers of several countries in Europe starting in 1938.

The radios and Movietonews began to expand filming news and reporting it in local theaters as added short subjects. Reporters and American journalists like Walter Winchell, with his eloquence and command of accounting activities of the war, cause people to know details of war throughout small countries and it bolstered our country's patriotism. Discussions by other journalists and newspaper companies led to daily continuous conversations over news radios, and what had happened was that a tremendous enlistment and draft was under way when America declared war on Germany and Japan.

The same pursuit was seriously prompted by British prime minister Winston Churchill and parliament that continuously requested America to send defensive military equipment and machinery to Great Britain from beginnings of the war and in anticipation of a world war. Shipments were set to sea in American merchant ships. Germans U-boats attacked American merchant ships with great intensity and satisfaction. Fear was roaring from east and west, and intensities of war were unknown in Europe; and even more, Japanese were fighting in the far east into China and Manchuria. The Japanese sneakily tried to trick America while planning the fighting. Then within a day or two of the weekend, the Japanese carried out an attack on Sunday morning on Pearl Harbor in Honolulu, Hawaii, at 7:00 a.m., with great force from their air force and sinking many United States warships. Overall killing included about 2,500 soldiers and innocent Hawaiian citizens all unsuspected of any attack. All these informative releases were commonly discussed among neighbors and businessmen and working women and women running their homes.

This attack on American possessions changed European people's weak-knee involvement now that the Japanese attack became a world-shaking personal affront. The pursuit by dominant powers in Europe tried to work appeasement without emphasizing a coming path of destruction or knowing how to demand peaceful coexistence within borderline nations.

As situations turned, they involved early expressions with new force by European leaders of disbelief with commitment to win at all efforts. It was so obvious with Hitler's pursuit after being amassed militaristic leaders critically interested in taking over the country and gaining overall control in Europe. The election implemented Nazi fascistic programs called National Socialism. His total power as a dictator was revealed within months, and World War II was dominated by Hitler in Germany from 1933 with the war full time starting in 1941.

This second attempt of world dominance by Germany with a critical eye was a revelation of his critical fatidic internal attacks on the Jewish people even to unexpected ordinary street assaults by the Stasi police beating some Jewish people to death and with no remorse or condemnation. The attacks on Jewish people were a foreboding paranoia of disastrous things to come and that Adolf Hitler had not only become chancellor but also led mass murderers of people of unchallengeable proportions. He was dead set on fighting for world dominance as well as total elimination of Jewish people.

America was alarmed at an increasing toll of people and with so many Jewish people wanting to immigrate and were accommodated because many had proper credentials so beneficial to America and England's military planning and pursuits. Along with strife in the world, from 1933 to 1938, even killing Jews were first attacks. America continued and increased immigrations through sending needed supplies by merchant ships and gathering certain people, especially Jews, with returning ships.

All people of years from young adults to midfifties at this time in many nations with valued "knowledge and experience" and even college-wise were already aware of what war meant, especially the Jews, whose lives were being valued less than nothing by Germans under Hitler. Hitler's leadership brownshirts were on the warpath wreaking human destruction with a solid intent to dominate the world; and as time passed, brownshirts even put fear of extravagant killings—that is, genocide killing—into minds of Jews.

The Jews of different classes in Europe thought threats of their elimination would stymie their leader Hitler's pursuit to dominate the world, but they were soon proven wrong. Germans, as though they never learned their lesson, fought against their fellowmen twenty years earlier. The German people were fully aware of hatred that their leaders and some people had sided with their distorted minds totally afflicted and wreaked havoc and death grossly. The end point in his pursuit of world domination was that Hitler wanted to eradicate all Jews so that Germanics would dominate as Aryan race Caucasian gentiles.

As killings of Jews in Germany continued after many years of war, what had never happened before was that millions of killings turned to total disaster called "the Holocaust." German leaders were responsible directly, and many were sentenced to death for savage brutal acts of mass destruction of people. These assaults covered even more horrendous acts and even larger total numbers of deaths throughout the world in Europe and the USSR during World War II of complete mass killing of soldiers.

As seen from a mature point of view, Hitler intends to control the world as a megalomaniac who envisioned an Aryan drive of German leaders to destroy and take over their country's enemies. Hitler's blind affliction being blamed on Jews. The coming Holocaust of unthinkable assaulting proportions with the intent of genocidal destruction was unthinkable to America and the allies as well. Genocidal destruction was practiced by previous leaders and had a long history in Africa, but to carry out the mass destruction in Europe was an unknown quantity.

During the time after the war, Frank had two other brothers, Eugene (Gene) and Edward (Eddie), and his only sister, Jane, born after Eddie. All of them were preteens. Jane, born after Eddie, was named after her grandmother Filippa, and in English, she was known formally as Phyllis Jane. Jane, however, was always called as Jane even before she knew her name was Phyllis Jane. However, Jane entailed her name for the continuation of her life because she insisted on being called Jane even to her own expectations from families and friends. The younger one, Bobby Jim, was born in 1943.

Within about four plus years, our troops and allies returned home with numerous warriors, the wounded and dead, some buried in different countries where they bravely died in battles. The honor of burial will never be forgotten every year, Armistice Day, on November 11, and on Memorial Day, on May 31. Our country from then to now had become the peaceable superpower. Because of our quick response, we suffered no or little significant people, property, and land destruction of America. The devastation of Pearl Harbor, with more than 2,500 members of America's military service forces and civilians who died at that site, was significant.

The regretful and saddened loss of our troops on foreign lands was devastating to our people and families, and their behavior showed the calamity. About 250,000 soldiers in total was a devastating loss of the brave men and women who had saved our world as we know it now. Our other protected islands were those islands in the Pacific Ocean islands including Marshall Island, Guam, and the Philippines. Battles on small islands like Iwo Jima and Okinawa and others became involved under critical fighting. Sometimes, the Japanese captured people living on the islands, resulting in torture beyond belief as instilled by the Japanese.

The Japanese, where the fighting was a continuous battle for life and death, had taken many as prisoners, and some were killed intentionally and unmercifully.

However, the leaders with the wisdom knew it was the beginning of a new era of peaceful coexistence, and intrigue scattered across the globe. One reason was that America had developed a weapon of mass destruction, the atom bomb of enormously heinous, even dishonorable mass destruction. After President Roosevelt's death in 1945, President Truman had truly explained with critical thinking not to use the atomic bomb to end the war with Japan. President Truman, with insisting demands, expressed critical pleadings for Japan to surrender with all means at hand. The Japanese had intentionally refused to surrender when America had requested, even dropping pamphlets, that defined the extent of the new atomic weapon beyond expectation of widespread damage and death and suffering to human beings as well as property devastation beyond all known means.

The first atom bomb was dropped on Hiroshima with no massive death and destruction with no surrender. The second bomb was dropped on Nagasaki, which showed continued destruction, and the Japanese leaders had come to their minds that the war's end is in their dying hands. The aftermaths were described under an enormous number of historical descriptions with expected responses of devastation under any set of conditions, and United States had explained details to the enemy. Many documents were from all human sources, some without taking consideration of the mourning cessation before all kinds of death and destruction will happen. The Japanese did not want to surrender and did not stop the warring until the second bomb was dropped.

After World War II, Dad and Mom had their last two children when personal excitement held a finesse of insistent happiness among our grown children and two new babies that shone a new path of life in the home with babies young enough after having added young Bobby Jim during the war.

Modern times now reveal new freedom after America and many other countries returned to a peaceable living. Our Divita family increased love of our parents and new progeny, while many other families moved in the same direction to mark *baby boomers* that had started during World War II. Renewed behavior enhanced our country's liveliness and reinstalled the pursuit of happiness. Our Divita family's three young children had a boom of delight that showed in their personality. The elder siblings did not experience anything but frightening behavior and despair during the war and were aware of death and destruction of people in the world.

Our pursuit was as stated, following taught *steerage* and *amour* as a continuation of developing minds in America. It was similar for new siblings, but their minds were at different mental settings. The elder ones had more respect for our parents but less fear of their teachings and compassionate directions. The trends of teaching more subdued methods were instilled simply by increased extended "knowledge and experience" of our parents. The teachings improved and led to enhanced individualism and realism. The personal people improvements showed even though they continued to teach *steerage* and *amour* the same way it was delivered with guidance daily.

However, as our mom and dad had said many times: "We have raised two families!" And elder siblings have said many times their raising was somewhat different from that of our raising in detail, but we got by with less fussing and more loving. Maybe it was more learning more! This time, Frank, Gene, Eddie, and Jane had our dad and mom giving us less "experience and knowledge" to levy *steerage* and *amour* from their minds into our minds because we also had gained some wisdom as a result of distresses during major world wars. The dose was continually levied by Mom and Dad into their younger siblings. They got by with more questions and requests, so maybe it was they learned more details about the *steerage* and *amour* teachings!

These three younger brothers relayed their thoughts and living practices as we inherited parts of it from Dad's interesting wit and humor. The system was almost undefinable in toto except that *steerage* and *amour* worked. And in their lives as adults, they extended help and loving associations as compadres and existed within all our minds even far beyond our places where we lived with *steerage* and *amour* as true love.

Some enemy's countries after World War II had accepted America's reconstruction help within their damaged country. Then afterward, countries became our nation's friends in ideologies and economic trade. Several Eastern European allied comrades who fought with America became our nation's antagonists certainly in ideologies such as Communism as professed by the Union of Soviet Socialists Republics and China. Their ideological behavior and actions were fully demonstrated as a coming potential adversary in newly formed United Nations and North American Treaty Organization (NATO). The continuation of NATO to date has helped people of the world to maintain mostly peaceful pursuits. Regardless of commitments, United Nations involved several continents to maintain peaceable ways. With time, potentially, several different countries in near 1950s had clandestinely and through traitors gained classified details of atomic bombs. The design secrets were deciphered shortly by Soviet scientists and, later, China scientists and then from other countries who had critical atomic warring weapons under way. This new assessment of our friendly nations and in anticipation of potential warring involvements became so much that Chinese Communists intended assault in South Korea via North Korea, that the Southeast Asia Treaty was why the United States of America became involved to protect, arm, and fight North Korea.

The strife and killings in Southeast Asia were in turmoil, and United States ended in war again and against a communistic leadership now fully surrounded by Asian and Soviet Communism.

After so many years of flags of stars displayed in country's windows, they were now forced again to go to war. American people wanted to know what was going on and how well were troops doing warring while fighting both military opponents and ordinary citizens in disguise.

American dads, moms, and sons and daughters were drafted to fight North Korea. America did not want to get involved in a new war. These involvements caused Communist North Korea to participate as associates in warring in other clandestine ways and wars. After several years, and much negotiating, peace was partially compromised to end the Korean War.

The America people, in its efforts of knowing difficulties, were also questioning miscellaneous wars and for what reasons by our leadership and difficulties that were rampant in discussions to gain a cease-fire. Then Communist Russia especially had agreed with America within assumed belief to practice détente (an easing, as of discord and disagreement between nations).

As bias, one of the Seven Wise Men of ancient Greece, so identified by Sir Francis Bacon, once said, "Love your friend as if he were to become your enemy, and your enemy as if he were to become your friend." Bacon further stated in "Advancement of Learning" [p. 96 of *The Story of Philosophy*], "Do not betray even to your friend too much of your real purposes and thoughts; in conversation ask questions oftener than you express opinions; and when you speak, offer data and information rather than beliefs and judgments."

This idea of détente started with Russians in the late 1940s and into the mid-'50s after the Korean War.

Before the Korean War, Frank was ready to make some important decisions. He knew that he wanted mostly to get married. Then within a short time, the war broke out in Korea, and he knew he was destined to be drafted.

What I'm saying here is that Frank always told me to ask questions when you want to get answers. This was the time I began to hear about his desires again to become a musician. Frank would grab my shoulder and say, "Ed, I know I wanted to pursue music. Of course, I also knew my father wanted me to become a doctor." Neither choice was a settled good or bad judgment.

Frank knew when it became his time to act on his desire that he could try to master studies of chemistry and biology to begin. He knew he would fall short of having the desired mentality and firm comprehension in his interests. And within his cognizance, he knew it would be beyond his developed and inherent capability of storing motivation for new scientific and technical knowledge to gain needed experience. He needed educational mental capabilities, talents to achieve directed goal related to health and welfare of the human body and mind; this complemented what he said, ". . . was not within his mind of desires."

Frank, in a quiet reserved way, assessed what he told me and must have collected a pursuit subconsciously from his mind and heart's spirit to believe that he was destined not to satisfy his father's grandest, highest-desired expectation. Along paths of cultural arts, Frank told me that he voiced his devoted intent with confidence and that he would need to cross his vocational stream to success by stepping on randomly spaced stones placed on the medical staff of life. His concern with stones may not be shown clearly or only slightly shown, and a potential of not being able to carry out difficult studies, failing was foremost on his mind. Frank told me that he devoted his time and might to satisfy his father and went into college to work on a premed curriculum and to see how he would come out. When he failed, he voiced, "I will have better understanding, and I must change my direction." Then while in a raging mountainous stream as a fish plowing ahead at breakaway strength and speed, he would be going at a slower rate than possible to achieve his desires. Frank had stopped the premed program when he reviewed his grades from the first year and they were poor. He said he wanted easiest stones sorted in his mind, step by step, to become a musician. With that choice in observation by my parents, their response was that he gained some wisdom from their teachings. Dad's answer was not just OK, but he answered with a resounding, "I knew you would be able to make your decision to study music."

Frank said, "I know you love music as I do, Dad, but when I listen and hear Caruso on the radio or one of George and Ira Gershwin's songs like, 'I'll Build a Stairway to Paradise . . .' on record, I know how much he has created in his mind. If I can handle the stress and strain to create music, my mind and spirit will only be held back by lack of study and achievement with help at the beginning. I may run into unknown musical details sometimes that I cannot overcome, but with others help, I can learn, as did George Gershwin, and he became even a grand classical musician."

I knew that the devotion must be as much as a worldly Jesuit priest expends to become successful as a preacher of Catholicism. The priest must appeal to common people and knowledgeable Catholics while voicing life's natural happenings more than enough to survive life's turmoil to generally understand involvements of natural mores.

Knowing there are even more complexities, Frank continued governing his personal power instead of religious power, and he spent inordinate amounts of time working on his music as intended.

Frank insisted to me that he knew in his mind that the initial requirements included not only talent but also innovation, but the lack of creativity is inconspicuously seldom contained in human beings. After all, God promised only "free will" to *Homo sapiens* more than a hundred thousand years ago to make their choices when created.

Here is what I thought when I studied philosophy of life. When discretionary thinking came to light, God had given "free will" to *Homo sapiens* in their mind with the complexity to make mentally determined choices with thoughts beyond survivability efforts. God also gave each of the human beings a capability to pursue a vocation and to expound specific and characteristic personal capabilities and personal mental demands within his mind.

Frank then continued his thoughts out loud for a few seconds and exclaimed to me, "I would have to earn money either as a virtuoso or, if not, as one especially being a good music teaching discipline." To do this, he continued, "I must be multifaceted—that is, I must study to be the complete musician with creativity as famous artists of the past. I would have responsibilities to do the same if I had mind power and had chosen to become a doctor."

Then Frank thought; as I surmised, he said with braggadocio, "If I go for music as a teacher, I would want to be recognized by virtuosos on a scale from the middle C to both ends, bass and treble, and in tempo and accent from keys top to bottom, always selecting scales of notice as one competes highly with newly composed music. That is, if I could publish classical or modern music with success with my creativity. The music I compose must be self-sufficient as a teacher in the field or be just as one Provençal lyrical troubadours of long past years like Sordello. But to fit the bill of an accomplished musician, which have infinite varieties and difficulties, would be enormously overbearing to become expert in musical compositions selected by self-direction that produces money along with fame."

Frank then, as I remembered, maybe coined something like, "My father is a man who would never admit failure. Dad accepted his promise knowing that his lifetime desire for his first son was always one to make a go of it under all negative conditions and peril. Even if this first weighted desire could come true under a surprised expectation. Dad, instead, taxed his mind's power and strengthened his body's endurance as if he were a freight train on a track as he devoted himself to his car business." Frank thought, *I am going to drive the same freight train that guides my mind. I may have to take a new track or a line of different tracking to my desired vocational pursuit.*

The next four years were more than Frank had expected after he graduated with a BA in music so that he could become a teacher. Frank knew that after his graduation from West Virginia Institute of Technology within a few months, he was totally smitten by the woman in his life; it was Betty Young, and she had also graduated as a nurse. Betty had studied nursing in our city college but at the Laird Memorial General Hospital. The two of them, endearingly satisfied, became engaged and looked forward to becoming one in their natural and spiritual endeavors.

They had been dating during his last year of college and Betty's last year of nursing school. They became very serious about getting married without much knowledge except that their growing love gave them a sense of devotion beyond expectations when sharing time together. They were experiencing happiness, and they expected to stay together for the rest of their lives.

Their marriage event happened with an average celebrated fanfare without any major expenses of significance. The family helped put it together as a special occasion to be remembered. The wedding was performed at the Immaculate Conception Catholic Church in the city of Montgomery. The celebration was within the home among families and friends.

After the marriage celebration, they left on their honeymoon and later returned. He was ready to work in his new career. Frank took a job as music teacher in a high school in the northern part of the state of West Virginia in Peterstown. After settling in the town with a nearby property, Betty set up the home in a rental apartment. Frank knew being a responsible man and getting a good job made it a good learning process for him and Betty. Things were going well until all hell broke loose.

Frank is essentially telling the rest of the story about his involvement with the military, to put it into his perceptive prose. Frank told me that he received an unexpected letter from the Draft Board Organization of the United States of America. Then he said the first thing he was forced to do was to answer a draft notice from the United States government saying his draft number was going to be listed. He needed to decide either to enlist in the air force or get drafted into the army. Without hesitation, he joined United States Air Force mostly with intent to stay out of the army. He knew the draft was a demand and a response had to be made. He knew he did not want to go into the army for any reason.

Frank knew he had to decide as to where Betty would live while he was in the air force. He planned that Betty, now pregnant with their first baby, was to go live with his mom and dad's family. Frank was going to be stationed in New York and could get leave after a while and would be able to see his family when on a furlough. Frank's duty in the air force after basic training was an assignment to be a member of the band for our air force company. So being in the band was certainly an assignment that could only help my future life as a music teacher.

For most soldiers in military bands when discharged, they might obtain jobs in orchestras or join local musical groups; however, only a few with a real musically instilled mental drive could become involved with orchestras. In a short run of the mill, his duty was accomplished after the Korean War had ended.

From what we were told, Frank was back to a new school to teach music, this time in a small town still in West Virginia where it looked like making money teaching band class was far from my grandiose sites in music. It took a while to resettle at a new high school, and this time, his job was closer to where my parents lived. This all occurred within little more than one year of scattered activities where he was strictly a band teacher and director so common as in every high school. The many who started first thinned down to those candidates chosen really with an ear, brain-mind control of sound deciphering and stamina dexterity with a superior capability to note mentally deciphered musical sounds. All this

Frank had learned related to timing and beat and usually made it into the fight to perfect his best, a complete piece of music, soundly in rote by repeating the play.

There was a time we had my only sister, Jane, who came as a visitor; however, she spent some time at our home, and she was very helpful with the family and the children. She gave Betty more stability and became a solid blessing, a boon to our new start with her association.

However, after a short year of high school teaching, he quashed his music teacher's pursuit, not because of competitive endurance but because of devotion to providing subsistence to help my mom and dad through rough times with their business that had evolved with times of economic despair in the early '50s.

Within a few years, we were back in my parents' home involved with adjusting to making accommodations for two-family living conditions and rearing one child and one on the way. Frank began looking at what could he do. Frank had told me that he knew, within a short time, he could really make some money to raise his family. It was easy because Dad needed help to run his business. Frank took the management position along with Dad and beefed up the business with some better Packard Company Cars as taxis that should draw new and old customers. Times got better, which was to our advantage, and his pursuits were better directed especially in our city where our name was well known.

Frank pondered his dad's business and family's problems, taking care of two children and in need for a job to earn money. Frank knew a better vocation had to be picked. It would have to require talents that I have within my being, trained by his father to first make sure he considered all options. He did, and it looked like at this time having been trained about the details of cars and considered himself a craftsman first, knowing his elder boys were taught by Dad to do account management work for his business, his bookkeeping, and technical things as I grew into manhood. The next step could be another right move.

Frank knew his mind had ceased to point to musically gratifying cultural arts direction. As a starter, Frank devotedly became interested in Dad's automobile business. At this time, with growing economy from a making-money standpoint, all aspects of car designs, performance, and making sure they ran as new designs are offered, the business is going to be stepping up in the future. This feeling of a total pursuit extended his ability to buy and sell cars as a business. He gained this fever when he was given jobs in his father's garage business partially years ago. Now, to really help, Frank, with a lofty business acumen, asked to help his dad, who was experiencing hard times but not failure. Frank's pursuit was to help keep Mom and Dad's family, who were still caring for their three adult children, especially because boys were considered mentality smart as students with a *steerage* impact inherited from all influencing relatives little by little over years. For a while, his eldest brother, Bob, worked with him at the taxi and moving business. After we restructured the taxi business, Frank became manager.

Well into the 1960s, the three elder ones Gene, Eddie, and Jane, had gone into fields of medicine, science, and literature. The three younger brothers, Bobby, Phil, and Richard, were getting their degrees in art, accounting, and finance. Things changed considerably in that time, and with the help of his brothers, Frank moved into a new business with Dad's friend's help. We also started to build a new home after the new business venture to be with an old dealership was settled. Highlights of their lives will be placed in family order interacting in new business with expectations and family support that amalgamated his siblings at major meeting times both at the family home and their individual homes.

Gene's children were born in Houston, Texas. Ed and family visited them in 1971 at their early age and saw the magic of their grand personalities in Gene and Peggy's girls and boys. They were raised the same as were Frank and my children. The girls had copious conversant things to talk about, and we enjoyed the stay, unforgettable, remembering their astute knowledge and experiences while expressing their good looks like young Italian Americans.

Within time, the new car business was successful enough to give the public some notice of his business acumen. With Dad's help, he became a friend of a man my senior by ten years who was the son of a good friend of my father. This man was also running a successful automobile dealership with his father, who had retired recently. Within a couple of years and because our dad had full control of his business, Frank was asked to join Montgomery Motors dealership through his dad's close friend. The sweet offer included a contractually agreed promise of a partial share of 20 percent of the company in three years provided the business could be doubled in that time. The company, along with his salesmanship and success in the garage, satisfied customers.

The business became more successful, and partnerships were put into effect with more than a doubling of the business. The time of an increase of the business was caused by the increase in the economy and because of good times in the '70s for new car sales. Times were changing in the country because a new pursuit was initiated. After few years, the business partnership rapport easily showed a significant public notice and increased breadth of clients, and the company made money. This was to Frank's advantage, and after five years, Frank bought the company from his partner because he wanted to retire for health reasons.

Frank became the man around town who had many friends who wanted to move my popularity to include a long-term strong involvement in local politics at various meetings. Close friends are now more influential and politically powerful in the city—that is, other business owners who had been successful for many years joined his interest in city politics. Frank's first run was a win of a position in the city council in the mid-1960s. The city council had observed his father over the years and heard and watched him wheel and deal with the local politicians for the people. Frank was able to fit the bill as an expert on knowing how to offer solutions to solve dominant social problems and worked to improve the city social structure, operations, and infrastructure. He voiced these ideas effectively and after a few years.

Then next time for the mayoral election, Frank was impressively elected mayor of the city of Montgomery. Within a short time, during the upcoming national election year, Frank became recognized as a statewide political force in our locally populated hub area that surrounded Fayette County and extended being known at the capitol building of Charleston in Kanawha Country. His job as mayor was primarily influenced by coal mining complements, metals and large equipment industries in two counties along the Kanawha River that goes from the eastern end of the New River and eventually ended at the western end, on into the Ohio River.

Frank told me that he knew he had the force of the county and city's influential and congenial friends, and people he knew cared about our town and state. These people included those mainly who had agreed with my political ideology, which was a majority. From curses of the day from his adversaries, he knew he could be elected and was destined for the next two terms. Nevertheless, he was not without excuses and penned one highlight, over adventuresome silence if not diligence, on wondering eyes that friends treated me with humor about attractive women's comments because of his inherited good looks and personality.

Mainly because of the one and only case that had been rumored by an untrustworthy woman who felt scorned but was unknown to others. All he could do was refute this accusation because a great deal of mental distress had reached my home and disrupted our compatible family life completely. He recognized his celebrity, and his job was no longer a job; it was his pride to extend his business. Frank grossed enough net profit, more than an adequate payday; making more money may have become his main pursuit. Frank never thought the more friends he acquired, the more money he made, would inundate him with gossip of a moral debasement of instinctive behavior as opposed to the grand level of his *steerage* he had gained from his family over the many years.

The happening might lead me to a practice of "will of desire," but Frank had embedded his mind with even more "knowledge and experience" because of his citywide position. Frank guarded himself from many chances of *amour*, and it was not only in his mind but also sometimes with critical effort to hold his sanity.

He continued to control the numerous personal and business involvements almost on a weekly basis at the business and continued to revamp and improve the looks of the company. As he told me, sometimes, he thought he was being pursued by women who were attracted to him and those whom he thought were even more attractive sensuously for sure. Then these attractions, which looked like a consideration, plagued his broadened life among the relationships of public exposure.

All the while Frank had reached his position of mayor, Gene and Ed had already pursued their higher educational pursuits in the 1950s. Gene had completed his premed at the same local college known as West Virginia Institute of Technology (WVIT) because, fortunately, it was inexpensive but with a great curriculum. He then had finished part of his time being accepted to medical school at West Virginia University. It was no surprise to our mom and dad, both on cloud nine that Gene's persona was a student at the medical school in Richmond, Virginia, finishing his last year. Gene had great grades and graduated in 1957.

Within time, Gene and his steady girlfriend, a nurse-in-training full of fun known as Peggy, had planned to get married, and the whole family attended the church wedding in Richmond. Afterward, they left on their honeymoon and then traveled to Houston, Texas, where Gene selected to do his internship at Baylor University. As time passed, Gene and his absorption of *steerage* and *amour* stretched beautifully to his patients and groups, giving them exceptional confidence as exclaimed by his major pursuits that followed as a medical doctor into psychiatry about three years later.

During that same college educational desired striving time for Ed, he followed Gene into WVIT after graduating from high school two years later than Gene. It was a given compatibility because Ed had spent one year with Gene in WVIT where they gained more appreciation of each other as full-on adults working together in college. They both continued to work to make money at theaters in Montgomery and to continue to help the family.

Ed, as a real thinker, with talents and creativity, completed his complicated engineering courses while continuously making friends at WVIT and meeting new student from other states and cities and those being friends from our hometown like forever. All the while, Ed was a participant in the student union and joined the Sigma Tau Alpha fraternity. His selection of subject work was a bit unusual being enough to get minors in chemistry and mechanical and electrical engineering, while learning about physics of the blossoming nuclear research and engineering work being taught by one of the professors having worked on the Manhattan Project. Ed earned his BS degree in engineering physics in four years. After several resumes being accepted, one by General Electric Reactor Company and another by Lockheed Aircraft Company, he accepted the offer at the Glen L. Martin Company in Baltimore, Maryland. Ed worked for Martin-Marietta for almost ten years and then was asked to join the Jet Propulsion Laboratory in Pasadena, California.

Following Ed as the fourth member of the first part of Benny and Jo's children, Jane was the last for a while but not the least of the educational achievers. She successfully graduated from WVIT with a BS degree in English literature and then moved on to Northwestern University to get her master's degree and teach to earn money. Subsequently, Jane earned a PhD in English literature from Michigan State University. Later, she married Robert Woody, and both pursued a move to work toward professorship careers. Both settled at the University of

Nebraska at Omaha as professors in their early years, beginning in 1975 with top-notch acceptations and positions in psychology and literature and eventually teaching clinical psychology.

During these later times, these four earlier siblings made sure they visited each other and Mom and Dad and the three younger brothers while they still lived in Montgomery continuously, and even when they moved to other cities and the families were in other states.

Our last three brothers did eventually become professional workers and raise families of some renown in the late '60s and thereafter. Sister Jane and her husband, Bob Woody, were prolific in teaching different college subjects at the University of Nebraska. They also wrote technical articles and were editors of books about psychology and added their critical subjects that were published and were editors and writers of published books. They each continued the value of their choices for life after commingling with their family, at times somewhat later where many Divitas attended yearly Divita family reunions.

As time passed, Gene and his absorption of teaching *steerage* and *amour* to his children exclaimed successful schooling in major pursuits that followed. Gene had stepped up his studies to become a doctor of psychiatry. Their exciting lives' ventures with family life and among business and social activities will be expounded later showing total influence that *steerage* and *amour* had extended influences throughout their lives.

Their exciting lives' ventures with family life and among business and social activities will release a show of influences that *steerage* and *amour* had extended behavior patterns levied in their minds throughout their lives. Gene's family confronted each other much later with individual personal problems that he was able to resolve with his expert advice, which was always taken as the right path. Gene would relate understandings of circumstances and did eventually manage good times as adults. As time passed, three sons and four daughters had married and became separated from their parents. Much later after, Gene and Peggy separated. They maintained in lonely situations and then parted. Gene and Peggy had been married for a long time. Then Gene, after a year or two, mentally lived alone and was lost and with lonely pursuits while working as a doctor. His elder children shied from him because they did not know the details of their mom and dad's divorce.

Gene later began making socially involved meetings with a woman who was a practicing psychotherapist. He had met her later while at his psychiatry office and seeing her doing psychotherapy with a patient. Much later, after dating several times, both decided that they wanted to get married. They communicated the intent for whoever wanted to be at the marriage and then added social visits with primary family members. For the most part, they accepted and enjoyed the family members and their new lives. Both Gene and Kathleen, as a psychotherapist, worked in medical fields related to maintaining healthy minds.

Peggy had left Gene and chose to be on her own until she later married again. Her second marriage was unknown to extended families and mostly was not disclosed by their siblings; however, she did maintain a relationship with her mother-in-law Josephine that allowed her to keep other Divita families and close relatives in touch with the well-being of both Peggy and Gene.

The relationships of the other five children, Ed with Patricia, Jane with Bob Woody, brother Bob with Arlene, Philip with Mona, and Richard with Nancy, were steady marriages and continued their ways toward pursuits of happiness. The Divita family always maintained associations with all members of the Divita family and were more than compatible and related by thoughtful true love with continuous visits.

CHAPTER II

New American Heritage—Values
Steerage and Amour from Divita
Family to Families of Millennials

*The triumph, of mind and will over illness and a thousand
obstacles, is one of the strong spots in the book of man.*
—The Story of Philosophy, Will Durant, p. 274

*Drama is a form of memorable truth and folklore—not just
entertainment. However, lies, hearsay, and allegations cause
disastrous situations, and, with many cases, the pursuit of happiness
never opens the door of well-being and happiness thereafter.*

Italian heritage has renovated new American heritage into *steerage* and
amour values carried over the years in a manner that our grandfather Francesco
and grandmother Filippa birthed their second group of siblings in America. The
four children immigrated with their mother Filippa, who were born and raised
in Sicily. These Italian children gained American citizenship with their mother
at Ellis Island and became first-generation Italian Americans in 1913. Then later,
living in America, Big Poppy Francesco and Big Mommy Filippa had born six
other children and raised their American-born children as natural Americans.

The new American births of the four siblings of Big Poppy and Filippa were
their three sons, Francisco, Charles, and James, and a daughter Katie. During
this same time, two other siblings, both girls, died during childhood, as did many
children during times of diseases in the 1920s and 1930s.

Big Poppy's four elder children who were born in Sicily as the three emigrant
sons and one young daughter, much later, were either married or had become
American citizens starting in the late '20s. Later after their marriage, Big Benny
and Josephine made sure their children were born in America. They made sure
their progeny were to be the same as the people as citizens of America. I am sure

that they, Liborio, Antonio, Giuseppe, and Maria, took on the same positions as Benny (previously named Liborio as the eldest son of his father Francesco and after his grandfather Liborio) and Josephine, who named their eldest son Francisco.

The teachings of *steerage* and *amour* were a continuation of the Italian method of teaching children to be of prime quality in each mind of four immigrants that traveled with their mommy from Sicily and had already started to gained natural "knowledge and experience" from Big Mommy, who especially implied that as new parents, Benny and Josephine, Tony and Catherine, Mary and Little Benny, uncle to Big Poppy, and Joe and Maxine later would follow the same teaching pursuits for their American-born siblings.

Benny and Jo's next three younger siblings' births started in 1943 as baby boomers, adding three more grandchildren, and by this time, the World War II was well under way. Within bounds, these children held on to sensitivities that demanded each would be taught *steerage* and *amour* to ensure good minds, proper care, and security. The significance was the way they pursued their lives, which was the same as the elder siblings.

As memories were revealed by their dads and moms about good times that dominated, with some snares and other traps left set for them to work, each sibling evolved and influenced their future lives in ways expected that were critically influenced by their fathers and mothers. In my mind's memory, they were as close in personalities as the four elder ones were brought up. The elder ones knew their moral and natural weaknesses and expanded their personality characteristics as they became older. My Divita family insisted on expanding our wisdom by using *steerage* and *amour* that would signal "knowledge and experience" more often than "will of desire." My mom and dad did not leave us short on the use of our minds' determination when problems arose. The continuation then changed, and maybe lives of younger ones had better family associations. The main point is they did not have the same behavior involvement with Grandfather Francesco as living children companions as did Frank, Gene, and Ed.

With a slow pace, Frank now moved toward the steps in his thought line that included a change from his business to include involvements with his children's independence that was saddled sometimes with poor judgment. He had less work time on his mind, no matter what diversion; he worked the next problem at work and at home. He told me that he recalled his best time of the day being around the kids in their early years. Even though it was short, it was having his kids in his lap and giving him their demands trying to force him into buying them things he never even knew would be on their mind. For example, especially his girls, who want to have earrings at eight or ten years old. The thought quickly disappeared as if he saw an image of his life as a kid who didn't have the nerve to ask or demand something from his parents, even a new pair of shoes, even when the soles were flip-flopping.

Their pursuit was one of keeping a positive mind working toward building happiness and being self-sufficient. In concert, my siblings grasped same pursuits of mental reactions to the nature of instilled Divita heritages and demanded that compatibility flowed toward human happiness for a lifetime regardless of problems with either moments of depression or anxiety as faced by all human beings as life is lived while striving for pursuits of happiness.

Frank's son Fran left with his second family when he was newly hired by a car dealership company in Erlanger, Ohio. At last, one thing that Fran told me at the last Divita reunion was that he still carried his dream to build a race car someday. I have no direct knowledge of any reaction to the world of dreams that he might gain except that he needed money to help him realize his dream, and his dad may help lead him to build a race car and compete in professional sports car races internationally.

The love of interests turns almost immediately into a constant family involvement. After settling in, Fran and his wife Dawn knew later, after many evening discussions over dinner, that both are convinced that Fran and his wife Dawn, the mother, both had devoted their lives to concentrate on raising their children on *steerage* and *amour*. Dawn has convinced him that he's the man that she has been waiting for her all his life. Fran's front-end genius ideas were detailed big time even though he was inventive and had his share of innovation and certainly was blessed with an adequate amount of creativity. All he needs is a position to extract his inventive genius into the industry, which is a large demand while taking care of his family. The admirations were exemplary as well for Fran, Dawn, and their children.

Unsuspecting, his brother Jimmy had left his father Frank's dealership after getting his degree from college, and he planned to become a builder of homes. During that time, he had let a precious chance of true *amour* come into his life with his girlfriend Penny. Being conservatively savvy, he had wooed her seriously without challenge so that the love in her heart would win her over. They both pursued different vocations as togetherness remained. After a while, they married, and the agreement was double edged at best and potentially provided Jimmy with Penny, who had just become a doctor, with a critical pursuit of the two of them as they raised their children, Jennifer, Jillian, and Jordan. All I know is that three girls were the pride of the family as beautiful daughters and were closely admired at yearly Divita reunions with references that they wanted to become doctors.

These compliments also are part of our memories of Frank and Betty, their sons, and their girls. The girls, Beverly, Cheryl, and Janie, who also were married now to Joe, Allan, and Bill, respectively, selected well-known, well-educated, and good husbands professionally involved with geology, education, and business investments that allowed them as much freedom as needed to raise their families. Each of the girls had their families. Beverly has one boy, JT, who is now a married man and following the way of life taught to him from childhood. Cheryl has Allan

Jr. and Emily Beth, both highly educated; Allan as a lawyer and Emily as a PhD chemical engineer. Janie and Bill have twin daughters, Emma Jane and Emily Ann. They are both college educated and are pursuing the sports field while still young.

Frank and Betty's girls all succeeded in pursuing different vocations. Beverly was educated with a degree in management and administrative business. Cheryl was educated earning a PhD in the teaching supervision and management. Janie followed her father's pursuit as she continued to work in the car dealership business in Virginia. We did at times see more of the girls because they had visited us several times with their children, or we visited them as a desire of interest to get to know them better as the families grew.

We did not know much about their details of living and had a great rapport with all of Frank and Betty's children. The details are assumed that they have recorded their ways along lines that were offered by their heritage from Big Benny and Jo, and Frank and Betty, and also to those within the family who had passed away in the Francesco and Filippa Divita family and extended families of renown but grandly had taught their kids with compassion as the Italian ways of life.

The words of insistence were, namely, use your mind seeking "knowledge and experience" before jumping at a chance to follow the instant instinctive ways of a first offer, which is "will of desire" as inferred within this story about "Steerage and Amour!—What's It All About!" to show that each strived using their real mind's decree.

The same extractions were taken from my mind as they related to the love and understanding of Gene and Peggy's children, Eva, Regina, Charles, Elaine, Vincent, Marie, and Marshall. And still following the same teachings that were taught to Jane and Bob's children, Jennifer, Bob III, and Matthew. Many Divitas were successfully educated in colleges and continued to pursue their endeavors and challenges to achieve careers a teacher and a professor and savor a scholarly life, except Matthew, who wanted to enter the business world and is currently manager of a major restaurant business and planned his next step to achieve a position in state and eventually national government.

The main thrust of knowledge came about, although we all were separated by many miles during times they grew to adulthood and were even less observed in those later times as they passed more because of our difficulties to travel and maybe somewhat because of interests to travel or being able to travel because of their controlled working modes. We did meet at times with Gene and Frank and their wives, even many times personally and at the Divita reunions. At occasions, there were times their children were not with them. We mostly met with Frank, Betty, and family because it was at their home.

Pat and I traveled to West Virginia to see my parents a few times after moving to California. One time, we met with Frank and Betty, who had traveled to California to be with us. As an adventure, we drove to Las Vegas with them to be at a General Motors Convention to show off their new cars. At that time, they had Fran with them. And then later, Gene and Peggy had traveled on the same trip another time with Frank and Betty. We had also visited Gene and Peggy and the family in Houston one time as a family at a time when our kids and theirs were at compatible ages, and it was a fun time for all. And by chance, I did visit with them several times when I had to traveled to Houston on JPL business.

Pat and I have enjoyed our lives both when our children were young and happy, and loved the times of our lives on vacations and every venture and good times to celebrate. After Joanne was married and settled down, she lost her first husband in a motorcycle accident. A few years later, Joanne married Jeff, and they have thrived in their lifetime both with his building business, and then, second, the two of them bought a full-fledge ranch and farm that has been successful for many years.

Edward Jr. and Julie were married about a year later after he had completed his BS degree in architectural engineering, and Julie had gotten her bachelor of arts degree in agriculture. Ed started work in Hawaii with a large building company and was making great success with his work in a large building company.

The saddest part of our life at this time was that our daughter Catherine Marie Divita was accidently killed in a car accident while, after leaving work on her own, driving from work in the early evening. It happened without knowledge when she apparently hit an animal on the road and slid into the oncoming lane that pushed her sideways into a ditch, and she was killed instantly. The remorse was intensely devastating to Pat and me with the heartbreaking loss of our youngest daughter, which sent us in despair and a change of life, more feeling the importance of our lives and the Divita family's lives, which some of them had also received when the bell tolls for the dead.

Within a short time, Ed and Julie married and had their children. Our children were descriptively admired when they visited our family, and we visited them many times form their childhood to their teenage years and thereafter, keeping track of Ed and Julie's family. Our children's love was always expressed to our grandparents, my dad Benny, and mom Jo.

After some time, Ed had decided to go back to school to earn a master's degree in construction management. Ed had achieved considerably in his endeavor and was offered to stay at the University of Florida. Instead, he had other plans. Ed and Julie then moved the family back to California and later was given a full scholarship to Stanford and decided to earn a PhD in computer technology for building construction. Ed's final pursuit was followed by two attendees in the building business, and while there, they heard him present one of his demographics working problems that he had had mathematically modeled and written with his computer and showed the results. After, the new presentation was recognized with a good applause when it was responded by listeners.

The CEO Michael gathered with Ed and said, "Would you be interested in working for my company as a partner?" From that time on, Ed has been a successful partner of the Discovery Land Company as a developer and builder of country clubs, golf courses, and new homes surrounding the complexes.

We have met with Jane and Bob a few times in California and their son Matthew several times as he visited us with his wife Tonja after they were married. They had visited to just get acquainted and later came for family compatibility event at the Divita reunions. They now live in the county of Los Angeles and at nearby Pomona where Matthew, while in the restaurant business, also ran for his first time in 2017 to see if he might become a member of the Congress of the United States of America. I think that Matthew might eventually campaign for a position in the House of Representatives next time when the voters in his district gather more information about his stature in business and his committed action in his life. We did see Jane and Bob when they were on business trips or at business and education functions in the Los Angeles and Santa Barbara areas and enjoyed the personal conversations and friendliness so embedded with family. We never traveled to Omaha, Nebraska. We had seen their children once in Baltimore when their first two children were young. We did see Jane and Bob at my dad and mother's home with the family at previous times.

All Divita families, from what I sensed, felt they must either resolve problems with exemplary conduct or follow a new path to resolve their ailments or live with angst. What we do know is that instilled learning, personally taught and inherited, provided more room to clearly resolve any type of living concerned with a grasp of choice ways to pull toward a pursuit of happiness.

The words of insistence, as I have said before to maintain Divita families, were to be true to each other—namely, use your mind before jumping at a chance of instant instinctive ways as a first offer of "will of desire" as inferred within this story of *Steerage and Amour!—What's It All About!*

Each of us were thinking and using the real mind's decree that last taught *steerage* and true *amour* to each of us by our fathers and mothers and the self-imposed heritage that our sons and daughters received to follow and to gain life's ways to successfully follow allegiances of the Constitution of the United States of America, savoring *life, liberty,* and the *pursuit of happiness.*

Of course, the *pursuit of happiness* may not be achieved by humans always; however, it increases decisions using one's mind as taught by personal teachers, mostly families that induced mentally *steerage* and *amour* by simply thinking with the "knowledge and experience."

That is this story's pursuit. Human beings should follow true love throughout their lives to learn how one might gain from mindful sources of determinations recognizing the need for kinetic modifications in personal behavior. The separation of the mind's choice is between affaire d'amour (a love affair) and affaire de coeur (affair of the heart).

The main problem is to store the understandings in one's mind's memory and use it to track life in a self-sufficient way and to be predominantly concerned with the right thing to do while pursuing or seeking *happiness*. This approach means staying away from the mentality of the mind's life's behavioral spectrum that could lead to mental health diseases of extremes of depression or anxiety. Follow this pursuit of *steerage* and *amour*—that is, *affaire de coeur (affair of the heart)* that brings *happiness* to modern-day *Homo sapiens* to celebrate life following the pursuit of happiness.

Without a doubt, there is emphasis that the younger ones were being put on the spot by longtime interactions with Mom and Dad because they were wiser and still in the prime of their lives and healthy enough to do their best as in the past, but still were decisive with understanding "knowledge and experience." The elder children might have gotten more than they needed sometimes because values of their teachings stayed in their minds to resolve values between "knowledge and experience" and the instinctively forced first thought of "will of desire." Having known our younger siblings and eventually that elder siblings were involved with them in many situations and incidences displayed complete compatibility.

The first of our younger brothers, Robert, was educated, as were the other two brothers Philip and Richard significantly, and has had several knowledgeable vocational pursuits. The dominating one, Bobby, wanted to become an artist, and, eventually, he became a teaching artist at a private art school. This happened as Dad had told him, "Do something in which you can make money and do your art at home and when you can get paid for your creativity."

The other two boys took a different pursuit while going to school and had earned degrees in engineering and accounting. They earned money to make these vocations achievable while they worked for their brother Frank while in college. Both told their dad Big Benny they were going into the finance and building businesses. Knowing my dad, that was his own values enhanced. When ready, they both finished college and gained graduate degrees. Phil became a financial engineer started as a builder for a while and then worked for the West Virginia State Police as a department head for their finances. Richard became a certified public accountant and was the parts department head for a major car dealership in Charleston.

The second progeny of the same family of Benny and Jo years later produced three children notably proud of their behavior. The next step of their progeny was started with Robert (Bobbie) James Divita when he was born in 1943 during the peak of World War II. Bobbie's life grew with the family along with special care during all the turmoil of the war even though America was not attacked on our land. However, everyone in America had their mind-set that was unfurled with expanded concern about families whose sons and daughters were fighting in Europe as American soldiers. Much later after the war, Bob and Arlene were married and, later, had their son Brian, who now was formally educated with a

PhD in business administration. Brian was married but later divorced with two children, and his career continued as an active college professor.

Next birth was Philip Ray Divita born in 1946, and his time was after World War II ended, leaving him in a different growing pattern of behavior, although the teachings of *steerage* and *amour* continued the same way as always with compassion and understanding. Phil did his schooling in the same fashion as his brother Bobbie, who also helped Richard jointly with all three boys to enjoy school during their growing time as younger boys. They did the same things that their three elder brothers had done, always studying and playing sports. Phil was the one that played sports in high school and was considered a strong and smart quarterback. All of us boys were good in sports, but I think Phil wanted to do it from his mind and heart. The three boys also worked part time to help the family at home and with family businesses with the same excitement and gain that added their good, and each has remained with their pursuit of happiness. Much later, Phil and Mona were married and, a little later, had two children. The eldest is Susan, who is now married and has raised four children. Susan earned a bachelor of arts degree in teaching and is now a principle administrator in the Kanawha County Education System. Phil and Mona's daughter, Anne, also became a teacher and is married with two children striving to continue to educate her children with a college education.

Richard and Nancy, the last and youngest of the second family of Benny and Jo's children, were finally married in the early 1970s. They have raised each of their girls, Treasa and Marie, with good friendship and understanding the teachings of *steerage* and *amour* to their advantage. The result was that after their marriages, both had met and married good-natured men who loved being in the Divita family fully. As time progressed, both girls, Treasa and Marie, finished college and earned professional degrees in medical fields, one in hearing evaluation technology and the other teaching speech therapy within the school administration, adding even more by helping people gain significant advantages in communication, and they did it with love of their work.

These younger families inherited and adopted teachings of *steerage* and *amour* from their elder siblings and from their teachers, both grandmothers and grandfathers and their moms and dads. All of Benny and Jo's children followed teachings of *steerage* and *amour* that made their siblings recognize the values of making good decisions. The mind's pursuits gained a heritage of making good decisions. What was obvious to me was the younger families adopted the same path of a simple loving life with compassion and accepted familial responsibility primarily so that their families enjoyed pursuits of happiness.

CHAPTER III

Steerage and Amour in Past Generations

I deduced from our next philosophers that God can overwhelm mankind
with disasters, take health and wealth away, but man keeps his privacy.
—*The Resurrection* by William Butler Yates, p. 589 in
1000 Years of Irish Prose, Part I, The Literary Revival, edited
with an introduction by Vivian Mercier and David H.
Greene, New York, the Devin-Adair Company, 1952

Steerage and Amour!—What's It All About! has been purposefully mentally devised within my mind that it evolved from heritage and developed in minds of *Homo sapiens* so modern mankind would use their critical capabilities to improve and to resolve human confrontations in philosophical ways, using wisdom, which continues to maintain living in pursuit of happiness.

When properly inherited and then taught, *steerage* and *amour* gained extended memory as always expecting to respond to an interaction from one's mind with a first response instinctive decision via the "will of desire." The mind's first step should be used only to make sure one survives. A second comparable immediate mind's response released quickly with the proper decision. Then within an infinitesimal strike, the decisive mind will fully react and make the next mental impulse with understanding to continue to resolve the mind's response via "knowledge and experience" instantly. In the past, people made a *steerage* and *amour* decision with hardly any personal family teachings about differences of *amour* or thinking about expected result. Eventually, as eons passed, methods of understanding numerous personal mind transactions was to first sense a warning that allows one to eliminate problems of illicit *amour*; when that occurred, some people would take a second thought to prevent it from happening even though instinctive thought was hardwired in the past from the beginning of *Homo sapiens*.

Interactions are critical starting points among individuals of all ages after adulthood, but memory has the mind's strength and capability even before one's teens, and it may be introduced to four- and five-year-old siblings when they comprehend by responding to actions such as when touching something that is known to be burning hot. The exposures are numerous, and in words, multifaceted explanations abound. Both informally and formally educated persons with normally sound minds and capabilities are designed to render primal decisions involving sensuous emotions based on "experience and knowledge" instead. However, more often, the bulk of people face a quick instinctive decision by the "will of desire."

The main thrust of the story's expositions covers commonality in minds that deviate from loyalty to gain illicit pleasures of sensuous desires leading to a calamitous aftermath. The detailed experiences of *amour* are commonly pursued by members of the Italian Divita family descendants who track their mind's reactions based on having been taught not to repeat mindless instincts that have continued throughout mankind's existence.

A tracing of widespread nature of sensuous behavior in the past with poor choices caused people of major reputations, both famous and infamous, to suffer aftermaths. Some of these people typically reveal and disclose behavior of all sorts of compromises that fall under reasons made clear to mankind. People easily know more natural and proper ways to respond, but, generally, they do not arise and may be left on the back burner.

This story takes advantage knowing details of Divita family's working minds. They initially want to satisfy their sensuous desires; but instead, they also want to help by knowing *steerage* taught values before following pursuits of *amour's* "will of desire" that selects immediately. It may occur properly when one decides that the first instinct is wrong because many options and interpretations are written on stone in mankind's mind for access to related disastrous aftermaths. Past leaders have recalled specifically with extended characterization in the book *The Man of the Renaissance*, by Ralph Roeder, that most aspects of proper decision-making from the mind were slow to meet the masses even with the new First Renaissance advancements in morality sensed by geniuses.

Ralph Roeder examined his book written about the "the men of the First Renaissance" about the nature of their times and then related it to the natural behavior and slowness of effects of *steerage* having so many improvements with the First Renaissance. The advancements improved morality slowly but took time in the First Renaissance in Europe and especially Italy in the late 1400s to updated talent, innovation, and creativity of few with wisdom that dominated technical advancements. The following is an extraction of *steerage* and *amour* mindfulness as expressed by those that implemented promotions of the First Renaissance beginnings. The way they felt about what mankind really needed was to continue combinations of cultural life's behavior including those that related to art, music, and development of science and new cultural and technology needs for the future.

For those people of the past who generally have a good reputation, they did not know how their daily behavior was conducted within their mind's eye. Their counterparts tried to improve mankind's behavior, which came with their heritage. The gain of any knowledge in detail by pursuit with related experience revealed that there is nothing new under the sun.

Details of *amour* that arises in this story of Divita family lives are specifically recalled by perpetrators with complete revelation, honesty in discourse, and solution. It was mostly opinionated from recall by all. The people included effects and episodes of partners in businesses, friends, and people who associated in recreations and businesses. A commingling of associates of men and women who became immersed in amorous situations when passionate embraces moved to kissing bodies was closer than magnets attracting fervently amorous bliss.

All this did not happen in continued fixed time but had gotten accomplished in so many momentously discrete events, and time was lost in count or simply did not matter. One can disclaim mental urges by climbing knowledge ladders to gain wisdom could defeat "will of desire" instinctive behavior objectively. People that recalled a second memory with detailed understanding significantly improved good behavior. Unless one wraps one's self mentally by using "knowledge and experience" of life's past lessons, it caused one to grasp rungs as mankind's animal magnetism holds steadily.

Other involvements occurred such that people in the past found themselves in rapids of sexual desires where mental management was close to a static disconnect. On the more dominant side of pending amorous capers, many people had personal desires and depended on the nature of evolving situations. Amorous situations typically involved their friends, new associates, or magnetically attractive personalities when brought into their lives. Continuation of common situations revealed influences when tender lives required an immediate abandonment of "will of desire."

The situations were based on involvements in past eras where significant country and even global influences such as world wars caused crucial amorous involvements with some human beings with despair. What I mean is when situations are immediately noticed and getting amorous responses, people made corrective changes of individual minds, as in cases of wars that involved America over a few hundreds of years. Changes in *amour* occurred at a much greater pace in the past, and people usually followed "will of desire" because ongoing concomitant of warring activity caused less faith and more doubt of continued intentionally discarded life of families and friends.

Despite being ceased with more shame with warring times, *amour* was always wrought while in the heat of passion until it transpired completely. A normal mode is the joining of many human beings under warring situations who are known to continue their association with true *amour*. As always, situations and personal lives affected mankind's mind control and social mores of individuals with control. People were influenced by their associated familial environmental upbringing. Depending on resulting chaotic events caused by *amour* situations of sensuous desire, rancor ensued and ranged from barefaced lies to innuendos, double entendres, and equivocations that intentionally mislead receivers under society's laws. In these cases, when more parties are involved, outcomes may lead to devastating results of depression or anxiety. Some only amount to personal involvements that could result in resolution to ensure their personal concerns: all at various levels of intensity and expected effects of unknown future aftermaths.

To accomplish this disclosure of "What's It All About!" involves everyday activities of three generations of common Italian American Divita families whose grandparents emigrated from Italy and lived during their lives and related progeny through two world wars. Newly imposed environmental and social changes exacerbated the period owing to next few years after arriving in America during global warring activity caused by Germany and Austria in 1914 during World War I. The war was won on November 11, 1918, after United States of America had gotten involved on February 18, 1917. Afterward, changes in behavior were unusually different beginning in the Roaring Twenties. Later, with new laws from national legislation such as Prohibition and gun laws, people, including gangsters and illegally distilled moonshine whisky, demanded new exciting times such as gambling and whorehouses galore in the United States of America.

This new evolution of American personalities of coming years passed to those people sensing different modern times leading to significantly different behavior patterns in family lives. The changes had several personal effects, especially during business involvements, increased political support, and personal patriotic work that led graciously with new military buildup immediately under way while uncertainty existed among all people. These adjuncts occurred in a concoction of recreational actions with major uncertainties about future world wars. Pursuit of sensuous amorous desires did not remain the same as had been for families of all mankind from the beginning of time during limited peaceful times.

This personal behavior continued under the same pursuit from its existence without following or using much of the mental "knowledge and experience" of the past. A multitude of amorous interactions both having beginnings and outcomes took place during these modern times of birthing new progeny under a variety of environmental upbringings and naturally different personal modern-day circumstances. The essence is that as it was manifested among human beings from many places in the world that it often led to significant disparate individual behaviors, but outcomes of aftermaths remained and even enhanced.

The behavior patterns most pertinent to this story is one of sexual desires stemming from human's instinctive will, which completely is expected to influence outcomes in durations of people's lives. Many occurrences are within an individual's life seeking interaction compassionately or defiantly as one being induced to be disloyal or being self-judged to be disloyal to their spouse or their known loved ones while away for long times. And in either of these responses, various reasons could be changed, and new paths were followed simply in the mind's analytical evaluation of expectations after changing instinctive desires.

The story of amorous events brought about by "will of desire" explores how related family individuals reacted to *steerage* differently owing to their overall character that natural ergonomics and conditions of life economically, morally, and socially, all while influential worldly imposed world war generational changes occurred.

There are different lifetime eras, or as what fits more appropriately, Zeitgeist—that is, the spirit of times in which intellectual and moral tendencies characterized different eras. These bearings on lifetime eras of family members involving humanity experiences, mental dispositions, and religious precepts were exposed behavior under personal Divita family conflicts in which the subject question is asked, "What's it all about?" Usually, perpetrators seeking some consolation and relief of guilt added to their actions, something from their one-sided memory—it's the times we live in!

What may be a more valid searching to methodically seek forgiveness from supporters who may likely want to defend people's position having not yet to see coming aftermaths, protagonists in search for an answer must let the perpetrator being a loved one, who may generically, consciously or unconsciously or by common nature as a friend, feel some grief of personal responsibility for instigated happenings. This feeling could remove blame or give solace to victims.

In each of the eras fantasized, where unconsciously induced thought through memory extrapolation via extrinsic family folklore, an actual knowledge of happenings must have been already experienced numerous times in the past. The actual character and behavior are usually based on memories about other family members, which in this story stemmed from induced heritage of *steerage* from immigrant Italian family. Everyone knows that *steerage* will have bearing on resolve and any expected aftermath that could occur.

I imagined that my brother Frank, after being born in 1929 and had lived through the Great Depression in the '30s, kept his memories. Frank inherited and mindfully embedded memories from his grandfather and father and his father's wife Jo, born in America but from an Italian family of immigrants. And he decided within his mind as a first-generation American specifically that he had no idea what caused his grandfather's depression. Later in Frank's lifestyle, he was told about corruption in the mines of Sicily and, after immigration, also corruption in American mines. Living as a young man through some personal depressions during Second World War left him with a loaded memory. With this memory, he followed his parents' natural teaching behavior, and it always left *steerage* and *amour* concerns within their decisions to be sorted more noticeably toward using his mind to make decisions.

In the end, being his father's American-born son, he sensed only good ties to his emigrant great-grandparents, who were characteristically sophisticated Italians of some repute in their times. Thrust of this mental outcome, being provoked with memorized decisions, was because he was Big Benny's son with direct relationship to his potentially critical situations. Frank's amorous pursuits were exposed in earnest and produced from recollections of his memory having to do with his good looks.

What an excuse! Frank later said something about the same to his two younger brothers with penned-up words like "I think all men have amorous desires at about this same time in life regardless of where they are from, either as to country, family, social status, environment and culture, or even class, creed, or race. Within this story, one can see how current-day individuals might react and respond to related conditions. The situation depends on how they were affected within the amorous passionate event and ensuing confrontational results. I also assume that this had happened with women who pursued passions of "will of desire."

The inference of heritage could dominate as it proceeded to successful revelations of human beings' desires of will when it affected other outcomes. No matter what the reason, lineage from person's genes would not be a sound excuse when it comes to abilities and having the mind of *Homo sapiens*.

Amour of the eras is revealed after reviewing lives from the great-grandfather's time and his family members to present day, based on overheard, relayed, and perceived opinionated information. As always, some knowledgeable information is hearsay in conversations carried on because life's plights, as juicy and emotionally exciting as they might be, wrought criticism to reveal lessons of good and bad morality for all even at an early age.

This is also true of many stories from historic and memoir discourse as eventually told from times of first *Homo sapiens*. It doesn't mean that those who received these uncountable sources of personal information had a clamp on the truthful parts. And in the same manner, this also applies to disclosures learned and hopefully registered in their minds especially in minds of well-educated great-grandsons who then can relay stories of *amour* to their fathers, revealing modern generation's excitement under unscrupulous *amour* unheard of before in their times.

The evolution of these familial lives is revealed by how they lived and as they lived in the times of the world's behavior and how they influenced new lives of younger family members so instilled hereditarily. God forgive me, some amoral behavior by Frank's grandfather happened concretely and then was exposed for family and friends to hear about his behavior ad infinitum.

Some members were different through remission of past times because of instilled cognitive characteristic changes owing to spirits granted by, we assume God, in eras of time as Zeitgeist—that is, "The spirit of time. Intellectual and moral tendencies characterize any age or epoch, such as The First Renaissance that started in the 1470s had revealed a revamping of *Homo sapiens* intellectually."

For continuity, one can easily associate these learned episodes of *steerage*, and sensuous encounters with illicit *amour* make one wonder actually, "What's it all about?" as a family's sensuous desires are so like any other family's true pursuit that is involved with lust for *amour* or Eros, the god of love, as many Greeks, and philosophers to boot, such as Socrates and Plato so fondly ejaculated with shown desire and confessed about it in torridly clear words with the betrayal or loyalty that follow unexpectedly.

As in many families, there is a simplistic account of heritability success including personal and proper choices in life that affected behavior such as powerful minds of wisdom and not just strength. The political, social, and knowledgeable philosophical evaluations were learned from books and during Socrates's seminars. Even pleasurable occupations and vocations in recreational activities and performance arts were part and parcel. Any one of these may be leavened with "knowledge and experience" simply when time to think it through is taken from second thoughts in the mind.

Of singular interest is that one and more of these endeavors may occur in lives of members of this extended family that makes members typical worldly contenders in legitimate amorous pursuits. It includes having a choice between following "will of desire" versus using "knowledge and experience" from mankind's history.

All the while, *amour* is insistent throughout lives of others, as it does in all lives, the world, as people go around and around practicing and preaching "the same ol' thing," taken from this full-fledged mountaineer. The continuity extends from these common families' daily living in their personal times and in their business lives, times where both activities are involved in personal desires and so devilishly and unrelentingly pursued.

During these eras, one significant influence that bears immensely on all having abilities to pursue *amour* in modern days to accomplish personal desires is the invention and ownership of an automobile. The reference of this immensely popular invention satisfied our first new generation after World War I to its exceptional usage. Cars have continued beyond expectation into the modern generations as foremost significant ways to pursue *amour, amour, amour!*

The automobile matches mechanization of mankind and their craving heart flowing fueled with zest within one's amorous endeavors be it moral or amoral as a *plus* to achieve one's desires. The automobile's interior and exterior makings become the single most demanded influence levied on mankind and on the socioeconomic and environmental conditions of global societies from the early 1900s to present days. The automobile industry thrived because it fulfilled personal desires of both men and women as well as children with a thrust of exposed gusto upon first sight from its beginning. The car shone, reflecting, glistening from everyone's eyes when owners show a full disclosure of public and personal achievements.

However, as has always been, "ideological and religious" influences affected everyone's nature of daily life, especially a display of amorous behavior. Specifically, religions account for a block of time most prominently displayed especially while in church on Sunday mornings and other days of meetings of worshipping their God with doubled interest in praying for needs and wants of course.

The prayers are for special religious holidays especially like Christians' Easter and Christmas and other enticing holidays, such as the Hebrews' Judaism that celebrates Hanukkah and Passover and Islamic religion of Moslems that celebrate their Ramadan that lasts days with contrition, more so than in modern times where faux images are displayed with intent of holding beautiful and good-natured expressions to family and friends. Ramadan is a time for thirty-day fasting for morally projected personal behavior, being the ninth month of the Moslem calendar.

For that matter, religions took root during critically good and bad times in the extended past, but more recently in the change of the calendar years coming by the Romans. The change did so with calamity during Jesus Christ's times and teachings as a rabbi that defined the religious philosophy of Christianity. Jesus thrived with equanimity in the short living life of only thirty-three years. After his hanging, the Crucifixion, by Romans, people of the time in Nazareth displayed demanding contention that arose to formation of Christianity. The documented evidence and practice of Jesus's religion during the next fifty years was found when many written records were made along the time of the Julian calendar, when years became anno Domini. Picking the newly defined time as the significance of Jesus Christ's birth and belief that he is son of God as professed by Christians.

Later, the calendar was corrected to the Gregorian calendar, now in use in the modern world today, with added day to February after midnight, December 31, and is called the legal year to accommodate time in the year deciphered by human beings. Much later time was related to Earth's rotation per day as twenty-four hours and cracking the time per hour as sixty minutes in count so easily and then breaking the minute down by a count of sixty seconds. All related changes to the source of mechanics of our solar system in terms of Earth's rotation around the sun, corrected every four years, make final accountings to accommodation years repeatedly.

That same Christian religious philosophy had its values strengthened during their bad times such as during war with Romans. The depressed social and economic times and environmental changes wreaked havoc on Christians as human beings and all others under control by Romans. The lives of animals, as human beings existing as *Homo sapiens,* means there is the mind's force to gain solace, meditation, and mental strength that build various forms of protection with peaceful living and happiness and little induced fear by leaders that recognize the gain as was taught by Jesus Christ.

A continuation of all life-forms until assaulted by mankind or when believed that they are acts of God with inserted earth received encountered devastations such as asteroids that could cause enormous destruction and number of deaths. After the first few eons of time, and presence of *Homo sapiens*, second thoughts from the mind's "knowledge and experience" were fashioned to force current mankind's beginnings to build solutions devoted to maintaining peace.

For many, there was no one else to turn to but accept belief in God with formulations of earlier religions. *Homo sapiens* adopted teachings of Jesus Son of God and seven sacraments of formality starting with baptizing babies after birth as Christians became members of the Roman Catholic Church. Three members of Trinity with God, Jesus Son of God, and Catholic people's soul and spirit are beliefs that their soul's spirit will have life everlasting. Modern days claim that many people believe in everlasting life of spirit, a fundamental belief until the universe ends.

These three proclamations combine the Catholic Church's mystery of the divinity, if so believed and enthralled as a plus to save souls as part of the Creator's intention signified to early mankind because it has always been the existing dominant belief. The entity of spirit and soul so govern the minds of all to live morally but with opportunity to confess sins that must be forgiven by God. This concept of belief allows all upon death to have an unknown path to become an integral part of God the Creator.

While this made sense to many living human beings so gallantly hallowed with their living spirit lasting forever, they also must be understood that mankind in these times enforce opportunities to those that recognized that sensuous desires abounded instinctively but should not happen more times as an impulse. Without any special knowledge, rather instinctively grasped, each person may be supervised by people who considered "knowledge and experience" as the guiding light simply by association. Being on the same side as God's will, who professed to mankind as a given, was that mankind was given "free will" to believe, and its influence on *Homo sapiens* mind is set for nature of life on earth. With the potential that a thrust into purgatory with some sort of spiritual suffering in preparation of accepting recombining with God in some nature with potential spirits living as a part of God was proclaimed by Jesus the rabbi as identified in his times as a teacher of God's ways.

Because of religious activities usually being notably less rewarding outwardly with physical actions, the expected rewards rise and fall because of moral achievements. The overall severity of morality wrapped in the mind's red warning flags relates to changing social, cultural, and mental dispositions of the nature of individuals. These natural or political changes in various time eras have influenced the amorous pursuer's wants in such a waning by any of these induced influences may decrease moral and natural behavior guided by the current world's revelations.

As previously predicted from remnants of longtime past eras, for example, during caveman times, men dominated life's purposes so much so that dominance was later defined for obvious literary reasons as inherently chauvinistic and Machiavellian behavior to gain end desires of *amour*. This control was forced by personal power that engorged emotional desire almost always with expedience of completing onslaughts and ignoring outcomes, especially when it comes to amorous ventures. The gain from a personal desire to win at any price dominated free will's pursuit. After all, man is the spear carrier, and from time zero, he has had to overcome his prey if he wanted to continue to carry the spear and live and eat with the family.

Now, in current times, many men of all descriptive faults and fancies want to have a car. It can be used as bait to attract their desired woman or person of choice. At any time, mankind may coarsely capture prey for *amour* with intent of satisfying amorous desires with ventures, the pleasure and the payback all within the same time span. Say, for example, now, man uses his unique car that he so idolizes or has used to puff up the story of his lifestyle so easily confirmed by his car choice with his expertise of showering lavish influential "goodies" on the one he wants to semipossess until fully paid, to gain *amour* successfully.

However, women's part as distaff has seen many changes that certainly continuously leveled the playing field of encounters with men through "seen that or done that" and the use of her added weapons of choice. The inherited desirable, sensuous attributes of appearance or earned woman's amenities of desirous ways through modern-day adjusted constitutional freedoms certainly in America, a country that gives her a choice, called in 1973 women privacy rights, under a decision by the Supreme Court of the United States (SCOTUS). Before that state of legal conditions, mankind as *Homo sapiens* is the only people directly related to rights as in the Constitution of the United States regarding abortion. Women's privacy rights were never written for women or men.

Importantly, property ownership, a right to vote, job acceptance, and equal personal expression and human being's inalienable rights were in the Constitution. The Supreme Court added in 1973 women's identified rights to privacy instead of including all human beings constitutionally have stated rights as being inalienable rights to life first and foremost. This precedence from SCOTUS was an overkill and should not have been allowed by gender. Mankind as *Homo sapiens* is the only surviving species of the genus *Homo sapiens* as modern mankind.

These amenities arose in America but initially were earned from the time when the Declaration of Independence was signed and passed to a position of completing the Constitution of the United States of America. The Constitution usually is enforced by enacted laws of United States Congress and, even its adherence, dominates familial guidance and personal actions under the law; while SCOTUS is only a precedence that does not fit ranking *Homo sapiens*. Even now, children are predominately piloted by women and teach family standard bearers to cover all forms of direction and access to entertainment for personal rewards.

This concept is not fundamental simply because women do not control all positions of guidance. While the man as spear carrier or bread winner is generally in hunting pursuits or actively gaining money to barter for materials, he also provides for family needs and goods as required by the law.

Women now can earn or gain access to money to purchase advantages, or they may use money to levy their passion and desire to one they may want to pursue or gain possession or control thereof. This sounds like "What's good for the goose is good for the gander," as any man might ejaculate. However, men always took that pursuit before women ever thought of it. From the beginning of *Homo sapiens*, man always thought that he had even more rights than women.

It is common knowledge that males of families gain disposition through their heritage from generations of persons who may be from various nationalities and mixed or nonmixed in marriage. For women as well as men, their amorous behavior is also determined from heritage. However, a more fundamental nature is that women control the extent of establishing a family; but now, it includes to an extent of their personal satisfaction of having or not having a child. The extreme decision of abortion, if so desired and now yet being promulgated as law of the land, within legal limitations and controls, women now have gained special rights beyond the right to life of one's progeny.

Again, and after all, women are the distaff members of families, which mainly means they control how personal satisfaction is dispersed, and when approved by husbands and when both agree, wives gain allowance according to current laws that may include murder of progenies. As well, associated women's sensuous emotions emanate mostly from their responses to male mates or significant others who influence both their mental and physical behavior, some with intelligence and some with simple heartfelt responses of love to gain needs within their desires.

In all events, this story steers standing amalgam of males and females who powerfully stand their ground. And they insist that their positions are righteousness no matter how amorous waves of desire flash on and off to a finality when killing a human being is the matter. This is common because pending simple attractions to unattached individuals or to complex individual involvements with others, both may face their pursuit as infidelity or loyalty, whoever may be the person as unattached receptors.

When the question "What's it all about?" is proposed and answered dramatically in each illustration of detailed lives of familial people, it opens eyes of those who have experienced amorous situations or those who are about to entwine in an amorous experience. But as historic experiences reveal, those who expect to have won the race are more than likely to suffer later in expectation with a harmful degree of disheartening.

The outcome being the affected future, even though gain was enjoyed, it may happen when the bottom falls out for lives no longer remaining together or recognized as an entity in each other's lives. The stain of even destroying a conception remains in memories of others until death of either one when in womb, a growing human being is killed.

After all, Ananias either was struck dead by God [so quoted in the Bible], who apparently took a stand against mankind's "free will" or committed suicide induced by his mind's "free will." The suicide occurred after Ananias was rebuked by Peter for lying, as stated in the Bible. This all happened for only lying about money he had promised to add as his full share from a property sale so that others could be aided as needed as determined by the appointed distributors recognized by Peter. As lives continued to follow their "free will," so much so that money and property have become the payoffs that dominate the "will of desire" infractions. In this set of personal episodes, which spans many aspects of magnetically compassionate desires, some outcomes may be good or bad depending on whose point of view is taken.

Explored in this story of memories of mind-sets, it is about lives of three consecutive generations of Divita family men and women all with complex involvements within one extended family and close associates encountered with incidents. Although simply put, these persons are mindful of moral and cultural commitments, but there are times that instinctively emotional passions may bring about joys, satisfactions, and happiness to some, and to others, heartbreaks, unhappiness, depressions, and even death as an ultimate disaster. Each of these gains or losses because of amorous ventures, in some way or other, automobiles may be initially connected as supporting influences; even though it was initially only intended to be the most phenomenal invention for mankind since fire or at least since rock wheels were rolled around by cavemen.

The automobile in its evolved attractive splendor of color and chrome, interior and exterior decor, operational devices and entertainment systems, accommodates personal desires of both species of human beings. With all amenities that propagate from its evolution, each car embellishes and releases one's display of their private heartthrob, symbolically gained in the mind's eye. The details of each generation of cars are exposed and then memorized for selected attractive features by practically everyone from young seekers to be like their counterparts. Even when one is a few years older than most men and all macho men and some macho women who are born dramatically afflicted with a sport-loving induced chromosomes, both types are hell-bent on driving their choice of new cars.

Getting a car and winning someone's affection or gaining positions of *amour* with all its attractiveness, even receiving praise as the display is admired, is truly a symbolic self-centered accomplishment of imprinted honor within the mind. The desire for a car is second only to immediate and magnetically propagated instinctive desires for sexually gratifying involvements among men and women. And more highly the car is desired and admired for its style, cost, uniqueness, and its use, the more one is willing to sacrifice just about anything or anyone for expected gains from *amour* that's likely to come about.

There are three classes of cars beyond use as a plain travel convenience that drive men to whatever victory they seek or as with the chaotic nature that the car can encourage, but never marking whatever disaster they might never be expecting to encounter. These are ultraexpensive cars beginning from early times as were Pierce-Arrows (and other old models) to present-day cars like the American Cadillacs and Lincolns, the English Bentleys and Rolls-Royces, Jaguars, Austin, the German high-end Mercedes-Benz, the Italian Maserati, Lamborghini, and many of the genres from numerous different countries; to name one more, the French Citroen.

Some of these cars are specially designed to meet specifications of governments for safety usage in crowds or for warring purposes. Even modern-day pope's cars are especially made with finesse but primarily for protection and little else fancy except for visibility for parades and prayerful speeches outside Vatican City (*Città del Vaticano*). The next most broadly desired and idolized cars are classic collector's cars after they have aged to an antique and then rebuilt "to the nines."

This type of collector brings many others to join the camaraderie so that now, specific car owner persons of means and especially by organizations that are spread across the globe are known to all through special displays for camaraderie and sales. Then collaborators politically display these cars with well-planned and widespread and even national viewing attractions for competition and awards.

The third and most important category of car for joy so pertinent to this story is the sports car, especially nationally and internationally acclaimed racing cars in such events as yearly Indianapolis 500, Daytona 500, the Grand Prix, and numerous other local American and European race events; internationally, the many Italian, English, Australian, and French roadway races such as the Grand Prix of great repute; also races dominate their presentations of racing fans and ingenuous young girls surrounded by captivating men and scenic views of the lay of the land, homes, and seaside in areas such as mystique Monte Carlo, entrancing Paris, royalty of London, and the preeminent historic Milano, the land of *amour* and pageantry, and all were gregariously dominated with "will of desire."

Within these types of places and events where persons seek *amour*, they have most significant impacts in common-day modern times where glamorously amorous situations arise widespread by owners of a sports cars, drivers of a sport racing cars, and those persons whose dominating desire is to own a car that they might use to impress one they admire sensuously. Cars, even more expensive ones, set classic and extravagant car owners at a position of aristocratic elitist levels that make them a special category of men and women. Many mentally aligned elitists are known to be talented enough to inherit the hunt for *amour*.

This inherent mentally stored ability of many owners or drivers puts them in brackets beyond achievement by those who feel just a little better than the next person if they can add this selected car to their accomplishments. They live it from day to day openly or in their minds for sure, as we all do without recognizing reservations, and many know how to advance their advantage to accomplish desires of their will.

The truth is in many families and with their friends, some people's lives get involved in amorous situations; but then, dissolutions occur either by lack of personality or by chance of a major distraction such as inherent loyalty. This generally happens especially when certain men and women's influences, including others, get involved in dominating environments affecting their innate libido's intent.

The desire wrought potential as infidelity steers strong sensuous desires to a recognition of an ending of a disastrous outcome. Under such a strain, yearning for the outcome, both parties are usually left carelessly dangling, frustrated with disappointment and with an emptiness. Neither parties have honor-saving guts enough to survive first temptations that are to remove tight grips of loyalty.

It's understandable that large numbers of these off-track amorous ventures of the past more than one hundred years usually involved cars in some way or other as an initiator. Those afflicted men and women afterward, so entangled with disgust because of infidelity, seldom achieve individual success beyond their distrust and that it mentally and socially complicates those lives that are directly involved.

There are times that these lives are randomly tormented by tragic human failings and abusive confrontations from family and friends. However, because of their desire to own a car of a certain kind, no matter what the cost, they also find themselves suffering the flings of induced money problems, as should be expected with extravagance that occurs with the instinctive practice of "will of desire."

This argument may lead some to distraught and force a move to gain new attention from another, which is usually using an affliction to an enlightenment of joy from above, at least it feels that way, but as it fades, the darkness pervades as the spoiler. Then outcomes are instigators and partners who seek pity or, if accommodated praises, are sought to gain rewards from their kind of friends who also have amorous natures.

Then all hell breaks loose when antics are disclosed, having acted as if they hadn't already experienced the same type of outcome more than one time. As the parting occurs after revelation by a person unidentified to the pursuer, blank stares dominate their vision toward where they might end up because of a mistrust. Sometime afterward, they either randomly exist in mind as a subhuman in a second time around or find satisfaction with living alone with their car taking the course as if driving along life's interactions and outcomes one day at a time but never finding the destination. Some are perplexed when looking for proper amiable personal support, which could provide comfortable solace when located. Even with proffered support from family and friends, most of the time, they continue to practice a pattern of living nearer disaster even though enamored pursuits are making gains. The lack of committed trust causes ever-present mental rejection and not a victory of personal compliment to neither one nor both paramours. The blend of ensuing amorous adventuresome exposés includes unconsciously recognizing the assault on one's personality as if it reveals tainted behavior, sometimes with intentions of comedic occurrences and reminiscences. Other times, with purposeful tragic fates, one never wanted to be shamed regardless of the behavior.

Even though some people follow new paths with proper mental attitude, an outside observer can recognize the change in lives of adulterers of instinctive desires. One humorously notes a subtle memory reservation that tags their minds, saying, "I won't go there anymore." All who experience rendezvous will feel the heart-wrenching reality of passionate slippery slopes that lead to a romantic pursuit be it tragic or comedic to the extent of their interest. Scratching surfaces of interactions, one groupie-looking guy with an egotistical personality practiced in articulation or even one with a laconic personality may steam up attraction. When committed, a joint-induced moving ardor complies with only a few choice words practiced, without a confrontational change or a justification enough to remove beginnings of critical incidences along the course, but it may never work out for either party. Again, when they honor their sacred commitments of marriage, a solution arises.

Those involved measure their luxury on a grand scale that could release money from the nugget bag by ounces, as did the gold diggers use dust to pay out for instinctive desires. Some of these buyers were from unknown ends of spectrum, and both were considered reprobates who sought and paid for short-term amorous epics. In bad times, it led parties afflicted to totally different ways of life in the future. For those who amorously pursued riches, changes inflicted initially may become a means to enjoyment and happiness. Others may become wrong to join future times because new changes are difficult to practice for a lifetime. However, to those with different reasons for involvement, it could also lead to mental, moral, social, or religious crises, even life-threatening outcomes when vengeance from faithful senses and ends in a moral crisis that pushes quickly to divorce or abandonment.

Each of these primary characters all with mentally self-centered personalities so different but initially with the same purpose pursues new car buys as an inheritance. Each buy is characterized with an emotional urge when the car is bought with a sparkle in the eyes. The cost is mostly not an issue except when customers are forced to their limit of means. In conducts of carrying out these emotional pursuits, buyers think they use their mind's eye, shrewd behavior in dealing, and will almost do anything to get their way. Guys give in one way and then try to make a gain from detailed car performance knowledge and its value. Usually, buyers come up with money needed to buy what they want.

On the other hand, some people insist sincerity with money but are known to lose personal composure because access to family members then is limited. They lose association and influence blood relations, and some may seek unsavory people to borrow money but drops it immediately at a high interest.

Many buyers do drift away from knowing that they have "free will" but now take a religious slant and ask for God's help or even that "God's will" be done as a last resort. This type of requisite prayer is too late to be granted. Mankind has no grand or encompassing solution to control instinctive behavior when needed unless each human being simply applies the thinking mind following "knowledge and experience" path. In many cases, power and position may be used by the individual's need, or it could lead to an unforgivable situation. The last few available pursuits to buy from power mongers include using legitimate boisterous fan dancing to hype one's desires.

In this story, outcomes of others' lives affected by disloyalties or loyalties are revealed through protagonists' specific interactions and involvements with closely related persons, good friends, and associates in his, her, or even a close one's life. What is more important is if one pretends a change of disposition in discourse, exaggerating sensuous pursuits with deceit turning to disaster as one is told, then one would leave and discover what *amour* is and . . . "what's it all about!"

The point is that when discourse occurs and after occasion has materialized, the protagonist has assessed it, one might have been able to realize the ability to see future benefits, or advantages might make newfound *amour* either worthless or of little value. On the other hand, new life might be a venture wasted because of stated distortions. All this is based on protagonist's understandings of mental, emotional, and physical disposition of confessor at the time that one's responding to the question, "Steerage and amour!—what's it all about?"

Amour is "what it's all about." The question is put to protagonist, or he puts it to one of his trusted comrades or relations as concocted under extremely difficult times especially having to do with his own amorous desires and their aftermaths. When one asks the question or answers it, the answer reveals pursuit through wit and wile; but facing consequences pressing for critical personal burdens or some gain of praise might arise from one or more of outcomes already intact and was recalled to one's advantage.

These plights so detailed to a confessor are commonplace, and many lives may be tainted up to a general disgrace until the end of their days. The disgrace may be influenced by exasperation of daily outcomes, losses of friends and relatives and associates that were always hale and hearty in one's company. Each answer relates to ongoing crucial involvements and incidents. The release of the action is critically influenced by generational era in which potential disloyalty or loyalty occurs but with damning hearsay. All know that regardless of outcomes, even as a new plight of life ensues; and one's future life is unknown, but its revelation with time is part of the new undefined destiny that evolves for both men and women.

The main thematic behavior encompasses man's surge to amorous behavior, and it usually comes into play about things, places, and persons. When it is new cars, sports cars, and singularity in plight of influence of race cars with implications of needs to win something, as well as one choice friend pursued, with position in society, money or looks of immeasurable worth then go to the winner with zest.

The automobile ("car," a word derived from Latin *carrus*) and all that has evolved with its use by people since its influence was thrust upon society just before earlier years of the twentieth century. The car has speedily delivered a blunt impact on people's personal and public conduct beyond any measure to date except modern-day airplanes and extent of space technology and exploration and all new devices derived therefrom.

The measure of car's value and influence on *amour* has never been exceeded. The collection of cars is fully available to researchers in archives. Company makers and buyers and users are inclined to buy cars to be winner of most amorous adventures. The car has significantly increased pride of goods ownership and showmanship to new owners, but with little real value in being able to satisfy needed physical and mental personality developments. It generally augments brunt of anyone's disloyalty, be it *amour* or imposed pursuit of *amour* at first sight.

I will include vignettes of several episodes identified previously, all involving related personal events; but so common as to truly represent any human behavior might involve amorous pursuits with cars ad infinitum. There are some that have been deciphered each as potential male and female betrayals or infidelities and with several, with guarded loyalties maintained; but in the long run, events have already been experienced many times no matter who the human being is, under any pretense of greatness or smallness of a representative of mankind. Another vignette will be treated as a convincing loyalty or a display of genuine loyalty to one's mate. All inclusively revealed as they get an understanding of meaning of the story's title, *Steerage and Amour!—What's It All About!*

Each episode of memories is an asset to potential pursuers of amorous desires, and it signifies critical detail of deceitful knowledge parlayed by instigators through revelations, disclosures of secretive confidential braggadocios, and confrontational involvements. The complexity of incidents herein overreaching with descriptions to perspicuity. The primary exposition reveals similar or associated vignettes, some of which may have happened in lives of these family members unintentionally. These incidents were influenced by the same old practiced typical amorous attractions that everyone would expect, yet they occurred multiple times in each of three eras of heritage, which span seventy-five years from the early 1920s.

As each outcome depends on whether options are earnestly or frivolously taken on either side of one who purveys infliction of disloyalty after a folly, it was recognized with wit and relayed by wry or humorous ejaculations. Usually, perpetrators generally feel they have high ground and discard feelings of wronged people and will dominate situation until cows come home. Then under afflictions of aftermaths, they fall apart as do so many. After all, what has been done has been done uncountable times in the past.

All humans pursue instinctive behavior uncountable times in the past with a uniquely large variety of outcomes that range from a path to new life to one that is hell-bent on destruction, and many of the "will of desires" do not involve exploitation of amorous ventures. Think, and you will surely recall we all follow irregular eating and drinking schedules, and sometimes we behave like animals and only use the instinctive mind-set.

When one seriously wants to maintain life as the nature of marriage inspires or continues as a personal closeness calls for, then one following past revelations can make or attempt to make a mental commitment that forces one to follow solutions of avoidance taken as a surprise in character demeanor and mindful thinking. One more obvious choices is influenced by morality or other unexpected influences that combat the perpetrator's propensity to stray into fields of infidelity or to not cross red chalk lines that define disloyalty.

The event and outcome surprises are woven with common thread of wit and pathos to reveal inherited personalities. Keep in mind that these revealed psychologically evolving characteristics dominate main characters from nationalities of old and new generations. In the end, a climaxing event that potentially wields a disastrous outcome that hounds Benny's son Frank in the modern generation was solved by being personally accountable to his family, especially his wife, and by following advice of his father Benny.

The psychological conflicts within each incident expose disharmony in families and their influence on extended family and friends. Disappointments and personal commitments eventually cause tragic or comedic incidences because of impulses about personal desires that may hurt one's partner about money. Some friends have inclinations to pursue any position toward betrayal or to begin secreted personal warfare on partner's infidelity. The patterns and influences of the characters of past generations are imposed sometimes as slightly knowable personalities that will be transferred to involved characters in families in their coming generation resulting in a stolid saying, for example, "Like father like son!"

For the life of me, I don't know why new-generation persons know how blank their minds think about old-timers when many lived their lives as rakes, womanizers, and hustlers, hell-bent on impressing opposite sexes or even the same sex in a macho sense. After all, we know this behavior has extended from time zero. Even though only few changes in how men and women carry out their amorous pursuits have resulted. The changes that have evolved are morally considered worse by older generation; but newer generations just added extensions to new amorous events.

The common ones are revealed with continuity in each main character's behavior through current-day humor and wit, at least those that are immeasurable in the eyes of the hotshot who can easily hoodwink many of surrounding people who don't give a damn about their behavior of either party in the long run. Some people revealed new and significant happenings that occur and are associated with outcomes psychologically pertinent but intensely sad or have calamitous pathos in those situations of affliction or great distress.

Although when these cases have been and are studied in detail by psychologists and psychiatrists, results and many solutions would be easily recognized as having been studied because of past occurrences of similar infidelities. But study is not enough; so-called patriots or clients are needed, and pre and post detailed treatments may be collected to alleviate the coming suffering. Back in the olden days, affected persons did not pretend to carry weight of mentality to influence other individuals' minds as it is today especially for women.

Many knowledgeable people from previous times may have connected with expected reactions in their own events or others of past eras, but even they usually are caught by surprise as responses aroused by victims' feelings that could beg for pity, sorrow, and compassion. In contrast, others might want to expose needs for a new sensuous relationship without any remorse—that is, taking on a new partner is typically persons in the modern-day era have different ways to meet with friends and also they behave differently. For example, there are times that aspects of life show positive outcomes in contemporary times but, later, may be savored with joy and contentment with family. The cause of turmoil by the person chosen may be after the friend's home or money.

CHAPTER IV

Poor, Rich, Powerful, and Royalty
Lapsed Steerage and Amour

*He knew before influential and congenial friends who agreed with his
political philosophy and from the crises of the day should and could
be solved, but he was not without experiences of sensuous adventures
some silent and only one, the one refuted since his great mental
distress, and lies first primary loss of a compatible family after???*
—Baruch Spinoza, Dutch philosopher

Frankie, as a young man, narrates thoughts, behavior performances, and interactions with family members, associates, and responses that he observed in other people who think they are from different classes when he started from an earlier age of seventeen. All this augmented by his father and mother's teaching familial needs of *steerage* and *amour* to ensure his pursuit of happiness.

As he would say to me many times when in my teens, "Some people waste away in misery no matter if poor, rich, powerful, or of royalty. Back when they lived under torments of onslaughts of black plague through devastating diseases caused by fleas from rats, engrossed with debased thoughts, in middle ages while dying. Despair darkens their existence with no thought in mind of affliction with virulent, highly contagious black plague. Some gasped as they died, and only a few survived and managed to find a path to recovery."

When I hear those words from within my mind, I gain an understanding to save others with whatever help to restart a new pursuit for modern man, *Homo sapiens*. Knowing what I have read advanced my thinking described in writings of the First Renaissance that led me to a new response to "knowledge and experience."

Although this group of *Homo sapiens* was still hardwired instinctively, many will still become afflicted with "will of desire" before groping for morsels of mental evaluation extracted from poor teachings. They will live without extended consolation, direction, and mindful attention from wise men's humanity from coming new heritage of the First Renaissance.

Years later, these human beings scattered aimlessly among daily squalidity intake like droppings of birds of a feather that splatter noticeably on nature's gifted palatial land; unless a proviso directly hits heads of society's individuals, there would be no responders. Then lapse of responders awaited an immediate collective gain from those who stress *steerage* emphasizing to all that they should follow paths to use "knowledge and experience" to adjust to pursue a life of *happiness*. When these changes occurred, governments had the responsibility to protect people's "general welfare and security" as selected by wise men.

Poor humans have no explanation why they were positioned in this world to suffer a degradation as severe as being engulfed in uncultivated syndromes. The poor were treated as if they had an association with a disease springing from sweaty, dirty, raggedly clothed bodies, exhuming odors of bodily excrement and urine, never suspecting one could infect those nearby without physical contacts. That was why they were constantly kept at a safe distance from people of all points of view, socially and personally disjointed, and not just because they were economically thrifty and aloof.

Being poor existed within vision by physical and mental attraction, which identified one's syndrome to respond to instinctively hardwired mind's immediate decision that controls their actions of alarm by sight. Those who understood a higher mentality of living mustered to remove stigmas in some way. First, they added thinking time to ensure they started with mental dissection of main problems of physical and mental disease. Sane poor persons with problems could be partially improved with more mindful work, which would lead to a solution using conscious minds as a next instant step to decipher via good linkages to "knowledge and experience" in human beings.

First transfer of their existing mentally visualized appearance had to be eliminated from surface exposure with a mind that decries manners, cleanliness, and proper dressings that could be obtained from almost any societal facility. Then one must revamp one's self to match other common normal human beings and take advantage of one's good features and work toward an effective way to be acceptable by society's most compassionate common folks.

Heritage sometimes often bestows good looks to human beings, but their displays of personalities must be used in a positive sense. It is important to reveal capabilities of people's minds by putting them forward with emphasis. Everyone's mind needs mental evaluation of actions, ways, and help with proper decisions. Another simple gift is that of having a sense of humor, so it should be used to one's best ability and it will get better. One must noticeably use some mind power to influence others to help bettering one's life.

Many pursuits result in one finding a partner for taking on *steerage* rather than *amour*. By being decisive in judgment, one further sees needs to improve daily and make sure they correctly establish legitimate amorous relationships. The helping approach is the solution. All it requires is maintaining the use of self-esteem and personal selection of friends and associates who follow natural behavior laws by using God-given common sense and controlling instinctive behavior.

Rich people, as do poor, gather to battle woes of life when led by "will of desire." Most certainly, all *Homo sapiens* are entranced with *amour*. Most people do not see clearly before pursuit of illegitimate woes of *amour* that might cause aftermaths. All of us feed on values with satisfying bodily desires for pleasures to be sought or bought, yet gleaming to reap even a touch of *happiness* even when not legitimately gained.

If a philanderer is one who seeks remedy, then one must expect some form of counteractions from harmed persons will proceed until resolved. Rich people having been gifted via heritage of position, but progenitors did not earn royalty life status. Everyone simply values life's existence goods. However, some people are dabblers in *amour;* many get nabbed under "will of desire" that lends little help in the pursuit of happiness. As do many, they may suffer sure-fired shortcomings when lowered in status by lack of use of mind power. Many others within communities suffer fulfillment of desires regardless of standing in the community, which is always a personal blow to rich people, but they may buy their way out of desperate situations.

Powerful humans always have collections of other humans that are or may become their lackeys, and as such, do their bidding of committed allegiance that usually includes cheating, lying, and stealing anything they can to relieve or disprove any argument as might be demanded. It is like actions and interactions of family members that use deception or cover-up, but power of familial demands direct descent to ensure the best of survival of fittest and if necessary follow "knowledge and experience." Those who survive have a new power in communities of business, society, and offices of control of humanity. Powerful persons via influence and leadership may succeed to be famous human beings unless they engorge selfishness in society and play to satisfy "will of desire" like animals to gain special treatment. The infamous of record have caused negligence *steerage* teaching above all by not mentally or properly grasping required instilled growth of "knowledge and experience."

As related to human beings living until a critical happening, good or bad occurs; but bad is always remembered, and people involved are never quite the same to families, friends, and strangers. The bad happening is offered to an enormous number of humans almost randomly and impacts their everyday life's thinking. During good times and bad times, both with heartfelt effects in wane may cause personal breakups. Sometimes, people lead different ways to continue living in a place unfamiliar with mental scars that still remain as if from a plague, but, obviously, they must adjust with intent. The mind aggregates processes that originate in or are associated with the brain's mind, even impacts with ever-present spirit or soul involving consciousness and subconscious thought, interpretation of perceptions, insight, imagination, "knowledge and experience" from memory. Recollections by people occur within their minds that they are the only unique genus of *Homo sapiens* in our earth's solar system and yet to be demonstrated in the universe.

First mankind accumulated little mental experience and knowledge living on earth, but as it happened, even up to now, a dominant belief in God's creation and continued evolution of mental growth would be most boggling even from when mankind first evolved.

The unforeseen happenings in the universe were never seen or even recognized until modern times after medieval times expanded into the First Renaissance with the start of Galileo Galilei's design of the telescope as a first scientific instrument to be a major creative invention after many thousands of years. The expansion of minds within the First Renaissance sparked coming into the minds with evolving mental life of *Homo sapiens* as modern mankind with definitive thinking.

Within the mind, new ventures were revealed to mankind, let alone many other unknowledgeable things that expand on earth now being defined and used in daily activities. These new and unexpected changes such as night and day are being defined by Copernican evolving ideas. The sad point is that Galileo was condemned by the Roman Inquisition and imprisoned. All things that followed advancement by creativity of modern man included other life-forms chosen to include other genus of animals and plants, and all that would derive from information granted from God in belief as part of human procreation and continued evolution.

When first *Homo sapiens* were viewed or even observed, many light spots (unknown only as bright, small, white sparkling balls) were above in the darkness during the late part of day. *Homo sapiens* were identified and had new life after the extinction of Neanderthals (the cave dwellers with unknown words for dark and light) for sure. *Homo sapiens* evolved after many eons after Paleolithic man, and *Homo sapiens* eventually, with personal macroscopic bodily actions, communicated actions and reactions personally and as well to surroundings of all things. As now defined and known as the sun as a yellow round object installed by God of creation as a starter, it was unknown words at their times, unknown or inferred with fingers pointing warmth in heaven from way back in time. Eventually, unknown maybe unidentified. God the creator and continued evolution evolved *Homo sapiens* with minds significantly moving toward talents, innovation, and creativity, saving in their memories "knowledge and experience."

Then at nighttime, they could see the earth's moon and stars at night as only spots of light twinkling (but not other planets or planets yet unknown). Earth's moon looked like our sun to them at nighttime, but not of the same brightness and often was of different shapes and various colorations. The same feelings passed through their minds looking for some grasp of elucidation. They had no recognition of significance about uncountable numbers of white circles, the stars, as they gawked into distance at night at the unknown universe. If even countable, hardly anything yet discovered in these early days of mankind probably were nameable in some fashion by *Homo sapiens*. They could see a brightness with their eyes, bigger white light unknown but like a star, which was a planet (maybe Venus) near the moon, an unknown light at different times. These sightings, by first of many mankind, were completely unaware of natural reality until the coming of *Homo sapiens*, who then must have started to gather fundamental "knowledge and experience" in their own evolving languages as history of the earth indicated when possible.

That knowledge was not present in first mankind morally and mentally without a planned learning culture. Learning must have at least begun when mankind finally inherited real mental discernment as a swallow of real influence of *Homo sapiens* new life. Even knowledge as it came had to be encouraged and dominated by *Homo sapiens*. The mindful knowledge expanse every day of their own continuous use of their minds must have ensured propagation of new life unhindered as was created by belief in a Source, God unknown, and to some eons later even identified a God unknown or whoever.

During these primeval times as they passed, the least of mankind's descendants should have collected a splattering gather of "knowledge and experience" to begin recognizing mankind's individuals' hardwired instinctive inheritances and to await some expectations of different reactions just by the actions and reactions and resulting aftermaths. However, in full measure, only bit by bit did instinctive behavior installation ever so slightly readily used with affectation. The instilled sensuous desires were engraved, as is quoted, "hardwired" in human beings' minds even to the extent of breaking man-made natural laws and morally opined beliefs as the Creator unknown—that is, one who has unknown mental power of creation and continued evolution of the universe in unknown beliefs. God sent initial reactions to assist as a first step toward "survival of the fittest" as bounded. The requirements that *Homo sapiens* monitored life's maintenances for value of human being must have happened from the beginning of a new life, starting in the womb of the woman.

All that really matters now and that happens into present day from the past time was mind's libido memory acquired a level of desire that essentially remained unaffected. When the first instinctive process took over, it continued, no matter what; it involved *amour*. The actual mental achievements gained by enhancing "knowledge and experience" of *Homo sapiens* genus to enhance evolution to use both conscious and subconscious minds store memory. Sensed discharges from minds along a practiced neuron path lasting with instant inherited nature that memory permits. Without continued recall, minds wane steadfastly when *amour* is in an amorous pursuit. What that means is it easily translates into firmly fixed memory identified as "will of desire" as first mental extractions.

Visionary mentality could be "called to mind" with fragments of past many ventures amassed in human beings that could be extracted from memory packets of "knowledge and experience." Then mind's brain would ensure the availability to be followed for all *Homo sapiens* to gain critical life, freedom, and pursuit of happiness, separately or together. This pursuit does become part of the mind's effort to follow *steerage* and propagate transferences as a heritage demand. If, indeed, neuron paths in propagation get added as one would suspect, then one could allow one to support the cultural development of mankind's mind and life. We hope that God had planned every construction of evolution from beginning to end of time ad infinitum.

This development all depends primarily on one's inherited intelligence quotient of time that might bring extractions of significance under trying conditions and situations, especially if amorous ones occur. The gain, however, is from past records that might instill a direction to pursue *amour*. However, we hope that the mind and spiritual building blocks that show *steerage* will subsist. The amount has not been based only on a level of one's intelligence level but the randomness of infused hereditary of *steerage* that will continuously grow in the mind.

After recorded eons into life of mankind that have passed, dominance of instinctive behavior proves why failure of completing life with a truly improved cultural grandeur is not only difficult; only a few humans have accomplished its pursuit over the eons. "Knowledge and experience" as a critical accomplishment in mankind today, being so slight, carries an unusual sense of failure of general populace. The reason is there has been slow gain in the evolution of heritable laws of nature that enhance minds to develop intelligence to evolve cultural pursuits.

The saving feature is in some *Homo sapiens* who impose and cause a mental response and trigger a valuable reversal of drive to achieve desire, and it happens naturally by taxing knowledge or is expected by the spirit's evocation of Creator's influence, the Creator's will, whose almighty power and will exist but not distributed complementary and may be extracted from one's mind with a will to clear the confusion of laws of nature on the earth. This gathering within the mind is assumed to be adopted unimaginably in the universe as supporting the prime Source's issue of the gift of "free will" and will show when new human life is discovered in other parts of the universe.

Among many scientific specialists and philosophical speculators, many modern members of *Homo sapiens* fit unique assessment of genus of modern man having wise extractions from their minds regarding decisions. Those with truly operational minds, when afflicted instinctively, reject paths that end in failure, or they react before the chase of sensuous and numerous personal desires satiate them. In case of sensuous desires, intelligentsia must use conscious and subconscious minds to spark a spot impulse that rings their memory's bell to curtail their libido from full force to an abrupt stop.

It must signal the superior mind's amygdala to concentrate on legitimate emotional desires or nature's phenomena requiring cultural mental pursuits to be loyal to one's self. The problem is, how does one whose mind is afflicted separately or by jumping on the "bandwagon" request the proper use of their judgment because the loss of response never sends neurons to the "knowledge and experience" mind areas of the individual's mind?

In either case, the normality of many minds must be vigilant and forgiving of facts that they do as others and operate with a primitive mental pursuit while clinched in the grasp of their mesmeric animalistic, statically and magnetically fascinated mind's mentality. These states of mind defeat obligations and loyalty mind-sets. When exposed, the mind registers inchoate transfers of promises of amorous enjoyment that scattered into the ether and may not be discernible in a superior normal mind engulfed with "knowledge and experience," let alone in one with a dominating instinctively hardwired disposition. The real situation is those learned people would be able to tell others what they had learned after situations of dominating sensuous desires prevailed, and then inform those knowledgeable and experienced. The problem that pursuers of sensuous desires had was what was known by the muse goddess (named after daughters of Mnemosyne, goddess of memory, and by Zeus, the supreme deity, ruler, of the celestial realm, who made her mother of muses). She was never understood by many of those who think instinctively and those who wanted to know what others could not understand by those who knew from "knowledge and experience."

People hardly ever talk about the historic story of *amour* among recorded humans whose plights were treated as delights until Samson and Delilah's love affair occurred and their eventual aftermath destruction of their lives and regal quarters later presented from extracted history. The historians and creative writers, however, spent inordinate amounts of time writing about individual stories of *amour*, researching historic documents about specific people and times in which they lived in past times when the "will of desire" prevailed almost as a domination of species. Little is exposed about those human beings practicing great care to follow "knowledge and experience" within their behavior with other's lives throughout the years. This pursuit did continue, but extraneous events caused it to move in a slow process.

Most revelations pertained to either life's critical conflicts and disasters, or accomplishments of invention, skill, talent, innovation, and genius relating to objects of life, be it persons, places, or things. Some human beings are also instilled with urge to pursue mentioned capabilities. Other human beings do not sit around discussing life's secret desires for a fantasized sensuous *amour* without considering their shortcomings and expected numerous aftermaths of illicit pursuits.

Advancements through new beginnings of *Homo sapiens* began to backtrack a few laps around the globe to evolve beyond getting captured by historic happenings of sensuous desires before experiencing occasions. However, firing of mind's pursuit is so instantly instinctive that open responses are ignitable for pursuits of illegitimate *amour*. People try to recall times when thriving emotions of prominent and classical high esthetic principles as ancient Romans and Greeks demanded conformist behavior by recorded history. Instead, they imposed upon each other many years ago to control behavior, especially morally. Approaches are the same, and *Homo sapiens* still follow amorous enticements of today's common vintage.

When one examines mankind's nature and his response to sensuous desires, it is easy to expose the historic race to *amour* by poor and common people from mankind's beginning using continuous multitudes near infinity with the same acts of modern days. Now, not to leave anyone out, all those up to the highest exaltation, which include celebrities, religious practitioners, leaders in dominating tribes, are powered by those on their high horses. The field of excited people, noticed by increasing their gallop, extended to those people in powerful countries with unbridled desires since birth of *Homo sapiens*.

With that known, why do we have to disclose embedded nature of mankind when people know how anyone will behave overall within spectrums of life's nature from a low of despair to the middle at happiness and then to a high-end extent of anxiety? Common mankind under this practice of "will of desire" reveals how it sometimes happens; and believe it or not, it sometimes does not happen even unexpectedly with a good start. A pattern going back to past times reveals nothing more than we know and has not changed in retrospect from back to the beginning. However, during past times in history, many things were unrecorded except on rock walls and then parchment.

Mentally rich evolved few and far between times when mankind had the wherewithal mentally and was sufficiently enough to tell stories during eras when languages were formulated. It started with soundings instilled as letters and words formulated and composed. Later, mankind deciphered as they talked words and composed sentences of mindful senses for communication. Mankind continued with man-made bass musical sounds from hewing devices when men stroked by hand against soil, trees, and stone. They used waves of hands toward stars sparkling after sundown with known words of emotions to create a musical composition in tones among tribes. Much later, people, as they were unknown, gathered and did innovate; but, later, tribal people added simple ballads and poetic stanzas. This personal quality flourished in the minds of Europeans, in the Britannia Isles of the ancient Roman invaders, and especially by tribal Irish of Ireland to allow musically inherited players to follow beats to the same tune. They must have heard their innovations chanted along with the melody. Then harmony with stories told engrossingly satisfied by mixed people who extended written prose beyond expectations. That was a revelation of *Steerage and Amour!—What's It All About!* by those who captivated instinctive musical mental responses. Each person's arsenal of mentally memorized notes obtained by mind-bending words eventually was transferred in stories that led to guidance of musical sounds inadvertently into their minds' memories.

Later in the next time era, going back to times when Greeks, who were glorious and great and documented many psychological case studies of philosophy relayed words from their mouths in stadiums of learned people, discovered truths and deceptions. Their scribes recorded on parchment into their burning minds of intellect memories to brighten philosophical revelations. The intent was to galvanize mankind with democratic philosophies embedded in their memories of "knowledge and experience" and continued through inheritance.

The ones most notable included collections of people such as Socrates, Aristotle, Plato, and other serious students to amassed philosophers of modern days who learned and deciphered, imposed, and extended Greek philosophy. They dug detail and stored ongoing extents of understanding to broadening society with intent to follow philosophy of the wise people.

All the while, Hebrews also concentrated on the same fundamentals with a different concept that God the Creator sparked their religion from past times, later, but before Jesus of Nazareth, the founder of Christianity. The unknown gain of words from Jesus as a rabbi to speak with the highest human corporal concept of the divine idea provided directions for people to grasp moral senses to retain and augment their lives in society. Teachings of the Hebrews established a belief as a melding declaration of life to pursue *happiness*.

Then God-fearing people explored the revelations of Jesus Christ's birth, so unusual from later times; a first formation of the New Testament Bible was compiled more than fifty years of archival data and personal information. The Bible was combined and engraved into a new man-made religion that minds associated writings with Hebrew religious philosophies. The expected coming of Jesus by one man known as John the Baptist, who told his devotees that a Messiah will be sent to aid Hebrews' religion, starting with propagation of his performance of baptism by John the Baptist. John also informed in received words, received mentally with religious minds. The compilation was transplanted into the minds of leaders by the Creator, called God at the time. God put messages in everyone's mind who accepted belief of Creation when written. To this day in our world, people scattered with enough divergences of beliefs that concoctions cannot be neither synthesized nor integrated.

Many warring times were expected solutions to gain peace through dominance in six or seven centuries later. Religious conversion by mankind leaders desired to convert religions even if it required warring in the name of God. Many leaders sacrificed fellow human beings to death as an aftermath.

However, mankind never reacted to agree on details of beliefs, so warring solutions proceeded as if on a schedule by fate from one generation to the next. It would be easy to count times it has happened in many countries across the globe based on political and religious beliefs. Many believed this happened systematically beginning from mankind's start to present day. Earlier, beliefs started almost mythologically with observations of sun, moon, and stars with interpretations of small-minded shallow beliefs.

Later, as it was believed or written in existing Bible compiled after Jesus's times, and later disclosed by mankind, man's life on earth will be involved in warfare. Most people could live in peaceable conditions as thinking human beings with power and control to follow "knowledge and experience" and not tend sparse beginning laws of nature and morality. However, mankind must maintain and follow laws prescribed by leaders.

From thereafter, new religions were man-made, comprised and devised as if demanded by the hearings of words from God in their minds. Leaders of mankind always needed a new denomination like fruit from different trees. Some religions are not viable or useful in a common way of religions when defiance of God's nature would be unacceptable. Each new promulgator answered his commitment to define natural, factual claims to words in the Bible as pretenders do thrones of royalty. This approach was nonsense of power control propagated by leaders of past days and sustained by their predecessors to present day. The self-service leader implied needs, desiring more respect, notice, and position, especially above others that evolved as *royalty*.

Where did they get religious ideas? Obviously, it was not from thorn crowning of Jesus Christ in his day of extreme persecution by nailing him on a large wooden cross, thrust with a spear in his side and left hanging until dead. Within that same ending week, Jesus, on Sunday, as professed, was believed by his disciples to be the son of God. *Christian philosophical* teachings were formulated in the *Christian Bible* as the son of God who arose from the dead after three days and consequently was identified and seen by some of his followers as a result of unexpected and unknown changes after the site of Jesus's death. Jesus had wandered noticed in a materialized body to some apostles who were unbelieving. Other disciples kowtowed to Jesus with words and sight. The Christian religion was propagated over the next few hundred years by Romans as Roman Catholic churches through formal continued persuasion were first led by unique popes throughout ages from Peter, as said by Jesus to Peter, "Upon this rock, I will build my church of believers." Second, Constantine I, the first Christian emperor of Rome, had substantiated the solidity of Christianity. The emperor Constantine I, called the Great Emperor of Rome, led Christianity during the 288 to 337 in Constantinople. The force of Constantine's devotion settled strongly among the people through the next few centuries. The Orthodox Catholics held on to their religion of the seeds of life's teachings, learning, and growth while towering with their parishioners with a belief; but as are all human beings, the entirety of mankind has their belief ranging from belief in God to atheists' belief in no God.

Starting at least by birth in AD 570? years, Mohammed was next to become a self-professed prophet until his death in AD 632. In his time, his new revelations of Allah (God) were collected in the Koran. He began his new profession of a man-made religion, started by creating spiritual writings by Mohammed, a desert nomad sheik. At the time, he was the leader of unidentified forces and means of little notice. After following his writings from existed Old and New Testaments of Christianity, he adjusted within his access and extractions personal singularities unknown to God. Mohammed also saw writings on the wall, so to speak, that led him to extend power by caressing pieces of Old and New Testaments into the Islamic Koran.

Much later in time, and when he finished his Koran of Islamic religion by interpreting writings from the Old and New Testaments that suited his vision, he thrust powerful forces on fellow nomads who were Arabs under his autonomous control as leader of Moslems. Maybe he wanted to be the dominating sheikdom king leader. He traveled with many fighters by his side to invade and convince other Arabs with force, making them settled upon his sea of believers in Allah as their God. The bevy of directions under his control as the religious leader with a threat of punishment was beginning with trouble because death was considered, if unfaithful, to anyone. He especially commanded women, who were specifically gauged by man, as those of the world's continents, as subservient to man in many interactions including religion, society, and leadership. The Islamic religion also eventually became under a widespread promotion in the surrounding areas in Mideastern areas of Indonesia and Malaysia by force to adopt the Islam religion or if in denial could be put to death as an infidel.

To the Christians, the Islamic religion became the first man-made religion by a nonreligious zealot, a nomad sheik, as defined, a self-appointed leader. This step was unique to ways Christians evolved their rabbi Jesus in belief as son of God.

Later, mankind followed or dreamed up new religious variations to be concocted to suit their desires. Now, even to this day and age, changes are consistent with man's beliefs, and under natural behavior, mankind's religions have been adopted under many circumstances with royalty of kingdoms devised. Other new religions have proceeded into modern times.

This is another instance of warring as Jesus Christ had said in his time that mankind's life is a warfare. I added we must include peaceable and happy times to minimize the warring as one might believe that God so delivered messages to mankind's minds. Man-made evolving religions, for a variety of reasons, move into medieval period and the First Renaissance period. The dominant religion of Christianity at that time was fully empowered. At times, Roman emperors such as Caesar prospered from its extent and tortured many human beings. The Romans showed more savagery than animals using fierce lions for the killings to dispense with the Christian believers. And it was done with wild animals to treat nonbelievers in Rome with beware of the inhuman potential treatment. During the next three to four hundred years, the same Christian religious activities prevailed. As was well known, Judaism religion was also practiced for many centuries. The isolated Hinduism and Buddhism religious faiths also flourished many centuries before times past throughout continents of Asia as philosophies for life's pursuits, all pre-Christianity far back in time but in the same span of what the Hebrews proclaimed as Hebrews Judaism religion. All tallied, mankind had a selection to make and many times chose not to comply with any of these religions by being identified as agnostics or atheists.

Now, beyond the medieval times, human beings became cognitive and inventive as they moved into the First Renaissance. Many leaders were concentrated on use of fear to control followers. They repeated past times with more same self-styled Bible claiming man-made religions, some out of whole cloth, which included those derived by royalties of countries.

The first one changed for England by Henry VIII during the First Renaissance in 1506, when he asserted royal supremacy over Catholic religion in England, giving birth to an independent Church of England, repudiating papal authority. Other new formations of churches were followed by mankind's good-sounding reasons of personal demands such as one started by Martin Luther, a Roman Catholic priest, by naming it the Lutheran Church. Then Luther was followed by Protestants and Presbyters, usually converted priests or parishioners from dominant Roman Catholic religion, to a formality of churches' names as defined by noted movements.

These new strongly supported religions led to origins of numerous other Christian denominations spread out today as several hundred denominations. Religious participants were so singularly inept from practice of religions that a diffuser of existing beliefs demoted time spent practicing it. Little more is chartered parishioner's expense, except those making money for its practice as leaders.

As people expanded, new lands were discovered, settled, and acquired. People were colonialized in part of other's homelands under expected human confrontation and potential warring. No one in modern days really knows what religious gain is to people except those whose minds prospered from its promotion and teaching, with repeated memories of teachings used as mental guidance. As a worthwhile offer to gain public attention and new members, all religions offer people of world charities of many kinds sponsored by giving gifts to congregates and church organizations.

No matter what was taught, all religions from the beginning of time are nothing more than a belief usually expressed the name of *Homo sapiens'* belief in God as the Creator. It is not a belief in personal opinions and extended discourse of people who promoted religions. Everything else is compromised according to mankind's justifications under natural and social laws.

Mankind certainly used laws enforced socially by organized governments politically set by laws of the countries in which some were based on religiously instilled morals. According to treatises on laws that govern mankind's nature, on earth, generally everyone knows what to respect. However, ways of carrying out respect depend on various incidents and events. The common laws are levied by nature on human beings, at least according to St. Thomas Aquinas, whose treatise of natural laws for people is a query that must be considered.

Philosophers and muses who offer principles to follow by practice in written critical analyses and reviews are understandable and usually followed. The concerns of man-made laws must take precedence with laws formally promulgated by laws made by the federal government leaders. In many occasions, imposed controls and regulations across the board minimized chaos because different mind psychology and wide levels of cognitive behavior include minds concerning interactive confrontations.

Why doesn't mankind mentally use their minds to determine how things were done during "good old days," to use a coined phrase, that worked? The changes of one with issue, whether it was better in past times or better now in modern days? If one changes pursuit of *steerage* and *amour* teachings and then apply attention as implementing "will of desire" automatically without recognizing aftermaths, then based on past, human beings would fail and their behavior would slowly become disjointed. This unnoticed loss of mentally insistence with instinctive tracking then pursues with bias, causing a loss of decision. Almost as an affliction unknown, this leaves learners a direct response of mental blindness when faced with illicit amorous pursuits.

Make sure originators of historically inherited *steerage* and *amour* were dormant in primeval original forest of God's mind from beginning of time. The Creator in his plan had continuous knowledge in the beginning and beyond knowing past, present, and future in all times. The beginning was recorded that the universe and God knew how to pursue wantonly desired *amour* driven by one's instinctive "will of desire" rather than use effective *steerage* gifted to *Homo sapiens* later with mentally induced memories of past "knowledge and experience."

In all minds of *Homo sapiens,* they should follow the mind's decisions. A few specific examples offered herein allow mankind to historic compilations that have tenuous amounts of truth that can be used to minimize turmoil in their lives. The latent, invisible historic knowledge for many years was what people had pounded into their brain's mind of modern-day mankind installing permanent records of unknown inheritances and memories from forbearers directly articulated.

Maybe from compilations from storytellers to storytellers to real genuine historians from the 5000 BC time era, even back to the far past where beings are not yet being found. "Knowledge and experience" of human discernment of the sun and thinking it is the Creator called God or something yet unknown. However, from the near present and on to future times, the current archeologist founded historical information that could be substantiated with findings of artifacts, scrolls of proof, forms of divinity, and with less belief and conjecture supporting it.

As it was during the First Renaissance at the middle of the fifteenth century and opening into the sixteenth century, seeking both *steerage* and *amour* was more aristocratic because of instilled genius afforded by teachers. But in pursuit, it was as recorded as instilled with dry wit among wise and shortsighted naysayers, and yet it was satisfying to creative minds and independent thinkers.

How it was deciphered by affected participants and their families is unknown unless written in self-written books. Only those affairs held within minds were assumed to be of modern-day behavior. However, behavior never changed the mental and good will of persons involved or even considered destructive behavior on individuals' lives.

Political and religious leaders exercised ardent control of nonassociates; common people were controlled by legally powerful people with significant punishment including imprisonment. This same class of officials adjusted to give casual relief enhanced with glow of achievements to immediate friends certainly, at higher levels of leading aristocrats and patrician families disguised, who were in favor of royalty.

Looking back further into the past times of the AD 1200 to the early AD 1300, ardor of early human beings before the First Renaissance but three to six hundred or five to seven hundred years after medieval times of the Dark Ages. Let's say during Dante Alighieri's time of writing. Alighieri's real surname was Durante. By the way, one of Hollywood's loved actors of comedic talent, song, and his own pursuit of love affairs was known because so many women loved him in their minds, not by his looks, but his social prolific exorable behavior. It was known that he sang and recorded love songs that became classics because he had a desirous following of fans.

History revealed those people seeking *amour* carried it out with societal positions, dominating their helpers in scheming and conducting affairs. The paramour usually had an ardent desire of will or simply wanted to pay back cuckolds for an interference or denigration of some making to their personal standing in society, with humor pasted in written words and with an aside of sardonic comedy accompanying pursuit. The nondescript stories of past times are referenced for erudite and true seekers of humor.

Back to the First Renaissance time era when religions impacted the practice of *amour* by followers that received harsh punishments causing continued reduction of bad conduct at times. Moral commitments were forced including ex-communication with alleged sinister or evil congregates personally driven ardor. There were times when some were burned on stakes as witches or imprisoned criminals. History implies moral commitments eventually originated from religious leaders and were imposed by people to control what was defined as evil behavior.

All action of control that was imposed was to combat sadistic and terroristic action as dictated by creatures of evil referred to as obsessed by the devil. The punishment usually resulted in death to insistently possessed offenders, many of whom were women, by fire or some other crowd-watching cruel death method. When punishment for defying God was installed, it came as the inquisition practiced at the beginning in Spain where a dominance of royalty prevailed. The practice was probably just as much in a widespread manner. This practice led, but to no avail except for heresy, broadly imposed religious controls, which led to rejection of religions. Ultimately, philosophically bent thinkers, decidedly unmoved by supernatural sources, would mentally change selected features of Christianity. They see judges with poor moral senses. It made those who break moral laws to be leery of men and woman.

The course of Judaism was held stalwart because within the sect, they were mostly satisfied with their adopted guidance from God. God's voice from above to prophets accepted Christianity. The real source of corroborating evidence was a big giant stone, enormous weight that opened as said by Christ, the son of God. Jesus was confirmed as guiding lights of mankind, and as endorsed by prophets of times, John the Baptist was one by words from God per the Bible if not in deciphering minds of mankind. Thus, foundational beliefs are extents of Source's interactions within minds of humans. *Homo sapiens*, modern man understandably accepted by religious minds, wonder about earth's origin along with paleontologists (those who study about prehistoric mankind such as Neanderthal and Cro-Magnon), including astrophysical scientists involved with mankind.

But alas! All of mankind has no idea of how time had passed over eons and distorted human minds into a little understanding of simple evolution that would have been easy to arrange by God, who created the universe. And God is still promulgated as the Source being spiritually believed through man-made religions. The idea and concept remain a mystery to believers and even to agnostics and atheists who hold on to their beliefs!

The pursuits of *steerage* and *amour* after the next two centuries from 1700 to 1900 were as always dominated in numbers by common people, but who are now enhanced with learned innovation separated by self-adopted qualifications such as part and parcel from poor people to royalty, leaders, and powerful of nations. The apparent ardor suddenly was beginning to thrive with mental gusto within groups of people who had status accounted more than aristocracy and those who propagated royalty since times past. The inhabitants of assumed royalty were promulgated in past times with power by powerful leaders who were successful in their acquisitions of land and control of people living on various lands in many ways. Those of royalty and their counterparts dominated people both socially and religiously with powers of imprisonment and death by enforcers to make serfs comply with demands no matter what positions they held. Most times, those of religious bents were treated as people who were against governments and were punished, some even to death for infringements of nonbelievers who dominated regal governments.

However, many centuries later, religions demanded domination as founded by the Arab sheik Mohammed, who practiced selectively the Islamic religion, which entailed forced compliance with threats of death as various sheikdoms were overtaken. Then for a time afterward when it waned, people spread ubiquitously to appear within upper classes of rich and powerful as they regained footing among the aristocrats.

The spread with royalty occurred as they imposed awards of related tenure such as princes and princesses, dukes and duchies, lords and ladies. The pursuit even counted down to royalty like knights, sirs, and proceeded in modern times to others. The spread of amorous affairs was boundless within royalty even more because there was no real control on upper-class citizens unless legal systems imposed specific laws as regulated by more powerful and higher levels of royalty. The control usually was set at king- or queen-named kingdom who had to apply laws to governed people of their kingdom under influence of rich and powerful. The thought was that they were special human beings and therefore must be admired and kowtowed to by subservient humans. All were born the same way, and as we were born, we inherited unique traits and have purposes and inherent desires as did all *Homo sapiens*.

And to this day, these same people of royalty are nothing more than common human beings that have no specifically selected different DNA other than by heritage and with no power to claim dominance. People's births were unique to all persons forever in their life as *Homo sapiens*. When other comparable life may exist elsewhere in God's universe, life of a dominant genus of families of mentally minded beings with decisive portentous minds must be categorized as the future unique species *Homo sapiens*.

CHAPTER V

Impact of Divita Family Living during a Second Renaissance Unassigned

The triumph of mind and will over illness and a thousand
of tasks is one of the ensuing spots in the book of man.
—*The Story of Philosophy*, Will Durant, p. 274

Advancements in modern times have mirrored the First Renaissance promises making the arts, music, and technology that evolved from the beginning to restart creative parts of the First Renaissance from 1474 into the 1550s. The new creation thereafter waned continually into 1700s, when a new beginning culminated with new advances with intelligence and culture and then related technology with mechanizations of new inventions. The personal evolvements included modern social and environmental behavior. The new thoughts of intelligence and new technical designs majestically being constructed showed unknown advancements have begun anew. The effects of these times were geniuses with intelligence and engrossed with creativity, innovation, and talent in technology, art, and music. The people, some wisest of beings, advanced with devoted teachings of art and music and teachings of *steerage* and *amour* within minds of teachers to enhance the mentality of minds of *Homo sapiens* to ensure making proper decisions. New human thrusts of behavior evolved with a new dominance in the human being minds' spirit, sensuousness, and compassion, which raised the bar beyond present and future expectations. The teachings had happened slowly as were beliefs in God's ways of his creation and continued evolution.

The top clergy of popes, Julius II and Leo X, and their teachers living during the First Renaissance expanded details of their troops that subtly displayed significations of warring to save their Christians.

Michelangelo Buonarroti, Mozart Wolfgang Amadeus, and Leonardo da Vinci, each, respectively, challenged new fantastic creations. Michelangelo created prime sculptures of the Pieta and Roman Catholic paintings on the ceiling composed of God's beginning glory in the Sistine Chapel, while being an architect and poet in his spare time. Mozart created classical music primly composed from his childhood until the end of his young life with grand continuation of his music. Leonardo da Vinci created new technology involving designs of new workable scientific prototypes that led to many new inventions. The telescope, which became the new prime major operating device of his making, continued development of telescopes into modern times for exploration in the universe. New technology and many drawings and paintings were best of all at the time and even in modern days, advanced new technology for the world.

The same teachings in Europe were enhanced with symmetry and rhythm instilled in the beginning of art of building, painting, and sculpture in Italy that also transgressed across the continent of European and beyond. The most noticed architect during the First Renaissance was the renowned Andrea Palladio (who lived from 1508 to 1580) with extensive broad scope masterful buildings, one of many of Roman architecture identified as Palladian Basilica throughout Rome and specifically in Vicenza, Italy. With the further teachings, the geniuses of those times who had continued to take colossal steps into the work in times of Galileo, Leonardo, Michelangelo, Mozart, and Palladio used their comparable genius, as did others in the same era of the First Renaissance.

The intent by firming beliefs with concrete information from the outcome of growth, many human beings continued discovery by pursuing both "will of desire" influences by *disloyal amour* and a lackluster pursuit of "knowledge and experience" influenced to make worthwhile decisions by following teachings of *steerage* and *true amour* that guide one's mind with discrimination.

New mentality marked transmissions from medieval to modern history as mankind's mind improved by untold increases of further decisive capability that increased needs for creativity, innovation, talent, and extended genius within minds of more unnumbered human beings. These refurbishments extended into the mid-1700s and brought on second newly inherited birthing of *Homo sapiens* minds that addressed *steerage* and *amour* from geniuses learned minds with inherited wisdom and understanding to fulfill needs of onslaughts of new advanced tools, electricity, radio inventions, and extensions of arts and music.

These steps require effectively thinking and wisest human beings to lead governments and societal improvements for countries, provinces, states, city statutes, and ordinances. The ways to decide to take care of land and all infrastructures and mass transit systems with controls are needed daily. The exposure of significance of what I have labeled as an unassigned Second Renaissance with many newly expected things enforced "the one of a kind" probability that much later, a Third Renaissance may start beyond mid-2000s that could gave birth to unknown entities needed by mankind that will capture a new approach into a new twenty-second century.

What! I say, thunderously grumbling, the car was not a cultural changer! However, I would never say cars did not have a cultural impact on explosions of unassigned Second Renaissance, if ever exclaimed. Khaire and other unknown archeologists with down slants in their learned eyes say same things when unknowns are revealed having significant values to mankind's lives in the future.

The act of buying a car alone does not go against what one holds dearest; it's for your sense of identity and what you think is appropriate and valuable. The ways radically new, culturally influencing products sometimes do unexpectedly; they represent grasping for new buys. The oil as a crude petroleum was extracted earlier by seat-of-the-pants wildcat derrick adventurers and increased oil drilling, and, eventually, the few geniuses developed fractional distillation. New oil engines improved conditioning and performed substantially better, bulking car industries with new oil and fuel for cars. Cars caused most singularly phenomenal cultural upgrades for human travel and even in modern times. The need for more cars forced critical even crucial pursuits of building large derricks resulted in hot debate, both détente and detest as noted but continues under government control of usage.

When women started using cars—cars alone did change the gender culture detest because women were well able to drive. Surely, it was a change enough because men did not think women should want to drive or even maybe they would not even be good drivers overall. Certainly, women were not known to be mechanical minded and maybe not strong and able enough to manage any kind of car faulting behavior. The change had uncounted effects on the growth of many mixed-gender drivers.

Then later, as the twentieth century proceeded during and especially after World War II, women, as did men, used cars to go to work, which in turn made it possible, even with widespread upheavals occurring by women at times, that working was a must for women. The car was the enabler. Modern pursuits now, as in the past, are a pursuit end use of oil and its derivatives. Much later, we moved on to more modern power sources, like solar, fuel cells, and batteries of unheard types and sizes, and even by electricity run by newly designed batteries that supply motors with alternators as chargers to give more distance of travel before needed charging.

Technologies seldom changed culture without mankind's involvement, but new creative inventors' minds enabled creative changes in significant ways. The creativity was formulated by mathematicians and electronic and mechanical engineers who knew mechanics of existing machines desperately, little about microelectronics before World War II. Communications was the driving force, and radios were researching frequency transmissions, and communications was going strong with electromechanical creations involved with ongoing needing radar systems warning assault attacks. The war brought on starts of mechanized codes. The next step was conceived inchoately about computers by inventing numbers methods of doing quick analyses. John Von Neumann, who was born in Hungary in 1903 but immigrated to America, became a citizen and a top mathematician. His first invention produced beginnings of computers. With new ideas, American people asked, "Is what we are doing right or wrong, and should it matter less?" "I will admit," Khaire continues, ". . . that most people don't like this kind of dichotomy." Then many new advancements in all fields certainly have made it easier to access more creativity and changed ways people would think about what we do day in day out living for America. An exceptional hurry for new inventions continued to be created in the '50s when the new transistor was developed and started development of large computers in mid-1950s with gusto from then on with new developments. Then by early 1980s, personal computers were developed by William Gates and Steve Jobs with different teams of creators that evolved separate computer types, and others were modelled after their computers. Both types were used in offices and later in homes that expanded enormously with great demands and costs.

Then Steve Jobs created the iPhone, and after the first production sold, it took off like a magic carpet of delivery to or bought by many buyers, pouring into Apple significant amounts of money beyond belief. Even to this day, new versions are produced, making his company a multibillionaire. The Information Pad (iPad) was next connected with Google and other companies and many other personal and business computers that have changed the way we think, work, and behave. They say, the iPad, along with iPhone, has certainly changed the way we live lives and our times. That is, relaxation and communication with each other both for personal and business reasons go on continuously and easily extend the need for advised steerage and amour knowing how the people's minds continue to behave with instinctive thoughts and easily lose making proper decisions requiring "knowledge and experience" so obvious in their minds.

I find it hard to believe that merely having an iPad will lead one to contentment that could change ways one thinks. I say, "If that is so, it may be sporadic unless one is solving a problem concerning or interacting with the iPad to ensure final decisions, confirmations, or compromises."

The business of innovation is a valued product among so few of those that have it, and they are always in pursuit of what they are happy doing, even having fun. Creating culture, if not only socially changing products and building industries around them, is difficult on any number of fronts. First, almost by their nature, they rub against accepted norms and conventions of appropriateness and values to people as well as innovators.

The very act of creating a market for new products that go against conventions and norms of what we value and of what we think is appropriate, which means ". . . that you must change what we think is appropriate." Take rap music and the hip-hop culture, which sprang from a world that few people knew or understood even after it was screened on television or in motion picture theaters. Hip-hop at times did not fit into anybody's conventions of what was appropriate and valuable. Khaire says, "It offended as many people as it delighted. But the fact that it sold is itself an indicator that somewhere, somehow, you managed to change people's way of assessing something as appropriate and valuable." Broad scope in this world of billions of people is that people can bring about adequate returns that may be cultural influences, but also might be insignificant, but could be deleterious.

The one legitimate to advance culture is a job for historians after extensive research. Loyalty is examined daily while historians often take much more time and planned time to continue to tell those who were embedded with infidelity refuting natural laws and implied religious morality.

One example of royalty-driven or a flaunted royalty and aristocracy is easy to point as a happening in times of great Shakespearean kings so written and highlighted after our times to come. What I read is the life's activity of Henry VIII, how he changed things with the use of his "will of desire" and even though consequences of changes evolved were insignificant, morally and naturally, because it continued under other leaders who wanted changes and did make a practice of changes. The indicated changes continued but lost its force as the rich humbly fell into palatable admiration of aristocrats above all by their unthinking. Fear of royalty's power and its immediate dispensation under many circumstances is always questionable. Others who were taught mentality enhanced "knowledge and experience" but *steerage* were ignored by royalty except when forced upon their meager considerations by pompous revelations as those who practiced it without exposure.

Church of England is just another of many man-made religions, and those that followed created newly claimed religious leaders that impressed crowds of serfs greatly. The religious leaders amassed money galore to control believers in God, using God-granted preaching methods to masses. These religious prophets in their minds are displayed with fool's gold cloth that gathered parishioners to maintain and fill churches. The real shepherds of God's creation of mankind should have demanded the devil's wishes to be outcast from minds of many, but God gave mankind their will by prayer of contrition with humility and compliance to be done at their own volition.

Pick one from Christianity and then one from an extension of man-made variations thereof (e.g., Protestants, Baptist, Presbyterians, Lutherans, Anglicans, Episcopalians, Mormons, Hindus, Buddhists, and Islamists), made to fit the bill and pointed professedly as a religious royalty. The main gist of the story is told effectively using Christianity especially involving Romans from days that were glories of Roma (spelled in reverse, "Amor") to which is now Italian people who critically inherited pursuits of sensuous desires by their nature and openly behavior exposure. They, as do most human beings throughout different religions, simply follow hardwired paths that dominated animals instinctively affected only, instantaneously, congenitally fully aflame sensuously in minds of religious people.

To reveal this observation of people of several ethnic groups and religions covering times past, one from Jewish, Buddhist, Hindu, and Islamic points of view, was disclosed in earnest to show similarities and likely natures of mankind across the globe regardless of beliefs in God's universe of his making and yet may be released to controlled explorations by mankind at some point in the future that continually changes.

In summary, the significance of end results of widespread amorous ventures all being close to sharply similar if not truly alike and all outcomes end close to afflicted aftermaths. The actual pursuits are now exposed with both good and bad endings based on following *steerage* and *amour* within needed training that come about via heritage. Those who had gained it as part of their heritage and passed it on to newly indoctrinated happenings almost unnoticeable except by ways teachers of *steerage* and *amour* live their lives.

I withdrew memories that I recalled from my brother Frank's life, my protagonist being the eldest son of our siblings. After many years, he had become the father of five children. This tie will give the reader character essences of Frank's life of recall by me from what he generally expounded during his childhood and later when he informed me years later about his life and how to live it by his teachings of his two younger brothers, Gene and Eddie, yet to become substantially fulfilled as adults with self-sufficiency. Their continuation to educate their own younger siblings followed the same way. The essence of his earlier life was revealed later as he took on teachings of *steerage* and *amour* mostly received from his father Benny and mother Josephine and his grandmother Filippa over ten years of his life and already got married to his sweetheart Betty Young.

Frank then, at times, voiced to me after being a married adult contented herein as an everyday occasion to reveal himself as he completed college. The next time I saw him at home, his eyes narrowly opened to view surroundings in Mom and Dad's home where they were staying until they figured out what he will do with a major in music and working on a teaching degree. Shortly in his midyear, Frank took a position in Peterstown, West Virginia, to teach music at the local high school, and Betty moved with him. What happened then was, within a short time, he was drafted in the army and made up his mind to join the air force.

Frank first looked back in time to recall their firstborn child, Beverly, now asleep in her bed as a teenager, as was Cheryl also. At the time, Janie was about six, and the two twin boys, about three or four, were the youngest. He pondered with silence in a whisper as he ejected mentally a memory's thought. "I always awakened when bright morning sunlight shining through windows." And then subconsciously, he thought, as he later told me, "Lights even undetected with closed sleeping eyes release my conscious mind." He then thought aloud, "Another part of my mind was working. When Frank gets up, he is dressed enough to have breakfast."

Knowing Frank, after, his venture was to help his mom and dad when they needed help; all the while doing his business as the owner of car dealership in Montgomery. His plan was while now working on his new home nearby across the tracks on Fayette Pike, expect him to be excited with his children now grown as much as himself. Frank usually thinks while taking a stand. Quietly, he walked barefooted to a closet, grabbed his robe, engulfed it as if a boxer leaving the locker room, and noiselessly waved his arms, creating a con brio sound beamed into air with a smile. He noticed his declining leg strength and shoulders on mirrors, as we all did. He thought loudly to himself, "I'm an Italian stallion, but I am retired from the ring." In this corner, hesitatingly again with words aloud as he passed wall mirrors, saying, "You've got to start exercising!"

Silently, he then reached under a carved dressing chair to get his lamb's wool leather slippers. He forced them on as his mind released a mental note, asking, "What job is on my mind today? I hope it's not me doing the same old things."

Betty had awakened with a twisted body and responded as she eased out of bed quietly. She saw all the kids sound asleep. Covers snuggled over most of their bodies with wisps of air from each as they cozied with love and security. She left the room. These boys, now up in age, during days, spent a lot of time fiddling with games and finishing homework.

It is now early morning, and Frank was on his own thought, as I would expect him, as we brothers were very alike. He worked his way into a comfortable place in the kitchen and then put on coffee and waited. While that unsought message was all that was on his mind this early, his words seeped out from his cerebellum to recapture his normal stance, activating important timely mental thoughts.

I heard his mind again in my memory, from what he had told me, in a light shout, "I'll go get the newspaper!" And without further thinking, as with only one purpose afloat in his mind, he drifted out to his carved white oak wood front door, opened it, and inhaled an intake of fresh moist air coming up the open driveway, looking out toward his highland about one hundred feet down the lawn and looking everywhere. He jumped when he heard his poodle bark at the door.

While looking for the newspaper, the cool breeze kept hitting his face. He thought the paper was never in the driveway and moved toward the glistening grass and greenery. His mind's thought process automatically released an unexpected message as he always would say, "Find the paper and get back inside!" He treaded down a few steps into the grass enough to see some water droplets scatter from the filled dewdrops, bent down, almost slipping, and picked up the wet but not soaked newspaper, raised his body, balancing, and circled to view the area, may be looking out for strange dogs, which usually leave a surprise for him.

Then he said, "I straightened, looking toward the east as I dodge the sun. I could see a few dewdrops stationary but glistening on the top of my slippers." And with a simple wonderment in his mind, out came "Dewdrops on my slippers! That sounds like a title to a song!" He turned and stared away from the radiant, almost blinding early morning autumn sun bouncing and reflecting off every piece of glass it could find at the front of the house. He was squinting with half-closed eyes at our lilac tree now in bloom, seeing reflected bluish-white petals and the red-dotted pistils from flowers and especially at its location where it grows in the center of our front yard. It was bordered with a few red roses also appointed with balls of dewdrops from the night's self-imposed condensation. The sun's reflection glistened off the pollen on the anther of the stamen; the glistening on the petals making them seem luminescent to his sight and my mind.

Then as a flower lover, he changed and let himself have it by saying, "I'm behaving as if I will have no problems to face today." As he turned, looking intently toward and across the driveway to the surrounding greenery, he saw an old turning brown newspaper under the neighbor's juniper tree's lowest branch. The scent of juniper tree, although not pungent, smacked his nostrils sharply. The evergreen spun his thoughts to Christmastime. Then he recalled, that's nothing unusual; with his mind's eye, he got the aroma every time he passed to go to the car. The aroma triggers an unusual response of past delightful times of summer.

All during this visiting time, we continued to talk while at home during times when everything else was ongoing by the family. Frank did ignore looking for the old paper. Then he changed his mind's thought train. He returned to a common place, thinking he would find a piece of paper in an unknown place under a hedge fragrant of white jasmine. The aroma was picked indecipherably when he noticed the newspaper was folded the old-fashioned way with a closed leaf squeezed slanted under the plant. He bent into a reminiscent position challenging his personal physical competence without words, but with a fussy twist of his jaw, he picked up the paper as he arose and paused to contemplate sunshine, warming air. He looked like he was reminiscing about what had happened these past few years. He said orally, "What have I done to deserve this blooming life that has blossomed into my family with my wife Betty?"

We went into the house and was walking into the living room as Betty entered the room. And we both obviously missed the constraints on the boys because it was already dished out by Betty with a hand chasing them. Frank grabbed her and gave her a big kiss, and she smiled and stopped the chase with an exchange of kisses. These types of family confrontations happened as the years passed. My early years flew by like I was a stallion prancing to show my stuff to no one or anyone that might be watching.

I saw the kids' faces covered with odd-shaped smiles staring at the kids and Pat and me. Two of the girls look up with mouths full of food. Then the two boys fussed for more bacon. Our children were calm while at the table. With my mind still in slow motion, we commented on how we forgot about how time flies when doing nothing but relaxing like an angel. At this time, Betty poured coffee to the adults and started eating. Then I thought, *Today she's early.* Betty, casually pretty and always with a mild-mannered expression of service, formed a bright smile. Frank said lowly, "Wow! Honey, how can this be? No one was in the kitchen when I got up, but now everyone is eating. And our two boys are really eating. How long have we been outside? The morning dew caused me to think about a few things that put me where I am today in the 1970s."

I sat down in my chair, looked at the clock showing 6:40 a.m., and said, "I'm about a half hour late." Betty put my plate filled with two eggs and several pieces of bacon on the table while I was scanning noticeable political headlines of the newspaper. I always look for jewels from the administration getting ready for the next election in a few years in 1972. God and I only know who's going to be the next president of the United States of America, and now it's very likely to be Richard Nixon now that Lyndon Johnson has decided not to run a second time with such a calamity over the Vietnam War, and that's the truth.

Thinking about my children at the kitchen table forced Frank's mind with a wondering thought that jutted into a reminiscent of what he could count on his hands without refutation about lingering times. Frank remembered when his family helped Mom and Dad with money before the current times in the late 1940s into the 1950s.

From the beginning when Dad rebuilt the home on 618 Third Avenue, Frank, with Gene and Ed, had helped Dad do a lot of practical fixes, things around the house from top to bottom. We did any form of painting and plumbing repairs both at home and at his business, while in school, and before he got married—who doesn't? Much later in the '50s, when by joint desire we were living in Mom and Dad's home after moving to downtown Montgomery, Dad could afford to buy a home. Mom and Dad's children always worked at supporting the family needs. We were a family that not only thought about our families but also knew what to do, thinking by themselves, for our parents as they grew up. Let me say that my dad did not stay around to do work himself; he had to go to work. Instead, he always taught us in his manner of detail that he had inherited via *steerage* that he learned from his mom and dad. Later, when he would come back home, he would check that it was done and was done right and then would give us compliments galore.

Back when I was a kid still in grade school, I remembered Dad always gave us a few nickels and dimes at times, and other times, we weren't paid and didn't ask why. Dad always said, "Why don't you ask for what you want instead of beating around the bush?" I'm not looking for credit, but we earned a deep appreciation for us becoming the men we are now by following his detailed *steerage* as he used it. What Frank had done, helped my family maneuver into modern days into the early 1950s later in their lives after expending their prime mostly learning from family peers, uncles and aunts, my sister Jane, and other relatives that made them inhale practices that solved weaknesses in our young ages.

Some of the details I had remembered as if they were captured as a motion picture show. Dad trusted his children and never failed to keep track of us using any means he could raise to his favor. With my memory and desire, I will uncover a more substantial piece of their living and my family's lives later when it imposes significance and meaning to the way we were brought up. It was easy to relay to my kids all that is good and truthful that came from their grandparents, and when I say grandparents, I mean my mom and dad; they were the real leaders of our lives, who did not shy away from interactions and demands. Each of our children had a mixed interaction with love and demand from their grandparents, and, overall, it worked throughout their lives. They were even more insistent as my parents for social correctness, and they used *steerage* to teach our children as needed, and it worked. My parents' efforts and teachings must have doubled their parents' influences on our kids' minds because sheer times of devotion allowed us as parents to teach them proper *steerage* and *amour* where hard work was so demanding. Just knowing this fact, I knew that Divita family progenies of Benny and Josephine Divita satisfied them sufficiently to continue to help our parents in their aging lives. We all adopted many of their everyday teaching methodologies, which began to lead to more decisively beneficial outcomes to our own children.

There goes my mind thinking into the past again, about Frank and Dad in particular. Dad was a businessman all his adult life. He always had time for his grandchildren while Frank's family was living in Mom and Dad's home. The grandchildren demanded to be seated on his lap every morning at breakfast. He was full of humor and love and responded to each of them with happiness and wit. They had personal fun interacting with him, and his stories were told with humor or rhyming words that caught their fancy. Happiness and smiles were commonplace love in the home of our mom and dad.

Then I recalled that Frank, in the early '50s, went into talking about different previous subjects about different wars to let me know how he felt about his life then. Now that his life is before him, I had known only a little bit about his times at my young age. I had only finished my sophomore year in Montgomery High School, and Frank had finished college at WVIT and then married Betty. Within the next year, he was drafted; but instead of being drafted, he joined the United States Air Force and was stationed at the military airport in New York.

He flashed back to times after he had married Betty; without thinking, we talked about the concern between Chosen under Japanese control from 1910 to1945. Within the next few years, Chosen divided into North and South Korea in 1948, when the America was part of the NATO treaty with United Nations and allowed these new countries to be separated, first, the democratic country Republic of Korea under an ambassadorship after World War II became known as South Korea and had their capital city as Seoul. Then the Democratic People's Republic of Korea became known as North Korea, which then became a full Communist-run country taken over by Kim Il Sung in the capital city of Pyongyang. The two countries became major enemies.

Frank was in the air force for more than a year. After his discharge, his next change of life guided him back into music as a teacher after the war had ended in 1952. A lot of local friends' and neighbors' sons fought, some severely wounded, and some local personal friends and neighbor boys were killed, and some died earlier in life after that war. For such a small war, many American and United Nations soldiers were killed, as were an enormous number of Koreans were killed and a great deal of suffering by the people of the Korea as countries. Many soldiers directly involved suffered depression, especially by our soldiers, who suffered mentally, and others were physically devastated with post- traumatic stress disorder (PTSD). Most troopers' injuries, be it mental or physical, now will never be the same or even treated the same as before the war. This is the usual aftermath of wars. Yet the warring remained unsolved by even visionaries in power in many countries, especially in Asia when North Korea and China became Communist countries.

What's more important is that when my father's taxi business was failing, Frank and family moved to our mom and dad's home to help. In a short time, he became a partner with Dad for a few years, and their compatibility was superior. Frank headed daily operations of the company because he had energy and time to make sure it's on course. In the small town of Montgomery, Frank ran the company with a strong hand to maintain his position with friends, associates and customers, and family members who work for him and bought cars from him. After all, he was one that did most of the real money work, at least that's what we all thought. His workers may have another opinion of him as he had mentioned to me at times, but he did get needed professional work from his two uncles Charley and Jimmy and several of Frank's children. The other Divita families and their cousins were always in the dealership to get any work on their cars as needed.

Frank, with words from my mind, did release a lot of discussion as time went by because he would go into details of buying and signing for buys and inventory and paying bills. We often talked about money and borrowings thereof. He was the man behind daily readiness every time he walked into his place of business with me. I tagged along when we visited our Divita family's relatives. The business has to do with automobiles, new and old ones; it can't be too complicated because car business is old hat now after his business grew into Topsy, as described, "she had just growed . . ." as in *Uncle Tom's Cabin*. Frank was well-educated in new cars for years before the middle 1960s and continued with whatever strife encompassed his time as it began to change his happiness as he put it in my mind that led to a future expose of extra consequences described by him later, appropriately.

The business of current times included car sales and detailed repair services in Frank's garage. He teamed with my father to buy cars, new and old, for his friends and for the taxi business. And they fixed the old ones to sell. We repaired all cars and sold parts needed to satisfy our customers. If there is any other business harder to manage people than car businesses, I'd like to know which one fits the bill. One thing for sure—you never know who is trying to do what to gain some advantage, especially when it comes to money and relatives.

First news that popped into my mind as headlines dominated pages continually about international war events. Within the next year or so, peaceful intents still existed with compromising demands for the Korea War to end. As the time passed, a treaty was signed in Panmunjom in 1953. Even now, United States troops are still stationed at the demilitarized line at the 38-degree parallel in defense readiness.

Frank recalled to me that he gathered thoughts about what had happened in those last few years, which was a different warring time. Wartime in Korea was against citizens of all kinds previously known as Chosen. Koreans mostly looked the same, and during war fighting incidences, many troops of the North were dressed as citizens with hidden weapons to kill our troops by surprise attacks. The ways of killing brought about killing fields of times for many Koreans; some needed to be killed, but others did not get killed but simply were captured.

Suddenly, Frank's train of thought ran off track because he heard sounds of little people's feet pounding on the floor quickly almost before he turned the front page. He was inundated with two kids in his lap and lost his thoughts. Later, he called me into the kitchen to let me know what he recalled several times to let me know what was on his mind at the time and how he was absent from the real warring.

With a slow pace, Frank now moved toward the steps in his thought line that included a change from his business to include involvements with his children's independence saddled sometimes with poor judgment. He had less work time on his mind, no matter what diversions occurred; he worked problems at work and at home. He told me that he recalled his best time of the day being around the kids in the early years. Even though it was short, it was having his kids in his lap and giving him their demands, trying to force him into buying them things he never even knew would be on their mind. The thought quickly disappeared as if he saw an image of his earlier life as a kid who didn't have the nerve to ask or demand something from his parents, even a new pair of shoes, even when the soles were flip-flopping.

There goes his mind again with internal messages to me as he mumbled and then broke in with his words as a query, "Is my breakfast on the table? I've got a lot to do today." He looked down at his plate and, within his mind, said something like, "I've finished!" He saw no bacon and eggs on his plate. He looked around and noticed that Betty was no longer in the kitchen. His coffee was almost finished. He quickly finished a last drink and left me in the room without a pause heading to our bedroom.

When he came back, our two girls were playing, full of mixed words and giggles, both still in pajamas, Janie happily clasping her toy teddy bear while trying to get around my leg to sit on her dad's foot. Cheryl pushed Little Janie aside with intent of doing the same thing. Now, both are on his legs. Then as he managed to sit down on his easy chair, Janie pushes Cheryl off, and she maneuvers so she can get on his lap with a wet and maybe a dirty diaper. As Frank moved her, he knew it was there, and he looked for the rescuer.

Both kids now gathered on the floor with an aroma that triggered escape. But they both still went out to their mom with their baby talk, whimpering unintelligibly, released but with a pleading face and hands seriously seeking a cleanup.

Beverly, the eldest, came in and said, "Where's Mommy? She didn't dress us yet. We want to go outside."

Frank softly said, "Here she comes, Cheryl. Tell her you want to get dressed. I am tuned to those two girls who showed a desire to be recognized and loved." He pondered with "How does anyone get to know kids, and how do they figure out what to do? How can they always seek a way to make a place for themselves?" As an expectation, I said to Frank, "Their minds release the expressions of their souls, and both work to their advantage. Sometimes, it's to their disadvantage depending on how they take in what they hear or how they pay attention to what they are thinking or have been taught."

Frank said, "I see a lot of different kids every day respond to personal interactions, social situations, confrontations, and environmental conditions, which always amazes me when I am observing them with an attempt to teach some specific useful behavior at their age with whatever amount of 'knowledge and experience' that existed at the time." For my own mindful ways, Frank wondered, "Do they use their minds around people that love them? And is their home life thought of as everyday activities that embellish their little minds with behavior patterns yet to be recorded in their memories, every single thought and involvement with an indelible path to their taught *steerage* primarily?"

Frank retorted, "That sounded like me, not the kids. Their time will come when the use of *steerage* and *amour* will remain embedded and guide them with what myself and Betty have taught them."

As I write this memoir, I find responses within my mind much later than Frank's family time to them now, but in my memories. Maybe some are easily recalled, but sooner than later, if paths of understanding are uninteresting, the memories could disappear. Frank makes a few final statements that I recalled along the same discourse. From what I recalled, he said he hoped they would grow up to fixate paths of mentality to common sense and use common sense every time it pops up. The most important ingredient is maintaining a heart and soul disposition of happiness within the family. We all know that our conscious and unconscious minds should work simultaneously to our advantage, but that instinctive impulse is always working when we do not use our "knowledge and experience." But when excited, the action is not collectively evaluated and registered. The action normally responds to general conditions of involvement. The mind insists, especially when at a choice of strengths, by responding by previous practice not in concert to aid or hinder the controlling influence that's principle with each other's pathways of disclosure but by body, mind, and emotional desire.

As time passed, Frank recalled that Divita families visited each other and have get-togethers. The interactions of these three young girls of Frank and Betty's left in our mind's traces of good judgment, but it is unknown to anyone's mind how the disheartened sincerity and soul emotionally exudes mental capability so obviously shown in concert by the families who have suffered warring times. Maybe it's none of the above. It could be my family prejudices smothered in blood inheritances but saddled with *steerage* and *amour* to gain true love and happiness. With thinking about influencing mental processes in a hereditary extraction, I am mentally trapped.

Then I hear within my mind silently but clearly as exclaimed one time by Cheryl, asking with an ejaculation, "Dad! Do you even know how your own mind works? With your great behavior and personality, how could you know another human being's mind's concerns in any situation?" Consciously, with a quick subconscious retort inwardly and still silently and unexpectedly, she ejected loud enough only for me to hear, "I know I don't know! I meant it. I don't know."

Frank thought about it, even wondered if the mind works in concert based on random heritage formulations extracted from his mind's memory storage and processed with exclaimed heartened sincerity that he said something like, "I would usually be relieved."

If minds worked on every given issue of moments involved and when it takes considerable time to extract input to guide or give direct orders at the moment, it should come to a knowledgeable decisive conclusion even when desire may be an alternative, especially under evaluation when one already knows when emotional or even sensuous desires might have potential effects on others.

This level of deduction should be avoided, be it personal and morally confined; no one wants to naturally develop mindful thoughts for different responses to diametrically oppose answers that reveal differences to children's average mind's intelligence.

This type of battling led to problems of smoldering contentions and court cases within the United States and as well confrontations in both Koreas that involved troops taken to courts. The Korean War was a long time over but never really ended except when North and South Koreas divided their country at the demilitarization line at 38th latitude between North Korea and South Korea. My mind continued to wonder what happened during the Korean War with our new military supplies and new training methodologies, some of which did not work well or failed to gain any advantage.

What happened at the beginning of a separation of two countries was the split because the two ideologies, Communism and democracy, had to be separated. Syngman Rhee was president from 1940 to 1960 when known as South Korea. South Korea was on America's side and under NATO protection. The Republic of South Korea in 1962 now as a separate country was a republic democracy with a newly elected president. North Korea, now Democratic People's Republic of Korea in 1961, became hardwired Communists, and all people who were involved or living in South Korea or potentially on a list were going to be killed in the coming war.

All this happened first because the United States and Russia had an interest being so close as a nation and knowing plans were already in place for North Korea to become a communistic form of government. Both countries agreed jointly to remove Japanese forces from the North Korea when they decided to split into two countries at the 38th parallel. Second, the fact that both countries had decided they could not reunify Korea because of political strife between the leadership of Syngman Rhee, who was replaced. Syngman Rhee lived only a few more years until 1965 in the Republic of South Korea. Rhee was backed by the United States during World War II. The Chinese paid special attention to evacuate him, and some of his people were sent to safe havens; nevertheless, some leaders met with unknown disaster.

The Soviets backed Kim Il Sung of Democratic People's Republic of Korea in new North Korea. Initial fighting was between South Korea's leaders located in Seoul and the Communist rebels in Pyongyang, who were in violation of existing treaties between United States and Korea as part of associations between United States and Korean leaders that were made after World War II. The United States already had troops pulled out from the country Chosen. Afterward, North Korea attacked the South Korea and the United States returned troops and commanded an authorized coalition military force under the auspices of the United Nations to push the North Korean back to the 38th parallel advisory positions.

This was all known to United Nations that was formed in 1947 after the war and organized internationally to ensure peaceful coexistence within nations. With the onslaught of Communist rebels, the United Nations Security Council passed Resolution 84 that gave the United States of America command of the use of UN forces in Korea of which during warring, America was the dominant supplier of all military weapons and materials, and American troops included the army and marines and navy ships, who were the main fighting forces. Initially, the goal of this war was to remove the Communist dictatorship that had overtaken the northern part of Korea.

If this could have been achieved, then United States would be instrumental in reuniting North and South Korea into one country. This vision was not accomplished because broad scope Communist support from China and Russia had collectively been supporting and supplying North Korea to prevent a takeover.

This became an American issue between President Truman and Gen. Douglas MacArthur that resulted in a strife of high-ranking military leaders unforeseen in our times and an odd retirement of one of the most famous, indefatigable, conscientious, and decorated generals in American history. More than fifty thousand names of our dead soldiers were carved into walls in Washington, and more glory was assigned to the Arlington National Cemetery.

After several years of fighting torturously personal assaults on American troops and citizens of the south, a compromised truce was led and negotiated by John Foster Dulles to keep the country separated as the two countries and as now known from the end of the war. The separation will be like all breakups of other countries that have occurred in other countries. The likelihood that they will be rejoined as one is highly improbable in our time, as have been all other attempts to restructure countries to establish a new country. In particular, the Israelis, who were a numerous collection of homeless refugees after the Second World War, continue to war with countries next to the new Israel.

The mess of what will be elevated next by the Communist pursuit was the begetting of a Cold War of the '50s, especially under China and Russia's domain. America placed shrouds of recognition over our dead soldiers' graves in Arlington to pay respects to those brave men who were not fully prepared to fight wars in Asian jungles. Later, the overall Cold War lasted until the '80s but with an ever-present clandestine entity on both sides of the fence. The Americans and our allies that survived the Korean War after honorable discharges, many soldiers uncovered a new life as social cultural pursuers, especially those who entered college with GI bills in America or maybe even in their own countries. Those lives were lost, and others had died for naught; no problems were solved regarding the two Korean countries, leaving the two countries and America with troops stationed at the demarcation of the demilitarization line at the 38th parallel.

These many warring times continued and involved America and the American people with continuous stress and personal concerns that current behavior patterns change significantly until Ronald Reagan became the next president of the United States of America.

This last recall in my memory's sorting directed orders jolted by Frank's memory about a recent time that he told me he felt mentally alone at odd times even when he was married. Especially when he was the mayor of Montgomery, he had to figure out ways to do the right things when peoples were told lies, innuendos, or equivocations with a slant versus what was intended to be the truth of the matter. As usual, it was spread to many families and friends, all for naught, and unbelievable to try to work out some problems. What had happened in his mind at that time that mentally seemed only an instantaneous moment ago, the same thoughts were significant to my nature to work out problems that evolved to a dominance of satisfaction.

In the next instant that passed, my recollection skipped to what had occurred two years later when he worked out a pursuit with his dad, in a way to help him restart Dad's wavering taxi business. My mind's functioning wanders; it ponders. Then in the mid to late 1950s, Frank's family had been living in his parents' home. He paid his share of household costs and daily care for the children mainly because he was working with my father as a partner in his taxi and transfer business. He had a small amount of money that he put into the business to revamp its attraction and increase the business. After this had happened, we two families were closer to how real living the common life felt, especially the daily interactions both in good spirits and sometime even discourteous encounters to ensure proper care of the home with young kids.

And now, by paying attention to family affairs of daily life, Frank told me that he determined how easy some form of *amour* comes into one's life without really pursuing it on a needed or directed basis. Sometime after a few years had passed, he began to keep a record of how amorous events made their way into peoples' lives, especially our extended family. This stacking and staggering revelation of "Amour!—what's it all about?" is also a question that released his observations during his remaining lifetime and those within my immediate and extended family and among family friends where familial contention existed.

Later, after about eight years more, my brother Gene was a practicing psychiatrist as he said to Frank much later, paraphrased: Gene told Frank and Ed that it was a good connection at the time, if not a better situation, when two families lived together to solve problems with compromise. Only a few relationships hinged within minds that later reflected on both families' lives with minimum agitation because of unlimited compromise with help from Mom and Dad. Why do I let my mind recall this event? It registers a stirring moment of personal gain and getting to know details that my other younger siblings might never experience for their own good simply with a lack of interest or with excuses.

Suddenly, beating hearts I heard mentally from the family. Frank, with a silent mind and pulsating heart, tried to trigger a response openly in a whisper from his dad's mind's memory, saying, "Wake up! You're about thirty-five years old, and you are on your way to bigger things." We both have friends. Dad had been asking Frank to go into another phase of life with a new career. His dad said outwardly within the family, "Your local friends and city leaders are interested in you as a person with a good mind and major concerns about our city!" The words have spread to important people in the city.

Frank was in awe of expectations. Remembering what he had at his early age, he thought he had been blessed or had earned good fortune staring at his face in the mirror. Certainly, he claimed he was blessed because his mom and dad raised him, and he will never forget them. And with the same heritage, he adopted this guide of his life, which will be responsible for his wife and family. It was his confidence that he explained to his family at different times that makes him feel purposeful, concentrated, and loving. Frank knew he could manage this common but big business and sizeable responsibility.

A responsibility that he called "taking care of my new family." In this situation, it includes throughout our being involved with some of his younger brothers, a sister, and my dad. Under the circumstances, I could have used my two elder brothers, who are within a few years of my age, to help, but they're out with their own careers and in other states.

Frank knew that Ed had a going career as an engineering physicist when he joined the new nuclear division at Glenn L. Martin Company. Now, he had already been working for the past eight years on portable nuclear reactors for the United States Defense Department for the army, navy, and air force. Martin Company was developing self-supporting portable reactor systems for selected emergency sites where electricity was needed or services for hospitals in poor areas or where troops would require more power for communications and operations. Ed stayed with the company about nine and a half years and was asked to join the research staff at the Jet Propulsion Laboratory under NASA's control through California Institute of Technology.

Gene was always in touch with Frank after he graduated from University of Richmond Medical School in 1957. He married the love of his life, Peggy, and the two headed to an internship at Baylor University Hospital in Houston, Texas. Frank said that he had let his brothers know what his plans were because he would be on his own with a new dealership, really changing his course for life. Both of my elder brothers were busy forming their own lives with responsibilities and guides, but all kept in touch so that they would have inherited required teachings of *steerage* and *amour* taught to well-educated men. They naturally followed *steerage* taught by their mom and dad casually during their younger lives.

Frank marveled as the next few years passed, almost skipping seasons, if not months when things needed to get done, but never got fully done without attention paid unrelentingly. The most important was using my work with my dad as a jumping point to gain a job with one of his friends in the local dealership. Frank wandered with might as if he knew much about where his life and memories were heading and would be in the right direction. Frank told families every time we visit that his new business is improving. He disclosed his heart's pursuit in words that the buildup was always active and positive, leaving his mind's memory fully thanking God. He gave his mom and dad credit for having made his first move to go after the dealership. He used his mind and personality and, of course, his salesmanship especially selling a quantity of cars every month. Frank's capabilities captured the essence from within his mind a "knowledge and experience" that he relished selling cars.

After doing same old work day in and day out, he plowed usually, with his draft horse strength, so to speak, or braggadocio, and continued recall of what was indelibly printed in his memory all wrapped up in words many had heard in his sales as time passed. He recognized neglect, regret, and redo, and with some achieved more progress in both natural and moral lives in the family. It was like a subvention had occurred without any great expectation. The money came from out of the blue heaven like stars that light up after total darkness occurred simply by earth's spinning.

Frank now had "knowledge and experience" after helping his dad make his taxi company come back financially. Later, Frank was offered the promised partnership of his friend Jay's because the business had become a successful car dealership and growth with more net profit after several years. This did happen when he was told that he had earned 20 percent of the company after only becoming a partner after four years. Frank was totally surprised even though the promise did exist in words. The Montgomery Motors dealership continued a consistent growth fortuitously in such a relatively small city with at least three other dealerships.

Then after six or eight years or so had passed, Frank bought the business through a bank loan from his friend who had worked as his junior partner. Jay's father William had aged and retired so he could care for the family's health.

Now, fully involved and having convinced the bank, Frank borrowed $100,000 to make a real competitive boost with new inventory, which caught zestful desires of new car buyers starting in 1968, while Frank started to build a new home for the family in Montgomery on the hillside on the college side of the mountain.

As other days came about, just as so many in the past were wasted, Frank was prepared to go to work as usual. The claim hit me later because Frank had described the area where the home was built and much more about the natural look. It hit me in the face with my mind reminding me what he had said to me. "I am still reminiscing about my successes every time I step outside of the house to go to my car."

Frank regained his external faculties, and as a regular nature lover of the land, he was happy to have chosen his home's property and design. He said he looked toward the sun to make sure we get the sunsets over the Kanawha River. My memory's lightbulb beam was intensely nondestructive. Frank instantly glanced at real results that had happened—that is, he said there were many trees on the mountain's back side. What I remembered from Frank was that when I had been there, we observed inchoate wind gusts brushing against laurel bushes along my path extending under my cuffs and imposing a slight chill. Then I see why—deciduous trees in nearby neighbors' yards were sending branches swaying from all directions.

I regained my senses. Later, he called me about the time they finished iron rail installation. He told me over the phone, "Thanks for the wrought iron railings. They looked great and were well installed." More importantly, he later told me that it turned out to be a time in his life like when cold wind made me shiver from top to bottom. He said it affected him like a nausea from bad food to which I have never been hypersensitive. Maybe it is an early warning to my human system that I may be neglecting some feature of his area. My thoughts registered in my mind with "Who knows?"

The winds of autumn set the course, and a year later, we visited their home, and Betty and Frank showed details of rooms, and then we trekked around outside areas. Frank expected an intermittent blow on the road's front side. Frank said the wind could range from mild to intense, and both speeds spread multicolored leaves in oranges, reds, browns, and yellows off the area that had planted sycamores and sugar maples and white oaks on hillsides just above hay-colored grassy berm adjacent to our side hill nearer the road. Some leaves already were variegated with yellow and red, orange browns, and all colors of stained greens laid entwined, while others, still green on trees, flared, waving in winds, manifesting leaves as related to plant life by flapping and fading to its last breath as I heard my mind saying, *We're in a rainbow metamorphosis of leaves!*

Even with this ever-present changes at these times of year, two evergreen juniper trees that maintained their whiff will be coming near Christmas from the sun and earth's winter solstice. It is almost a spiritual nature that excited me as harvests and holidays approached and winter proceeded with low temperatures.

Still in a mind-set of wonderment, Frank walked back toward the door and opened it as he thought about hinges that hold it up and wondered if his hinges would continue to work for years. We followed as he entered the house, and as he expected, he heard voices of my twin boys, now ten or eleven, and many times louder. Betty and three girls were in the kitchen with their granddad, laughing about his cooking, where aromas were everywhere emanating from Italy to Greece. The oven was baking his famous recipe of black olives in olive oil and red-hot pepper seeds.

Frank, now a public servant, has gathered much more sensibility of ways West Virginia will have to advance socially, culturally, and expand its goodwill and natural environments being highlighted by visitors. He thought a spurt of joy and personally spoke within his mind as he passed through this mountainous riverside city enhanced by being near the capital city of Charleston. Mountains galore with exceptional plants of grandeur are covered and separated by the city, river, and surrounding watersheds into the Kanawha River. His mind organized his memory along ways as he made many observations mentally so he could voice them to his family. Ed and Pat's family were visiting, and that is what he recalled with excitement. All this only a tiny fraction of wild and wonderful sites in great coal and industrial sites in West Virginia.

The Appalachians also have plentiful farms and mountain spreads, valleys, and rivers so peculiar in full extent of the eastern face of the state. Now, many years after World War II, West Virginia was reckoned as a dilapidated state with a lack of manufacturing. However, in more modern days and age-critical innovation and development of state, amenities had been soaring from their roots through massive amounts of coal, one dominant source of heating and electric power for other states.

In recent years, with both political prominence and as a major coal-producing state that used electric power plants, West Virginia has become one state that has gained respect in the eyes of believers in laws of nature and maximizing control of deleterious byproducts. And its sights certainly contain some wonders, such as its gorge in Hawks Nest, an area and expanses of Appalachians with signs beautifully designed and claiming, "Wonderful West Virginia!" Nostalgia of sites along the highways showed coal strata from creative evolution and thrusts of life in old coal mining towns as one travels from peaks of its mountains to valleys where rivers flow majestically toward a collection and eventual paths to the Ohio River and then eventually to Mississippi River flowing into Gulf of Mexico.

And what's more, people, poor, middle class, rich and powerful, have started to feel their oats with their sons and daughters storming into colleges to seeking professional educations that will remove stolid stenches of inferiority being from coal mining and farming people. Nevertheless, we people still needed to advance state's amenities and gain complements from others in remaining states of United States of America.

At this time, Frank had professed that he would be heading for success. He told me when he was in his mayor's activity that he made sure he worked on solving city problems or sudden confrontational incidents that need to be resolved. He said he knows his heritage, and it does carry suffering, and, usually, it's not subtle; but he feels he can handle anything that comes his way. After all, he said, as an Italian, he will have a great deal of fighting spirit, both morally and lawfully, with a good share of mental vigor, loyalty, dedication, and integrity for our country.

Frank reckoned mentally, both subconsciously and consciously, and would say at meetings, "West Virginians are not hillbillies. We are mountaineers." His words so commonly referred stopped ad hominem, signifying squalid uneducated impression. He would say, "We are of the countenance of mountaineers." Frank's word implied, and we know it in our hearts, we're expressing our values to rescue the rest of our country's people's destiny.

Frank explained to me how his life was evolving as he got older. On one occasion, he said he drove into a parking lot from Route 60 to his business. He said, back when he parked the car and then walked to join his wife Betty, who was with our three girls at the main front entrance of the business, he noticed kids scuffling and having fun in motion and shouting. Then as he approached, people talking and music playing aloud beyond belief were coming from all directions like a flock of birds landing in Kanawha River's backwater.

Within a few feet after entering our new car display room, he studied banners flying with flickers of sunlight reflecting from the windows. His mind responded silently first and yet loudly from his heart emotionally. He thought aloud, "This is a real classy celebration. It looks like more than what had been ordered." He knew it was happening, but he was shocked. This is the home of my new business, and it's a big-time celebration with more people than he knew. With deep concentration, he said to me, "Ed! Now, I will sell cars and trucks to some of my relatives and friends and even to those I don't know from Adam. That's my job!"

We as a family who suggested this celebration walked toward all who were enjoying our sweet smell of success. Some reservations, as always, were disclosed out of corners of my eyes; our two elder girls, because of boys and school friends, were shy until they were greeted by several of their true friends. Frank was relieved and turned to his wife Betty.

Betty and Frank steadily complimented each other with beginning conversations with joint decisions to do it big time in this small miners' hub town. Frank told her she was as important as he is to our business. Frank knew she knew numbers and values of money. Betty finally realized what we have burdened ourselves with and gasped excitedly, "Frank, I hope you make a million dollars first year because you are going to need it to keep this place running!"

Frank said to a few of us around him, as he was captured by a sucked-up stressed moment, "I feel like I have already spent a million dollars on this ambitious customers' party!"

Then we, starry-eyed with specks of tears, gleamed at new cars, model designs of Buicks and Pontiacs metallically decorated and colorful with shiny displays. New flowers in pots caught Frank's attention, leaving a whiff of springtime, refreshing, but it made him think out loud, "You're damn right, Betty!"

The last words of which came as an outward expression and gained a questionable response from Betty, the love of his life, as she continued with "I didn't say anything. Are you saying I'm right about hoping you make a million to pay for this grand extravaganza?"

Frank said dumbfounded, "Uh-huh!" Then he looked at the walls and other places with new paint and pointed for her to pay attention to his disclosure with "What do you think of our new decor?" New paint and plaster dominated our eyes until our minds were captured and his mind so engrossed. Frank graciously smiled with an odd twist to acknowledge anyone looking and wondering what he was doing pointing, as he turned around and could easily see that events were pleasing to all and viewing was well under way.

Betty noticed his face and read meanings of his smiles as she said, "I'll say! What have you done? I thought this was going to be a small celebration with a few of your local friends."

Frank turned in surprise with a red face as he gasped for air that floated out of his mouth. He mumbled, "So did I! The celebration was modestly announced in local papers."

Frank whiffed, moving his nose to gain an aberrant aroma coming from his new air-conditioning system. He sensed it as it spread very lightly outgassing metallic coatings or be it some form of lubricant, including plastic and leathers outgassing from new cars. Many people behaved as he did and looked to Ed for a response. Ed's mind screeched to his memory's pursuit of external cognition and asked with a simply shout, "Who bought all these new cars!" Frank was in limbo and had no vision as he cringed to take cover with an internal anxiety spurt. He was saved by his wife, who knew his facial contortions by heart, and she saw the need for a little comfort and relaxation.

Betty hugged Frank with a warm merriment touch and smiled as she said, "You've made it up to now, honey. Your next step is to sell these cars. I know you can do it!"

With that instilled confidence, Frank's inspiration level popped noticeably. He knew he was on the right path. He smiled back lovingly at Betty and kissed her on the cheek. His timing was right on time with "Honey, I can't believe I bought all these cars and trucks. I do believe you," and then face-to-face emphatically said, "I know I can sell them!"

By now, many people had set eyes on us and were drifting toward us while they were eating whatever in hand and or looking to expect their share of small talk and hopeful praise. They were into everything from hors d'oeuvres and special canapés and attacking soft drinks. There was wine drinks selection but in a special room. Being mountaineers, they were probably wondering why no real whiskey was out for adults, which was obvious with children running around ungoverned.

The tables for goodies were set for braggadocios par excellence in a glamorous rococo occasion with real flowers to be enjoyed in comfort and with freebies of value. The snacks and tidbits included small Italian cannoli stuffed with pistachios and lemon cream for sweet-toothed, Italian provolone, mozzarella, and a dip of Ricotta cheese spiced with small chips of red peppers, not intentionally hot, celery and carrot pokes, and Risotto balls with shrimp centered and inserted.

The sandwiches parts were set easy to make with basil-seasoned stripped short ribs, turkey, specially baked and sliced, baked prosciutto ham, and choices of cheeses. Hors d'oeuvres were of asparagus wrapped with Italian prosciutto ham and Italian baked sweetbreads for the hungry.

It was like a fete at an Italian wedding celebration, with bells and whistles, and glamour imposed on bride and groom. The mating partners of this day were new cars and trucks and families, who every which way turned and readied to choose one they desire with excitement jointed for joy of this part of their lives. Frank's mind quickly repeated aloud, "Promises, promises!" To me, it was like a celebration of a famous person or a happening that grasped minds of one either making a hero in the eyes of beholders or solidly embedded in the crevices of Frank's mind with memories of others to see him happy. Frank, who sees himself as a hero at the dealership, hoped that he would continue to do what he had done in his life so far.

Frank suddenly realized his company dominated businesses that were within twenty-five miles in all directions just short of the capital city Cadillac dealership sales with bells and whistles. General Motors Corporation, especially Cadillac division cars, within limits of good prices, also puts on no less expensive cars and trucks to celebrate with their friends.

Then we saw Frank being captured by a friend grasping for attention to give him a compliment about outstanding decor. His friend pointed fingers at flying banners and flags spread across high-ceiling areas and small crepe paper borders of cutouts of realistic cars, detailed enough to hold for a while in the garage as a keepsake. Other display areas near exits had colorful tubs full of giveaways, limited to only one small car that was given to each child that wanted one. Most models of larger cars were for sale as a souvenir for the rich kids when they leave. What he noticed even more outstanding was the number of people and friends already on the display floor, which was clean as a whistle for new cars, especially sports cars and one 1946 Indy 500 old racing cars perfectly rebuilt and sent to him on loan to his masterful party.

A crowd was surrounding my father Big Benny, and the main attraction was a green-and-cream two-color Buick Roadmaster, like one that my dad had given me back in 1958. This one was lavishly appointed with more chrome than on a Rolls-Royce. I parted my way and went to my dad with a few tagalong friends. I noticed he was impeccably dressed, which, of course, was his forte from many years of practice as a middle-class businessman in a mining town hub. I might add, my father left coal mines at a young of twenty.

After I had grown into midforties, from my knowledge, he was always dressed in a well-made suit wearing a white shirt with a grand tie and a sparkling shine on his shoes. This was his dressed stature before when he started his business doing construction work on roads in northern parts of West Virginia near Buchannan. What happened thereafter, as I recalled from happy memory, after about two years, he married his first love. That all happened through an unusual invitation from one of my mom's brothers while working on roads near Adrian.

The story is yet to come in detail. After his marriage, I know he didn't shine his shoes. I do know my mom did them for him after he started his bus line business. After they were married many years, some of her sons were old enough and also got jobs to proudly shine his shoes. Every one of them did it with joy. He made sure they got credit for it with an almost unique praise of performance and many times with a nickel or dime or more in change.

Being the eldest, Frank got first praises because he always wanted to be like his dad, especially since his first primary admiration was when he first saw Dad's face expressing in features and words so proudly that he was one man in town who was able to put together a buy through his friend at General Motors of a new 1946 Cadillac Series 60 Special Fleetwood first out for new sales since 1941 models were stopped because World War II had started by December 1941. The crucial point for him was owning Divita Taxi and Moving Transfer Company. He owned it until he sold it to buy more taxis. Frank, being like his dad when he started his automobile business, parked a white Buick Roadmaster convertible in his garage at their new home, and many times, he used it during the '70s parades in Montgomery.

Then another past memory popped up, with a new subject that fits with my dad's times now getting close to his old age. I'll start with what I remembered when World War II ended and patriotism was dominant. It was after the wake of World War II, which created a havoc of admiration and totality patriotism flourished in our hometown. What I recalled from Dad's memories about what had happened as the war ended was peoples' stresses that the atom bombing of Japan loaded enormous concern on minds of all Americans. Many friends had listened to him but with uncanny excitement. This dominating feeling was especially so, with stories that were saturated with hyperbole and praise when veterans and patriotism flowed in streams all during news about how World War II ended.

After all it was the first major thrust to work in Kanawha Valley Industrial Plants using new materials to fabricate new military equipment in concert by patriotic people from our town since World War I. Even in the late ''30s, everyone knew businesses were picking up and especially new cars on track to move this town back as the hub of south-central West Virginia mining districts. The factories along Kanawha River and adjacent valleys extended for miles and reigned output of warring materials and machinery including major systems such as tanks and Seabees equipment for attacks on battlefields in Germany and on Japanese islands.

World War II had much to be discussed and laid out for the reader to grasp enormous impacts and changes in America during those four years plus of war when we enter the fighting in Europe as a member of the Great Britain Allies and other countries with England such as Australia.

My dad quickly stepped up to remind people what was foremost in the minds of leaders in America. What he said about it after the war was that troops' readiness and grand heartedness by their tough action helped save large numbers of lives and helped many countries to recover. The good ol' USA was on its way into a greatness, so unsuspected; later after the war, two prime American generals started the Marshall Plan for Western Europe, and Douglas MacArthur, as chief of the occupation forces in Japan, critically aided renovation that showed metal of the United States of America.

My dad released his memory, and I added my heard words: "Greatness is when one meets the promises of liberty for people of America setting examples in other countries who were proud of America for allying efforts and fighting the war to its end." Before it happened, the Japanese would not yield a final complete surrender with President Roosevelt's pleading. The bombing took two times and, after such mind-deafening terror and death, was wrought by explosions of two atom bombs when the first one on Hiroshima, August 6, 1945, and the second on Nagasaki, August 9, 1945, had to be done to end the war completely.

Frank later remarked to me many times about World War II when he was about seventeen years old. Everyone in America started celebrations that included relief of people's minds. Frank was usually by his dad's side listening as Gene and I were also by his side.

As he pointed out to us a few years later, at a parade in Montgomery, he told us that he saw Betty give him a special facial glance that he had never seen before. It was like a high school aficionado smiling with "I want a kiss or smile." Betty joined her lips and snapped them against his cheek. Neither of us said a word. Betty continued and later told us that she was lucky on that special day. Later when they were dating, she said nothing like that had happened to me over the last few years. Then Betty said to Gene and me, "Don't interrupt him. Frank sees his father, and I know he's headin' to give him a big hug!" This was the start of their dating, and it led to their marriage in 1950.

Later, after a year or so, Dad was in his garage and had the hood up. The car he was describing had new a main feature with power steering on the new Buick Roadmaster that quickly gained onlookers. He had his finger on the power steering assembly. He called to my brother, whose nickname is Gene, "Gene! Turn the key on. Now, turn the steering wheel!" He told all watching, "Watch the wheels turn so easily!" as the front tires made a light screeching on terrazzo floors. The power steering assembly made a squeaky air pressure hydraulic sound. Power steering was being developed two years ago.

Dad had his way of showing people how a car worked; this time by so much better than before, showing his boys that movements make noise in its housing. It was astonishing. Frank let him finish as I stared in awe at surrounding people. I saw a pause and one that showed he accomplished what he had planned and showed a great big smile, looking for applause for the lesson. Ed reached him with both hands and gave him a hug and said, "Dad! It looks like you are a mechanic when you are under the hood of a car! How do you do it?"

He was about to be questioned by an older man. Frank turned to face the man, interrupting with "There is nothing my dad does not know about cars. He's always owned a few of them since the mid-1930s. He learned about them by reading owners' manuals he bought for taxicab repairs. Dad fixed them no matter what. And," he emphasized, "God only knows how many he fixed when engines would not run!"

All this remembered conversation began springing from each of us like it was from my memory. Dad said it was the same way it was said; it sounded to me like, "Everything I know I learned from reading and doing the work like a recipe. When I cook, I don't need a recipe. Learning how to live is another story. I learned firsthand from Big Poppy and Big Mommy about how to do craftsman things and how to cook. The main thrust was to be happy in what you do." Then he continued. "My Big Mommy was the one I learned most from. She taught me to think about what needed to be done." Then Dad said, "You must do things right throughout your life as long as you can control your mind. The rest of the ways of life came from my mom, who had a sense and always got a response when she used *steerage* and *amour* as our guide." Then Dad said, "The way your mom raised you guys after you were babies started with her mind of goodness for her children. She had a sense of what normal personable good-minding meant to child behavior."

Frank thought for a few seconds, recalling how all us kids in Mom and Dad's family absorbed formal education, starting at grade school, becoming capable of full-on English. When they became older, they were self-taught to be good in math to make good grades but to pursue math techniques for everyday activities in daily life and in business. In many cases, each one of us amassed enough knowledge to have fun conversing about many problems with people far more formally educated. Dad taught all of us how to keep accounting books, especially what we had to reevaluate to be correct—namely, fix mistakes.

His teaching ways generated an interest to pursue more education. Teachings of Mom and Dad were a mental pursuit embedded in each sibling without influence, only via osmosis from my dad and mom. Now, all I ever noticed was Dad reading newspapers. He had significant interest in the way the country was being run. He would lay criticism on anyone of us, whoever was present, even though he was a dyed-in-the-wool, maybe even a diehard Democrat. Dad told his friends reasons that they must take time to think about politics. However, they had too much to do chasing after each other just trying to earn a living.

Ten years later, my dad Benny was still involved with his taxis, but the business was waning. Frank decided to get involved with his dad's taxi business that was having trouble with by-times. Frank helped specifically by moving in with Mom and Dad and doing things he knew he could work and uplift both families. Frank and Dad, as reported earlier, after the mid-'50s, were back to work making money. Frank had become mayor of the city of Montgomery later with many years thereafter. He had set good ways to run the city of Montgomery, and he was well known by the people because he made sure things got done. At that time, he was a friend of Jay, who was running his dad's Montgomery Motors dealership. They became friends, and Jay knew that Frank was a good businessman. With needed conversation, Jay told Frank that his dad was ready to retire. The two of them conversed about his running of the business by himself and that he needed help. The idea was inviting. Frank was considering getting into the car business.

Frank got in the automobile business with Jay as previously described. After a while, Frank became a partner, and Dad joined with Frank to operate the business of the selling used cars. The overall joined families made a quick success of the businesses. Frank then bought the dealership. It happened quickly as the business had grew.

That was a few years ago when one of the Divita family members asked Frank about an idea of setting up a surprise party at the dealership. He offered, "If it isn't one thing, it's another coming to a head at the dealership. Remember, if you display your success, you will not have to worry, and you will increase your business."

One of the charmers from the local college standing beside Frank smiled and interrupted Frank with a touch on the shoulder and said, "The people will be excited to see your cars and friends. My plan is to buy one of your cars." I was also seeking his answer with a stare, asking, "What are we having for Italian foods and desserts at the party?" He then seriously responded in my vernacular, something like, "Your dealership looks like it should be in Charleston. I'm from New York City, and this is the way top-notch dealerships look there!"

Then my aunt Aline, whose husband Charlie worked at Frank's dealership, chimed in with her humor, "Frankie, my hero, who is going to do the decorations?"

"Aunt Aline, my whole family will do it. Who's that with you?" as he grabbed one of his cousins with the same name as his dad, Charles Leigh, and Uncle Charlie got the response, "Let Frank do the planning."

Young Charles Leigh shouted, "Big Frankie! What did you say? You must be one rich guy to buy all these cars!" Charles Leigh, a little more formal, grabbed the hero's hand to shake and squeezed it and with a hug said, "Where's my favorite car? The Cadillac!"

Three days later, two aunts, Mary and Katie, several family members, and three of their girlfriends from Smithers came in with the crowd. All at once, seeing Frank, one of the girls, Angelina, almost my age whom I have known almost from birth, embraced and kissed me on the cheek and said, "Your aunt Mary told me you are going to have a great celebration of new cars. That never happened in this town! I'm ready to buy a car! I'm going to need one. I'm going to have a baby!"

Frank's dad moved toward Dr. Stallard, who had entered. Dad greeted him with a handshake as he said, "We got just a new sports car for you, doc, but it has to be ordered by you. It is a Corvette! It will have all the bells and whistles! Just tell Frank what you want! I'll get you a flyer on it."

"Dad, I agree. But you stay. Your sisters want to talk with you. They know you so well! I know he will follow your advice about what you said about the coming election and this celebration. I got lost in conversations about a celebration in the dealership."

Dad walked to his sisters and asked, "What's on your mind today, Mary? Is it the big affair? Frank did guarantee specially prepared Italian food. I know it's got something to do with Frank putting on a big event, Cosa Italiana!"

Dad came by as he said, "You do the event with good help and you know you will get the best. I want to reach back to times when I was in the mines as a young man." His dad paused and thought with an expression that he was about to reveal changes in our lives but changed his mind and said, "I was going to say something about my old times in the mines—"

Frank quickly interrupted to register his mind's thoughts when he heard others talking undecipherable. Dad then asked Frank to go to the office with him. Once there, Dad jumped in and started with "I remember the times when mines were having cave-ins and miners were being beat up by dozens of Rednecks. The company let it happen. And then they blamed the miners. There was only one doctor in town. The union was hiring thugs to beat complaining miners. The companies hired tough guards to control miners raising hell with the union instigators."

Frank tossed in his two cents. "Dad, you told me about mine troubles, specifically about your ventures at your times being so roughly controlled."

Dad jumped in again, repeating concerns after so many times, "I know the one! It was when a bunch of Poles, Germans, and colored miners were chasing some Italians. Sometimes, it was vice versa, out for other miners who only listen to their bosses. Most women's boyfriends and wives were frightened and worried what might happen to their man." Instead, Benny blurted out, "You both know when disasters occurred. One kind or another, we all helped to save miners and provide food and places to sleep when families needed it."

Frank said, "I knew it. What do you think? People always want to help, but sometimes, they don't know what to do."

Dad said, "Sometimes, they waited until it was an obvious disaster."

Frank continued. "We learn how to help people before things turn into disasters." Everyone knew that owners had to make sure working conditions and miners were following safety regulations. They had to make sure mine safety codes were in place and workplaces inspected. The two men walked out to another side and left the crowd in their various unheard conversations. But they only wanted to go to another gathering to see what's happening during people's interactions.

Benny continued to a more recent time with Frank, bringing up, "America stopped fighting in the Korean War years ago. Troops are still manned at the— what the hell do they call it? Uh—the demilitarized zone. Our troops were waiting for someone to take the first shot. President Eisenhower did not want to start military action no matter what. The people never learned the lessons of World War II."

Frank said, "Whatever happens, there's always significant differences in how governments are run. The new generation expanded other divergences into more warfare."

Benny said, "It must be the new hippie generation. Look how quickly liberals moved from licensed marriage to living together or shacking-up."

Frank retorted, "Dad, I don't believe generational changes influence all families. It's society's behavior that identified it as occurring within the experiences of various family members. You must remember you are talking about people who have been to war and worked in manufacturing new warring materials and weapon systems all during the war. These complicated personal involvement at times caused more amorous associations especially with opposite sexes."

"Frank, are you saying that men and women are wrangled with their thoughts? Or are their minds looking for love in all the wrong places by chasing after hanky-panky?"

"Dad! Records are in the courts. The numbers were confirmed. You're right! That is, during the war, numbers of court cases for divorces doubled, and now percentages increased."

I looked into Dad's eyes and saw a wanting out of this conversation. Then Frank said, "Dad, amorous adventures were happening even before these modern changes."

I say in this story of remembrances of my current days of society, things that are illicit are much easier to get away with whatever anyone wants to do. God only knows how men and women attained togetherness in distant pasts even after the First Renaissance. It was every human being for himself or herself. The rich did take from the poor, and powerful people took from the rich. Back then, it happened to those amorously attracted from kings' royalty to serfs, however it came about. God only knows who, when, how, and why royalty still accomplishes its attention for naught!

The doctor moved over to Frank and his dad and chimed with knowledge of having studied and being involved in cases of disloyalty revealed to him by patients. What I thought I had heard and remembered was "Let me say a few words to confirm what Frank said. What was critical was how different times back a hundred years ago manage marital infidelity. People had different interests in another's life. When people start to think about different ways of living their lives and changes that cause separations and loneliness, they decrease desires to make changes."

Benny, puzzled, paused and made a mental response. "It's simple," smiling and then a short laugh. "Doc! Life is just a bowl of cherries. Most people and the cherries end up in the pits most times."

What I know, as in my mind, is that attractions relate to both persons' admiration, and it springs gingerly when two sets of eyes meet! It's all in how one makes it happen and how personally the *steerage* that we used to teach children to use their mind's "knowledge and experience" figure when they should or should not take wrong paths to disloyalty.

These two may have made a legitimate mentally astute contact of meetings of their minds and revealed something that works like maintaining one's "knowledge and experience" to not to pursue illicit *amour*. It makes no sense because the Italians know that it will turn out bad.

Frank, in response, said, "Dad, I think you are convincing enough when you relate how we full-bred Americans seek *amour,* which is different from how Italian emigrants and first-generation Americans sought *amour.* Italian ways of teaching *steerage* versus how it has continued in contemporary times still linger delicately. Your people were those who dominated perceived embedded amorous behavior as a main part of European lifestyles, and you learned how to handle outcomes to a just advantage in America."

Frank then went off on a tangent with "Dad, your people lived and walked paths that family sexual desires were with societal and religious morality generally kept in mind, and not relayed as common conversation under excitation of feelings. All these types of feelings were within eyesight and hearing of children or their parents for easy understanding. I'm not saying that people from other European countries didn't do the same, but if I were to pick an example, it would be Italians in my book." Maybe I think that because Italians initiated the First Renaissance.

Then his dad popped out with "During my time, son, men were expected to hold on to their wives. They did not in any way submit to infidelity, although it did happen in all European countries anyway, but not as frequently as it does in today's world."

Frank slightly raised his eyes, but knowing his father and his demand for respect, his voice came out almost in a squeak. "How do you know that? What do you mean?"

Dad said it like something I remembered, "Son,"—as he stared me into my eyes, I felt a cool flash over my face—"now, when it's the husband, God help his wife or others from whom she might seek help because it's going to be a goddamned dragged-out fight to get money out of a womanizer. And when the wife knows it, she follows suit and fools around. She may be snubbed and, many times, plain thrown out of the house with maybe some force and certainly with little pity. She usually leaves without money and is never to be seen again."

Frank responded, adding close to what I also remembered what Dad said, "Dad, what are you saying? Is the way men of your generation handled women's hanky-panky mostly through domination to prevent marital infidelity?"

Each incident that occurred in my dad's era was a classic. It is defined from the family's point of view and from the partner's point of view when minds discriminate the situation to anticipate an interaction and aftermath. All this action with underlying wry wit, sometimes it can cause truly disastrous reality.

As analyzed by me, with this memory recall, disloyal incidents, to my knowledge as an adult, were caused by men usually of known low morality pursuing women in a hush-hush way. They would hold it secretly even among close friends with facts that whether they were a rake or womanizer. Even under this crassness, they were not generally criticized by their partners just so they could maintain family continuity with disgracing deception. Men that you may know as rakes are usually also known to others that he's a womanizer!

What became even more common among first-generation American men and women is their practice of secreted infidelity, as it is now easily accommodated in our modern times because no one believes excuses for time delays or business requirement excuses in any way or form to use morally corrupt words to gain relief. Looking back into my younger years, at times, I will tell you what I convinced my mind to do, which is, always evaluate the mind's decisions to eliminate making an easy illicit *amour* pursuit instinctively.

Frank paused for thought about his two brothers who had entered professional positions in other states. His thinking transposed to what he knew they would follow to completion. He walked to the window and got zero registration of concern from his mind thinking about how Mom and Dad were doing at home the past several years. He then stared through windows as rain was pouring down and wind was beating on windows and walls of the house, with pulsating spheres of water exploding against windows. He turned quickly and walked up within a foot to a window as he snapped out of his mind's daze. Then he motioned as he thought about his mom and dad's life.

Dad, somewhat amazed, returned a response wittingly. "Son, that's because you think you're going to make money and fall in love with your automobile dealership business!" Both laughed, and then Dad continued. "Making love is not considered when one's setting up a new business or even investing in a new public offering of stocks priced with a good expectation to make a profit. But just the opposite occurs when looking for love in all the wrong places. The mind engrosses one instinctive pursuit, and that's when no additional consideration of others bounces around in one's mind."

Then his thoughts changed, and I heard him say, "Dad, you must be exhausted listening to my psychobabble!" Those words shocked me especially coming out my conscious mind audibly. My ego was triggered to release my mind's true knowledge.

More out loud but with clear facial respect, Frank said what I recalled from memory, something like "Dad, you know that many people know what's going on when big deals are being consummated. It doesn't interfere with ongoing business. However, when it looks like an easy divergence to cover, run-of-the mill business transactions come to light showing what is going on. My attempt to set the business up to make money is doing it right for a payoff, and sometimes, it does not always make money."

Dad retorted, "I think that's a good example, and it sums up the way most cases of infidelity get started. Why, they usually turn out for the worse, especially in your case where your wife fares well enough to withhold bad feelings because a lie might be told for some suspicious reason and it's not the first time she felt it." Dad signaled with his head in a nodding motion, with modest agreement, but still with his hands in his pockets. Then he retorted something in words like "After all, money makes the world go around, and it also buys many forms of happiness.

When odd times are spent, depression or anxiety may bomb your wife's mind freely. More common folk, so-called middle class and lower class, may make out OK for the short time, but in the long run, it is a toss-up."

Frank rattled with "This makes my moral conclusion easy to repeat. God only knows that women usually encounter some form of depression or even disaster after five to seven years into a marriage. When infidelity is against the man, he's going to try to do better than expected. Usually, the rich or upper class, both men and women, uses money to continue their lives, and most of the time, it works. Dad, how many times have you said the rich have it made no matter what!"

It's a critical mistake that leads anyone into a pending disaster when most people would know that woman had followed me into towns where most popular restaurants were known, as in the Glen Falls Hotel and Restaurant in Glen Falls West Virginia. That's the main street where people hobnob.

What had happened previously was a woman known in town as a local worker in one of the ladies' goods stores intentionally revealed amorous intentional greetings to Frank at the table. As Frank and Rose met, Rose sat down. Then in full voice, she stated, as Frank recalled and what Frank told me, something like "I'm so glad we decided to meet here for dinner," as she added an attractive touch to his shoulder. As the mayor of the hub city of Montgomery, an announcement of such a pleasure could be mistaken as a planned get-together by anyone's sensibility. However, an instilled assumption revealed in people's mind that it was a planned amorous meeting. And for sure, almost a conviction that Frank's pursuit was one of taking advantage of a younger woman.

Dad responded with bravado to stay away from convicting situations so prominently set up, "Son, you had plenty of time to stop people from thinking you had an amorous venture under way. You should have stopped it before it got out of hand by excusing yourself and leaving the premise!" That was when he decided to talk about the situation as he encountered it to see if it made sense.

Frank sat down with my dad to follow up on what he had said. "Dad, I didn't know she was there to meet me, and it was already under way by her joining me at the table. Nothing had ever happened in the past to me before when I was being nice to a woman even before I knew her purpose."

I then relayed it all to him and later to my brother Ed in a phone conversation, pretty much the same as it was with my dad. What had happened was that he had made it home that night about an hour later than usual because he drove her back to town and chose to drop her off at her home where she lived with little conversation.

The next day, it was all over town. She in her own words had responded to questions by locals in a way in which she helped to place me in a compromising position, one of doubt and one that I told her I would be at the diner in Glen Falls. As he told me, "Your friends and family all thought I crashed into the *amour* tree unknown to my wandering amorous emotions.

Then Frank's brain computed, he thought, maybe he had succumbed to an infidelity charge that was never levied by a reputable person who said she saw the incident as an involvement. Everyone thought he was disloyal to his wife and family. No one questioned either of us if any sexual involvement ever actually happened. Without any legal consultations or advice from members of the family, he was served divorce papers, and under pressure of being wronged, he held his ground and simply said he never had anything to do with the woman and she knows it. She never denied it, and so it was left in minds of those who thought him an instigator. The extended family eventually agreed with my wife because of her remorse, and they knew she was convinced that he had wronged her and the family.

Frank almost lost a good wife, which he didn't want to happen under any circumstance, and God knows that he had withstood various complaints about his whereabouts and actions during and after work. He knew it looked like his desires overcame him at a moment of total enticement, but he only did what he thought was the right thing to do—that is, he took his acquaintance to her home because, otherwise, she would have had to walk six street blocks if he dropped her in town on his way home, and it was already ten o'clock. Frank felt he could not escape the responsibility, and it was as he told it to me his trusting brother. With such a steadfastly "pat" excuse, it made me look concerned for him, but I knew he was telling the truth as we had always made sure to stand our ground when we were telling the truth about serious issues.

The eventual misunderstanding left him remorseful as a husband. Frank's thoughts of entering a new life's plight so changed because of a potentially doomed marriage. What his brother told him was that he should have expected an unfair exposure that had turned his wife and children against him because he knew he was known as an attractive man about town and involved politically with many people, so he said apparently that he had no way out with finality.

The bottom fell out before he could have the woman corroborate his reasons and action with a justification and an admission to the fraudulent impression of illicit involvement. Guess what! Later, when she relayed her account of the meeting, she never said anything but innuendos and intimations she had exposed and didn't excuse him from trying to arouse a suspected sexual exploitation.

Frank changed the subject without a comment about his time in the late 1960s, but as a spark of a past memory registered, he had gone when he was still mayor of Montgomery. He knew what was in store for his future if that was the way he was going to be treated with such a minor infliction that was really nothing related to an affair.

Much earlier, Frank, as the mayor of Montgomery, West Virginia, knew the country was seeking the ennobled John Fitzgerald Kennedy, who recently was revealed as an intelligent keeper in the Senate. In the eyes of his peers and new wife, all knew he was amorously attractive to women, if not personally involved with those whom he was desirously attracted. He was young at heart and with a great regard having served during the World War II as a navy lieutenant commander for America's strength and patriotism. His credentials appeared to be impeccable as an ex-navy officer and hero on his leadership of his PT-109 in the pacific during World War II, the son of a high-level Roosevelt political businessman, Joseph P. Kennedy, who was chosen to be England's American ambassador and confident diplomat. He was, however, later recalled because of his odd support that diverged from that of President Roosevelt.

John Kennedy was the first candidate for whom serious consideration brewed even with doubts by religious zealots who visualized him being controlled by the Roman Catholic Church's Pope because he was a Roman Catholic. John Kennedy himself was held in high regard as a new and especially unusual candidate, one with political brains somewhat unique in this time when the Cold War was at its peak of consternation. The prophets predicted that voters almost single-handedly convicted rich Democrats and Catholics with talking money and promises that might cause a close race against his opponent, Richard M. Nixon, who was vice president under Pres. Dwight D. Eisenhower. Richard Nixon's record as a Republican was gold starred from the beginning, first, as a congressman and then a hardworking member of the House un-American Activities Committee investigating German spies and producing convicting information on Rudolph Hess on microfilm found in a pumpkin put there by Whitaker Chambers and who was sentenced to life imprisonment in 1946. Nixon's critical standing culminated as an active investigative America senator.

Kennedy had his work cut out for him, and it was a challenge to be a master who controlled a lot of footwork and demanded a sharply appealing patriotic campaigning through his worker horses under the auspices of his younger brother Bobby Kennedy and Dave Powers, the man who never stopped pushing the good in the campaign. JFK did so with Irish charm and with American pride to have the opportunity to run for the office of president and commander-in-chief to lead our country.

With little cooperation, especially when nearby Cuba secured Communism that ended in a disastrous situation for JFK at the beginning of his presidential career, the failure of the United States planned military support to rebels during the assault known as the Bay of Pigs War was poorly planned militarily, and the president as commander-in-chief was blamed. The finality happened; the rebel people's army and the United States failed to regain control of Cuba, and the loss left a black mark on Kennedy's presidency. The political tempo was allegro and crescendo increased as it created presto tempo in political ideological mind-sets.

Richard M. Nixon was known for opposing global Communism, but John Kennedy had the same perspective on Communism; however, John Kennedy was a head above Nixon with an unchallengeable and dynamic charisma and closely won the presidential election with an added increase of popularity from his book *Profiles in Courage*, a militarily inspired dynamic hero's personality, and especially the hard work of his devoted election team.

After all, Al Smith was a presidential candidate running as a Democrat, but he didn't make the grade; he notably had the popularity of the New Yorkers. There was little doubt of prejudice even though he was the first Roman Catholic to run for president of the United States of America, but times were different looking retrospectively at the person's personal versus later at a strongly overwhelmingly heartfelt patriotism as John Kennedy becoming a naval hero during World War II.

The now famous senator John F. Kennedy during the campaign had transformed into John Fitzgerald Kennedy, a.k.a. JFK, vying critically for the number-one office in the country. In all respects, with personality being a significant gauge, the trend moved the people toward listening to him, and most had no doubt that his Catholicism would influence his allegiance to America.

Some few thought it might have some unknown religious ties that may have a bearing on his political decisions, especially ones that could be influenced by the Pope of the Roman Catholics. These concerns were discounted in several speeches after his earnest words that the country's security and defense would dominate his decisions. His words gave the people confidence that there would be no bearing taken from the Pope or any religious figure under any circumstance.

Even his workers, who have their own lives, and my new lady friend as one of his campaign media specialist showed that he had instantaneous control on my attraction for whom Frank had spied her at first sight. Being of sound mind and sure of myself, I felt I was there for a good reason. I was loyal for several years, but after we talked several times, our affair lasted only until the next day.

John Kennedy had given a message to all campaign travelers within a few hours of that very same evening; orders that the campaign team was to leave within the hour because he had to be back in Washington on Senate business, and the order was "All staff members and campaign associates must get ready immediately."

Her response, being especially attracted to me, was convincing, but Frank noticed when she gave him details that she didn't hesitate to immediately respond to his direction to vacate premises and, so she did leave, and there was never "an affair to remember."

In the stories that Frank told me that happened under my parents' tutelage, our children were directed from an early age to study meticulously about details in school and to pursue advanced education that thoughts remained motivated be it inherent from parents setting examples and/or sibling pursuits to gain "knowledge and experience" through *steerage* worked when it is mentally absorbed.

Nevertheless, hardheaded ones—that is, those children within extended family who do not accept scholastic study—usually did not listen to insistences of their parents. The *steerage* and *amour* were levied so graciously that words of advice dribbled down enough to impose a mentally determined and self-decided thought path. Usually, the decision led them to a higher level of thinking beyond commonplace or a humble lifestyle. Within the extended family, many progeny also acquired higher educations. If not, at a minimum, they sought steady middle-class jobs to maintain an Italian lifestyle influenced by Christian principles of belief. Being taught morals that they learned early in Catechism outlined principles of religious creeds with asking questions and getting answers.

As parents recognized pursuits of their children, especially toward higher education after several formative years had passed, they loved the way their children's minds behaved after teaching *steerage* properly. The real buildup was so noticeable after World War II because they wanted their children to even seek education with an intent to gain a proper understanding of wartime life. The parents made it known to all their children that they take notice of their children's good abilities no matter how minor they may have seemed.

The same set of noticed abilities was performed for neighbors' children closely involved with our family, and it worked as do compliments for recognizable accomplishments. Even the poor took advantage of low-cost collaboration that flowed from secondary and higher education facilities with personal contact with teachers. This type of contact was carried out by the good lead of parents and teacher meetings and associations of modern-day times. However, in opposition, it caused an inchoate and clandestine support of training for trades. Young men and women take political science subjects in any university classroom to be mentally aware of positions as public bureaucrats, especially in state and federal governments. As each person gained new capabilities, the thrust of college graduates was to use their minds to make decisions following "knowledge and experience" to gain positions.

People who married usually have children and maintain a family. By staying together with driving intents, marriage remains; unless the same ol', same ol' happens—namely, infidelity or disloyalty at various levels by those who operate under their own power of deceit.

Whenever people or parents separate, entity divides. Disheartening is a sure sign that all involved were on a path of losing the race for a successful and happy life. And it is often said, parting sometimes is such sweet sorrow . . . as Shakespeare proclaimed in the 1600s . . . and more often than not, it is disastrously mentally and socially debilitating to both parties and siblings. The heartbreak of abandoned mothers was pervasive in the site of family and friends. Only in some cases, those who had the most to lose, did it leave areas to escape from involvement shortly thereafter.

For men, breakups were mostly sour grapes, blaming something like an excuse that she couldn't keep my motor running or she never had interest in my needs or "hankerings." Never would men say, "I just ran out of gas," or any other excuse that would lay blame on him. For many men, an increased depression might follow. With time, however, most men always tried a new pursuit of loyalty toward women.

The trial run usually materialized into a race to recover and seek an amorous bliss that could involve one as if selecting a new car with a different driver training course that plies a new road or pathway to follow a proper behavior. God only knows if this next race for companionship ends in marriage. A second or third time around the course, it makes no promises of winning the next lap no matter what pursuit is exhibited by the driver. What mattered as an analogy was how easy would old drivers change old habits or buy a new car for themselves as a new driver with life-devoted attention.

After each child's education was completed at the college level, Mom and Dad's siblings usually left to take a job away from home. When the mother's little darlings left, spending the next four to six years becoming adults, then they started their own families. Loneliness dominated this familial remorse partially and caused change in husbands' and wives' daily interactions. Sometimes, siblings stayed in local areas to watch their marriage race start the first few laps; but then, they were not involved in using daily trials and tribulations to qualify and cohabit as parents until the race ended when they left to be on their own and make their family lives be together.

Those siblings who left and then returned to visit on holiday occasions displayed their own events. Interactions and disruptions with each family usually caused dissention, neglect, or, at least, inconsideration. And outcomes were the choice reason to accommodate aloofness among all members of the family and even extended families. The main pursuit of families in America was education at all levels of cultural, societal, and technical classes regardless of wealth or position. When this personal goal was pursued, it led to broadening many new product developments and integrating major new infrastructures for people to gain more joy in association, communication, and travel and respect for environments with exposure and social ability.

As new family life progressed, love from newly evolving families is grafted within new generations predominantly as heritage, dominated by presence and not by interaction except when disaster or calamity happened. Absence of real personal contact can make communications close to impossible because one could not say or ask what was really on one's mind. Thus, familial depression smothered many familial ties, and a lost love would be broadcasted and with time exacerbated the heartbreak. As new life reflects only an atmosphere of family ties, members of extended families mystically disappear into thin air, the more distance afar family ties that lose and miss association and acquaintance.

In extended families within a fair distance to maintain personal involvement, compatible member always maintained contact in casual and familial ways. Visits were timely, and friendships grew when interests were similar. For example, with man talk about cars and sports, and women talk about shopping, cooking, sewing, or social gatherings of many kinds; even going to movies or watching television is some relief. Until mostly someone's marital disharmony raises its ugly head through innuendo and sarcasm; this pursuit of mental attacks must be eliminated in each of their minds by thinking sufficiently enough to keep one's mouth shut orally before making stabs that minimize associates or eliminate them from activities at unfortunate times.

Sides were either chosen, or a nonposition caused separation. Friends knew whom they could or could not take into their confidence. The ignored party began seeking knowledge of other partners whereabouts, starting with relatives and close friends. After marital frays, real signs of contact by relatives and friends occurred casually by chance meetings and with inconsequential greeting cards.

However, the immediacy of genuine support happens when self-righteous friends, usually men, look for someone of stature in the family to help him out of his incompatible family situation. This pursuit happens most often with those having marital problems relating to infidelity. If a parting man or woman sees that he or she is in line for some harm, he or she calmly attempts to resolve conflicts immediately by telling the truth.

In this case, it might have gone away for good unless the partner sees a chance to make a clear break and stop it in its tracks. If one is not so inclined to use humility, the harmed party may leave via exiting the home and finalizing it with a divorce. If it turns hateful and harmful to the suffering person, then she or he may be dragged down by his or her mind as a wrecked person destined to netherworlds of mental destitution. This spiteful insistence may lead to any form of havoc that they could wreak upon a former partner with legal confrontation as a potential workable compromising decision.

From worldwide experience, most people that encounter these marital infidelity situations spend their remaining lives with new partners and ventures. New moves usually included counting their blessings or residing with heartbreak but expecting some form of restitution from their new partner, who has no idea what is due. On the other hand, if two individuals bare some causal responsibilities, they may gain back a recovery to normality. If not, they could get involved into a similar or worse than previous situations that plagued one or the other and might add to their depression and cause faulting ad infinitum. An indication of how this type of marital commotion on life's track either resolves in a man's or woman's favor or builds up animosities that tear down intimate feelings of many associated lives, especially family and close friends, is revealed within the humor of this story that always says, "Think first with steerage and amour that you must have been taught."

In each segment, influences of unique physical and mental heritage and the dispositions of modelled minds as life proceeds are revealed, as we know within our mental capabilities that overall *Homo sapiens* are unique. Confrontational but poor humor or witty behavior leaves only surprise of what next generations wrought to inherit. The practice of mental heritage pending behavioral influences waits to be levied by unsuspecting next generations and coming generations. These approaches are repeatedly exercised in modern days with emphasis on declaring with wit and humor differences and effects that may related to economic and environmental changes affecting marital problems explicitly in the modern generation. One's disposition always becomes an influence especially if the person is rich and self-centered; the gain required is to keep funneling into one's life's self-sufficiency.

CHAPTER VI

Italians Immigrate to America's Ellis Island

Birthing produces uniquely different individuals via heritage as descendants then absorb from their minds or are taught Steerage and Amour to the inherited mind's uniqueness. Instilled behavior becomes limitless because evolving babies from conception are born as Homo sapiens. *Babies as all birthing of the Animal Family occur, are born uniquely and within a baby's developing body, mind, personality and the personification are accomplished continually.*

All Human Beings within this planet earth assume best and worst ways and suffer when critical judgments are levied unjustified. Therefore, minds must discriminate pursuits to be undertaken as is common with the mind. Heritage guarantees the timeliness as one ages into a significantly resulting personality with a significant brain and mind beginning with conception. Randomness is not an imitation; it is the dominant feature of uniqueness in details of mankind's makeup at the beginning in order to keep it going until birthing ends.
—Steerage and Amour!—What's It All About!, Edward L. Divita Sr.

The essence of a new life visually appeared in America when Francesco Divita, earlier in 1910 and a few years later his wife Filippa Divita and her four children in 1913, traveled over the Atlantic Ocean on the SS *America* from Palermo and deported from the ship to doors at Ellis Island, after eventually getting all the immigration papers approved and physical checks accepted, with little or no help in understanding papers that were given to them to complete their immigrations.

Francesco had only a little English-speaking capability from his previous stay as a worker in America when he immigrated in 1910. On his return trip back to Valguarnera, Sicily, in early 1912, he planned for his family to immigrate to America. About a year later, Francesco returned to America to prepare a place to live when the family arrives and eventually make way to a place to live and work. By chance, once back in America, he saw a friend from years back who was a teacher in Sicily in the town where they lived. As he approached, he was recognized and greeted. After much discussion, Francesco made sure his plan for his family was going to be secured so would be accepted in Ellis Island as emigrants. He also made sure they had friends until the final trek to West Virginia would begin.

For clarity, Filippa and her children were ready to travel after the planning was explained. Liborio, the eldest at thirteen, was born on February 10, 1900. Antonio was four years younger, Giuseppe about six years younger, and Maria was the youngest at only two years old. Their mother and four children, after being on board two days, were under continued unknown stress unimaginable and needed traumatic personal persistent care. Daily pain was an unrelenting torture while on board good and bad for about eight days before entering Ellis Island. The coming early morning dark was like seeing the sparkling star of Venus while entering the Verrazzano-Narrows Bridge area near lower gateway bay to observe the Statue of Liberty, an initial inviting grandeur of America so clear in their friends' minds. As Filippa awakened that early morning and positioned herself and the family to see the famous Statue of Liberty, her smiles and words were electrified with laughter, and the kids were romping around insides of Ellis Island to gain their checking in as emigrants. Filippa was prepared for all receptions with love, but she knew in her mind that English-speaking people dominated. She knew study work will be required in next few years of learning English, which would be a burden fully rewarded.

A first step is a poetically driving intent to explain how it came about as it did for so many people wanting an enhancement of collected words of praise to become emigrants in America. Only very short stories were ever told about their trip, and one could understand why they never wanted to talk about the trip.

The question-and-answer situations were unfathomable to express their discussions about unexpected behavior along the ship's trip. With degrading mental and physical sickness-induced suffering, Francesco revealed his counterintuitive mind sided with his demanding commands to his wife and children that he did it for them twice. When he talked, he interfered with ongoing conversational commands to stop criticizing what he says. He did not have a clear understanding of what he was being told about unbelievable mind-striking travel time.

It was repeated for him to gather his family and to go to New York City where appropriate services could directly help him and his family. In this conversation, he revealed his character, both the inferior part and his backup superior mental hold knowing his physical strength.

Nonetheless, his insistence on remaining friends with his practically minor acquaintances was demonstrated with a smiling and accepting face of thanks but always prevailing as a man seeking help while bolstering his strength and convincing his children to increase their strength. Big Poppy used facts that this new land held promises to fulfill his and the family's hopes for a renewed life. Francesco and his brother Paulo's intent was to take the family out of living under strife and in poverty in Italy, and now that it was happening, his mannerisms have subsided. At least for this time, some redeeming qualities of character in Francesco showed, and his associates were compatible when they had returned to America on board ship SS *Sicilia*. Many friends had a different sensitivity to the Americans now that they were already involved with Americans.

From their heart and soul, he made sure his family would have a much better chance by moving to America living under his fathering's power of mind and strength and by working daily under a constitutional democracy of elected representatives of the three federal government branches that served people in America because they were chosen. The representatives, chosen and elected, became representative members of the federal government, as did some within the states that fulfill three branches of the federal and state governments for America and similar officials for cities and municipalities of states.

Yet he remembered that his first trip over was a use of his inherited *steerage* far more than he needed so that the family settled easily having just traveled. He knew, to say the least with a smile, even though the trip was a torturous impact to persons of all ages unsuspecting the worse being that even a young man of great endurance such as Francesco could hardly endure when he had traveled two years before. His might was built for his current second trip.

Francesco had already been through one of great disgust and mental and physical pain receiving trip with no relief or even when or if relief was offered by the captain's mates completely unknown or ever seen up close involved the collection of human beings so remarkably known as the *steerage passengers*.

The *steerage travelers* were typically and intentionally compared with cattle on ships, but as humans, they experienced great physical and mental pain; a product that wore off after making their way to America, landing in New York at Ellis Island with implied values for life. This understood message also applied only a few years before when they had squashed dreams of Italian miners Francesco and his brother Paulo to head to America in the prime of their lives.

During Pres. Teddy Roosevelt's time, Italians were used as hard labor to build roads, towns, and cities in New York, and many were thankful for the jobs, even with nominal pays that keep their families with room and board and time for leisure life with little expected after their workdays.

Francesco sensed the reason why he made the trip in the first place within those three years with the grant of freedom and "free will" with little or no force imposed on the workers. No one in the immediate area where he worked or wandered among authority ever bothered him or his brother. Francesco had been married to Filippa (La Spina) Divita in Valguarnera, Sicily. Even after the marriage, he was constantly interrogated or prompted about his whereabouts because he was originally from Palermo, Sicily, some two hundred miles away and in a much more complicated city at the time. Big Poppy remembered being in Italy for a short time but had moved back to Sicily in late 1890s to mine sulfur.

After maturing to the ripe old age of thirty-five years, living through such hard times and being challenged carefully, he did not show a frown on his face about anything that had happened in Italy. He knew he had done the right move, and without a doubt, he knew he didn't know how to explain it to his wife and children. Francesco had so imprinted in his memory that he must leave. He never expressed the mining job having imposed a little less self-esteem for himself but not enough to change his personality.

Now, he awaited the arrival of Filippa and the children as immigrants departing on the SS *America* from Palermo, which sailed on December 5, 1913, and would arrive in eight days. Francesco waited at Ellis Island Office until their reception and interrogation allowed entry to the United States of America. They thanked God for the kind treatment and help with settling down and finished signing papers and medical investigations.

After much of the day passed, Francesco saw them walking with her family. Suddenly, all his children saw Francesco and Paulo. They rushed to grasped each other with a loving expectation at the sight as Francesco's family satisfied their dreams and hopes. Francesco hesitated to talk until he finalized their future life with "Thank God!" He used loving and hugging care with might and conversations so warmly conversed in Italian.

From an Italian person's description, overall observations covered a critical aspect of Italian heritage that showed what they expected and what they could see both as the poor *steerage passengers*. The way rich people displayed their new cars with servants waiting was easily showed to surrounding people. The differences among these ranks of people were enormously varied and within their minds with different expectations.

The interactions among Italian families traveling *steerage* on the ships were total responsiveness to the expected immigrations. Their reactions came about when the initial caring included sharing good personal attention and then once they were taken where their new friends lived and were graciously received. For most of the people coming to America, it was like a celebration, and their lives in these accepted time spans cherished moments in memories with attendance and care.

Francesco and Paulo had their minds made up. They were going to head for the mining country and West Virginia because they were told the mines were specially chosen for the type of mines in the mountains that are not nearly as deep like the ones in the Sicily sulfur mines.

The influence of old-fashioned Italians is relayed and taught to the new first-generation American Italians so that they carry that same moral and legal faithfulness to those families that pledge allegiance to America. Loyalty is first and foremost, and it must be defended and respected by all in their work actions and behavior. Italian family members work as required and follow known legal requirements.

The other side involved criminal elements, some of which were inherited or just plain came over on ships among crowds of new immigrants. Those socially working in concert tried to minimize prejudices within the variety levels of families, and those associated within business levels, as one might expect, included favoritism. This behavior quietened when the World War I broke out in Europe. The bulk if not all European emigrants predominantly considered themselves Americans in 1914 after Germans engulfed Europe in World War I. The most important was Americans, when they joined the fight, being Italians, had already welded their minds and hearts to support Americans in battles in World War I.

Disposition always becomes an influence especially when people are rich and self-centered; the gain required is to keep funneling into one's mind's self-sufficiency.

Chapter VII

World War I Affects Americans' Steerage and Amour

When the poison reaches the heart, that will be the end.
—Phaedo, sections 116–118, tr. Jowett, p. 13

What I have recalled from categorizing thoughts along times of how we grew up as Dad and Mom's children was that we studied for improvement toward better and more harmonious livings. They practiced sibling competition and worked their way into a moral culture of being dominant mentally and using their minds intelligently in society. Many of these first-generation American children, as they became adults, sought formal education toward professionalism in business administration, medicine and science, some becoming entrepreneurs, some mastering arts and crafts unexcelled by blue blood counterparts.

Here is how I explained how my family lives as new generations of progeny of *Homo sapiens* as God's continued evolution moves to immortality as he defined. All of you must be on your best behavior and carefully mind yourselves starting from World War II and still propagating into the millennium.

The Divita family, as were all Americans, in past times, had demeanor significantly influenced by their taught behavior, first during World War I with Grandfather Francesco and Grandmother Filippa and their living progeny. Then much later during World War II, three of their sons fought during the war during prime development of their lives. World War II had started with the next generation of Francesco and Filippa's children into their teens and early twenties for the elder sons that then married and produced new progeny as Americans. The same for the progeny from the first immigrant children, and the first American-born Italian descendants had been taught how to behave during critical times by following the teachings of *steerage* and *amour*.

Now, the new generation of the 1950s came into vogue and the societal changes in America's society and cultural living new times with lighter less influences because the wars were smaller and only in one or two countries at a time. Piecemeal wars were personally different to children in many ways. They ventured into a "live and let live" daily behavior, being positive and beneficial to all who lived unencountered.

As Benny aged to adulthood, his life was involved in every detailed thing his mom and dad did in their early lives. That experience our dad had gained by his father's opposite personality by his poppy Francesco. However, his mother Filippa was what led Big Benny mentally to become a peacemaker par excellence. Filippa was a mentored easygoing teacher of *steerage* and *amour* as so defined throughout this story. After immigration, the Divita family settled, and more children were born over the next ten to fifteen years, and each sibling received Filippa's teachings while living, and the continuation came about from new well-trained teachers as moms and dads as they made time for children living nearby.

Grandfather Francesco was a smart man who had evolved ambition from his previous experience as an emigrant in America before returning to Italy to bring his family back to America. After they returned, he invested his money wisely in land and amassed resources over a twenty-year period while working in the West Virginia coal mines. He was smart enough to start an Italian delicatessen butcher shop and store in Montgomery around the 1930s with the help of his sons. Because of the times, it was a store that also sold beer, soft drinks, and various sundry items. Benny and two of his brothers worked in the store daily. The boys concentrated about a total of eight hours at the store, always taking time off with substitutions for dinner and interaction with their children. Sometimes, two eldest boys, Benny and Tony, would return home in the late evening; and if they had a beer from the store, they were ready for either bed after a little snack or a bit of radio and a doze in the club chair. They also worked at the Fayette Bottling Company part time to make money along with helping his father in the store's deli areas.

I imagined what it was like at the family compound where several of the children lived with other young families. Big Mommy had more individual responsibilities for the children at home and started out with more than a dozen children from different families. Sometimes, devoted mothers spent their days with common household duties with spare time while cooking or preparing three meals a day and rearing children every minute of the day.

At night, Big Mommy's first job was feeding Big Poppy when he came home from the mine. Then her next job was one of getting her husband into bed if he does not do it himself. All the mother's night ends after finally getting a few hours of child-uninterrupted sleep, usually sometimes partially awake, until early morning sun appears through windows creating a joy for the exuberance of her younger children.

The baby in the crib, her son Jimmy, was so comfortable in the same room that for this one, he looked as if he was guarded by the king's guard all night long. As days sped by, Filippa visited various places nearby to see other family members.

Often, elder children would return at odd times for a renewed boost either for food or conversation with their momma Filippa about their daily learning and involved activities.

The stories of the day involved relatives and friends, and sometimes, elder brothers and sisters offered to help to do daily chores. Other family members were continually coming in the house as uninvited visitors and have some, or at least in their view, important things to discuss usually with Big Mommy. They might be with other members of the family, especially if they were looking for companionship for the day or asking for solutions to everyday problems.

Each family and children visited the other extended family members of their ages. No doubt children got together for meals and family celebrations. Katy and her three younger brothers, Frank (also named after his father Francesco), Charlie, and Jimmy, as they grew up, likely had friends and eyed the pretty girls in town. Later, the same was done when we, the Benny and Jo Divita family, moved to Montgomery in the beginning of 1941, and Tony and Catherine moved to the Yaquinta Farm of her father's in a separate home. Then some elder families moved to Montgomery, Smithers, and Glen Falls outside of the *OverHome* area.

The remaining activity was Big Poppy's ventures into and beyond ordinary outside living time, which was associated with his sons nearby, business counterparts, and many recently new people and friends that were becoming his associate partakers at Al's Place.

Only two events were covered to explain the nature of this generation's American heritage and choices of behavior. The first and most important was that extended family interactions of these strong-minded and physically adept men were ready to go after new jobs and later even after new businesses. Their social personal behavior being a new generation of Americans fitted like clockwork.

There were weekly gatherings at the *OverHome* of their paternal grandparents, usually on Sundays, in Smithers. At their grandparents' home, the *OverHome*, the visit was expected if not demanded. It was especially one that was understood for every Sunday that culminated with dinner and conversation of sorts, sometimes overcontrolled by Big Poppy and his mind's well-being based on his days during the week and what he wanted to do preferentially, like maybe having a few drinks with his sons.

It was more than dinner because it started usually a few hours after some siblings and their families might have attended their Catholic church in the local or nearby city of Montgomery. At midday time, certainly around 2:00 or 3:00 p.m., was a must time for all his family members to be at the *OverHome*.

Women gathered as a team in the kitchen and talked in mixed Italian and English, and God only knew already what each of them would discuss. Then cooking starts. Most kids were playing in yards or sitting on porches. Some were in the living room with elder children being ordered to go get treats, which was always a mystery to the little children because it was so easy to do, especially candy-coated almonds. They were too busy playing and scuffling to worry about it. Getting a taste of food was good.

The part about getting money interested them because they knew at times, money was coming to them when families engaged kids to show off their specialties such as singing, dancing, or drawing by those who had talents. There was always talk and care about kids. On a whisper from the old grandfather Francesco of their well-being, the devil's disciple, to all who had seen his wrath, the response was that they were well treated. He could get away with feeding babies somewhat in odd ways, but he was there to give them physical and medicinal aid. If an accident had occurred, he was the first one there to give aid. His medicine was sugar; in my case, when I was about five years old, he put sugar on my forehead when I fell out of an open chair seat on the front porch and clobbered my forehead.

Every member of the family knew that get-togethers were a direct order from the patriarch. He didn't give it a thought. Francesco just expected it, and if it didn't happen, he raised hell with whoever was late or who had to be found and brought in by his eldest son, Benny. The attendance was demanded. If neglected by one, all faced chaos, sometimes directed against the grandmother regardless of celebrations. Also included were special meetings that involved usually elder sons who had to rescue the Big Poppy from himself or someone who was about to get clobbered by him.

On my mother Jo's side of our family, we intermittently took special yearly trips to our grandparents' home in Adrian, West Virginia. These gatherings were different in that relationships were loving, peaceful, and enjoyable. Francesco's experiences were as different as night and day in the *OverHome*.

The differences occurred mainly between the grandfathers. Our mother's father Alphonso was a hardworking miner from an Italian family from Cambria, Italy. Her mother was of the same caliber as Grandmother Filippa, showing a graciousness and love for all of us, as did our uncles and aunts. These two were man and wife who immigrated earlier in the late 1890s. I mostly remember visits from my mother's brother Samuel (called Sandy by friends and family), and at times, we visited Uncle Al and Baptist (called Buster by friends and family) and their families. In every way that I can recollect, we were included as a family of Marucas with their siblings. We all met the family several times there after our mom and dad were married within the year and later at least visited them or they visited us yearly and less times as time passed. Members of their family visited with us a number times throughout the years, and earlier, some of the uncles worked for our dad and even stayed at our home for a short time over the years. Even Grandpa Alphonso stayed with us several times in his older age at our home. Later, we would get visits from their individual families, who mostly lived in the New York area.

But there was also tragedy that struck my parents in their early marriage. Frankie was the first born in September 1929 and was very strong. The togetherness and love surrounded her two boys, Frankie and Alphonso I, who were living in both good and bad times. The worst disaster was the loss of my mother's second child, a boy born in April 1931 who only lived almost five years and died after having diphtheria in September 1935. Later, two boys, Gene and Eddie, were both born in January; Gene in 1933, and Eddie in January 1935. Later, one girl, Phyllis Jane, was born in October 1936. All three also lived through bad times and sickness without proper medicines during the 1930s. However, the next child, Alphonso II, after Jane was born in November 1939, only lived for six months and died in May 1940. Both boys that died were named after our maternal grandfather, having been named after their grandfather with the name Alphonso I and Alphonso II for lifetime memories. They lingered in our love and in despair and heartbreak for years, especially for my mother and dad and their grandfather and grandmother. The solace that gathered relief with time was that their souls were taken to eternity in heaven eventually with God as we believed. Benny and Josephine were modest parents and friendly as a big family and with neighbors. My maternal grandmother was also named Josephine, which was the given name to my mother Josephine; both were named after their parents.

The Maruca grandparents had a position of great respect with their children and our family. Even at Grandmommy's age, she was called Mommy! She always showed concern for children in every way. The Marucas had raised four boys and five girls. Our visits took place almost yearly, but as the children grew older, they did less visiting; but the memories remained. The remembrances included ventures on their farmland with a flowing creek and plenty of vegetables. The one place that I can still smell was the cellar where smoked pepperoni, sausage, and ham were hanging to cure.

Grandparents Alphonso and Josephine made sure their children were cared for under situations or circumstances that might indicate that they needed care. There were times when some of our grandmommy's family visited our home in Montgomery as individuals, or there were several in-laws who visited us for a few days. This familial behavior evolved through regular communication that, in a sense, I recognized an accumulated inheritance evidence with my insight on heritage methodology—that is, the Maruca family had a strong grasp of teaching *steerage* and *amour* so gifted by both families, and it continued through both our mom and dad's lifetime raising their children.

These added teachings from contact with my mother's family were positive, as was our mother Jo's constant teaching of Divita children par excellence. Usually, traits were revealed by us through our personal behavior among each other, and it was displayed to other wives and husbands as they interacted together being of Italian descent. As all know, it was not as common as it was sparsely done.

The families of first-generation Italians born in America always propagated influences of their heritage in a typical psychological way, as it does for all human beings that had emigrated. In Italian families, men are masters psychologically when they know how to prescribe dosages of mental discourse; it was done by both mother and father. It is their inheritance from people of Italy that practically all have creative minds.

However, depending on dominant heritage traits, some men may be different as night and day within a given family. The dominant Italian influence from each generation also evolved a few men and women from long lines of reared Italians with confrontational behavior way back to Romans and Etruscans as separate heritages.

This story reveals instilled associated humor and pathos unequaled after the melding of several, if not one or more, nationalities, especially Italians, English, and Irish people. This was the case after first- and second-generation Americans immigrated and then, thereafter, procreated and evolved in America, where freedom of life, spirit, and love resides. Nevertheless, the same thing happened during the First Renaissance so proudly exposed; but many people did run amuck without care and using their minds at times, as do human beings in everyday living throughout the world.

Benny, as Liborio, was the immigrant son of Big Poppy, who was raised until he was thirteen, brought up during the early 1900s in Valguarnera, Sicily. Benny, as my father, always had a good story to tell his children at home. Benny was wrapped in wit and humorous sayings. One of the first that I recalled was a whimsical large-scale incident that he brought home during 1949 after we moved into our completely remodeled home at the lower end of the city. It was near Easter, so he brought home a goat for Easter dinner, still yet a few days away. Now, with excitement, there was a lot of things that he could have brought home instead of a goat because it looked like a pet to us kids, not a pun. Of course, that was so because it was the way they played with it. You know what Dad had to do with the goat—he returned it to the owner's farm and said, next time, he will bring one home that was ready to be cooked, as do so many people on farms who eat goat. All of us kids laughed and said out loud in unison, "We like ham, Easter eggs and candy, and a bit of Mom's baccala codfish in her specially made soup!"

The next time in the early '50s, our father was known to bring home many items of food including balls of provolone cheese, a dozen pepperoni sticks, a ten-pound box of Italian sausage, fresh hams, and live turkeys and chickens in cages from some of his farmer friends and from Cavalier's Store. It wasn't a mystery how he managed these feats of gifts. He used his connections as a businessman well known for miles around for his acumen gained from his father years before, who had an Italian delicatessen shop in their hometown of Montgomery.

For any family member, being around live turkeys and chickens was enough; but for young kids, when they get to know these animals that were going to be killed and prepared for dinner, sometimes it turned out to be traumatic. Keep in mind, my dad Benny was the firstborn in Francesco and Filippa's family. After leaving Sicily and immigrated to America, Liborio, now called Big Benny, acquired ways to survive and to maintain peace among the families. What's the big deal? Well, I'll tell you: It was "Steerage and Amour!—What's It All About!" It's about the family or individuals gaining position and power by learning to do things that everyone should use in the new country of America. Following this method of being taught that they would fit into society and adapt new ways of life, which, as always, included men and women participating in marriage and teaching their children with compassionate language. Excuse me, infidelity also takes place in all cultures and countries even though we are the only *Homo sapiens* on earth.

But for Benny, in his new endeavors, he took a wife in a religious ceremony about the same time as several of his siblings of Francesco and Filippa, and their Italian cousins also married. I think my dad wanted to raise his family with significantly more finesse than what was used by his father, and certainly with more compassion as his mother had insisted. And I really mean they did raise their siblings with much more finesse and a great deal of being able to make sound decisions.

All while under the pressure of having formed habits and ways that had come from his heritage or simply the gifted sense of "knowledge and experience" to make a good decision or good judgment, Dad knew he had to control himself as much as the children and do it with love and calmness. With a new family started, he established his business at his home base, and he helped various people over the next few years to get a start. This was a time in the mid-'30s, although not good times in the country with the Great Depression well into riveting a pan-poverty-producing stage in America. He gained a position of respect and was a benefactor to members of the family. Benny made decisions for himself and others upon request no matter how decisions they might have thought his words could affect their lives, and they did, and it was to their wants usually every time.

Dad told us about how uses of foreign languages were generally undecipherable by different nationalities, and even so by Italians of different dialects, especially between the northern and southern parts of Italy. Some people were even noticeably different in tongue speeds and pronunciations between the Sicilians and those people raised in Calabria on the bottom eastern side of the boot. However, Italian people, within less than a minute, could manage to understand most of what each other would discourse with a different language accent, speed, and pronunciation.

Without thinking, Europeans of different languages made America the gold source of lingo so unexpected even from state to state, including accents and sounding dialects in English. We all noticed different ways Italians spoke their languages to my dad as he told us. He kept us informed on many things simply because he ran into so many things and happenings.

In America, and especially in West Virginia, small adjacent properties were finely kept in lawns and bushes; and most other people's homes had only small gardens. Grandfather Francesco's property had flowers planted all around his homes and a vegetable garden in their side and back yards. The backyards in homes were small spaces. The one part of the duplex opened into a dirt alley where trash was burned in backyards unless alleys ended on a backyard. That was the place where we played when we were young kids living in the *OverHome*. Many children played in alleys and yards and in roads and vacant lots for games such as baseball and football and got very dirty.

In the first neighborhood of Smithers life was a simple way of living. A few adults were always around various outside areas in mixed conversation because they knew each other at their work or as neighbors. Most elder people relaxed on porches sometimes in conversation or meditating half asleep. The Kanawha River was on the other side of the road and behind a single row of homes that bordered the road. The homes across the road were more expensive and on larger lots. I imagined neighbors were always wondering what was going on at Big Poppy's where excitement filled the day's activity. Many adults, children, and their families and close-quarters friends visited his site, and children usually played in his big front yard.

Adults and children were always on the go with disruption ensuing. The children were afraid to question their fathers but had no problem conversing with their mothers. Some children were afraid to challenge their mothers because they might be exposed to the wrath of the father when he gets home. In Italian families, most women dished out discipline with simple demands or a whack on the butt. You got it and you took it with nothing but a whelp or a slight cry! Usually, a wooden spoon or cooking utensil was available and kept near to minimize the chase and ensure a strike on the bottom.

Some truly American women felt uncomfortable with positions of authority when faced with a problem of dispensing a paddling. At times, friends nearby could see that kids would be taken into the house and put in the corner. Usually, after a while, the child shows remorse or promises to settle down.

Other women let it reside with husbands to level punishment when they come home, which, psychologically, causes stored mental disorder. In all cases, in my mind, this was a barbarous approach to let the justice be meted out by a nonobserver of the committed misdeed. So many men obviously devised a way to gain a reply like, "I will never do it anymore!" Then, at least, the punisher would be diminished, if not relieved, and qualify it as, "Good!"

During the era, most women's time is devoted to childcare, and mostly when they are youngsters. Beyond that time, children learn, for the most part, proper behavior, except when a few individual children are overactive in ways unexpected, mentally or physically. During most times thereafter, mothers spend significant time making sure youngsters are being good in play times, while mothers spend times with children for various personal reasons or preparing daily meals, especially dinner for kids and the dad.

Our mother Josephine, wife of Benny, had respect for and from the Divita family. It was a given because of her husband's position in the family. This farm girl Josephine knew her husband's ways from back in the '30s, so things he would do for the family never surprised her. And she knew when he was up to something with surprises that were expected no matter what; she didn't mind challenging him to his face and win sometimes. However, in confrontation, he always did whatever was the right way to compromise with her and solve any problem in the family. This was just one way both Benny and Jo predominantly remained happy in their lives even under difficult times when death in the family and despair changed their lives in many ways, with details of managing their siblings' lives by living with more knowledge of morality with all *Homo sapiens*.

CHAPTER VIII

Mankind's Behavior in Society with Cultural Extensions Dominated by Wars from the Past

> *A moment of revelation comes, it must be admitted, practically*
> *to everybody and not to Italians alone. A day comes when men*
> *of all nations understand that life can be pitiless and ugly. Each*
> *has his own way of reaching maturity [during world wars]. Some*
> *need the imperceptible passing of the years. It takes but a tiny*
> *incident for others; like shaking of a kaleidoscope it precipitates*
> *an abrupt change of the picture indecipherable. Or it makes a*
> *great event that awakens him: he sees his country defeated . . .*
> —*The Italians*, chapter 10, "The Pursuit of Life,"
> Luigi Barzini, Atheneum, New York, 1977, p 176

Most common in recent past times was the continuation of mentally instinctive behavior pursuits that react autonomously in mankind's mind at a flicker of eyes that attach and seek sensuous desires. Everyone's yearning for *amour* is always engaged. Changes in mental messenger minds that signal the Four Horsemen of the Apocalypse, flagging chaos by death in world wars, is eminent. Critical decisive thoughts stop or seize responses from good decisions that come from the heart and soul when following teachings of *Steerage and Amour—What's It All About!*; but even now, sometimes, it becomes distorted toward the instinctive "will of desire."

Part of this story reveals general changes of men and women's nature and behavior regarding amorous pursuits especially when under warring action and mostly sensing survivability. The effects may be embedded memory practices that flog mind's nerve cells encased within neurons that place more caution on workable mind-grasping sensuous, if not patriotic demands. The dominating calamity of wars yields different responses in people when choosing between "will of desire" and "knowledge and experience."

Therefore, in mankind's concrete memory bank, mixed with growing self-asserting personalities, minds create changes as often as they respond to "will of desire" or to "knowledge and experience" stored by normal mentality. Most people become excited before thinking to decipher expectations related primarily to *amour* when it is related to illicit *amour* or a natural heartfelt *amour* accounting for immediate joy, versus potentially living a short lifetime. One should be able to instantaneously translate memory's "knowledge and experience" that spurts into the amygdala without delay to force an ejaculation of "will of desire" to block initial instinctive pursuits. The blockage reaction happens in a flicker of mental time it takes to hold instinctive resolutions, extracting a decision by any *Homo sapiens* because, at home, it would be less than abroad during wars.

This mentally mindful maneuver to advance government troops and personal lives in warring society does not happen without strongly striving for cultural extensions with time. However, through exercises of access to one's mind's memory of "knowledge and experience," the mind will shift to ensure increasing potential to change to a known decision. The inherited and gifted taught *steerage* infers that ability by teaching families for one's own good. The result, eventually, after mankind's many reactions to informative drives, will then be enhanced by habit and will quickly respond. Even though it had happened over eons on a regular basis, it is less likely to gain dominance because humans have always first maintained forced amorous responses with instinctive will. Thus, instinctive reactions were never intended to accept any such change except at the instance of measured happenings such as life changes of expected critically measured threats even to death.

From the beginning of mankind when it had responded under God's planned evolution and belief in God's creation initially, an immediacy of survivability would have been a major occurrence with propagation of the species. At those critical early times of life-forms, large and destructive animals would have easily defeated mankind. The mind would have interfered with survival of the fittest from the start of mankind's initial behavior. Then when *Homo sapiens* mind proceeded to the initial path of current status as genus *Homo* as modern man qualified with sapiens when they exited the Cenozoic Quaternary times. Mankind during Cenozoic Quaternary times happened unknown millions of years ago when God had started to include a qualifier of being wise within the mind's brain. God's creation and evolution must have provided coming advancements when it all started from the initial creation of the universe. Whatever your choice may be, *Homo sapiens* only by birthing is autonomously now ingrained with a functional mind, and its usage is instantly accessible and must be used to complete decisions.

Then all amorous and sensuous events that have occurred in the far past might have been hardwired to be passed as a selection before being passed morally or naturally. At least the instinctive resolve is maimed enough so that the conscious mind should have countered it with recalled knowledge accumulated. The first thrust of experience directly through hereditary evolution was dominating at the expense of instinctive behavior. In this modern day, we know that, without a doubt, the instinctive behavior is still hardwired, but the mind has its second decisive thought displayed for use.

What I mean is more than enough is known about sensuous evolvements, actions of happenstance and planned encounters arise, but responses would be that the mind instills cautionary conscious pauses against instinctive directions. As we know, the mind dismissed the touch of dangerous surfaces such as things too hot or too cold within the mind's memory over the years of teaching or plain life experiences; the mind usually causes pause to react before walking on thin ice or fighting fire. From study and tests, scientists know so well that children do not sense the danger until it is recorded in their memories as "knowledge and experience" yet to be triggered by any one or more of the seven senses.

Personal *amour* is released uncontrollably by a multiemotional code of lust that vibrates continuously to spark an emotional fire in minds of any human being instinctively. Whether they are received and returned has to do with one's personal inheritance, societal influences, and inherent environmental and cultural trends of the times. The actual practice that comes with "knowledge and experience" may shadow the decision to do the wrong thing.

Steerage and Amour!—What's It All About! reveals how human beings can be dominated by amorous influences of behavior; but once inculcated, and as one gets lost in desperation, parents attempt to instigate *steerage* to crucially defer personal family warring conflagrations. Each person's actions and reactions cause perpetual changes in mankind's nature that changes society and culture critically at times because extensions of behavior are dominated by *wars*! When that happens, the evolution of changes reveal people's behavior in cultural and sociable behavior among people who controlled decisive influences and then recognize disloyalty that latches on to unforgiveable disgraces and immediately trust their minds to the "will of desire."

Situations like these were pervasive in early Roaring Twenties. However, during mankind's innovation, talents and creativity evolved many years before in the past during the First Renaissance of beginnings in 1450s and dominated with a thrust of life changes for more than fifty years and continued to extended society, behavior, and culture morally as time proceeded into the 1700s.

Impacts of living during the First Renaissance after the Middle Ages was historically recorded. In my mind, I think a Second Renaissance started in the early to late 1700s when various wise men worked using their minds to gain more peaceable times both for free people and slaves. The times were brought by England, who wanted to colonize the New America, while the living Americans wanted to obtain America as a free country. The Revolutionary War was started by England to continue their colonization. The Revolutionary War continued until America won its freedom from England. The dating and accounting continued from July 4, 1776, to 1789 with all proper documents, and American as a country continued to formulate their laws for the existing states following the Constitution of the United States of America.

Then within the next seventy years, changes had been needed to free slaves and indentured servants to make all people of America free. Finally, during Abraham Lincoln's time as president in the mid-1860s, the North's Union demanded to free slaves, and the Confederate South wanted slaves to remain. This was the time of America's Civil War. This war among the American people caused untold death and destruction. Lincoln had commanded his generals and their troops to expose and win most of the fighting, and they eventually won the war by forcing his mind to win the war. After settlements among states were brought together, the congressional union statesmen had the Senate win the vote for the Emancipation Proclamation.

This action convinced Americans with first intentions to secure the social and political declarations for all people to be free. The new pursuits in society, culture, arts, and technology expanded and continued in the United States as it grew and blossomed during the industrial revolution after the war with recognition of new wisdom involving mankind. The nineteenth and twentieth centuries later revealed new and unexpected cultural improvements, developments, and technologies unheard of except from the same kinds of minds as those who primed the First Renaissance.

In my reading and formal study about many times of wars in America, starting with the Revolutionary War when Great Britain wanted to colonize America in the late 1700s, warring continued with the Civil War of 1860s. Later into the 1900s, wars continued internationally worldwide until World War I was started by the Austrians and ended up across several continents, causing a tremendous amount of death and destruction, and in which America was involved as an ally with Great Britain. After that war, the Roaring Twenties began to distort unruly and unorderly behavior by many people, and those times depressed the '20s and '30s, causing unrecognized suffering of the people during the Great Depression. The climate added further personal depression, causing unusable land for food-growing environments, and people's businesses were penniless, but the government of United States of America helped poor people across the country to survive bad times.

Later in the '30s, Germany brought on World War II, starting with England and the European continent. Then the Japanese led America to war thereafter while tending their secret but final interest by bombing Pearl Harbor on December 7, 1941. After the American forces won the World War II and things settled down, the next war was started in the '50s and followed into continuous warring in Asia with American forces. Then America continued as they followed by extensions into African countries to this very date in modern times when significant technological and social advances were dominating world advances and new means of living and controlling nations as a team of the United Nations.

Remember, as I do, the unqualified version from Jesus in his time vocally had relayed, "Mankind's lifetime will always be a warfare."

The United States of America had also thrived during the extensive Cold War with Russia. Détente was watched and maintained during the Cold War, and it ameliorated, except with an advancement of Communism in Asia extents in China.

Several wars in Korea were then started when Chosen was separated into North Korea and South Korea. Those wars caused America to honor the Southeast Asia Treaty to protect South Korea. After a few years, the Korean War signed a treaty. Then a new war continued in Vietnam. Need I continue as to what is now going on in modern days related to the warring of countries that the United States of America had been in or were still fighting in the Balkans in the late 1990s and then into Africa from 2011 to current days 2019 facing little if any détente in the Mideast and they were always under arbitration?

In the late 1700s, one might think back that a Second Renaissance had proceeded but concluded with its warring ventures; all the while, warring might be the major cause of what I called the Second Renaissance that started by expanding into wars from 1800s into the 2000s. These new scientific and fortified technical accomplishments could lead mankind to many advancements such as new creations starting with trains and cars and, within mid-1940s, jet airplanes, nuclear power, and horrendously destructive nuclear weapons. Nuclear power began in the mid-'50s, and later, within a short time, America had nuclear-powered submarines, carriers, and battleships. Then in 1960s, space travel started with new developments of newly designed space vehicles circling the earth with prototypes named *Mercury* and *Gemini* and eventually the *Apollo* spacecraft traveling and landing on the moon. The finality included NASA's shuttle vehicle to carry various scientific subsystems to do experiments and the International Space Station, which stays in orbit using supply vehicles developed to carry supplies and new astronauts to rotate stays.

All the while, artificial intelligence was taking off with the modern electronic devices and radio and remote controls to advance toward building effective robots for multiple mechanizations and health requirements such as artificial part and organs put into human beings. Television and iPhones and computers have advanced beyond radios and were extended with natural colors that created plasma and LED screens showing significant realism of new ventures into leisure time.

The giant surge of microelectronics significantly created new electronic systems and information storage and transmission systems of different wavelengths adding new memory storing and programmable developed electromechanical computers of significant capabilities. Telephone innovations were now completely revamped and given mobile access. Thereafter, every three years led to new ventures complemented by new technical communication bands and radio communication access to capabilities in spacecraft to follow such extensive space rocketry for science exploration of our planetary system. The rise of the *Voyager* spacecraft with different means of information transmissions, communications, and power sources with computer technologies using the near infinite extent of the broadband and X band frequencies allowed transmission beyond our solar system. The ever-working Hubble Wide Field and Planetary Spacecraft has presented many new photographs of various neutron stars, supernova stars, and even black holes of features of enormous density with a microwave outer layer and defender to project incoming large matter.

These new inventions happened in only one hundred years soon after the railroad trains and automobiles were fully under production in the early 1900s. The next surge of new inventions included new architecture including new bridges and extremely high-rise buildings in major cities. New societal and environmental improvements surged, and many unknown contraptions were placed at the edge of new cultural advancements. Their usage of new mechanizations was daily, spread across America with global interactions through communications.

The next inventions led to new computer development that changed the 1960s with augmented scientific capabilities that genius individuals increased the leading edge of modern technology. The technology explosion, mind-boggling and complex, and within individuals' wise minds, continued to evolve current inventions with full flow of complexity.

Living in this assumed scientific and technical Second Renaissance ensures a probability of a Third Renaissance will follow in the future, and if so, a continuation of Renaissances will arise while the universe exists. At best, this kind of expectation makes mankind's future advance in mental and physical life with natural creative improvements expected to be evolved from God's creation and continued evolution. What could happen regarding the invention of nuclear weapons may be a major concern with an owing potential of the involvement of nuclear warfare on earth.

Mass nuclear warfare is potentially a stone's throw away when one dreams of a new renaissance mankind's pursuits at home with talent, innovation, and creativity, yet unknown as of now, how to devolve nuclear weapon systems. When a next renaissance blossoms into light of genius from heaven of new minds that would devise a concert to combine countries to revert nuclear materials threat chemically and mechanically and convert to a methodology that destructively changes the elements by eliminating uses of weaponized elements under no circumstances to recover, the intent would be to dismantle all nuclear weapons from all countries.

This kind of expected genius will aspire to destructing their warring nuclear weapons for humanitarian reasons. Also, these gifted people will explore destructive methods by molecular, elemental, and isotopic separation analysis and eliminate the capability to convert the elements by converting them to nominal use. This look into future efforts to do the above changes will most necessarily conflict significantly with the nature of "Mankind's life will always be involved with warring."

I add much more detail of the warring in the current modern times because it will highlight what is intended to continue as current times progress with major conflicts of war. The following are exemplified herein as they follow timelines of our lifetime involvements in wars among many nations of people who have a hyperbolic differentiation of why choices for war is wrong and is no way to establish peace. The following expose to exemplify the concerns and also has much to do with making mankind understand what has been going on over the thousands of years and must gain insight on how to stop warring. I will cite herein highlighting critical times for the reader to absorb what has happened in the last half of the twentieth century into the twenty-first century to store an understanding blast that will affect people's minds.

The North Atlantic Treaty Organization (NATO) had already been signed in early 1949 after World War II, mostly with the United States of America, Canada, Great Britain, Australia, France, and later, Union of Soviet Socialist Russia (USSR) and Italy were against European countries and nearby countries of Italy (aligned first with Mussolini), Turkey, Greece, and North Africa as a military and naval alliance against all potential foes under agreed to declarations of war. Especially since such critically unexpected behavior was owed to experience gained during the past many wars including World War I that ended in November 1918 and World War II that ended in 1946 with great success.

Only less than five years after World War II, the Union of Soviet Socialist Russia installed a Cold War with the United States of America in the 1950s. The general thrust of the spread of international Communism was warped by NATO into those peculiarly different wars involving Korea, Vietnam, and the extension into Laos and Cambodia from '60s to near '70s as if someone as a source needed to see what would happen in the next ultimate move of mankind as expected from treaties like the one the United States signed with many countries in 1954 after the division of Korea into North Korea and South Korea with disastrous treatments of prisoners and intentional killings of all people in their paths. The finality of limited peace left the two countries at odds because of potential great might of the North Korean warmongers who wanted to make the country one again.

NATO met with leaders for peaceful negotiations in concert with the United States of America and other members predominantly from the European countries. President of the United States Dwight D. Eisenhower participated in the new treaty with Thailand along with the United Kingdom, France, Australia, New Zealand, Pakistan, and the Philippines, known as the Southeast Asia Treaty Organization (SEATO), having no binding for joint military action or no formal organization other than secretariat and consultative council in 1954. As a treaty, it was firm to all members as protectorates when required, and when North Korea signed the treaty, so did South Korea, and they were supported and defended by America with NATO.

Then later, all hell broke loose in the South Vietnam and North Vietnam and Cambodia and started a horrendous extension of warring. The assaults continued at extreme levels as do most wars. These wars were still fighting even after the assassination of President Kennedy was assassinated on November 22, 1963. The front-end agreements came to play, and within the year, Pres. Lyndon B. Johnson continued but was desperately unsuccessful and decided not to run for the presidency in 1968. Afterward, Richard M. Nixon was elected president, and he continued the warring until he ended it in 1973.

Only God would suspect the previous ultimate killings in Asia as onslaughts continued. People who have specific intent knew how the Asian minds worked. Steerage was not followed by people who were at war because "will of desire" changed the way the people lived; the leaders preached for war and against associated and involved religions. The exception is the Islamic religion, now whose leaders operate with a demand that citizens must change or convert to Moslem. Moslems deny it, and then they do nothing about those who have it in their every thought.

Those Islamic extremists knew better but meditated on what preparations of clandestine destruction plans that they may work to gain spiritual rewards. The concept was an assault on the marine barracks in Beirut, Lebanon, in the Mideast, where over two hundred marines were killed by terrorists with a truck bomb in 1976. Then in the 1980s, several attacks were made again by Islamic terrorists again with a first strike at the newly constructed World Trade Center in 1993 during Pres. William J. Clinton's first term. Only little response by the United States was pursued. Repairs were made with no understandable assault, let alone an attack against perpetrators. Instead, an open warring support from the United States was switched to the Balkans, where warring combat was under way to the extreme with attempted genocide conceived by both religious members, Catholics and Moslems.

Within eight years, a second strike was at the World Trade Center on September 11, 2001, and totally intentional by the Islamic terrorists. The bombardment was set up to learn and use hijacked large commercial American airplanes. The individual airplanes dived into the World Trade Center's two buildings, and another one unexpectedly headed toward and crashed into the country's Pentagon, where the United States Department of Defense for all Military Operations was, in Arlington, Virginia.

The attacks were effectively carried out by Islamic terrorists via a plan to secretively hijack commercial airplanes with unity of the day. Once terrorists were on board each airplane, they immediately overtook passenger-filled planes from major East Coast airports with force enough to fly. The planes were loaded with people and fueled fully as they guided into their targets by diving into their selected sights with intent to kill all aboard.

The suicidal terrorists headed to their targets and kamikazed the planes on three targets but missed one because Americans heroes on the plane prevented them from making their target. The fourth airplane was interfered by heroic passengers that caused the flight to head in a different direction, and it crashed into a field in Pennsylvania, killing all in the plane, and a memorial was also built to honor those brave people in the plane.

Overall, more than three thousand ordinary fellow Americans citizens and international persons from many countries, military personnel, and the rescue personnel, all at or nearby, were exposed to destruction and death from scattered heavy concrete and under rescue efforts' dust. Many police and firefighters continued to help save people's lives. The major problem for all helpers on site was that people's lungs were being damaged, and many died unexpectedly after a few short years.

The deadly effects lingered during rescues and the long-term effects of personal recovery caused by the World Trade Center twin buildings being destroyed. The aftermath of deaths continued with exposure to the harmful dusts and actions in the cleanup that caused many to suffer and affected people later from induced injuries and diseases.

Many multiphased meetings related to United States of America National were to be discussed under Pres. George Bush as commander-in-chief. The meetings were both while he was on site and later with his organization of secretaries. He and the Defense Department military strategy planned what should be returned in might of power against known terrorist countries with major grossly deadly assaults. Details of the planned warring attack was initiated against the dictator leader Saddam Hussein of Iraq. Discussions are extensive in Wikipedia.

After much reconsideration about rebuilding, architectures were selected to team individually and perform detailed designs to rebuild a new World Trade Center Area as a memorial to honor the innocent people from the world. The historic site was eventually completed after about ten years as a major presentment of respect for the free people of the world.

After much discussion of how to react to this enormous secretive murdering of free people by terrorists, considerable compromising decisions and reactions of America leaders were undefined and unknown to American people what had happened to their country of those that carried out monstrosities of killing innocent people from many countries.

Instead, only follow-up was conducted by Pres. George Bush, who took on an understandable plan to attack the country of Iraq with a primary reason to rid the country of the dictator Saddam Hussein and to lead their country into a democratic election of leaders. The limited success was meager. Hussein was captured and was eventually hanged for crimes against people of Iraq. Involvements in Iraq are still under warring but initially was under way to build anew as a peaceable country with elected leaders. Simply put, war in the Mideast is still going on, and warring is a ring of thorns on heads of free leaders in the world for each that has been involved righting warring efforts because it has not materialized for America's advantage to bring peace to the Mideast.

The overall influence of the nature of response and behavior of other countries as influenced by an emboldened pursuit of the close-knit and homespun Islamic religion revived its potential to spread it wings of people into other countries, and it worked secretively until the religious extremists recognized the destructive terror strikes as a means of infusing fear so that it changed methods of attack to analyze and discriminate terror attacks in many countries to show a hatred or a disgust for being ignored as both a religious power and one with clandestine warring capability.

The warring involvements by Islamic leaders in the Mideast has been under way since 1950s, which was when all this had its beginning to establish a homeland country for the remaining Israelis decimated by Germany during war. With that change of land, it enhanced widespread countries' despots who had even hated Jews more being nearby as planned by America with help from Great Britain. The Mideastern Arabs and some African Islamic people worded many times, "We will eliminate the Jews from earth." The hatred was further revealed after the world under the United Nations, led by the United States of America in 1947, had made changes in the old country of Israel so it will become a new country of Israeli people.

Some of these Islamic despots who followed their extreme elements of leadership were ones who instilled genocide into minds of their people. Many were influenced by extremist Islamic teachings by Imams with Allah Almighty's leadership of Ayatollahs, again preaching their own deciphered, mind-twisted versions, as some say, of that religion founded by Mohammed in the late 600s that resulted in two staggering forms of practitioners or Islam sects from two different extended families; one called the Shiah, who was cousin to Mohammed and was his son-in-law and first Imam referred to as Ali and was the successor to the Prophet, and the other sect called the Sunni, whose leaders acknowledged the first four caliphs as rightful successors to the Prophet and accepted the orthodox creed Sunna and Koran as equal authority. Islam as a religion for Arabs started through family ties. The different sects such as Sunni and Shiah claimed rightful lineages to Prophet Mohammed, the Sunni having claimed the Orthodox Moslem creed professed by Mohammed.

The above was offered to all people as religions proceeded and formed to a widespread of followers. The pursuit of Islamic conversion was that it was conversion without refusal. That was when Mohammed had the power, and he used it to ensure conversions even within his own family and his in-laws. These

Sunni verbalize, as a means, actions that were carried out instinctively after mind-tarrying was on its way to another version or more like the Shiah religion. The two sects, among themselves and for all others, were against all nonbelievers. What happened to their coming heritage was that lives who practiced the Islam religion were acceptable. The Islamic religious teachings, now a variety of types as Shiah and Sunni, continued those pursuits in these modern days even to warring against one another in their Arab nations and other countries.

Does this ring a bell in one's mind? The world has found one singular use of Moslems that respect Islamic mankind's minds. But they were saddled with minds of ordinary people that strive for specific moralities of their desires—that is, to develop religions based on beliefs and stick them down the throats of the concerned, weary, and weak, and those afraid of death if they did not receive the calling. Some gain of power in gatherings and participations did suit Arabs to adopt this inherited or given nature within their belief in a soul or spirit that also is inherited and firmly expected to be transferred back to their God's entity Allah. This step is one belief that might make sense because believing in God the Creator of the universe does not leave another God called Allah to create religions.

Devising human spirits in belief as a part of God's doing but unknown to mankind is potentially ad infinitum; and in beliefs by God's election, the future will exist forever joined in mankind's minds, hearts, and spirits or souls as believers.

The puzzle that must be solved is why this religiously induced warfare continues to this day against many ordinary religions and nonreligious living people of millions proceeding from day to day within family and friends and broadened to live in any country, which is more of a mystery. The mystery of religious belief itself started from beginnings of mankind and propagated into the acceptance and was factual evolvements from pseudo-illusory, or apparently not genuine, mentally deciphered inputs.

Most human beings with similar beliefs as propagated seek and express love in one form or another of *amour*. But those in this Islamic linking to do religious assaults also may even be pursuing this love but without *steerage*. Many of them may be in pursuit of a secret or suspicious pursuits of *amour*, be it appropriate or illicit and be it in vogue. Also, it may be under any circumstance existing in times while at the same time sweating out an amorous affair that potentially has devastating aftermaths to themselves and those infatuated.

Immigration occurred with indentured service from all races at a cost to expire services and with bought black slavery from Africa sent for pay to other countries' rulers until America's civil war, when Abraham Lincoln demanded the Senate vote for the Emancipation Proclamation on April 14, 1965. The Emancipation Proclamation gave all slaves and indentured emigrants that had been sold in America both after being bought from African kings and European countries freedom to all in America.

Many countries have imposed human-originated morality laws controlling association for marital involvements, sexual acts, adultery, and in some controlled class, enforcements was under power of punishment by patriarchal members of families of classes as in India and other Asian countries of current days. Even outcomes, at times, those who are subjected to personal punishment, end with unfathomable consequential punishment of persons who commit for example a sexual offense. No matter how broad scope it might be levied on those as ones marrying within different races and especially in a lower class under government constraint of known individual families. A marriage usually results in a situation that is critically judged by family and relatives and even ostracized by neighbors. Many unknown citizens who become privy to class information are accepted morally as classified religious sect law.

Some self-denying regimes imposed religious morality laws and politically prudent and wise laws. Others under provisional conditions to command individual's actual virtues practice or pursue *amour* on the sly or in a totally planned deception. While characteristics of such individuals may be subject to outsiders who demand extremely gross punishment, it is unexpected from modern mankind. The new *Homo sapiens* outwardly express gregarious morals, but many are common as believers' actual virtues and usually eliminate commonplace sensualities than what must be allowed.

However, those who have lusterless moralities that prevailed without any sign of having virtues want a finality to the answer to the question, "Steerage and Amour!—What's It All About?" as if they don't know their lives' future are at the edge of the cliff. The torrential backwind of the instinctive will blow potential remorse at their backs under great pressure, while they suffer a last thrust to complete a push into the abyss of no enlightenment and repent after death.

Intimately related to the above are people who pursue *amour* relationships without a doubt. The behavior of those who are different yields to amorous Amour-pro-pre attractions relate to self-respect in walks of life. Even those engrossed in world's advancements and culture—that is, pursuing studies in scientific knowledge and research advancements—also seek various types of amour.

These "goodies" of innovation affect many whose lives follow cutting edges of moral and social convention. People see it by exposure and enhancement as it takes notice of attention gained through such innovations as telephones, cars, airplanes, jet airplanes, even space travel while using personal computers and discretionary spending that enhances personal communication. Opportunities once enhanced with new supports to pursue *amour* fit into lives in a democracy or any other societal ideology, with some lit more than others having a senseless finality.

New places where common interests of social subjects say a revitalization in arts in a new civic center or social gatherings like a convention widely dispersed among unknowns having common interests, even gatherings of the dominating politically controlling environments and different interactions in life's daily behavior among strangers of attraction. For example, younger people have become well versed in the practice of sexual involvements simply as divulged by common means with mass communications pronounced via Internet or phone text messaging.

These methods enhanced knowledge especially of younger persons attracted by advertised influences of new inventions and societal improvements so common to mankind and detailed specifically and provided internationally to promote global communication. The influences were adapted as a practice and exposed herein as it relates to behavior of broad samples of human beings all within one critical Italian immigrant family, and their offspring chomping at the bit to gain citizenship during early 1900s America. The family of immigrants and those new generations as American-born children show what they expected were advantages guaranteed and practically follow the laws of the land.

The exercise of European lifestyles among immigrants was pursuits, not social fringes or odd elements of behavior. Instead, they showed thrusts of life, being working people, wanting to improve living life under the United States Constitution. In the frontispiece of the Declaration of Independence, "All men created equal . . . endowed by their Creator with unalienable rights that among these are Life, Liberty and the pursuit of happiness. That to receive these rights, Governments are instituted . . . decreeing their just powers from the consent of the governed." The pursuit of happiness takes many forms. Many are seeking *amour*, be it by legitimate desire or morally or legally wrong. Using instinctive "will of desire" has little basis to invoke control without selecting "knowledge and experience" decisively in the same path. This driving promise has guided many immigrated people creatively coming up with new wants, needs, and desires to spend their lifetimes pursuing happiness.

In minds of muses, discourse drives home an understanding of personality defects that helps to extract answers to the question of "Steerage and Amour!—What's It All About?" Response is generally expected based on one's experience with past sensuous accounts, which remain only as a memory exciter of a needed train of thought stored collectively indelibly imprinted stress on the mind's overall control and processing system of memory storage and access. At the very least, advice from human beings' minds tracked within the mind's directed operational gray matter to release common sense knowledge, not inherently uncontrolled instinctively illicit amorous human behavior. Then disloyalty is never expected during the rest of their lifetime.

That is when problems of value become questionable because responses given as advice relate to times that human behavior might dispel adherences because of social changes. Whoever gives the advice or being one that receives it depends on how the expressed information is understood and characterized by people with recent past generations that cover general plots of lives, nature, and behavior of known Italian migrants that immigrated to America.

As a reference, the first major migration of Italians that immigrated to America as well as many from other countries because of poor economic and social times and expectations were offered by Americans at Ellis Island.

The second period of immigration from 1920s to 1960s, starting with post-World War I, included learned immigrant adults and children that visualized what America had to offer. Then, also, the coming immigration in later years led to Americans born during World War II, who were called baby boomers. They being immigrants were referred to as the second era, but their new progeny were first-generation citizens of America. New immigrants are still often referred as Italian Americans but are not only from the European continent but also from all the other continents that were involved after the Second World War.

Then several life stories that followed later within the new generations occurred later in the succeeding time that covered 1965 to 1985 and included some families and added some new generations of American-born citizens called hippies and flower children as they appeared after two critical wars on the Asian continent. By their actions and social negligence, these modern generations generally obeyed existing laws more than social mores. They mostly favor music, "recreation drugs," and drinking, which were so common in the '30s. Now, the modern progeny are referred to as persons that are strung on continued habits of liquor and drugs.

The last story also covers periods from 1985 to present day, including generation X, and as the world approaches, the new millennium generation of 2000 is already under way. Most of these new modern people are not yet at critical ages of influence except by the few entrepreneur front liners saddled with monies to burn. They have come by business ventures, ones that try to seep money from plain stupid people via mobile phone users and handheld computers constantly grasping for information, generally nonsensical, or game playing with amounts of money to be gained. These businesses' methods of advertising by millions of people unbeknownst to whom it benefits except to proprietors of new ventures such as Internet companies like Facebook, Google, Yahoo, and Amazon. Even now, the evolution of an enormous number of "apps" that go along with the near infinite number of programs are levied daily on easy prey.

Bring a critical point of times into play such that social, economic, and environmental behavior was part and parcel as to how assaults by terrorists achieved and performed terrorist activities, predominantly their religious zealots and extremists, moving toward gain positions in America and other countries. After many years, they are now settled within the many countries, and they practice their personal behavior and religion as a starter almost without interference by the countries' governments. Some of their emigrants have in their minds for the future as Islamic Moslems and then even consider overtaking in some fashion or form by force areas by Islamic religious zealots in massive takeovers of countries.

As a means of keeping track of specific personal narrators of these past previous times to modern days, the ones who have the most have collected mindful details—that is, "knowledge and experience" of Divita family stories of sensuous desires ad infinitum that settled during dominating wartimes. Illicit *amour* exposed the invaluableness of decisions of previous knowledge and overwhelming experience in which we lived over the past sixty years. These modern years were also common in contemporary times that now, from predictable general circumstances, the people with working minds have evolved a maturing as it seeds thoughts beyond our past expected pursuits into realms of generating no more deadwood. These new people might gain more genius and fill creative gaps that could bring on a coming Third Renaissance.

From experiences of the past of many notably famous and infamous persons like President McKinley's amorous pursuit in 1900, who was mesmerized, would make clandestine rendezvous with the exciting Gibson girl with whom he was notably fascinated. Even other presidents that followed with great achievements— men like Franklin Delano Roosevelt, elected in 1933; and Gen. Dwight David Eisenhower, later elected president of the United States of America in 1952. These famous men had their baggage of illicit *amour* revealed to no avail but was archived, and it so continued. Those famous men who came later as I have showed as top-notch leaders during their warring times definitely were affected by the war, even while so demanded to do their jobs.

These giving and country-serving men had their experiences unveiled in complete sense, but the revelation for each was of a semi-unknown nature. The reason was not identified as being so significant in historic books that these men in past times with saturated major concerns in their human minds holding ideas that related to *amour* pursuits while families were personally and morally constrained. The mixture at times of important men's lives while devoted to military service sometimes would branch off to illicit activity and later lived with aftermaths. Similar amorous endeavors were cancelled more numerously than their minds could comprehend because they did not think future times would last for them.

Naming names of comparable infamy would only bore readers and would show whimsy of a mind's choice to assume that anyone needs to specifically name those that include the most common names under the sun's history. It would be like observing different tales encrypted each day and remembering specifics of each such as its DNA from evolving genes of the only surviving species of genus *Homo sapiens* as modern mankind. Both genders would stay in their minds when they learned each tree's nature is only for the genius tree expert. Otherwise, we common folks don't give a damn what fellow human beings do with their "will of desire" because it gets neglected as do many pursuits fail in life.

Their knowledge and work toward improving our country's well-being applied a sizeable source of "knowledge and experience" that was toward their composed decisive good. What else could one expect from common people if not rampant pursuit of *amour* during these latest critical wartimes? Many people simply suit themselves without thinking that all behavior leads to an aftermath of human interaction. We know that evolution of human beings related to everyday common family life in homes was in disguised wreaks of distortions because some military people are easily trapped in amorous ethers of sensuous involvement during wartimes. Some people believe their fantasies were of no consequences to others because they were not reported. The truth is that money and prominent people are just as involved with their amorous desires. They are usually always susceptible to be found out each time. The common people involved in trysts happen even when uncommon and unexpected extreme disheartening and desperation occur daily among the partners.

A critical point of disclosure was so obvious much later when Pres. William Jefferson Clinton had a past well known that started in the state of Arkansas. Then when elected president, he held the public's amoral attention for four years in his second term. This event of instinctive attraction, of course, happened to this Democrat president during modern times between 1992 and 2000.

His habits had him stuck in the same amorous pursuits before his election even though during his campaign, he was thrust into the turmoil of past affairs; what was critical was that there was little influence on the electorate until he was caught groping at the band of sheer panties so revealed. With some headway, he continued his habit to pursue his specifically offered sensuous desires even while in the Oval Office. It all happened during the administration of our country's prime security and defense and the economic and international business regardless of the criticality of personal issues.

This one inchoate woman of desire, a newly hired intern, likened to a hidden burden of lust that she revealed within a private passing, led to his eventual impeachment because he lied to a grand jury and the Congressional House of Representatives. Except by one Senate vote under the Supreme Court's jurisdiction, Mr. Clinton was not found guilty. Even this action was supported within law but with an implication tagged by the thinking mind that a greater loss to the country was in the making if he were saddled with the guilty conviction.

Ms. Monica Lewinski, when she arrived to serve as an intern, could have been innocent to pending amorous circumstances by our rake president Clinton so known for many years before gaining the office. Maybe, as so inferred by the media's judgment, Ms. Lewinski was "still wet behind the ears" but thought her sexual attraction might gain a partner in conjugality for life. All she really knew was that she was hired by the Clinton Executive Administration to be a menial "gopher" at every beck and call. But her main "boss" had upon his observation a much more titillating job for her, and with one flick of a thong, he could sense that he could easily get his way with numerous promises undisclosed; and if not as confirmed to this day through an impeachment charge of a not-guilty verdict by the Senate by one vote.

The judgment let him remain as any other rake with some repute. Most people and especially Democrats didn't care as to what he had done against his promises cited in words on a Bible to the country's Constitution of United States and the laws of the land.

All this happened at the time when the law for sexual harassment or any form of oppressive behavior levied on an employee was on the books of laws written by the federal government and distributed to all public servants of leadership and companies throughout the country of legal stature to apply to all persons of power in business, be it public or private who took advantage of a subordinate inherently and intentionally susceptible while under their direction of complete supervision. This law was in force but was never measured to see if it took effect to the extent that an American president at the time it happened had violated the law when being a rake out of control using his instinctive "will of desire" on the intern, willing or not, in the White House at his volition.

At the end of the twentieth century, he crashed into impeachment and was lucky enough to not be submitted guilty by the Senate. The one and only William Jefferson Clinton thought that he should be treated differently while pursuing his amorous adventures, being president. He especially had need in his past political positions and ties with the "good ol' guys," and he continued pursuits as a free man into society with riches unrecorded. Regardless of his public position or any consideration of his complete family, it was obvious that he did not continue to make attempts to control his sensuous tries for illicit *amour.*

CHAPTER IX

Mankind's Behavior Litigates with God's Immortal Life with Continuous Propagation of Progeny

*Human knowledge had become too great for the human mind. All
that remained was the scientific specialist, who knew: "more and
more about less and less," . . . and the philosophical speculator,
who knew, less and less about more and more . . ." ". . . Perspective
was lost. Facts replaced understanding; and knowledge, split into
a thousand isolated fragments, no longer generated wisdom." ". . .
The gap between life and knowledge grew wider and wider; . . ."*
—*The Story of Philosophy*, Will Durant

The American people, especially the young, who are on the edge of
culturally not accepting demanded involvement in morality and paying little
attention to nature's laws, should examine mental compliance details that exist in
Homo sapiens. *Homo sapiens* are the only and ever human beings that God created
in his plan for immortal life through birthing progeny.

The significant concern of ensuring new life must be reworked to eliminate
the assault of the Supreme Court's landmark decision ruling under *Roe v. Wade*,
410 U.S. 113 (1973). This is the issue of abortion that rubbed red into the eyes of
God and those people who understand the minds of truly mentally healthy *Homo
sapiens* who fundamentally know human beings are unique and would not kill any
Homo sapiens and especially the least defenseless yet to be born human beings of
the same genus no matter the demanded intent for any makeup reason.

The Supreme Court had ruled simultaneously with the companion case, *Doe
v. Bolton*, decided in 1973, 7–2, that women had the right to privacy (which was
never granted under the United States Constitution, except for the above current
precedence by the Supreme Court) under the due process clause of the Fourteenth
Amendment, which, had it been properly converted to a new law promulgated
and defined, would have included man as well to the same right to privacy. They
stated precedence of compliance minimized only to gender way overstretches to a

breaking point decision that then included women's decision to have an abortion at their volition and with no interference from or by any man, even the husband, doctor, or impregnator.

The missing of the total Supreme Court judgment not accounting for *Homo sapiens* must recall the precedence that did not give man his right to privacy under the same Fourteenth Amendment. The existing precedence is unfair and should be allowed equal challenges within all court levels, especially by highest federal court with proper court reasoning necessary to counter the existing decision. The decision to maintain the baby alive in the womb to be properly cared for and delivered by doctors and any *Homo sapiens* that follow laws with legal court protection until delivery.

Afterward, the baby is the responsibility of parents both of *Homo sapiens* to properly maintain the baby's life or have the appropriate court of law to determine a place in a home of accepted foster parents and adoptions, which should be crucial in all countries. When necessary, the new life must be continued even with adoption laws, the same as parents with proper care as do all babies deserve to ensure continued life from conception. No person can deny the baby's life, the same as all other people's life are protected by the federal government. The states must follow the same unified law of the land without exception; with some caveats, one being that the right to life is first and foremost in the Constitution of the United States.

The laws must consider legitimate control and enforcement in performing life-threatening abortions: protecting prenatal life to finality and protecting women's health sufficiently enough to deliver the baby. The Supreme Court must not allow any legal abortion unless a life-threatening medical decision is made by a combination of doctors in control of approval.

The Supreme Court accepted the trimester framework that limited abortion to women having a right to abortion until viability is shown where the Supreme Court decision in *Roe v. Wade* defined "viable" as being "potentially able to live outside the mother's womb, albeit with artificial aid . . ." In this case, the Supreme Court added that viability "is usually placed at about seven months (28 weeks) but may occur earlier, even at 24 weeks . . ." (with confirmation by legally demanded examinations by doctors in control of approval).

In disallowing many federal and state restrictions on abortion in the United States, *Roe v. Wade* prompted a national debate that has continued ad infinitum about issues to cover who has the right to make abortion decisions. Why shouldn't it be a legality as above so that persons involved with the pregnancy with loaded affectations would not make excuses to eliminate any baby for any reason?

Those being both the man and woman while gestating the baby should when a human being is being procreated. At that point, the right to granted privacy of birth should be required by the authority of the implicit laws of any human having legal authority to complete the birthing.

A human being by law throughout the creation of *Homo sapiens* is the only existing modern man. Better said in common language, human beings have implied legal protection of prenatal life. In America, the Constitution of the United States of America guarantees when life is first identified. The life of a baby in the womb are all human beings specifically and must be protected under the laws of the United States Constitution, the Bill of Rights, and compatible precedencies from the Supreme Court of the United States (SCOTUS). These afforded laws regarding this defenseless human being as a life continuing birthing, and it must be demanded that the care of its life is maintained by the federal government's guaranteed complete protection. The need decrees for a constitutional amendments to clearly satisfy the Constitution of the United States of America for our country at least.

Did the Supreme Court in the past come up with laws to apply to all forms of human being life without allowing abortion and then decided to change it? When the Supreme Court justices were wishy-washy with an extremely sensitive law, they had to take it as a Supreme Court proclamation first and completed by the Congress and president, who make the laws. As with all other previous human beings that insisted on using medieval methods available to allow the life to be born as did all those who existed in past times and from the beginning until eternity, those people whose instinctive "will of desire" demanded abortion secretively will thereafter indelibly receive memory imprints bouncing from anxiety to depression daily until their death.

Why didn't the Supreme Court use constitutional adjudication to demand that the life of a human being starts from inception of egg and sperm joining to start splitting cells to form the embryo and to naturally evolve within natural laws of probability related to the end of a birthing life? As do we all appreciate the gift of *life, liberty, and the pursuit of happiness*, as promised when it was our time for birthing.

A Supreme Court solution using "knowledge and experience" knows that issues of rights and wrongs serve human beings same mental powers including judgments about abortions, be it private, socially implied, or religiously unacceptable as in many decisions under the laws of the country. The decision should be to beseech people to add a new amendment to the United States Constitution . . . *stating the law to be bound by all people without influence of any kind related to* Homo sapiens *mankind life and all religions to ensure progeny to continue unaffected ad infinitum.*

The formulation of an expected new constitutional amendment simply would be one that would guarantee life with laws for punishment of criminal assault and death that would preclude and certainly minimize intentional or clandestine interventions to induce abortion. The laws would require creators of human beings initially in the right of either one or both to keep their human being to complete its birth or instead give up their right by granting its due to foster parent(s) or to be adopted by other human beings with justifiable legal strings within the court system for adoption. Otherwise, they could have required people of the United States of America to vote on a change to the Fourteenth Constitutional Amendment to cover this needed right to all human beings so deemed within the United States Declaration of Independence and the Constitution of the United States of America with amendments that refer to rights of all citizens of America judiciously under all situations and cases.

The role of peoples' religions and moral views in political spheres would have the say of their own religious decisions but within compliance of those of the United States federal government with no interference or any allowance to impose religious laws by states. The legal role of mankind's natural laws must prevail as we are all within God's control as encompassed by mankind's minds to honor our laws of the land.

Without due extensive man-made and natural law considerations by SCOTUS, decisions referenced above divided for United States of America must divulge the former evolution of a "pro-choice" and "pro-life" ideologies that activated grassroots movements to become political, religious, and secular viewpoints. Without that option, the natural way to select life as specifically stated in the United States Declaration of Independence is "All men and women [*Homo sapiens*] are created equal, . . . endowed by their Creator with certain unalienable rights that among these are Life, Liberty and the Pursuit of Happiness." This is clear and fundamentally emphasized as everything within peoples' control, naturally as evolution, the environment for life of mankind to maintain its inherited guardian of assigned natural laws.

All the while, up to more than forty million babies had been aborted since 1973 and by 2010 because of gained private rights of women stated in SCOTUS decisions without definitive allowance for rights of men having the same power of concern as women: per the Constitution of the United States of America . . . *because how it is stated as the rights of human beings as* Homo sapiens *and show no gender discrimination.*

Those living human beings who made it through birth now were heading to their teens, or some were even in their twenties. With the communications boom, many of the young were given openly new secrets of sex and sexual behavior. Also, they were assured by their president that they should be allowed to not claim what was their personal moral responsibilities. This allowance has help to continue the country's young people to adopt a less moral and more liberal pursuit and have caused more young people to stray from real life's purpose, which is to generally advance the culture of human beings. Instead, about half of the people have chosen what comes as a joy of gratification even though it was instinctively chosen with intent of guaranteeing *survivability* without the need of the first instinctive thought of "will of desire."

As already discussed from the beginning of the 1900s, family life predominantly centered on happy times until about 1910–1912, when many countries had been experiencing poor times economically and a recession was ahead in Europe.

Poor employment after World War I inculcated the Roaring Twenties. All that was needed was money to rebuild all of Europe. The few countries that had some monies to help sustained a minimum thrust during the next ten years. In the United States, a considerable diversion was pursued on establishing a more common mankind level of society. The main efforts were to take advantage of others, either with Prohibition laws or deporting organized gangsters arrested for illegal activities, all to control businesspeople and power-mongering to the citizenry activity during the Roaring Twenties.

Nevertheless, in the beginning of early 1920s, many common families were dysfunctional to some degree, and a smaller fraction was pursuing illegal or amoral actions that were detaining, if not confrontational enough, to cause trouble for police within the major cities of America. States like New York, Los Angeles, San Francisco, Chicago, Philadelphia, Detroit, and Boston, and even in major cities in Texas, Ohio, Colorado, and especially in Washington DC were caught in a distress of wildness. A lot of the lawlessness was induced by blacks from the ghettos, white lower class, and a larger number of immigrants. Only some of them who were from Europe were now bad apples as was the case to be like all in the '30s.

This was worse than a recession; it was exacerbated with large unemployment. What also exacerbated the dilemma of despair clouded individuals' lives with hazy vision of only a doomsday way out. This feeling was dominated by the induced pressures levied by crooked leaders in politics and business. This despair was augmented by the few people in the federal, state, and local governments not knowing what to do, and so, typically, the wrong things were done. Many of the religious people thought that they might be getting punished by God, except what God had proclaimed at the beginning was that he gave mankind "free will," as was assumed to be received by the early members of *Homo sapiens*.

Things such as aggravating aristocratic leaders, certainly elites, were negligently responding to the poor as if they put a blight on the country. None of that hype helped poor people or their neighbors. The impact and aftermaths led to many disasters, but all the while, amorous desire seekers were spending their time chasing their magnetically attracted opposites at home fronts, at work with friends, or even strangers at nighttime. Many people more responsible conveniently found people who were building nations' cultures the same way self-sufficient people pursued researching new lands in America.

After World War I, too much disjointed thinking led to behavior patterns that existed in intrinsically abnormal by people who were puzzled how to control their personal behavior after so many killings during the First World War. Aggressive individuals and families during the Roaring Twenties significantly changed their behavior to have more openly exposed personnel activity.

CHAPTER X

World War II Impacted Intuitive
Steerage and Amour

*We have had our last chance. If we do not devise some greater
and more equitable system, Armageddon will beat our door.*
—Douglas McArthur (1880–1964), September 2, 1945.
Thom Hartmann, *The Last Hours of Ancient Sunlight*,
Mythical Books, Northfield, Vermont, 1980.

To curtail these anxious people's activities, the national government promulgated the prohibition of intoxicating beverages with the Eighteenth Amendment in 1920 as a law to eliminating liquor of any make or kind to be illegal in any way, made, sold or used by the people of America. However, many people with their desires enhanced sought and stayed in speakeasies, finagled to hide and get bootlegged whiskey, and also chased sexual affairs of all kinds, and the gross activity helped develop, expand, and enrich gangsters of the new century.

This subcultural pursuit enhanced illegal widespread purchases of whiskey and kept affected people tongue-tied, sometimes self-induced with a bellyful of mind-knotting tonics obtained from clandestine moonshine makers of whiskey products. From back in 1920s, after a few years, the national government formed a special team of experts and a few FBI members and local police to attack places of hidden liquor, which further extended their uncertainties of life and high living with little interest. After teams destructed many whisky sites and arrested gangsters during attacks, some were killed and jailed. Team assaults continued with pursuits until the United States national government, under the stress of the onslaught of the Great Depression, repealed the Eighteenth Amendment of Prohibition law in 1933, and they entered the new depression with a great patriotic effort to give relief to the people. The starting of World War II pressed firmly to impact more mind-forming decisive behavior and maintain the best of decisions from individuals who have settled their patriotic minds on people's lives both at home and soldiers at war.

Then within a few years, the American people moved toward the last years of the '20s, and by October 29, 1929, almost immediately, grosses of saved money within the stock market declined, and people fell into a massive depression that became the Great Depression of reality in 1929. When the disaster occurred as imposed by the unseen demise of the stock market, as if the ticker tape machines lost its black ink and only had red ink to randomly bleed over each declining value of wealth, the stock market collapsed like a bobbling beached whale trapped for hours and inescapable.

This pursuit was an invitation to the oncoming recognized and analyzed 1930s Great Depression, uncontrollable at the extent of economic disaster widespread. The spread of the Great Depression had already started in Europe, where ensuing worldwide recession had been under way for years.

The Great Depression spread like a plague of despair on American city streets and throughout the dust-blown fields of farms unrecognizable throughout the Midwest all the way to California. The Great Depression was global as well, although cited for America, because of the extensive influx of a variety of personal wealth devaluations and onslaughts of powerful and rich depressing people in all walks of life. As characteristically notable with some exceptions, solidly money-rich people whose money continued to grow with everyday running of the country were unaffected. But the ones not solidly rich, the market investors, panicked and started off mentally by whelping and even jumping to their death going into the deep end of the Great Depression.

Shortly thereafter, some people mindlessly leaped from windows of high-rise office buildings. While noticeable to many, also on streets completely disordered with trash, others, apparently if not vaguely unconscious, were walking the streets for money as if mummies with unknown directions, sporadically voicing gibberish, mocked by the poor whose shoes had soles that flip-flopped like the poor hardworking farmer's clodhoppers who were mocked in jest previously over radio on comedic stations and in sublimely powerful movies such as *The Grapes of Wrath* by John Steinbeck, who won the Pulitzer Prize for his novel in 1939 that showed to an enormous number of people as a classic the overall nature of the people.

The imposed depression spread a sickness of despair that was exacerbated with lines of beggars seeking food and lacking personal hygiene, who excreted on city streets through the night. This "poorsville" expansion extended to people of wind-blown farmlands in Midwest without precedence but impounded with gross despair.

However, during that same time, the Nazi, National Socialism German's Working Party, was overtook by Adolf Hitler with the claim that America and Great Britain devastated their land and the Versailles Treaty. With grand complaints, he gained the backing of powerful industrialists, and he was voted and installed as their chancellor in 1933 and was called der Fuhrer immediately and given full dictatorship control in 1933. Hitler, now chancellor, without hesitation, immediately told his powerful members that he plans to overtake the world.

He then set up his first team of brownshirts initially assaulting Jews. After he joined with his first few prime leaders, they organized and ordered a fifth column in America and in England into a devastating power pursuit to keep track of ally activities.

After gaining many new weapons, he then started wreaking havoc of death and destruction as if he was the full force of the Four Horsemen of the Apocalypse. From the early '30s until the instigation of the pending Second World War was well under way by 1938, Hitler's military had conquered Norway, Holland, and Poland and took over control of Paris by early 1940s. The cost was excruciatingly conducted, and even death to their own people, and other people were taken out of common social living, and many lives were secretively lost unknown, because they were totally unexpected to be controlled by so-called Hitler brownshirts and Nazi storm troopers, who, when desired, ravaged and killed Jewish people without cause or punishment.

Many statesmen and politicians knew what was happening because Hitler's vision was known, how he planned to eliminate his evil people from the very first onset with malice aforethought and did not use caution or halt to reconsider. This position of mankind's nature was known by the astute demonic Adolf Hitler, whose mind was set on gross eliminations of all Jews and other challengers against world domination. He demanded all people must adhere to his commands.

From the start in early phases of the depression and recession, it was also exacerbated by leaders worldwide not knowing what to do to improve businesses, as famine went rampant under drought conditions. And it became widespread when associated service jobs declined significantly within the businesses of America including stock market investors and people's care and needs for services.

President Roosevelt did get the government involved with large public-funded work programs and, to some extent, providing some relief for craftsmen and experienced building and fabrication business companies needed immediately to build warring equipment, but in an expanded view of accommodating people's needs. The needs had gotten high level, but American patriotism was shown by the multitudes, and the president acknowledged, and experienced people of the times who move American mass-production industry to limits beyond expectations began buildups of war machinery to a recovery with unflinching fervor. Many, if not most, people were never able to let go of their sensuous desires. Across the globe in European countries, at times of elitist meetings, people were very copacetic with ardor.

The stock market failed so severely in the United States along with the peoples' opinion or even belief that God imposed drought on America because of irresponsible behaviors of both rich and powerful people. For the next five or six years, the Great Depression cooled to a reality to all levels of people; but the few wealthy needed and wanted more workers to be employed in Government Work Programs Agency (WPA) and Civilian Conservation Corporation (CCC) jobs across lands and others in construction and manufacturing workers for special private projects. The notoriety was spread about the building of massive mansions such as the Vanderbilt Home in the Blue Ridge Mountains of Asheville, North Carolina. Other business buildings were under way and even much more after what President Roosevelt knew in his mind during mid-1930s to begin gaining manufacturing critically needed warring equipment in appropriate places. Building of superstructures like the Empire State Building in New York City and the Golden Gate Bridge in San Francisco and bridges and insurance companies included new building centers elsewhere in other major cities of different states. The country secretively gained new products and many patriotic people of great technical minds. Many citizens lived in contained and centered happy times with both wife and husband and several children for a few years because hard times plagued them in their hometowns since marriage.

The people, poor, middle class, and some rich, not all, were part of the many dispersed in fields of dust and squalor. America was for a long time immersed in an overwhelming tsunami of poverty's turmoil that flowed a destruction on life and mind unrecoverable. The world was thrust into an unsolvable global depression that moved to California and other states along the Great Pacific Ocean, full of threats of earthquakes unfathomable in size along the Pacific Mantle.

First-generation Americans immigrated earlier in this story during the early 1900s, particularly those of Italian and Irish descent. The *amour* predicaments abound and included other nationalities; some small life changes occurred that characterize family life at home and at their business or places of work. Many Americans were more friendly and sociable with new products and a more common adaptation of advancements in homes to accommodate their then modern civilization. This pursuit happened by historic influence instilled by thrusts of America's success during World War I. Not only were other countries thinking critically, but also their cognitive thinkers were considerably slower than how America was run politically. America started building its warring equipment to globally get involved as early as possible to support our known allies, especially England.

The emphasis was in everyone's mind to do their best for the country, and it was the same imputable dominance that was the essence of a fundamental drive of nature that started the First Renaissance, and the people with great determination and wisdom already had taken what might have been a Second Renaissance in the late 1700s, materializing with a great deal of development and technology as discussed about unknown outcomes of effective capabilities.

Many who lived through the wild Roaring Twenties gained a head of steam after being fizzled through Prohibition that ended in 1933. Then the country had slipped into the Great Depression that dominated the remaining '30s, quickly following an onslaught of an expected new world war. By the late '30s, patriotism grew enormously and brought all people closer together to help the mechanization of new ships, warring equipment, and weapons.

This started quickly within the United States with mechanization and military buildups to support Great Britain and France with supplies, with Americans knowing that Germans attacked us in the Atlantic Ocean with U-boats, and in Europe by Germany before World War II was declared. America had already instilled larger patriotic mass production in the mid-'30s of all types of weapons. The extent of patriotism pumped up a capability with super devotion, and workers enhanced mass production of new and dominating military weapons beyond expectations and even toward war's end, when they created a nuclear weapon of mass destruction.

Historically viewed, combined allies were victors in both world wars. Communication methods with war reports stimulated all individuals and, by visionaries, the right outcome; although complex in nature, the peace treaty eventually worked well. After World War II, a rise of dominating communistic power by the Soviet Union was now imposed in Europe with military force in East Germany and much later in Hungary in the mid-'50s. The intent was to set the people against United States, which caused the Cold War to supervene. What happened was that Soviets induced communistic ideology within or surrounding our allies imposing Communism, socialism, and undesired dictatorial principalities in Poland, Hungary, and Czechoslovakia. Sheikdom regimes gained in smaller countries and in states throughout other continents, especially Africa and Asia.

About midway of the ongoing World War II, a beginning with a new generation of children known as baby boomers was initiated with increased vigor of patriotism throughout America as well as other countries into the '60s. This surge in population also followed a surge in military weaponry at all levels of defense and assault. The buildup, especially in present days, increased detection capability through computers and communications systems both miniaturized and hardened scientifically.

One of the guiding concepts was to allow the promotion of amorous interactions of the troops and the ranking upper class to enjoy partying and *amour* in any fashion in taverns where they could gain the pursuit. The buildups of military, police, and secret police, and the political buildup of supporting operational appointments were swiftly accomplished, and they showed themselves at the local pubs with a dominant influence, and it worked. The people that complied were then further enticed to do their aggressive pursuits of illicit *amour*.

Hitler's thugs' mentality afflicted by his hype so detailed was also a camaraderie of men who savored their menial senseless fearmongering to enhance their desires for taking advantage of sensuous situations and the abnormal level of Eros that markedly increased when individual amorous situations arose. After they had control and even before when it was convenient, Hitler brutes enforced their demands to fulfill sensuous desires as a form of racially accepted dominance that included all forms of distorted *amour*. They set up many associations that engendered obligations by those who did not want to be identified as seekers of sex and obnoxious sexual misbehavior, but a prominence began to be revealed in Berlin first and then in other cities across central Germany.

The brownshirts aggravated the Jews after their formation, first, with fisticuffs and personal assault, and much later, life-threatening assaults. Getting away with this approach without any specific complaint by the townsfolk, who, within their minds, knew they would be next in turn if they chose to speak against the German chancellor. The brownshirts added more force to intensify the elite Germans' hatred for the Jews. This threat of retaliation, no matter who might supply aid, made it an easy start.

Hitler was pleased with pursuits of control by the brownshirts. It pleased the abject deranged leader now gaining central power of the country within the organized government. He had his henchmen add more select brownshirt troops and enhanced them with the Hitler's German-designed swastika.

Then many more personal assaults with battery denigrating and vilifying the Jewish "nationality" and religion occurred and resulted many times in murder without police involvement. These personal and intentional attacks caused some to escape before they were identified as potential victims. The brilliant Jewish professors, well-off businessmen, and technically adept Jews used power as successful teachers, inventors, and investors. They saved money to leave the country as soon as possible or move to seclusion outside Germany's boarder. The ones that managed to move out of the country were those that lived. Others, those without money and direct useful intelligence except socially, thought they could be hidden in secluded quarters or even in squalor by friends or even into homes or places of those of way lesser means and would become assumed dead or gone from the country.

The Nazi Party members or their nonconformists appearing uncritical would quietly and slyly in secret give words of locations of Jewish families. The investigating gestapo, after the war started, or the early enforcers known as the Nazi Party brownshirts did their dirty work in the streets. Many Jewish people, when this was told to the Nazi police, were picked up in the middle of the night.

Within a few days, they became physically and mentally displaced from their homes and society's activities. German citizenship was cancelled at times when Jews were incarcerated. Random attacks occurred at night, under induced alarm by cowards who lay hiding in the dark like carnivorous animals to devour their unsuspecting prey.

It became evident with a gathering of crows cawing a critical beckoning across the nations that the Jews were under attack by the Germans, known by personal exposure; all this even happened before America declared war. The irony of the behavior devastated the Jewish ways of life because the good and capable people of Germany and those with considerable influence continued to let the attacks happen without criticism and no concerted action. The lack of action by good people pulsed old practices to a high bias toward Jews reminiscent of that held during times of Moses. As we know from the Bible, the same bias was practiced by the Romans with the killings of Christians.

In these modern warring days, the Jews were removed from their homes and sent via trains to places unknown. They were encamped with no care except torture, and some were executed to satisfy the Fuhrer. What added in humanity beyond human expectation was that those mentally disturbed or disabled in some ways were lost in the herds and used as experiments to satisfy their inherent belief that a good might be revealed from odd, unheard-of euthenics medical unraveling of life by these mad-hatter doctors who used humans as guinea pigs.

Those of sound mind and expectation quickly began scheming to extract themselves from Germany. The impetus came from families afflicted foremost, and as they sensed and saw these atrocities, they moved parents and relatives to safe havens in Great Britain and United States, but in some cases, they moved into countries that would become easy targets for rapidly building German forces, exacerbating more deaths to nations of Jewish citizens.

The Jews suffered unwanted abandonment because they were constantly haunted and taunted by Germans as if prey of disgust and disease so much so that people wanting to help were in fear of their own lives even though they were near in friendship to those physically and mentally waylaid. The Jews had no one to turn to for help except those people in the fields. Many Jewish businesses and their associates in businesses in major cities were ravaged, and rural town areas were closed to Jews, especially owners of businesses because ethnic attacks put fear of assault, and non-Jewish citizens were also killed. Beggars and turncoats were everywhere, and very few people were trustworthy under a threat of critical harm if they were caught lying to German enforcers.

With the force of Hitler's new army, they easily had overtaken several border European countries with great force, including Poland, Norway, and Holland. The takeovers were clandestinely implemented without much notice into France, the French in Paris, whose submission was expected from within. A committed collection of French guerrillas and intelligence officers supported French people in Paris and sent information to England that saved many lives.

The main elements of Europe were still against their turnover, and many people of means left for England or went into hiding, and some organized guerrillas fought Germans in stealthy ways. The personal dominance of invaders was enhanced because Germans had forced control over government officials, especially in what was called Vichy France, who had no voice in what could happen to French people under circumstances of incompatibility, including spying for allies or being informers about enemies.

Women were mostly used as targets of desire, and little could be done about it without confrontation that generally led to severe punishment or death. The plight of *amour* had taken on a force that had previously been worldwide but only practiced mainly by joint decisions of persons involved, many times, with faux promises. Now, no promises were even made, just demands or else, and many suffered consequences.

Hitler's dominance over his own people, and now those in countries overpowered by the initial invasions, led to a continued pleading and cajoling to the British that he wanted to make only border country occupations to ensure that countries were properly run under trying circumstances of suppression worldwide. While France was occupied, the sham no longer worked because Germans were in control through the Vichy government, who had kowtowed to minimize deaths and destruction at least initially to Vichy citizens.

The accommodation by Great Britain's leader, Prime Minister Neville Chamberlain, was addressed by inner circles of parliament's leaders. The overall parliament saw writings on the wall but with more criticality than that of Chamberlain, who thought a negative response might turn the situation into a full-blown war. In combination during meetings, Chamberlain and parliament did not have the courage to act immediately, and resultant outcomes were that critical decisions had to be made, and it was almost immediately when the message of a declaration of war was pending. The neglect of the actual situation arising was ready to explode. After all, the world knew about two plus years of Hitler's actions in disguise and the beginning of the holocaust yet to amalgamate. The British parliament, then in 1940, quickly voted out Chamberlain and formally selected Sir Winston Churchill of the Labor Party as prime minister.

Churchill quickly changed his reactions from an indecisive plight of vacillation almost witlessly to a clear reaction with a vision of what fed Hitler's purpose to dominate the world. Within minds of many could see that Churchill promised that he would do everything within his power and beyond to not only prevent this haywire vision but also establish allies in a united effort so that it would never happen again.

France's opposition had continuously beseeched Britons' help even though the English had been conned by Germans under Chamberlain. A complete turn was implemented after Churchill was chosen as the British leader. Churchill and Americans were now involved directly in the war, and the French general Charles de Gaulle, now in England, worked with France's allied leaders to quickly to set up a guerilla network. The treaty of France's occupation by Germany in 1940 saved France from full domination, and it minimized property destruction but caused a divisive nationalism with its people. All the while, the combined secret service of allies was used to gain intelligence, attack German clandestinely, and confuse their warring in France until the coming invasion.

France as a partial country much later began warring with Germany on the sly. The French leaders under Charles de Gaulle, as part of the allied effort controlled from England, had to reconstruct their opposition to occupied France, while more than half of France was under Hitler's occupation. The irony of this odd way French people reacted was that a complement of French leaders decided to remain under Marshall Petain, who had signed papers to cooperate with the Germans. These leaders and followers known to many were identified as Vichy France, and many of those that opposed Petain's position remained and worked in concert with guerilla operations.

The French people in the country and large cities were taken into control, and some cities' officials became compliant to maintain their lives, which were considered less than a bullet away from a word said in opposition to Hitler's demands that continued his annihilation of Jews. This was complied with by the Vichy to a great disgrace. Many of known turncoats were punished after the war with some French Vichy leaders and were severely sentenced for war crimes. With the resistance under Gen. Charles de Gaulle, those leaders in Great Britain who worked through secret agents and clandestine spying guerillas housed in secreted farmhouses and in basements of abandoned buildings and unsuspected homes of the towns continued to carry out their guerilla's assaults.

As was already prevalent in Germany especially conducted in Berlin and mayoral cities of other countries, involvements of its people in sexual amorous trysts and worst, including rape and all forms of sexual assaults, were well under way. It looked as if nothing but an enhancement of a new pursuit of out-of-whack sexual behavior that would continue during the war, as was always common practice by warring nations as it did occur with the nature of Germany's dominance.

A gripping effort was initiated by Vichy leaders to control the behavior of its women and men, but some estimates show that as many as 10 percent became prostitutes to support their families. This warring in France changed Christian behaviors, and it didn't improve until after the war, as did many who have a cowardly disdain of existing life.

France's dissidents under Vichy control took to guerilla forces tied through Gen. Charles de Gaulle in England with aid from allies to reconnoiter German activities. And now, within a little more than a year, America was building formidable allied forces in England. In addition, pursuits of active combat increased and helped to advance allies' war efforts to strike targets of crucial sources of military activity.

What began as a storm of Hitler's territorial troops trotting through Europe in a few small countries with a deadly force takes a turn and is now engaged in an assaulting gallop of mass killings envisioned as genocidal carried out by various insane leaders who chopped their way through continents and countries within Africa, Europe, Asia, and India. At first sight of counteraction, totally innocent citizens, at that time in bitter conflict and conquest of nations, these innocent people were at wrong places at the wrong time on God's unique earth in towns and cities of industry, and many businesses became German targets for destruction by massive bombings and invasions.

However, numbers of sacrificial genocidal mass killings were more noticeably skewed to an actual thrust to eliminate Jewish people. The Poles also were Hitler's targets, where long-term hatred had boiled for many years, so evidenced by gas ovens used for uncountable human being killings in German-built ovens built by those who labor to gain their death.

Then killings worsened. Hitler's henchmen, of little if no sense of decency, created a genocide as intended to petrify humanity's complemental continents of allies so conferred by symbolic comings of the Four Horsemen of the Apocalypse so emblazoned as the worst calamity ever. The characterization of the spread of the black plague during medieval times involved poor and depraved human beings who did not have a fighting chance to survive from diseases.

Backtracking to a time shortly after the war began in border countries, America, for a short time as a country ally to England, began providing support both with equipment and supplies and warring machines sent via merchant ships. Almost immediately, Germans put these activities under surveillance using U-boats in the Atlantic Ocean. The Germans, although, were not equipped with a fully planned navy because Hitler thought it was not a naval war and did not need a big navy with precision destruction of ships on seas suspected of carrying military aid to England. This all happened when United States took the assault seriously.

As is known historically and politically, World War II was aggressively implemented by Germans with a total surprise over most of Europe. The United States knew that Germans' prideful, dominating nature and impressive strengthening of attacking capabilities could lead to a world takeover. This expectation must have hidden in the back minds of the allies' visionaries as might assemble from scorned women whose wrath has a fury when their children are attacked. Unknown were German responses, especially since they lost and suffered a crucial surrender under the Versailles Treaty after World War I. Hitler's mind while in prison was dominated by a massive mental affliction that guided his pursuit that was to be nothing less than world domination. However, it only existed in close-associated Germans' minds, the same instinctive survivability that grossly gathered among powerful Germans and led to untold millions of deaths.

American leaders at the front end of war were dumbfounded when supply-loaded military equipment and basic purchases were put on U.S. merchant ships that were being sunk like in target practice regardless of the cargo. America was caught with its pants down while Hitler planned U-boat attacks that were turning the Atlantic into a cauldron of disastrous fireworks. The U-boats destroyed ships with supplies on their way to help the British. America also had other international problems brewing in the Pacific Ocean, which from the immediate frontend knowledge, it looked like we were being fooled from all fronts; but President Roosevelt was aware of working both problems with Germany and Japan. The shock, however, was the unexpected attack on Pearl Harbor.

War was part of life and caused continuous interactions among human beings with intensive traumas. Some men joined with brassy cheap insolent shines to get involved in personal amatory affairs on their own. Other military personnel when abroad had only one kind of *amour* in their minds, and being alone made it easy to jump at pursuits. Even military meetings led to a small part of groups of men who were with partners and would pair off with their girlfriends, and as expected, some few joined with their wives as high-level officers and diplomats. Even those few associated in-service soldiers, predominantly officers, were blatant and zestfully on the chase during their time off duty from warring but actively in their pursuit of *amour*. These war-fighting influences changed many peoples' lives' patterns of behavior.

When Uncle Jimmy shipped to a new area of combat, he had told my brother Frank years later that he initially followed the same pursuit of illicit love, but it never appeared during his time in war, and after he came home, he married a sister-in-law of his brother Joe's wife. The marriage did not last, and a desired divorced from his first wife was wanted with no reason but to go back her home to Virginia. Sometime later, he had some neat ideas on how to win a woman's love with a proper coeur de heart. He felt the same insult as many men do when they were forced into divorce without a cause. He completely changed and married a second time. From that time on, Uncle Jimmy was the most believing and compassionate man that I have ever observed. We know he was latched on to *steerage* that sunk in from his mom, and he did not let it go until he mastered its use.

These same sensuous ventures were widespread in both France and England, and many, if not everyone, knew these same pursuits were rampant in Italy. What was going on in African countries and Asian countries were yet to be discovered. The scrutiny surely would be with declarations of war against Japan, who already was in pursuit of dominating China and most of Southeast Asian countries.

All the while, United States increased its involvement with Great Britain's buildup of military might and its people who, under Sir Winston Churchill, pleaded with Pres. Franklin Roosevelt for more support. The two leaders had direct mind-sets to do whatever was necessary beyond the call of duty, as if fathers making inhuman effort to save a child from a storm of quick disaster.

President Roosevelt immediately devised a plan with Secretary of War Henry L. Stimpson, a devoted record keeper. Secretary of War Stimpson ordered the U.S. Navy, Army, and its associated Air Force to put equipment and soldiers on the ground in Europe within the year. Roosevelt responded wholeheartedly in agreement and with zest, his infamous smile so engaged while smoking a cigarette in his classic holder. The American people loved Roosevelt's quintessential facial expression full of confidence, as was Churchill's during the war.

The American people enlisted in various branches of the military service, and those who remained at home became workers who complied with rationing and increasing production of warring equipment as if guided by bees to deliver everything with gusto and patriotic flair that was unsurpassed. As an all-out effort, in every nook and cranny, our country's people were on high in America.

Within the year, American military and civilian attachés were fully involved in many parts of England, especially London along the coast facing the European mainland of France. The American leaders, active with people of London on duty, were responding to Allied commanders with more than considerable preparation under way and making emplacements of strategic ship locations, military equipment, trooper might, and proper weaponry.

Officers and operations personnel stayed in the politically complex and military genres on occasions because they were socially involved as said; a few expected and courted with amorous intentions were allowed throughout bases in England. Only a few of these pursuits lasted during the extent of the war and after the surrender of Germany; at which time, some came back married. Their lives in return were compromised or suddenly changed to distraction when the end of the marriage of illicit love burgeoned into hate and divorce with existing wives.

This type of nearness and interaction led to close associations with both service and diplomatic men and women. And as usual, the sparks of amorous desires sighted many targets and experienced direct hits including sexually attractive invitations that involved discourse and intercourse as such events matured. Only a few military men followed this manner of interaction. The American and British troops were always on a path to support and led the allies in every way for up to four years. The pursuits were always within personal *amour* seeking involvement; some with political pursuit, others with military pursuits. Many serious personnel made legitimate amorous attachments as they trekked along proper trails heading to intercontinental marriage.

The need for a combined effort brought us to our proverbial feet to take a stand but did not cross troop lines of demarcation of military might. All military personnel knew what had to be reckoned with after crucial political awakenings of the ongoing spread of takeovers of many European and African countries.

The United States, in concert with Great Britain, had to establish a positive aggressive posture and defense with both countries. The supreme leader for the planned attack was Gen. Dwight D. Eisenhower. America, in a short few weeks, significantly increased their shipments and provided weaponry on board ships to maintain supplies with ample military physical and mental aid. The United States took a reinforcement stand that bolstered their national home fronts, especially with our European allies, 100 percent confident.

The allied European countries needed our associated intervention with troops and military equipment and their beefed-up Office of Secret Service (OSS) action, which was already being provided; but now with driving impetus to relay information on Hitler's smartly and broadly planned strike force, OSS got our warring rolling like a phoenix ablaze in flight rising up on the sea and on the ground. America's mass production geared *high-drive* pursuits and exponentially increased enough to match needs of allies on both ocean and continent fronts.

The thrust in America was to stand our ground with little need for conferences. The need to act was forced upon President Roosevelt because of earlier sneak (assumed by some) attacks on Pearl Harbor on the morning of December 7, 1941. Roosevelt and his military leaders, cabinet members, and their close associates as strategists were quick to declare war on Japan and used gained espionage, which needed a concluded and presented yes by the Senate. Even Herbert Hoover had insisted that an all-out effort must be imposed on people of America to protect our home front and help our allies the best ways possible.

President Roosevelt, after consultation with Congress and with consent, responded to the country's surprise attack on Pearl Harbor the next day, on December 8, 1941. The United States Congress declared war on the empire of Japan. It was formulated an hour after his Infamy Speech that Pres. Franklin D. Roosevelt relayed his address to the American people via radio and other means such as national newspapers and film released by Movietonews immediately to theaters across the nation. As voiced to people by President Roosevelt, "It will go down in infamy." The Japanese airplane attack destroyed our naval base in Honolulu, Hawaii. The number of injuries and deaths included killing more than 2,500 military and civilian personnel and sinking numerous docked ships and planes on our airfield. And within a few days, Germany declared war on the United States America on December 11, 1941, and shortly that same day, our American Congress, with voting approval and with President Roosevelt's agreement, declared war on Germany.

The dominating air attack on United States' ships at Pearl Harbor base and many fighter planes and bombers at the airfield were damaged or destroyed. An enormous number of military people stationed, living under a peaceable Sunday, did not have any warning of a pending attack until the Japanese sneak attack began to appear at the site, and the attack was reported without any formal declaration of war by Japan. This, as we were told much later, was not the intent of the Japanese high command. The attack should not have commenced until thirty minutes after Japan had informed the United States that it was withdrawing from further peace negotiations. The intent was that the Japanese would uphold conventions of declaring war while still achieving a surprise attack. The attack began before notice could be delivered and some immediate steps to make people feel more secure. The military there with equipment and ships would have been ready to defend against such a major assault.

Tokyo had transmitted a five-thousand-word notification (commonly called the "Fourteen Part Message") in two blocks of transmission to the Japanese embassy in Washington DC. The story was that transcriptions took too long for the ambassador to deliver it in time. Even so, the notification was worded so that it neither declared war nor severed diplomatic relations, which was peculiar behavior with a severe attack on the total base and killing more than 2,500 personnel and local citizens. The following description of the declaration of war against Japan and Germany after the attack on Pearl Harbor was extracted from a compilation taken from Wikipedia as composed and stored on the Internet. Some exposition was edited to fit the sense of tremendously serious times and proper responses.

As composed, the Seventy-Seventh Congress of the United States of America at the First Session was held at Capitol Building in Washington on Friday, January 3, 1941. A joint resolution declared that a state of war exists between the government of Germany and the government and the people of the United States, making provisions to carry out a complete and major military effort, and United States of America became allies of Western Europe, already in the war with Germany and in a massive warring defense to fight and defeat the Germans.

As stated before, details of the declaration of war on Germany were accounted with the action of Congress: "Therefore be it resolved by the Senate and House of Representatives of the United States of America in Congress assembled, to define with a high number of votes that a state of war between the United States and the Government of Germany had thus been thrust upon United States and is now hereby formally declared by the Senate."

President Roosevelt was hereby authorized and directed to commit entire naval and military forces of United States and resources of the government to carry on war against the government of Germany. The intent is to bring the conflict to a successful surrender with all resources of the country pledged by the Congress of the United States. The document was signed by Sam Rayburn, speaker of the house of representatives, signed by H. A. Wallace, vice president of the United States and president of the Senate, and was approved and signed by Franklin D. Roosevelt on December 11, 1941, at 3:05 p.m. (EST).

Great Britain also declared war on Japan nine hours before United States did, partially because of Japanese attacks on Malaya, Singapore, and Hong Kong, and partially because of Winston Churchill's promise to declare war "within the hour" of a Japanese attack on United States.

President Roosevelt formally requested the declaration in his Infamy Speech, addressed to a joint session of Congress and the nation at 12:30 p.m. on December 8. The declaration was quickly brought to a vote; it passed the Senate and then passed the House at 1:10 p.m. The vote was 82–0 in the Senate and 388–1 in the House of Representatives. Jeannette Rankin, a committed Pacifist and the first woman elected to Congress, was the only vote against the Declaration in either house as recorded by the vote.

President Roosevelt signed the declaration at 4:10 p.m. the same day. The power to declare war is assigned exclusively to Congress in the United States Constitution, and it was therefore an open question at the time whether his signature was technically necessary. The president's signature was symbolically powerful and resolved any doubts in minds of patriotic people in the United States. And with the president's insistence on undivided personal patriotism, the Congress supported and defended the president's position for a declaration of war on Germany. There was only one objection, and it was from one senator from Montana whose position she should have defended, but it withered and later was unfounded, unimportant to reason but identified in the Congressional Archives.

American patriotism had filtered down to each family so much so that unrecorded achievements were made in production rates throughout all items of equipment, making weapons; and all along, shipping needed supporting armaments to England at great costs to America. By doubling the dollar devotion to the effort including patriots building of our military made it well worth the cost because the early motivation moved our patriotism to on high and increased production in many states who were geared up to make mass production work even beyond the German's belief in pursuit of world domination at the first onslaught.

All during the festering European military conflagration, American troops were drawn into a Second World War with the determination to go into Asia against the dominating Japanese Imperialist and longtime emperor Hirohito, whose diplomats while on site in Washington DC had displayed false intentions. They assumed that we were American fools, as the leaders in Japan planned, and within days, carried out the sneak attack on Pearl Harbor on Sunday, December 7, 1941. The American government, among millions of citizens, was shocked severely with fear of war that, Sunday morning, uniformly demanded a declaration of war. What happened was an all-out overwhelming swelling of patriotism that soared and to the defeat of the enemy after many years under the rising red sun's flag.

Then President Roosevelt and Congress immediately formulated a declaration of war on Japan with every intent of our minds and strength to defeat our enemy. The war-mongering premier Hideki Tojo had inherited from a young age an intensely megalomaniacal mind-set directed on overtaking the United States of America and all of Asia. The Japanese leaders must have formed a plan for expansion based upon the assumption that America was responsible for the depression of the '30s. Political minds felt they needed more land and control because of the smallness of their county.

Our patriotism gained the support of European forces as we had shown in like kind our support to their plight in Europe. Many allies including Australia and Canada strongly supported us in the warring that we were forced to conduct in Asian countries that were pro-American throughout the Pacific Ocean Rim to rid these countries of this now powerfully manned and militarized dominating assault, a feat that was to be an atrocious achievement after so many years of almost bestial fighting in the Southeast Asian island jungles.

The critically demanded military manufacturers drastically invigorated president's pursuit of patriotism. Increased mass production already under way in high presto tempo because of our support to European allies was needed because of German's war efforts to gain control of all of Europe, and then the domination of the world was singing its baritone shouting pursuit, and it was dynamically working. All American businesses and other ally countries moved with a zest using all classes of society as full-on patriots to achieve the machination of warring machinery and weapons, be it for offense or defense, including tanks, warships and boats, large guns, logistics trucks and jeeps, and fighter and bomber planes.

The initial subterfuge used by Hitler's emissaries to cover his prime intent for world domination was so brightly flashed to organize Europe for Germany's dictator Adolf Hitler that it blinded the British prime minister Neville Chamberlain's leadership capabilities and decision-making mentality. Chamberlain's early insistence clamored that Hitler only wanted to take over and guide minor countries in Europe. The eyes of England opened after the flash of death and destruction even before United States declared war on Germany. Great Britain's Parliament quickly set Sir Winston Churchill as prime minister.

Hitler sold his pursuit of dominance of Europe to the Russians by entering in a treaty early to prevent their involvement. Russia agreed, but then Hitler reneged and attacked Russia's giant border at the time of a cold Russian winter. As the German troops with their mechanized armaments moved along the hundreds of miles of frozen and snow-covered barren farms and wastelands many miles from major cities, the soldiers and equipment bogged down and wintered in a coming doom of death by nature. Unknown to Hitler was that Russians could take the coldest weather, but Germans could not. The movement of Russian troop reversed the drive and gained monetary support by the United States with added supplies and warring equipment. Russia then was able to stop the German front that finally would lead to the invasion from the east from England and a definite plan by allies.

Churchill was a man with enormous warring experience on front lines. His knowledge and experience were wholeheartedly devoted to England, and he demanded that his country stand its ground and defeat their enemy. The British primarily, and French afterward, recognized that their country needed the allied complex agreed only after a slight resistance by the Vichy French now under control by Germany. Vichy was occupied, and but shortly afterward, the French underground operations began to fight for their country.

Many local French citizens organized with all that they could muster at home and in concert with allies' spies to challenge Hitler's gestapo's pursuit of brutal punishment and death sentences of public people not even involved in any counteractions against the Germans. The German army in every way intended world domination by National Socialism. The main pursuit by the United States was at first a standby, but within a few short years, when 1943 began, the development of the greatest weapon ever built under the now third-time elected president Franklin Delano Roosevelt and where Harry S. Truman, the senator from Missouri, was asked to not delve into monetary requests at the behest of the president. America secretly began creating job types to be performed by improved mass production techniques and methods so that factory workers could quickly accomplish individual military weapons tasks as work items passed to the next worker.

The same type of improvements was adopted by family owner enterprises and large corporate businesses with demanding organizations spread out and filled new and old sites throughout the country with production by patriotic people. Preparation was secretive in clandestinely located sites, especially new weapons projects. With little suspicion, the unexpected happened, and some Americans were exposed as enemy spies because most Americans did not think any American would want to help Germany or Japan to win the war.

Shortly, with the Federal Bureau of Investigation (FBI), newly formed Office of Strategic Services (OSS), active overseas and various military intelligences at home were actively uncovering by surprise many more spies who were being observed as they infiltrated our classified work and our logs of weaponry. These spies in America were especially groomed by Hitler to be his elite order of spies and his German citizen cohorts still married to their mother country when they immigrated to United States in the early '30s. While Hitler's actions were sparse, his intent was devout as the almighty parent image who has strongholds on their papers in the homeland. They were revealed as planted Germans and German American supporters who hated what the American-guided Peace Treaty at Versailles demanded after World War I.

The allies could see that America set gears in *high drive* and sped toward mechanization of warring machinery even before the Japanese shammed President Roosevelt with phony intentions. Even the expansion of the patriotic demeanor and pursuit added many opportunities for people so associated to pursue *amour* as an added thirst to the increased level of an unknown future, and to some, they simply did what comes naturally, especially since they could cite the caused for companionship with unknown demands during war—that is, it was just plain time spent with each other during working hours or thereafter. In addition to their already existing commitments to marriage and family life, those left back home and those who emotionally felt out of sight, out of mind and heart, had a neuron tingling in the unconscious mind until a prevailing instinctively gnawing signaled—this could be their last days. What an easy path through the near infinite number of sensory receptors to raise the inborn animal magnetism of attraction to the height of a mortar blast and of magnitude of a quickly win over by the "will of desire."

The owners of businesses in the USA smoothed racial bias to some extent, certainly on the surface of interactions. That sort of usage of easy ways existed during wartimes based on power of military or diplomatic position, money, and individuals in pursuit of *amour*. All others outside of this bill of credentials would always be ready to take what they could get at this time and did it effectively but not at any real dollar costs.

Many other subterfuges of personality and unfathomable cunning linked couples until lights were turned on. The physical and mental cost to individuals was put on the back burner until the resulting cost of being found out by word of mouth was too much to bear. As always, the secret lovers couldn't figure how the ether of their fling spread while displaying an air of abandonment with their low spirits. The class structure related to power and money of position no longer dominated the local society to the same extent so obviously as with the indoctrinated signs for Caucasian and Negro citizens prevalent in many countries but more naturally in the USA. The racial differences were inscribed in the minds of the young almost religiously by breeding bigots, and it was rubbed into the minds of many young who had a mild infection of the bigot ideology. Many teachers with a maliciously bigoted intention sought to keep the practice going. However, some racial bias continued in certain walks and endeavors of life especially in early military actions and during associations in public places and facilities.

The invasion sped up our positioning to lead the onslaught in the European theater eventually with the leadership of five-star generals Dwight D. Eisenhower and George C. Marshall in the European front, and Gen. Douglas MacArthur was the leading force in the Pacific Islands and Japan. Gen. Douglas MacArthur had a dominating personality, and he personally impressed it on all Pacific allies' forces. He relayed the same message as intended in my words: Gen. Douglas MacArthur said we will succeed no matter what commitments may require, and we must be fully devoted by troops to win the war. Selected other generals were all deeply devoted and later with archived recorded in history as leaders, such as Gen. George Patton. Many more generals were also archived in history books. This grand complements of leaders were well trained in our military academies and forts in concert both in the Pacific and the Atlantic conflagrations. Valor was spread to those deserving with spoken credits and decorations.

CHAPTER XI

Amour Behavior during Wars in the '50s to Present Times

John Fitzgerald Kennedy's historic words from his
inaugural address inspired children and adults to see
the importance of civic action and public service . . .

*Ask not what your country can do for you, ask
what you can do for your country.*

He challenged every American to contribute in some way
to the public good. In this lesson, students learn about
the talk in President Kennedy's inaugural address, civic
action, and consider how it applies to their own lives.
—Pres. John F. Kennedy during his Inaugural
Address on January 21, 1961

Civil rights among all were still yet to awaken public acceptance even into 1950s. It wouldn't be levied until much later as civil rights by federal congressional lawmakers after Pres. John F. Kennedy was elected in November 1960 and pursued equal rights untethered. However, civil rights were enhanced, especially when it blurted nationally about political bigots who were exposed with an aura of simple education bias justifiably. In the education arena, American men and women were more insistent to attend and were to go to state universities because they offered fantastic curriculums in some southern states and lower tuition costs.

The upper class always liked to attend performances by real actors in stage productions and operas because it satisfied goals to protect their self-recognition and status in society. The so-called middle class and even those in a lower class, because of lesser wealth who were as productive and with some reservation, were up to par with everyone they knew. Their main problems were lack of money. Most people at the universities listened to the more common folks on radios for music, talk about average daily life, because sitcom television programs were easier to follow. The political news from radios and from those who had early televisions in the '50s mostly covered news of the day repeatedly, making it hard to be at a television to hear and view details. The final one was religious preaching shows depending on interest in selected ways of life or even with expressions of the hereafter.

Many of these same people attended local theaters to see Hollywood movies of fiction and nonfiction stories and, before the 1905s, a relay of bits of on-site film about Movietonews of the day and sometimes included animated cartoons.

More significantly were unabashedly revealed forms of humanity in our society to make up countries broad scope humor in daily newspapers with artistically devised cartoons that became a dominantly recognized entry that gropes kids as well as adults not yet used to ascribing to directions for unknown works.

The lower class and even the less fortunate, some also known as the poor and some below the poverty level, owing to monetary or personal losses, were currently living off the land, beggary, or government welfare. Even these people full suffering life's woes as they piled up like the garbage of dilemmas of despair. There was a resurgence of many men with American patriotism that came with John Fitzgerald Kennedy's aggressive political personal knighthood about new ventures into space with a manned flight to the moon. JFK flagged American people with "Ask not what the country can do for you, ask what you can do for your country!"

Then while his space venture was actively making real progress, things in his backyard were going astray. A fury of turmoil arose with Cuba when Fidel Castro decided to overtake Cuba with his strong rebel militia and did it with aplomb. Castro then met with JFK and his military leaders. After many conversations regarding Cuba and America, Castro essentially told him he will not support America. Later, Castro chose Russia's Communist country, and he formed a socialistic dictatorial government in the late '50s. The next venture by JFK and his brother Robert Kennedy and his military staff was to plan a retake of Cuba with an advanced set of American troops and local Cubans against Castro. The Bay of Pigs, as it was called, was struck, but the next onslaught by Castro's military was powerful enough to force the rebels to surrender. This debacle left JFK to eventually set up an Atlantic Ocean embargo of any Russian ships near Cuba no matter what they might be carrying. The standoff was later solved by Americans; but demands by Castro continued to claim his country as a Communist dictatorship and he continued to side with Russia even though Russian military ships cruised back home.

Early in the '60s, new technology accelerated the evolution of commercial jet airplanes and research to investigate the practicality of space exploration. Then in a short time, it became a must to compete with the Soviet Union, who beat us to the punch of delivering their Sputnik before our Vanguard into earth orbit as the first man-made satellite. Pres. John F. Kennedy, shortly after his inauguration, thrust a formulated decree into the laps of our country's best aerospace companies and universities via the newly renamed NASA that he wanted to put a United States astronaut on the moon by 1969.

A new unexpected event happened, which was disastrous to the hearts of American people when JFK was assassinated in Dallas, Texas. It happened in the afternoon at about one o'clock, while riding in an opened-top Cadillac, driving slowly along Dealey Plaza parading through downtown Dallas. The assailant, Lee Harvey Oswald, was located on the fifth floor of the storage area in a library building. The aura of cowardly assault covered America with subterfuge, all within the reach of Russia and Cuba. Later, the pursuit included covering the globe with conspiracy exacerbated by the Cold War. Years afterward, the Warren Commission, the United States House Committee on Assassinations, concluded in 1979 that Kennedy was probably assassinated because of a conspiracy, but evidence indicating conspiracy was subsequently reexamined and rejected.

Citizens' personal thoughts pervaded the ether of the good times past and a spread into melancholy as they took jobs that boosted their psychic of our country first. The investigations were pervasive and broadly covered by any persons of intellect; but nothing significant resulted. But many other deaths and despair of nothing more than simple solutions led to Lee Harvey Oswald killing President Kennedy as he had planned, all stemming from his inadvertent siding with Russian Communism after having been an American marine.

The man, Jack Ruby, who loved JFK, was a local businessman and friendly with the police and the station. The very next morning, while Oswald was being escorted to the county prison, he was shot and killed by Ruby. Ruby casually walked into the transit path of Oswald while exiting the Dallas police station to be incarcerated elsewhere and walked up to him and shot him in the stomach unsuspectedly on November 24, 1963. The event caused more significant investigation; but it also left a mystery of a wonder never to be cleared, except the love of JFK by Ruby.

Oswald, first a marine serving in combat and then later spending time in Russia, had essentially become a Communist. While there, he married a Russian woman and returned to America and secretively planned his ploy to kill JFK while JFK and his wife and entourage traveled in Dallas along the highway in a motorcade in an open Cadillac limousine with Gov. John Connally and his wife Jacqueline that proceeded along the Dealey Plaza to speak to people to gain failing support and concern in Dallas at the time.

The strife continued and was conducted as a court case even though Oswald was shot and killed by a devoted Democrat known as Jack Ruby. Ruby was familiar in local taverns and knew some police almost as friends so had easy access. The sincerity of the president's death was twofold; some few thought it was great, but most, if not all, thought it was a loss that Americans will never get over our president being assassinated. The extended result culminated with many books about the assassination and a story of the whole assassination as a popular movie.

As the recognition by the government gained vision, the slightly biased people waned and made strides but significant gains in the mid-'60s after President Kennedy was assassinated and Vice President Lyndon B. Johnson replaced him and then was elected president in 196 and the Civil Rights Act was passed by Congress and made the law with Johnson's signature.

The pursuit of new technology had taken root with all the new college graduates and ventures into science. New college graduates ventured into science and technology, medicine, and psychology, which led to significant inroads in space technology, both in the commerce of the countries and the delving into space. As an aside, especially profoundly newsworthy was child-rearing as voiced by the many and started by or given credit to the visionaries Dr. Benjamin Spock and his cohorts of pediatricians and pharmaceutical companies, who saw the need for upgrading care and treatment to children from an early age. These new changes predominantly caused families to concentrate on specifically guiding children from kindergarten learning toward college education. The doctor's primary intent was to mentally implant interest in mathematics, science, medicine, and new technology, all with innovation. This new technology revolution and those directing it led to the transistor and a new edging into the visionary methods of travel in all forms, such as jet aircraft unexplored because of misleading aerodynamic calculations.

When the next generation, generation X, was just getting under way in the late 60s, world powers were sending spacecraft into earth orbit after five years of government-concentrated and scientific and technologically devoted development. Within that same generation, as it matured, it became known as the flower children and hippies (and druggies) sometimes identified as the generation who had no more than music, disobedience, and dysfunction on their minds and in their actions. These contrarians as an entity were always in pursuit of liberal ways as if the promise was one awaiting for a date with the girl next door no matter if she's married; but portrays herself in a sensuous way so that desire of the will displays attention and the man's the pursuer is as certainly as a gift in offering.

Young liberals, when in step as a devoted mob, almost always concentrated on demonstrated disobedience, and as a people in concert, they thought that they could link with and display any form of sex, if at all abhorrent to the locals anytime and anywhere. All this happened while the United States of America sent astronauts in a one-of-a-kind capsule, the *Gemini*, to the moon. The country was on a high even under Pres. Richard Milhous Nixon's leadership, which shoved conservatism down our throats like a rampant father who knows what is best for us in the long run but fails as the mind's intake dissolves admiration and honor as expected.

The United States continued to develop and boost unmanned spacecraft on grand tours to the planets and even beyond to outer space with the *Voyager II* spacecraft. Critical and new details were gained immediately during nearby encounters about outer planets. The Hubble Space Telescope, although suffering a short delay because of the shuttle launch failure afterward in 1986; but within a later time it was launched into earth orbit around seven hundred nautical miles. During the mission, the Wide-Field and Planetary Cameras revealed the unforeseen universe, relegated galaxies and their contained many bodies of large variations of stars, their nature as stars where some star systems might have capabilities of homing planets for life as we know it today.

The results enhanced the understanding and theoretical use of characteristic measurements to further explain black holes that Albert Einstein had theorized years earlier. Recently, more elaborate telescopic investigations have revealed their presence in simple detail and structure. The next step is to detail characteristic predictions of universal constants and theories to further understanding the phenomena of universal gravity. The tenure of exploring the capability to live in space while conducting experiments inside and outside of the International Space Station and Hubble Space Telescope and newer telescopic systems "just growed," like Topsy said. This feat as international joint experiments of great scientific pursuit of many countries resulted in accomplishments from the USA shuttle and Russian spacecraft docking capabilities and advanced new space telescopes from American space systems developed by NASA. These achievements led to significant experiments being replaced with more modern designs. Many technical instrument systems were farmed to other countries such as Canada and several European nations. USA astronauts and Russian cosmonauts and invited scientists and medical doctors experienced living and working inside and outside space stations, and it became a practice. Little seminal excitement engrossed scientists and explorers except at hometown levels where they are considered heroes, in museums where their story is told, and all opportunities exposed to space-enthusiast followers.

Each of these pursuits resulted in the building of large infrastructures that extended development of jet airlines starting in the '60s and '70s and produced computers and miniaturization of devices that led to the unexpected creativity that has resulted in communications surge that now envelope minds of world's people in everything from everyday business to whatnot while allowing significant personal travel via many new automobiles of all makes with scientific devices and especially what is provided by satellites in orbits above earth that maintains visual information with Global Positioning System and camera systems for protection and safety of others.

These accomplishments spread knowledge and mass behavior across countries by globally adding to the nature of many new ways of seeking amour, and it worked. Of course, all this was unexpected by government leaders, be they self-identified visionaries or politically benevolent or dictatorial heads of state; this was done by the almost lightly identified scientific visionaries of whom most are poorly identified unless a great deal of money and power evolved with them from inventions and innovative ideas for making great deals of money such as Bill Gates of Microsoft and Steve Jobs of Apple and George Lucas of Pixar, notably large businesses that lead to fame and fortune.

The social and political extravagances of the '90s caused a lot of the computer-savvy brains to become so engulfed in the personal computer and software continuously being developed. Within a few years, e-mail and the Internet evolved and sucked up the dominant portion of people who did whatever on the computer. Then the pre-bloggers used PC time to use the combined documentation of the search engines to examine the U.S. federal government by collectively studying and understanding of the Constitution and the Declaration of Independence of the United States of American in its entity and relate it to modern times during election time.

Their thrust was to evaluate what were the policies regulated and implemented in the country within each federal branch that made sense. The details of additional parts make sure the laws are clearly written when put in place by interpretation by the proper branch of government to fit fundamental laws of the land. And just as important, what are the activities of these high-level elected or appointed federal employees? We American citizens hope they are copacetic with oaths given by judges as directed by our Constitution and its amendments to only deal with truth.

The personal computers (PCs) were running full stream of electrons and photons into every band that was exposed on a time and frequency band. When the e-mails kicked in via the Internet, the global discourse abounded in semi-wireless signals as transmissions in the upper ether. All this happened at the beginning of the millennium while the federal government pursued continuously into President Clinton's second term, where he was revealed by evidence of his ongoing amorous behavior during working hours and any other free time he could muster. No matter how much the citizenry expected, disappointing results occurred, and numerous learned people produced formal paperwork critiquing several branches with significant emphasis on the executive branch, but at that time, without a grave disclosure or result to save face as if we were the Indians who were cheated.

The judicial branch didn't help much at all in reacting to problems of the day and had no truly knowledgeable record after *Roe v. Wade* and *Doe v. Bolton* cases continued with progeny abortion, cases that resulted in allowing the government to control the allowance of all abortions for unfounded reasons or a lack of sensitivity to human life, unguarded with no self-protection.

Although shortly thereafter, Arab countries were inundated with leadership turmoil. The exposure to the real outside world caused them to be religiously righteous. The old-world Islamic Moslems were known to be grossly defiant against long-term settlements of their adjacent lands of which a small piece was diced after World War II. The problem was the land of Israel in Africa was given to displaced Jewish survivors of the Holocaust. This decision of a new Israel gained through the United Nations with strong inducement by the United States. The United States, with unending purpose both in maintaining their stature in the world and helping develop the homeland identified as Israel, had the strength of fairness on their side. From the past, as history showed, the Jews were driven out from their land by the Egyptians. Their return was promised within their minds through religious belief so many years ago and was now renewed.

The confirmation by Allied Forces leadership, real decision makers at the time, intended to gain freedom and become peacemakers of the free world, who were led and succeeded by the United States of America and European nations as members of United Nations Security Council after the war even with other nations dead set against its fruition. When finally confirmed in 1947 by the United Nations, the confrontational demeanor was enforced with boarder infighting until it turned into war in the Middle East as it was inevitable.

Miscellaneous wars among the Arabs and Arabs against Israel picked up in the late '50s and '60s and continued to critical incidents and several wars with Israel and among various Arab countries such as Iran, Syria, and Iraq that continually escalated to this day, all of which in some form involved United States of America and continued confrontations with United Nations Security Council.

Shortly thereafter, the Soviet Union set on acquiring Afghanistan using its friendly neighbor in power but only to contend with oppositions. The Soviets wanted a border country as an ally to counter Iranians and Pakistanis, who were currently friends of the USA. But the USA interfered and provided further opposition with forces to counter Soviets after a long stay. By that time, Soviets had its problems with leadership and were in turmoil both within its own house and outside in Germany's East Berlin and eventually left Afghanistan.

The dissolution of Union of Soviet Socialist Republics (USSR) countries was inevitable as the nation experienced internal strife and national incompatibility. The Soviet Union's influence on dividing Germany was ready to end in disaster because there was only one solution, the recombination of Germany as a unified state and its reconstruction back to the historically known European nation. During the '80s, USSR continued fighting in Afghanistan for what was at least ten years, but why—God only knows!—and I'm sure he was happy to see them leave. Then a bit of détente grew with some roots edging throughout Russia during this period, and it began to break up over the next ten or so years into separate states that even extended into parts of Asia.

The influence of détente was especially taken as an advantage in China although soaked for many years in communistic domination and on its way to becoming a world power both militarily and economically. With its great population, it has a world of problems to solve to please its people. The main pursuit was to establish trade with the USA and develop negotiations of peaceful coexistence with the USA and other democratic nations in major trade agreements.

For all those years, China now was a communistic country of dominating influence in few previous wars that continued to show a friendliness for trade while developing a warring capability as one of a more than a billion people could with communistic control. China's main plan was to establish long-term buildup of their military power while sacrificing their multimillion of proletariat, many of whom are living in poverty certainly including the low-class workers, unemployed and poor peasants indigenously forced to begging. As China built its military power and nuclear weaponry, they have become one of the many threats to world peace. Their approach usually was held at bay if needed, just knowing the unending suffering of a nuclear war or knowing that both Russians and Americans have dominant nuclear weaponry deterrents.

All during these trying times, new trade agreements were in negotiation throughout and among many countries. The most accommodating one was North American Free Trade Agreement (NAFTA), which was with the United States, Canada, and Mexico covering both environmental and labor conditions and common regulations. However, the USA still has Cuba's embargoes and sanctions, which have remained these many years. Cuba continues to remain Communist under Fidel Castro and his military thugs, all to the amazement of many of their citizens and the whole of the North American continent. Shortly after Castro's coup in Cuba, it began to decay socially and economically but always maintained a military force. Regardless of the support from the USSR, the country has been inundated with widespread poverty and scattered with human injustices, which prevailed in grottoes of the Cuban liberty seekers who continually try to make their way to America and once on land are received with sanction.

Back in the mid to late '80s, mutually strengthening the pursuit by the United States president Ronald Reagan and Pope John Paul II led to the collapse of the cold war, and their eventual dissolution of control of Union of Soviet Socialist Republics' communistic countries led to a new era in Europe and especially in Germany, where reunification of the country occurred. This outward thrust of peace grew, at least into a form of progress, coexistence, and intellectual freedom, as so written by Andrei Sakharov in 1968 in the book *Progress, Coexistence and Intellectual Freedom,* to impress upon people of leadership that there are enormous fears of nuclear weapons. The same intent is in Aleksandr Solzhenitsyn's book *The Gulag Archipelago* with subjects of communistic mistreatments of political prisoners in the USSR.

Closer global ties enjoined countries, and settled ways made way for oil conflicts and terrorists' pursuits against many countries by Islamic extremists from Middle East-enriched leaders with oil export and a need for a concerted effort to convert people and countries to Islamic religion of divined Mohammed, the tribal leader and sheik of the seventh century. A pursuit by the people of Islam evolved with the intention to dominate the world with this religious embellishing the belief by using threats offered in substance as do or die. To the rest of the global population, the threat from those that would die to overcome infidels so naturally call Islamic extremists by all as they infiltrate into other countries. The unexpected violent bombings and killings are a close second to that of the propagation of the bubonic plague back in the mid-1300s as a threat and fear of death as put to infidels by its extremist religious leaders.

Finally, during eras of personal computers and new communications systems dispersed into the ether of the '90s at federal levels, the pursuits of *amour* were so ubiquitous to even main politicians; one was William Jefferson Clinton, who had become president, and he continued his same raconteur ventures that he had pursued in his early years to gain *amour*. With the widespread knowledge and disclosed behavior under the critical eye of the people, he didn't care enough, although with a claim of some brains but much less wisdom, who knew how he got it even if it was just to get his jollies off? This debacle turned out to ruin his second term in office, and he still survived to maintain a personal appeal to his people in modern days even though he suffered the embarrassment of impeachment so honestly placed but released from a guilty finding, thanks to Arlen Specter, the "nay voter" Pennsylvanian senator.

The country was semishocked because citizens continued further expansion of global markets through daily communications and using new personnel computer systems. Their lives were hardly noticed except for evening news events. Good times were a boon to President Clinton's tenure. New personal media and methods of communication combined with the Internet captured people by bucketsful with cell phones, cameras, and simultaneously used numerous business software programs. Digital capabilities of personal computers constantly were looking for daily responses, and any little thing was given serious thought.

This all happened through revelations via television as the media and press made prime politically astute servant leaders of government recognize libido levels rising comparable with many men, be they wise men or fools and anything in between. This includes those with journalistic credentials who staved off with an ounce of secretiveness and anonymity after hours. And because many innocent parties were afflicted and clamor revealed no assaulted concern or remorse of William Jefferson Clinton, he continued his time in office as president.

The total incident having coursed a few years with loss of government cognizance of our country's well-being, little judicial sensuous malady occurred. The major player, Pres. William Jefferson Clinton, waylaid with equivocation that minimized his effects of suffering a uniquely libido-induced presidential impeachment. Under best conditions he afforded, by the journalistic mentors,

Clinton colored the action as hanky-panky. The claim was essentially denied by the president's wife, discounting it as a right-winged conspiracy in the face of media. It was roughly ignored by senators after the impeachment, and just by the skin of his teeth, he was politically exonerated both by his check-and-balance peers and in his mind to a relief by the not-guilty vote.

As for new technologies, they were extracted and used by many countries and have since been evolved into many different products. They were proven by use to be successful and needed technologies. In close relationships experienced by the worldwide population, it accomplished as much science and technology that the research continued with spacecraft experiments that eventually were sent to the moon, Venus, Mars, and outer planets, Jupiter, Saturn, Uranus, and ventures to observe Neptune and Pluto set in place during Pres. Ronald Reagan's Strategic Defense Initiative.

The impetus of the strategic initiative led many NASA shuttle and International Space Station missions that revolutionized the technology of modern days. We will not cover amour opportunities that were added to world's population grabs that were mesmerized to implement new ways to infidelity or loyalty with untold numbers of outcomes. Any responsive family of humans' *amour* fit bills of laden that sufficed explanations to questions regarding "what's it all about?"

Cooking, so to speak, "the world's people's soup for their minds" during the new 2000 millennium produced a consequential potpourri of technical and communications inventions that influenced many family personal lives and business pursuits worldwide. It was after almost fifty years of piecemeal wars in which the United States of America and coalition forces from Europe, Australia, and Canada had fought Communism in North Korea supporting South Korea only thirty years before and then in a war against the Vietnam Communist insurgents known as Vietcong in the mid-'60s to the early '70s where significant killing was caused with fire spreading that killed anyone caught in the napalm fluid bomb fires. Wars of that use of weapons were stopped with some lingering that involved the United States completing our troops' return home.

The war was stopped just before Lyndon B. Johnson decided not to run again for president. At that appropriate election time, Richard Nixon ran and won the presidency. He then continued to stop the warring with Vietnam insurgents. Then as president, he recalled the American troops that remained stationed within some allied countries for the assurance of demilitarization line where American troops continued to show commitment to ensure fighting was stopped. However, the American military demanded that troops that were killed be returned to the United States, and that action continued for a few years, remaining while the countries settled their life-devastating losses and as the people in the Koreas and Vietnam worked to build peaceful living.

After many years, new car manufacturing companies delved into hybrid electric and electric and fuel cell-run cars, and, eventually, we expect some form of cars may eventually run on separated hydrogen and oxygen from water as an additive to fuel all types of vehicles. Then among all the broad pursuit of new technologies, researchers continued development in the long run so that cars might eventually be long-term operated on microwaves, lasers, or even radioisotopes or controlled thermoelectric nuclear power that could be designed to be separated when not operational, and when operating the new materials, would only have the ability of proper particles to be absorbed within the container that would be easy to control and use for times within five or ten years as made to disintegrate totally with proper isotope disintegration. Future cars and trucks may eventually be augmented by microwave and laser power when researchers figure out how to convert microwave and laser power into electric energy and add increased power and control of conversion.

The racing car competitions had continuously thrived after World War II with advanced military improvements and new, more powerful and designed for effective antiair interference sports cars. The racing fans after World War II ended have multiplied by people and in all car sports activities. Each new racing car race has increased monetary prizes and carried with it the reward of more powerful engines and transmission-thrust improved fuels. All these changes have added to more fame and increased accomplishment among racers, owners from various nations who have means to fuel their libido, and spectators and fans inspired and so immersed into sensuous desires with this living exhilaration on the sidelines.

What does this mean as my story exposes continuous natures of the Divita family, while only a few, maybe the few geniuses, inherited enough wisdom that they needed from our ancestors? I will expose what follows and what was relayed to me from memory and hearsay about their behavior while at the famous Indy 500 Race in 1941. The next race would not happen until the war would be over and would start in May 1946 revealing their choices of usage of *amour*. One meaning of *amour* is affaire d'amour (an illicit love affair), and the other meaning is affaire de coeur (affair of the heart). Both dominate the way *Homo sapiens* live within their own minds with beliefs and pursuits of their desires.

The expected intent was minimal with morality as defined in *The Man of the Renaissance* during and after the First Renaissance. I'm going to tell you about what they now do. This is *Steerage and Amour!"—What's It All About!*

Knowing the Divita family, they would want to know why morals appeared better before the two Indy 500 Races and previously during past times. Much after the times from the '50s to the '80s, as read in chapter 10, they were astonished how perpetual warring changed their behavior patterns, and it involved any of the *Homo sapiens* who would take little care within their minds when involved with amorous ventures. Chapter IX delves into the related subjects of what really discards the true meaning of life from the world's point of view as was created by God, who funneled into *Homo sapiens'* minds to understand his nature of the definition of immortality. Simply stated, each new progeny from *Homo sapiens* with propagation starting from conception moves the birthed progenies the next step into continued immortality.

Chapter XII

Mentality of Adopted Steerage and Amour Heritage

*I have opened my heart to you more than I thought to do. There
is a reason for me to expose my soul, my body and all the learning
God has given me for love of him and for my salvation and else.*
        —*The Man of the Renaissance*, Ralph Roeder, The
        Viking Press, 18 East 48th St. New York, NY.

The way of the peacemaker is hard.
        —*First Principles*, part 1, 1862

Frank recounted to me many times that he observed his life's behavior
during associations with families and relatives and associates during various
involvements with close common friends. Frank released words of good feelings
and understanding about the commonality that the appearances of people, both
men and women, shone differently with discourse expressing their facial reactions.
His persona had its unique body, facial expressions, and in his normally ejaculated
words of expressions both flared with sincerity and in tone. At times, with some
misleading verbosity, he used different words discharged by actions of their
behavior. For Frank, the exchange was so difficult to be noticed because he
explained with grandiose inflections depending on whom he might encounter.

However, with some women, he would sensuously accept a propensity for true
amour, although he was sure that some ladies had been saddled in disloyal *amours*.
A complete mental image of attractions and compliments of any sweet talk that
surfaced to win the argument of true love became historic in Frank's attractions.
He mostly instilled *steerage*, and it worked almost every time. Gravitating notices
in his father's ways was the path that Frank followed from his parents leveled with
married grandparents who had lived a long life together. They usually had joy
within their minds because they maintained the pursuit of happiness.

As in the past, people desired the grasp of illegitimate *amour* even at the
expense of suffering a lingering depression if not worse when it did not happen.
However, infinite ways and means divulged common paths to illicit *amour*, and

he knew it would lead to an aftermath. The same methodology was always expended when amorous pursuits of times past were consummated, and he knew few continued to survive especially after notices had been exposed to deceive people.

This intent was obviously the way many things occurred from first existence of *Homo sapiens* mankind on earth. The sacrifice was grossly deserved because knowledge of end states was not judiciously released during happenings but with unknown belief that the Creator knew what the complete story of love was from beginning to mankind's end. When mankind evolved into *Homo sapiens*, they should have realized that they must believe the Creator had produced this universe that would force the wisdom of mankind in the direction toward immortality ad infinitum.

Disloyalty was characterized in mankind's mind usage. Everyone knows the instinctive part of minds that maintain survivability first as it was hardwired into the *Homo sapiens*. When a lesson from history was not learned or adhered, the expectation of results from history that one knows the aftermath will be repeated. That revelation to those who know teachers who continuously taught *steerage* and *amour* to nonbelievers did not use the mind's decision path that followed the teachings.

Yet I say, many, if not most, humans take the course of living a mentally normal, natural life and lived within the belief of the spirit of God the Creator. A moral life with companionship will not fault loyalty no matter the significance. Human beings feel the good life when they displayed their advantage on an even ground. When they falter and recover without failing significantly, they hold on to the positive while trying to reconcile their lives to partners. Many good but faltering human beings had to revalue themselves.

The deceits that plague some with mental distress and affliction jump into known amorous situations with unsuspected ramifications. Many are known as their memories later recall clearly that it led them to calamity. It's the mind's eye that triggers the unrelenting emotional response. And at times, it can be the sense of smell of ancient animalistic pheromones or a response to some sensed physical behavior even extrasensory perception within the mind. For example, if a man or woman's scented aroma attracts another with invisible musk seeking within the mind's sensory, it causes a seeping into open pores and releases unharnessed senses of musk to readied receptors. The musk creates an event that may or may not work depending on receptor's mental receivers. The mind's final approach includes insight; also, it is driven by "direct instinctive behavior" that follows first. Then minds have tendencies to discard self-preservation and are pushed toward "knowledge and experience" judgments that raise emotions that can be mollified with thought.

When humans are aroused in whatever sensory way, but whether one or a next one remains in a stable and controlled way depends on their overall reactions. All humans have listened with amazement to stories told about *amour* and mentally store those that made wrong decisions. The innocent ones maintain mental composure. The actual joy of ventures into a realm of sensuous emotion is considered by many to be as expected. But as they gain pleasures and conquest, they lose sight of unrecognized mandatory conditions imposed in mankind's mind of aftermaths.

Frank kept a tight rein on his prancing passions by quickly using a crafty cutting of pending desires with his mind's fiery slicing and deleting impassioned words. Members of families quickly recognized one's absurdities, especially when one is making a fool of one's self. Everyone who is about to get involved knows, as do the rest of the world, that it is fools who embark on more common simpleminded paths when sensuously emotional attractions are enhanced as they are released. Warnings are taken in the mind to no avail. Frank would say to me what he had may have said, "I'm not simpleminded. Will you listen to my point? Amorous incidences bring on the mind's timing to a decisive matter on how it comes about." Then he said to me, "Every woman and man want committed partners to have loyalty and integrity, but to find one with devotion who makes careful decisions and one who thinks in a wise way is rare."

As his best associate in the family, I was with Frank many times as he recalled his living time being with ease. He told me that he walked the whereabouts outside his new home on a regular basis in the early mornings. After all, he built the house because he loved the land for himself and Betty and his children's happiness at home while in the local schools.

One time, he said to me that he sees the early morning mountain fog clearing as it divides the mountains into layers of different visual atmospheres. Also, he said he was distracted by a deer. It stunned me as he walked into fields of soft overgrown grass heading to a hillside of pine and white oak trees and low-lying shrubbery behind the home backing mountains that extend high toward backlands of West Virginia mountains. He paused to notice discolorations of greenery that had been changing to golden yellows and scattered reds, all stressing toward oranges prevailing.

With some mental strain, he sensed me with more talk and words about his memories. He felt consciously about my writing previously two different stories about Mom and Dad to unveil some of the main characters of this new story to establish *rules* for this creative memoir. Frank wanted to know if the story would be confabulation of our lives' behavior over our lifetimes. Frank's involvement as the helper in his times has told mentally extract memories of this story to me that should present arguments and activities of natural behavior, however informal, in a manner that his words commonly made clear rather than complex or ambiguous to readers. The answers to his questions began to expose my new composition, *Steerage and Amour!—What's It All About!*

Keep in mind there were times when other elder family members might personally recall memories and provide details about my father's life as a boy while in Sicily. At that time, he was named Liborio and even referenced his name after his grandfather Liborio Divita. Little would be known about Liborio except how he behaved around his momma and poppa. Later and much later in age after immigrating to America, he was renamed Benjamin Franklin Divita and was called Big Benny. There were times when he responded with memories of times as Frank's dad recalled and expressed certain life ventures and their influences when he lived in Sicily. Later, after our father's marriage, he continued to follow his momma's teaching on subjects related to "Steerage and Amour!—What's It All About!" He learned from his mother Filippa, who loved the life he lived.

Frank also accomplished this poised venture from his father after their siblings were born and had changed his name in mid-1925s; he was called by many as Big Benny. Being the eldest son, he overheard things by his nature of inquisitiveness or he was told by family members and people close with detail including our mother and dad's brothers. When it comes to divulging behavior of my father himself and his immediate family, this was a chore of family *steerage* and *amour*. It was mostly from my father's point of view, and his "knowledge and experience" was gained by being self-taught because it was in a different era of peoples' behavior.

Frank only had a clinging grasp in his memory in his early years. Then during teen life in the mid-'40s, he had not only lived through the Great Depression but also knew more about beginnings of World War II from simply interacting with his dad at home listening to news and following his dad's associated patriotic and political interests with constant conversational uptake when together. In his mind, like others, it affected his emotional shock of a major war and a tug of his heartstrings because Italians earlier in the war were fighting with Germany. This only happened for a short time, but it upgraded his interests in being an American. Dad knew that he added truth to himself as a self-guide, having become an Italian emigrant that enhanced his mind-set as having been taught by his momma Filippa.

Frank's memory after experiencing his young life as a kid was surely attentive. After reaching a mature sixteen, his mind predominantly went from good to stable with grand storage of related memories of the war. Frank's memories stored in his minded detailed good behavior during the war. What he remembered most was that his dad was immensely engrossed with his amiable ways and adopted a gainful expressive personality daily from friends and acquaintances. His behavior with people encounters was always under control no matter how trying circumstances abound. As a qualified quote, he would say to friends, "My dad was secretly known as a peacemaker within his extended family and friends and with regular people and always greeted new people." This quote in my mind fits his demeanor.

As in the past where it all started, Frank recalled within the story of these stimulated exposés of my dad about his paternal grandfather Francesco, by being his father's eldest son, from his humble beginnings with his wife Filippa in Italy and eventually to their emigrant family's ambitious and substantial life in America. With a finality as Dad proceeded into a much more present time, I observed Fran, one of Frank's twin sons, years later, also an eldest son; but I am more critically knowledgeable about his three girls, all older than Fran and Jimmy.

And as I let Frank relay part of his memories of this story, some of lore from his memory to my memory primarily related to incidences of familial *steerage* and *amour* as told over years piecemeal for good done by Divita family elders.

As for continuity and later, Frank confided in me for reasons and concerns about his life's times taken in context while gaining an understanding of fundamentals exclaimed in the titled story *Steerage and Amour!—What's It All About!* I was involved with him at times, being six years younger than him but old enough to understand what was going on. I delivered and then sold on sidewalks downtown the *Charleston Gazette Extras* that was about the war's end. The city folks, while standing on the corner of his taxi place, were totally gathered with my dad in grand conversations.

I could see it in my dad Benny's smiling face and swinging Italian arms in gestures that he expressed his happiness. It was his speed of storytelling as humorously relayed to his excited gathering of crowds. He ejaculated words about gearing up with a new suit and shoes for the big Indy 500 Race that had happened back in 1946. The reason was that this next race was the most important race to him because it gave him self-stature with friends that he thought he might never make from his humble beginnings. His achievements had little beyond normal ratings but mixing with people who loved the same things he loved. Conversations allowed him to mentally inject, using his quite capable brain, a sense of a great deal of ongoing national significance with unending charm and having experienced reliving his memories of the people killed caused by the megalomaniac Hitler. From his facial expression and movements of his body, he loved the action of times as he relished talking about happenings in America and throughout the world when this grossly significant World War II ended.

I will save details of my father's trip to the new extravagantly renovated Indianapolis Speedway 500 Race in 1946 for your full edification later. Keep in mind, this race was attended by him and some friends for the first time since the 1941 race. After the Indy 500 was stopped in 1941, the World War II was declared by America on December 11, 1941, against Germany and Japan, but the overall war was already under way by Germany.

The persons involved in rebuilding the Indy 500 Speedway Facility amalgamated stature gained all sites immediately after the war, along with the current owner, Mr. Anton Hulman, and solid devotees that included Gen. Eddie Rickenbacker, a famous aviator in World War I. What all will remember is it was restarted after the end of World War II under a highly received revitalization of one of the most famous car racing sites of the century for the United States of America. The revelation of coming races will be phenomenally conducive to new and unknown venture for owners, drivers, and teams of new cars, and a revamping of the complete Indianapolis racetrack center. The hype that every race car driver is expected to excel beyond past records was broadcast across our country and Europe. The planned enticements to new and old race car drivers and previous devotees and fans were trumpeted in every newspaper and on every radio across the country.

The rejuvenation of the 1946 Indy 500 Race had significant undertones of "hurrahs" from every direction across the globe with the complete win of World War II and, of course, the *new track design* that sparked and ignited unprecedented anticipation and planned attendance. Unknowingly instilled would be an excitement of youthful fantasies of *amour* if not *steerage* in the minds of many. Even matured men of power, substance, and accomplishments will have aims unexpectedly at women at the race, some with good friendly involvements and others with illicit ideas.

My family's hyperpersonal behavior caused by newspaper reviews of past events of the Indy 500 1946 Race was exacerbated by my dad in conversations. He relived his manifested self-ingested memories of onslaughts of conflicts between professional car racers, ones he knew or that he had met during the last races in 1941 by chance.

Later when he told excerpts of his experiences, he essentially put news in his children's minds and especially in vogue in town that friends tagged along in his company to hear vented vignettes of the race details. And among a few if any associated amorous expectation stories were implied in conversations, or he may have told amorous stories about the Indy 500 Race that he would be able to reveal. His extravagant comedic excitement imposed in tales increased risks that listeners with instill mentally experiences of *amour* to the point of criticality in minds of entranced young persons with facial writhe that showed a bend spontaneously as he ejaculated with humor.

The outcomes of each new amorous venture reached a parallax crescendo as if in a revolutionary change of the sighting of stars. A later revelation under protected privacy conditions, several of life experiences of our racing devotees, adult friends who were at the race, were herein exposed as folklore without sources. The changes as hearsay, which leaked out with added humor if not hyperbole, could make told complexities reveal dishonesty, infidelity, and, oddly enough, confirmation of loyalty among amorous relationships, but, typically, they were more sociable.

The critical event is one that Big Benny identified unexpectedly early but one that magnetically drew individuals to enjoin within the mind a mighty desire to race cars whenever the chance of the experience may reboot from memory. Thank

God that the fright of dangerous perils surrounded a sense of potential damage to life, limb, and property with unbounded personal and economic cost penalty.

Based on what Frank knew later as a man—namely, what was prying memories from his mind—was that he will eventually see his son's detailed experiences with cars inherited unrelentingly. Frank knew that cars were driving him in a direction in which he might go down in flames. Dad's newest sayings when at professional races, where timing is so automatically voiced mentally, were that some cars might crash and burn. From outcomes of precursor experiences within Frank's memory list, his dad mulled over whether to help his son solve his self-weaved problems of *amour* instinctively while gaining little money in his childhood days. Then out loud, Frank shouted to me, "Wow! What a potential happy outcome headin' my way."

Frank thought he knew later complications would develop from his heritage and his emotional drive might challenge his wife-to-be's well-being as a partner in his life's follies. Even when Frank was told about a pending partnership with a woman who was involved, he knew without trying to figure the reason that his newly formed partnership might disperse his amalgamated childhood dream of designing, building, and owning a race car. Frank much later had told Fran to remain working at the dealership in Kentucky where the money that he gets paid will take care of his family.

A good example of an old memory of a confrontational brouhaha between Frank's dad Benny and his brother Tony was the disposition of the Blue Ribbon Bus Line deal that my father had originally owned. However, our dad, the peacemaker for family members, showed his giving the total Blue Ribbon Bus Line from his heart. He gave his brother Tony his half via a shake of hands and turned it over to Tony lock, stock, and barrel when Tony was down and out. How Tony could have survived even for a little while was questionable, but it was never a point of contention between brothers. The Blue Ribbon Bus Line did not make it into the late 1930s, but two brothers moved to other working ways. Tony got a job being a policeman in Montgomery, and Dad put together his taxi and transfer services, and in the next ten years, there were difficult lulus including World War II and new advancements in technology and creations of new devices and many upgrades unknown into the late 1940s.

Now, up to 1950, Frank had wondered within his memory as he told me, "How do I fit being married and being a faithful husband? I know I have a strong family credibility, a sensible and strong business acumen, and always was suspiciously interested in politics and wondering how to help the city grow socially as Montgomery, where it was so positioned among potential expansions being the hub that maintained good businesses." Beyond that, Frank pondered. He left it up to those who knew him, and then he left because he was drafted into the Korean War; but with some personal knowledge and with a family started, he decided to join the air force. My explanation of the differences eventually contrived situations and a position that led him to join an air force band in New York.

Two years later, when he was out of the air force, he gained a teaching music in Peterstown, West Virginia, that had been concocted for and against him for the next few years because the pay for a small town was low. The spread of expected involvements critically influenced his generational and cultural opportunities supplemented by his attractive disposition and achievements. What must he use as a first opportunity?

His choice happened after he moved back to Montgomery and moved in with Mom and Dad to help improve his taxi business. This was a gain in presence and demeanor with loyalty to the family and city. Within a few years, he was voted in as part of the city council and later as the mayor of Montgomery.

Later, a second story from what I had been told by him several times in his job was when he was at a business dinner meeting in Kanawha Falls, and he explained surprising results—that is, at that time after the dinner, he was totally pleaded by a known woman whom he had inadvertently met to drive her home. As he said, "All I did was made sure she got home. Then I drove to my home without noting it, but to no avail, because I thought it was not noticed by anyone else." Frank also knew that a significantly different result happened because he had heard about a friend who made up allegations of a so-called amorous portrayal of which he was falsely accused. The whole matter did not contain a hint that an amorous pursuit was initiated, and especially one in which he did not participate.

My goal was to be the listener of Frank's continuous revelations and delivery over the times in our togetherness during his path of life that he conducted in a clear and decisive way. Frank, at this time, recalled a bit of "Will Rogersesque" humor from his days because he was politically minded. He talked about existing major government members that inadvertently revealed their political behavior, even when chasms were apart in truth, especially his grandfather Big Poppy, who was beyond a light-year's distance to understand the potential of criticism.

This fancifully capricious tragicomedy is about lives of these four genetically related multifarious men from a common extended Italian family plagued with sudden changes of mind or action all exacerbated mentally and physically with emotional commitment, even while well able to apply their intelligence based on God given "knowledge and experience."

I am sure a woman's instinctively unquenchable amorous passion and desire found it difficult to ignore Frank in conversation. Some of the men his age were instilled with chauvinistic lifestyles regardless of their marital status, moral and religious convictions, ideology, and expected social and cultural deportment. All these men types do not disclose their secretive steps in common discourse. Instead, he used compassion and sensitivity even though, obviously, sexism and prejudices are revealed in their dominating personalities. Even some were laughable, but mostly, regrettable allegations turned out to be falsely spread.

This family's story is one of abundance of love and lacking marital betrayal, maybe the latter word is too strong a word; but it steers some partners to distraction if not to a terrible family life in the long run. Many times, instinctively passionate pursuits by men who are professedly in love with their mates do not mentally support an adequate motivation to stray. Sometimes, stray is caused by a whim taken on as a lark in a frivolous associative adventure where coalescing sparks enhanced inadvertent pursuit. The pursuit can be exacerbated with drinks or drugs during a hilarious time at a party or a gathering even of family and friends. In some families, both men and women in the past have been under the influence of alcohol or stoned with marijuana, distorted by cocaine or an opium pipe, heroin and lysergic acid diethylamide (LSD).

Now, in present days, senselessly immobilized people use methamphetamine, and in extreme cases, an amorous pursuit could spark use of ecstasy or comparable drugs. Under any of these drug-caused frailties that cause a personality distortion, sidetracking a reasonable mentality, ones that indulge may innately and magnetically become an easy mark by a woman or a man under any of these mind-changing drug influences.

When the man is under a physically or mentally impaired situation involving infatuations, one may be in a hush-hush situation or he might take a sublime pursuit tasking his wits or assumed mental control to achieve desired results. And under some situations, he might use seat-of-the-pants emotions with little thought that usually don't payoff. In the end, the man either succumbs to better judgment by following sound moral or social principles, which is difficult under impairments, or, as do most men, most times, seeks amorous adventures and lives with the aftermath that follows.

The traits of women in these same assisted amorous but psychologically mental mood changes are similar but usually have less discernment and event exposure. However, when ventures are disclosed to many, resulting amorous outcomes are pretty much the same, and many times, the woman is a victim of self-debasement and a change of her way of life dominated by a lack of self-esteem.

As Darwin projected in *The Origin of Species*, his natural selection theory as the dominant way of life has progressed to its current state, even with aside induced mutations both mentally and physically randomly inherited distortions. The evolved processes add to and subtract from the brain's mind capability, and capacity will slow growth within the known nature of evolution by the Creator. God's plan included instilling it as part of continued evolution. Under the prime belief that God created the universe, it would be a simple accomplishment for him to extrapolate to let evolution proceed randomly by the Creator's intended creation in the making of detailed life-forms for the *universe* down to all beyond and even smaller microforms of life ad infinitum.

PART 2

EMIGRANT FAMILIES' LIVES AND TIMES ENABLE CHANGES

Note 2—Prudence is the proper rule of conduct.
Then he said all men have, and have had, a different purpose. For
Christians their purpose is Christ, for other men, both present and past,
it is and has been different, according to their persuasions.
—Friar Savonarola, in *The Man of the Renaissance*, Ralph
Roeder, The Viking Press, 18 East 48th St., New York, p. 108

But the past is rarely known, or the lesson
of the past is hardly followed.

Khaire says, "You don't manage the
creative process, you enable it."

In part 2, inherited *steerage* and *amour* in the first-generation American Divita family continued teaching their progeny as a first gift to their American-born children. The abled Italian-born Grandmother Filippa and to a degree some specifics from Grandfather Francesco in his unique ways taught by his demanding his way or the highway. A starting from Francesco's eldest son, Liborio, now called Big Benny in the United States, was Francisco's first birth from his loving parents, Benny and Josephine, in 1929. In this situation, Liborio was Francesco's grandfather Liborio, who was born in Sicily. Francisco's mother, Josephine Maruca, was born as a citizen in America on May 5, 1912, as were all who were born in America.

Josephine was raised in Clarksburg, West Virginia, and later, her family moved to Adrian, West Virginia. She was fully educated and accomplished in both Italian and English languages. Josephine had inherited the same methodology of teaching *steerage* and *amour* from her Maruca family. Josephine learned the teaching earlier. After their marriage, she continued the teaching discourse of *steerage* and *amour* the same as her Italian parents, as if emulated fully as Americana patriotism—*Cose il Italiana*.

Francisco, called Frankie as a child with his Americanized first name, involved some of the narrative as the protagonist from what he had recalled and what he relayed and revealed to me as the writer of this story as close brothers' incidences taken from his mind's memory of what had happened during his early personal life and the lives of his father and mother and the details of the same values that his siblings inherited. Frankie was an astute observer and mindful and, as a boy and the eldest son, certainly inherited the induced wisdom from many of his mother and father's ways of life and social behavior. He was taught as was his father, being the firstborn to his father Francesco. He even ignored occasions of opportunity to take the path of "will of desire" for minor misbehavior actions as a child; but instead, he concentrated on "knowledge and experience" taught by his parents. For the most part, he was the muse for his newly birthed siblings. The nature of his actions during their childhoods was commonly followed with a continued improvement through his relation of expressing his self-gained taught *steerage* and *amour*.

However, much later in his life, after he had gained public recognition and positions, one revelation primarily heard by hearsay occurred and continued to plague him in his married life. Later in life, after being happily married, he was brutally informed by his family members and friends that he was directly involved with a local woman that they made the infraction seem surrealistic, almost dreamlike, even an overexaggeration. Although against his teachings, much later, a somewhat refutable incident again arose that he was trapped by himself with whom he had spent some evening time mostly at a diner out of town that eventually led to a disastrous aftermath of disloyalty that was never proven, and unexpectedly, it led him to a finality that ended in him being the one who wanted the divorce after suffering from an exasperating disease.

During his many years of married life, the family's life exposures were continuously examined. The lives of his children had an obligation to follow his guidance of his gathering and expounding his regular words of wisdom on *steerage* and *amour,* as would many from day to day be related as if they had his inherited skills. It usually was not perceived by others and was not easily released from others' minds. The inherited wisdom flowed as if an ether of inescapable of inhaling was the extent of an unrecognized wisdom when decreed from his father and mother's guidance from early life to adulthood.

Being the eldest son, Frank, at a young age of ten to twelve, had revealed his thinking to his brothers and his one and only sister. He also would advise close family cousins and friends as they experience his life revealed in truth when together. What may have followed as hearsay was probably abandoned. Even when a third party proclaimed emphatically that it is the truth, he, with his mother's guidance without journalizing in records, until later in life, suspected it would end up being closer to his memories, and with little doubt.

The more he exclaimed the truth of his story, the better it was believed. The catch was an inordinate way that events turned out to involve closely related new friends and their dominating influence who were fascinated with his activities with cars as was his dad Big Benny, a fan of international race car events. Their actions were engulfed by these two self-made men of excitement and adventure.

Big Benny was associated with preeminent men and women friends in his taxi business owner's endeavors. Many of these past early personalities were in the minds of many people across the country, as are entertainers in art, music, motion pictures, and radio.

Much later, as Frank's life continued beyond the '50s, and Mom and Dad still self-sufficient and happily married, their experiences always had some involvement with cars. Then in the late '50s, the invention of television, which had delivered via reporting anchors and performing stars of sitcoms, and from newspapers of those days composed by popularized knowledgeable and experienced persons. People were educated and trained as professional journalists. Some political pundits were professionally educated in law, political science, and social environments of government activities. Newscasters were more factual and independent about politics; however, reporters are nowadays generally highly opinionated.

People of the past claimed former newscasters made factual daily revelations that reporters get corresponding inputs from newspapers, magazines, including books and popular pertinent publications. Even media and newspapers and other perfunctory methods of communication via opinions and editorial responses including line services, speeches, and prepared compositions were used to enhance personal usage of *Homo sapiens'* minds that also had the ability to inherit or to teach "Steerage and Amour !—What's It All About!"

The first step was Francesco, known as Big Poppy, always had the mind that the Divita family would relocate their children within several miles' distance from the *OverHome* that Francesco had started building earlier before the World War I and afterward again in the 1920s. He followed; his plan was then to complete buildings within two or three years to house his adult and growing children.

Many years later, children got older, and their two eldest boys almost in concert helped his brothers Benny and Tony's families move to Montgomery and to the nearby farm of Catherine's mom and dad, respectively; and away from Big Poppy's *OverHome* commune in Smithers, West Virginia. The distance was only a mile away from the city; familiar to families but far enough to gain significant privacy. Nevertheless, families had to respect primary teachers, primarily the matriarch Filippa, who kept the pursuit to instill *steerage* and *amour* by association. The continued teaching was by spending odd days and every Sunday when Filippa conversed with the children much of the day until dinner overtook the *OverHome*. Big Poppy and most families and Mother Filippa kept him in his good graces. All these changes happened up to the mid-1940s.

The need for education was noticeable during the next ten years; college time was by the elder ones. Each sibling jumped to participate in the real world of America starting with eldest children. This step was expected with grandiose teachings by Big Benny Divita's family. Frankie took the first step. Then other siblings followed the same path, and all earned professional college educations.

CHAPTER XIII

Peacemakers Conquer Steerage and Amour Heritage

*I have opened my heart to you more than I thought to do. There
is a reason for me to expose my soul, my body and all the learning
God has given me for love of him and for my salvation and else.*
— *The Man of the Renaissance*, Ralph Roeder, The
Viking Press, 18 East 48th St. New York, NY

The way of the peacemaker is hard.
— *First Principles*, part 1, 1862

Frank recounted to me many times that he observed his life's behavior during associations with families and relatives and associates during various involvements with close common friends. Frank released words of good feelings and understanding about the commonality that the appearances of people, both men and women, shone differently with discourse expressing their facial reactions. His personae had its unique body, facial expressions, and in his normally ejaculated words of expressions, both flared with sincerity and in tone. At times with some misleading verbosity, he used different words discharged by actions of their behavior. For Frank, the exchange was so difficult to be noticed because he explained with grandiose inflections depending on whom he might encounter as a man that tries to model after his father Big Benny.

However, with some women, he would sensuously accept a propensity for true *amour,* although he was sure that some ladies had been saddled in disloyal *amours.* A complete mental image of attractions and compliments of any sweet talk that surfaced to win the argument of true love became historic in Frank's attractions. He mostly instilled *steerage,* and it worked almost every time. Gravitating notices in his father's ways were the path that Frank followed from his parents leveled with married grandparents who had lived a long life together. They usually had joy within their minds because they maintained the pursuit of happiness.

As in the past, people desired the grasp of illegitimate *amour* even at the expense of suffering a lingering depression if not worse when it did not happen.

However, infinite ways and means divulged common paths to illicit *amour*, and he knew it would lead to an aftermath. The same methodology was always expended when amorous pursuits of times past were consummated, and he knew few continued to survive especially after notices had been exposed to deceived people.

This intent was obviously the way many things occurred from first existence of *Homo sapiens* mankind on earth. The sacrifice was grossly deserved because knowledge of end states was not judiciously released during happenings but with unknown belief that the Creator knew what the complete story of love was from beginning to mankind's end. When mankind evolved into *Homo sapiens*, they should have realized that they must believe the Creator had produced this universe that would force the wisdom of mankind in the direction toward immortality ad infinitum.

Disloyalty was characterized in mankind's mind usage. Everyone knows the instinctive part of minds that maintains survivability first as it was hardwired into the *Homo sapiens*. When a lesson from history was not learned or adhered, the expectation of results from history that one knows the aftermath will be repeated. That revelation to those who know teachers who continuously taught *steerage* and *amour* to nonbelievers did not use the mind's decision path that followed the teachings.

Yet I say many, if not most humans, take the course of living a mentally normal, natural life and live within the belief of the spirit of God the Creator. A moral life with companionship will not fault loyalty no matter the significance. Human beings feel the good life when they displayed their advantage on an even ground. When they falter and recover without failing significantly, they hold on to the positive while trying to reconcile their lives to partners. Many good but faltering human beings had to revalue themselves.

The deceits that plague some with mental distress and affliction jump into known amorous situations with unsuspected ramifications. Many are known as their memories later recall clearly that it led them to calamity. It's the mind's eye that triggers the unrelenting emotional response. And at times, it can be the sense of smell of ancient animalistic pheromones or a response to some sensed physical behavior even extrasensory perception within the mind. For example, if a man or woman's scented aroma attracts another with invisible musk seeking within the mind's sensory, it causes a seeping into open pores and releases unharnessed senses of musk to readied receptors. The musk creates an event that may or may not work depending on receptor's mental receivers. The mind's final approach includes insight, but it is driven by "direct instinctive behavior" that follows first. Then minds have tendencies to discard self-preservation and are pushed toward "knowledge and experience" judgments that raise emotions that can be mollified with thought.

When humans are aroused in whatever sensory way, whether one or a next one remains in a stable and controlled way depends on their overall reactions. All humans have listened with amazement to stories told about *amour* and mentally store those that made wrong decisions. The innocent ones maintain mental composure. The actual joy of ventures into a realm of sensuous emotion is considered by many to be as expected. But as they gain pleasures and conquest, they lose sight of unrecognized mandatory conditions imposed in mankind's mind of aftermaths.

Frank kept a tight rein on his prancing passions by quickly using a crafty cutting of pending desires with his mind's fiery slicing and deleting impassioned words. Members of families quickly recognized his absurdities, especially when one is making a fool of one's self. Everyone who is about to get involved knows as do the rest of the world that it is fools who embark on more common simpleminded paths when sensuously emotional attractions are enhanced as they are released. Warnings are taken in his mind to consider. Frank would say to me what he had may have said, "I'm not simpleminded. Will you listen to my point? Amorous incidences bring on the mind's timing to a decisive matter on how it comes about." Then he said to me, "Every woman or man wants committed partners to have loyalty and integrity, but to find one with devotion, who makes careful decisions, and one who thinks in a wise way, is rare."

As his best associate in the family, I was with Frank many times as he recalled his living time being with ease. He told me that he walked the whereabouts outside his new home on a regular basis in early mornings. After all, he built the house because he loved the land for himself and Betty and his children's happiness at home while in the local schools.

One time, he said to me that he sees the early morning mountain fog clearing as it divides the mountains into layers of different visual atmospheres. He said he was distracted by a deer. It stunned me as he walked into fields of soft overgrown grass heading to a hillside of pine and white oak trees and low-lying shrubbery behind the home backing mountains that extend high toward backlands of West Virginia mountains. He paused to notice discolorations of greenery that had been changing to golden yellows and scattered reds, all stressing toward oranges prevailing.

With some mental strain, he sensed me with more talk and words about his memories. He felt consciously about my writing previously two different stories about Mom and Dad to unveil some of the main characters of this new story to establish *rules* for this creative memoir.

Frank wanted to know if the story would be confabulation of our lives' behavior over our lifetimes. Frank's involvement as the helper in his times has told mentally extract memories of this story to me that should present arguments and activities of natural behavior, however informal, in a manner that his words commonly made clear rather than complex or ambiguous to readers. The answers to his questions began to expose my new composition: "Steerage and

Amour!—What's It All About!" Keep in mind there were times when other older family members might personally recall memories and provide details about my father's life as a boy while in Sicily.

At that time, when Big Benny was named Liborio, and even referenced his name after his grandfather Liborio Divita, little would be known about Liborio except how he behaved around his momma and poppa. Later, and much later in age after immigrating to America, he was renamed Benjamin Franklin Divita and was called Big Benny. There were times when he responded with memories of times as Frank's dad recalled and expressed certain life ventures and their influences when he lived in Sicily. Later, after our father's marriage, he continued to follow his momma's teaching on subjects related to "Steerage and Amour!— What's It All About!" He learned from his mother Filippa, who loved the life he lived.

Frank also accomplished this poised venture from his father after their siblings were born and had changed his name in mid-1925s; he was called by many as Big Benny. Being the oldest son, he overheard things by his nature of inquisitiveness or as he was told by family members and people close with detail including from our mother and dad's brothers. When it comes to divulging behavior of my father himself and his immediate family, this was a chore of family *steerage* and *amour*. It was mostly from my father's point of view, and his "knowledge and experience" were self-taught because it was in a different time era of people's behavior.

Frank only had a clinging grasp in his memory in his early years. Then during teen life in mid-'40s, he had not only lived through the Great Depression but also knew more about the beginnings of World War II from simply interacting with his dad at home, listening to news and following his dad's associated patriotic and political interests with constant conversational uptake when together. In his mind, like others, it affected his emotional shock of a major war and tugged at his heartstrings because Italians earlier in the war were fighting with Germany. This only happened for a short time, but it upgraded his interests in being an American. Dad knew that he added truth to himself as a self-guide, having become an Italian emigrant that enhanced his mind-set as having been taught by his momma Filippa.

Frank's memory, after experiencing his young life as a kid, was surely attentive. After reaching a mature sixteen, his mind predominantly went from good to stable with grand storage of related memories of the war. Frank's memories stored in his minded detailed good behavior during the war. What he remembered most was that his dad was immensely engrossed with his amiable ways and adopted a gainful expressive personality daily from friends and acquaintances. His behavior with people encounters was always under control no matter how trying circumstances abound. As a qualified quote, he would say to friends, "My dad was secretly known as a peacemaker within his extended family and friends and with regular people and always greeted new people." This quote in my mind fits his demeanor.

As in the past where it all started, Frank recalled within the story of these stimulated exposés of my dad about his paternal grandfather Francesco, by being his father's oldest son, from his humble beginnings with his wife Filippa in Italy and eventually to their emigrant family's ambitious and substantial life in America. With a finality as Dad proceeded into a much more present time, I observed Fran, one of Frank's twin sons years later, also an oldest son; but I am more critically knowledgeable about his three girls, all older than Fran and Jimmy.

And as I let Frank relay part of his memories of this story, some of lore, from his memory to my memory primarily related to incidences of familial *steerage* and *amour* as told over years piecemeal for good done by Divita family elders.

As for continuity and later, Frank confided in me for reasons and concerns about his life's times taken in context while gaining an understanding of fundamentals exclaimed in the titled story, *Steerage and Amour!—What's It All About!* I was involved with him at times, being six years younger than him but old enough to understand what was going on. I delivered and then sold on sidewalks downtown the *Charleston Gazette* extras that were about the war's end. The city folks, while standing on the corner of his taxi place, were totally gathered with my dad in grand conversations.

I could see it in my dad Benny's smiling face and swinging Italian arms in gestures that he expressed his happiness. It was his speed of storytelling as humorous relayed to his excited gathering of crowds. He ejaculated words about gearing up with a new suit and shoes for the big Indy 500 Race back in 1946. This race was the most important race to him because it gave him self-stature with friends that he thought he might never make from his humble beginnings. His achievements had little beyond normal ratings but mixing with people who loved the same things he loved. Conversations allowed him to mentally inject, using his quite capable brain, a sense of a great deal of ongoing national significance with unending charm and having experienced reliving his memories of the people killed caused by the megalomaniac Hitler. From his facial expression and movements of his body, he loved the action of times as he relished talking about happenings in America and throughout the world when this grossly significant World War II ended.

Notice that I will save details of my father's trip from memories told afterward to me by Frank about the extravagantly renovated Indianapolis Speedway 500 Race in 1946 for your full edification later. Keep in mind this race had been attended by him and some friends for the first time since the 1941 race. Afterward, the Indy 500 was stopped in 1941; the World War II was declared by America on December 11, 1941, against Germany and Japan, but the overall war was already underway by Germany.

The persons involved in rebuilding the Indy 500 Speedway Facility amalgamated stature gained all sites immediately after the war, along with the current owner, Mr. Anton Hulman, and solid devotees that included Gen. Eddie Rickenbacker, a famous aviator in World War I. What all will remember is it was restarted after the end of World War II under a highly received revitalization of one of the most famous car racing sites of the century for United States of America. The revelation of coming races will be phenomenally conducive to new and unknown venture for owners, drivers, and teams of new cars, and a revamping of the complete Indianapolis racetrack center. The hype that every race car driver is expected to excel beyond past records was broadcasted across our country and Europe. The planned enticements to new and old race car drivers and previous devotees and fans were trumpeted in every newspaper and on every radio across the country.

The rejuvenation of the 1946 Indy 500 Race had significant undertones of "hurrahs" from every direction across the globe with the complete win of World War II and, of course, the *new track design* that sparked and ignited unprecedented anticipation and planned attendance. Unknowingly instilled would be an excitement of youthful fantasies of *amour,* if not *steerage,* in the minds of many. Even matured men of power, substance, and accomplishments will have aims unexpectedly at women at the race, some with good friendly involvements and others with illicit ideas.

My family's hyperpersonal behavior caused by newspaper reviews of past events of the Indy 500 1946 Race was exacerbated by my dad in conversations. He relived his manifested self-ingested memories of onslaughts of conflicts between professional car racers, ones he knew or had met during last races in 1941 by chance.

Later when he told excerpts of his experiences, he essentially put news in his children's minds and especially in vogue in town that friends tagged along in his company to hear vented vignettes of the race details. And among a few if any associated amorous expectation, stories were implied in conversations, or he may have told amorous stories about the Indy 500 Race that he would be able to reveal. His extravagant comedic excitement imposed in tales increased risks that listeners will instill mental experiences of *amour* to the point of criticality in minds of entranced young persons with facial writhe that showed a bend spontaneously as he ejaculated with humor.

The outcomes of each new amorous venture reached a parallax crescendo as if in a revolutionary change of the sighting of stars. A later revelation under protected privacy conditions, several life experiences of our racing devotees, adult friends who were at the race, were herein exposed as folklore without sources. The changes as hearsay, which leaked out with added humor if not hyperbole, could make told complexities reveal dishonesty, infidelity, and, oddly enough, confirmation of loyalty among amorous relationships, but, typically, they were more sociable.

The critical event is one that Big Benny identified unexpectedly early but one that magnetically drew individuals to enjoin within the mind a mighty desire to race cars whenever the chance of the experience may reboot from memory. Thank God that the fright of dangerous perils surrounded a sense of potential damage to life, limb, and property with unbounded personal and economic cost penalty.

Based on what Frank knew later as a man—namely, what was prying memories from his mind—was that he will eventually see his son's detailed experiences with cars inherited unrelentingly. Frank knew that cars were driving him in a direction in which he might go down in flames. Dad's newest saying when at professional races, where timing is so automatically voiced mentally, was that some cars might crash and burn. From outcomes of precursor experiences within Frank's memory list, his dad mulled over whether to help his son solve his self-weaved problems of *amour* instinctively while gaining little money in his childhood days. Then out loud, Frank shouted to me, "Wow! What a potential happy outcome headin' my way."

Frank thought he knew that later complications would develop from his heritage and his emotional drive might challenge his wife-to-be's well-being as a partner in his life's follies. Even when Frank was told about a pending partnership with a woman who was involved, he knew without trying to figure the reason that his newly formed partnership might disperse his amalgamated childhood dream of designing, building, and owning a race car. Frank, much later, had told Fran to remain working at the dealership in Kentucky where the money that he gets paid will take care of his family.

A good example of an old memory of a confrontational brouhaha between Frank's dad Benny and his brother Tony was the disposition of the Blue Ribbon Bus Line deal that my father had originally owned. However, our dad, the peacemaker for family members, showed his giving the total Blue Ribbon Bus Line from his heart. He gave his brother Tony his half via a shake of hands and turned it over to Tony lock, stock, and barrel when Tony was down and out. How Tony could have survived even for a little while was questionable, but it was never a point of contention between brothers. The Blue Ribbon Bus Line did not make it into the late 1930s, but two brothers moved to other working ways. Tony got a job being a policeman in Montgomery, and Dad put together his taxi and transfer services, and the next ten years were difficult lulus including World War II and new advancements in technology and creations of new devices and many upgrades unknown into the late 1940s.

Now, up to 1950, Frank had wondered within his memory as he told me, "How do I fit to become married and be a faithful husband? I know I have a strong family credibility, a sensible and strong business acumen, and always was suspiciously interested in politics and wondering how to help the city grow socially as Montgomery where it was so positioned among potential expansions being the hub that maintained good businesses." Beyond that, Frank pondered. He left it up to those who knew him, and then he left because he was drafted into the Korean War; but with some personal knowledge and with a family started, he decided to join the air force. My explanation of the differences eventually contrived situations and a position that led him to join an air force band in New York.

Two years later, when he was out of the air force, he gained a teaching music in Peterstown, West Virginia, which had been concocted for and against him for the next few years because the pay for a small town was low. The spread of expected involvements critically influenced his generational and cultural opportunities supplemented by his attractive disposition and achievements. What must he use as a first opportunity?

Frank's choice happened after he moved back to Montgomery and moved in with Mom and Dad to help improve his taxi business. This was a gain in presence and demeanor with loyalty to the family and city. Within a few years, he was voted in as part of the city council and later as the mayor of Montgomery.

Later, a second story from what I had been told by him several times in his job when he was at a business dinner meeting in Kanawha Falls and he explained surprising results—that is, at that time after the dinner, he was totally pleaded by a known woman whom he had inadvertently met to drive her home. As he said, "All I did was made sure she got home. Then I drove to my home without noting it, but to no avail, because I thought it was not noticed by anyone else." Frank also knew that a significantly different result happened because he had heard about a friend who made up allegations of a so-called amorous portrayal of which he was falsely accused. The whole matter did not contain a hint that an amorous pursuit was initiated, and especially one in which he did not participate.

My goal was to be the listener of Frank's continuous revelations and delivery over the times in our togetherness during his path of life that he conducted in a clear and decisive way. Frank, at this time, recalled a bit of "Will Rogers-esque" humor from his days because he was politically minded. He talked about existing major government members that inadvertently revealed their political behavior, even when chasms were apart in truth, especially his grandfather Big Poppy, who was beyond a light-year's distance to understand the potential of criticism.

This fancifully capricious tragicomedy is about the lives of these four genetically related multifarious men from a common extended Italian family plagued with sudden changes of mind or action all exacerbated mentally and physically with emotional commitment, even while well able to apply their intelligence based on God-given "knowledge and experience."

I am sure a woman's instinctively unquenchable amorous passion and desire found it difficult to ignore Frank in conversation. Some men his age were instilled with chauvinistic lifestyles regardless of their marital status, moral and religious convictions, ideology, and expected social and cultural deportment. All these men do not disclose their secretive steps in common discourse. Instead, he used compassion and sensitivity, even though obviously sexist, and prejudices are revealed in their dominating personalities. Even some were laughable, but mostly regrettable allegations turned out to be falsely spread.

This family's story is one of an abundance of love and lacking marital betrayal. Maybe the latter word is too strong a word, but it steers some partners to distraction if not to a terrible family life in the long run. Many times, instinctively passionate pursuits by men who are professedly in love with their mates do not mentally support an adequate motivation to stray. Sometimes, straying is caused by a whim taken on as a lark in a frivolous associative adventure where coalescing sparks enhanced inadvertent pursuit. The pursuit can be exacerbated with drinks during a hilarious time at a party or a gathering even of family and friends. In some families, both men and women in the past have been under the influence of alcohol or, much later, even stoned with marijuana, distorted by cocaine or an opium pipe, heroin, and LSD well into the late '60s to the '80s.

Now, in present days, senselessly immobilized people use methamphetamine, and in extreme cases, an amorous pursuit could spark use of ecstasy or comparable drugs. Under any of these drug-caused frailties that cause personality distortion, sidetracking a reasonable mentality, ones that indulge may innately and magnetically become an easy mark by a woman or a man under any of these mind-changing drug influences.

When man is under a physically or mentally impaired situation involving infatuations, one may be in a hush-hush situation, or he might take a sublime pursuit tasking his wits or assumed mental control to achieve desired results. And under some situations, he might use seat-of-the-pants emotions with little thought that usually do not payoff. In the end, the man either may succumb to better judgment by following sound moral or social principles, which is difficult under impairments, or he may, as do most men, most times, seek amorous adventures and live with the aftermath that follows.

The traits of women in these same assisted amorous but psychologically mental mood changes are similar but usually have less discernment and event exposure. However, when ventures are disclosed to many, resulting amorous outcomes are pretty much the same, and many times, the woman is a victim of self-debasement and a change of her way of life dominated by a lack of self-esteem.

As Darwin projected in *On the Origin of Species*, his natural selection theory as the dominant way life has progressed to its current state, even with aside induced mutations both mentally and physically randomly inherited distortions. The evolved processes added to and subtracted from the brain's mind capability and capacity with slow growth only within the known nature of evolution by the Creator. God's plan included instilling it as part of continued evolution. Under the prime belief that God created the universe, it would be a simple accomplishment for him to extrapolate to let evolution proceed randomly by the Creator's intended creation in the making of detailed life-forms for the *universe* down to all beyond and even smaller microforms of life, ad infinitum.

CHAPTER XIV

Americana Patriotism—"Cose Tutto Il Italiana!"

Socrates said: "Know thyself. Many philosophers before
him . . . had sought for the physics of nature of external things.
That is very good, said Socrates; but there is an infinitely worthier
subject . . ., and even all those stars; there in the mind of man.
"What is man, and what can he become? So, he went about
prying into the human soul, . . . [Asking]. What is it?

"What do you mean by honor, virtue, morality, patriotism?
What do you mean by yourself? [Socrates tout de suite]
definitive answers to two of our most difficult problems—What
is the meaning of virtue? And—What is the best state?

"If for example, good meant intelligent and virtue meant
wisdom, . . . The intelligent man may have the same violent and
unsocial impulses as the ignorant man, but sure he will control
them better, and slip less often into imitation of the beast.

"Surely the management of a state is a matter for which men
cannot be too intelligent, a matter that needs the unhindered
thoughts of the finest minds. How can a society be saved,
or be strong, except it be led by its wisest men?"
—The Story of Philosophy, Will Durant, pp. 9–10

Frank narrates behavior within his family as he observed his extended
family's behavior during the inherited Italian teachings of *steerage* and *amour* with
continuous guidance and associations with the Divita family. Big Poppy and
Big Mommy's family started our first-generation Americans and continued to
produce educated and productive modern-day families with relationships and

close friends. Italian descendants say, "We are what we are!"—that is, "*Cose Tutto il Italiana!*" (everything Italian), but we are Americans now and forever.

Some Italians that became American emigrants gained or lost from their heritage because of personal conflicts, emotional desires, and personal common sense without circumspect, be it man or woman and whether they plan to go back and stay in their homeland of Italy. Immigration is difficult at a minimum, and most people are likely warned by intelligent leaders or friends to stay in their countries, but to no avail. Therefore, early emigrants mostly treated their interactions and confrontations or an immediate pursuit, be it instinctive, mind-bending with words that might inflame or with a quick wit that brings laughter. The young and some older, for sure, knew Italians could be worse than expected, but resettlement likely satisfied the new gain from poverty or worse with the opportunity to work in a free country.

With a lack of respect, one knows when an amorous desire is offered with perfidious action when a desirous act is pugilistic. One sizes his opponent like a boxer at bell time fulfilled with fight. At other times at work, with a deciding mind like Frank's would clear the confusion and friendship would remain. This observance blended with unconscionable disregard of one's religious faith, although many Italians are typically still practicing Christians and simply fares rightfully to continued Catholicism ardently in America.

As mentioned earlier, seafaring immigration trips to America came about. Travelers needed some mental understand of traveling hardships, but they also had stored an expectation of what their reward would be once in America. In this story, the Divita family was first to leave Sicily. Francesco left with his brother Paulo trekking to Palermo, Sicily, in clean clothes not pressed but certainly looking like an intended and dignified men but will be installed as a *steerage* traveler. During their walk in a semidark foggy night, it soon followed with a light rain in the evening on that epoch day, July 15, 1910, both, with only a sense of what was intended, never suspected what was to be expected.

What was more to the point, they were without any close friends but later met Maria Divita Smeraldo (Smiraldi), a married sister of the two men, being Francesco and Paulo Divita. After all the talk and planning of many associates at work, a group of Divitas immigrated, and two sons of Liborio Divita Sr., my great-grandfather, maybe had lived with the Smeraldo family in New York. Everyone knows Italians had the same intent embedded in their minds to go to the United States of America to gain a fair and better living and to eventually bring out their families.

Along their way to the seaport city, business and residential buildings changed from small nested houses to industrial warehouses and more activity than had ever been seen with a continual immigration activity. Francesco said in a low measured voice in Italian with a slight cough, "Siamo sicuri di ciò che stiamo facendo? Abbiamo solo una piccola quantità di lire, non-molto denaro in America." (Are we sure of what we are doing? We have only a small amount of lira. Not much in America money.)

Paulo laughed and was quickly more serious again with facial lips' corners contorted downwardly in an imagination of recognition as he said, "Se questo è solo quello che stiamo portando con noi, è meglio che torni a casa, Dio e tutti gli altri sanno quando lasci il tuo paese non ce l'hai per portarlo con te. È quello che puoi fare quando arrivi lì che sarà continua così!" (If this is only what we are taking with us, we better go back home. God and everyone else know when you leave your country, you don't have it to take it with you. It's what you can do when you get there that will keep you going!)

Large cranes were clanging and ringing with loads of steel beams moving to safely hold back dirt taken out for sewer lines. Francesco snidely said, "Che cosa hai detto? Tutto quello che riesco a sentire sono le gru che muovono grandi travi di acciaio e scatole di corde in bretelle. Uh! Camion che trasportano e scaricano merci tutto il giorno." (What did you say? All I can hear are cranes moving big steel beams and roped boxes in braces. Uh! Trucks carrying and unloading goods all day long.)

Even with noisy cranes, some cranes were hanging idle, some with men smoking stogies. The surrounding area where eyes could see within the dusk, workmen were ready for lifting action to move things into place at a moment's notice. They both looked at each other and in unison said, "Siamo al molo!" (We are at the docks!) Within a few hundred feet, many more Italians and wanderers from nearby countries gathered into paths toward ships, a plethora of undirected human beings unknowing of what *steerage* on ships implies to a journey on the sea. The travelers are saturated with one thought only—that they are heading to personal freedom in America.

All are observed unknowingly by their God because they appear heartily satisfied. The intended position expected to be taken on board the ship along with the trip cruise time in the Atlantic Ocean will take its toll on both mind's content and personal body safety, navigable ocean passable behavior, and seasickness treatments and suffering. For some adults, it could be vitally painful, if not critical, with critical concerns for children who will suffer among the travelers.

As the two men stood in line, they met with several friendly Italian men who were laughing and bragging on the cloth sign displayed as they deciphered it. "American leadership is for freedom" is a symbol that the United States is the ship's destination, and all who have tickets already know the destination. The christening name imprinted on the ship SS *Sicilia* is plain to them that it's an Italian-owned ship. What they did not know was that all boarding was to become as *steerage passengers* for the next eight to ten days heading to New York. Few if any of these emigrants have seafaring experience on crowded liners. They were in for a critical tossing and turning unlike any nausea ever experienced. Most will suffer enough so that they will recall it for a lifetime. And as well, the experience will be recalled in detail, grimacing for all who simply ask about the trip and gets snowed with sickness complaints unfathomable.

After four or five hours, even with the light beaming as the sun began to rise, each man, woman, and child beamed with energy with excited characteristic facial expressions of depression with head and stomach pain; hand gestures galore as they talked and recollected times of the past as if the future was not only a change but also a new beginning of grand expectations.

Their manner of display made it possible to understand each other without hearing the words, a mental transference if not induced telepathy. Each one could tell when various Italian dialects became clear. Their mentally ostentatiously oral ejaculations were Italian plain enough so that each person's plan was simply understood. Everyone wants to get a job. In their hearts, they are on a venture to seek the freedom to express their life in America. The words translated come out as each almost simultaneously said, "Posso fare parte del lavoro America tener que offrire." (I can do any of the work America has to offer.) Each man had a will to carry out their feeble plan with most of the time spent simply knowing, as said in Italian, "Si voleva ottenere una casa per la famiglia." (They wanted to obtain a home for their family.) They do not want their families controlled by governmental aristocrats.

As they entered, the port area was full of machinery driven slowly to dodge people scattered throughout but to move supplies and baggage to the ship. They were ordered with many others to mark their baggage, take tag receipts, and put bags on specific stopped trams. That was the last time they would see their bags until they made their way to the *steerage area* of the ship where they can claim it. Now, they were moving closer to the ship among an enormous mass of Italians of all classes engaging odors of life from perfumes in vulgar Italian, as noted by many out loud, "Perfume and escrementi or merda." As it was in the fog and evening, one could not tell from who it was coming.

The mass of people began boarding bumping and rubbing against each other with numerous Italian dialects of ongoing conversations and complaints, some of which may not be understandable to each other but not to all. Many were shouting at ship's sailors to make sure they understood directions they were giving the people. After making it up the ramp of the SS *Sicilia* headed to New York, they gained a sigh of relief. However, with no known prospects of a continued life under the pending trip, they stood in awe gaping at the levy full of loneliness.

Hours later, everyone was on board, and the ship was tugged from the Tyrrhenian Sea to the open Mediterranean Sea. Each passenger of all status or class was on a new venture across the Atlantic, and with great enthusiasm both understood and expressed by all in Italian, "Este que vive?" (This is our life.) It is in captain's hands while they were making the voyage.

Many of these new venturous passengers were aware that what America was offering had to be better because they were living in squalor. People who were pursuing freedom could see no way out. The political strife had become a mess in Italy even before the 1900s. People were mostly confounded and confused and bewildered with all of Europe's political ideology and practicing royalty and aristocratic control by the self-ordained patricians of the vitiated countries.

The ones who had quasi-good longtime jobs were fluent enough to know what was going on, and outside of Italy, they knew that several miner friends had written to their families that opportunities, especially for hardworking Italians, were waiting for those with special skills and that numerous jobs were available because of the growth of the country since the industrial revolution in the mid-1800s.

The point of immigration presented by the United States government to be relayed by the Italian Immigration Agency was that there was plenty of work in New York and other major cities in the country. It was true, but unknown to the hungry job seekers, it was primarily hard labor that involved the grunt work needed to build new buildings in the city and to replace dirt roads with hard surface roads of macadam surfacing material, which was flourishing across the country as automobiles were now budding in the spring of life. Major cross-country railroads were in their midlife expansions all the way to western states.

The two Italians, Francesco and his younger brother Paulo, now full-fledged emigrants, were innocent if their future might offer better than the life they were leaving, which was potentially extended despair and poverty that started around the late 1890s in Italy. With such depression and lack of good government, they conveniently ignored what was in store for them in America. Their minds were saddled with a bright-eyed, deep breath of joy that positively caused the emotional seeping of hormones from the adrenal glands to make the move and then make it work. No questions were asked by wives who had let their lives begin with raising newborn children, so, typically, subservient as common women in this past thriving age of patricians. The common folk were desperate and could see America as a better future in the only country on the horizon, as their starter families only had help of their peasant parents of little means who had less than poverty-stricken people in America.

That being the situation, the time to make a move had dawned. Francesco tried pursuing the best thing available but with the most uncertainty with the hope that a new life would be better than that currently being endured now that he was newly married. Any man who had a normal allegiance to his new wife could see going to America as a genuine way of reshaping their lives; although of even minimal well-being, some would jump at chances even to leave their country. As newlyweds, they were proud Italian patriots, and their homeland was never the question; it was personal well-being for their children.

Italy was confused and full of political consternation at the highest levels of leadership and those who plot to gain leadership. The times of distress had imposed economic recession, and hard times were pervasive on the peasants' daily lives. The disastrous conditions were worsened because money was undervalued in Italy's inflationary conditions, and from the beginning, peasants had very little money. The peasants left in droves as families when accepted. Many Italian men left, even sacrificing family life to go to America because the *dream* of a job and making *money* was the only thing the poor had to hold on to knowing the family will continue to suffer Italy's woes until they could immigrate.

Once in America, the men easily found work; it was hard work, but the pay was well above what one could expect to earn in Italy. What was the work? That's easy; it was daily hard work on roads, and every day, the same thing with overseers demanding that more be completed. The management imposed stringent working ways and friendly reminded us not to waste time in conversation except a lunch stop time.

Most of the men shared living quarters and their daily victuals. Little time was spent in the evenings, but at an odd time, a few drinks or some wine at home made life better the next day, and we worked harder than the day before. Our jobs were secure because the labor was hard. Saving money was difficult, and sending money home to the wife was even more difficult. That is where friends had the know-how to make it possible to keep in touch and hold on to promises of return to bring the remaining family to America.

Francesco, two years later, returned to Italy with earned monies and an expectation as a citizento return to America with his family for a new life of freedom. His younger brother Paul was with him at the time and planned to return to Italy to be with his family. The first time Francesco came to America in 1907, he had left his wife and four young children, Liborio (later known in America as Big Benny, the first born on February 10, 1900), Antonio (Anthony, born 1904), Giuseppe (Joseph, born 1906), and the baby Margarita (Maria, born 1910). Maria was born after Francesco had gone to America in 1910.

Francesco, while in New York, was introduced to many local friends, some Italian emigrants and some people whom he had worked with and enjoyed their company. He made a point of getting to know each personally with offers to help with local home tasks, or he would make gestures while in conversation in his own now broken English that he was available to help, aid, or do a good deed for them in their lives. This way, he got to know many regular people within his own neighborhood. He continued his habits having lived and married in Italy. The habits were ameliorated by his wife Filippa that curtailed his wine drinking, and whiskey was used only during sociable situations.

What was just as important was that he got know the people and even relatives in New York City and surrounding cities. He learned about eastern states beyond where he worked. The most important one was West Virginia, where many coal mines were, and he was continually told that there was plenty of work. He was told by many that it was steady work because of the demand for coal by industries for heating and creating new electric power systems and transportation shipments to other states. Train's engines burned coal, new dams were being constructed, and the new electric plants were being designed using coal in various states where it is needed with inventory always being shipped where required.

After laboring at building roads in New York, Francesco planned his return to his homeland, Italy, to the town where his family lived, in Valguarnera, Sicily. When the time came for him to return to Italy, he knew how to handle district prejudices and to obtain papers for his family to process in Italy. He spent the next two years readying and teaching his family for an unknown future and an incredible cultural experience in America. He worked in several jobs but mostly in the sulfur mines of Palermo, Sicily, until he completed the necessary savings to return to America.

The authorities knew of his achievements through his references in his papers and knew that his family could travel under his stewardship when immigration papers for each were completed. The whole intent was to bring his family, well and in good keeping, to become full-on citizens of America.

He had developed a shrewdness socially and could display proper mental and sometimes physical strength to show his control of capabilities and to use them to get jobs easily. His doctored résumé, voiced by himself and penned by knowledgeable friends in America, complimented him on several jobs in America that he worked for over two years. The pay for such hard work met his saving's needs. While his family grew with baby Maria, he had gone back to New York. Now, Filippa had four children when he returned to America, and she had to get ready for his family going to America.

Filippa (La Spina) Divita was about four years younger than Francesco. She was young and attractively endearing for an Italian farm girl. Filippa was typically, genuinely submissive and surely a dominated and devoted wife. She was expected to have sexual activity at his beck and call, and it was expected. The family increased by one—namely, Margarita—after Francesco returned to Italy to prepare the family for a complete family immigration.

For the intent of the potential horror the children would face, those on board ship were, by age, Liborio (now thirteen), Antonio (now seven), Giuseppe (now five), and Margarita (now two), and all became the immigrating part of the family, which occurred in 1913, much similar to what occurred in 1910 because immigration to America was still in full force even though many suffered total sickness, some died, and others were tormented with seasickness. In those past five years, they lived in Palermo, Sicily, having moved from Valguarnera, where Big Mommy's parents, Antonio La Spina and Maria (Costa) La Spina, lived. When he returned, they moved to Naples where he could expect more money because he had skills of a miner and a road builder.

As I pointed out, my grandmother Filippa Divita was about four years younger than Francesco as shown on her record of birth and her marriage certificate. Filippa was born in the province of Valguarnera in Cattonnetta, Italy, on November 9, 1875. She was called Phyllis by her peers and neighbors in English much later after she arrived in America and she settled down in West Virginia. By the early 1930s, she was sometimes called by her grandchildren as Nina or Nona, but Big Mommy was more common. When talking and referring to herself, Big Mommy was the way she was addressed by her own children when they referred her to their children. Her children and daughters-in-law all called her Mommy.

Palermo was Big Poppy's birthplace and where many were told that was where his family for years assumed he grew up with his family. Real governmental evidence was uncovered that confirmed his birthing place, and the parents, whose names were obtained from Sicilian government offices, were Liborio Divita and Margherita Veviata (or Vivattene) from the earlier times. The Divitas had five children, whose names were Francesco, Paulo, Giuseppe, Maria, and Cristoforo. As I said, the rumor hovered in my early years that maybe my grandfather was an orphan because there were times when his behavior was in question based on all other Divitas. The only records were those of the SS *Sicilia*, which showed up on the ship's records that his younger brother Paulo traveled with him on his first trip to America. Many years later both were in their 1920s records, maintained by Mormons who archived records in Utah that indicated that they had settled in a small town of Smithers in Fayette County, West Virginia, certainly by 1920.

His brother Paulo Divita and family were well known by the first-generation children, who also settled in Smithers, and they lived nearby and had close relationships as first and second cousins as families propagated. Francesco's biography as a young boy and after he entered manhood is partially folklore because little archival accounting has been extracted to date. As surmised, around early 1912, Francesco Divita moved to the port in Palermo, Sicily, where, in Italy, he registered with a family from Sicily to immigrate to America.

Francesco, on his first trip, left from Palermo, Sicily, and was already an America emigrant for at least two years. Francesco shortly returned to America by himself in 1912 and when he arrived, he worked on road building as a gainfully employed citizen and was granted permission to request his family's immigration upon showing a capability to support them. He sent for his family to get ready. He had set up a starter home in New York City with some friend he knew in Sicily. Francesco had sent them money and made arrangements that their travel was firm. The travel started in December 1913. The family traveled as practically all emigrants do, boarding status as *steerage passengers*.

These emigrants sensed a new beginning in a new country. It was confirmed as a way and had already happened when the ship passed under the Verrazzano-Narrows Bridge exiting the Lower New York Bay at the opening of the Upper New York Bay early morning with an all-encompassing view of Brooklyn on the right and Staten Island on the left full of numerous levies and storage buildings but predominantly open land on both sides. As the ship proceeded toward Manhattan into the spread of the bay, all travelers delightfully awakened for the moment when the Statue of Liberty's reflection was indelibly imprinted on each traveler's mind for an infinite number of reasons as joy was mindfully recorded as freedom. The ship closed in on the Statue of Liberty so eloquently, as it prepared to be docked by tugs near Ellis Island for travelers' deployment into the divided arenas for reception of the status of different passengers. The waits began; even the privileged were impatient.

Those people having minor interactions were continuously gawking into the New York Harbor with unnerving observation of the Statue of Liberty sculpture as a magnificent, spiritual savior of freedom that flashed sunlight through the hearts and minds of the onlookers and continued to make an indelible imprint on their long-term memories of its design effectively portrayed. The expectation of so many past years, shipped along its journey by French sculptor and friend of America, Frederic Auguste Bartholdi, and built by Gustave Eiffel, was unveiled in 1886 in New York.

The Statue of Liberty has an inscription on a tablet in the left hand in Roman numerals as July IV, MDCCLXXIV, identifying United States of America with its official name "Liberty Enlightening the World" and as remembrance that forefathers signed the date of the Declaration of Independence. The meaning promises freedom and independence in America for the emigrants in their new country. However, it gives a sincere view of hope and desire and also promises that a righteous pursuit to gain stature and economical satisfaction will be part of gaining love of the country and devotion to being part of working people following paths of freedom. Only a few had any idea what was stored in minds beyond unthinkable by all emigrants, which was, will it be different and better than our homeland without our families?

Francesco continued to save money even after bringing his wife and a family of four to America. What was his plight in his daily life, only a few knew, from the time he gained a few days from Ellis Island's medical tests and inspections of belongings. To be specific, the few traveling were his wife Philipina (Filippa and later in America called Phyllis) and his eldest son, Liborio, who was now thirteen, and for a boy who mostly grew up with his mother, he was manly and astute with an inquisitive mind and considerate; he was the one who always watched and helped his two younger brothers and sister during the trip.

Being responsible for younger siblings revealed Liborio's character, and it was noticeable by many, even on board ship where he continually kept close lookout for his younger siblings. The revelation was obvious; he had his mind set by his mother from a young age. As a woman with four children, she was young at heart but statuesque in size, sensitive and compassionate and fully aware of morals and natural laws of the world created by God. Not one of her children ever ventured beyond her sight except on board the ship but was always sought and found.

It was almost four years after their arrival and having lived through the bulk of World War I's news that started in 1914 in Europe about the daily fighting in Europe for the first few years, which involved all of Europe and their homeland, and by early February 1917, the United States was fully involved in Europe, and disastrous reports were nerve-racking.

Francesco decided that he wanted to leave not just because of the hustle and bustle of the big city; he wanted to get settled down to a job that would be steady and have a peaceful time at home. With the talk that had occurred, he knew he had to take his family where coal mines were in the south. He knew this kind of work, and he was good at it. Some of his friends and his brother Paulo knew he meant business and understood his feelings to leave. His plan, although simple, was to leave New York City via the train where they could have full control of the kids and hear about areas as they traveled. Both knew people who not only were thinking of the same thing but also were having about the same intentions and thoughts to leave New York.

They planned to travel together to maintain good decision-making and to convince each other to do it as a last resort. They all wanted to raise their families in undisturbed and smaller surroundings. When final decisions were made, the group included his younger brother Paulo and his family and two other families not too well known but who were compatible and had children. Because of the near coastal train travel to get to the city of Philadelphia, each had an easy way with children especially since it was the trip's beginning.

Then Baltimore was the next stop, and it was full at every corner with a variety of foreign life and places called the Polish settlement; next door were Little Italy and Irish Town. This was no place to stop, so onward to Washington DC, and as expected from all, the conversation was about the war and the excitement of the nature of how great the American people were to win the win. Washington was almost as crowded as New York.

A few men on board the train when they were at Pittsburgh told them that the south-central part of West Virginia was almost empty with big valleys, rolling hills, and mountains of coal. The several families tentatively decided that they would continue traveling to the coal mining state of West Virginia. Francesco knew he could get steady work in coal mines because he had experience in the sulfur mines of Sicily where he worked as a young man after he returned to Italy in 1910. What was more than noticeable was the fact that Filippa's two brothers, Chris and Joe, had already left New York about six months before to move to Ohio, where they became strip miners. From their memory of a letter and earlier family talking and looking at maps at times, they had an inclination that her brothers had to travel through West Virginia.

Francesco and his brother Paulo's family settled in the small mining town of Smithers, West Virginia; other children, those who lived to become adults, were born as citizens of America: Francisco Jr. was born in America in 1915; Katherine, also known as Katy (Katrina), was born in 1917; Charles was born in 1920; and

James (Vincenzo) was born in 1922. All the while, his eldest son, Benny, helped his father with his work at the mines.

When he acquired property for the *OverHome* as an associated "compound," maybe even in modern days, it could have been called a commune for his family and friends. Big Poppy's sons helped him build homes treated as the *OverHome*, which included Big Poppy's large home, a second two-story home next to their home, a second one side by side for his daughter's home, and two duplexes end on end for his eldest sons. The complex was noticeably well done and featured his home on the corner of his lot having crossing roads that one could view across Kanawha Avenue to see edges of the Kanawha River from the main residence.

The other buildings also had good construction and utility and were well-kept. During the Divita family's early years in the small town of Smithers, as grandchildren arrived, he was called Big Poppy, and Filippa was called Big Mommy. Big Poppy worked for various mining companies in nearby hollows named by the coal companies, such as Cannelton, Morris Creek south on Route 61, and on the other side of the Kanawha River was the town of Deepwater north along Route 61, where the Eagle Coal Seam resided since the eons of past Carboniferous era about seventy-five million years ago. Most settlements nearby different mines were mine companies who owned the business and generally were worked by emigrants of several European countries but with different nationalities and languages and some from African countries.

Many of the ethnic families meshed because of common ties. While under the stress of making new lives in their own ways, they were harassed by local people and treated as subservient by mine owners and different ethnic groups during the 1600s to 1800s, mostly English-speaking people. Many Italians had formed what is most commonly called living in ethnic areas; say, for Italians, the large cities areas were called Little Italy, as were other European countries so identified when the adjective of dominance preceded their signified country. This was adopted as formed across the East Coast in many major cities to identify peoples' origin and to this day is still used with a revered attraction of foreign specialties although almost unmentioned in modern days.

Regardless of internal strife of the different ethnic groups, they were all under the forceful workload levied on them to mine their assigned portion of coal to satisfy the mine owners and their supervisors who controlled their work status. As emigrants, their lives and other people's lives who fell within this labor mix proceeded in menial jobs and some even degrading; but some suffered duress and terror that newly forming unions used to gain their support and ties as members with promises of future benefits and higher pays. The union bosses displayed socialistic comprehension of equality in numbers. Workers had a comparable way of interacting with management to make money for themselves.

The unions insisted that they were the ones who wanted to organize workers to mentally and physically arm themselves by numbers so that they could negotiate with company owners. This led to mining company owners organizing with strong-arm people and tactics while trying to gain government support in the middle of their confrontations. The unions used comparable methods and political ways to show their strength against companies.

Perhaps it's normal not living a life like others that came much later. Yet Divitas had every right to have a realistic desire to be as one could expect in the good ol' USA to strive and realize the American dream. Every day, miners walked toward their homes up the dirt alleyway, gully-ridden and sometimes muddy and other times with small fires burning or smoldering with gross smells of changes in life. As are many towns in West Virginia, Smithers is a small town named after a man who has a name among common names in the world; but it's not a woman or a man who identifies themselves as one who uses their first name initial and a mother's maiden name as his Christian name.

Dirt roads were normal road types in almost all towns at this time, but many now have some concrete or macadamized roads and mostly new buildings and homes unrecognized as when Big Poppy built his *OverHome* as a commune. They were buildings that were significant improvements since cars had been invented in the late 1800s. Back to alleyways, which are only pathways worse than a dirt road to gain access to Big Poppy's land. As I said, alleyways are full of ruts and mixed rock sizes mostly brought in by neighborhood kids randomly kicking rocks and following nature's laws when God cast the die before man's leveling into pathways. The spring rains and torrents mostly produced a natural beauty of green growth and flowers on local mountains in such a mixture unknown to minds of mankind who try to mimic garden beauty in confined spaces.

After rains, torrents of water were still flowing rapidly finding new ways to flow that please kids racing in gully streams with odd cut wooden boats with stapled, pinned old handkerchiefs as sails. Sometimes, after a spring rain, just walking in streets, running in fields, or skipping down boarded sidewalks was fun while frolicking and breathing clean air, for a while uncontaminated with coal dust from boxcar train traffic. Rain brings out creations of simple games such as hopping over puddles without getting wet shoes or finding some clay-filled soil to model. Other times, dirty "fun" jobs were digging newly found boulders revealed by rainstorms.

But in the sun, we prided ourselves by jumping from dry spot to dry spot, splashing mud on roadsides and each other as we ran full pressed in streams of water still flowing as a challenge to the ones behind us. Street repair guys quickly would chase kids away, shouting as they would say, "My god, look at the messy roads. Don't make it worse! The deep ruts and wheel ridges took lots of time to fix. You kids know it's hard work. We have to fix it so cars can drive over streets without getting stuck." I knew that it happened because my dad said it enough times after a big rain every time he drove us to Big Poppy's house where he usually hit a deep rut.

Big Poppy's home life is a story not told because it was known only to times of his marriage in Italy to Filippa. There is no one who ever relayed his young life's happenings in full detail about his life until his early twenties. After his marriage, Filippa never divulged what she knew of him because she as a subservient woman who lived in fear of unknown confrontations.

Francesco's life really started as known from the time after they moved to coal mining areas of West Virginia. His life and lives of family members really were noticed and recalled by family members who lived within his self-run commune that Big Poppy owned. To my little notice, no one living there was unhappy to be part of it as memories flourished and primarily became folklore of Francesco's emotional pursuits for years. His eldest son, Big Benny, was his first knowledgeable son that created a stability in the family as the other siblings followed his course of life. Each of the other sons and friends used their mentality to store happenings in their minds to relay details that allowed the propagation of "Steerage and Amour!—What's It All About!" The source of emotional desires was based on hereditary and especially *steerage* so classically taught by Filippa to Francesco's children when interacting with the Divita family, especially their momma Filippa, who made sure they were fed as days passed while working under Big Poppy's demands.

Big Poppy had all homes of the *OverHome* commune built under his masterful direction and critical eye. He made sure that professional contractors would not get paid if the work was not done to his satisfaction. In those times of early '20s, in their free time, his sons helped build the *OverHome* by working themselves to save money.

His first home was constructed with a shiny glazed cinder block, which had the surface appearance of randomly wavy surface toned purplish brown reflecting as an unusual stone. At the main entrance was a large concrete porch floor about twelve by fifteen feet square with a smoothed concrete finish by troweling. The porch was bordered at the same level with a complement of blocks that were used to build outside walls of houses. The outside of his porch was lined with blocks to prevent rain from gathering, but later, some blocks became chipped and partially filled with things from wherever.

During one of the many times when I was there as a kid, one of the other kids was always digging into one or more of the blocks. My trouble was that I liked to walk along while standing inside a broken basket-weaved chair. One of the times, I fell and hit my head on one of the border blocks. Big Poppy rushed outside when he heard the scream. Big Poppy ran inside and quickly put sugar on it. It did leave a scar but healed very fast. Keep in mind, after it was built, however, any child could come up from broken block insides with something, even if it was a worm or snail.

The actual home's entry was at the kitchen's entry about twelve feet wide and twelve feet long. The entry to the dining room was on the left, and the master bedroom was next door about ten feet wide and fourteen feet long. The dining room had a straight through opening to the living room that was fourteen feet long by twelve feet wide with an entrance to a small bedroom on the left. The living room had an outside door that exited to the back porch. The steps were two and about level to the ground. A swing and swinging couch with a few chairs could be moved for talking purposes. Food was also an easy mark, and it was taken to and from the kitchen to the dining room with ease. Most times, the women that cooked were under close Italian watch enjoying grand cooked food odors beyond belief.

Looking up the Kanawha Avenue that fronts homes, the next one was a home Big Poppy built to rent to his friend Dominic Cosentino and family after it was finished. It was a two-story house because it needed several bedrooms with their four children, Dominic, Angie, Oscar, and Johnny, plus parents. While we were there during the 1930s and early '40s, they were still living in the home. Back porches were made for every home on Kanawha Avenue that faced one line of homes in the back where the Kanawha River was close to the land about ten feet above the water.

Big Poppy fenced his homes for safety and so families could find a view of the Kanawha River along pathway openings about two hundred feet toward the old Baptist Revival Church on the corner of Rosa Street. The walkway on Poppy's land was narrow but could be adequately maneuvered along the flat land above the three- or four-foot-high hillside down along Kanawha Avenue.

Before the hillside where dirt paths make a slight bending right turn at my dad's home, one had to make sure they could negotiate a flat wide walkway against the fence with little or no slipping on the hillside to gated and fenced properties. The areas were widespread between homes, which made walking easy. The parking in front of Big Poppy's entry side of his home was at least enough for two cars, especially in front of the home and intended for his daughter Katy's home when finished.

There will be more about Katy and Sam Argento when they get married. Uncle Sam was my mentor when I was a kid and the best father and family man. Sam was a genius in fixing mechanical devices. He could make anything work, and he had the ability to make any car operate. At this point in the yard, one could see Uncle Sam's old "Tin Lizzie," which he rebuilt and painted to perfection but used it only for short family trips. Most of the time, when we were there in daylight, he was under the car with a set of wrenches. Kids played with a yard full of enjoyment, and it was noticeable; but no one ever paid attention to them except Sam, who tried to interest them in cars and fixing them.

No one ever checked on kids or wondered, "What in hell are they doing?" Some of them were under houses and some around a fire burning in alleyways. This joyful behavior continued into late evenings with games of some sorts, like Indian Trapper.

Back to the homes on the *OverHome* area. My mom and dad's home was at their property's end along Kanawha Avenue. A duplex, as it is called nowadays, was Uncle Tony and Aunt Catherine's home at the other end. I know because I was one of the kids in and out of both homes. Uncle Benny and Aunt Mary's kids later lived in Uncle Tony's duplex after Uncle Tony and Aunt Catherine moved to the mountainside off Route 61 at Cannelton Hollow. Aunt Mary's home had a gate at their front entrance, and the Donleavys lived along the back alleyway to downtown. Most kids were Divitas, and they were certainly noticeable on Sundays because their ages ranged from babies to ten or fourteen years old during the late '30s and early '40s.

One day, a bunch of kids were playing in the alley when Big Poppy was seen coming up the alley. I shouted, "Look out! Big Poppy's coming!" He's waving to all, and we mostly would stand still. Someone else would say, "Big Poppy's coming home!" Someone must have said it ten times. In my mind, it was echoing or being said by all kids following his first shout because in their little brains, they projected their sense of fear and made sounds warning with impending concerns.

Uncle Sam slid out from under his old jalopy and looked at kids running. All Big Poppy wanted was Jimmy, and he got everyone's attention. Jimmy listened and hightailed into the pathway heading straight for his poppy's desire. Jimmy was about ten. He knew what his poppy wanted him to go for! He didn't have a choice. Things quieted, and everyone went about their own business. What Jimmy had to get, we did not know.

Some mortar slots needed new concrete to be replaced between glazed cinder blocks with fill. So Big Poppy wasn't worried of any potential danger to children who could come up with numerous ways to flail themselves or maybe even poison themselves with rancid matter that they might find in the block holes. The other houses appeared newer and maybe just looked older but well-kept. They were built a little cheaper being walled exteriorly with clapboard. Misdeeds were intentional bangs or pounds with any tool to which kids might have had access. Many kids were commonly in and out of yards and homes during the week with dirty little hands and showing food marks on the little mischievous outside eaters. Added to buildings was a light cover of gray coal dust on buildings of many materials unless they were painted or washed within the past year.

The biggest home in surrounding areas was the Donleavys', located at the wire fence but well abused by climbs and, as expected, rusted and torn wire. The home is a big gray-green craftsman's home, a two-story where the fence was opposite Big Poppy's home. The Donleavys' home was constructed with a large wood frame covered with horizontal boards nailed front and back. Porches were attached at both top and bottom floors. The mansion appearance was due to its largess, but because of wear and tear against aging wooden construction with missing boards, it was obviously run-down, and the occupiers were negligent. One could see that it was built with a lot of utility but with little continuous care and a lot of use by at least four or five children being raised by several sets of parents and their mothers and at least one set of grandparents.

Most other homes were unnoticeable, but people were always leaving and entering at right times, and many times, families were visiting kids that came over to play with some Divita kids. The home most noticeable to families was the home across the street where Roger and Mary Ann lived with their parents. She was the good-looking girl on the block, maybe except for a few Italian-descent girls who had charming good looks. What her father Tony and brothers Mickey and Sammy did were noticeably working at his dad's restaurant. Both boys were exceptionally good sportsmen on sand lots and became members of the high school football teams. All the guys played ball in vacant lots nearby the alleyway that ends at the site of Divita homes.

What was most important to the Divita family was that their children were accepted by all neighbors, and all of them were achievers in grade school. I know it was my parents who had taught them that the way; to make friends was to participate in all activities and make good grades like the smart kids of the neighborhood.

What was unique was the existence of Big Poppy in portrayal as a close, totally unexpected individual, at least as one man in a million whose looks and build, along with his manly size, made him appear overweight but strong. His physical characteristic signature was typical of Italians even in America. He had a handlebar mustache that, without words or facial reactions, appeared normal, even to children. However, he was the overseer of his total land and buildings, and all knew it. His family and one miner friend including his family with four children lived in his homes that he called his *OverHome*. By the late 1920s, his four sons were grown boys. The eldest daughter, now called Mary, was only about ten years old at that time. During the same time, Momma Filippa lost two daughters after shortly after being raised. However, three younger sons, Frank, Charlie, and Jimmy, and daughter Katy were born in America. Within the next ten years, two eldest sons and eldest daughter, Mary, were already married with children in early 1930s.

The work confrontations became the foremost topic during this period and continued until John L. Lewis and his cohorts managed after several years to establish unions with bargaining positions, some of which were good for miners and some were not. The disparaging animosity continued even during these days among unions across America.

The United Mine Workers Union (UMW), founded on January 22, 1890, in Columbus, Ohio, had merged two old labor groups of miner and trade unions, modeling its policies after the American Federation of Labor to develop mine safety; to improve mine workers' independence from mine owners and company stores and provide miners with collective bargaining power.

Working in mines caused many health issues. One problem was that areas being mined were, on average, five to six feet high inside as they got deeper. As a result, some larger-size miners worked all day without standing upright. Because mines were hard to access by an average man, demands for young boys to work in mines grew. More inexperienced miners led to more accidents. Another health concern was that dusts of dirt and coal that miners breathed each day caused some miners to suffer black lung disease. In the '20s, few miners in Matawan, West Virginia, were involved in mining activities. They were contentious with management forces and continuously combated union leaders' infractions. During one of these incidents, twelve men were killed in a gunfight between town residents and Baldwin Felts Detective Agency that were hired by mine owners. This was the story depicted in John Sayles film *Matewan*.

The Redneck War, which occurred in 1920–21, was generally viewed beginning with the Matewan massacre. This conflict involved struggles to unionize southwestern areas of West Virginia. It led to the march of ten thousand armed miners on the county seat at Logan, ending in the Battle of Blair Mountain in which miners fought state militia, local police, and mine guards. These events are depicted in the 1987 novel *Storming Heaven*, by Denise Giardini, and the 2005 novel *Blair Mountain*, by Jonathan Lynn.

The Herrin massacre occurred in June 1922 in Herrin, Illinois. Nineteen strikebreakers and two union miners were killed during mob actions on June 21–22, 1922. John Llewellyn Lewis, forty-two years old (February 12, 1880–June 11, 1969) was an American labor leader who served as president of UMWA from 1920 to 1960. In 1933, government organizers spread throughout the United States to organize all miners into labor unions when the National Recovery Act was passed by the national government. Combinations of this change provided safer and better working conditions and higher wages for such dangerous jobs in and around mines.

John L. Lewis was the driving force behind organizing millions of other industrial workers in the 1930s. As a leading liberal, he played a major role in helping FDR win a landslide in 1933. Lewis was a known political isolationist, and so he broke up with Roosevelt in 1940 on foreign policy.

A little history is needed to show the extended power of men who rescued the miners. Lewis was born in Cleveland, Iowa, the son of Thomas H. Lewis and Ann Watkins Lewis, both of whom had emigrated from Wales. Cleveland at the time was a company town built around a coal mine one mile east of Lucas. His mother was a Mormon, and her son adopted her rigid views regarding alcohol and sexual propriety, but not her religion. He attended three years of high school in Des Moines and, at the age of seventeen, went to work in Big Hill Mines at Lucas. In 1907, he ran for mayor of Lucas and launched a feed-and-grain distributorship. Both were failures, and Lewis returned to coal mining. In 1906, John L. Lewis was elected a delegate to United Mine Workers (UMW) national convention. He moved to Panama, Illinois, and in 1909 was elected president of the UMW local. In 1911, Samuel Gompers, head of the AFL, hired Lewis as a full-time organizer.

Lewis traveled in Pennsylvania and West Virginia as a union organizer and troubleshooter, primarily to keep things safe in coal mining towns.

After serving as statistician and then as vice president for the UMWA, Lewis became the union's acting president in 1919. On November 1, 1919, he called the first major coal union strike, as four hundred thousand miners walked off their jobs. President Wilson obtained an injunction, which Lewis obeyed, telling the rank and file, "We cannot fight the government." When Lewis was elected president of the UMWA in 1920, he became a dominant organizer of the biggest union in the country.

The next step much later coming into the new century was to solidify the union with a plan for a three-year contract between UMWA and coal operators, providing for a pay rate of $7.50 per day. President Coolidge and then Secretary of Commerce Herbert Hoover were impressed with the plan, and Lewis was offered the post of heading the union.

And to be clear, relative to long times that had passed, the adjustment to current times in 2009 was about $93.29 per day. When adjusted for inflation today, it would be quite a bit larger.

Mining company stores had their own methods of handling money to pay wages. The mining companies had a way of controlling miners' families' pay by using "script" as was approved by the government and predominantly devised coal companies to allow miners to buy in company stores at cheaper prices but at a profit to coal companies. The major fallback of this perk was that the "script" was only worth seventy-five cents on the U.S. dollar. When the good ol' American dollar was needed, the exchange was made by miners, and anyone having script could buy in the company store including at gas stations owned by coal companies. The ethnic prejudices fueled by each person's insecurities and fears of potential harm to their loved ones set ethnic barriers that continued to exist even for future generations.

Even during the early 1920s, more than fifty years after the Civil War, America was granting citizenship to people from many countries. The newcomers still feared that they could be controlled by the strong, smart, well-educated, and powerful people. They were also told that rich mine owners, so-called bluebloods whose sires were part of early immigrations in mid-1800s and earlier, would try to force them from gaining land with mines.

The English, Dutch, Spanish, and French who explored in 1600s and 1700s also stayed in America so much so that they, early birds, thought they were American blue bloods. Every so often, people still heard it mentioned when one takes claim that they were here before the American Revolutionary War. Most remainders after the mid-1800s were Spanish explorers and their mates who migrated to islands below America and went to South America and Mexico. Some then moved to western coast territories of America and a few even into Alaska to dig for gold.

It wasn't until the late 1700s and early 1800s when some of these eastern emigrants and many others with much more wealth moved to the western areas and became settlers and homesteaders along with those who were fortune hunters of gold, silver, and copper; but those who were cattle barons, fur traders, and started local businesses had built homelands to gain large areas for their cattle.

The hard work within families, their love of freedom, and a passion to earn rights and monies made way for vague but lasting cultural steps for next generations of siblings through education, in art and music. Italians as well as emigrants from other countries concentrated on learning their jobs and making sure their children learned ethics of working for a living. In this era, emigrants were motivated by the American industrial revolution in the later 1800s. Furthermore, their intent was to make sure that their kids got more education than what little they got in Europe. For both good and bad, ethnic thrusts instilled new cultural contributions to educating the poor throughout America.

This story embraces a family that significantly influenced many families the way they lived in small mining towns and eventually throughout America. It is an epoch of early formation of future creative thinkers. It covers their progeny as first-generation Americans with impetus-guided minds with an energy and motivating force. In addition, changes made in lives of these emigrants after social and cultural improvements include the fact that they were accepted and melded into the new century of America, some as rugged individualists.

This is also one part of the epoch of *steerage passengers* of emigrant families that come from other countries that want to be truly new citizens of America. As new American emigrant families, they understood that they promised to accommodate federal, states, and territorial rules of law and become part of the country as citizens of America with committed allegiance. It was obvious that some knew the right things to do, and a few had other ideas how to get ahead using unlawful practices that were already in their minds. This is an expected behavior, and these few unwanted emigrants managed to get through inspectors at Ellis Island.

The real *steerage* taught to new emigrants comes about through the cultural heritage of those emigrants and their family's teachings and experiences as practicing freedom-loving individuals. These new people of the twentieth century accepted by America are still striving for love of freedom and equality. They value free exercise of economic rights as individuals or groups to pursue education and arts. They knew how to live socially among each other without strife or any type of insurrection against all forms of governments. Their everyday living among all Americans were searching for companionship of one form or another, be it business or friendship to those next door.

The story explores impacts of personalities of first-generation Americans on their evolving offspring and the *steerage and amour* of coming generations being a new generation of procreated Americans. The psychological behavior of Big

Poppy and Big Mommy, their siblings and new members born in America, released actions through their sons and daughters and eventually with their second-generation American siblings from their children's offspring. The general trend was that emigrants accommodated times and people of bad times in the country and throughout the world. Later, even during World War II, the demeanor of Italian families was overboard patriotic.

Big Poppy, and maybe his generation, found that he had to change his hardened and dominating behavioral pattern that he had developed during his mining experiences in the '20s and '30s in conflict with unions and management alike. His domination was practiced excessively at times especially if he was under the influence of alcohol. There were times when this was good and times when it was under worst conditions, especially when he launched threats at family members with demonstrating action. Many aside comments included that even meanness within his spirit was direct by induced spells made by enemies, or as Italians liked to call it for those that had poor times, a spell of the evil eye was attached as the cause. The evil eye was placed on persons by another as assumed by one's self or another person who has personal knowledge under recognition to cause a known discontentment or worse. Even at his death, the family kowtowed almost to his every wish and command as how he was to be laid out for his burial ceremony.

This same demanding approach was used by his father, who, during the Great Depression after the repeal of prohibition of liquor, had his deli store that including a license to sell beer. He continued to work in mines, while his elder children helped to make the store profitable as an Italian delicatessen. Big Poppy profited enough to build several other homes on his property and buy places where the delicatessen was located in the nearby town of Montgomery. He rented some of homes but also built homes in which he let his married children live for a price, all of whom were working at jobs or owned their own businesses. At this time, Benny and Tony owned a small bus line, and Benny was trying to get a taxi business started. The deli was stopped after a few years of hard times because of the Great Depression, but Francesco remained employed at mines. Then as the year 1940 began, he continued to work in mines and with his steady earnings. Big Poppy had maintained his funds before World War II to live satisfactorily during the time of war somewhat above average. The mainstay was that he owned his property and gained some support from his sons, who paid to live in two of his homes, giving him a feeling of prosperity.

A year and half later, some of his elder sons moved from the *OverHome* area to nearby towns or cities. His *steerage* continued to occur even though it was isolated within small mining towns. Francesco maintained access to his sons and daughters and families by his insistent regular Sunday dinners in his home where he exercised his authority and domination that lasted mostly after diner with conversation, a day that usually emboldened him by drinking whiskey of his choice provided by his sons upon entering the *OverHome*. Sometimes, *steerage* got out of hand because Big Poppy might not be satisfied with his boys' behavior, especially if he heard bad words in Al's Place about him. This concern by Big Poppy, certainly his girls, from a father's point of view, should it be their personal behavior or their gifts for the dinner or even what or how the food was cooked, would cause him to roar with praise. And for the most part, get-togethers were friendly, and conversations abounded because concern about World War II was ominous. Within a short time, three of his sons had joined the army.

The coal companies continued to mine large coal deposits in the surrounding counties. West Virginia was known for its coal deposits on both sides of the Kanawha River, which ran for many miles across the southern part of the state. Practically, all of West Virginia had coal deposits sometimes observable just by looking at seams in hillsides during winter snows and rains. Of course, many other precious minerals were also being extracted or processed along the valley for military industrial purposes. Steel and alloys were made in local areas using coke made by overheating coal to generate hotter byproducts. Many other byproducts were prepared and fed to industries throughout Kanawha Valley and shipped to manufacturing plants across the country to produce military products. The Kanawha Valley was noted for its industrial complex especially during World War II. Products were produced and sold throughout various states that needed coal to produce electricity, steel, and other industrial materials.

After his first nearly twenty years passed in the early 1930s, Big Poppy was addicted to alcohol, and his belligerent behavior worsened his rough behavior even in fun. He would become inebriated when he felt like it. Benny, with the help of his mother, Big Mommy, who had suffered Big Poppy's dominating and incorrigible behavior, usually knew how to appease his poppa. When he would not be incorrigible with Big Mommy, who was a solid and devoted wife of true compassion, my dad would protect her mindfully until the fussing stopped.

Big Mommy knew from her early years in Italy that Big Poppy was a loner who lived in Palermo, Sicily, with his family before moving to Valguarnera. How Big Poppy behaved overall as a young man was that he might have been self-centered with a personality operating without much formal education. In the light of how Sicilians behave under dominating autocratic conditions in the late 1800s, he could only see that domination worked for him as it did for many.

Vindictive treatment was one of the main thrust why the Sicilians and Italians and, for that matter, others from many European countries immigrated to America. America's laws allowed a peacefulness for peasants, certainly in favor of socially elite and government bourgeois who felt only slightly above common people. In this era, the only good treatment one who had suffered abuse was self-treatment. When fortunate, the help given by intimately involved loved ones maintained a goodness that relieved their mind's foremost. Big Mommy knew what to do to instill a sense of manly value in Big Poppy to make him recognize importance of his family under incidents that arose within the family so that he might interject comments for the good. Sometimes, his comments were off-site or too critically sharp, and he became aggressive. Turmoil resulted, and it languished until it was settled in some fashion with an apology usually by the one that criticized him.

Back to when Big Poppy's eldest son, Benny, was thirty-three and married to Jo for five years and had three children, he was a completely opposite person with behavior about his father. The outfall, however, was good with *steerage* teaching simply from the start, as he had learned from his momma. These children were born in America and were first-generation American children who were more thoughtful, respectful of elders and their postulated intelligent behavior was bolstered by teachings from Big Mommy and the way her children had been nurtured from childhood. Big Mommy made sure *steerage* and *amour* were clear from within her heart and used to make children think about life and being happy.

Big Poppy's personal behavior instilled the essence of his sensuous heritage into the progeny of this story. Although this heritage is dominant, it has ameliorating influences that not only lessened imposed desires but also gave their minds good things that had been sparked by his family's heritage. At times, there was some critical debate that came as the learning cycle was not used, and an involvement was attached from childhood to adult life. Who did this amelioration? It was instilled by the women, mothers of close involvement with the progeny stressing mental improvement. Big Mommy was the first in the family to seek answers to questions about the secreted, mentally hidden, accepted stress and sensuous desires among children. It was Big Mommy who first asked her children when stressed, "Che è tutto?" (What is it all about?)

Big Mommy's personal behavior was mostly with words of encouragement while providing a teaching behavior with thought figured by the mind to make sure the thought answered the question. The catalyst was interest to satisfy Big Mommy with happy satisfaction that molded minds of children from their first steps, and she encouraged it in free America.

The upbringing of her grandchildren was also influenced by their parents having experienced benefits, and impediment sometimes caused deprivations of mentally anxious or low periods in their lives. Big Mommy was supported in the encouragement of each of her elder children, already adults, by using *steerage and amour* for her siblings and her daughters, sons, and in-laws anytime she was around them for the joy of conversational *steerage* to be mentally stored. Mothers and the children of each family always recognized and maintained induced loyalty and fidelity as it related to true *amour*.

During Big Mommy's life, her influence ever so lightly manifested throughout with friendliness as she would tell one seeking the answer, "Questo è ciò Che è tutto!" This is, what's it all about! Even during early lives of grandchildren, Big Mommy and her daughters and daughters-in-law as mothers simply explained types of personalities such as those being self-sufficient would lead to disowning life's stresses and poor intuitive judgment to refuse getting their way and making a good decision. Her daughters and daughters-in-law adopted Big Mommy's legacy and practiced it with each of their children.

The premise that Big Mommy's emigrants and first-generation children and their families upgraded their valuable heritages from Big Mommy for the most part. She cashed in on the good psychological values related to normal social behavior, but throughout ages, some do not make it to an effective level and will undoubtedly suffer slings and arrows that accompany their plights. Each sibling family instilled a new level of behavior and desire for cultural achievement, although with rough edges, starting with Big Mommy's children and especially with their wives and husbands that provided significant fidelity.

The eldest son, Big Benny, vitally intelligent when teaching children, assumed the role of peacemaker from early in life, common in Italian families. Under every experience, he was always involved with bringing about peace with and among extended Divita families. During these critical times, before World War II, after a few years, he headed his young family during the time when my dad was age thirty-six heading to forty-two. He had the mind and gusto to work. He was frugal even with his savings. He started a small Italian delicatessen in the same manner as his father, but after his time was not supportable to both businesses, he remained with his taxi and moving transfer business.

Now, as postwar modern families, each member of extended families acted decisively, and it resulted in mixed outcomes in which all involved suffer confrontation and certainly the results of poor decisions. So that as siblings gained age, Benny always took the first look as the firstborn and isolated the idea that he would be the peacemaker even to his children. With his decision-making being astute, he generally followed to maintain the comradeship expected even within his enlarging extended family. In some incidences, feathers flew in consternation and strife was rampant usually among brothers, even among some family members, but his workable solution with truth survived.

As the eldest son, Big Benny set an effective pace and was a role model for his brothers, who used his interaction skills with their children. His demeanor and societal behavior and honesty told his lifetime partner Josephine that he will be a loyal husband and family man. The one change from his promise was it left him with a minor addiction to alcohol while living with diabetes. He could only drink a small amount of whiskey as a relaxant under stresses of hard times during World War II. The relief he gained, although lightly used but ineffective, was the fact that he suffered from diabetes, which had harmfully occurred after a major car accident that nearly took his life as a passenger, and he and the family suffered while he was in anguishing total pain from head to toe, physically incapacitated by poor health, but within six months, he was back to work at his business.

After a few years, my dad Benny was set for his primary enjoyment, which included his special time when going to the Indianapolis 500 Race that came up the year after the war had ended in 1945 were his interest and love of race cars, he had once before was asked to attend the Indy 500 Races before World War II started. He knew that races in Indianapolis would be cancelled until a later time. After the war, the immediacy of refurbishing the racetrack facility was planned for 1946. His most recollected highlights stretched his desire to return to the first one due in 1946, since the last one that occurred before the war started in December 7, 1941. Benny had met his friend Mauri Rose, who won the race in 1941.

As my dad moved into the '50s after that time, he was not able to devote enough time to control his business, and the business began to fail. The problem stemmed during an economic recession in the early 50s. His work capabilities diminished, and tough times with the economy left him needing support. He was grandly helped by his elder son Frank, who had married Betty and was drafted and joined the United States Air Force. After the Korean War ended in compromise, Frank and Betty were settled with two children living nearby in Peterstown, West Virginia, and he was not happy teaching music to high school children for past year. Dad had contacted Frank by phone and asked if he would be interested in helping with running this taxi business and getting into selling used cars. Frank and Betty both thought that going back to Montgomery to live in the family's home for a while seemed better than what they were doing in Peterstown, where he was not able to make enough money to properly maintain his family.

Dad, of course, became effective in business with his son Frank, and with his share of effort, he made significant improvement in the business. They bought several Packard Models that people liked and especially enjoyed comfortable rides. Dad was happy working with Frank. And especially with two businesses, he began increasing passengers and making money. At home, they managed with two families well enough to keep going. Dad did continue but had shortened enjoyable drinking times with his friends and family, more as a taster than as a drinker. And the family, sometimes in the late evenings after being on site, and he would leave his manager sometimes enjoy sports and card games such as BriSCA, casino, hearts, or mostly poker as the choice when they had free time. These card games that they could bet a token amount to strengthen the enjoyment were their first choice.

Other times, mixed friends and family members encouraged dinner celebrations in his Deluxe Diner next door on his taxi property. Mostly with his brothers but at times a friend or two would be included and get freely fed and treated.

However, the main thrust with the taxi business led Dad and Frank into a more compatible business and a new relationship with close friends who were interested in looking for a friend with capabilities possibly to get involved with a dealership who was a close friend of his dad, who was planning to retire. When Jay

Ricciardi's dad decided to retire from the company, Frank had discussed details to both of their advantages. Jay asked Frank if he would be interested in joining him in the business as the manager and eventually becoming the future business partner when the business becomes successful. This led Frank to become a new member of Jay's management of the dealership. Over the next two years, Frank worked masterfully and became a partner of the dealership. After a year or so, he was elected to be the mayor of Montgomery and eventually bought the dealership when Jay wanted to retire.

CHAPTER XV

Family Thinks about Life's Teachings of Steerage and Amour

*Propagation [natural reproduction] of progeny dominates
our future paramount beliefs in the Creation of life with
the minds of* Homo sapiens *must decide to live with good
behavior under all actions to maintain Happiness.*

To acquire nature's philosophy of life within the mind of a Homo
sapiens, *human beings must cogitate analytically and examine
themselves for answers why God designed mankind's lives to
continue immortality of human beings until ad infinitum.*
—Edward L. Divita Sr.

That people tend to behave in ways that are consistent with
their mind's thinking that is fairly well known when they
know the teachings of "knowledge and experience." What is
not so well known is that the reverse also occurs. Many think
in ways that they justify the behavior of "will of desire."

The eminent English scholar Dr. Samuel Johnson explained
the two tendencies as follows: *Not only our speculations
influence our practice, but our practice reciprocally influences our
speculations. We not only do what we approve, but there is danger
lest in time we come to approve what we do . . . for no other reason
than that we do it. A man is always desirous of being at peace within
himself; and, when he cannot reconcile his passions to conscience,
he will attempt to reconcile his conscience to his passions.*

—Samuel Johnson, as quoted in *The Quotable Johnson: A
Topical of His Wit and Moral Wisdom,* edited by Stephen C.
Danckert (San Francisco: Ignatius Press, 1992), p. 39

All this mental regard comes about instinctively simply because it started at the creation of God's beginning with whatever such as microscopic details of deoxyribonucleic acid (DNA) that is fused into a molecular formula within the egg when inserted by the sperm and begins making the mind and body development to birth new *Homo sapiens*. Its *Homo sapiens* beginning of progeny that needs the mating contribution of the egg and sperm made at conception to continue, which is undeniably unique. The human being from that point on is the only genus of *Homo sapiens* on earth. What is commonly said as a reason or excuse to combat what follows the perfidious one's human example often exclaims, "I can't help it! It's in my genes!" This transfer is thereafter promulgated in the resulting progeny including mental dispositions, physical looks and behavior actions, emotional reactions, and embedded temperaments.

The gifts of skill from nature's genes such as inherited talents, innovation, and creativity more than make up for other shortcomings. Each of these inherited attributes in various amounts are in all human beings. They inherited an encompassment of mental containment and wit and through Divita family teachings that gained fixed shares of cerebral capability based on where one's mind evolves in the spectra of the mind's two sides, right and left, respectively. The mind will thrive on the right side with ability to recognize the creative emotional glory of art and music resulting in potentially familial inherited gains of culturally personal demands, and on the left side, hardwired instinctive behavior might favor vocations of critical analyses and details that may drive for desires and survivability, or at common times, minds revise mentality to show wisdom that is diametrically opposite mind's pursuits. In procreation, this hardwired instinctive innate tendency is essential to any of human being's existence, development, and preservation. For both left and right minds, results are hell-bent pursuits to seek one's desires instinctively no matter whose life or lives are at stake or who might be heartbroken because of prevalent social mores not being practiced as a matter of modernism.

My mother and dad picked the time to begin my birthing of my life at due time for my being a *Homo sapiens*. I was extracted by Dr. Moore personally, full of life and with embodiment and a mind instilled with happiness coming from my mother's womb with excitement even in one of the small homes by Big Poppy's *OverHome*, where we lived. I could hear my mother's voice with vibrations of pain. Several people that were in the room felt the cold as I did and as I appeared into my new world exposed to natural life. More importantly, I knew that my senses stemmed from my mother's nurturing, but I felt it in my head a sensation of my mind's state of life. I knew that the life sensing was brought on by her from her natural ways. The only unrecognizable action was when delivering me, she was under her stress and strains with grunts mixed with unfamiliar sounds to me as I appeared.

After delivery and on first sense of my openly active mind, I especially sensed the midwinter cold. I then realized that I appeared as a completely grown human being, unknown in name and words from my mind. I assumed all others that had been produced on the planet earth as my mom and dad's siblings wandered in full of excitement as well as the large fully grown people interacting with me of little action.

Later, after hearing what transpired from my memory, I was wrapped and was placed in the warmth of my mother's life with my life being a member of genus *Homo sapiens* with contentment. And much later, I was told in so many words that I eventually understood how difficult the extracted birthing compared, but I knew the quarterback was my mother and the rest of the team was on the field waiting to tend to my life.

Several years later, I, named Edward Lee Divita, was told many things about my birth, even the day, Thursday, which was on January 24, 1935. This was told by the time I was talking, and as it later happened, it was within my mother's heart that the words came out as they occurred when we were riding in a car approaching the underpass where Carbon Creek was generally proceeding in torrents to the great Kanawha River. I damn near could feel that the frozen creek had deducted a few more degrees from my ambient temperature. What kind of life was I heading into, and how would I be able to withstand the cold weather? My mother then covered me with a warmer blanket. She did it without me giving her an answer, but the joy offered was shown by my smiling and my cooing.

Well, a few more years later, I found out the answer—the earth does have different seasons all the way from cold to hot and anything in between that goes with its behavior. Then again, I realized this was not about me, but it was about my family all the way from my grandfather Francesco, whom I have seen frequently by his choice, but I did not converse with him. Rather, he touched my hand and lifted me and claimed what a beautiful Italian boy, claiming to my brothers and all the other kids as I viewed my lifetime growing achievements of a personality, height, size, and capabilities to speak pleading, thanking, and surprisingly happy within my self-sufficient manner that I inherited from my father after a few years.

I also carried out many functions just simply because I observed continuously my elder brothers, who fortunately taught me what they knew in their own words. I did understand most of the words intuitively from actions and playful ways they treated me. It was more about my eldest brother, Frank, and many added expectations from my second-eldest brother, Gene, who was a whiz kid from his start. The two of them told me over many years about our family, and anything else made me understand my choices in life and emphasized it all by my mom and dad.

I stored "knowledge and experience" in my mind for future use. I thought they were toying with my mind because it took a long time for me to remember what I had stored in my memory even with a multifaceted thoughtful mind of the yet unknown detailed memory. As time passed, my memory gained a boost each year, and my recall spontaneously reacted as I pondered daily about the past and applied my reading skills to sharpen my access and working efforts to ease my mother's time that was devoted to us and our dad, et cetera.

I did interact within and as the story progressed, but all of us, in some fashion or other, recalled from memory and gave me associated knowledgeable teachings of *steerage* and *amour* that left a recognizance of our personalities that evolved using their teachings by progenitors. We were always in our early times in Smithers under some condition or demand, and this was one of the times that I recalled what was told and how my elder brother Frankie felt about the job handed to him from the beginning as a teacher, and other jobs were handed from other families, mostly their eldest ones and their moms and dads. As the years passed, Frankie would every so often tell me about our family from times past in such detail that he made me think he knew everything that happened or at least told it as he heard it and never forgot it, no matter what the crisis or outcome.

Frankie recalled in his tidbits of words how he saw things in the town of Smithers, WestVirginia. About that time, as he told me close to his words later, "Every time I go to town, I see the towering water tank outside made of wood steel-strapped constructed next to railroad tracks where trains, mostly B&O, operated coal carriers. Sometimes, trains would stop to refill their steam engines."

Later, I used to explore the total area around town. And eventually, in time, with cousins, we would go all the way to the mountaintops. We were surrounded by mountains, which were close and, obviously with me, starting sometimes from road surfaces of U.S. Highway 60 on one side and other times from road surfaces of Highway 61 on opposite side of the Kanawha River. I always sense myself as a camera on top the large water tower viewing the steel-trussed railroad bridge, and to the other side, a poorly paved and hardly ever repaired asphalt road and stone inlaid at the underpass with stone walls along an old concrete bridge.

The rest of the personal story I will relate later about what Frankie had told me from memory without interference but with words of others or so characterized by Frankie himself in his lifetime. Much later when he was called Frank, he had less than a little genuine folklore embedded in his memory but with imposed repartee and arguably some incited truth exaggerated after living his grand life.

Frankie had walked tracks through Smithers so many times as a kid that his close-up view was one that there must be many small mining towns in southern West Virginia that suffered losses as businesses failed during the Great Depression. As a young boy, Frankie, about twelve years old, was living in our renovated home in Montgomery in May 1941. Some people were still under poverty levels from the Great Depression, even though my dad had plenty of work because World War II was ongoing in everyone's mind. England and France were insisting on our military help, which was given and under way with merchant ships loaded with military equipment and warring machinery. As for me, his brother Ed, I knew very little about the United States helping with the fighting in Europe at that time because I was only in the second grade.

My dad sure knew what was going on, and he raised *hell* with anyone that did not back the country as a patriot. Then after we had moved to Montgomery and when the declaration of war happened after an attack on Pearl Harbor on December 7, 1941, America within the week declared war on both Germany and Japan within a few days. This was the expected involvement; country's citizens began enhancing their patriotism beyond high devotion and were even more devoted to doing critical jobs. Everyone helped with everything, and it included kids searching and gathering scrap metal. It was a job I enjoyed, and I was good at collecting scrap metal.

Dad was always critical of us doing odd things that might lead us to get involved with dangerous activities where we might get hurt. This thought lingered forever on his mind after his two sons, both named Alphonso after their maternal grandfather, had died of sicknesses during the Great Depression. The first child died after he was almost five years old, and the second child died a few years later after only being a baby about six months old. This devastating time during the Great Depression was a life-changing and heartfelt disaster especially for my mom and dad. It took their life of love and turned it into an unprecedented close watching care time for their children and increased teachings of compassionate *steerage* and *amour* to ensure minding bound memories of "knowledge and experience."

Afterward we siblings were in school for a few years, we were mostly around the home or within a block of our home. As we got older, Dad allowed Gene and me to walk to the Montgomery Bridge, but we could only focus on actions of townspeople crossing the Montgomery Bridge heading toward Smithers, looking west at the bridge's end where the highway above railroad tracks where U.S. Route 60 Highway was toward Charleston and at the opposite end east toward Cannelton.

After begging for a visit to Uncle Tony's home, we sometimes got Dad's permission, and off we would go, and, eventually, we even walked across the Montgomery Bridge; the distance was only one mile. Sometimes, we would go into Smithers for a short visit to stores to see what was for sale. For most trips, we went straight to Uncle Tony and Aunt Catherine's home for an overnight stay on the weekend. We loved being with their family. As weeks went by, we mostly liked staying overnight at Aunt Catherine's on Saturday. We romped around low parts of mountains with my cousins Frank, known as Bert for a nickname, and he was also named after Big Poppy; John William, named after his mother's brother Bill; and Junior, named Anthony after his father Antonio (Tony). Once we were together, they took us hiking to the Devil's Tea Table Mountain. I talked Gene into gaining an OK from Mom, and she did the rest.

For years to come, we cousins were usually together throughout school including Aunt Mary's children, mostly with her boys, Paul, Franklin, and

Tommy. We had family interactions and sociability and comradeship continually, always at work and even while in college. I loved my aunt Mary and uncle (Little) Benny, who was a miner all his life. As during my schooling that lasted forever, I was usually with Paul, Johnny, and Bert on a daily basis in school and at work. We had a repartee that continued for years, and after marriage, we had separated because of departures to other states or places, and yet we visited many times thereafter when we visited Mom and Dad and went to Big Poppy's *OverHome*. The level of our involvements in our lives after passing the 1950s is yet another story about our lives including our children making our way pursuing *happiness* together as we worked steadily at our jobs.

As I continue these earlier associations, I walked along the highway looking at the train tracks and the river. Usually, there were no B&O trains on the track, but a tram pulling into nearby Smithers was bringing home coal miners after a day's hard work unknown to all but themselves. The tram, a double loader with two cars, stopped and dropped off miners. I turned to look at the tram carrying miners but just stopped as they jumped with their gear and lunch pails. This time, by chance, Gene and I noticed one old miner as we stared to concentrate on the barrel-chested man leaving the crowd. We were distracted only for a moment as four miners removed the tram from the track under supervision of the driver.

The man directly in the grasp of my eyes was our grandfather Big Poppy. Coal dust covered shoulders, elbows, and knees, all drying but still darker with sweat stains on his shirt underarm pits and across his chest.

Big Poppy looked back from under his black steel miner's cap toward Carbon Creek as it roared down past mountains to the valley cascading toward Kanawha River at a distance. I noticed several people and miners also eyeing him in anticipation of his next action. Big Poppy is an impressive man, rough-hewn, dirty, and old-looking, even though he looks younger than his nearly sixty-nine years. Gene had that facial expression of pride that his grandfather was still able to work in the mine. Mine workers all look like they aged as if under great stress in their work, as does one who works so hard mentally on difficult thinking jobs. Isn't that odd?

Gene said with a comment, "Big Poppy must be happy doing what his job demanded and as his life goes, but he does not show that happiness releases him from a stress of age-related demands." I just listened to what my brother Gene's deep-thinking mind said, and I gathered it as a memory.

Big Poppy, who has been working in the mines since he was a little more than a kid when he got his start in Sicily, demanded respect. Francesco did not expect anyone to erupt from their minds when all were within hearing and sight distance of his stance. In build, Big Poppy was a stocky five-foot ten inches in height when he was a young Italian. One difference is that he has a white limestone face for an Italian, supposedly from the south of Italy because it is more common for northern Italians. His strength was revealed in a wide stride complemented as a demonstratively mustachioed proud Italian.

In stature, he was distinctively different from other miners, young or old. He exuded a threatening image. We did not want to cause him to get a sense of displeasure when he beckoned and later to explain everything to Mom and Dad why we did not go directly to Uncle Tony's home. We decided not to head to him. Gene simply said, "We were on our way to Aunt Catherine's and had gone far enough to recognize him, and that was enough." That let all know he has achieved what he set out to do from any point of contention in his life, and that was what he did the rest of his life.

What was strange at this time was that Frankie was in town at that very time, and he later told us what he had seen Big Poppy do after he returned from the mine to Smithers where the train stopped at the water tank. I know Frank liked to talk and did intensely about what Big Poppy did during his daily walk from the water tank to home. He kept in mind his age, and many times, he repeated his habitual walk home. He was a man of means and prosperous enough homeowner and family man and should have been retired. He owned five homes within nearly one acre in the nearby Kanawha River at the bank on the corner of Kanawha Avenue and Rosa Street.

Big Poppy was with several miners as he walked, stepping slightly bandy and forward heading for wood slats laid as sidewalks that headed him to the road to his home. A few of his close friends now surrounding him as other people on the street and miners dispersed sneakily when he approached. He crossed the main street and stepped upon the wooden sidewalk, which was raised above the ground level. The thick slats had about one-quarter of an inch spacing as a necessity to keep the rain off when the street flooded. As he passed people, he reached out and slapped a dodging friend on the back with a laugh. He shouted, startling him, to show a jester of strength more than friendship, but the man being a longtime friend was copacetic.

At the same time, the train engineer in the approaching freight train blew his whistle, which added another jar to Francesco's friend. Now, Francesco was known to his old friends as Frank. He got a big hug from his friend, and in his own mind, he sensed a fear as he said, "John, a neighbor, don't be afraid of train. The whistle tells you it's a close, uh, warning you. Anytime you are warned, then you, uh, must notice or you must move fast to save your life."

Big Poppy looked into John's eyes and asked, "You, uh, OK?" Both men looked around and saw that no one was having any kind of problem. Many people in close-by areas took heed and looked astonished to see that all was well. The whistle was just a warning with several actions around the track area. The engineer saw a collection of people on the grassy berm, weed-encroached hillside.

Several of the other people, some friends, cringed as Big Poppy whistled with his two fingers in his mouth to mock the train.

John jumped at the chance to pose a façade of a response with a slight whisper in his voice. "Hey, Big Poppy! Good to see you and that you're out of that hole in the ground once again."

The appeasement took several more men of Italian descent gathered around Big Poppy, and conversations rattled, some in Italian, one with a mentioning of his name Francesco.

Big Poppy doused it all with a shout, "Ho seniti tutto." (I hear everybody.) "Uspata!" (Wait!) "John, what you say? You no like me pat you on the back?"

John, shying to a shiver, quickly said, "Francesco, I love your hit on my back! It tells guys I am your friend. Nothing, uh, better." All the guys stared at John and then smiled to signal an approval to Big Poppy.

A few miners and some local people gathered behind and followed the two men now walking side by side to see if something was going to erupt. This went on for about twenty or so seconds, and Big Poppy pointed to Smithers downtown area and the dilapidated theater, exclaiming, "Look, uh, what the hell is this smelly theater showing? Cowboy and Indians movie. How come they don't show miner's shows?"

John interrupted with "Questo è il grande cibo di Hollywood per gli Americani, tutti pensano che siano dei cowboy in Occidente." (That's Hollywood's big feed for Americans. They all think they are cowboys in the West.) Big Poppy paid little attention, and he gestured with his hands like holding a deck of cards as he said, "We play, ah, casino! Saturday, usual time! At Al's, eh? You be my 'Little Bossa'!"

John Cosentino OK'd with a smile. "Qui! Frank, you the Big Bossa!"

Big Poppy, with a thrust in his voice almost ready to fight, shouted, "You goddamn right! But you gotta win beer, eh, John?"

John said with great respect, "Yeah, Frank." He left Frank's company with a wave and entered the shoe repair shop.

Big Poppy continued along his way on the boarded sidewalk thinking out loud, slipping with sound as he walked about, "What a shitty town! This is where I live, and this is where I will die."

Michigan Avenue is the only business street of downtown Smithers. An eclectic design of early 1900s now prevails, and its growth remains small, old facades of buildings blackened with coal grit; business buildings are on one side of the road. Old parked cars on both sides of the street are covered with coal dust, and only a few are washed. Several cars in parking spots are in a dilapidated state or broken down. Buildings are only on the one side of the road because the B&O Railroad Company railroad tracks are on the other side of Highway Route 60, with only about twenty feet between the road and tracks, and the area is mostly surrounded with shrubs, small volunteer trees, and weeds.

Beyond the main Highway Route 60 was cut out from the bottom and into and adjacent to the imposing mountainside, revealing scattered seams of coal parallel in strata that reveal the age of when undercuts were cut to gain flat road measurements. This geological revelation showed the extent of maybe fifty to seventy-five million years ago of what had occurred in carboniferous conversion times. It all took a million years within Paleozoic era during Devonian times that began the formation of coal.

One would think that it must have been God the Creator that selected to put these Italian people of past times in Smithers. Big Poppy never knew to say God was the planner of both creation and evolution or anything else in the universe. Big Poppy set his knowledge in action as it came along to support all living people and things and especially lives of Italians because he imposed his opinions as they were mentioned.

Then on the open existing slanted surface of the climbing mountain, plant life flourished with lush greenery to the top of the mountains at least three or four hundred feet high in great Appalachian Mountain expanses where they were on both sides of the Kanawha River and beyond all unaltered except in mining areas. Back along the city's buildings included a lumber yard office at the edge of Cannelton Creek along where it flows toward the Kanawha River. The cleared field at the backside was an old oil storage site and distribution center for Eastern States Standard Oil (ESSO) so popular at early times throughout the Eastern Seaboard.

Beyond storage sites in Smithers but not toward the river, a large vacant flat field lies for about a half mile and is used by kids to play any kind of game they could devise. Baseball was ever so popular in times starting in 1920s when famous Babe Ruth and Lou Gehrig's exceptional performances for New York Yankees, which made it America's most popular sport that has carried the moniker to modern times. Almost every kid and young adult played it during the season in schools and college including several sponsored semipro and minor league teams, by who, I don't know?

Going uptown on the east side of the creek toward downtown Smithers is the old theater next door to a small beverage shop and a shoe repair shop. Giannini's Hardware is located a few doors up and carries numerous home building supplies and things needed on farms, such as seeds and garden tools and mining tools and supplies with a display of all kinds of shovels and picks outside. Further up from Giannini's was the pool hall, later bought and run by Al Falbo after World War II, and he called it Al's Place. On the next block, where the walkway is raised with an additional two wooden steps, was Cavalier's Groceries. Various other services such as barbershops, grocery stores, even delicatessen and bakery, street vendors, and sundries are opened for miners even though they have little monies for discretionary goods.

The locale and environment had degraded, as do the state's small towns under these poor times. They were dragged into the Great Depression era. Little or unnoticeable changes will be made to the buildings from this time until many years after the World War II. Suddenly, Francesco felt *depreso* (depressed), although he didn't know why he held thoughts about a woman that had just passed him. He almost gushily enticed his mind to bid hello with a smile and tip his miner's cap but didn't because of his miner's appearance and behavioral constitutional fortitude as a sober man coming home from work. What went through his mind was a sensuous attraction that disappeared in a few steps as he clumsily bumped a few passersby on the street, touching one with a dirty elbow, who lightly shouted, "Be careful!"

Francesco lipped an, "Excuse me." He tipped his hat brim to expiate to the lady having already passed by. Then he saw children playing, shop owners at their doors, and even some groups that were walking miners look seriously. John was still looking for the reason for the whistleblowing, anticipating danger or an accident. With no answer, onlookers all silently settled down as Francesco's gate increased to get on home. Francesco encountered two young miners as dirty as himself on their way home along his same path. He singled out one young miner as a neighbor of a long time and shouted, "Tony, where's your poppa?"

Tony saying and whistled while pointing at a girl and motioned to his close-by friend as Big Poppy walked toward him and looked at the girl. He knw Tony knew him, but before he can say anything, he heard Tony shouting as he pointed at Dooley, a guy with whom he grew up, saying, "That's the girl I'm gonna marry."

Dooley touched his heart and formed half a smile. "Hey, Big Poppy, help me with this guy? He's making fun of me and my new girl." Bill Dooley saw that Big Poppy knew why his friend whistled, and Bill gallantly shouted, "She's a sweetheart! Yes! And you know she's married to me." He execrated to the height of disgust, shouting at Tony, "You should join the Union. Tony, you would get a raise, but with your brain, you would have to be a lackey for Union bosses. After you fail in that job, then you can get a job in another Union—he John L. Lewis' United Mine Workers or a Marital Union, which your wife would run! And it would be you that would cause her to run out of town!"

Big Poppy, a longtime Union man after the fighting in 1930s, cannot take anything negative about the Union. He shouted at Bill Dooley, "You put down the Union! You no talk about John L. Lewis like a that! Get him, Tony! Punch him!"

The two men were half wrestle, half jostling but with an eye on Big Poppy to gain his interest. They grabbed and spun each other and bumped four or five other miners. Miners then chased Tony for fun. Tony threw his gloves at Bill. Bill ran and grabbed his wife and lifted her, giving her hugs and kisses. The other miners laughed jokingly. They did sexy whistling and sang, "Tony! Here comes the bride."

Big Poppy broke in and manhandled both men as he put them in shock with his strength of the grab and smiled as he said, "Dooley, you love, eh, your wife, and that's a good. She'd like a that! She's so sweet!" Then he whispered to Tony. "You're OK! Hey, Tony, come over here," as he pointed to the Smithers Hotel. "I know where you can get a good girl. It's located on the other side of the street where the railroad has a slightly raised embankment. The *cilindrico* (cylindrical) wooden water tank needs the black metal funnel, but it is difficult to find one."

Francesco pointed at the base of the tank with a mean expression, saying, "That's a where hobos hang out. They use it as a place to eat, drink, and sleep. And anything they can get away with, eh? The police tell me they catch women there sometimes. Most of the time, 'hobos (*disperde*) scatter into the hills and behind trees. No one goes above the railroad to the main highway along the mountainside." What odd thoughts must be going through his mind as he stared at one of the girls nearby that knows Tony.

I was told that miners and local laborers mosey along track groups of hobos shouting obscenities as they pass other hobos along stretches of tracks. The agitation sometimes causes fights, but one seldom happens because working miners have advantage. They were looking to beat the hell out of the hobos, who do not have the physical strength as do workers, or they run for the leaving train. The workers move quickly to disrupt hobos and discourage them from stopping and staying in the town. The sad part is that some snide words were used under their breaths but were not understood by me. When I saw lingering shallow looks on their faces, the workers didn't give a damn what they did; they chased the hobos away.

The congestion of people in areas was so narrow that the land presents people, old cars, trucks, and miners scurrying to board them, whoever were lucky to own any one of them. Miners board cars and start revving up their smelly, loud engines, producing smoke fumes and gasoline smells that repulses nearby townsfolk coughing and complaining. It's the same thing every day when they drive off to make their way home. People in concert were shouting out in several European languages including Italian, Polish, and German so constantly and consistently that it enhanced mixed noises that roar in towns, which brought police to handle ongoing confrontations.

Now, Big Poppy was just a block away as he continued his trekked path on the wooden walkway directed at accomplishing his daily ritual. He looked toward the end of the street where he lives. From within his subconscious mind, he was looking for the alleyway, a shortcut to his home.

The alley path is about one hundred steps closer to his home than the roadway home. As I was always accustomed to the way his mind works, his subconscious mentality guided him with the thought that it's the right path where he would not run into any more people.

Alleyways were a site to behold with home trash burning or old smoking fires glistening with embers and especially when children were kicking up trash and extending smells and mixing gross aromas but with the intent of finding a nickel or dime. Big Poppy looks at dogs playing with kids for whatever trick they wanted while running and barking after sticks and even hot tin cans. As for cats, they usually were running and screeching to get away from kids because cats never do anything for kids, especially when kids throw bottle caps, pieces of burnt wood, and small rocks at them.

The children and mothers were usually somewhere out in open areas, being part of families that live at various houses that back into the alley. Mothers were on the lookout for their husbands and sons who work with their fathers or at the same place or in some cases in another job. All the while waiting, mothers were in common gossip conversations that were about neighbors and families with local interests among young girls and boys who were excited about each other so that they know what was going on. Most younger kids were roughhousing and playing kick the can, maybe kick the fire to spark lighted ashes or even playing marbles. Others were jumping rope or passing balls in the alley. Its proximity after having already passed beyond the gathering area. A train started as Big Poppy turned to look toward the trestle over pass. The train engineer blew its whistle again as steam exited, rose, and spread into the direction of the sunset high in the horizon against the mountain.

Frankie remembers when he looked toward Charleston into an array of a massive extension of clouds in the sky of oranges, magentas, and deep reds mixed with a multiple of yellow hues. Frankie wondered where colors come from. He said he just gave up thinking about it almost as soon as it entered his mind to be recorded. Many years later, his chemistry teacher told him, "It was caused by the way the sun's light scatters in materials and changes wavelengths when it scatters." At that first disclosure, he said he thought, what the hell does that mean? He still didn't really know. That was because at that time, he was putting most of his interests thinking about his coming education and paying attention to music, playing, and writing; nothing else and certainly not science and not medicine.

Frankie sidetracked his thoughts and grabbed Gene and me and started to describe young guys playing ball in the big field next to the Italian hall where meetings and affairs were held. They were all in a huddle and looked like they had never been washed. Frankie was standing on the slight hill at the main track area across the street but directly in front of the alley watching Big Poppy coming up the sidewalk.

We just listened. Odd sounds were emanating from railroad tracks area, beside their jargon, slang, and hideous but hilarious profanities, an obvious haggling with screams by a couple of them. I knew they were hobos that ran to jump on the train with excitement mimicking train noises raising ambient sound level about thirty decibels. Then the train whistle blew the second time as smoke sprayed from the stack. Both puffed smoke and the engine chugged at a rapid pace. And in broken English with a blessing by all shouting, "Holy smoke!" He saw the smoke ring. One of the less-engrossed hobos pleaded. "We've missed our train!"

Frankie turned and put his eyes back on Big Poppy. All he saw and heard were hobos settling in the grass with God only knows whatever, them shouting and scattering in all directions. Frankie then gained our silent attention, and we moved toward the building as he saw Big Poppy walking toward the door of the corner beer garden, which is Al's Place where people drink beer, play pool, and talk and bet on sports.

Frankie, Gene, and Eddie moved closer. As Big Poppy stopped at the doorway, he saw Frankie, the other two behind him, as Big Poppy said, "Frankie, *vene aquia* (come here)!" Big Poppy took his hand off the door, knowing men and boys at younger than eighteen could not play pool. They both got out of the doorway. Frank turned to observe what's going on in Al's Place. He turned to Big Poppy with the intent of a limited and shy conversation and asked him one question, "Big Poppy! Are you going to Al's? We gotta go home!"

Big Poppy gave him a hug and told him to go home. Gene and Eddie ran home. Frankie took off toward the main road home. Frankie being a well-versed camera user panned by eye the beauty of West Virginia's hills looking toward Boomer. From what he told us, he pointed his camera toward company houses dispersed on both sides of the town as miners disappear up the road and into homes. Then he focused on the highlighted paraphernalia, decor, and people who happen to be in town. Frankie then went home by himself.

I am now guessing what Big Poppy did, because after seeing him do the same thing so many times, we know his routine. I have composed what might have happened. Big Poppy probably opened the door and bumped into Al Falbo's boy Sammy. He then grabbed Sammy's hand and squeezed it to where Sammy showed pain and pulled it away with a smile. Big Poppy grabbed another young Italian man maybe with thinning hair and pulled a few strands to gain a squeak. Larry turned and recognized Big Poppy and gave him a hug. Larry smiled and laid his arm of peace Italian style on his chest. Big Poppy also got a hug from Chris, one of his brother's sons that everyone knows. Miscellaneous background noise in the bar area increased just from the spinning would nearly make movements. Old spilled beer odors from new but minor splashes and aromas of smoke from Italian dark brown stogies just being lit and chewing tobacco and to spit hitting spittoons.

Miners and pool players were talking gibberish with slang words and known gestures with their hands to complement obscenities with limb expressions and tidbits with four-letter words tossed among each other. Big Poppy answered guys next to him, waving his arm with a fist and pumped from the bend at the elbow, whispering, "Ah *fongule!*" which by the way, we did not understand the words, being children.

Without another word, he shook Francesco's hand. Big Poppy put his lunch bucket on the bar. So let's hear what he has to say as he continues his practiced ways. Big Poppy usually pointed as he hit the bar with his fist, shouting as vibrations move all heads toward the sound. "Goddammit! Who's a runnin' this *peshitu* (piss) smelling place?"

Little Sammy, bartending for his father, crossed over to Big Poppy. One of Big Poppy's neighbors joined him, demanding his favorite beer, and said, "Sammy, pour two Miller's, one for Francesco and one for himself."

Big Poppy looked a little excited to the boy, but without a blush of red in his face, he firmly said, "Goddammit, Sammy, also fill up my sonnabitch bucket! What's matter, Sammy? I'm your friend. You don't like a me? Every goddamn time I come in, I gotta ask for beer! Where's your poppa?"

Sammy was frightened but bravely replied, "Eh! Poppy, you're my godfather. I love you." Sammy looked off to the side and found his dad and shouted, "Hey, Pop!" as he touched Big Poppy's hand in friendship, "Big Poppy wants to see you."

Big Sam interrupted customers. "Excuse me." He shouted as he walked with excitement, "Francesco! I'm coming. Big Poppy! I'm here!" Big Sam took the bucket from Sammy and filled it to the brim, sensitively saying, "Sammy, move over and take care of those two guys at the end of the bar."

Big Poppy said, "Sammy's a good boy. He, uh, makes me *soberbio* (proud). You like me, uh? You give me beer, *qui?* Ah! And give a me Baby Ruth candy bar." Big Poppy hit his chest, hugged Big Sam, hit Tony next to him on the head lightly with a knuckle pop, grabbed the lunch pail and candy bar, and left. On his way out, he directed a boy playing pool to open the door quickly and bumped into several miners as he left. They dodged him and his aura of fear respectfully.

Two miners, remarked after Big Poppy went through doors, "He's . . . one . . . tough . . . sonnabitch!"

About five other guys ejaculated in unison, "You're goddamn right!"

Big Poppy exited the sidewalk at Main Street in the late afternoon as the cloudy and cold weather hit him in the face. He knew he's close and continued toward the alley.

Frankie told me at the time and many times thereafter in his own words, "Most of this is what I heard many times when I followed him home and listened to his words. Sometimes, I was close enough to hear him talking to friends. By the way, I've done this several other times when it occurred by chance because it mentally allowed me to understand him, and maybe someday, I will know him as well as my dad does. Maybe not, but I still am able to gain knowledge of his common actions. I know he likes me, and sometimes, he sees me and calls me over to walk with him especially in summertime. That's when I get his tight neck hug and he lets me know who's the boss, and an extra squeeze makes sure I get the message."

Big Poppy bumped into a nonminer friend, Sam Giannini, who owns the hardware store. He quickly brought up the cloudy weather coming back after the big rain last week. Francesco made it a point that he doesn't care about the weather for the most part because he spends the day in the mines. Francesco only sees it when he has had lunch and when he leaves for home. Francesco directed Sam to deliver eight four-by-fours to his house on Friday morning. They parted after Sam OK'd the order. Francesco continued walking toward the alley. They walked to the outside door of Cavalier's Grocery Store. He stopped, shook hands, and looked inside a display window at Italian sausage and soccer-sized provolone cheese balls hanging in the window. He said to Joe, "My son Benny will buy Provolone and sausage when he comes over, uh!"

Big Poppy headed home up the alleyway, bundling up in his jacket because the early evening wind increased. I would do the same. He put his hand on his forehead and smiled as he immediately saw five kids acting cold, rubbing hands and holding them over the heat from the fire in the alley. They are red faced from activity and now huddling around the small burning and sometimes smoldering trash fire. Each boy looked up, appeared frightened, and stared away and down at the fire away from Big Poppy as he walked up alley, sidestepping holes and trash with concentration on each big boot's place. One dark-skinned kid touched his pail as he went by.

Big Poppy responded roughly, "Tu sputa. Tu bruta basta, poco! (You wait. You mean little bastard!)

All the kids scattered except one.

Big Poppy exclaimed, "Here, take da Baby Ruth. Share! Or I'll smacka your head!"

One kid grabbed it to share. The other kids gathered again nearby Big Poppy. The littlest kid shyly said, "Thanks, Big Poppy!"

Big Poppy said to the other kids, "Here's another one. Share it!"

Other kids said, "Thanks!" He tore off the paper, and both boys were sharing the Baby Ruth by handing pieces to three other kids and smiled, and one said, "Take some. He's OK!"

Big Poppy continued on his way past kids but heard one kid as he said, almost in a whisper, "Sometime, you have to watch out for him. He doesn't care who you are!" Big Poppy smiled and knew who's always the boss. He proceeded walking, and one kid turned and walked behind, pretending to be Big Poppy. Big Poppy turned and kicked dirt back toward the fire, shouting, "Watch outta! You think you're a tough? Wait when you grow up. You'll find out who's tougher than you, and you will know it. Learn to take care. Don't start nothing and there won't be nothing."

The little kid smiled with an expression of fright, his hands near his mouth, so easy to notice his dirty nails. He went over, took Big Poppy's hand, and thanked him for the Baby Ruth. Big Poppy grabbed the kid's hand that looked so dirty and said, "Wash those hands when you go home. You look like a miner. When I give you candy, it's as good as you'll ever get—remember, it's a Baby Ruth!"

Big Poppy kicked the surrounding burnt rubble into center of bonfire and proceeded up the alley behind the Donleavy's, who lived on the left of the alley, an unknown family on the right, and the Bakers, who lived at the end of alley next to Big Poppy's duplex at the far end of his *OverHome*.

Frankie remembers that the Bakers owned a bakery in downtown Smithers. The Bakers are an Italian family with an Americanized name taken at entry at Ellis Island. The Bakers had popular children and several good-looking girls. And as Frankie told us later, he asked one of the girls to go to a movie with him, and she did. He said the eldest two were knockouts. The family who lived about halfway down the alley in which the back of the house was exposed usually burned trash in alley and many times. They also had two girls, and they were there observing the fire while young boys were talking with them. Big Poppy kicked ashes away to reveal a brown-blackened edge and shiny silver face of a dime sparkling on ground. He motioned to a dark-skinned Italian kid with his hand by pointing to the hot ashes, saying, "Use a stick to get the dime out!" He rotated his head, contorted his face showing signal to be careful, and said, "Use a bigger stick so you don't get burned." He smiled and left kids all intensively looking at the guy fishing out the dime before anyone can say anything to him.

Big Poppy continued toward a metal chain gate in his fence partially hanging and mating with the one attached to Donleavy' fence and entered his yard. He closed gate. His homes are newer where Big Poppy lives. It's obvious the houses were maintained. Located beyond the gate was one of his duplexes in which two of his sons' families live. These homes face toward Big Poppy's house, at the end about sixty feet away. Big Poppy passes each home in his *OverHome* every day as he walked toward his own home at end of the site. The surrounding outside grounds were kept neatly.

Frankie said my dad and uncle Tony, now grown up and married, lived there with their families. Mary, his eldest daughter, lives with husband, Little Benny, Big Poppy's nephew in Upper Smithers near Boomer (next town east). Katy, Jimmy, and Charlie, the three of his other children, lived with him and Big Mommy in their home. Sons Joe and Frank Jr. rented in Montgomery where they worked. Big Poppy's home is the *OverHome*!

Big Poppy walked toward the front porch. Katy ran out to Big Poppy at the door, greeted him with a hug, and exclaimed, "Poppy! Poppy!" Katy kissed him respectfully but as a fearful daughter. "Poppy, you work so hard! Mommy's got your bath ready."

Big Poppy handed the top half of the lunch bucket to Katy almost as if she were expecting it as he pulled it away and smiled as he let go. Katy looked inside and smiled, saying, "Poppy, you saved a piece of piece of cake for me!"

Big Poppy dominantly frightened her as he shoved the bigger bottom half of the bucket to Katy, and she knew what to do as she took the handle carefully and watched her poppy give directions. "Take, ah, the beer, put in icebox. Don't, ah, drop it! A piece of cake for you then. Eh!"

Katy carefully took both parts of bucket, walked kid-fast into the house, watching so as not to spill any of the beer, and proceeded to get the task done as told. Frankie was behind Big Poppy at some distance this time and did not want to interfere with him or my aunt Katy. She was much older than me, and I know he will take care of me another time with some sort of goodie.

Even at this age, thoughts that were spiraling through my brain mattered; I listened to him. He made me think out loud about what he was saying, so I interrupted him at this time to express what I had heard after many years later. "Frankie, you know what's it like at Big Mommy's on Friday nights and payday. You should have fun! You know what it was like on Saturday, the next day, all day and then on Sunday, more fun, until late evening when it's our bedtime. You've lived it for the past five years since you've been big enough to know what the hell goes on in the Divita family under all kinds of conditions and confrontations good and bad. God only knows what's next to do, but then he said, "Everybody knows who's going to start it!"

Frankie then said, "Big Poppy is the boss. It's his home, for that matter, in anyone's home, especially his children and Big Mommy." He's the honcho, no matter what the subject is or who brings it up. He usually starts out dominantly because he wants everyone to fear him. Most of the time, he was not serious, and the incident was easily resolved and with some sound reason when less alcohol had been imbibed. His personality used divisiveness to gather his forces or reduce strengths of his adversaries about family matters. Most confrontations end with abusiveness as a run of the mill directed toward shortcomings of women in the family, his wife foremost, and most of the time, she never complained. This was a characteristic that he must have developed as an abused kid in Palermo, Sicily, from his early days. He was, at times, thought by many family members to be treated like an orphan. This assumption was highly doubtful because his family birthing ties having had a sister and three brothers known to his own father Liborio's and mother Marguerita's family as noted members is well accounted in past archival records. Big Benny, the eldest of Francesco's children, must have known his own real grandparents whose names were known and archived. Big Benny was named Liborio after his grandfather. Beyond those times, little is known about the Divitas.

This is a transfer back to their intentions to go to America. As a start, Francesco left Sicily on July 1910 heading to America, and when he arrived, he got a job to work in Brooklyn, New York. He wanted to work for the next two or three years to bring his wife and children to America because his family had already been married and had three children still living in Valguarnera, Sicily. He stayed in Brooklyn to earn monies to bring his family back to the States. And remembered, when he returned three years later, his father had passed away. Big Poppy's plan was to bring his wife Filippa and children in the family to America. After one year and at nearly within the next year, he would go back to Valguarnera and get the family ready to leave for the United States of America on a different ship. Big Mommy had told him that his poppy was hard to handle, although he was the firstborn in his father's real family.

The combined and remembered story continued with many exchanged words archived in many memories. Big Poppy may have lived under tough familial or peer behavior in his early years, which was unknown to all. After he was fully a man, no one ever would have dared to attempt to abuse him, after he became an adult, under any circumstance. He had a difficult time with allowing people to ignore his wants, orders, or demands. His adulthood, first, in Sicily and later in America, was under extremely hard times and conditions where the force both physically and mentally always acquired control over weaker natures.

Only Big Mommy really knew him when he was younger, in his earlier teen age, and from the edge of manhood when they married. She could see value in his strengths and on the front end forgave his weaknesses. When they first met and later married, he had to work many hours in sulfur mines to make sure they could live as he was expected to provide. Times were very difficult for all people in Italy during the late 1890s, and to feed one's family was a major achievement. This was his driving force that plagued his mind, and the more he heard about America and the country's differences regarding life, liberty, and pursuit of happiness, the offer to immigrate and make a good life, the more he discussed it with his wife.

After a short while and during this time, he was never a drinking man but was one of great mental and physical strength. Francesco had made the decision that his family would venture with hope in their minds and love in their hearts to jump into a new life. It was cast in stone by Big Poppy, as old sayings goes, "Things do not change easily."

His family, one of many poor families, left Palermo, Sicily, and moved to Valguarnera, Sicily, where they had lived after their marriage about eight years before he left for America. During this time, Italy was a depression-stricken country. Overall, Italy was under aristocratic oppressive times that left the common people as serfs who were at the disposal of the wealthy and were almost treated as beggars. That was when the Divitas knew they had to leave under the strained conditions of having saved only a little money to start on their journey of immigrating to America.

Big Mommy knew how to get along with him most of the times especially in the early years. In the later years, even after going to America and much later when he became addicted to alcohol, he was difficult, rude, and derogatory; and when at his best, a domineer human being to the family. Sometimes, he would psychologically attack Big Mommy or anyone by degrading them with their shortcomings. Big Mommy, in a compassionate way, always greeted Francesco when he lived, and he worked in the mines in Smithers, West Virginia, to appeal to his sense of her love for him, and one could see it in her eyes when she greeted him in Italian as he entered the doorway every day, saying, "Papavero, bene a casa tua." (Poppy, good, uh, you home.) She hugged and kissed him, with both respect and uneasiness, saying, "Sembra che tu abbia lavorato così tanto oggi. Hai fame? Ho formaggio, peperoni e pane fresco per te sul tavolo. Quello che ti piace." (You look like you worked so hard today. Are you hungry? I have cheese, pepperoni, and fresh bread for you on the table. What you like? She walked into the dining room and placed a chair open at the table where Poppy always sits.

Big Poppy pulled the chair and sat and then shouted, "Cheese! Where's, uh, my pepperoni I bought at Cavalier's?"

Big Mommy quickly replied, "Sul tavolo nel piatto coperto, Poppy! Come faccio sempre. Si strofina la schiena mentre si sforza, dicendo, Questo ti farà sentire meglio la schiena." (On the table in the covered dish, Poppy! Like I always do it.) She rubbed his back as he strained, saying, "This will make your back feel better."

Big Poppy grabbed a piece of cheese, took a bite, forked a cut piece of pepperoni, bit it, and followed with a chunk of fresh bread. He looked at Big Mommy and directed her, saying, "Non parlare più." (Don't talk no more.) Signaling to her, he waved hands, pushed food in his mouth, and ate pepperoni wrapped in fresh bread as she, with a sad expression, left the dining room and went into the kitchen.

"Papavero, il tuo bagno è pronto con l'acqua calda fuori dai fornelli." (Poppy! Your bath is ready with the hot water off the stove.) She, as usual, went into the bedroom where old furniture was grandly set, walls decorated with religious pictures, with a special cross with Christ sculpted in detail showing sorrow that would wake any mind viewing the scene with remorse of the agony. The bedding cases and spread with an embroidery were handmade. On the floor a decorative Arabic wool rug covered most of the floor in front of the bed.

However, the setup was pretty much standard every workday. I always remember seeing the area many times, always before Francesco would get home and Filippa would have his tub ready for him when he was ready for a bath.

Frankie also had seen similar bathing actions many times. Frankie told me everything about the bathing from his stored memory with anything he might have added to make it clear in prose. I reduced the thing that he said to me as Frankie help his grandmother Filippa do whatever he told her.

At that time, and with Francesco so young, this is not unusual for many wives or mothers to do hard bathing because it was a must to get Francesco clean including the bedroom. Otherwise, the home will smell like coal dust as well as look dirty no matter what is done to clean the house after a few weeks go by. Modern-day wives think they have it tough. Wow! After a few minutes, she would take boiling hot water from stove to front bedroom to pour it in the tub. Big Mommy returned to the dining room and said, "Papavero, il tuo bagno è pronto con l'acqua calda fuori dai fornelli." (Poppy, your bath's ready.) She did her final heat test of tub water and asked, "Poppy, you want a touch to see if it's OK?"

Poppy said, Ah certo, lo sai per certo Uspata!" ("Ah, sure. You know for sure. Wait!") Big Poppy, still eating, moaned and signaled to Filippa that he was not finished by waving a pausing hand shaking in the air. She went into the kitchen to sit quietly but despairingly at the kitchen table. Within minutes, he got up from the dining room table and went to their bedroom. He shouted for her even though she was already on her way. "Filippa!"

Big Poppy began to strip off his miner's work clothes, pointing to her for help, saying, "Ora togli la maglietta." (Now pull the undershirt off.) With his mental attitude and motions in his hands, she did it with a soft finesse that quietened him for the moment, and then he directed his attention to the day's work. He fussed saying some words in Italian about the day's work. "I padroni che siamo animali!" (The bosses think we're animals!) He stopped and continued to remove the rest of his work clothes with her help.

Mommy said, "Che succede a Poppy? Che cosa è successo?" (What's the matter, Poppy? What happened?) Big Mommy knows Italian, and oftentimes, she would say things to Frankie, things that were said in English. Frankie told me he made up some things Big Poppy and Big Mommy would say simply by putting them in his own words to make the story sense the actions of a coal miner's bath with me adding for the story the Italian language. Frankie had memories detailed in his mind, and I listened to everything he told me.

He began complaining using his hands about having a dry mouth from the coal dust. He pointed into his mouth and then said words of intent that continued, "Uh, tutti si lamentano, lo sai, mi sono lamentato della polvere di carbone, i supervisori eh, non me ne frega niente, pensavo che fosse mio amico, quel dannato ragazzo ha detto all'azienda Boss." (Uh! Everybody complains, you know! I complained about the coal dust. Supervisors, eh, don't give a damn. I thought he was my friend. That goddamn guy told the company boss.) He came back and said, "Gliel ho detto, ma so che non farà nulla." I told him, but I know he won't do anything.) Then he said, "È un lavoro da minatore e tutti dicono che succede ogni giorno." (That's my miner's day's work ends after taking a bath. "Everybody says it happens every day.")

Big Poppy's clean clothes were laid out on the bedroom armchair, towels on metal rack and the extra-large oblong galvanized steel washing tub still sitting on top of an eight-by-eight-foot-square cotton rug to absorb water that splashes on the rug.

Frankie returned to Big Poppy in his bedroom the next day to see if he needed any help. He's very interested in the way the bedroom area is laid out and paused in detail looking at the pasta on wax paper on the bed.

Frankie noticed it's the only thing out of place or that looks abnormal. He said to me, "That is when I see the newly made pasta strips drying and organized so carefully on wax paper on a clean sheet. They will be ready for the kettle for Sunday's dinner." Then again, it's a normal household job related to being responsible for meals when the whole family would appear almost out of the woodwork and under direct orders from the patriarch Francesco.

Dinners on Friday evening also happen when family members, still in some of the *OverHome* buildings, including some sons and daughters who live with the family, come in to see Big Poppy. He never refuses to offer food or even a sample and, for sure, may offer a beer or a glass of wine. Frankie continued to recall activity in the kitchen no matter how hard it was because his awes around Big Poppy gets him involved with poor responses.

Two hours later, Katy was in the kitchen stirring meatball sauce for Friday night's dinner. The radio was playing music. Katy was singing lightly to herself the song that was being played. It was one of her brothers Benny and they were excited, the boys laughing joyfully. Katy paused as she finished the song "A Foggy Day in London Town" and turned down the radio.

It was from one of George and Ira Gershwin's musical, *A Damsel in Distress*, that they had completed when they first went to Hollywood, California. At that time, the song was popular simply because it was great, and it was wintertime across the country. Katy had seen it at the local theater with her girlfriends. The music was on the radio as background music was being played. Katy turned, took a few steps, and opened the front door at the kitchen. She then walked to the front yard with the same excitement as she always showed when Benny and Josephine and the kids came to dinner; her personality gleamed. She was a great help to her elder brothers and sister and watched kids galore when shopping had to be done.

Katy ran to meet Josephine, gave her a hug and one for her brother, and touched the faces of the three big boys, Frank, Gene, and Alphonso, and baby Eddie. Katy pleaded, "Josephine, give me Eddie. I'll hold him," as she greeted the other children by names. "How ya doing, Frankie? Give me a hug, Alphonso, Gene!"

Josephine inquired, knowing that something was on Katy's mind, "Is it Poppy? What's going on in there? Is Mommy all right?"

Katy quietly responded, "Everything is good now, but when he came home, he seemed like he was upset with his supervisor friend at the mine. Mommy gave him something to eat. He's back sitting at the table. He's expecting all of you because it's Benny's birthday." Then she changed the subject. "Poppy was in the bedroom in the tub an hour ago, but he's now dressed and flaunting around the house with his hat on looking for something to fuss about." Katy, still excited, revealed, "Mommy's got supper cookin'. " Katy asked Jo, "Are you gonna make bread for Sunday? Your bread is the best!"

Big Poppy waited until everyone was in the house, and that includes about two or three families who come into the house after Big Benny, Jo, and the kids. Two of his sons still living home were walking down the front yard. This is what happens most of the time on Sundays, but since Friday was Benny's birthday, it looks like Sunday, when it happens every week.

Frankie later told me about that time with emphasis when I was only five years old, "You ain't seen nothing yet, but you will as you get older. When Sunday comes, especially as time goes by, I saw it from the beginning as a kid." What really happens on that Friday at dinner was Big Poppy described his day at work to his sons. They were very attentive and added curses to the supervisor to offer support as he latched on to his glass without looking for it and buried it in his mouth with the last swig of red wine along lasting on his bottom lip. The sons drank from their glasses at the same time.

By the way, his boys usually bring the wine or, for that matter, liquor when he asks, and bottled beer. Poppy also has his own wine that he makes in the basement under one of the duplex homes. While at dinner, they mostly eat and enjoy a gabfest in English and Italian. About one-half of the conversation is confrontational and usually aimed at one of the sons. Sometimes, it comes in broken English. When Big Poppy asks in Italian, he wants an answer from his boys in Italian.

Discussions were about his conflicts with workers almost getting into a fight over the small amount of progress made so far by the United Mine Workers Union. Even after 1937 and over the past two years, complaints were made. Complaints about the whole year of delay to get the Union involved in the local mines in the area was always discussed but went nowhere. He singled out miner's problems with breathing and sleeping. And he especially relayed with damnation a post support failure that happened today in mines and points out the company's neglect.

He's ready to protest with union guys joining together and fighting industry owners on their own territory and politically. Being an old-timer, he understood what was needed to make things work for workers but never saw reasons that unions make money for their leaders. His personal brag was a comparison of his age and strength with younger miners when he was in Al's Place. He made a point to say that he could work twice as fast as them but won't because he wouldn't get paid for it.

He wondered in words what he might do in retirement now that he's in his early sixties (time now is late in 1937). He knew he had a drinking problem, but in simple terms, he had no remorse for or knowledge of his ingrained caustic personality. He ended it with a voice of strength of how he had helped many miners and their families and had received no help in return.

Big Mommy was a woman of great sensitivity and mentally had inherited common sense education, which was gained while Big Poppy was at work and she took care of the children. Big Mommy taught steerage and amour daily as circumstances and confrontations arose. She read magazines and newspapers and listened to the radio. She shows love to and for her children and her grandchildren just as she held them or fed them and always had a fun gift for them. Both gathered their type and share of character from simple and short involvements with all grandchildren, especially elder ones.

The mothers were more concerned about the younger ones because Big Poppy wanted them to be tough, and he let them know with his tough behavior. Big Benny was a true character personification of the influence his momma had during his development into a known and accepted peacemaker for the family. Later, you will understand that alcoholism and sickness with diabetes had effects on Big Benny, being overweight and used to eating and drinking whatever he wanted. Even as his life changed, it did not change his peaceful personality. The alcohol robbed him of much more, the time he could have spent with his wife and family with all the little confrontations related to how he handled his health.

Bring in three of their elder children revealed what children could sense in Big Poppy and Big Mommy. Each sibling recognized that the gift of advice from parents move them to a higher level of culture for the family. We all could measure that Big Mommy's children will do anything for her. Benny and Jo's children were taught they would do the same for their mom and dad later in life for any menial work. They ran searching through the house to find things even when they do not know where to look. What really happens on Friday nights was what Big Poppy wanted to happen.

Does he play cards with family and friends at home? Daughter Mary typically goes to *OverHome* and greets her father, Big Poppy. She always brings something to him. At this time, some chicken in a spicy tomato and hot peppers sauce that any Italian would stub his toe trying to get to first; but no one touched them until he got his and made offers to others.

Josephine also would go to the *OverHome* mostly with sons, Frankie, Gene, Alphonso, and the baby Eddie, only a few months old, to check on Big Mommy, especially her well-being. She never trusted Poppy when it comes to dishing out abusive words or actions especially to women or when the children were around.

On one past Friday evening, Big Poppy took Frankie, his first grandson and namesake, pulled him to his chest and gave him *un bacio come si pizzicò le guance* (pinches both cheeks as he gave him a kiss). That's him telling me he loves me as a proud man. Big Benny came in and gave Poppy his sons and daughters, who call him Poppa, as they gave him hugs and kisses. Big Benny then told Poppy that he will bring some sausage for him on Sunday. Big Poppy said to get it at Cavalier's. He then kissed Frankie on the cheek and touched Alphonso and Gene's heads as they ran to their dad for rescue. Big Mommy showed an inherent peace of mind seeing her eldest son with his children and knowing that their mother is one of the best Italian girls she had ever met and got to know.

Under conditions of times during late 1930s, she appeared well able to do whatever she wanted and managed to care for her three children with run-of-the-mill problems that plague these times. The main reason was medications were sparse and treatments were skimpy. Doctors told families to keep the children in bed and make sure they don't run a temperature and keep them cool with a compress on the forehead, mostly waiting for the children to heal.

Usually, they responded to various epidemic afflictions as did so many children during the Great Depression; however, many did not survive. Benny and Jo had their fourth child, Edward, in January 1935 and was very happy with the new baby, and as the months improved with the weather, the children were doing fine. However, by midsummer, Alphonso I had gotten sick and was afflicted with diphtheria. Within a month, on September 22, 1935, Benny and Jo's son Alphonso I died from diphtheria suddenly. Both Benny and Jo were shattered with grief and heartfelt despair. Jo had suffered heartbreaking depression all the while taking care of baby Eddie. The grief lingered until she became pregnant again and had another baby. The new baby was born a little more than a year later. This time, the baby was a girl named Phyllis Jane Divita, and as nature demanded into their years of marriage, it was the only girl in the family. The next baby was born on November 30, 1939. Significant care was devoted by both the mother and father, family, and doctors; but the winter was harsh, and diseases were rampant. Alphonso II suffered in his early life and died after five months with pneumonia.

This dire and dreadful loss of a second baby in the mid-1940s was an assault on their Christian beliefs. Only the lack of medical care that was unknown left the baby only under the watchful mothers helped as the day and night goes by until either they get well or as the case would be another child expired, and the heartbreak was enormous; it changed these parents' approach to continually offer close control of any of the children to any kind of danger of affliction.

With all the turmoil and grief, our mother survived with the help of her religious beliefs always on call for a sense of memory and a need to continue raising her living children. She lingers with a living happiness as she holds and talks in a teaching manner to the children in both endearing Italian and clear English. Special care and help to her were always offered by Benny and the elder children. Even the women of the Divita families were there for Jo anytime she would call for one of the sisters-in-law, or if they knew she needed some to help her get through the day, they would contact her. Each family provided various necessities and gifts as if each day was special.

CHAPTER XVI

Divita Family Moved to Renovate Larger Home in 1949

Asceticism
When people are suspicious with you, you
start being suspicious with them.
—Aldous Huxley, *Brave New World*, p. 47

People who are prominent in the town easily covered their sensuous behavior using social importance to resolve the stigma of disloyalty that some had experienced. After becoming a citizen of America, Liborio had been named Benjamin Franklin Divita in 1925. Many years later, my dad had become known as Big Benny, a well-known businessman in the city of Montgomery. Even more people knew him simply because those who knew his story after he became an emigrant in America as a child knew enough about Liborio and even then acknowledged him as a self-sufficient boy with knowledge and experience. All during his early life, he was educated with *steerage* and *amour* that his mommy Filippa continually taught him during the voyage and continued throughout his young life.

Benny Divita, after a journey in the coal mines with his father, then worked in Big Poppy's delicatessen for about another ten years. Then over the next ten years, he had built his adult businesses. First, he started his road building business, and at that time, he found the love of his life while building roads in the farmlands in Adrian, West Virginia. Within a short time, he married Josephine Maruca. After their marriage, he started a taxi business in Montgomery where he settled and had his proud family of children beginning with his first child, Francisco, and then Alphonso I, who died within five years. Eugene, Edward, and Phyllis Jane were next, respectively, and, finally, Alphonso II, who also died as a new born after living only six months. The trauma and the loss of the two boys left them with remorse and sadness that never dispersed. The future children came much later even after World War II had started and at the beginning of 1943. The new family included Robert James, Philip Ray, and Richard Allen in a three-year sequence, who all also followed the teachings of *steerage* and *amour* and became morally and natural educated brothers and one sister, having minds above average and saddled with "knowledge and experience" as strengthened by their parents.

At this time, with his success now living beyond the Great Depression, Benny had decided to go to the fabulous Indianapolis 500 Race in 1941. During the session at the races and meeting friends of great repute, he had the time of his life because he was so interested in sports cars and the racing men who liked his technical knowledge of cars and grandiose personality. The excitement lived with him and his friends and as his business continued to grow.

Later, however, in 1943, one night after the war was under way, he was a passenger in one of his taxis, and the driver was involved in an accident with an unlit parked truck over the edge of the road by at least two feet. Many friends had become compassionate observers and even more than friends and explained the details to the state police. The accident occurred when he decided to go with his driver to deliver lunches to the night shift in the metal ores amalgamation plant in Alloy, West Virginia, a few miles over the Montgomery Bridge heading east, traveling on Route 60. The report stated that the tractor trailer was over on the edge of the driving road about two feet parked on part of the highway with no lights on the tractor trailer. The cab hit the back side of the truck and sent both the driver and him to the hospital. Benny was the one significantly injured being in the front right seat.

A court case was involved, and little amount of real damages were paid, except that the company paid their hospital bills; and it took about six months for Benny to recover and get back to work. The psychological dispositions of the two men, Big Benny and Bill Sergrato, relative to their work and social positions and their loyalties remained and gained praised from both families and many friends.

Everyone in town knew where the most dependable taxi stand was even though there were at least two other taxi businesses in town. The reason for the competition is simple—it was cheap to ride taxis, and only about half of the people living in the city had cars.

Frankie recalled from his times working in Dad's garage that he also owned and told me from his memory about things we did because I also was one of the helpers. Frankie was older by six years, a lofty and almost fourteen years old in the mid of 1943 when I was about eight and was one of the baby cleanup guys. The two war fronts involving World War II were expanding beyond control in the Pacific with most of the Asian continent involved, and in the Atlantic, all European and Africa continents and any adjacent land with military action under way. Our allies critically need more soldiers, weapons, and warring equipment, and the warring capabilities were improving. Significant demands are being made of every nation, and the United States had implemented the leadership in mass production in every industry to the surprise of our allied nations, but especially to the surprise of Germany and Japan as we were beginning to turn the fight to our advantage since the middle of 1943. The patriotism was exacerbated simply by the people who were enlisting and being drafted to fight patriotically for our country with every mindful drive and strength of body in their desire to win the war against the demon dictator in Germany and imperialist in Japan and the Pacific Islands that they had overtaken.

With great interest, I noticed new pursuits of my dad, Big Benny, mostly to eliminate confused relatives where several other Bennys were around when doing family talk and referencing activities. To all others, he is known as Ben or Benny depending on who is addressing him and for what could they expect from this man of peaceable behavior and practical knowledge.

Back in the mid-'30s, my father and Uncle Tony also had started a small bus business that they bought on their own after slyly drifting away from responsibilities of helping to run Big Poppy's owned delicatessen over the previous ten years. It turned out to happen without much fanfare because it had to be closed because of bad times caused by the Great Depression in a small town where Italian specialty foods business was not as active as in New York, which was also in a recession of unusual bad times.

My dad paid for the bulk of the costs of the bus line. With his level of personal and familial generosity, he treated Tony as a full and equal partner as one might expect of a big brother. The bus line's main use was for passengers traveling in and out of town locally, and because of the times, no plans were in the making for an expansion to other towns and cities in the county. Businesses were slow in their own towns where Montgomery was the hub for many nearby towns, but people did not travel much by bus; instead, they hitched rides to go to Montgomery, the hub, to do their shopping. Most of the time, they would end up in Benny's taxi service because they knew that Benny was a fair man with his costs to ride. Benny gave his share of the Blue Ribbon Bus Line to Tony to see if he could make a go of it, but it fizzled out within a year because it was too short of people riding buses in town. The idea, however, was good, and my father had started his taxi business about this same time, and the specific places to go to do business and then take home in a taxi were more required.

The main reason for Benny's decision was to minimize the influence laid on him as the eldest son and to increase separation distance between him and his demanding poppy after work ended for the day, especially since the taxi service could run into a demand of his time from early to late nighttime. The two eldest sons now were not able to see their families remaining in Poppy's *OverHome* commune during the important parts of their lives. This gave them more time to be at their homes, and it was agreed to by their wives. However, that decision materialized, and both men had new addresses beyond local interaction after dark, so to speak. Big Poppy showed a little less respect for both sons because he had lost a degree of control that he could not exercise.

Then over the next few years, more familial migrations took off on a yearly basis as the birds whose habitat is in North America would fly to South America where life was calm. Once this leaving of the *OverHome* had occurred several times, then, finally, younger brothers also departed from the *OverHome* commune especially after they were married. Then the families of the youngest sister and the eldest sister both moved later to distances within the next town; Boomer for the younger one, and the elder one moved much later to Montgomery, a mile or more away. The eldest sister, more invigorated because she had a larger family, moved closer to her eldest brother. It took about a year before the personal responses returned to normal interaction; even with many visits and, of course, a continuation of Sunday dinners at Big Poppy and Big Mommy's almost every Sunday as far back as I can remember even during the mid-1940s.

Because Big Poppy, personally upset, saw less of the families, he made it his business to go to Montgomery more often than any family member expected. He, with a personality of dominance, made it a point to confront each of them when he would find them in town. He knew where to look as if he had conspired with those in the know the whereabouts of his family members, and he would pay a visit. Benny knew his father's mind as one who works it overtime to make sure he gets the right answer to things that he pursued. Therefore, he knew his father's pursuits were ones to force his ways on each of them, and he thought the only way it would work on his boys was to show his might and maybe threaten reprisal. His boys always had to be on their guard if confronted when anxiously encountered. Nothing could interfere with the heartfelt sense of delight and contentment without his presence. Nevertheless, his appearance could lead to a mind filled with an infinity of expectations as if when each soldier in battle is in suspense of the enemy's whereabouts and how they are conditioned.

However, Big Benny's bliss of joy dominated to show that he knew his expectations were not common, but a new home properly located was his next desire. Each one expressed their love at first sight for their new home, and the plan for a normal family life was in the making. Of course, excepting regular family problems, those that usually spring on each member following the "will of desire" could initiate an unexpected move into amorous or unallowed situations of staying out late, and even the young ones were attempting to smoke cigarettes by the time they moved in 1949.

Frank knew his dad would seek and find out about family interactions that were under way within the extended families. He also found out who and what was causing the uproars in both towns. Dad knew from the past that he was the first team to keep watching his children and even of his poppy's activities. Sometimes, he needed his brother Tony's help. This one critical situation involved Big Poppy, who was willing to argue with a vendetta to get his way, especially after being disappointed when his two sons' families left the *OverHome* commune. Big Poppy could not accept that they would not want a lot of time with him. He thought they needed him because they were taught to ask him what he thought of what they were doing in their businesses. Of course, he felt he must be able to tell them that what they were doing was not wise. He didn't give a damn. He used Italian curses imperatively without an ounce of consideration in front of Benny's friends.

This kind of demanding and aggressive meddling was why Benny put some real distance from his father's family as well as to keep his father away from his home when he was not at home to eliminate potential involvements with his wife and kids. And if anyone had good reason and understood why my dad did this distance thing, being the eldest, Frankie knew it was necessary. It was because Big Poppy's persona was always with a mind-set to argue the situation or the outcome under question. After all, Dad's father's twisted slant on his boys was that he is still the boss of these full-on adults. In his mind, not only must they do what he wanted, but also he was prepared to threaten them even at their age and had a record of carrying the threat out, at times, to mentally or physically abuse their mind-sets. Even with this full mental knowledge so deviously distorted, Benny had the chutzpah to resolve the pending action before it could happen.

Benny knew that it will be more difficult for his father to interfere with his family's life if he's a few miles away, especially because he doesn't drive the taxis. On his own, with a well-adjusted mind, he simply thought that the overall separation by distance maximizes time to gain interaction, and it was a good idea to trade distance with time, either one depending on the situation—namely, time and distance, something naturally basic.

In a simple example, Albert Einstein planned his early exit from Germany in 1933 because he figured the writing on the wall that Hitler wanted to head into a new world war. The theoretical information was strongly exposed to the world by his genius, who had already developed and devised in detail his special theory of relativity to a reality at the time around 1905, as $E = mc^2$. Yet he needed a continuation of his mind and other physicists' minds to extend the general theory of relativity in 1915 with principles of nature's interactions between universe fields and stellar bodies.

Werner Heisenberg, a well-known German physicist born about twenty-two years later, had been evolving his theory of the principle of quantum uncertainty and had defined the nature of an extension of relativity that gave him position in Germany. On the other hand, Heisenberg decided to stay within Germany as a German Jew and experienced with little aplomb unassociated devastation and killing Jews. Einstein was more venturesome and left for America because he had a special feeling for being a German Jew. Einstein had enough practical sense to recognize the total hatred of Jews because Hitler's pursuit was to destroy Jews, starting his widespread Holocaust already under way. I believe that my dad had a similar type of mind, and we experienced it as he mostly made sure he knew what we were doing when he was not around.

Now, after thinking about it, the move made sense and Dad's plan was to buy the house in Montgomery that Big Poppy once owned and used as his own Italian delicatessen, which kept his father thinking it's a good idea to buy. Also, at least on the surface, it was a good idea. No one knows what was going on in Big Poppy's cunning mind. Dad knew when Big Poppy thought he has lost control of family members that he unconsciously had an indelible vendetta rolling around in his myriads of memories and concentrating on abnormal neurons whose dendrites have receptors ready to receive neurotransmitters to stimulate any one of the modal memory strikers of recall as instigators ready for mental combat.

As Frank always told me about Dad's thinking, he reminded my memory to release in words related to him, like, "Your dad is a mechanical-minded man from early years' upbringing by his mother's influence and teachings of *steerage* and *amour*. He tinkered with any invention that came to his mind. Then he usually figured it out or he bought one when he was fascinated with its workings and could show it off." As time passed, the new progeny of his immediate family was also of the same mind-set, and he loved it when he could show any job well done to friends.

Each of his younger children had similar talents; most of which they had gathered from their big brothers. With their added innovation, they experimented jointly being dominated by brothers who had the know-how and would take initiatives to direct various projects but with a generous amount of camaraderie.

Dad always took the serious and sensible approach throughout knowing nothing will change as long as he follows his mind's decisions based on his thinking. He was a genius at knowing current situations, and he would review weighing his experiences in his mind's eye. In most situations, he primed people's memories to release reality in such a way that one would imagine the extent to which one would reveal one's self. He had the sense to anticipate changes with thought of expectations as they have come out of others, maybe after the millions of years or when much more than twenty thousand years had passed. Within what we know, maybe it happened much earlier when the *Homo sapiens* had evolved uniquely mentally different as modern mankind.

Fresh images of new mind activities coming from *Homo sapiens*, metaphors oozing to translate feelings, music rose to unify and create blissful thoughts of lyrics to begin compositions of early words yet to be improved by the *Homo sapiens'* minds. Various senses of mind and body in action often repeated sounds and words instilled from memory that deliver messages to spark forgotten memories with new thoughts almost making expected new images once imprinted to be revealed to each other. Most early human beings never thought much of sounds from hearing except when exposed to fear as even now heard. The evolution of words must have started the creations of languages, and, eventually, reading of it with associations and meanings came much later.

This revelation lets readers reflect about their own reality, their thoughts about persons, and important things going on in the world. Dad wittingly relayed to his children something like, accept every day that passes will add to your "knowledge and experience," and the mind builds intelligence and imagination. Many people thrive on happenings of interest to readers' imagination even though thousands of years have passed. He made sure that each one's mind was always capable of selecting to either follow the path of "knowledge and experience," knowing the collection of life's changes and habits. After considering the hardwired instinctive "will of desire," stay off mental tracks that lead to amorous primrose paths. He warned his children that the mind knows troubled waters so clearly that people sense mindful thoughts that continuously buck shores of water when a revealed disloyal *amour* would be the offering.

It was easy to see outputs of Dad's vision from my mind because his first projection had to do with the five homes that he helped build his father's *OverHome* commune land in Smithers. From the time after completion of these homes, they were fully used as homes, and it made Big Poppy a significant amount of money and set good protection for his family for years. However, after their marriage, Mom and Dad were very happy living in their part of the *OverHome* until the birthing and loss of their second child, dying from the disease diphtheria after living until five years old. The real breakdown of Mom and Dad came when the sixth-born child had died of pneumonia about six months after birth. Benny and Josephine suffered the deaths of two of their children, both named Alphonso I and Alphonso II, one in 1935 and the other one in 1940. They and families suffered deeply for many months of heartbreak. Benny had to make changes from the home where it had happened.

By the beginning of 1941, Benny refurbished a large building in Montgomery that he bought from the bank, once owned by his father, Big Poppy. To make it pay for itself, he converted it into a remodeled home on both second levels for his family and at the back end of the building on the upper level. When finished, he had converted it to apartments designed for two different rentals. The remainder, a large basement at the ground level in the front and above his living area, he converted it into a large storage garage, which was under the whole building with a small office on Fourth Avenue. The wise choice was that Dad rented it to a mining company that had seen value in the location to distribute equipment to local mines; this refurbishment all happened just before the Second World War started.

Benny had many needs for this business venture rental in mind for part of the building in which the family would live. What I am saying was that he knew that continued money would increase because of the enormous garage area for storage of mining supplies for various companies. Dad also refurbished back two apartments for people, mostly his friends, who needed living quarters and would be a good location in the city, and rental money would be needed for his businesses.

As Frankie had said, everyone knew that poor times in the last ten years had left a lot of people out of jobs. The depression had subsided because the United States had begun to beef up its military might and was supplying British weapons and fighting machinery and trucks for the war that had started and now added new jobs with the coming war.

From Hitler's beginning, he had revised his interests in the old National Socialist German Worker's Party (Nazi) founded in 1919. Then sometime later in the '20s, he was jailed, serving five years in prison for treason, while he wrote *Mien Kampf.* After he was released at the beginning of 1933, he formed brownshirts, uniformed police-like men, to implement his nationalism to impress people about a form of militarism identified as National Socialism. Hitler, after a short time, was elected chancellor of Germany with a strong pursuit by German political bosses. Immediately, he continued with extreme militarism, racism, and totalitarian directed with all political domination heading Germany toward world leadership, which is total dictatorship. Adolf Hitler, within a few years, began touting his torment on Jews and Germans who did not agree with his planned world domination.

Initially, it started with sneak personal attacks until his party gained full power with him as the chancellor almost by edict with the promise to make Germany the most prosperous and powerful nation in the world. And as it continued even under notice of the German so-called Aryan race, the German hierarchy had relinquished power to Hitler. With this plan, his first direction was to eliminate Jewish people by making them enemies of the country's people in all their endeavors. The new regime developed means to carry out planned annihilation of Jews as if a right had been decreed to Hitler from devotees preaching an Aryan race heritage, which, of course, was a lot of bullshit fed to German people vehemently by Nazis who didn't give a good goddamn for Jews, and everyone in other countries knew it from the beginning no matter what excuse was offered.

Among newspaper reports on the war, Benny Divita knew the idea of an Aryan race was preposterous; after all, people in existence were all from *Homo sapiens* with no differences except environmental conditions on the earth that changed their features over the many years during their existence. It was a psychological ploy used by Hitler knowing it to be a phony decree that might mesmerize the bulk of German people just with their innate pride, but not at all levels of their people. The ones that knew it to be a hype lived under terror because they could see how heartless German military forces even under a suspicion of disfavor. Those in the know and involved with the Hitler, the chancellor, knew they better kowtow for whatever reason or most likely would be destroyed from within or killed by Nazi members of the Schutzstaffel, SS Troopers, the Blackshirts that were called Hitler's personal bodyguards, and the brownshirts that were Hitler's street assassins secretly involved in uncovering dissidents in local governments, especially Jews.

The effects, being immediately, made enemies of people who disagreed, and their minds overtook as an infecting psychological disease. The leaders controlled all people and assigned their pursuit as if laws of nature had it planned for the domination of the world. Then the war was full blown and now most critical for the past two years into 1940; its continuation was now an apocalypse. Germany's intent was to take over the world, and the English and French knew it, and so did America.

Hitler's Germany had ravishing border countries in mid-1938, such as Poland, Norway, and Holland. Later, his troops marched into Denmark in the north and Czechoslovakia in the south. He also occupied Austria and Belgium with overpowering troops. All the while this happened, the English did not realize that Hitler was gaining control by increasing his forces. He as the leader commanded his field officers to use tanks, artilleries, and assaulting soldiers to kill people of cities with machine guns who didn't comply immediately to surrender. The gathering of any dissidents and most especially Jews were foremost in their captive and on the gestapo list, which became a nightmare of terror and death.

The automation of European train systems in various countries was overtaken; and within two years, Germans implemented and directed freight train schedules to makeshift internment camps first. Then Germans rebuilt camps to provide capabilities to conduct continuous multi-deathly methods using gas and ovens to eliminate many lives that they defiled simply by their racial environmental birthing. He stressed racism, and he convinced important people of the country that he should be the totalitarian leader directing and controlling all political activity, including economics of the country and cultural activities of people whom he saw fit to project into the position of fame, power, and control.

The French, through the response in the city now called Vichy instead of Paris, already made the provisional capital of France by Germans during the declared war by the end of 1941 and had many Frenchmen supporting German efforts to win. Without a doubt, a part of France had essentially surrendered, but not all. The French underground was active in many clandestine and destructive assault activities with British spies, American's Office of Secret Service (OSS), and directly headed by Gen. Charles de Gaulle. Nevertheless, many officials were ready to accommodate Third Reich demands as if the war was won. And under anyone in position of power among allies where the war was being fought knew it was heading that way with deaths of soldiers and civilians totaling into multimillions. The United States of America, in concert with Great Britain and eventually Russians, began to plan an assault of dominant offensiveness. A major assault was planned to be launched over the next year from a different point of entry into Europe in Africa, Italy, and from Russia.

The Russians from early on had first signed a treaty with Germans (early 1942). Then they were turned on by Germans in late winter 1942. The Germans had attacked Russians but were caught in a desperately cold winter without supplies and suffered great number of deaths of its army. With the winter, Germans in the battle had lost control of its supply lines and were forced to retreat. The Russians being winter people attacked all Germans as they retreated, and with equipment, military, and money help from America, they turned events as an assault along the eastern front, giving American troops an invasion plan and an assault along the western front.

Even with early American declarations of war, attacks were so severe over Europe that at its beginning, some feared that even with America in the fight world, domination by Germany had become so widespread that a loss still could happen. The allies, with headstrong determination, prevailed, and after the next three years, Germany was defeated, and the aftermath was severe and critical within Germany.

Even in Japan where the war was still going on, Americans warned them that they had a new weapon that was a consummate destructive bomb and had asked them to surrender. The Japanese would not surrender after many warnings. The war in Japan ended in a disaster of the first use of the atomic bomb, devastating first the city of Hiroshima without surrendering, and within a short time, the second bomb destroyed Nagasaki, leaving both cities in enormous continuous disaster from radiation effects and caused many to suffer living deaths. The Japanese officially surrendered on September 2, 1945.

World War II ended. The *boys* started home, and the glory and pathos guided by hometown people's prodigality of wholehearted thankfulness and love surprised them. Among the "Italian Mountaineers" were the three younger brothers from Big Poppy's family that were in the army, and the three other elder sons were too old to be drafted and did their share as patriots at home. Katy had said closely with a smile, "I got one from Vincenzo. I read it to Poppy. Jimmy was driving a big supply truck in Italy. He called it the Red Ball Express! He said nothing is happening now. What a funny name, Red Ball Express." Katy said she heard from Charlie and quoted him as saying, "My company is still at the campsite in England, but we do get to go into town sometimes on leave."

On one occasion after the war during a Sunday dinner, when families continued to go to *OverHome,* this particular Sunday, Charlie and Jimmy had made it home while on furlough but at the end of the war wanted to be with their mother because they knew she had been sick. Big Mommy was so proud but frightened, and so were their sisters and sisters-in law. However, at dinnertime, the family was full of emotional love and gratitude.

Later, Sam and Katy got married, and the traditional Italian "Belling" was highlighted at the *OverHome.* The excitement and the mutual friendship were truly Italians full of happiness that the war was over. The excitement was enormous and many people mostly the Divitas' extended families were having fun and were full of joy. Some of the music was played from old records as I remembered; but the music was surely Italian, and as required, and the singing and sitting was for the lifetime of effects of *steerage* and *amour* that was good and tiring as from times that had passed and forever will remember.

The "Belling" was highlighted with a "Deh vieni, non tardar," a grand Italian aria by Mozart. Another Italian aria was used via a Victrola from the opera buffa (comic opera) *Marriage of Figaro*, also composed by Wolfgang Amadeus Mozart in 1786. The opera tells how servants Figaro and Susanna succeeded in getting married, foiling efforts of their philandering employer Count Almaviva, who came to seduce Susanna; but she taught him a lesson in fidelity. The aria from Tatiana's Letter scene was from the opera *Eugene* Onegin composed by Pyotr Ilyich Tchaikovsky. Eugene Onegin was a well-known example of lyric opera, and to which Tchaikovsky added music of a dramatic nature. The story concerns a selfish hero who lives to regret his blasé rejection of a young woman's love and his careless incitement of a fatal duel with his best friend.

A libretto from London created by Andrew Lloyd Webber, "Aspects of Love," also carried the extravagance of love. The wedding and traditional inferences of Italian wedding music that involved gifts and special gifts from close family members that were beyond expectations with the homely marriage of customary ventures with dancing and Italian music. The lighting for the evening and dancing were typically Italian that occurred from late afternoon to late evening with wine, hors d'oeuvres, and dinner par excellence. The married couple did not go on a honeymoon, but they did get the master bedroom of upstairs of the Cosentinos' home.

The three major conversations that fully describe the heritage and emotions of the wedding party and couples included grand family of Argentos and their families, who were already closely associated with Divitas as family friends. The main actions were how many children had joyous fun being involved with their aunt Katy, who had every bit of her love for her nieces and nephews from times that they were born. The children were affected without knowing it with the inheritance of instilled *steerage* and *amour*. They showed how they reacted to the pageantry by continuously interacting with their friends and senior members of the marriage. Katy and Sam for the time being then lived in the *OverHome* commune in Smithers for a few years and much later moved to Montgomery, where they raised their children.

Even at that time, much after the war's end, Big Poppy still talked with his sons about the war with Mussolini siding with Hitler. He hated the mark of association with Hitler for the rest of his life. He expressed a strong turn against Italians that supported Hitler, but his father and Big Benny and his elder brothers also had already turned against Italians from the beginning. Yet all knew many Italians were in their country that also hated Hitler and Mussolini, and they mutilated him in streets in a tied and drawn action by a driven wagon.

After the war, two younger boys told him that Italian people loved turning against Hitler and Mussolini. This is an extremely moving time, and the scene fills with awe as demonstrated with both Italian and American languages being spoken. Big Benny and his brothers, at that time with great pride and love, had grand feelings living in America that showed in all sons and their parents and brothers and sisters. Most Italian families would not let Italians be spoken to or taught to their children from now on, especially Benny and Jo. What we do know now and later is what we were showed done by Italians who did not fight with Hitler. It provided proof of cultural pursuits of Italian emigrants. The change to the uniform will change our presentment and deportment to the world. The garb of the industrial worker now changed his disposition and character in the United States of America.

Big Benny did not allow the Italian language to be spoken in his home; nor did he allow his children to be taught to speak Italian even though it was the real time to start at their early ages. This is a remembered shortcoming by his children later; none ever became fluent in Italian. He hated the Italian government under the fascist Benito Mussolini, who joined Hitler in pursuits of world domination. This, in my mind, is the only psychological release that he was originally from the poor provincial Italy in the early 1900s. Benny felt that what they did in siding with Hitler no matter what was promised was a black mark on Italians, their character as human beings. His children were told not to tell anyone that he was originally from Italy. The Italians, after surrender, got the brunt of criticism and prejudice as expected, and serious writings about planned destruction were distributed to lighten his burden. The Germans in the surrounding towns did not stay, and, eventually, Italy returned to its stability as a long-standing famous country.

Big Benny also had set his personal family goals always on the upswing being a well-known citizen in the town of Montgomery, West Virginia. After his son Robert James's birth on April 23, 1943, he called Bobby one of the early World War II baby boomers, as did the country, and the name was adopted. His family grew, and he was ready for another child named Philip, who was born on October 6, 1946, as his business prospered after the war and new times of behavior were happening, and he lived it up with his friends. He had planned within the year that the war ended, and within his mind, he would plan to attend the Indianapolis 500 Races with friends and brothers in May 1946, about a year after the war ended.

Big Benny and Jo took in Charlie, with him just out of the service, and Aline, his wife, afterward for a short while until they could find a home. Aline was going to be expecting a baby, and it would be called Charles Leigh after his father. Shortly, Uncle Charlie got a job at the Greyhound Bus Station and was able to rent and eventually buy a home for his coming family. Big Poppy made an invasion of his own as he proceeded into Big Benny's home looking for trouble. He frightened Jo and broke the front door window because of something Frankie had said to Big Poppy with the wrong Italian words. This was the straw that broke the camel's back. Jo wanted nothing to do with Big Poppy anymore, and she said she will never set foot in his home again, which, of course, wasn't true. With some details, Frankie had used a bad Italian word while talking to Big Poppy. It caused a calamity in Dad's family because it was aimed at Benny's eldest son, Frankie, as he was still so called. In his relay to cover it up, he lied, saying he never used the word. He used a word that sounded like *puttana*. He chose one that had a redeeming quality, and as Frankie said, he tried to explain that he wanted some (*panni*) bread. The lesson learned from all three, Big Poppy, Benny, and Tony, is beyond explanation. It was not accepted. Frank got the belt on the seat of his pants.

Back to the people in the United States and in the major patriotic efforts that the Kanawha Valley Industrial area pursued in 1940s to supply America and British military with major warring equipment. The area of Kanawha Valley manufacturing continued to produce many products and materials and equipment after the war. The associated stores and other companies had hired workers in mining city's hubs where most shopping was conducted because people didn't have cars to travel to the next closest major city some twenty miles away. The reasons for the buildup of business activity was that President Truman knew in his mind what was happening, and he created a steady increase in military warring equipment production that was already under way even under critical objection by peaceable organizations.

Big Poppy got almost nothing but a weekly Sunday dinner in his home with his sons' families, and most of the day, it was with the complete family. His sons were interacting with many of their woman friends, and it caused him to digress his strengths as an agitator to them, and he blamed elder brothers for their absence. Nevertheless, he makes sure he gets to elder sons by a little walk or taking them on a short trip to his special places like Al's Bar.

Business was booming. Soldiers were in and out of the town needing taxis. Life among the street people and the gregarious towns people thrived on patriotic behavior. Frankie meant in all areas of business. Improvements and repairs were always being done on houses. Benny and his brothers and sisters had the money to repair their homes in late1940s. Music was still foremost being played by adults and children playing music and continually out in the fields and on the streets playing ball and games until nighttime. Art was being taught in schools, and some of us really got interested in art especially patriotic art, such as drawing American airplanes and coloring them. Children were busy working on homework and school activities, and parents were making sure they did their lessons. Benny's children were venturesome and loved learning, doing drawings, playing board games, carving, and sawing wood to make handguns and rifles to play army.

Music, law, and science also were on the minds of the elder sons especially when some new discovery was accounted in newspapers from industrial companies, and an urge of excitement was exhibited to a few interested children in town. Interest in music, medicine, law, architecture, and engineering seemed to be subjects of late-night talk at the kitchen table and when the witching hour appeared—that is, when Dad came in at an odd time, he also got involved and, within minutes, told us to go to bed with a sleepy smile courtesy; unless you still have some homework to do.

Several of the remaining Divita families moved from compounds as the next few years passed after the war. The sadness engulfed Divita families when especially after Big Mommy passed away in 1949, a loss of the foremost love of all her family. She was the solace of Divita family's lives ranging from comforts in grief, trouble, and calamity of a lifetime supported by mitigation with all. Her sons and daughter and daughters-in-law and their grandsons and granddaughters missed her enormously. And the family felt the loss of Big Mommy for many years, recalling memories mostly those related to her teachings and good-natured ways of treating grandchildren with her homemade *steerage* and *amour*. Big Mommy was the perfect grandmother, and the loss was despairing to all; missing her being and getting her words and love. The homes they mostly bought were affordable and were well able to do some décor and finishing touches to live in improved homes. Two brothers had already moved across the Kanawha River into Montgomery, and one stayed on Smithers mountainside of the Kanawha River.

Benny and Jo's children are always busy either playing or, while in school, concentrating on their homework without too much urging; it was almost a self-satisfaction or maybe even with a passion knowing within each child's mind that they were competing for what I don't know, but a few kudos always appeared out of the blue. All Benny and Jo's children, at one time or another, were at the home many times while their dad had it remodeled inside and outside; this was another learning curve that they were on, and it continued for about six to eight months.

PART 3

CHANGES IN ITALIAN HERITAGE OF DIVITA FAMILY VALUES AND LIVES

It is not the strongest of the species that survives, nor the most intelligent that survives. It is the one that is most adaptable to change.
—Charles Darwin

In part 3, heritage values and times about our lives are recalled from my protagonist's father Benny and my brother Frank from within their intensified minds' memories. From the nature of my life, I was chosen to extract understandings and write about my Divita family lives from when I was younger and until a man of many years. What I present from memory and hearsay covered many family involvements that caused significant adaptable changes by the Divita family that lived a family of happiness. My dad and Frank knew because they understood what happened as their time past with related life's pursuits, they would maintain loyalty to their wives and families while pursuing vocations of business following the personal teachings of *steerage* and *amour!* That's what it's all about!

A few suspected disloyal, amorous activities from hearsay expositions in unknown versions and, even more unconvincing, involved spiritless allegations about unfaithfulness without any concrete foundation. Frank had his own self-enforced acquiescence—that is, obeying authority; but at times, he had practiced friendly persuasions without gaining twists of amorously instinctive incidences.

Frank remembers relays of teachings from his grandmother and his mother Jo and father Big Benny from early childhood teachings. His grandmother Big Mommy was predominantly different from Big Poppy Francesco, who was almost less than a transfer of vaporous knowledge with discontent. For Frankie's loving grandmother, the essence of "knowledge and experience" came from her instilled meaningful, compassionate, and defensive learning.

The survivability teachings were owed to his grandfather's heritage, who was stuck working in sulfur mines known as the devil's way to hell or God's purgatory in Sicily from an early age. It was an awful job of working with the powder sulfur and digging continuously under dangerous conditions and exposure to chemicals in the air. The chemical fumes were many times worse in Sicily than in America, where he had worked after becoming an emigrant.

In Sicily, paid amounts were worse than discounts for making mistakes, even though there was no comparison because any mistake was treated as a careless act. Sulfur mist and smells affected lungs and body of many miners both as inside and outside body contaminations. The mines at that time were closest involvements to being in hell as part of Sicilian underground for those young years that he worked before immigrating to America in 1910. For relief of mind and body, he would take freedom with submission to amorous adventures he steadily pursued at his volition.

As Grandfather Francesco got much older with more confidence in his manly pursuits after many years in America, his outward behavior was extraordinarily examined so that he would treat women with strong persuasions that might be somewhat dominating. Francesco's dominating personality—that is, his mind-set—mostly followed the instinctive "will of desire" instead of making demands with significant use of his mind's thoughtful tract enhanced with age through his gain of "knowledge and experience."

As Frank had said to me many times, he had followed Big Mommy and her son Benny and his wife Jo's teachings of *steerage* and *amour* by mentally demanding the use of his extracted learning about how his mind closed bad pathways. With instilled mindfulness, he would reject his desires, eliminating his personal expense of going down the Primrose Path.

The Primrose Path so familiar to Grandfather Francesco was unattractive to his timid wife Filippa, who feared his retribution if she criticized him. He was vindictive if not a vengeful man who might take out his abuse on anyone in the immediate family. That vindictive way, if needed for man or woman, was inferred or voiced concern about his ventures as they came about as did some one-nighters later in his life. However, Big Benny when he was a young man, his father Big Poppy's behavior suspiciously was disjointed by not following *steerage* and *amour* and more commonly followed the sensuous "will of desire" as shown by his reactions to daily events. He may have ameliorated with aged forces, but it made him make only minor changes as he aged. However, he was not always on the path of "will of desire" instead when practical things related to achieving his daily work at work or at home to maintain his desire to live with respect, and he generally used his mind under his strong moral control.

Nevertheless, he continued in his later years; even though he was more serious, he still followed Pollyanna ventures that included chasing after paid young women lovers for sex in his older age. With other members of the family, Big Poppy essentially lost his patriarchal position in the mix of family lives. His dominating ways garnered a loss of respectability among his family and peers. Loyalty and infidelity critically change family values, lives, and times after many years living as married adults. Frank and his brothers and sister and his own children related his life's pursuits and with his mom Jo and dad Big Benny. It was easy to see how Big Poppy's revealed personal activities in which he was involved demeaned his own Divita family personal achievements and self-esteem of mentally emotional desires as a businessman and business acumen to his driving pursuit with great ambition to excel in the automobile business as a showcase even beyond what was later mentally accomplished by their progeny.

CHAPTER XVII

Frank's New Life's Pursuit—from Music to Cars

A married man is seven years older in his thoughts the first day.
—Letter to Lord Burghley, 1606, *The Story
of Philosophy Will Durant*, p. 90

*My praise shall be dedicated to the mind itself. The mind is the man,
and knowledge is mind; a man is but what he knoweth . . . Are not the
pleasures of affections greater than the pleasures of the senses, and are
not the pleasures of the intellect greater than the pleasures of affections?*
—*The Praise of Knowledge* (1592) by Francis Bacon

*No doubt one can in this manner dictate the future;
and play royal highness to the Universe.*
—Francis Bacon in *The Story of Philosophy*, Will Durant, p.?

*Music and measure lend grace and health to the soul and to the body;
but again, too much music is as dangerous as too much athletics. To be
merely an athlete is to be nearly a savage; and to be merely a musician
is to be "melted and softened beyond what is good." (p. 410).*

*The two must be combined; and after sixteen the individual
practice of music must be abandoned, though choral singing,
like communal games, will go on throughout life.*

*Certain of the desired pleasures and instincts are deemed to be unlawful;
every man, woman and child appears to have them; but in some persons,
they are subjected to the control of law and reason ["subliminally"].
The better desires prevail over them or they are either wholly suppressed
or reduced in strength and number; while in other persons these desires are
stronger and more abundant. I mean particularly those desires which are
awakened when the reasoning and taming and ruling power ["mind's*

sensor"] *of the personality is asleep; the wild beast in our nature, gorged with meat and drink, starts up and walks about naked, and surfeits at his will; and there is no conceived folly or crime, however shameless or unnatural-not excepting incest or parricide* ["Oedipus complex"]—*of which such a nature may not be guilty . . . But when a man's pulse is healthy and temperate, and he goes to sleep cool and rational, . . . having indulged his appetites neither too much or too little, but just enough to lay them asleep, . . . he is least likely to be sport of fanciful and lawless visions. . . . In all of us even in good men, there is such a latent wild beast nature, which peers out in sleep* (quote, see pages 571–2).

First cars were ushered in by earlier attempts of exploiting car inventions through associated transportation creativity that added speed and ease as advanced from conglomerated knowledge gained to expand excitement. The car, as were all inventions, was derived by innovative geniuses that used newly developed ball bearings and case-hardened steel fitting of gears made with machines set with precision measurements.

The step-by-step experimentation and seat-of-the-pants development evolved working systems from rough experiments that had minds of many creative scientists and artists detailing similar devices that had been explored in smaller sizes and simpler devices. This was the main pursuit of mankind from the beginning, and the legacy continues in what history has defined in phases, but each phase was unique and what came about was astonishing and soon was needed for whatever the demanded use arose.

This wonderment of invention came after the industrial revolution and proceeded throughout early 1900s until the beginning of the First World War, which was started in 1914 in Austria by the German Kaiser Wilhelm when emphasis kicked in, and by 1916, new warring machinery and many weapons of great mass destruction were in production, especially mustard gas.

Around twenty years later, mankind from around the world was forced into a warring mode by Germany and Japan. It was called World War II. In a time of warring, four plus more years still in the mid-1940s, inventors and scientists made quantum jumps, settled down, while many people lived with critical internal and personal strife, established in their secrecy and spy-filled action that led to total distrust of enemy combatants. Eventually, warring was rampant and on an extended and large scale, which is a manifestation, and one acceptable within a short time because people were being killed by millions on all sides during more than four years of war.

This happened after the beginning of the century when the affliction blotched solidly in the minds of followers even after losing the First World War. The Rising Sun people and the dictatorial German people both were afflicted mentally. The

German and Japanese people as leaders did not consider the people of the world who were being sacrificed with imprisonment and unrelentingly killed because of politics, race, and creed. The German people contemplated and dwelled on expected previous total losses to their people in the First World War. Their country's affliction caused Adolf Hitler, a megalomaniac who was imprisoned for condemnatory judgment of political standings but released in 1933 and then was elected chancellor of Germany. That was much later, when all hell broke loose as it was relayed in World War II.

The car inventors, designers, and builders experimented, tested, and then incorporated the newly proven to be workable advancements in technologies with many tries to put them into existing car designs. What these adventuresome, knowledgeable men wanted to do was to increase speed, performance, and endurance. New designs added long lasting with less wearing. New designs also made cars that could be put under enormous pressures and forces of nature on the track and especially on famous racetracks with gusto.

This part of the story expands innovations, and creative designs even now are used in modern-day cars. At the same time, when significantly improved racing cars came about every year thereafter, added thrust was abound after World War II. The positions and connections between common mankind and those of achievements in contrast between moral standards and worldly achievements having enough knowledge that each will lead most people and countries toward accumulating peaceable nations. However, when other's minds are self-centered with positions to dominate, the finality could become devastating; ending this insistent pursuit must be the finality.

Recovery back to normal was the new pursuit as was done previously by those who introduced new pursuits many years ago during the First Renaissance. Now, I contend that a similar start of a Second Renaissance began after the most critical resolve started with the American revolution against the British. The gain of freedom for the new America from Great Britain's colonization led the trekking of research and technology in all fields from improving culture and the wisdom to ensure Americans' freedom through the dominant use of one's talent, innovation, and creativity. The governing men, our forefathers, and most of the citizens had achieved the freedom from the power of their country with a newfound wisdom. Many leaders when selected by vote formed a Republic, a representational government of the people, by the people, and for the people. The laws of the United States Constitution and the Bill of Rights dominated value as human beings, versus those that supported with lies and deceit by previous royal kingdoms of domination should have been stopped.

I picked the time to follow our country's early revolution in the late 1760s as being the start of the Second Renaissance, and appropriate persons were so born and were called our forefathers. The forefathers showed characterizations of significant wisdom that caused improvements such as individual freedom for human life. It was easily recognized by the evolvement of wise minds of *Homo sapiens* as a quantum step for humans being equal and being unique. Each person had the ability to evolve new talent, innovation, and creativity that could expand improvements beyond 1800s, and it did with intense pursuit.

A total worldly stop of the fanatic extremism happened at the end of World War II, and the new beginning was started with the buildup of new technology and research that was a must for achievements as related to the potential next step toward another new venture into a Third Renaissance as would be expected. This new pursuit now looks like what one could expect as time passes—and that is, that a quantum leap will happen under certain circumstances, and what evolves will tell the story when history reveals the next renaissance cycle that could start with the rebuilding of the war-torn countries and peaceable action and mostly respectable culture needed in all countries. Now, with many countries at the end of 1945 needing new relief and rebuilding, the United States of America set a new path under way to encourage people to build exemplary cultural pleasures in arts and music that began building America and many countries that were much older and vastly damaged.

This story's protagonist Frank isolates values of *steerage* and *amour* by using his mind's decisive pursuit to maintain "knowledge and experience" while only deciphering the "will of desire" to fit cultural mental pursuits for the future and good of mankind. Knowing that many human beings make mistakes or choose the wrong course of action for mankind inadvertently or even deliberately as was done in the past two World Wars. With conscious knowledge, American leaders set goals years earlier that forefathers created three branches of national government for the nation as the executive, legislative, and judicial branches, having access to conduct checks and balances to resolve any governmental problems arising because of a lack of proper and a rightful potential discourse that was commanded by the Constitution properly developed for the country with constitutional amendments as a Republic that continuously defined fundamental laws and principles that govern and control personal inalienable rights to life, liberty, and the pursuit of happiness.

This pursuit allows each branch to investigate and legally resolve false representations and hidden conspiracies by officials so that they could reveal and maintain truths as uncovered to one and all critical people of the nation. The transparency can be issued in letters of government authorities by the stable and wisest members rendering truths in newspapers, interviews, and court testaments using candor and practicality to extract deception that can be debunked or loyalty where it occurs and that can be pridefully relayed. Where necessary, psychoanalyses divulge the extent within one's mind or another's thoughts to be thoroughly investigated so that the influences to carry on the association in one's life and its influence on another's life happens. Go back in time to review happenings of pursuits of *steerage* and *amour* that historically fit and which occurred in early times of the twentieth century for the Divita family and has continued to modern times, unfailing.

Structuring fits themes of this story in that relationships between concepts of teaching *steerage* and *amour* from the menial to supreme pursuits as it might have led others into a razzle-dazzle of choices when actions were less encouraging as one expounded in this story about the new Indy 500 racetrack being refurbished with capabilities to add improvements to mechanizations of automobiles, trucks, trains, and new sports cars from inventions produced during World War II. Modern sport cars have new creative innovations taken from engineered and scientifically developed seat-of-the-pants ideas to evolve micro- and macro-electromechanical devices with computerized controls and sensors; and these computers use sensors with macro-servo-electromechanical subsystems optimized to detect and operate under required performance parameters with driver's control.

And modern times of interactions would be grandiose and could maximize worldly pursuits of amorous adventures properly. This path has distinguishing marks making easy sense of limiting disloyalty; but instead, it reneges *steerage* and *amour* by detracting loyalty and truthfulness in their behavior to their loved ones. Appearances of sensuous and excited men and women radiate differently in judgment depending on whom they encounter. Under what conditions and how their mentally tuned-in libido undertones become excited and flash accelerando or moderato desires expressly. Triggering amorous odors are easily sparked because sensuous melodic stanzas of human beings' propensity musically drive pursuits of instinctively dominating *amour* into other's human minds. *Homo sapiens* as a species and as demonstrated from primitive mankind throughout was destined by God to become a mind-sensing *Homo sapiens* species. A force upon the axon as central processes touch neurons within mankind's brain should guide impulses to one's mind. The action gathers in distinguished lobes of minds to differ from sensuous desires that are hardwired; but without *steerage*, instead the mind grasps lustful *amour* pursuits predominately.

As mind's "knowledge and experience" have long-term memory recalls, the instance that a direct instinctive response may lead to an expense of suffering or a lingering depression because it had been recorded by situations where disloyalty pursues the path. "Knowledge and experience" of those times past were a simple recall task for minds to compose because it characteristically repeated genetically induced memory traits as experienced living human beings bear out. Take the course of living a good moral life and its continuance. In part, Frank's father as a young man in his forties narrates some of his life's ventures with cars to Frank. As well, he also sometimes got more than enough from his uncle Tony. With this decisiveness of his mind's ability, he revealed transpired thoughts, never released to naught, valid behavior patterns, interactions, expectations, and observations of and about his father and his buddies.

This was the first established characteristic of his personality, one instilled self-sufficient being and the one only responsible for his callings in life. As Frank recalled within his thoughts he added to his memories. Frank implied that he had only slightly smaller goals than most mindfully self-taught people, especially his dad. Frank's foremost goal was to serve his family and to establish a good rapport with our extended families and friends and make sure, even under stress, that no concerns were left unresolved.

Later, much of his personality was mindfully expanded with associates as a businessman and a promoter of people's pursuits. Frank hoped these desires were embedded and would accompany his words in detailed discussions and advice on how the community should be developed per his opinion and inputs. Frank forever guarded his children and made them know in clear terms that he expected them to be good Christians and to do their best to use their minds and knowledge to expound on interests of ongoing social events at many levels. He always told his children to be mindful of their thinking and knowledge so that they could lead to culturally improved ways by their own interactions. He further demanded that the ways they conducted their lives should be an example to many on a small scale, if not on a much larger scale, in literature and science and even in cultural art fields. Simply put, he impressed upon their minds that what they do must be important to their lives as rain is to the soil for growth. Then a harvest is what would satisfy them in their older times.

Frank hoped in his lifetime, as did his father, that he would know and follow the respectable outcome and be reasonable about unseemly parts of others' lives that preceded and followed the good of their lives. What he meant was that helping a human being, even one, would make a difference in their lives. The doing good would be enough reward to satisfy them and would allow them to pursue more important achievements. Of this expectation, both Frank and his wife have used hints and maintained a mild insistence that they would be achievers. It was always an intended message that he taught to his children in conversations. Even with his shortcomings of good knowledge of natural things, he told them that when taking a cultural step in the right direction, one should think beyond immediate mental responses not to blame others. As a man, he often said what his dad told him, "Frank, you should be able to make changes in your life with the gift of freedom after he became an American citizen.

Frank later said to his dad that it was easy for him to see how some things did not work for him with a string of personal failings. Noting as all human beings, he had one, two, or more that plagued him throughout his midlife. He added based on what he told me much later that Dad's failing health because of diabetes added to his disheartened fight to discard his drinking liquor for one and his overeating for another. Both binges affected his health more than a little as he aged. This made him doubtful of others and sometimes not compatible with those who loved him as I knew I loved him.

Frank trusted himself to gain as much knowledge of business workings under his own business interests and control. At times, the automobile industry was on his mind. He always knew that the functional sales system was most important done with truth and compassion. The buying and selling parts became his main thrust in versatile times. The operation of two businesses, one the new automobile dealership, used cars sales, and his Firestone Tire Service Station and Store. It was unusual, and he was unaware of those that knew his casual personality, and this was just one of them.

Frank's one lack was that he only had his dad to advise him about details of business. Frank's father's advice was essentially the same as he had experienced with his own car garage and taxi business, all a part of the car business. The only mentor he had to expand was his spiritual feelings, which was what he had gained in wisdom from his mother and his wife Betty.

Frank gained from his dad a self-taught understanding of math and uses it to analyze things related to managing money of businesses. He knew what path to take to solve problems related to cars. Frank's experience was important knowledge from his dad to follow, and he was good at using it along with being patient. As it turned out, it was more than enough to get started in car businesses, and he continued for many years as he refurbished his dealership to an outstanding achievement in the city.

Frank had little interest in pursuing unacceptable behavior even when under stress that many times quashed his day. A night's simple sleep would bring him back to normal under his guise of a family leader. He was sure he gained a mark of mind disjointedness because those who noticed his stature, either family or friends, did offer opinions that he could be ignoring his loved ones at times. Under no circumstances did he ever divert from a strong standing for truth; just ask his children, wife, family, and friends. He learned critical mindful directions from his dad's guidance, including how to be self-sufficient as I have said many times. He was commonly wise in judgment and knowledgeable, most of all, to use guides of good behavior instilled by his mother, and her ways improved his pursuits in life as he became older and wiser.

Frank, backing up to his times past, in a way that I remembered, said, "I should take a peer into my expected future lifetime to make sure I know where I am heading." Then Frank's narration is augmented by the Frank, who remembered his love of music and his planned devotion to study music. Now, current utterances characterized his business and friendly pursuits from his past while among his friends and conducting his business without any major interference and chastisement. When he doled out advice to close friends in jest, he paraphrased something like "We pay for our instincts giving others his good advice. Sometimes, we have to use our minds as a God-given tool of intelligence to give charitable gifts to the poor."

Frank sensed his lackluster as he was getting older, but he hoped he would have a tough time permeating his mind's memory to open sensuous nerves that trigger ardor within his mind. This event always was automatic—that is, instinctively; but in his mind, following general *steerage* now preponderantly controlled his pursuits. His propensities depended at times on negative mental "vibes," be it a look in one's eyes or a contorted sensuousness beaming in his face that could cancel the ardor payback response. Stabilized enough with control, Frank would make witty comments about a woman's hair with a smile, saying, "Your auburn hair suits you!" He then listened in silence but with an easy smiling distraction, waiting her answer.

She said from what he remembered, "I've never heard such a sparkling compliment. I think you are trying lead me on or maybe to buy a car from you."

Frank showed no interest in taking the lead on this slight put-down. He knew that no matter what words were said by both, they later would have little to correct or even recall. In Frank's mind, the burden of desire might entice him as her body graced her shape in her dress. Then he slipped mentally to one of true love enlightenments of the *amour* with an expression that created a happy expression with a smile, as he said, "My feelings for you," he chuckled, "are like when I see my anticipation in someone interested in buying a car. It's a joy, and that's a good sign." Frank continued in what I thought he would end up saying, "It's a guide when good words come from you to expose your interests in my cars and even buying one." Even those of us trained and educated to pursue knowledge but then experienced persons sensuously aroused, one may not be able to extend a general expression of happiness instead of desire. More likely, most women might overreact to that statement.

Then Frank thought she might seriously retort with a witty dismissal or by an ejaculated emotional strike of a wordy insult or personal assault on the lack of attraction of the novice. And then if challenged, Frank, with extracted wit or with a thought-up humor, lightly, when put down in words, said, "I was only kiddin'. I particularly like you as a friend."

After feeling a bit embarrassed, she retorted, "I'm not simpleminded. Are you flirting with me? I like a man when he negotiates business in a prudent way—it is rare. I think I am going to buy the car as soon as I gather the down payment." Francis walked her to the door with an expression of appreciation for the planned buy. He greeted her good-bye as did she with a smile.

Things unexpected like television and stereo systems had become available in the late 1950s. Many more new inventions that Frank knew about were being developed throughout the 1970s as his dad's health was declining. Then afterward, he needed care, and his dad and mom knew they wanted to visit Ed and Pat and the family in California.

Frank had helped his dad as much as he could. Dad began to wane in his health in the late '60s, and more decline was in front of him. Mom and Dad were living with Francis's family at that time. They also were able to travel to visit their families that lived far distances away. We only found out that Dad was declining when Mom and Dad visited us in California. After that visit, we did return to Dad's home where he was under a doctor's care, and the next time we visited, he was in the hospital.

Mom told us about his ways as he was declining. She said things like he always said very little about his health and mostly remained silent about his health. He told her when it is my time with serious ailments that I will be ready. What followed was that he died from the cancer that plagued him for the past few years. From my family's recall, in my mind, from the very end, we knew that he would be properly buried by my family. All Divitas voiced that he would be off to heaven as a good, self-sufficient, and happy man. Our memory was that my dad left us with his instilled strong will and spiritual wit. My dad Benny was the ultimate self-sufficient man of our times. He caused an indelible imprint on his siblings' minds with instilled importance of their mother and father's *steerage* and *amour*. It simply made them think about the man and their mother's standing strong with contrition, unvoiced and depressed with her love of life expressed in their daily activities.

There is an art in dying well. Savonarola preached on *the art of dying well*. "Death, he reminded his hearers, [what] was the measure of life and the guide to its conduct. Death is the solemn moment of our life; It is then with man all his days, waiting for the approach of death to checkmate him" (*The Man of the Renaissance*, p. 78). Even if the assaulting disease is horrendous, the mind overcomes the insult of death. My dad's service was profound, but because he never complained about his health made it feel he died unexpectedly premature. The attendance of family and friends' appreciation were foremost filled with gravitas and comments about his good nature because death is the final moment of one's life of involvement.

Many things changed as Frank ventured into the 1980s both within his family, the country, and the associated new inventions and new technology that expanded. These times do acquire an effort to recall because the wearing out of lives is not only distracting but also depressing to see kindhearted persons like our mother wear out over the next few years, who passed and died on April 1, 1994, during Good Friday.

The continuation of how life in our family as well as the other extended families will be expanded from memories of specific activities through family meetings and the times we visited, sometimes jointly, to see our father and mother. Jane has presented her memoir as a book titled *Ed*, which will expound on the Divita family as a compassionate family of parents and as a grand set of progeny coming in a later time frame including members of their grandchildren and extended members of the Divitas covering times of the twentieth century. The remainder of our time will then be accounted in their times and ways by my three younger brothers, Bobby, Philip, and Richard. They will continue to follow the *steerage* and *amour* as inherited and taught by our progenitors until what might be a nearing of the beginning of the new millennium.

First, let me back up to expound into the 1980s, starting with the new mobile phones and the many new adventures into outer space and the finding of many cures and vaccines for many diseases. As did the First Renaissance miss out on obvious things that newly birthed people made little of newly disclosed values of personal advancements. The essences of improved cultural additions, social behavior among each other lives, and praise for their mind improvements were defined and written in *The Man of the Renaissance* by Ralph Roeder. The First Renaissance fostered environmental care, morality of life, and new churches followed by savoring new discoveries to improve lives, well-being, and living times.

I never expected, without identifying an unknown Second Renaissance, new devices that incorporated new materials such as the developed magnetic shocks and piezoelectric surface sensor controls with sensors dependent on forces, amount, flows, and system motion can be responded to at the same speed as a detector that gains, records, and transmits the information to faraway people.

With considerable thought but certainly with some devoted psychological analysis, it was easy to understand how the front-end thinking of my parents had lived. With changes in Mom and Dad's age, Mom, after Dad's death, was living on her own, in a new home that her sons had built for her in Montgomery. Her living conditions were grand, and she had many friends and relatives that gave her care and love of times and conversations. Her personal involvements including her religious beliefs abated under less activity with more time to lull or calm and savor social living while gaining some wisdom as others may have not noticed her personal gains because most add wisdom was her wanting. As before, we each have captured wisdom from the heritage procreation changes and eco-systematically induced differences.

These senior men and women, family members all from the same line, were now living with children and grandchildren in the 1990s. The firstborn as namesakes, all known, starting with our great-grandfather Liborio, Grandfather Francesco, Father Liborio (but Americanized as Benny), my brother Frank and his son Fran; and then Frank's brother Edward, and his son Edward Jr. and then Edward Jr.'s son Edward III, all in their times had admired living expectations for themselves and their families. The expectations of adding these men's useful lives to the world's culture in a positive sense are potentially enormous. These different times, especially with adding their wives' influences in the times of Edward Jr.'s father, did teach their children eventually with inherent and known ways to educate them with *steerage* and *amour*. Previous knowledge learned from these families, along with fate, claims each of them was saddled with their major hereditary social, environmental, and religious uncertainties and those unknown behaviors almost daily. Their lives to us revealed added worthy cultural and talents, innovations, and creativity, as have many of the new millennials. The modern changes brought about by their personal interactions and their use of making proper decisions continue the path of *steerage* and *amour*.

While lovers of life loved the way they are living in modern times as well, many remain unquestioned as they did not pursue infidelity. Instead, they are living happily with an affinity for the new family members who have experienced comparable lives generally with good will. That may be the expectation because it's amalgamated primarily related to the fact that they will be ones who are quick to ask questions of "What's it all about?" when they face the difference between "knowledge and experience" and the instinctive ways of the "will of desire." And when faced with options of either following the instinctive "will of desire" or taking the path of "knowledge and experience," their proper decision will maintain their pursuit of happiness; the choice is obvious with all the teachings impressed into their minds. The questions are either asked and answered within their minds or simply shrugged off. Either way, answers will affect their lives mentally or at moments of decision and choose to act consciously or subconsciously to enjoy their lives.

What's more in the question is, do average mentally in normal person's associations, behavior, interactions, and confrontations with others along life's endeavors have effects on others' individual personalities, and would the behavior enhance effects of inherent heritage? As a place to evolve these influences where each can be initiated for all involved, Frank's son evolved gradually and later was aware of pursuits when his dad's son Fran's life was divulged with only blurted-out hearsay.

At that time in the late '70s, Frank was miles apart in disposition and later became engrossed in personal interactions and reactions from a severe health disease that led to a separation as decreed by Frank. Then he divorced Betty, who had problems. Both Frank and Betty were left in a marital aftermath. Their lives directly interacted after their many years together as they became more mature adults, and Frank and sons and daughters had had several major disappointing even critical ailments and diseases in their lives. However, the relationships between Frank and his father Benny was always copacetic and one of personal respect. I hope the same had happened with Frank as he lived in confusion, but it continued to lighten his mind until his death about the happening of the divorce with Betty, his loving wife.

Years earlier, Frank had remembered a memory told by his uncle Tony and his dad about the Indy 500 Race in 1941 and more recall of 1946 as was recalled from memories of their friends that traveled with his dad and uncle Tony. From memory of what they related about and what I had coined in my understanding from input was the uniquely impressive trip to the newly reinstalled and refurbished 1946 Indianapolis 500 racetrack and facility with phenomenal postwar superstructure and environmental improvements. He covered sensitive and sensuous actions, situations, and incidents with added clarifications. All men ejaculated as they were told many things that happened, but some may have been padded with exaggeration undefined. The race was world renowned, and critiques were from noted men and women across the country and even from around the world in newspapers and magazines from times when refurbishing began. The word from local men in one of coal towns in West Virginia was not only about the trip; it always ended up moving uplifting with humor about and toward how many pretty girls would be at the race site, in restaurants, and in hotels.

Each one with spontaneity, he recalled only a few things at his young age about events associated with what had happened five years prior at the Indy 500 Race in 1941. As you know, the Indy 500 Races stopped because of United States was now in World War II with Germany. Critical thought was remembered and with his added age and living experience especially save much in my memory after our country was in World War II. What is more is happenings were assumed to have changed significantly with people's behavior patterns and critical concerns about their family members fighting in the war in Europe and other outside countries and in the Pacific Ocean on an island of Japan.

After the war of four plus passing years and following the after next new trip was critically influenced by values of greatly improved automobiles and new sporting race cars. The actions of conversations and behavior were padded with some mixed folklore because many quick discourses were finally put to my narrator who, as the eldest son, had given many stories about the race and for years memories was rehashed by Uncle Tony and my dad.

Was this attitude mentally searched out in Benny's conscious mind, or did some confusion occur as it was told? Benny is a self-sufficient man; many were significantly aware of his stature and analytical mind's extraction of truth even from his memories. After all, he did his teaching of *steerage* and *amour* continuously with his children over many years. No matter what he knew about their steaming expectations of hidden desires now will never be disclosed with genuine truth. However, the guys that attended did know that choices of potential illicit *amour* were close to infinity, and that was enough to wonder, "What's it all about?"

After making it to the racetrack, a group of men from Montgomery reacted especially to study sports cars and racing cars on display in local civic centers. Many people are captivated with new 1946 race cars they have seen from a distance, gaining position as close as possible when they arrived in Indianapolis and commented with admiration and love of Mauri Rose and Rose's racing car. Meeting with Mauri Rose, Big Benny was primed to renew his associations with the past race in 1941 personally with the winner being Mauri Rose that led to a continuous association because of racing car knowledge that Big Benny had displayed to Mauri Rose after the 1941 race. Big Benny also had been in company with George Robson in 1941 at the very last race time five years ago.

Benny and Tony and his friend Charles and Bill in their minds are floating about one foot off the ground being car aficionados plus knowing from Benny how race cars are designed and constructed to win races. The renewing of this past association brings about the future relationships with Mauri Rose's new friends and an appreciation from a few women beyond comparison. Within the various family members as lifelong friends of Frank's father's new associations that happened and continued years later with phone calls to Mauri Rose.

Years afterward in the mid-1950s, Frank had become recognized because of his involvements with cars and having continued new in-depth details of taking cars apart and putting them back together. All that evolved from working in his dad's garage as a young man. By the late '50s, he eventually, through his dad's friends, became part owner of a new car dealership, and as it continued operating for over twenty years, Frank became the owner of the dealership in the mid to late 1960s. With his interest and being the eldest, he was the one I selected to relate this story as collected by me, the narrator, about the Indy 500 Race in 1946. I told the story's existence continuously with glamour and interest about the racing people and fans he knew intimately and interacted with more than any of the Divitas as fascinating stories are told.

These pliable empathetic but self-made men are mesmerized into becoming potent protégés of their elders who have time to burn on racing cars discourse, the selling of new cars; and with sons and uncles even doing the repairing, adding design improvements, refurbishing cars, and gaining the excitement driving new cars. The combination of these desires symbolizes their love of sports cars. While among associated crowds at races, new sports cars enhanced their sensuous desires as amorously expressed in conversation and action especially among women without an ounce of detection or suspicion that they might be destined to an early rake's life.

As Frank likes to repeat, he said, "My dad Big Benny, the eldest son of my paternal grandfather and grandmother, has a recognized Italian stature, wavy black hair, and his deportment exuded a finesse in his height and size being about five feet ten inches and about two hundred pounds." Both his attire, even with a mild overweight in the stomach, and his looks fitted the way he dressed in a suit with a white shirt and tie daily. He would leave for work with a smile and sometimes even with a laugh after a bit of humor with his youngest son. As his first son, Frank, also said to me, and I saw the features many times, "I studied the way Dad walked and talked with authority in diverse situations including humorous ways while telling engrossing and witty stories." His storytelling as well was with authoritative directions emphasizing to receivers the need to respond without excuses so that it could continue.

Frank returned to include the effects at times during and after the World War II ended and especially how America changed when we returned to a peaceable country. The next thing on my dad's mind was what he had heard from a friend in Indianapolis about new efforts to refurbish the Indy 500 track and facility. All the while, it was foremost on his mind but did not reveal much verbiage to anyone about trying to go to Indy500 Races in 1946.

What was dominating the current worldly involvements was that the Russians were already trying to agitate United States about recoveries of damaged countries. Of course, they never paid what they owed to America. America did help many countries with money to refurbish homelands. Then what was started was repairs of foreign backgrounds. These efforts were exposed to hard country rebuilding. Many Europeans saw reason enough to become new emigrants by immigrating to the United States of America. Other countries only slightly destroyed tend to destruction, but mostly savored peaceable living.

The next year, business continued to be good. Dad and his friends went to the Indy 500 Race in 1946. After their return, the stories popped up and jumped from one story to another, usually different enough by men who had attended to maintain valued attention, but to some, it was usually an exaggerated braggadocio exposition. Frank, much afterward, was often at the police station in Montgomery where his uncle Tony was on duty after the champion race.

He loved hearing about what happened because he watched his dad and uncle Tony when their two friends took off to the race in his new Cadillac Super 60. His uncle Tony started with times they were at the Indy 500 Race and different yarns about good times in hotels and at the track that continued for many years with odd memories disclosed as it came out in retrospect.

By the time Frank was about twenty years old, he generally was stopping by or hanging around the police station and the firehouse with his uncle Tony. And as the time was often full of nothing to do, Uncle Tony, at an odd time, started to impart how wondrous and mesmerizing the story trip and races were with known friends during each day driving and spending three days at the sight of the Indy 500 Speedway, which was done to give the people a freedom of what they were fanatic about including the overall site.

Frank listened to his uncle Tony in a casual way that William's close friend had told someone that Benny was claimed to be involved with a woman friend of Mauri Rose. From little bits that Frank had heard at home from his dad after the trip, it was denied in a conversation that it was an exaggerated opinion. This one comes out of nowhere quickly to be falsely contrived by William's overstretching his opinion. Dad's friends had taken the liberty to disclaim the hearsay by William's friend.

As usual, with little thought, Frank thought his uncle Tony knew more about what his dad did most times than anyone in the world. And more appropriately and significantly more than William's friend because he highlighted an amorous pursuit might have been made, and my father was casually having dinner and conversation until Mauri came back. From what Uncle Tony told Frank was that William's discourse was totally untrue. Tony was to be believed because he was mostly with his brother Benny, and later, William and Charles joined them for dinner. It was simply stated again as he repeated in words as comparable, "William told me that your dad had been seen with Lily, the woman under the personal care of Mauri Rose for whatever the reason. William's pretentious boasting was not only unfounded—nothing of the like even happened except that your dad made sure she was looked after at the request of Mauri Rose while he checked out his sports car for a few hours that afternoon." Tony then knew that he had convinced Frank of the type of man his dad was when among his friends, both men and women.

Tony brought up and reminded Frank about an incident that had happened a few years before. The family found out about a week later as Benny had already told everyone that Rosy had a fall while working on a machine in the plant and that she broke her leg. Rosy called Benny telling him that she needed to go to the hospital at Laird Memorial General Hospital and had no one else to call. Uncle Tony then said, "Your dad took one of his taxis to the plant and brought her back to town and put her in the hospital and then informed her dad Sammy over the phone. Sammy later cleared up rumors when he was the last to hear about the situation known only to a few, which is always the case. That was the last time Uncle Tony said that he ever heard of any hint of your dad fooling around."

Then other guys had revealed inchoately stored memories of their amorous activities that oddly made them look like a hero in the making. They simply voiced those recollected and glorified events that reveal incidental and understandable effects on members of their families. Benny directed his conversation to each man who had no story of infidelity. He mentioned his father's good nature and his son's good looks that make him vulnerable. Benny had said everybody already knew his poppy's whole story of his playing aggressive wildcatting with men without concern of family, neighbors, or anyone.

The men William and Charles were close with Frank's father, and each man knew Frankie as a kid hanging around his dad's garage doing whatever he was told to do. Tony and the other two men in the garage were seen almost daily by Frankie.

William and Charles, longtime business associates of Benny, interrupted by passing comments asking for a change of subject. William had the closer association with William and Charles in these current times. William was more interactive within subplots that reveal amorous situations about each other but not pertinent to themes of "Steerage and Amour!—What's It All About!" In the current times of their gatherings, these characters revealed relationships, dialogues, and expressions that revealed personality traits of William being a lawyer and Charles being an owner of a dealership in the city.

The metal of each character in their environment on the trip to the Indy 500 Race in 1946 was disclosed later for a complete display. These four close friends were typical people each who have their good points and shortcomings as in John Marshall's writings of critiques; he revealed that it be known that each person has two personalities if not more based on their personal encounters.

Tragicomedy of the essence of personalities and moral turpitude is used in other parts of the story because of what may be called good for some and bad for others. The following covers main thematic paths from the beginning and must be compatible with and throughout conflicts of life that may or may not lead to a resolution so passionately desired, as in some cases, for the main characters and in other cases such as Frank's case when young. That is later when Frank was seeking a new life starting college and gaining his newfound love, Betty, near the end of the '40s, when both were casually in love. What happened in a short time was that both turned serious, engrossing within the year of her graduation and Frank dropping his pursuit after finishing his complete first year of preparing for a premed vocation. As stated and expected, within a short time, they were married. Major changes of their intentions included Frank completing his degree in music and being ready to become a teacher.

Then things changed with the warring that started in North Korea and left Betty under stresses with being with her first child, causing their married lives to be exacerbating over the next few years because he was drafted in the air force for two years. When he was discharged, he became a schoolteacher of music at a nearby school, and they were living in West Virginia, where they restarted and gained some needed happiness.

What happened later then, his mom and dad's family needed help for his family at home and his dad's business, which had become much slower with taxi business. Eventually, Frank, with the help of his father, became a partner in a car dealership and later the owner of a Montgomery Motors dealership, as was characterized earlier to show his special values. Frank achieved his goal under pressure and worked hard and long hours while collecting grand memories about his love of the car dealership business. But at the beginning, Betty resisted and added more stress. Betty wanted to spend more time with Frank so that she could be safe with the two children.

CHAPTER XVIII

Rambling Eyes "Rev" Men's
Engines, Not Women's!

The secret of peace is not to make our achievements equal to our desires,
but to lower our desires to the level of our achievements. "If what you
have seems insufficient to you," said the Roman Stoic Seneca (d. 65
A.D.), "then though you possess the world, you will yet be miserable."
—*The Story of Philosophy,* Will Durant, p. 76

The opening of this segment of the story relates to men of Italian descent that grew up enjoying their lives within the Francesco Divita family even under trying conditions with their father Francesco. Francesco was relieved by his family's desire to settle in America. And as they did, the country gave them freedom and the pursuit of happiness openly. The appearances of these men Big Benny, Tony, and Joe and their sister, Mary, when they were so little, she only saw the good that came to be. As they reached Ellis Island, each radiated with bright eyes and smiles that appeared on their faces when they got off the ship without sensing their intense suffering while traveling late in the year across the Atlantic Ocean. They had the right to make different expressions depending on whom they encountered, and to them, everyone was happy to be on the land of America.

For the brothers and sisters of Francesco and Filippa, as they matured became married and were living with freedom simply by being in America. The freedom gave them one total expression of happiness; and after marriage, their freedom was an instilled love among the new American Italian families that included Josephine with Big Benny, Catherine with Tony, and Mary with Little Benny, who was Paulo's son, and his uncle Francesco. Their sensuous propensity responded to what drives their instinctive pursuits to remain the same as always, love of family and a life of satisfaction with constant associations and grand Sunday dinners, even though at early times, there were consternation and unusual excitement usually caused by Big Poppy after a few drinks of wine and sometimes even whiskey.

All family members desired *amour* from the heart when they sensed a potential grasp that may randomly miss the proper signs of an outcome that may be simply unexpected or at the expense of suffering a lingering depression. So the teachings by their mommy worked, and so did Benny and Josephine as it was identified as teaching *steerage* and *amour*. A sight that has been viewed as it was the case in times past. Every member of the family knows that human behavior characteristically repeats sensuous histories of living human beings. The pursuit should be to take the course of living a good life and make it a life of integrity and happiness.

Big Benny, Tony, and Joe were closely related as kids under their mother Filippa's control, and all were handsome little brothers. After their marriages, they engrossed the *amour* of their wives as do all men become attracted to women in their mid to late thirties and beyond. They never waited for invisible musk from their brains to seep into pores, which opened and unharnessed its pheromones to hit the sensuous base of ardor. From what the families knew, each must have had an event of love at first sight that they did not care whether pheromones worked depending on receptors and receivers. From what we were told out of my dad's memory and knowledge, whether they might have been aroused, but stayed stable or controlled, Big Benny and those two brothers, Tony and Joe, and his cousin Little Benny had about the same time and behaved the same way after chosen their women, Josephine, Catherine, Mary, and Joe's wife, Maxine, a little later. Our men, with mindful intent, planned to live their lives fully with the same women until death. Their story after this time had been told at times of late 1940s on into times when our kids were going to college. The strain of a baby being born in anticipation of a mother taking the baby up into her arms is a joy that never leaves. All Jo's kids let her kids know how their mother felt about them.

Frank, much earlier in the late 1930s to 1940s, recalled how things were at different times. They were forever under a repeating nature of living vivaciously during times of the difficult '30s. Later, other Divita families included Uncle Joe and Maxine, and their children were in Dad's home frequently. Joe, who had joined Hooper's Funeral Home in the city, generally stayed close even after several moves and often visited Mom and Dad's home.

Frank, having noticed the table in our home after many years, cited the blue Formica and chrome trim on edges, a few nicks randomly placed, with some big ones and a few scratches so the age shows. In the center, a visible space reveals two openings showing two white edges, the borders of the separation section that marks the pullout edges of worn enamel on the chrome; but when the attached item popped up, the insert fits in place. The insert was already snapped in place with plates and utensils in a pile.

He remembered how his mom and her sisters-in-law always gathered at the kitchen table in our home. It never changed. As I recalled later in life, I could see my mom Jo standing at the oven engulfed in an aromatic Italian spicy tomato atmosphere with a heat of expressed delight from sausage, onions, and peppers frying in olive oil, as her sister-in-law Catherine looks on with enticement.

My aunt Catherine usually would be sitting in Jo's kitchen at the old blue metal table with her back to the wall for ease of talking. She was in a women's powwow with Jo about life's duties and family's responsibilities. Catherine's time was to be with Jo for the day because Tony let her off when he went to work. Some of her time will be spent up town shopping, but she expects to see Mary and other relatives as the day goes by. Tony, when he gets off, will come by and take her home.

Mom already had made some fresh bread, baked cake, and when she came in, she made coffee for the two of them. The table was later set for some big eaters—namely, her boys—due from the local nearby high school marking time for lunch.

Jo huddled a little closer to Catherine, leaned over her shoulder, and slightly whispered, "Many women see marriage as a stabilizing bond that holds partners to personal commitments. You know, like the spectacular feats that Connie claims that needed to be done so that my brother Bill (Dooley Yaquinta) will give her the car to go to town. Marriage in time usually improves the husband and wife's pursuit of happiness in life's every day. Live and let live makes it easy, although it's only by habit."

Both still alone, Josephine remarked, extending her personal feelings to Catherine something like a woman would, "Sometimes, I feel Benny has or may sense an attraction to women without really thinking about it beyond notice because he is so easygoing."

Catherine hesitantly responded with interest, "What are you whispering about? There's no one here to hear you."

Jo raised her voice a little and retorted, "I don't always know where the kids are." She continued with mindful exposure. "I've seen Benny a few times, how some women look at him especially when he was trim and well dressed. You know looking good was his main thing. He is tough but well dressed and confident. He never took any baloney from anyone. Insults against the Italians as a people was a real no-no."

Catherine interrupted. "Tony is the same way."

With her feelings then, Jo said, "From what I can see, Benny has his business on his mind. After all, you have been married for years. Remember the old days—Tony and Benny told us they made money in the store."

"What I was trying to do is recall his words heard by his friends. With men, most of the time, they do the right thing. It usually on their minds. Getting together and eating and drinking are back-in-the-mind ways. By watching Benny, I could tell he meant what he wanted to say. Then last week, he said, 'Men try to control their wives so that they can find a way to smoothly live together and keep the peace.' Benny does the same with laughing wit with our younger children, but when he gets a chance, he fancies some humor with good behavior with his elder kids and friends at his business."

Catherine chimed in, "Jo! We run our homes with good words and with a spanking when needed. If it is worse, I would never wait or get Tony involved. I know you do it the same way."

Jo inserted, "For me, if the little rascals run, I try to catch them. Otherwise, I give it up, but they know I catch them sometimes. With Benny, he tells them, 'Come here and it won't be as bad.' The kids always said it wasn't bad. Family control by talk is what Benny uses, and it works. Kids have a fear of easy whacks by Benny. It was the training he used to raise Big Mommy's kids through their early years, and they knew what life was going to be like."

Noise outside distracted the two women. They smiled to each other and said in unison, "Here they come!" They saws the three kids through the screen door making silly sounds with their mouths like a whistle and noises like animals at the door. They rang the bell or banged the backyard screen door as they went through laughing, with Gene screaming with glee, "Mom, we're home!" They caused clamor and disruption in and around the home day in and day out.

Jo shouted, "Settle down. Wash up for lunch. I'm ready to put your food on the table. Did you say hello and give your aunt Catherine a kiss?" More noise, door slams, water running, and towels snapping. Jo said, "My kids are all the same. Each pays attention to each other, and they know how to pay attention to us."

The three younger brothers, when they came along in the '50s, knew how to behave and help around the home from watching elder ones as they grew up. We did the same as our elder brothers, but we got away with more than we had coming.

Then when the two younger brothers were in Montgomery High School during the mid-'50s, Bobby and Phil heard Mom interrupted Aunt Catherine with "Where have I been these past few years? It seems like every time I stopped by to see you, you had different children in your home for lunch."

Catherine attempted to break in with "More including my children . . ."

Jo exclaimed, "I know! You know how many women like us Catholics hold in their minds the intent of marriage is mostly a religious promise 'till death do us part . . .' as everyone who repeats the oath procreates new babies. And if you believe what you read, that soon fades from their memory that signals a reminder." That memory becomes a background shadow consciously delivered maybe only on Sundays for a moment or so. Marriage is more of a promise to accomplish procreation with joy. Maybe different to men as a gratification of their desires. Both try to pursue or maintain personal happiness within the continual camaraderie of satisfying each other enough to maintain a visible peace of mind.

Catherine responded with wonder in her eyes, almost a tear, quietly as she said, "What goes on in my mind is usually hardly ever revealed to anyone, except to my husband. Sometimes, family members hear the message through the thin walls. I'd never reveal it to friends and others in my life, except maybe you. We are close from the beginning." Catherine made a smile so obvious from a deep friendship. My mom returned the smile, eyes on eyes. Then Catherine changed her inflection in unexpected words. "What about all those who don't marry in church?"

Mom made a move to console Catherine with "Civil marriages carry the same legal and moral intentions for all of us. However, they don't hang in the same place with morality if one breaks solemn beliefs in the religious union."

Catherine responded with a thought of the actual situation, "But, Jo, civil marriage licenses are only contracts that show that we are expected to comply with society's regulations. Some people have problems getting married in church. Getting married is the right thing to do even if it only records the status for the fully intended use of domestic laws."

Jo put two cents in with a smile. "That is the way of life. It's acceptable to others in the natural sense. It is what nature lays out to human beings. The civil laws provide ways that allow married people to break their contract using divorce in the courts. We know in both cases marriage is a belief that was cast in stone by God's Ten Commandments. It was recorded in Genesis from the beginning of mankind's known human relationships. Only a few know that as a Catholic Sacrament, it was cited as . . . 'It stands until death do us part . . .'" Jo paused and took a breath to finish, "The Bible's compilation time is a record of the nature of marriage, but it goes back even further than that." Then she sighed as she included a facial agreement and said, "Look at those children eating. They don't care what we're talking about or aren't even listening to us talking." Jo's kids were totally unaware as they shoveled down the food as if an aphrodisiac. And in between forkfuls, she said, "They ask for more milk or bread."

From my personal experience with marriage and what I learned at an early age, all kids know that critically mind-bearing promises were made by their mothers and fathers when they married. At their immature ages, they simply see nature as family's interactions and form their own opinions and ways of understanding, interacting, and responding while living at home under parents' guidance and teachings without thinking about it. They see light and intent of marriage as they observe their moms and dads and families of communities in a broad sense, mostly in personal and social activities with little action on how to improve and upgrade our cultural pursuits. From what I gathered, these normal wise words spread common sense understanding that becomes engraved in children's formative memories. The storage comes from brain's capability to operate mind's storage area that guides extractions from memory releases.

These imposed memory bits are semifixed or may be refuted after their conscious minds evaluate the nature of arguments from different people through exposure to their behavior from family members to complete strangers of repute. Memories may be registered with memory recall, but it must be under proper discourse sense instead of by subconscious releases. As an example, what marriages of mothers and fathers mean to birthed siblings as a joint pursuit or as seen from a personal view gains from mind's massive compilations of memories in unique ways. That is what ensures that we all are unique mentally as well as physically.

This memory recording goes from beginning of life to grow about four years more intensely and even continues after puberty. Each personality is dominated by what registers with memory associates, their parents, families and friends, and others who become involved in conversations. Normally, most children modulate and adopt normality enough to get through high school, and some with concentration make it through college. These two learning ventures gain wisdom increases ever slightly beyond thirties. Others run into complications that ensure their lives as years go by with mostly hidden reasons for abnormalities in judgment. This effect causes a lack of use of "knowledge and experience" over "will of desire" without thinking and cogitating about consequences of life when following instinctive pursuits.

Frank pondered as he told me that his intended ways were to wander in his mind to gain selected memories. Frank, on his own, would recall things that my mom said to Aunt Mary another time before. To the best of my memory, he made grandiose comments using his knowledge when he wanted to extracted memoirs something like—after children reach their teens, they're generally not interested in real family life, instead more just like himself. What children want was to be personally satisfied. Afterward, when each person was older, they want more than ordinary rewards that go with their married lives and experience, beyond compromises and rejections.

Much later, when Frank was a senior, he said to all of us that Aunt Mary and my mother had an agreement to keep in touch with each other as days passed and, on various occasions, it would require a visit or phone call to check on their current well-being. That is what I call friends and family love.

What was obvious to me as Aunt Catherine makes her point to Jo was that during this early time, parents spend most of the time interacting to get things done for their children. Some families had easy times with having plenty of money, and others live with stress of needing money to make sure they are living a normal life without daily problems. Others find times are more trying because self-imposed circumstances, usually excuses, lead to being forced to live under extremes such as making whatever they could muster from day to day. Children don't like to be forced by their family to live with extreme conditions that parents face, unless parents' problems are laid in their laps such as when they get older and debilitated. Most children look for an allowance usually ill-deserved; but some earn it, and some half-hearted make their response look good enough to get some spending money. Many children use these instilled mindful gifts to fund themselves through high school and college. Stepping-stones of achievements will be followed if well placed by parents. The mind responds to achieve their own family and self-imposed goals.

I know you'll ask, "Why has the author chosen to reveal this way?" As you read along, I will describe how my opening story revealed Frank's character and how he would introduce himself to nemeses that were a combination of, be it men, women, his business associates, political adversaries, or family members who gained an incline of happenings with very little knowledge. The newly anointed paramour might ask if or when it would be too late to look for an answer for "What's it all about?" This question is usually asked by someone who very likely knows little or nothing about situations being mounted. A few had some understanding of subject matters, but the words were ejaculated into a continuing blame because even questioners knew knowledge was meager. However, after being given a little more information, some people may have known more than he or she both have a right to know. From rumored knowledge or actual self-experience with the revelation that the truth of the answer is simple but agonizing.

In this case, it's the man's knowledge so deeply embedded that typically might steer him (or so it would be when a woman is involved) toward infidelity of which he never at the time had given it a thought. The paramour was referred to in the olden days when an infidelity was placed to his blame because he received the thrust against his normal way of married life unexpectedly.

To the questioner's surprise, this learned and mature person—namely, my brother Frank—is fully knowledgeable of subject matter because he has considered aftermaths of several kinds. He was the muse who has been in the same race or was offered the run of it and has experienced both choices. The outcome that Frank graphically describes as frailties of tainted love's commitment lies in Frank's suspected as the paramour. However, the questioner is surprised to hear that his learned friend or relative has the knowledge to disclose his actual coining of words such that it did not happen. There may be others knowledgeable of both sides regarding actual circumstances, but to Frank, it is not known. If the learned friend knows his revelation of the answer was at its worst unsuspected by the so-called good-looking man.

Frank proceeded to address one of the dinner parties he attended, and the confrontations were like some of his experiences and knowledge of similar situations. He insisted that he was the paramour and that he knew it was a critically poor decision to pursue amorous desires while being constrained in a marriage. Frank needed two ingredients in his discourse to relay this tie of minds to establish communication and compliance. He held the attention of his first son, Fran. He used wit and humor that he had acquired and then extended it from his first incident as was addressed and when he was told what he learned, the girl was involved with drugs, which finalized the expected answer. Then he had to give no response when no acceptable answer was proffered.

The first incident was covered by Fran's father. As another example, the second incident was about the approach taken by Francesco. Big Poppy, under strain, with a comedic and tragic exposition with ensuing action, was trying to attract a much younger woman and to use his money and home to plan to marry her. Further complications are not needed. Francesco is personally vividly expressed in a confrontational manner and was harrying to those involved. During expectations of the coming incident, the comedic event happened. Just before the pursuit, Francesco could have sent a signal that the affliction should have been ignored. The woman had a baby at home, and the situation was abandoned. However, the tragedy had devastating effects on all members of the family. The family revealed the answer that was only slightly but obviously discussed as to "Steerage and Amour!—What's It All About!" The outcomes were caused by serious human follies when one is self-centered. Depending on degree of believability of these mental affliction responses, answers might lead to a disastrous ending.

Francesco's third incident was or maybe should have been expected. The loss of a natural mother's love by death and within her mind was stored. A mentally imposed abandonment happened by following her husband to seek a new life in America. This occurrence and lifetime personal seclusion, being unable to attend to her in Sicily, mentally sent Filippa into a sad depression. Filippa's mother's death was a seclusion of retirement being without her family that caused her ensuing death although naturally occurring at her age within a few years in the late '40s.

Another incident that also occurred earlier but being the latter was one that involved Francesco's father Liborio. As expected, other Italian emigrants and other southern Europeans who migrated to America were also experiencing similar traumas of surviving the trek on the ocean and with a tough time in Ellis Island's worthy standards and medical inspections beyond discrimination. The situation required a bill of health for all physical health conditions and mental health capabilities and assessments. With this inflicting onslaught, many within a few years learned that their homelands were devastated, and families suffered. Big Poppy's father, who had died in his fifties while still in Italy, was a major concern. An ominous despair occurred as expected because they did not take time or have money to go back to Italy and bid him farewell; all exacerbated with loneliness to an extreme. But as usual in Italian families, they did their best, and all knew the problems involved.

The last incident, however, that occurred much later is revealed here to exacerbate influences of the next episodic answer to titled questions that clearly changed responses that contained resolutions comprised in a joint modernistic manifestation. After yielding, an immediate surprise was the only one that occurred in the late 1970s. It was associated with critical personal subplots that subjugated Frank in his marriage for true love with a person he was attracted to with amorous desire. At this time, Frank was afflicted with a liver disease that caused his mind worry and maybe an eminence of impairment or even death to choose a different and easier life's pursuit. After which, he continued in their married life but never as he told me that he had consider any illicit amour, nor was any ever taken as root.

Frank insisted that he was a businessman and was fully involved with only running his car dealership business. But within a few passing years, Betty's feelings turned to a lack of trust in Frank. She could not see a continual renewal of her love while he was afflicted with a low self-esteem. Betty judged and felt in her mind's observations that he was less attentive amorously. Betty felt that Frank was diverting his desires maybe toward others to gain attention of a quality of aspiration that he could not define.

That was when Frank sanctioned his personal behavior and mentally deciphered his daily behavior. Frank's actual behavior included involvements that revealed a desire for smoking more frequently. He intentionally did not show his gregarious personality as usual with friends and associates but continued his family daily associations as usual in his free time and during business. Frank never suspected that anyone observed this behavior until it began to plague his personal well-being under normal situations.

Even worse under abnormal situations, it was noticed by his workers. It was like he kept his business ownership's position while using assumed perks or substitutes for time allowances such as off-site lunch, several coffee breaks both in the morning and afternoon, and in conversations in his office as if to waste time of day. Even with these nonallowed perks, unhappiness surmounted his daily conscious mind and moved to overload him with poor response when confronted about the company's work performance. Work-a-day problems were things that come in one's mind's individual composure. Poor bedside manners in both words and deeds are noticeable to others but almost unrecognized by the doer.

Some of these habits that dominated incidents at selected times might be treated with true wit but with intentions letting wisdom prevail when the message was received with full awareness by the doer. The wit that hits revelers reveals expected enlightenment brought about by knowledge of one's superiority or by one's counterintuitive personality at the time. In most situations, it resulted in good changes, while a few times, it mitigated damaging effects on the friendship of others. In this case, the man of dominance was augmented with a continual expense of his chauvinistic traits of attachments to new people instead of lifetime friends.

Also included in an earlier incident are undertones in personalities when exposed and subplots such as a phony display of cultural advancements and religious revelations. These occur under strained circumstances such as when Catholics, Protestants, Born-Again Christians, Evangelicals, and Charismatic Christians, along with Eastern and Mid-Eastern Islamic, Buddha, and Hindu religions, are more aggressive and sometimes honestly dole out severe onslaughts of advice.

These confrontational encounters occurred with different eyes on others' theologies or even those that practice specific religions but were more naturally oriented toward dealing with human beings and not amoral zealots that must be resisted. Selected mention of specific historic events of *amour* were used to match current national cultures and religions of those with whom they are involved. This allows one to solidify comments within expected answers. Even groups of men who criticize their religions, especially Catholics, generally have lingering responses of remorse for comments they had made in crowds or among friends.

Similar characteristic behavior to be judgmental and confrontational was practiced by politicians in a hurting and colorful manner at gross high and low levels of insult by, for example, mean-spirited liberal zealots or ultraconservative extremists as related to questions about candidate answers to "Amour!—What's It All About?"

The pursuits by male and female may gain long-term amorous mental trophies regardless of consequences that permeate the humor if not cut with dry wit using involvements and excuses. These characteristic traits also prevail for obvious reasons, again as related to conveniences of time and the nature of worldly goings-on. And the reason why is that it is hard to change inherited behavior patterns even with social, moral, and cultural education and personal psychological training no matter how hard a mentor or even professional psychologists try to convince others to change. The mind's components are structured to continue to collect information inherited in this case of Italian *steerage* and *amour* so that one can control workings of their conscious mind and even subconscious minds as well, which is a formidable task.

CHAPTER XIX

Headin' to 1946 Refurbished Indy 500 Racetrack

*Only the countenances of men change and the extrinsic
colors, the same things always return, and nothing that
we suffer but has happened to others before us.*
—*The Story of Philosophy*, Will Durant

*Epicurus says, . . . "Nature leads every organism to
prefer its own good to every other good—We must not
avoid pleasures, but we must select them."*
—*The Story of Philosophy*, Will Durant, p. 77

In 1946, the Cadillac division of General Motors Corporation in Detroit, Michigan, released the Super 60 Special Fleetwood Cadillac, initially to selected best GM customers across the country. After World War II ended and several months later, the new year of 1945, the automobile was released with zest and fanfare by patriotic dealership teams. General Motors' main idea was to put out the innovations by word of mouth to all that the car was manufactured with a finesse so well developed over the past five years using the associated inventions created during World War II. General Motors strived to meet the grueling schedule to make the first new advanced car issue since the start of World War II a success. The number of vehicles made at this high-class Cadillac would be limited as a first special edition because of the revamping of manufacturing systems that slightly preceded the war's end. The actual preparations and testing for advanced capabilities were on a break-neck scheduled pace.

The persons involved in the rebuilding of the Indy 500 racetrack garnered an amalgamated stature and gained the site immediately after the war, along with current owner, Mr. Anton Hulman, and solid devotees, including Gen. Eddie Rickenbacker, who was a famous aviator in World War I. What all will remember is new racing was restarted the very next year after World War II ended under a highly received revitalization. The change was the making of one of the most famous car racing sites of the twentieth century for the United States of America.

The revelation of the coming race was phenomenally conducive to new and unknown ventures for owners, drivers, and teams, many with new cars, and a revamping of the complete Indianapolis Racetrack Speedway. The hype was that every race car driver was expected to excel beyond past records, and the broadcast was sent across country and Europe. The planned enticements to new and old race drivers and previous devotees and fans were trumpeted in every newspaper and on every radio across the country. The rejuvenation of the 1946 Indy 500 Race had significant undertones of "hurrahs" from every direction with the complete win of World War II and, of course, the *new track design* that sparked and ignited unprecedented anticipation and planned attendance.

Unknowingly instilled excitement of youthful fantasies of *amour*, if not *steerage*, in the minds of many, even the matured men of power, substance, and accomplishments will have aims at women at the race.

My family's hyper behavior was discussed previously in the *Charleston Gazette* of past events of the Indy 500 in the 1941 race. Dad, who manifested self-ingested memories of onslaughts of conflicts between professional car racers, ones he knew or that he had met during the last race in 1941 by chance, and new racers of acclaim, caused much local talk in his Divita taxi stand.

Later, when he told excerpts of his experiences, he essentially put news in his children's minds and caused more friends to hear vented vignettes of race details. Among a few, if any associated amorous expectation stories were implied in conversations, he may have told simple stories about Indy 500 racers that he was able to reveal parts of their stories from memory. His extravagant comedic excitement imposed in tales that listeners did hear experiences of *amour* to the point of criticality in minds of entranced young persons, facial writhe showed shocking expressions spontaneously as he ejaculated with humor.

The outcomes of each new amorous venture reached a parallax crescendo as if in a revolutionary change of sighting stars. A later revelation under protected privacy conditions, several life experiences of racing devotees, adult friends who were at the race, were herein exposed as folklore without sources. The hearsay that leaked out with added humor, if not hyperbole, could make the complexities reveal dishonesty, infidelity, and oddly enough confirmation of loyalty among spot relationships.

The critical event was one that Big Benny identified unexpectedly early but one that magnetically drew individuals to enjoin within the mind a mighty desire to have race cars whenever the experience might reboot from memory. Thank God that fright of dangerous perils surrounded a sense of potential damage to life, limb, and property with unbounded personal and economic cost penalties.

An early release of prototype models was planned to meet market demands. Early discrete advertisements of the coming luxuriously specialized Cadillac were whetting the whistle of what was in store for America for years to come. News of when this scheduled release process would occur made its way to a few outsiders who had charisma enough to promote sports cars locally.

Big Benny was one of the lucky ones known to General Motors and lived in a strategically located small town in the United States. He was personally located within twenty miles of the capital city Charleston, West Virginia, where many cars were displayed. Dad had gained his notice when he had attended the Indy 500 in 1941. He made friends with Mauri Rose, the winner, and kept in touch with him and privately interacted with General Motors managers about cars that he bought from the corporation as a businessman. As he gained his business during the war, he included phone contact and close relationships with Mauri Rose. Mauri and Dad were both Italians and had a good rapport with his new friends and associates, who were told how much knowledge he knew about cars. By receiving phone calls with knowledge, Dad continued to relay how much better he does with General Motors. During one phone call, he asked about whether he could buy the Super 60 Special Fleetwood Cadillac and take it to the Indy 500 Race with several top-notch friends and his brother Tony. The general manager gave him a yes and would let him know within a few weeks.

The three guys, as planned, only knew that they would be leaving soon for the newly refurbished, bigger-than-before Indianapolis 500 Roadway Race with Benny. However, they did not know that Benny was chasing after an approval to buy and receive a new Super 60 Fleetwood Cadillac vehicle without telling any of his friends even before the trip, let alone on May 26, 1946, Sunday evening, when he would take ownership of the Cadillac at a General Motors dealership in Charleston.

It's now Monday morning, and all four households were beaming. The sunrise peeked over tree-filled mountains, splitting the valley between two towering opposite north- and south-facing Allegheny Mountains. The inland evolution of midlands straddled down to the Kanawha River. These mountains are more than several hundred miles from the East Coast of the United States, and some are as high as few thousand feet. The local mountains are somewhat lesser mounds but still monumental along Route 60.

First out of bed in an exercise dance, as he would say to all, was Frankie, who was nearly seventeen years old. He dressed and made his way through the outside door and meandered down concrete steps and went searching where the newspaper was hidden by the delivery boy. He looked in the Mossaus' home next door where greenery was spread with mixed flowers, a variety of roses, and honeysuckle on the walls wet with morning dew. Almost immediately, he saw his youngest brother, Bobby Jim, and his sister, Jane, about nine, coming from two directions. Jane, about nine, opened the door still in her pajamas. Frank shouted at his three-year-old brother quickly, "Get back in the kitchen!" The two elder brothers, Gene and Eddie, thirteen and eleven, were fully dressed in pajamas and walked and sat at the table with Dad and Mom, who had joined the daily action.

Frankie got close, handed Dad the paper, and whispered words especially to his dad, evoking, "Daddy! Can I go with you?"

His dad pulled him closer and said, "Another time when you are older. The people at the race will all be much older."

Gene accepted his answer and said to Eddie, "Dad will take me next time."

Dad, now reading the newspaper while drinking his cup of coffee, let Bobby Jim climb upon his dad's lap. Frankie said to baby Bobby Jim, about three, "Get off Daddy's lap and let him drink his coffee. He's got to eat and then go on a trip." With all this domination by Bobby Jim, Frankie said, "Dad, can I tie your shoes!"

Gene said, "Daddy, I'll tie them!"

Mom was standing in the kitchen at the oven. Young Bobby Jim grabbed his mother Jo's legs, pleading for attention. "Mommy! Mommy!" And continued!

Jo was now frying eggs and some sausages on the range top in a different pan almost ready to serve. Then Jo looked at Janie and told her, "Janie, get the milk and put it on the table." Jo cautioned Bobby Jim as he went back to his daddy quickly. Jo made sure plates and cutlery were placed and condiments and bread were on the table. Jo shouted, "Eddie, go get the cheese out of the refrigerator."

Each child quickly took their usual place at the table without turmoil. As the elder boys do, they were interacting with each other, mostly talking and pretending scuffling and listening. All had reduced the commotion to plain kids' talk almost unfathomable by their parents. More important to the children is portions while they stare at the servings being placed on their plates. The only difference in this day from every other day except Sundays is that usually, only some of the children would be eating at the table at one time, but today being a special day for their father, everyone in the house was ready to eat. All they knew was that Uncle Tony and two friends were going on a trip with their dad to the big race in Indianapolis, Indiana.

Everyone will be gone for at least a week. They were preparing to leave their homes with quick good-byes and kisses and promises to the kids, who were all romping around full of excitement, some in turmoil, and sounds of words mixed with giggles and shouting.

Eddie grabbed onto his dad's leg, pleading, "I wanna to go with you, Daddy! Let me! Let me!"

Jo jumped in and said, "Eddie! Go to the empty lot out back and look at the car." They almost attacked the new Cadillac with every door opened and bragging with smiling shouts on the color and inside details even in the backseats never seen with such excitement about the design. The comments splattered from each about a new detail or with a "What is this?" Jo came out and shouted, "Don't touch anything. Enjoy your dad's new car. It's a beauty! Wait for your father! He's gotta finish eating."

In Italian families, wives always declare that their husbands must have something to eat, and when they're off, they let everyone know that they have fun just like the kids. And the fun is granted, of course, and with an inferred admonition in their tone but with an added expression like "I love you" shows with shining eyes and smiles.

Dad finished and went to Jo with his smile and hugs and a few kisses. Then Dad gave Jo his best kiss as the children laughed and hopped with excitement. He said, "Good-bye, honey! We'll be back on Sunday or Monday." The kids, still excitedly hanging around outside, followed him after he left the inside. He was still excited with them. The elder kids took his bags and put them in the car's trunk, and the two both shouted to their dad that the bags were in the trunk.

He begged off trying to get into the car so that he can start the car. He was in the car with the window opened. He smiled and waved and left as the engine purred quickly. The Caddy disappeared with glistening glass, and the car's body reflected sunlight and sparkling silences from the engine, as Big Benny headed downtown modestly. Frankie thought he lived through this circus of kids full of excitement as he prepared to make his move to see the final drive heading toward Charleston.

What was more important was that his uncle Tony had later told him stories of the trip many times. And by the time he expelled his memory of the overall story, he had remembered details in composed order. Frankie even remembered how guys got ready to limit details expected or added makeup for continuity as they gathered. The front end was observed by Frankie as he made his way downtown to several places where the guys will arrive before leaving.

Let's surmise that at homes of the guys departing were typical, and with a few words, Frankie made up actions at each home and family and finally ended up at Montgomery Motors dealership. The actual trip departure from General Motors dealership was not observed by Frankie.

Frankie knew what he was told by his uncle Tony as he left the bathroom with the aroma of shaving lotion and turned to Catherine as he asked the wife, "How's the shave?" She answered with a touch and gave him a kiss. Tony gave her a pat on the hip. Tony sat at the kitchen table, and his food was served. Tony, as usual, dug in and enjoyed both the taste and smell of the sausage. Usually, one or two dogs would get excited with the meat smells. Tony shouted at them to get outside. Boy, do they run! Tony said, "Katie (does not call her Catherine), you are the best. There is no better cook than you." He tasted the sausage, which was a little burned, and said, "This is just how I like it!"

Aunt Catherine looked at the pan and said, "I used the old pan by mistake. Here, I'll give you another piece that's not burned."

Tony continued eating his egg, and he made a sandwich out of the new sausage and headed toward the door with jaws full. Their children were just as excited as any child would be knowing that their father was going to the Indy 500 Race. They might have been quieter than those in Benny's kitchen mostly because

Tony is more of a disciplinarian and their kitchen is smaller and closeness rings with noise and commotion. Otherwise, kids followed the same pattern as their cousins. The talking and screaming for attention activity in Benny's home was about the same, except Tony had a smaller dining room.

Aunt Catherine did a quick job of satisfying the kids with food as they would eat having fun and good talk. In concert, the children left at the same time to go down to his car with smiles and a swagger and a sense in their voice, saying, "Daddy, have a good time!" As Tony entered his car, each cried out, "Bring us a surprise! We love you!"

Tony watched the boys kiss their mom Catherine lovingly. She is a great woman, and he shouted, "Good-bye, Katie! Good-bye, kids! Katie, make sure my boys get the work done in the garden areas."

At the same time, Charles, one of the partners of the Chevrolet dealership on First Avenue, was doing his preparations and had already shaved, bathed, dressed, and had a breakfast of pancakes and bacon. Charles wandered into the living room, as it was told later to me with memories galore by his dad's friends when they talked about leaving expressly the same when she went with her two children to shop. He said to his wife, "See you all sometime Sunday, and I'll let you know if it's going to be Monday, but I don't think so with Benny in charge!"

He kissed her and gave her a big hug with a smile as he said, "It's been a while since we've been on a trip for a few days. Think about it and we'll do it this summer! By the way, please go to the dealership and be yourself. Look like you know what's going on and say it to Jack. He'll hop to doing his job!" His bag was in the backseat. He made his final good-byes and hugs and then entered his car. He sat down, took a cigar and wet it, and then he bit the end and put it in his mouth. He purposely did not light it. He started the engine and left from his fully exposed yard so properly cared for with hedging and flowers in bloom and the grass so neatly cut. What a view of the mountains. He stared at the white clouds at the top of the mountain that was so green below. His wife turned and captured the view and smiled. It looks like a good day!

Meanwhile, William is a lawyer whom Dad has been involved with for many years, and he was doing the same preparations as other guys as Frankie assumed. From what I've have heard from my dad later in my life, William, being a lawyer, many times talked about how he was treated special at home. I guessed what typically went on was a lot of conversations between these guys that saw each other almost daily. I assumed that William had finished his breakfast. Then he must have had his last cup of coffee in hand, pointing toward his wife, requesting a special effort because being a lawyer, he doesn't trust anyone as he must have asked, "Is the office locked?" He asked his wife to check on it tomorrow and every day until Friday. And he said, "Everything will be OK on the weekend because police will check for me. I don't know if anyone knows how long we'll be gone."

Almost within minutes in, each guy packed their suitcases in the back trunk of their respective cars. Keep in mind, they didn't know whose car was going to be used for the trip.

Tony's car was taken in order in the drive as paths of other cars diminished in perspective, and atmospheres of gas fumes and oil spills from other cars were sensed. Each man commented to each other with concern that oil thickens. They hustled attendants, and they moved out quickly to clean up the area.

The guys drove through town where they passed breaths of hedges and other flowers. They gained attention from neighbors nonchalantly watching as they picked visions of waves and smiles. In Tony's case, one neighbor was digging a new garden area near the mountain road and shouted at him, "Have fun!"

In Benny's situation, he was late getting home that night and parked his Caddy in the backyard of his home on Fourth Avenue because in the morning, there would be only a few people on the sidewalk for whatever reason. Benny did not want people looking or peering at the brand-new car with gasps and shouting unknown words for sure.

Within minutes of each other, their cars pulled up to the Chevrolet dealership, where they stopped along some parking spaces. William pulled inside near the work area. Charles left his car outside in a parking space; he must have thought he would be taking his car on the trip. They exited their cars and went outside the car dealership where others will meet and send them off with flair. Then in came Tony. He casually parked on their lot. Then he told Charles that he put his car out of the way of business traffic. Charles easily OK'd it with a wave.

Benny drove up last and proceeded to park in front of the main door. He exited with a smile and with a wave of grandeur, pointing at his new 1946 Caddy. With "above and beyond" simple words, he said, "This is it!" In panoramic exposure, the viewers took specific notice, chanting, smiling, and laughing with words of exclaim, surprise, and compliments. Onlookers, excited by seeing nearby garage workers scurrying to look at Benny's new car, made their way with compliments. Benny said, "This turned out to be a surprise to me also. I got a call yesterday that it was ready. I hitched a ride with Belle and picked it up last night."

The big surprise was that only his family that night knew it was Benny's new Cadillac. The guys and groups of workers and local people nearby were at the dealership admiring the new car as he drove up. When the men saw Benny driving, they were totally surprised that Benny had a new Caddy. With great laughter, comments continued as detailed looks and some touching were made with excitement of his supernew Cadillac. Then bags were packed in the car so carefully. The men simply talked about what they saw that was special. Some time expired to settle the joint admiration. Finally, the guys that were working said they needed to get back on the job.

Frankie, off to the side and down a way, watched the men as they reflected or observed through the window at a distance in one of the side mirrors. Frankie knew each of these men very well and paid special notice while around them today because he's always looking for odd jobs. He had a special position because he knew their sons were all about the same age, and especially his uncle Tony when he spent time at his home with the family on some weekends. Frankie and his cousins on occasion stopped at the police station hobnobbing with officers and firemen who were more than a few years older than Frankie.

He learned a lot from these guys because they revealed character while dressed, but the men at the garage were in work uniforms describing their skills about work with pride in the work they do. No matter what, each of the men was pretending to be readying for their trip. All workers had a necktie on and pointed to it conservatively.

The travelers' suits were well kempt but used, with a slight aroma of dry-cleaning fluid after just being dry-cleaned for the trip. Even Charles, the rich one in the group, had a new suit with the aroma of new material. William said to Charles, "How's this sport jacket? I'm going to be in the car most of the time, and it will be off. I could easily slip it on when we stop to eat."

One of the girls outside said, "It's a great selection. If it's easier for you, the better. It takes quite a few hours of driving to get to Indianapolis."

Frankie now appeared on First Avenue near Charles's dealership. He found a position where the reflection of crowds of guys in the corner window appeared and faced other crowds as the morning sun beamed over the mountains. He observed the men in conversation outside of Charles's Chevrolet dealership.

Frankie had already seen the car and had almost a love affair in his heart's mind just by standing at the corner of Kroger Grocery Store, about one block from our home. The store was so encased in red-clay high-fired glazed bricks with medium-sized plate glass window exposures of sundries on horizontal inset boards. Taped inside was a set of special buys painted on brown wrapping paper in red, white, and blue characters and highlighted cost values.

Frankie sneakily watched his father Benny as the cold morning mountain air almost reddened his already fearfully pink cheeks. Emboldened, he approached a closer concealed pillar at the front of Kroger's Store at the corner of Second Avenue and Montgomery Street, with his face into the wall stealthily to ensure that his dad hadn't seen him because he had sensed that his father had too many things on his mind. Within Frankie's mind, he must have asked in thought, *Why so secret?* But he did not pursue questions or ask for answers in his mind because the thought could make him realize that his ass would be booted if he were caught after being told not to follow his dad to the Chevrolet garage. Frankie felt that the demanding answer would be in his dad's mind. That's when his dad said loudly, "Go back home, Frankie! What in hell are you doing down here?"

He must have said to himself something like, *I'm close and hidden. How did my dad see me? I was against the inner wall and out of sight of the dealership.* I could partially hear combined conversation, and then in particular, I heard Charles loudly say to his three buddies, coining new words about the war's ending. It sounded like, "We wouldn't be doing this if Eisenhower hadn't put an end to the war. I don't give a damn what the Russians said about how they helped the Americans get ready for the invasion. We kicked German's asses before going into Berlin."

These words in retrospect gave me insight regarding World War II and its ending with the V-E Day of surrender on May 8, 1945, because his brothers Charlie, Jimmy, and Frank were happy with expectations for America and the rest of Europe with the complete win. At my time, being Eddie, I was only ten years old. I had been a newspaper boy for some time with my brother Gene. I recalled that I was selling extras with great demand at the war's end, and I was exposed to the hearts and minds of the common patriotic Americans on the main street as they excitedly bought newspapers and screamed praises.

Frankie quickly pondered a mindful of thought that needed to be exposed with recall. After all, he had read the newspapers and pamphlets on World War II details that were given to him in American history class in spring. Frankie did not get much about the Indy 500 Race venture from his dad or uncle Tony until they had settled down and were back to their jobs or running their businesses.

I am adding a rendition of what Frankie had told me later about soldiers' efforts and their lives sacrificed in combat. Each of my brothers later wrote papers about the end of World War II and how the continuation of peace came about while in school. As for me, once in high school by 1948 and even in college by 1952, I wrote about the real meaning of peace in the aftermath and how the new peace will affect countries of the world, even those that were our hated enemies. I only surmised at my age, using as little of the detailed knowledge that I thought I had, that it was already obvious everyone wanted a peaceful movement. Simplicity of demands by victors might choose paths of intent with negotiations that eventually could end up in contention among allies and axis countries. The first direction was that the Jews were wanting to leave Europe, and the United States wanted to move them to Israel with maximum force predominantly by the United States. Again, their experiences are likely edging fiction based on their ways of reporting total outcomes of behavior, except factual outcomes of the race were at once lived in Israel back many years. I was sure that these four good men of unique leadership, President Truman, Gen. Dwight D. Eisenhower, Winston Churchill, and Joseph Stalin, would be discussing outcomes of the war as they traveled much like what followed as told to the people of their times. Outcomes of future times still live through unrest, extreme danger among countries near Israel, and at times warring conditions uncontrollable.

The surrender of the Japanese in the Pacific came later. It made things even worse from a recovery point of view because America had to devote a great deal of time and effort to rebuild Japan so much so with its people and its country's utility after such horrendous destruction, although warned that it was coming, but the nuclear bombs had caused unbelievable destruction and deaths and pending death to the Japanese and also lingering death caused by the fallout of radioactivity infecting those still standing.

First, the Russians had been a Communist dictatorial country under Joseph Stalin for years, and that meant that they were against our democracy and had been trying to get a communistic foothold into the United States even before the beginning of the war. During the '30s, local cells of Communist zealots and trainers of their ideology dragged socialist thinkers that were poorly treated by capitalism and purveyors that dominated America in the mid-twentieth century.

As a country, the bulk of American people were against known Communist movements since the 1930s. God only knows that it went on for years with spying and underhanded movements by Russians after the war. Thank God that during the war, Russians knew which side to fight on even though they had thought that Germans had an upper hand. Russia made a pact with Hitler until he wanted more than they could chew. It is well known there was a time that Hitler was at a peak. That was when Russians ruled by Stalin were joined at the hip with Hitler in a pact or treaty of some kind, but then Hitler double-crossed them royally. When the Germans entered Russia heading to Moscow, Stalin broke the pact. The Russians became England and American allies, and it worked out. Even under best conditions, we never trusted them on their words and pursuits in the war and the way they treated their lumpen proletariat.

The subject as a revelation of the "Men of Peace" first in tradition is treated as it related back traditionally to critical allied leaders who had to lead and fight wars before, such as Prime Minister Winston Churchill and Pres. Charles De Gaulle on the allied side against Germany. Then following tradition, those men led and fought during World War II, such as Franklin Delano Roosevelt and Pres. Harry S. Truman as presidents of the United States, Prime Minister Winston Churchill, the two strategic planners of the pursuit to victory, and Gen. Dwight D. Eisenhower, the supreme commander of the Allied Forces and commanders who carried out the plan. The story relates as it continues within homelands causing significant changes with influences on local behavior at sites with recollections from Movietonews and its dispersion to Americans and European allies.

With the ever-needed diplomacy, words go deeper to those who interact to negate wars or to maintain detente through negotiation or peaceful means. It meant persons encompassing, who are active politicians, economically, socially, and morally successful business leaders, societal civil servants, and the world's moral religious purveyors must use wisdom to fix political problems. Many try to solidify their beliefs into dire needs of mankind's more under of warring circumstances, which is natural. During semipeaceable times, some politicians are masked as pretentious impostors in these endeavors. They hand me down discourse with a finesse that easily gains a following, yet so easily uncovered by self-directed, wise persons as know-nothing braggarts or despot-minded with gross lack of valued judgments and consideration for the betterment of the country.

At this point, it was easy for me to go back to travel myself in a new Super 60 Fleetwood Cadillac polished to the max and with all the bells and whistles inside and out. The floor in the back area had a set of footrests. One would have to see it, and you might get a picture of one as a cutout when I insert a picture of the Cadillac in chapter 17, "Headin' to 1946 Refurbished Indy 500 Racetrack."

Now, I will continue getting back to writing about their trip to the new 1946 Indy 500 racetrack. All I know is what I have been told. In my mind, gathering memories may have involved some fictional elaboration or close to it regarding conversations and actions that became their renowned adventures while at the 1946 Indy 500 Race. What continued to be relayed to me as time passed carried some folklore about the new Super 60 Fleetwood Cadillac trip by my father, his brother Tony, and their two friends William and Charles being at the new Indy 500 racetrack speedway.

This is my revelation of how they behaved. I am imagining what they talked about and what usually was provided as conversation when people are on long trips. They also casually opined and then discussed their happenings day in, day out for five days to each other and their professional racing friends about the exorbitantly welcomed new Indy 500 Race.

These four married men were on their way to Indy 500 Race in Indianapolis, Indiana, leaving a few days earlier to settle down before Memorial Day on Thursday, May 30, 1946. I assumed that in the new car, the morning cool air filled their lungs after the night cleared by moonlight. A little later, they left, and the rain had started as they entered Huntington, West Virginia. The travelers continued and began looking for the road heading to Cincinnati. They expected to be in Indianapolis within time to spend the night in a hotel.

The next day, they took off with quick coffees and doughnuts. By lunchtime, after one o'clock, the guys were hungry. Charles voiced to Benny, asking that he stop as soon as he could find a good place to eat lunch and where there might be some exciting people. Uncle Tony always told us that he liked eating in small restaurants and usually liked small eating areas because it would be relaxing for him. Bill suggested, "Let's stop at the next place we see and eat. Look! We're in the outskirts of Ohio now. Face it, it's lunchtime, and we aren't in any hurry."

Tony said, at the same time as Benny agreed and he started to slow down, "There's a hotel with a small restaurant just a few miles down the highway. I'm hungry too. We are all hungry."

Tony chimed in, "I just want a big hamburger and some fries." After a few minutes, he said quickly, "Look! There's a Bob's Big Boy Restaurant sign on the roadside."

Benny checked the distance to Bob's where the billboard was within a minute. Benny signaled and pulled the Caddy into the parking lot. Bob's was across the road where he had to drive off. The turn was hidden, and Benny hit rough dirt and rocks at the shoulder, and rocks scattered almost everywhere on roadsides except at the sharp turn into a driveway near the restaurant. Big Benny turned at the corner as he saw where Bob's starts at the main entrance to the city about several hundred feet away.

Apparently, as they exited the car, Tony said no one gaped details of grasslands at the hotel except him and Benny, who were looking simultaneously but suspiciously at the front door of Bob's. They nudged each other to look through the front window. Both men noticed unexpected movement through windows. Benny and Tony signaled each other with their eyes but taking no notice of their friends or people inside Bob's to open their stride and widen their path like nothing had happened.

What had already happened was a robbery had just occurred in Bob's Big Boy, and robbers were about to exit the front door. Tony and Benny quickly moved away from the Caddy and walked toward the door as if they knew nothing had happened. Both nonchalantly were carrying on a conversation. Benny was right beside Tony. Their buddies were behind and talking and walking but didn't take notice of anything.

Tony suddenly noticed the front door was pushed open with a bang. In observation, Tony saw two men's faces covered with makeup and sunglasses. They started to increase their pace out the door. Tony, strongly suspecting what was going on and knowing what to do offensively, with surprise, quickly pulled his small blackjack from his pocket and cracked the two masked robbers immediately in the head with the blackjack as they approached him from Bob's entrance door while they concentrated heading toward their getaway car.

Because everyone inside had hit the floor as told, they totally did not see or suspect any physical confrontation from anyone in the parking lot, let alone just outside the door. Benny, seeing the initial strike of the two guys by Tony, quickly helped Tony keep the two guys on the ground. Benny quickly hit one of the robbers on the ground, disarmed him, and held him down with his foot and his two-hundred-pound body with a threat of face punch with his own gun. Charles and William quickly ran to help by standing on the guys. William went into Bob's and told them to call the police. The four guys held the robbers without incident until the police car arrived within two minutes. The police quickly cuffed the robbers and secured them in a police car with instructions to take them to jail. The crowd then saw that Bob's Big Boy manager, service people, and customers were seriously bragging on the guys.

The police thanked the guys but with a warning to be careful with what they interfere with. Tony said he told that he is a policeman from Montgomery, West Virginia, and that he had subdued crooks involved in quickie robberies of businesses on a weekly basis.

The travelers, after an hour or so, were back in the Caddy heading to Indianapolis with only a few hours to go. They pulled off as whirling dust surrounded the car and caused Benny to stop immediately. He stopped, but there was more clutter flying than at the garbage dumps in the West Virginia towns. Benny probably parked close to minimize the dust and waited until it settled as he put the Caddy in an area with some tree shade. With this surge of nature happening, only minor conversation arose about the robbery.

The heat got to all as the dust subsided. As expected, Chuck agreed and shouted, "You're damn right!" Bill would feel the heat the most because of his portly build and probably shook his head with a shout of "Yeah!" Benny drove the Caddy without stopping for at least three hours or more on a good highway.

Benny said, "It looks like everything's green especially trees, with leaves wavering in the wind probably caused by a big rain maybe just a few days ago. Let's put windows down a few more inches before we pass out."

After a few hours, Benny said, "Thank God the car has cooled down! We'll be getting to our hotel soon, and after we get registered, we'll go eat."

Tony pointed as he touched the windshield, saying, "There's a fairly new restaurant down the street! Let's get dinner now. I'm hungrier than a black bear comin' out of hibernation!"

Benny said, "OK!" He looked at the gas gauge first and said, "We'll eat first and then get gas, OK? Let's hustle into the restaurant before those other two cars unload."

Charles said with a yum-yum smiling face, "I'd like a good steak dinner. I don't want any kids' stuff! We still have two days before the race. We don't know what the hell we'll be eatin' at the brickyard tomorrow with the crowd rolling in!"

Benny said, "Don't worry, there will be plenty of new and good restaurants in the local hotels. The whole town will be different, especially after five years and the rebuild of the track by Anton Hulman.

A police car pulled up beside the Caddy as all looked into the black-and-white with no flashing warning light or headlight on. Casually and with friendly faces, they showed effects of the hot uniforms, so wet underarms and beads of sweat at their temples and on sides of hair where hat rims rested on their heads. But a friendlier greeting we never got on the road.

First policeman shouted friendly, "Hey, guys! Are you here for the big race?"

Tony, being a policeman, responded first, "Yeah! Are you guys going to work it? We're on vacation from our hometown. I'm on the police force in Montgomery, West Virginia. These guys are involved with a dealership, and the other one is a lawyer. I'm Tony! This guy's my big brother Ben, and I mean that in age also." Nobody talked about the robbery at Bob's Big Boy, and to my knowledge, little was mentioned about it during times that stories of the trip were relayed.

All others acknowledged greetings with facial approvals and small talk about food that was served in the Indiana Hotel Restaurant. They followed each other inside the restaurant and were amazed with crowds and seated people. The walls were full of large pictures flashing visualizations almost in real life,

life-sized photographs covered with previous racing cars and winners, pit stop photographs in full 1930s to 1941, and in some cases, fingerprints on various persons of professional sports car knowledge. Some were hand-painted artist's colors and best pictures of winners in their cars as a flagman waves with gusto. The trim wood guiding us was scratched and covered with imposed smears so noticeable.

The two policemen, noticing the stares, commented in unison, "This place has attracted customers like this for years. And at the same time, the owner, Mr. Hulman, is with celebrity crowds who would come through to salute men who were soldiers on furlough, and especially local people who brought business to his restaurant by droves, just to hear old racing stories from horses' mouths. The two local policemen separated and headed to the service counter. They sat down and ordered two coffees. The men, in an excited gait, had eyes wandering to cover all the paraphernalia and art deco miscellanea as they headed toward the hostess for service. The group continued to stare at the old counter at the register's gold-framed lightly darkened glass encased with God only knows what was stuffed in shelves other than smokes and candy. They could see it was surrounded by a variety of collectibles for sale with large white price tags.

The hostess grabbed an arm and shuffled the four men heading to a cleared table as they passed the register where two women were paying their bill. Then she seated the men at a table as she said, "How's this table?" They all seated themselves.

After a minute or two, a waitress approached and greeted all with "Welcome to the Winners Restaurant! We got everything your little hearts desire—in food, that is!"

Charles sweet-talked the waitress as she handed them iced water. Music was playing—"True Love Can't Live in a Heart Full of Shame." The melodious jukebox blared in flashing colors of light with the singsong voice of Ernest Tubbs, a performer known worldwide for country western songs, and he lives in West Virginia.

Tony chimed in, "Are the griddle-fried steaks tender? Do french fries come with them? These specials show beets as a side! I don't eat beets. I don't like the looks of 'em! But I want a steak and fries."

The waitress twisted and smiled. "You got it! French fries! Beets are good. Just say, no beets!"

The other guys quickly ordered steaks, one prepared well done, and the others prepared their plate side orders the same way. Benny then remarked with a humorous quip, "Remember! No beets on my plate."

The waitress said with a wink and another spin, "If they're on the plate, just don't eat them." And she laughed as she said, "They won't be! Just take it easy! Listen to the music!" The next record was Frankie Sinatra singing "Home in

Indiana." She said, "You'll like it, and you can enjoy others that you know as you eat your dinner."

A minor inside delight occurred with the waitress as Benny smiled and said to her, "I wish I had someone like you working for me. There would be more people in my Deluxe Diner, and they would be friendly!"

Tony butted in, polling each guy as he turned and smiled, "Do any of you ever eat beets?"

All said, "No!"

Another Frank Sinatra's musical rendition started playing—"It Had to Be You."

The waitress left. Tony and Charles looked at her body from the back as she walked away and said with a subvocalized purr, "Wow!" This exclaim was lightly heard in the nearby area. The guys shook heads and waved hands, laughed, and then quietened down, taking a sip of water, and some finished their coffee.

William said to the side, "Tony, you raised hell about beets! You should taste this coffee. Better still, you should be askin' about desserts, especially pears the way you were lookin' at the waitress! Did you see those tits! I couldn't believe what I was seeing while she was talkin' to you!"

Benny, with a slight alarm in his voice, emphasized, "What in hell's wrong with you, guys? We're strangers here! Act like it!"

The two policemen also turned their heads and smiled as the waitress passed. Tony looked out the window at the Caddy and recalled, "I was thinking of Big Poppy. One day, I asked him after he got involved with a woman in Sammy's Saloon, and he almost hit me on the fly, but he intentionally missed. That is how I know he was successful." Then Tony mentioned his son Frank as he relayed an odd question from memory, "I get questions from my eldest son at thirteen. He asked me, 'Why do you look at Jasmine when you go in Murphy's? Does she owe you something?'" Tony smiled. "The clock spins. 'You Can't Stop Me from Dreaming.'"

CHAPTER XX

Technology Overwhelms Steerage and Amour at the 1946 Indy 500 Race

*The ignorance of the crowds, that is when the plebiscites of any
city seem to have the same behavior patterns and it is known proof
by count. Those most ignorant of natural phenomena are under
worldly trust and may cause the destruction of mankind's life form;
but not eliminate its continuation. The question becomes will the
distorted version of plain simple-minded people and not the wisest
public servants elected and appointed to properly run the country
have the capability to survive or simply move toward completing
entropy, a randomness and predicted continuous evolution of mind
matter will disorder the country and send it into disaster.*
—Anonymous

*Barrum, Barrum, Barrum taps of the drum, creating the sound before
the beat as if in cycles and when in harmony is a messianic cry without
words as is the bugle that clamors knowledge of death as it tolls the doom
it created in irony as sequences of a collection of simple notes. A high
streaming keening joy rings on the New Year from a staccato of cheers to
expressions of common and amorous love wrapping the chilling to decline.*
—Anonymous

The new technology created electromechanical systems that had been designed and implemented in new cars of all kinds including racing cars and trucks days after World War II. The racing cars were predominantly critically improved in speed and performance, but some racing cars made by seat-of-the-pants inventors with significant improvements. After more than five years, newly educated engineers graduating from universities in America caused a new beginning, exciting the wisest of *Homo sapiens* to advance my unknown Second

Renaissance that appeared to circumvent the world of major countries with new talents, innovation, and creativity.

Other countries have shared new improvements and how they could be installed for performance. The new inventions are generally recognized and detailed by inventors. The new systems and devices were tried on new sports cars in this race of 1946 by businesses having contracts to develop better performing and more proficient assemblies and systems for automobile transmissions, new brake designs, front-end alignment control mechanisms, hydraulic power steering, and included methods of improving the speed of racing cars. The car companies have delved deeply into research, technology, and new designs related to driver operational support of car's climate control, driver display systems, and more detailed control features in engines, transmission, tires, braking, and exhaust systems.

The main electromechanical systems designed and implemented in new cars and trucks in the days after World War II were predominantly critically improved, but some were continued to be made by the seat-of-the-pants inventors. With the aid of newly educated engineers graduating from universities in America, a new beginning has occurred to excite the wisest of *Homo sapiens* to advance the beginning of the new Renaissance that has appeared to circumvent the world of major countries with new talents, innovation, and creativity.

The front end of these innovations began advancing as research achievers devised assemblies and system indicators such as gauges for oil pressure, gas amount display and mileage indicators, battery charge indicator, brake lights with anticipated new electromechanical devices having electromechanical response by the driver, windshield wiper with multiple on-off controls, and directional turn signals, which are really safety devices brought about by a new technology born during the war and afterward improved in the late 1950s. The changes significantly evolved inventions of transistors and associated devices capacitors, electromagnetic devices, and more powerful detectors and eventually sensor systems that were designed to identify problems before they come to disastrous happenings. Most important, new hydraulics in both braking methodology and hydro-drive systems were first tried in the 1946 Oldsmobile. By the 1950s, power steering was implemented on the larger and more expensive cars.

These new inventions were modified and tested and then were incorporated into the new large earth-moving trucks and tractor trailers that became an eye-opener for the farm boys and mountaineers that were fascinated with using the endurance mechanical technology developed for war vehicles.

Standard trucks and smaller pickups were being revamped and some rebuilt by veterans. The new younger generation, just getting their driver's licenses, added newly available items to old cars and to boot old pickups. The new pickups were being incorporated into businesses for local deliveries and for the conduct of private businesses, which were on the rise. This widespread pursuit was foremost in my dad and brothers especially their learning in the same path of mechanization. It was a boon for my dad because he was just short of a genius to fix cars and trucks, and people knew his capabilities in repairing engines and other systems of cars and trucks.

Personal trailers like the Winnebago, equipped with new inventions such as built-in kitchens and vacation vehicles all about the time of the surge revealed that motels were making the trailer look like a way to save money with gas being so cheap. The trailer was like a home where the owner had almost complete control of his day and night life. The demand leads to many new trailer builders, and the new company that built Winnebago trailers and eventually fabulous motor homes from a variety of manufacturers soon dominated the vacation spots and national parks during the next generation.

With new monies cropping up among individuals and some of these new automobiles, trucks and trailers and their sponsoring companies and dealerships maintained a new replacement parts for the companies, evolving infinite detail based on the new America's industrial revolution created by World War II. All the while, mechanical geniuses entranced with speed were developing new racing cars. They started by totally modifying old sports cars, making the much older, newly rebuilt sports cars in vogue even among the country folks, Westerners, Southerners, and many along the East Coast.

In this postwar era, one of the new top-of-the-line luxury sedan car designs is the new masterly attractive 1946 Series 60 Special Fleetwood Cadillac, which is the mysterious car that has guided the lives and destinies of the main characters in this story as well as the many people in America fascinated by the Cadillac. Its influence was astonishingly dominating. This new Cadillac so influenced his dad, his son Frankie, and his son's son much later so that they would be involved in the car business. In one way or another, they spent the bulk of their lives under the domination of cars in their businesses.

In the initial setting, the one that so impressed the first son, the immigrant Liborio from Italy, was his father's powder-blue Caddy that lived up to its name of beauty and performance. As part of the influence and heritage, his son had a precious white Buick convertible, spectacularly appointed car that dominated a space in his son's personal home garage. And it was used for special occasions both private and public by his first son many years after its initial buy.

As a memory and one enhanced by many stories, it significantly influenced Benny's two first sons' behavior and final decisions to have a special attraction to cars when each had come of age to work in their dad's garage. He relaxed in his hotel room and thought about his life coming along as planned. He started with his marriage, but when he and Jo had their first two new sons, when each had come of age, it caused him to reminisce how he came about to this point with a love for cars.

At an earlier time, starting in 1928, however, Benny Divita recalled that he only had a small crew of hard workers doing minor county jobs building back roads in northern West Virginia. Because Benny was so easy at making friends and taking on new pursuits when necessary, he followed his way to work in Adrian, West Virginia. At that time, Benny happened to curtail his dreams of a taxi business while working roads, and by chance, he was in a local restaurant when he met a friend who worked in a local mine who invited him to Sunday dinner at their home. The family's father was also a miner and a farmer who lived on a nearby back road. Al told Benny that he would come by and pick him up midday.

Benny, now on his own in his room for the night, started thinking and reminiscing about the time while working on the roads near Adrian, West Virginia. He felt good about the invitation.

As Sunday came in his mind, he ventured to the restaurant where Al took him to their home. As he entered, Alphonso Maruca and the many women and men were all happy to see him and to talk and hear about his life and theirs in the living room and around the home. By the time dinner was getting ready, he had become friends with all and were accepted by both the mother and father. At the evening meal, he was introduced to the family, all recognizing the familiar behavior and personalities, both being Italian emigrants. As did happen, my dad was especially attracted reservedly, as was his typical personality and manner, to one of the shy daughters just by chance because the men were seated for their meal while talking. Without a word but a smile and a nod, he knew that he had met the love of his life even though she had said nothing, and she wandered off to be with her mother. Benny didn't have any idea that a successful pursuit would prevail. This recall is developed from my mom's journal in part and the stories that evolved over the many years and visits. I am accounting in discourse from what was given by my mother later to know about their early lives and what I had also read from her journal.

However, he observed the way her father showed a protectiveness that goes beyond even a hint of an indication of an interest, let alone approval to pursue the young lady beyond the introduction, nor did he think he would be given a chance to see her again. Benny was told by Al Junior that Josephine's father and mother were emigrant Italians from the old country. Josephine let Benny know later that her father and mother were farmers from the area of Calabria at the lower part of the boot. He did think he might have some chance because he knew, being a kid in Italy for his first thirteen years, that his regard was not going to be one of trust without knowing what he really did for work and where and for whom he did it. And he knew was that it would take some time for Poppa Alphonso, at this time usually called Big Al because he had a son called after him for the namesake of his grandfather, as was the Italian tradition. Benny had to gain his attention with clearly voicing truths and with devotions of loving care so that he could be a contender for Alphonso's daughter Josephine's life. While away, he wrote her, and the two communicated with love thoughts and ideas of sincerity.

All he could think of at that time was that he wanted her to be his love, wife, and their lives to be beheld in the old-fashioned Catholic ways of life. Without guidance but buried in his mind, all he could think of was that his mother had taught him that it must be done in the Italian Catholic way of life. Even before involvement of any kind, the marriage, a Catholic one, must take place, and an assurance of substantiation in the use of his mind to love, honor, and care for his wife-to-be is a must.

With all this floating within Benny's mind, he knew this was his main pursuit to start—that is, one of convincing her father of his self-sufficiency so ingrained by Big Mommy over the years. And he knew that solutions were required and that he already knew how to handle their immediately demonstrated amorous affections in association with her father and mother. He was told that her father might erupt into action because he was told by his friend that Benny was one of those outgoing characters, an expressive character; not learned as a farmer like him being from the extravagantly green acres of vegetables and fruits grown on the land of Calabria, and even now as a miner, he farmed his gardens of vegetables, and in boarded areas, he had some animal stock with pigs and chickens. And what was particularly noticed was his underground built-in smokehouse used to cure and make storage for hams and pepperoni.

Benny's mind had wandered back to his earlier life pursuing a venture into the business as a road builder's helper with his dump truck. But with a quick reaction to a word from his brother while listening to the other men, he unconsciously returned to visit the family. Once there, he pondered their behavior patterns, but her brothers, especially one named Samuel, a true friend of Dad, exuded inherited traits of the home-grown Italians of the farmlands and their in-laws for those past many years. And with the good fortune after a few visits, Benny achieved his pursuit and planned to live for the remainder of his life with the love of his life.

Now, at long last, after being married eighteen years, Benny's experiences were predominantly an integral daily part of his taxi business. And as told by my brother Frank, we were always helping him with whatever he wanted us to do either at home or at the taxi business. The one thing that set in his mind the first time he attended the Indy 500 Race in 1941 was he was new to the people at the race and his racing friends. After being there for four days, he and Tony amassed a few well-known friends.

He gestured with his hands in praise all the way from indistinguishable conversational idiosyncrasies of the Italian vernacular so particularly used while in his newly bought car. The car had completed the full day's drive yesterday, and the guys stayed in a local hotel in a town outside of Cincinnati on the way to Indiana. The next day, they were on the road early, and the guys were relaxed to the point of little conversation except responding to each other's words, mostly words about the car and the war. Those many years later, Benny had bought a few new cars, but all were used as taxicabs. Tony had a feeling of admiration and delight, if not pleasure, to be with his brother.

The questions about the cars, while in restaurants, at the hotels, then to be allowed in the circle of racing friends in the car pits on the track and at the Indy 500 Race 1941 during race day, they were springing up to a few days of expected fun and enjoyment with the treatment and yet gained ten times as much as was provided by Mauri Rose, the race winner who became their friend with intent. And as the first trip shoulders its way with only a little hoopla in 1941 because of the timing of the coming war, the real essence of the coming Indy 500 in 1946 will be the gregarious intent of the middle-aged travelers, knowing that Big Benny would have been involved with Mauri Rose over the years. As a group, these guys know how to gain fun and enjoyment unrelentingly with a simply impressive way of life with exhilaration for the coming week.

The next Indy 500 Race did not restart racing until after World war II in May 1946. This is where the recollection has the most appeal and extreme rebuilding and a new owner. The memories told to me during the time of my life at home were discussions so characterized by my elder brother Frank and uncle Tony and very lightly by my father Benny; and the extolment that happened later was pulled from within their memories.

At the races, as related by their two buddies Charles and William with facial twists and pet expressions, exposed traits of their heritage of sensuality and might reveal minor infidelities, or each more typically had insisted that they were loyal to their wives, especially when their natural humor, emotional desires, and tempers were dramatically highlighted even if sometimes their weight was tongue in cheek. However, several of the revelations encompassed loyalty outcomes, leaving most of us with a slight jaundice eye of disbelief and a pretense of seeming belief because the times of repartee might be ripe for braggadocios in the company of real men.

In 1946, Cadillac created the Series 60 Special called the Series 60 Special Fleetwood. Benny had pointed out from his reading knowledge some of the features in dialogue with old-time braggadocios about a best radio, power of the engine, and riding comfort.

On occasion, Walter Winchell, while on radios at home reporting the news of the day and the nature of things, the world was in overtly urgent needs because the words portrayed were devastating as they related to the damage in the assaulted countries. He critically asked with the same emphasis, "What will America do in Japan after such an indescribable amount of nuclear-induced death, damage, and pending death to the people and property in Hiroshima and Nagasaki?" As an escape from guilt, the American reason was that the Japanese leaders refused to surrender regardless of the warnings of unexpected mass destruction, significant death; and with extended death of many human, charges would be accounted to their leaders and that their leaders would be responsible for sacrificing their people.

Dad never had a difference with President Truman. He knew a great deal of killing by the Japanese was hell-bent to overtake a number of countries like China, Malaysia, and Burma, and massacred our troops on the South Pacific Islands simply because they said they needed more room to expand.

The deaths were living death to the people and the tortured, burned innocent children expected to be inflicted and many living while dying from the radiation effects. With the destruction, no matter what the provocation might have been or the saving features of sparing other human lives, America was forced to suffer a leaf of legacy caused by the horror of war. A deterrence was imposed, but the proliferation extended.

Other countries conspired to gain nuclear weapons, and as time passed, spies gained the inevitability of evolving existing nuclear capabilities. Now, the society of the world's people will never be the same, and it will add horrendous fear mentally and physically as life continues.

The leaders on both sides will never be the same toward their own leaders. The people will eventually remove those who claim royalty and will eliminate those who want to dominate the people without a voice in the conduct of their national and international conflicts and the daily lives of individuals. The building of Japan was with the grace of the help from America, who saw the suffering that helped make the Japanese people's recovery with more understanding to move toward peace. God, as in one's world's belief, only knows the amount of the Japanese compassion for forgiveness.

Benny admired Will Rogers's type of humor and wit or even quotes from him as heard in radio conversations and from newspapers to fit conversation to the necessary work of our Congress and sensible spending and the effectiveness of President Truman's global sense via the United Nations to demand peace and strive to ensure peace among warring nations.

Now, we are in the Caddy where we have previously commented on the way the war ended and getting to what was happening along the drive. The road traffic was gathering with the view of my new 1946 Cadillac Series 60 Special Fleetwood being driven along the Tolsia Highway on U.S. Route 52 out of Huntington, West Virginia. The traffic was easy to maintain at the speed limit, which I follow always. Everyone in sight, be it in a car, truck, bus, or on a train, burst with facial expressions with a revelation to their traveler friends' view of the Caddy. The guys in the Caddy were about twenty miles beyond Cincinnati heading along the major Highway 74, viewing and, with their minds, exploring features and faraway features of the mountains as they left West Virginia as they turned to the rolling hills of Ohio. Tony looked close up at billboards off the road as his head rolled around almost ninety degrees to try to read one that advertises the 1946 Memorial Day Indy 500 Race at the New Indianapolis Motor Speedway.

Then Charles looked out the open window with the slightly warm breeze as his hair fluttered. He opened his collar, cooling him to a sigh. He sighted the farmhouses inland and one highlighting a red barn with "Mail Pouch Tobacco" painted on only one side. Just as they passed the barn, some old cars and a truck and one new car, about five or six years old, were near the home. On the road, a few old frame trucks passed in the opposite direction, both covered with dust from way back when and one large coal-carrying truck was breaking the speed limit of 55 MPH, as was our car, but Charles knew it was only slightly because Benny was the driver.

The guys were comfortably seated, and one was smoking, but very carefully and very seldom and neatly and using the new large custom-made designed ashtrays to suit the overall appointments. All were in their white shirts with loosened ties but with coats neatly snuck in the trunk as seen upon their departure. They were well out of Cincinnati, Ohio, which was only about four hours from Indianapolis, Indiana.

The men were dressed in white long-sleeved dress shirts with ties loosened or pulled down and with some windows slightly opened; at this time, there was no air-conditioning in cars.

The two Italian men, Benny, about forty-six years old, and Tony, about forty-three years old, were up front. Benny and Tony were always with their children as caretakers when going on trips. The two men seated in the back are longtime friends and associates. One is a full-blooded Englishman who traces back to the American Revolution and is a descendant of a British army colonel whose name is Charles. Charles owns a Chevrolet Motors dealership in the town where First Street was kept up-to-date better than Fourth Avenue. The main reason was that businesses and travel activities were regularly frequented to travel on Route 60 rather than Route 61 on the Montgomery side of the Kanawha River.

The other man is William, a first-generation American Lebanese whose parents, from many years past, were Roman Catholics and continue to be so in America. William is a practicing lawyer in the local counties and the capital city of Charleston with a notable reputation as a business and corporation lawyer. The state capitol building is in Charleston, about twenty miles away, and is the biggest city in the state. However, William was well known in the capital city. This connection leads me to say this is where he made his reputation and money that he tells no one about. Charles, as a longtime citizen of Montgomery and a well-known businessman with money, has William as his lawyer.

Benny, the father of Frankie, with his memory source in this part of the story, gets the idea embedded in his mind so much so that it was an easy step to think about what his dad had told him to think—that his future might be in music.

Benny also had close friends being in the taxi and transfer business for years.

His personal retained friends, having been at the Indy 500 in 1941, had contacted the general manager, whom he had met in 1941 at General Motors at the Cadillac division in Detroit. With this tie, Dad secretly bought with a down payment the new 1946 Super Series 60 Special Fleetwood Cadillac. Benny took delivery at its destination in Charleston after being transported by a train from Detroit back to Montgomery, unbeknownst to all locals and closest friends.

His close friends touted the new 1946 powder-blue Fleetwood Cadillac when they saw it the day they left. When he got back, he was told that conversation was about its beautiful appointments and the way it looked. Charles said to Benny, "I give you an A-plus credit! How did you know when to put your order in so early?"

Benny smiled and commented, highly satisfied, as he must have responded, "I saw the brochure and fell in love with it! I told the general manager of the Cadillac division who knew about our good relationship at the 1941 Indy 500 Race." That started the talk about buying a new 1946 Cadillac from a dealership in the capital of Charleston, West Virginia. The general manager knew about the rich coal companies and the large industrial areas along the Kanawha River. The general manager said, as best as Benny recalled, "I'm making a note of your expected buy. We'll keep an accounting of potential sales starting in Charleston and around the industrial area of the Kanawha River Valley."

Charles responded with a slight air of richness but with disappointment with his own standing with the General Motors that had happened just two weeks later when he had called for his delivery of new cars. He said, "I was told by my sales manager that there were no 1946 Super 60 Cadillacs left for this year's delivery. We only got back orders, and the one that hit the famous town of Montgomery in time was yours, which required only a simple request—I guess to the right person."

Uncle Tony said, "Chuck, Benny does nothing simple. He knew who to call. I'm sure his timing was right on! That's my big brother."

Benny, however, had called him with a praise of their business in Charleston and the nearby cities. He placed Benny's personal order with money, and then it would be shipped on the day so that it would be in Charleston by mid-May.

Charles, with little retort and a lot of jealousy, said, "Well, I should have placed an order myself at the same time. I did not know Benny was jumping the gun! He only said he saved the down payment money."

Tony responded, "When it's necessary, he knows how to negotiate, compromise, and make the deal a firm contract!"

Benny said to all, "I will not keep the Caddy when we get back in Montgomery. It would interfere with my business. I will sell it to one of my doctor friends."

William butted in, being from a large family himself, "Well, he better! He has got a lot of kids to feed." William noticed a change in speed and questioned, "Benny, why are you slowing down?"

Benny pointed to the roadside landscape up toward the mountain. "Tony, look! You bought your old truck from that farmer two years ago!"

Tony peered and quickly reminisced and asked, "Benny, why did you remind me of the truck incident?"

Benny stopped and said, "I wanted to look for the farmer's daughter in the field! Now you know, Tony! If you could see her, you'd end up with her in the field and say, 'Hello!'"

Tony laughed, William patted Benny's back, and Charles just smiled.

Benny defensively pushed him on the shoulder, saying, "Tony, you always tell the same story, but nothing happened!"

Tony laughed again with hands moving in praise as he said, "Last time she showed me her lambs!"

The two guys in the back voiced with little sound, "Lambs!"

Tony pushed Benny's arm with a smile and said, "I thought you told me she showed me her gams! Just teasin', Big Benny!" He pointed out of the opened car window, saying, "I know gams is the word soldiers used when they talked about the Italian girls' legs."

Excitement flared in laughter as the car approached a set of Burma Shave Cream post signs. Tony, with excitement, digressed to read out loud as the car passed each of the signs.

"Big mistake . . . many make . . . and rely on horn . . . instead of . . . brake . . . Burma Shave."

(The letters are clear and obvious with white letters on red board on large posts.)

Charles shouted as Benny rounded a curve on the road almost taking the straight path, "Hey, Benny! Do you know where the brake is on this car?"

Benny said, "Some of these curves need to be straightened! I slowed down and straightened them out." All laughed. Charles, excited, changed the subject and attempted to tell a corny observation about Benny's driving as Tony interrupted.

Tony commented, "I remember when Benny and I were heading to White Sulphur Springs for a few days to have some fun just hobnobbing with the rich people. I was going to learn to play golf, while he was meeting a friend from Washington that was going to be there. He wanted to see what's going on with the General Motors because his friend said the company was going to step up the plants to put out new models. Then at a small party and dinner, he got the skinny on the econ—"

William then interrupted Tony but then pumped out loud with a hee-haw laugh! "Are you kiddin'! Tony's going to learn to play golf!"

Benny retorted in a few choice words, "It's my new car, and I want to keep it in one piece!"

William said, "Take it easy, Benny! You're the best driver, and we all know it!"

Benny tapped the brake a few times with caution to make his point. Then Benny said, "At least there will not be any mistakes with me driving!"

Seconds later, they passed the next road sign that included a Barbasol Shave Cream billboard, a business that started in Indianapolis, Indiana. When this one was passed, Charles kept up with reading the signs. William saw him subvocalize the words. But as he finished the shave cream billboard words, William's attention was turned to several Clabber Girl Baking Powder billboards, also noticed by Charles. Neither Benny nor Tony made any comment. Both men had seen many types of billboards in their jobs as truck drivers and during his taxi and transportation business, and even Tony, being a policeman knew they talked about them at odd times just to extend their wit.

William observed and commented, "I never saw so many baking powder billboards in my trips chasing after business in West Virginia."

Charles knowingly continued to educate William. "The baking powder factory is in Terra Haute! It meant we're about fifty miles past Cincinnati. And we're about a hundred miles from Indianapolis." As he paused, looking at Benny's head and almost asking for a response, he said, "Here's a good one! The baking powder guy also bought the Indianapolis Speedway." Charles was a businessman and has money; and he had traveled through many states. However, William, as a lawyer, always had his mind on his next job while driving.

William, refreshing his memory and letting all know he has a lawyer's education, said, "You're right! I read it in the *Charleston Gazette* last week! The guy's name is Tony Hulman! He bought it from the most celebrated war ace in the U.S. Army Air Corps, Col. Eddie Rickenbacker, after the war. Eddie had everything going for him when he came home."

Tony said inquisitively, "Why the hell would a guy making baking powder buy the big-time Indy 500 racetrack?"

Benny answered as a guess but not knowing what's going to come out, "Hulman is a businessman, and what everyone has said, he must be a lover of racing cars and high-power sports cars. He's a lot like us but smarter about what's coming that would make money. Plain and simple, he's got brains! What's better, he loves racing cars as much as we love our cars. Tony, you know, like some of us, love to look at women!"

After Benny finished, Tony squirmed and looked back at the guys for their response. He shoved his hand into the backseat area and got a shake from William as he said, "We're gonna have some good times no matter what! Am I right, Chuck?"

William made a funny ending statement, "Chuck loves chatting up women and makin' money! He's our best man for setting up good times."

Charles proudly moved his hands to express himself posed with a shy look of desire as Uncle Tony said something like, "Billy, you're my lawyer, and what you know about me is confidential." He sneered with laughter.

William ridiculed, "Don't make me laugh. I might pee my pants! Let's make a pit stop! I really mean it!"

Benny looked forward and pulled off and up to a billboard. He slowed the Caddy to a stop to shut out William's view but with the engine running. He observed the big oblong red, white and blue Eastern States Standard Oil (ESSO) sign, so common a filling station sign. Benny pointed to the station as he said, "We need gas, and we should get something to eat." William got back in the car, and they took off.

As they approached the station, all they could see were scattered car parts and engines and old tires that looked like they intended to throw them more to the back area, some totally busted, base cords, split, and threads torn in several parts like they were caused by a blowout. With the window down, the smell of gasoline and old tires was only snuffed out by the grease odor from the old engines and transmissions on the ground nearby as they drove up and slowed down.

He looked at the station with an attached garage and cruised slowly over to the gas pumps. The station was simply equipped with two in-line gasoline pumps and an air compressor next to the station's side door. Benny heard the pump's noise caused by the belt on the motor and the rackety screen protecting the belt from the public as he lowered his front window.

He then spied a small nondescript restaurant almost next door to the station but about a quarter of a mile away. Benny looked at Tony and the guys in the backseat, and without asking for an OK, he nodded and said, "Go to the toilet while I fill 'er up." He filled the car and paid the old attendant. The guys came back to the car. He pointed to a restaurant for some food. Then he pointed to the billboard advertisement also at the station.

All gathered back into the car. He slowly pulled off the road near enough to read the billboard advertisement about the Indy 500 Speedway Race. Tony read the race, especially the race date orally, "Thursday, May 30, 1946." And words were written that it will be the first new race since 1941 because the facility stopped during World War II.

William and Charles nodded to each other, and Chuck tapped Benny. "What are we waiting for?"

Benny said, "I wanted to see how many cars were at the restaurant down the road at this time of day. You can always tell a good eating place by the number of cars in the parking lot." Benny gave it gas, tipped the brakes at the road's edge, took off when road cleared, and went only a short distance and stopped. He pulled in a Bob's Big Boy Restaurant so obvious with its sign of the Big Boy's in the checkered blue and white overalls.

Charles squeezed out a snobbish slur slowly about Bob's as he said, "They feed the kids hamburgers and hotdogs or worse. Maybe this one's OK! I think we could do better a little closer to Indianapolis. Aw, it's not worth wasting time because we had to stop for gas. Let's do it! Look! There's an apple orchard next to it. Some good pickings!" Charles laughed and cooled the situation and eliminated any further remarks. The guys all nodded with OKs to signal that they were ignoring Charles's smart-ass comments on the front end of the lunch stop to accept his elitism. And what was recalled and exposed were these comments made by the guys from their memories with a gusto!

Benny locked the Cadillac with his key, and they walked along the rocky and scrappy ground area. The men flanked Benny, one commenting that Bob's food was mostly done to accommodate children. As the men entered, the sunlight spectrum's stream exposed the interior of the restaurant, apparently a newer one with beautifully appointed leather and premium-grade navy-blue carpeting.

They stretched and peered as they adjusted their white shirts into their waists but did not touch their ties. Benny said, "This restaurant is now the sign of the times. It's the only way to go into the food business. I know my Deluxe Diner is too old-fashioned now, but it still has a place in the city, and old-timey customers use it all the time. The diner has a Pullman train coach look, and people saw it every day as the passenger trains passed through the city and stopped at the depot."

All the new children that were coming from all the soldiers that have gotten married were going to need a place to go for snacks. In a few years, there will be dozens of these quick-feed restaurants in every major city in the country. They get served and eat as they continued to talk about the critical times of the war and good words about some of their past friends who were going to be at and in the races.

After getting under way, Charles started with "The war ended up giving people more spirit, gusto with pride to go into business. The soldiers are now in homes where living conditions had improved. Everyone knew that children will come along." Then Charles said, "We've already experienced that, and the city has the kids to show for it."

Benny peered and pointed at a smaller and different sign about baking powder that can be bought at a local A & P Food Store. Benny read aloud slowly, "Baking soda powder is also good for heartburn!" Benny pointed at the sign and said, "I've used baking powder to settle my stomach a time or two."

William laughed and sneakily said as he kicked dust over the spit, "I can see why. It's big enough!"

Benny said, "Keep it up, big-time lawyer. You'll look funny walking to Indianapolis. Anyway, I take Stanback! They're for anything including a hangover headache after too much Jim Beam on Saturday night."

William apologetically said, "What the hell is a Stanback?"

Benny continued his remedy as he remarked, "It isn't nothing special. It looks like baking powder in a slip of wax paper."

The neat part about the trip was told so many times that it gave me some insight to offer about their trip, sometimes in my own words. For example, when Charles brought up the fact that he had met George Robson at the 1941 races.

Charles and Benny had previously met Mauri Rose earlier at a General Motors dealership convention in Flint, Michigan. Charles looked forward to renewing the old friendship to become a closer friend. Benny had said a few times before, "Mauri and I kept in touch by phone a couple of times during the past few years. Mauri knew in 1946 that we were heading to the racetrack." Benny turned to make a point to Chuck, "My friend John Campbell, your General Motors dealership competition, also knew Mauri Rose. He told me John met Mauri almost the same time on the race day. He saw him when he got out of his car after winning the race in 1941."

Charles, with interest, relayed a little knowledge to the rest of the guys. "John's son Junior, now twenty-five years old, still behaves like a spoiled brat. I was with him when he met Mauri's friend's daughter. Junior also had met one of the other drivers, George Robson! That was when Junior was around the driver's pit. I also met George's daughter. I think the woman's name was Maria." Anyway, he mentioned to Uncle Tony that she came to Montgomery a few years later while on a special trip to be with Junior. There was some rumor to her experience in the West Virginia wonders at White Sulphur Springs' Greenbrier Country Club. Charles said, "I was told that she was very interested in the life of the people known as hillbillies but were locals who recognized themselves as mountaineers. The way they were dressed in overalls or work clothes was their natural way."

William said, "You know, the young people do not think of anyone but themselves. In the future, I will write a book that will make all of us the laughing stock of the East Coast."

Benny turned to Chuck. "Chuck, one thing for sure, you do know a lot of the race car guys because you are an insider and you go to conventions any chance you get. Charles, we'll see George Robson. He's close with Mauri. I got to know Mauri Rose through a friend from Pennsylvania when we spent two days at his race car garage. He told me in a letter he's looking forward to meeting me again. We're going to have a great time, especially because both Mauri Rose and George Robson are among the favorites this year!"

Tony, slightly under his breath but enough to be noticed, said his piece to interrupt, "Speak for yourself! I'm more interested in viewing the women and winning some money on the race. With these two racing, it might be wise to bet on either one or both to protect your bet."

Charles was still tuned into Tony's thoughts, almost as a lonely teenager with his own thoughts about the pretty girl next door as he said, "George's daughter is good lookin'." He paused and moved both hands to his lips and smiled, yielding an extended kiss to Tony.

Chuck making the praise of George's daughter emphasized his point with a concern. "I wouldn't trust my daughter with Junior Campbell as far as I could throw the hustling bastard! I saw the two of them together at the Indiana Home Hotel, and he was spending his dad's money like he was a millionaire."

Speaking of bastards, Chuck changed the subject back to Hitler's takeover and blurted out with "That's what I wanted to tell FDR about Hirohito about both Hitler and Tojo. If only he had contacted me before he listened to the Japanese emissaries, I would have told him don't try to deal with either of those bastards or any of the tricky slant-eyed snakes in the grass. Those guys were trying to work a trading deal while the emperor had the USA in their gun sights. President Roosevelt should have known better. My god, look what the Germans were doing right under our noses before we declared war on both countries on December 11, 1941, after the Japanese attacked Pearl Harbor."

Benny said, "FDR knew within his mind that the Japanese were up to something other than offering to import and export trading agreements with England. President Roosevelt knew that the Germans were sneaking around our states looking for information to send back to the German brownshirt secret police and the gestapo. He noted them for their brutality against people including many deaths and under the NAZI regime even many years before Germany's declaration of war on European countries before 1938."

Charles, waiting to respond while in a shuffling, shifting, and scurrying action, edged out his response. "You're right about Hitler! He was a maniac hell-bent on becoming a dictator from his early life after the World War I. Many throughout the world knew during his time in prison that he eventually wrote *Mein Kampf* as a discourse in many words about his worldviews and what he planned to do to become Germany's chancellor and then take over the world. If only he had followed his earlier days as a paper hanger and a would-be artist who went unnoticed even though he had made earlier attempts to become a professional artist but essentially was not recognized. Too bad he wasn't a top-notch artist because he might have succeeded. Later, he would have died from hunger while trying to sell his paintings to Berliners during the '30s."

William chimed in with, "His general demeanor was to hate anyone who got in his way. He behaved as a real biased criminal with the Jews. Hitler was the one who brought on great bodily harm and death to millions of human beings who attempted to disagree with him."

American men intermittently were known to discuss times before, during, and after World War II with friends and locals in their small towns. The thrust was imposed on everyone's mind because the American people had gone through the Great Depression and then even more devastating during the tough times of the war.

As what I knew about what was going, I recalled times during the war when many citizens of Montgomery worked in the alloy metal mills. My dad sometimes would tell Frankie more than usual about the weapons plants under way earlier with reference to World War II from 1938 to 1945, the dominating influence of the expansion of the factories into weaponry and tanks and trucking vehicles that would be shipped and used for moving troops and supplies needed in Europe.

Later, as the story of Dad and Frankie progressed and the years passed, young guys and gals, brothers, sisters, and neighbors' kids who had been in the service remembered the value of their duty and sacrifice because many soldiers came back; some critically injured, and some were sacrificed in battle and died. Many were buried on foreign soil. Those few who were found were sent to the National Arlington Cemetery to be represented as proud soldiers who died serving their country; and the honor for our troops continued yearly.

The conversations jumped from one another and were interrupted abruptly. The changed reports were based on observing the bulk of humans and then concentrated on radio where newsmen were giving daily news. Many people were involved in daily activities and were busy with their cars, work, and solving family problems.

My memories now digressed to continue their coined conversations of current thinking as they drove toward Indianapolis. Racing and sports competition were interests of the general population, but a few of the rich participated only in small active groups, especially the people who have time, money, and acquired the accommodations where special events were advertised along the way.

These men's conversations stimulated them with exhilarating moments in the lives. These four well-known mountaineer men from the West Virginia coal mining area were true patriots.

Before the two friends knew the Cadillac was going to be delivered on time, they had offered their car and had it serviced, washed, and waxed to the nines. After all, Charles, who had the best car available, had said it was not up to a vote; his car would be used because they needed the comfort for four big men. Tony proudly backed up what Charles said with, "We Italian Americans hated Il Duce, Benito Mussolini, even more than the patrician aristocrats. That bastard should've remained running the trains for people on time."

William, questioned Tony, "Why would you say that?"

Tony looked up at his face and said, "Don't you know? He put Italy's trains on a working schedule. Italy should have never sided with the Germans! It was disgraceful to the Italians, and he changed our heritage. Everybody knew that a few of the American Italians were involved with the Mafia in the big cities on the East Coast and in the Midwest, especially Chicago." That was bad enough.

Charles motioned with his hand to Tony, changing the conversation by pointing out the window and saying, "Look, another Burma Shave sign!"

Tony read the next Burma Shave Cream post signs separated about every one or so minutes. "In Cupid's little . . . bag of tricks . . . here's the one . . . that clicks . . . with chicks . . . Burma Shave."

Benny, still thinking about the farm and the farmer's daughter, questioned, "Charles! What are chicks?"

Charles laughed with a puzzled facial expression as he exclaimed, "The girls you're always gawking at! Good-lookin' women?"

William jumped into the conversation. "No, Charles. It meant a good-lookin' girl! It's young people's talk. You and Benny are too goddamn old to get it!"

Tony, as a know-all with a satisfied smirk on his face, clearly insisted, "Wait a few years and you'll wish you got it!"

Benny, puzzled and wanting to stop the conversation, asked, "Got what?"

Tony showed a laughing face this time and fitted in, "OK!"

The other guys shouted, "Twat! That's what it's all about!"

This comment led to the instinctive situation of *amour* as to "what's it all about!" It really shows that when it comes to amorous involvements in Italian families, nothing stands in the way of family protection, even when personal jealousy is activated. For example, these two brothers quite often displayed brotherly love over jealousy when either one was exposed, compromised, or threatened within the family. The guys now notice that having been driving for a few hours, they were near the hotel where Benny had called days before and got the reservation for two rooms for four to spend the night. Benny pulled into the nearby parking area and went inside where he confirmed their reservations.

Then later, during conversations that continued about the war as the two brothers Benny and Tony walked into the bar, they all said hello to two policemen at the entrance. The four guys decided to take a short stop at the bar for a quick drink with some snacks and then later get dinner. They knew that they had to settle in their rooms for one night and try to get some sleep, for the new venture tomorrow would take some time meeting their old friends and the new racetrack and the overall facility.

The next day, the guys left the Indianapolis Hotel after breakfast and took off for the racing area where they had gotten reservations over the phone a week before they planned to leave; and at the same, for their digs for the next four nights near the racetrack facility. They drove the Caddy quickly to the highway to make up some time to be early. After a while, they were near the racetrack, and the atmosphere changed, blending the new place with the morning sun and loads of May flowers recently emplaced to further the décor overall.

The evolution of the excitement exposed the nature and behavior of the men enjoying making it out big time in the coming atmosphere of the refurbished Indy 500 racetrack for the 1946 race with a new jubilee for this most famous American racetrack that stopped racing after the May 1941 Indy 500 Race. They are revving up their macho to stay tuned to the crowd, mixing with different personalities with a smile or wave or a West Virginia howdy; all ebulliently excited about sports cars, races, the drivers, their associates and teams, and the new fair-weather friends and the sensual arousals that dominated telling the reader with ravenous and sensuous desires that scream to account for their steerage and amour, and yet get to know "what's it all about!" in every way.

This combination of personal interactions with new cars and their performance influences their minds that figuratively caused an explosion of personal desires that were unrivaled. These men from a small city in West Virginia clearly portrayed their nearly fanatic interest in the new Indy 500 Race that will finally occur after World War II. The new owner of the racetrack and the new racing cars and drivers, old and new, regarding this Indy 500 Race expressed its new background completely. The needed refurbishment was provided by the new owner, Mr. Tony Hulman, so that coming future years would be full of fun and excitement. Among all that was added by the team participants concentrated on letting the people about unknown changes. Expectations of installed capabilities were outstandingly new first for this refurbished world-renowned Indy 500 racetrack facility as a foregone conclusion.

The expectation of the winner, how well he would have to do to win in his new car and the accolades and prizes due for being a champion, was unimaginable for the winner and especially for the gifted bettors when they picked the winner! The nature of the influences of the winner and what happens later in concert by the fans were highlighted with a great spirit of success. The affinity at the conclusion when the award would be presented was about the winner, and every word goes back with the winner's memories unforgettable.

This new race led to revelations added and oversized so that the enjoyment transferred among close and old friends how the very popular race drivers, especially George Robson and his friend Mauri Rose, the 1941 winner, introduced each fan to new acquaintances of both guys. Many would have already had Mauri Rose in mind and some mentally visualized self-made meetings made at the several Indianapolis hotels that could bring about amorous adventures.

The sensitivity and parting after the trip from the race site while the mountaineers were driving back home to Montgomery was a homeward trip of excitement full of embedded memories. The experience was a step above having a variety of various memories of personality attractions. For these guys, just knowing George Robson, who won the race, was a unique feeling of pleasure because he was already known by all of us. While there, each man concentrated on the behavior of their lives; however, regarding being men in the Super 60 Cadillac was fully praiseworthy. These men were really exposed in their daily lives and had shown renown in their later lives under different family situations. Some of the guys had gained a self-sufficiency themselves or while with others as well, to account for numerous versions of memories that would be related to friends and families later that they were fascinated with the true teachings of "steerage and amour" as part of "what's it all about!" in everyone's life

CHAPTER XXI

"Gennnnntlemennnnn, Starrrrrt Yourrrrr Ennnnngines!"

Moments of silence are part of the music.
—Unknown. From *Words I Wish I Wrote*, Robert
Fulghum, HarperCollins Publishers Inc., 10 East
53rd Street, New York, NY 10022, p. 203

Many racing aficionados were already at the newly rebuilt track and facility. The men from Montgomery, West Virginia, saw crowds gathering toward their seats or positions of choice where tickets identified locations. As critical turning points in this story, it is imperative that the story of infidelity and loyalty was both tied to these types of events with money! Money! Money! Money makes the world go around and causes many unfortunate happenings. The people interacting may behave from shortcomings to extremes on a grandiose racetrack of life, and any one of them could have picked the one and only place where they might supposedly be able to charm women into a voluptuous quiescence with amorous attraction on nights before the critical race.

In the last race of 1941, with regard to Mauri Rose's involvements, he made his car a winner of the race at the 1941 Indy 500. He became a winner in life because he used his "knowledge and experience" that he inherited and was taught, and he learned from muses who commonly relay, "As we live let others live, and do unto others as you would have others do unto you." And with good judgment, that resulted in Mauri Rose's behavior with his friends Benny, Tony, William, and Charles when the second time together came. From two pursuits as longtime husbands, they followed the way to cultural development and desired improvements more like persons that relied on *steerage* rather than illicit *amour*, which had been attempted to be taught to all through heritage.

After World War II, personal behavior with both natural and moral laws and society behavior were more expressive, if not at some time even unprincipled, when ties were mindfully concentrated on *amour*; the one that is separated is the affaire d'amour (an illicit love affair) instead of an affaire de coeur (affair of the heart), which is the one that should dominate ways *Homo sapiens* live their lives within their own minds of beliefs and pursuits of happiness.

That sunny morning, the four enthusiastic guys, in their hotel, dressed well in newly cleaned suits currently in vogue personally and shaved with a man's scent, maybe Brylcreem and Old Spice shave lotion. Each man's hair was fully combed, and their suits with smartly matching ties revealed their fine looks as if readily made to be observed as elitist attendees with a flair. They walked through what I recalled the Back Home in Indiana Hotel on their way to the race. They knew they were going to have a day of great fun full of chatter and grandiose interactions. As the race day began, they moved from one place to another with delight and held conversations of choice with their favorites. Over the next four or five hours, new facilities made it a relaxed venture into a world of manly glee, but many were with wives and families. The excitement at the finish would be a commemoration, being a new first start, and would enhance the Memorial Day remembrance after losing five years of racing enjoyment mixed with excitement and associations with people in the same frame of mind now that the war ended.

The Thirtieth International 500-Mile Sweepstakes was held at the Indianapolis Motor Speedway on Thursday, May 30, 1946. Tony Hulman of Terra Haute had bought the facility from Eddie Rickenbacker and his associates, Wilbur Shaw and Homer H. Cochran, for a purchase price of $750,000 on November 14, 1945. Wilbur Shaw was named president and general manager, and Tony Hulman was the chairman of the board. Mr. Shaw then presided over the race in 1946 and guided the personal and practiced updates to conjointly treat fans, participants, racing teams, and facilities' employees par excellence. Their board of directors reviewed rules and kept them mostly the same, and new cars could be used when possible with some minor new devices installed with caution and approval because of demands on the nation during World War II.

He insisted on hiring many past employees, and the refurbishment was instantly pursued. That was a must because the facility was terribly dilapidated. Many new construction techniques evolved over the past five years of World War II warring, and new designs were used in buildings with upgrades of materials. This included new engineering and testing devices. Assemblies and designs improved car speeds and maneuvering over a new faster track so much. An invitation was offered by Indiana's lieutenant governor Richard T. James to European racing teams to be allowed to enter the race.

At the opening day, James Melton performed the song "Back Home Again in Indiana." It was the first time this traditional song had been produced before the start of the race. As well, new facilities continued with Tom Carnegie as the speaker on the speedway public address system from 1946 through 2006. Spectators were invited to view ongoing test drives and practice but at a price of fifty cents each. The people came from local areas and from all over the country to visit the facility. The count for attendance of race day was 165,000 attendees. Fifteen racers were expected, and by the end of April, the current list included forty-four cars so far but ended up with the traditional thirty-three cars allowed by design.

The final prize was listed as $60,000. After doing test runs against rain and other types of mishaps and parts failure, the race was ready to start. All racers had paid $125 entry fee and were not sure whether they would qualify. The final qualifications ended with thirty-three entries gathered at post in assigned positions. Mauri Rose was originally in the ninth position, George Robson in the fifteenth position, and his brother Hal Robson was in the twenty-third position.

This chapter's title tells the story in lightning flashing pings and roars of the engines when the race starter Tom Carnegie shouted,

"Gennnnntlemennnnn, starrrrrt yourrrrr ennnnngines!"

The revving was masterful and as loud as it could possibly be that all the racers had positioned to be ready at loudspeaker's signal for the pace car to start the race and to end with a winner after more than four hours of racing.

In the pace car, president of Ford Motor Company, Henry Ford II, was sporting a Lincoln Convertible Coupe with Wilbur Shaw in the shotgun seat, wishing he was the driver knowing that he was a three-time winner of the Indy 500 Race. The pace car went around the track one time and then led fastest qualifier cars into the race. The entire field crossed the starting line at full throttle as the pace car pulled to the left to the apron safely in front of the pits. The drivers were then positioned in eleven rows of three cars each for one complete circle of the oval.

Then the race started immediately, cheering for Mauri Rose, who led in the first lap and tied the record starting from the ninth position and continued through eight laps. He later had a crash and left the field after forty laps.

The next thing that happened to West Virginia fanatics was that their friend George Robson took the lead for good on lap ninety-three and led the rest of the way. He achieved a phenomenal position into a leader of laps with 138 laps and eventually won the race after more than four hours. George's car was a six-cylinder Sparks, a first six-cylinder winning car since Ray Haroun in 1911.

Note: A photograph of the winning car is inserted in chapter 20 for show.

I can imagine the excitement of four guys being in the middle of this sports car-loving racing venture. They had both bet on their two friends Mauri Rose and George Robson and won money.

Henry Ford I was a known force for the race from the beginning years and continued throughout with the involvement of his family and many known members of his business. He was honored by the president of the raceway, Wilbur Shaw, and selected Henry Ford II to be the pace car driver in this 1946 Indy 500 for helping to make sure the new refurbishment was accomplished.

An image of the winning car, as photographed and described by Doctorindy, an always member of keeping records, and driven by George Robson, was on display at the Indianapolis Motor Speedway Hall of Fame Museum during May 2001, at the one hundredth anniversary Ultimate Indianapolis 500 Winning Car Collection.

After the Indy 500 Race, the men ran full of glee and excitement especially because of winnings from betting on both Mauri Rose and George Robson, who won the race. They would be able to embellish their stories by claiming friendship with the winner. The saddest outcome is that in the next race that George Robson ran, he was killed in a race just months after his victory at the Indy 500 in 1946.

The race has continued for the more than seventy-two years starting from May 1917 and is ready for next year.

PART 4

MODERN ESSENCES OF STEERAGE AND AMOUR

*Don't exaggerate rhetorically, under your lack of natural and
general beliefs of people who are sincerely educated and with
a good amount of wisdom; although not all knowing such as
prophets of religious beliefs who profess a methodology of beliefs
from past gains of factual evolvements from God the Creator
of the Universe and Continuous Evolution; but in documented
words of creationists [. . . all that remains is a belief].*

—Anonymous

*Chronic remorse, . . . is a most undesirable sentiment. If you
have behaved badly, repent, make . . . amends . . . behave
better next time. On no account brood over your wrongdoing.
Rolling in the mud is not the best way of getting clean.*

—Aldous Huxley, *Brave New World*, foreword, p. vii

Loyalty and infidelity may critically change family values, lives, and times after many years living as a married adults. Frank narrates different parts of his related life's pursuit and what he knows about the Divita family as he reveals how his personal activities sometimes demean his personal achievements and self-esteem. As a businessman, he had concentrated his mind's business acumen to his driving pursuit with great ambition to excel in the automobile business.

After many years and different critical events had happened in his family's life, he decided thereafter that he would sell his Montgomery Motors dealership and retire with his second wife, Wanda, and carry the remainder of his life under uncommon circumstances after his divorce. As time passed, Frank did sense a quota of amelioration that allowed continued friendship with members of the Divita family and friends. All the while, Frank had maintained his associations with his mom and dad, his brothers and sister, and family siblings of grandchildren and great-grandchildren, especially with their careers that many used minds to live in pursuit of happiness, and especially that they recognized the need of proper steerage and amour. From what Frank knows, as do his initial Divita family members, they all have used their minds to gain careers as professionals within major professional businesses and universities.

CHAPTER XXII

Reminiscing after a New Start in California

*You have your ideology, I have mine. Your ideology is that which
enjoys the protection of the coterie or the pleasures of life. My
ideology is the thought of every wanderer in his own country,
and the feeling of every stranger in the country where he lives.*
—First American edition published 1995 by Frog Ltd.
North Atlantic Books PO Box12327, Berkeley, California
94712, *The Eye of the Prophet*, Kahlil Gibran, p. 20

Many years later, whirlwinds changed to a quiet time at the beginning of 1965 as if it were a new birthing on earth for Frank's family. After a family visit to West Virginia at Christmastime to be with the family for the holiday and to let the family know that we were going to move to California, my decision, they understood why Ed wanted to continue his career in a new job with one of the best space systems facility in the world, identified as the Jet Propulsion Laboratory (JPL), operated by California Institute of Technology (Caltech) as a laboratory under the control of the National Aeronautics and Space Administration (NASA). I had worked at the Martin-Marietta Company (Glen L. Martin Company had changed the company's name) for about nine and a half years predominantly in their new nuclear division to develop, design, test, and fabricate. The company's output were portable nuclear reactors and thermoelectric radioisotope nuclear power sources for the military.

During the last two years at Martin-Marietta, for a significant time, I worked on research projects and on proposals for advanced space exploration from the beginning of the projects *Mercury, Gemini,* and *Apollo* manned spacecraft research. Part of my work was modeling the radiation belts around the earth, evolving radiation requirements for survivability of subsystems and science experiments in environments and developing computer programs to analyze and design shielding requirements for unmanned spacecraft heading into space of our solar system and eventually to beyond space within the nearby universe.

These new ventures in pursuit of my career in engineering physics was to work on unmanned spacecraft projects for the Jet Propulsion Laboratory (JPL) under NASA programs. The reason for the transfer to JPL was that detailed unmanned spacecraft were already in flight and new ones were under way, especially to the moon. I was hired to do needed analyses for their missions and prescribe designs for radiation shielding for sensitive subsystems and science experiments to operate while exposed to radiation such as proton and electron radiation belts trapped in the earth's planetary magnetic field identified as the Van Allen belts. Also, there were other planets that had radiation belts that needed analyzing and predicting proper design with factors of expected control. The ever-present solar wind and unpredictable solar proton events from the sun were continuously random, and the range of fluence (flux multiplied by time) was at times high orders of magnitudes.

My group at Martin-Marietta initially worked on making sure the radiation levels would not be harmful to astronauts in early earth orbit missions. After going to JPL, we modeled designs for the science and engineering equipment on selected spacecraft. Eventually, JPL had a long-term mission that planned to use a current design of a thermoelectric nuclear radioisotope generator from Martin-Marietta as a long-term power source to maintain the new Voyager spacecraft systems during the mission identified during research as the grand tour of several planets demanding a significant amount of cruising time and even allowing the *Voyager I* to travel into outer space beyond billions of miles while maintaining communication.

On the front end of the planning of Pres. John Kennedy's first leadership desires, he began his term to increase new research and development to achieve designs starting with space orbital travel around the earth and eventually to land on the moon by the end of the decade. The president's goal was achieved with the most popular pursuit of supertrained astronauts landing and praising the country.

The sadness was that our president John F. Kennedy was assassinated on November 22, 1963. Within five years, his brother Robert, who was his attorney general at the time during JFK's presidency, continued to work as a United States senator. Somewhat later, Robert decided to run for president of the United States in 1968. During Robert's campaigning, he was assassinated in Los Angeles by Sirhan Sirhan, an Islamic extremist who thought Robert Kennedy, running for president of the United States of America, was planning an attack on his country.

The two brothers of resounding combined knowledge lost their lives, and the future of their expectations disappeared from site and recognition of their pursuits for the country of America and, maybe, good for other countries; but the times quickly changed. The vice president L. B. Johnson took over JFK's presidency as second in command and survived the detailed loss of JFK and maintained the country and the continued work for space ventures. Even though LBJ was heavily loaded with internal strife, many small wars of contention in Asia, and Vietnam particularly, put him in a political depression trying to figure out how to change the course of these wars. As a result, President Johnson did not run for a second time possibly related to warring turmoil and uncommon warring and strife within

China's threats and the competition from Russia among their space achievements and power of forces with differences between democracy and Communism.

After the time of the halcyon, seven days before and after the winter solstice, had passed, the thought was to breed and bring calm and peaceful times, if not only weather but also at least a period of peace and quiet guided by Pres. Richard M. Nixon. Instead, many things like contention in Asia and Vietnam settled down as wars were being stopped. My family's lives changed for good since we made the significant move to California in 1965 to work at JPL on new research projects.

Within a few years, we were deeply saddened in September 1968 and traveled to Baltimore to be with Pat's mom because she was critically suffering from cancer, even though she had remained in our minds because she had traveled to California to visit us for a while in her first year after we had moved. In her second year, 1964, Mother Kelly went to Dublin, Ireland. After Mother Kelly came back from Dublin, we did not see her because we traveled to Montgomery to spend Christmas with my mom and dad's family. Two days after Christmas, our family had moved everything in the house and headed to Pasadena, California. When we arrived, we stayed in a motel in Pasadena, and for the next few days, we were in La Crescenta, California. On Monday morning, January 5, 1965, I showed up at work, knowing that Pat and the two children needed help from the beginning of 1965 after traveling three thousand miles and was carrying a baby since December 1964. Pat's new baby Cathie was born in August 1965. Mother Kelly decided to make the trip to Los Angeles, and I collected her to our home in La Canada, and the love and excitement rushed in. We had a grand time with loving care of the new baby Catherine and the two children who had not seen her for two years. It was special, especially for the children, who loved her very much from her first day's venture when Mother Kelly immigrated to America in 1962.

Pat and Ed and our children, Joanne, Eddie, and Cathie, all talked about when we might head to Dublin. The worthwhile venture was that within the year in 1967, we and our three children had traveled to be with Mother Kelly in Dublin for visits with Kelly family members Danny and Maisie, Pauline and Dave,

Dorothy and Lar, and Jim and Joannie's families at their homes. The visit was forever remembered, and during times in the country, we visited excellent sites, especially the treks through the New Grange, where the Irish reveal that releases of the dead leave spiritual souls in the winter solstice episodes. We also visited many famous Irish buildings of renown such as the Dublin Post Office, Dublin Museum, and Trinity College, and the people were so friendly in the country.

Then later in 1968, we were told that after Mother Kelly had returned, she had become intensely sick. We left quickly to be with Pat's mother and the Kelly family in Baltimore while she was in the hospital. We stayed with the Bernie and Jim's family so that it would be easy to be with Pat's mom and Ed during her hospital stay with a serious lung cancer, which had required an operation. The operation was performed, but the prognosis was dire. We were happy that we had decided to travel and be there before the operation. After the operation, we visited Mother Kelly several times. Mother Kelly died later with complications, and our despair, even with our children, dominated our personal depression. Pat and I anguished with heartfelt sorrow for Mother Kelly, which totally lingered with despair for a long time.

The service was heartbreaking with all her friends and sisters and doctors educated in psychology and psychiatry that Mother Kelly taught daily similar *steerage* and *amour* compassion and tailored words of personal praise to do better and treated unwanted children in their care, all from her work at Villa Maria, Towson, Maryland, a place for care of unwanted children. The acknowledgments and letters sent to Mother Kelly for her efforts were given to her with enormous love and thanks and appreciation while taking care of the villa's children who loved Mother Kelly. My dad, with Pat and Ed's family, attended Mother Kelly's service for our Divita family. The day of the burial service, rain poured continuously.

The visit by Mom and Dad happened three years later, when my mom and dad came to our home in 1971. We spent some of the time with my dad, and he appeared as well as he could be with his ailments. He did not talk about or suffered his medical problems that plagued him unknowingly, but he continued to maintain his self-sufficient ways with humor for all of us.

Visits had been few and far between, and our children were full of anticipation with love. Suddenly, it was what was on my mind—that is, knowing about what had happened to my father over the past few years even though he looked rather strong and moderately healthy the last time we saw him. Mom and Dad called us to let us know when to expect the visit. They were due to arrive in early February 1971, just before my dad's birthday. Within a few days, we celebrated Dad's birthday on February 7, 1971. Excitement in the family was pervasive. Our children were full of anticipation and love daily.

From what I had gathered from my mom, my father's health was on our mind even though he appeared moderately healthy when they came. Mom told me he had been bothered with his ailments, especially with continued problems identified by the doctor with his pancreas.

My dad had his physical stature but not the whim and wham of his teachings by the man of whom I always knew the strength and mind during my early life. What I had heard these last two years was his desire never to see a doctor if he could get away with it. It is easy for me to say that I've trained myself not to ponder over every little thing about my family because unusual things happen without notice unless it was specially told to me. I was never told unless it was critical. I only have good feelings toward my mother and father and always with their minds' words of praise. Knowing my dad, he was likely to deny his health condition through humor; even though he had aged, his humor survived even under stressful earthquake conditions that happened near our home. Even while Mom and Dad visited us in Glendale, California, in 1971, with great gusto, fun, and plain love of all, a major of earthquake happened nearby with frightening excitement and concern for all. Dad did things that settled all of us after seeing only a little damage in our area. We knew that he was not well, but he continued his way of life for the next two years until he was in the hospital. We attended his service, and the honor of the Divita family was ours to send a man of peace to heaven.

After they returned home sometime later in 1972, Mom noticed that he lingered continuously. Mom told me that she could see that Dad's life was slipping away. It was her devoted attention to Dad knowing that she had been living with his ailments for forty-five years. Our family boarded the plane to fly to Charleston, and we were easily picked up and taken to our Divita family home, and Mom took us to the hospital for visits. Pat and I visited him with good praise and conversation of loving in late December 1972. Dad took the kisses from his family and extended families that visited him at times. Later, I flew back and went to Dad's time of death, January 26, 1973, and the funeral service. Dad died near his last birthday time and was laid to rest at a grave site near his family members in Montgomery Memorial Park in London, West Virginia. The service was a Catholic ceremony with a deep feeling of loss by both the family and many friends in the city. His memories will remain with us for the rest of our lives and be bandied around at times when humor is required to open the hearts of the people who knew him and those who voiced him for this truly self-sufficient, peaceable, impeccably dressed real man.

For me at that time, I was speeding into my vocational pursuit as if in a wormhole-like space travel to the stars; but instead, I continued my work on scientific details for the National Aeronautics and Space Administration Voyager Spacecraft Research and Technology Program since the program had started in 1969 being the research as the environmental requirements engineer doing analyses to define documented requirements to meet designs for *Voyager I* and *II*.

My memory calls up all extraneous family problems in our daily life; as an example, when we came home and had moved into a newly built home that I helped design. When finished, we worked in managing the move and furnished the home. The children dominated our time, and we finally settled in without any trouble except for the weather. It rained seventeen inches from Friday, January 17, 1969, to the next few days. The storm caused a large amount of damage throughout local areas of Los Angeles County and the city of Glendale, where we located in Verdugo Hills, where both mountainous areas overall suffered up to ninety floods of mud and rock racing into homes. The destruction was along streets and some roads and freeways in nearby homes in Glendale, California.

I was completely involved with my work at JPL and managing my own business known as Space-Topics Industries, which was a small iron works fabrication company that I hoped would eventually do custom work for big specialty jobs. The iron works produced products like gates, fences, and special projects such as screens for fountains at business sites; sometimes with little profit.

My children gained some mental broadening just being at my iron works on Saturdays when not open, but my children helped me with paperwork and cleanup. My being with them was a delight, and they were given doughnuts after the few hours of cleanup. I sold the iron works within three years after gaining some experience in business and learning as a designer how to develop designs to minimize finishing work and maintain good relationships with employees.

I returned to work after the New Year where I had already been working for five years at the Jet Propulsion Laboratory before buying the iron works.

Almost everyone in California, except the predictors of earthquakes at California Institute of Technology, where seismologists monitor earthquake activity, had reported specific measurement concerns at within a short time. They did, however, as always, let the people know that they have methods of predicting earthquakes but not precisely a time for a major earthquake.

Mom had said several times to me that he was strong in his views for life and knew that he followed them whenever he could to make it work for the family. Now, I had been told that he is ailing badly at his age of seventy-one. Mom and Dad's visit in California in February 1971 was a great time together filled with memories and love of our early lives. Our kids loved being around them, and conversations were continuously directed toward happiness and ways of showing love for us.

The only problem that occurred in February 1971 was that on the day of their arrival and in conversation, Pat, with a smiling face, had warned them that night that we do get small short-time tremors, but the ground shakes at times unexpectedly, but not to worry. It had been sometime since an earthquake had happened in our local Los Angeles County. The very next morning, at around six o'clock, all of us were quickly scared out of bed, afraid for our lives because we felt significant shakes and later saw destructions even to our home and many following tremors. Everyone talked in disbelief, but we calmed them with our humor of having experienced earthquakes before. Dad's humor was on spot too as he said, "Is that what you call a tremor!"

It seems every time I felt a soothing relief overall, my mind would impose concern for our new house's stability. I commented, minimizing the brown concrete block wall that had gotten a few cracks. Mom was silent, but her face expressed great distress.

In my mind, I then returned to an event earlier in 1958 that was a different personal, potentially critical event that happened. I remembered what happened in February 1958 before Patricia and I got married. We had driven to Mom and Dad's home and had felt at ease while driving a few hundred miles.

The next day, we had decided to drive to visit my brother Frank and Betty and their young kids where they were living in Peterstown, West Virginia, about seventy miles south of Charleston. The weather was good when we left but after the latter part of the day darkened; it was snowing. We were driving along the highway on a mountainside at a reasonable speed because of the weather. With little notice on a turn, we ran into large rocks and piles of snow on the road. As I slowed down to stop, we slid into rocks, and the car turned over off the road. The car stopped when it turned over, and the state policemen were there in minutes. We finally gained relief after getting out of the car with little harm. I was told by the state policemen that it was good that the car stopped. We were fortunate that the bank was shallow and wide. It was only one turn, and we were able to take ourselves out of the car. We thanked God for saving our lives.

We never made it to Frank's home. The state policemen drove us back to Montgomery to my dad's home. When we were returned to Mom and Dad's home, we were given special care for two days or more.

We needed a car to go back to Baltimore; because of the accident, our car was totaled. We were fortunate with little personal damage. I recalled that the next day, Dad had a car, and he took me for a ride to a friend's local dealership. The recollection breezed through my mind as Dad finished parking the car. I stared at the car, and all I could see was a Buick Roadmaster, two-tone in green and cream with all the bells and whistles and more chrome than any two cars. I bought the Buick through my dad from his good friend William, his buddy for years.

Frank having driven to Montgomery the next day and walked into the dealership's front door as he shocked me with an "Hey, Ed!" I quickly turned because I didn't know anyone was behind me while I was lost in my thoughts of the accident. He greeted me, grabbing my arm. An electric shock happened against a big nerve from my back. I smiled, hugged, and kissed him with a strong embrace. We shook hands with another hug and a kiss like nothing ever happened. Then we continued into shop areas where everyone was already at work. This startled him because he was concentrating with intent on how to gain my attention. I knew it could not wait until we made it to his office. He said with a plead but as always with an assurance that there will be a yes, "Let's get some coffee before we go at it." Then he popped out with "Your car was a complete wreck. I'll take care of getting rid of it."

Later the next day, Frank took me to the dealership looking for Dad, who was already in the shop. Dad was solving a problem because his mental concentration was on detailed areas under the hood, pointing with a ratchet wrench and setting it to screw in a loose bolt. I heard Dad as he said, "This is what General Motors calls a close fit! It's about how the fit of the battery cable was forced that they had to find or make a wrench to remove the bolt and put it back on."

My dad was always saying what could have been done better. And many times, he showed us that his way was the better way of doing things. I remember the time he got me involved with the outside mirror's side-to-side manual movement that had a wider range, and he wanted to make a big deal that the automatic control of the mirror from the inside on a Buick Roadmaster had less play than the outside manipulation, and he wanted to know why. Benny turned to Frank with a big smile and called him over for a minute. "Frank, come here. I want to show you something that you may want to design better than what they have. You could get a patent if you spend some time with it."

My mind leaves the past again into more recent times as I get back together with my Divita family years later. This time, Pat and Ed, with our three children, stayed at Frank and Betty's new home in the early 1970s. The turn in my mind was that years had gone by, and we had completed the work on the two Voyager spacecraft. *Voyager I* was sent on its way on a grand tour of planets Jupiter, Saturn, Neptune, and Uranus in 1976. *Voyager II* was sent shortly afterward heading on the way to outer space into the nearby universe, and current knowledge let JPL know that it spent many operational years in outer space.

CHAPTER XXIII

Later Reminiscing about Unexpected Critical Incidents

Unselfish intellect rises like a perfume above the
faults and follies of the world of Will.
—*The Wisdom of Life*, 34, Footnote: 108, Schopenhauer
in *The Story of Philosophy*, Will Durant, p. 251

I now realized it was 1977 and that we had a few visits during these past years. We stayed mostly with Frank and Betty at their home, with Mom now living in her new home in Montgomery that my brothers built. Philip, Mona, and family often visited Mom on short trips from Charleston, and at times, she stayed with them for good company.

Years had passed since we had a visit with Gene and Peggy and family since 1971. Our children were teenagers, and some of Frank and Betty's children were adults except for the twins Fran and Jimmy, who were both near nineteen in 1977. However, I did visit with Gene and Peggy every time I had to go to Houston, Texas, on JPL business.

Frank's car dealership had been an enormous success. Frank now was the owner, and after a number of years, he had newly refurbished his dealership. Around that time, Frank also owned a Firestone Company parts and service business. After the bulk of my work on the Voyager spacecraft had been completed and launched, we decided to visit the families in West Virginia by starting the first Divita family reunion in 1990, which was planned mostly by my brothers in the nearby Montgomery area.

After making our way to Charleston via a commercial airplane, we drove to Montgomery in a rented car and decided to stop just a half block down Fourth Avenue after crossing the new Montgomery Bridge where the dealership was located nearby. We surprised them with a grand appearance of excited happiness and fun. Pat and I and our three kids walked from the car to the lounge into the dealership's showroom. Then they walked in the garage just to see how it looked.

As it turned out, Frank and his son Fran were in the newly upgraded dealership, bright and clean and sparkling, and greeted us with sheer happiness and surprise.

Fran made some quick friendly antics with the kids, and they enjoyed the action and tagged along to see what he was up to. Fran did all he could facially with a formed smile as he retorted to his father, "The radiator's getting all my attention." With filler, he said with gusto, "The radiator is filled."

With a shout on a different subject, Fran said to all there, "I will be graduating from high school!"

His dad showed pride as he said, "He's a great student and a winner with his father and mother."

Fran ended with "I have a new design to inject fuel to cylinder chambers instead of carbureting the gas spray with air. Dad, I'll show you my sketch. When you have some time?"

Back to the showroom floor, the cars are exquisitely detailed with chrome polished to a sparkle in floodlights to ceiling heights. Each car was tagged with their suggested manufacturer's price and information sheets on impeccably clean window glass. What is neat is several Divita families including my family were there for various reasons. Pat and I went to the office for comfort and talked about our trip. We saw my cousin Tommy, Aunt Mary's son, who was complaining about his new Pontiac having skyward raising doors not fitting right.

Frank waved and said he will be up in the office in a few minutes. He shuffled for a hug with Pat even though he knew he was going to get a fussing comment from Tommy. He saw his son Fran in front of one of new cars, and he approached his grandfather's son, Uncle Jimmy, who had taken care of Tommy for the second time. He commented, "Tommy, I am sending your car to a General Motors assembly plant. They will fix it there!"

Frank begged off to leave Pat and Ed in the office with all the excitement of the family. As he left, he suddenly slowed down and mentally visualized his son as a boy and years earlier getting a squeezed hand with his grandfather Benny, who had died from critical operation in 1973.

Then Frank's mind wandered even further back many years ago as he recalled the family's *OverHome* in Smithers on Kanawha Avenue in front of Mom and Dad's home; at the lower end, Big Poppy's *OverHome,* which had given our dad the same test of strength. Then unconsciously, he told me that he visualized his grandfather's image and then it disappeared. Now, he thought to himself but in open words, "Now I'm staring at my dad's vision in my mind, missing him in this crowd because he was responsible for everything that's now showing." The thought escaped him as he saw his boys up ahead.

Frank, with his sons Fran and Jimmy in sight, returned to reality. Jimmy appeared together with Fran, and they verbally voiced a joked about how many old cars his grandpa said he had in his garage on Fourth Avenue in the golden times, which was with his wit as voiced. Their dad told them that cars were taken apart either into body parts, motors, or when tires were off and stacked for each car.

Jimmy said to his dad, "Where are Mom and Aunt Pat and Uncle Ed? I know you went to the office." Our kids smiled and wondered how Frank and Betty's kids knew so much about cars.

Fran smiled and said to his cousins, "Dad always told me he could fix any car because his dad taught him how to fix cars. How come you always have ten or more cars in the garage that looked like they were in pieces?"

Ed and Fran, being beside Frank, both turned to hear him laugh as he spurted something like, "You don't get it. That was for customers to allow me more time to fix their cars knowing I had others to fix. You got to learn all the ins and outs of the car business so that people you deal with, when it comes to making money, would agree and appreciate your efforts to do the best job on their car."

Fran said, "I washed the two cars you told me to wash today!" Uncle Jimmy grabbed him and gave him a little strong-arm wrestling, but he quickly broke loose and ran laughing. Fran broke his vision with a great big hug of his dad and said, "Dad, how do you like these new cars? Aren't they great? I've driven every one of them in the showroom. Dad, you even let me drive one of the sports car out on the road." When he heard Fran say that, his dad turned shallow. Then Fran said, "I was scared shitless!"

Frank shouted, "Hey! Watch your language. Don't be a smart ass. You younger guys try to get away with everything. If I had said that to my dad . . ."

Fran interrupted with, "I know exactly what he always told you. He would have put his size 11 up your butt!"

Without hesitation and a smile on his face, Fran's dad grabbed his shoulder as he said, "Now you know why and how great your dad was when you two were little kids." Frank turned with a slight knowledge of what Fran and Jimmy heard. He shone with pride and looked at his two sons, who now were stout and big.

Jimmy said, "Dad, your little bit of gray hair makes you look wise, but the way you show pride is almost like you are about to cry. So what are some of your other disguises? Quickly. Just kiddin'! When you were mayor of this city, you had advantages of enforcing decisions."

Frank smiled with pride and felt his eyes with a tear to hear his son say such a practical-minded thing. Then he responded, "If you only knew what people who elected me thought my job was, you would be surprised. I was the fix-it man! That means they want me to fix anything including what they thought was wrong with the city and people who live there. That would have been a full-time job for God, but he's already told everyone that listens, 'You got to fix your own problems.'"

Frank told all who called or captured him on the street or in my office, "I managed the city but not under their direction. If you thought they've got time to think about buying a car from me, it was the last thing on their minds."

The boys drifted away. Uncle Jimmy and Frank pointed to the office, and Frank said, "I'm going to take Ed and Pat and their kids to my home and settle them in. We still have some work to do." Frank said, "Betty will go with them." He proceeded, and the family gathered with hugs and kisses and all headed to the car with Aunt Betty driving. Frank slipped away toward Uncle Jimmy, who had been listening to the daily jargon and told him that he was taking everyone to his home.

Eventually, Frank and his children and Ed and Pat's children made it home, and excitement at dinner time was as one would expect in an Italian family; mostly laughter and continuous conversation about the past came to their minds. The next day, everyone loved being in the home. The inside was walked through, and they talked about the building design. Frank's brothers had worked on the home continuously to finish the building. His brother Ed's input was a set of iron fencing that he built to Richard's specifications and was sent by train from California. He later took Ed to the dealership for some man-to-man conversation about the house that he loved among other things, including the iron rails around the house porch area.

Later that day when they walked into the dealership's office, he hugged Ed's shoulder and said, "Ed, I spend more time trying to escape from a few great-looking women who come into my dealership to do everything but tell me they want my affection." That was a surprise to me, but Frank wanted to get it off his mind. I listened. Frank said, "Sometimes, it happens when I don't have energy enough to even read my mail while I'm in my office. Usually, I was in the city police and jail building in the assembly room over the fire station conducting special meetings on a need for a new fire engine. And one time later, I was due in the same building at a party in my honor for my second term."

Frank went into an explanation to me one at a time. He started with "One time, I was at a dinner in the Glen Falls Mountain View Dining Club while speaking at a conference for a Transverse County Mayors Conference to review city changes. It was an event with lots of time for fun and associations as one would expect for people running a city. I knew one of the women many years ago, and she had an innocent dating affair with me when I was in college. Nothing ever happened at that time."

Then he said to me another time, roughly catching the drift of what he went into about women. So I only remember the overall stories and made what I remembered. What he covered was something like, but in my own words writing about what he said. Frank told me he was trapped on the floor in his mayor's office late one evening after he thought he had already sold a car to a woman from his office, but expecting her to come in and sign papers in a few days. "Just before getting ready to leave, I got a call from the woman, who requested one last time to see the new car. She wanted to finally make up her mind. Later the next day, this very attractive woman came into my office and approached me closely. All I could see was the shape of her legs in her dress. My mind sent a message to my eyes and left me awestruck with a mental question of, *Why is she here?* I knew what was traveling through my brain."

A little earlier, Frank's son Fran had seen me as he came in the front door to see Frank. He shied away, apparently thinking he was unnoticed. I only pretended not to see him because I know Fran; he wanted a chance to prepare himself to come face-to-face with his dad with his new business baby. Fran brushed his hair and looked to my secretary for an OK. She smiled with a kiss from her hand to his face and said, "You can see him later."

He went through the display area and met and greeted his sisters. He paused and then stopped to talk with his sisters. He hugged Janie, who was actively involved with the business. Janie returned the hug with a kiss and restarted her conversation with her secretary. Fran said, "See you later maybe for lunch?"

Janie shouted as she smiled, "Yes!"

He knocked on the office door, and his dad's voice penetrated the area. "Come in!"

Fran approached, and after a friendly hug, he asked, "How are you, Dad? How's the business? Looks like you're making money if you can afford to have Janie working for you." He laughed, saying, "I know! I know! She's the best salesperson you have. You look like you're on a mission."

His dad said, "Are you hunting for a new girlfriend? I haven't seen you in a few months."

Then Fran said, "Dad do you remember what we talked about in February? My plan was to start my own business."

Frank said, "Yes, but you didn't say when. You never supplied me with details. I'm not a mentalist! You gotta give me written plans, and then I would see if it's workable or not."

"Well, I have it now." Fran followed with "I want to discuss some details with you," as he grabbed his head to show complexity of mind. Then out of the clear blue sky, he said, "But, first, let me make sure I know what direction I am coming from and am tuned in with my mind. What I really want to know is 'what's it all about!' Every time I start to do something, there's someone like you, Mom, Grandmom, or something was needed or in the way or someone has clobbered me with a surprise neck chop from behind, and it always related to money. Usually, it is not mine or even money that I had helped someone gain." Fran let his dad know that he was looking for help. His dad was listening to his son about his dream that sounded like it was about to go up in smoke.

Frank interrupted to get out of a continuous pursuit by saying something like, "Let's talk about family since you wanted to know 'what's it all about!' You may not have heard much of this story about your granddad and grandmom's teachings of *steerage* and *amour* to you and your brother and your sisters, but it did happen daily during your younger times. Part of it was embedded in your ways of running your life. The *amour* part and how one sees it when it is appropriate and when it registers in one's minds, I can give you a path to follow so that you will know 'what's it all about! Here it is."

This is what I had gathered as I received steerage teachings from my childhood. I think it came about appropriately as my belief and has been applicable and considered by many members of the Divita family. It was evolved as my belief over my years, and I evaluated and measured the values of the teachings of *steerage* and *amour* with the other members of our family and other Divita families that came along at the same time.

As the narrator of part of this memoir and the exposé, I generated information making sensational declarations of what methodology evolved from my parents and what came about previously from my grandparents. The inference of outcomes with supports that had been promoted within the lives of the Divita family progeny worked because they understood the essence of teachings to live a happy life.

Frank proceeded with the best that he told me, "Let me take you back to a time in the mid-1950s when I was in business with Dad. He was actively helping me to gain position in the city and eventually wanted to turn me into a successful car businessman and maybe a dealer because he had close ties with his friends J. W. and Charles, who had owned their dealerships for a long time."

He again changed the subject to get on with the story as he said something close to "After a little time had passed in my time as a married man, no involvements ever happened. Nevertheless, numerous hearsay information about my activities were put into the forefront as local gossip by people. I thought I knew what was building to use against me, but maybe only some who were my disgruntled friends. As I recalled, it was the kind of information that was given to other people as hearsay, but it would be released to show how life can change a person's life and family if it is claimed as the truth."

Several years later, that same collection of information distributed vehemently, and it was the main reason Frank became disjointed with his wife Betty. In the late '70s, Betty had heard so much hearsay about his distrust instilled by others that it caused significant angst. Betty discussed a divorce with me over the phone many times because she thought Frank had been disloyal. The concern was heightened by people who expressed that Frank had been seen with the same woman a few times. Frank could see that his mom left him without any recourse. And so did his family with rumors that were believed. This jolt of lightning struck Betty, and she extended her depression and suffered through an expected divorce. Betty could not live with the depression, and it caused her to surrender her life to despair without resolve.

The loss left Frank in an extremely low personal desperation of despair. Among his family, relatives, and friends, they were not able to regain his true personification. Frank continued as if he was in a pursuit of a life of self-reliance. He started making decisions that led him to more despair with his business with a loss of discernment. Before these mind changes had happened, Frank had been sick for a few months, and he lost true ties of his future life enough to warn him to change his life's future. After he got well, he began to change his behavior that existed in past times that were in his previously known happy life. He even felt within his mind that he effectively maintained his business and had proven him to be a doer and straight shooter.

Frank found it very difficult to relay his feelings of the love of his life without Betty's trust and believed suspicions. Others had let it be known that their opinions and beliefs, all to his disadvantage, were a loss of familial life to a large extent. Frank did not recover soon enough to remain with Betty, while she lingered with suspicions and deception and feelings of lost trust in Frank. Frank tried his true communication about his simple plan to help a woman he knew only by sight, to no avail. Instead, the Divita family and extended families more than shunned his person. After the divorce, Betty lingered with Frank's heartbreaking mind, knowing that he was finally on his own. Betty continued suffering her depression for an extended period until she died.

Frank's car dealership business continued to decline in the early 1980s, while times in his life were seriously changing. He began involved with Wanda. Frank sensed this change was his way of hoping for a special resolve to change his true feelings about how he might want to live the rest of his life after being challenged many times with allegations of disloyalty within the family. He later married Wanda, a woman he knew for several years who had worked for J. W. at the dealership and with Frank when he was the mayor in the late 1970s. Frank was still popular politically and well known in Montgomery but was under a continuous struggle with his personal life under strained family personal conditions. He had a great deal of responsibility with the business, but he continued with a great name. He decided to sell the dealership. Complications with the sale caused a significant amount of added inventory costs and a lower sale price of the business, leaving him in further distress of behavior among family members.

Usually, when family members like Frank had a high political office, their position would have influenced future generations, and their family's environments would be more sensitive to social activity. With Frank's family, he knew he had some influence on his children overall, but that was years ago. Later, after his second marriage, he did not look like he had any influence with his extended families, and even grandchildren's involvements, behavior, and pursuits except while with large numbers of family members using casual compatibility and modest association.

I want to go way back to other memories of an earlier and enjoyable time in my early life during Christmastime in the late 1940s. Frankie was much younger, and so was his mother. They were living in their home in Montgomery after fifteen years of life's endeavors. Mom and Dad were muses of old times who coached Frankie decidedly and instilled in our minds more good expectations now that the war was over. In essence, Mom and Dad did insightful teachings of "Steerage and Amour!—What It's All About!"

What then happened later after the 1946 Indy 500 Race had already been exposed by tales from memories and much added hearsay and maybe some folklore. "Let's discourse about things that had happened much later and after you had become the man you are today as you continued to be more impressive with your grown children."

Fran, at this time with his dad, exclaimed, "I am not what I am today as what I was a few years ago to my family and friends. They saw me with my heart on my sleeve and a devil-may-care attitude. Go at it, Dad!"

His dad came back with quick and friendly lines of a famous quote. He attempted to convince his son Fran to listen to an old story of what happened after Frank and Betty's marriage and years after his birth in 1959. "Your grandfather and friends had already been to the Indy 500 Race in 1946 as the time moved like a photon to Mars into the early 1950s when my dad and I were working together."

All the while, the men running Frank's business were in a word fight that was brewing, if not had risen, over a discussion of James Bond's Aston-Martin in a 1968 movie in which he was the star. Several men were insisting they were right, but Benny at his age knows when he's right. He had actually studied the Aston-Martin and then said something like this: "I have had an old Aston-Martin apart in my old garage. I remember when a man, an Englishman and a citizen of England, challenged me." He paused and said, "I told him that something was not true about the Aston-Martin and followed with, 'You don't know the details.'"

The Englishman said, "What does a Tally know about racing cars!"

A fight like in a John Wayne movie almost broke out, but Benny, with his peaceable control, quickly stopped the assault and apologized to the Englishman down on the floor. He then quickly picked up the man and apologized again for the shove and fall. Then he brushed dust off his clothes. Benny said, "I have a bad reaction when someone calls me a Tally. I made the push before I knew I pushed you." Then he told him that he became an American citizen when he was twenty-five years old.

The man said, "That was stupid of me to insult you. I also am sorry! Let's get back to talking about one of the first new Super 60 Special Fleetwood Cadillac in Frank's dealership. I've been trying to buy the Super 60 Special Fleetwood Cadillac and am willing to pay $20,000." He claimed aloud, "Do you realize the cost to do the rebuild is more than double that!"

Frank entered as he heard the man talking about the price of this Super 60 Special Fleetwood Cadillac. It was one of the first Cadillacs produced for delivery to be bought for the Indy 500 Race. He butted in and told him with a straight face, "That's the price!"

The man told Frank and his dad, "I think your dad is trying to make a killing on the sale."

The wife of the man stepped into conversational frays and started to explain with, "We need to make another apology." The man was startled. He saw that he was being caught in the wife's crossfire.

He said, "I guess I'm too excited to discuss this buy at this time. Could we do it tomorrow?"

Frank saved face for the man by telling him more about detailed add-ons and use of new Super 60 Special Fleetwood Cadillacs when it was bought for the 1946 Indy 500. Frank then said, "My dad is the type of man that when he buys special cars, he knows where every nut and bolt goes with all specials attached. This car is a Super 60 Special Fleetwood Cadillac built for Benny F. Divita. It is unique and was uniquely cared for by my dad and myself." When he finished, the man fell in love with the car. Then he thought, studied, and refused it!

The wife expressed her understanding, and the man stood down. As the man left, he kicked tires, and his wife stormed away from him in a fit, causing attention pointing to the man. And then two boys near the car, in unison, called him a son of a bitch under their breaths but slightly audible. The man quickly ran frighteningly through the doorway to his car.

Frank had a second sense as to when to laugh with Uncle Tony as both were listening to the story. They both caught on, and he laughed with Frank. When Frank sensed the comedy of the situation was displayed verbally to all, he commented, "Certainly, it was good judgment by Benny when he said, 'If the man would buy the car, would it haunt me!'" It would be expected for someone like my dad to preach only the good points of the car. What Frankie said he saw was the contrarian position when faced with his problems. Tony said, "Benny, this time, you were emotional about your Cadillac within your unusual instinctive mind."

Family members were quick to recognize absurdities when the man made a fool of himself even in front of his wife. Everyone knows the earth is simply composed of billions of people throughout, and each person as a *Homo sapiens* operates uniquely as usual with little changes set up to respond randomly for the most part at the tail end of poor judgment. Every woman wants a man of loyalty and integrity, but to find true devotion and be a careful decision maker to boot in a prudent, prognosticating way is rare. A mental urge with a moral bent from within as a trained way of life usually first prevails, and if not, more wisdom will be effectively gained for the most part.

Pigeons are fowl that are easily frightened but extremely useful to humans in many ways. My brother Frank is artful in using his gained reconnaissance wares stacked with attention in getting information and running his business.

The Cadillac was fully rebuilt, which had refocused the Super 60 Special Fleetwood carried on from the Fleetwood Brougham that took over Super 60 Special Fleetwood as positioned with new developments. This model is a collector's item. It pays off as a customer attraction and conversation opener to give customers recognition for their old car knowledge. As I recall, Frank also later had owned a 1976 model convertible Cadillac El Dorado that was on the floor as décor, and he kept his white 1970 Buick Roadmaster convertible in his garage at his new home that he built with the help of his brothers.

Benny had said many times in the past, "As I have told everybody, there was no affair or anything at times when I was with the woman especially at the 1946 Indy 500 Race. The guys just liked to tease me to have a little more fun about the race and involvements such as at dinner or lunch by creating some not-so-funny gist. They liked her, and being with her during the day before the race, they would kid me even though he was doing his friend Mauri Rose a favor. None of that happened at any time during the whole time I was at the Indy 500 Race."

From what I heard later, Dad told his brother Tony something like, "In my mind, I would never give up pleasure to pursue impending pain! Making my mind refer to light of day to clear my mind using an amorous pursuit would be poor judgment. I have noticed that when a man is attracted to a friendly woman who may have other desires, so to speak, makes the involvement an intensely compromising situation, and it should not be chased."

Much later, my mom and dad, as the grandfather to Frank's children, were gathered at Frank and Betty's home in the late '60s with his family celebrating his dad's sixty-ninth birthday. Around the dinner table, he openly talked with good conversation about his early years before coming to America. Benny added, saying, "Frank, I never thought much about my birthday, but your mom and all the grandkids give me joy! Let's eat!"

Grandmom Jo said, "Who's going to say the grace!"

Granddad Benny retorted, "I will!" paused and exclaimed, "In the name of the Father, the Son, and the Holy Ghost, the one who eats the fastest eats the most!"

Frank's kids laughed and waved to their grandfather. Grandmom Jo squeezed out a smile and a light chastisement, "Ah! Benny! You think you're funny! Wait until I tell Father McDonald!"

Granddad said, "Father Doyle was the one who told me he says grace every time he has to cook his own meal!" This story advanced with love as gifts were given to their grandfather, and he opened each one with a praise. All had finished Granddad's Sunday dinner birthday but were still around the dinner table as is common for Italian families that keep talking about things that make love spread within their minds, hearts, and souls.

Frank's son Jimmy said, "Granddaddy, that was an easy story that you told us about the 1946 Indy 500 Race, and you know the winners. What about the first one you went to when you said you had met Mauri Rose and other drivers? You know, back in 1941! That was back when World War II was already under way in Europe. Were you just bragging? Did you have much fun and wine! Who was the winner? What was the prize?"

Benny said, "Ah! Let me talk! Do you want to know, or do you want to ask questions? Don't get me started on asking me questions about just living until you get married!" Benny was making fun as he hugged several children jointly as they squeezed around him for more stories. He said, "I met Mauri Rose at a meeting in Philadelphia before we went to the races in 1941. I went over to him and told him who I was and that I knew every detail of cars and even some of the sports cars made by General Motors. This got him interested, and he asked a whole lot of questions. I dreamed up answers that he liked. That started our friendship, and it was one that was never revealed much to anyone in West Virginia.

"At that time, Mauri Rose won in another car owned by Lou Moore. His Maserati was placed in the 'pole position' but lost power after sixty laps. Moore gave Mauri his other car from his teammate to hold his position. It was a Wetteroth/Offenhauser. I don't remember the winner's purse but maybe more than $100,000. In those days, it was like a million dollars. The team's two drivers, Rose and Floyd Davis, each won over $50,000 because they split it after the race. The car was a beauty. You ain't seen nothing until you've seen knocked-loose hose clamp in Moore's first car."

Frank asked, "Did Mauri Rose get the trophy?"

Granddad said, "Sure! And car owners and sponsors got sales boosts and advertising for their goods. Anyway, he won! And we had a great time!" Granddad gave them a little more detail. "Because it was to my surprise that Mauri told me he was with a man I worked with building roads in West Virginia that remembered me.

"He had been working on fixing one of the racetracks in Pennsylvania. When I saw him, I went over to talk while he was talking with Mauri Rose, who was checking on the Indy 500 track conditions. Mauri introduced us. Mauri always liked to know about details along the track. He was a car engineer. We became friends because I knew something about cars."

From what I recalled about the 1946 race, my dad Frank had told me that he had met Mauri Rose several times in Pennsylvania before going to the 1941 Indy 500. Then at the 1946 Indy 500, they shook hands and renewed old times. George Robson came over with Charles, whom he knew, and we all had a few drinks. Charles knew George Robson from his dealership meetings. When we left, Tony had so much fun he got a little tipsy. I don't think drivers ever drank anything but soda pop.

We were excited being with race drivers. We were just hillbillies from nowhere. Mauri left after a half hour, but George Robson told us, "Let's go to dinner," if we're able tonight. Only God knows what happened after that get-together! Indianapolis was full of people and excitement. Going to the Indy 500 in 1946 made four men's day. It was even a greater celebration because United States America and our allies won World War II.

Frank thought after reading a registered newspaper information for his mind that those Japanese sons of bitches bombed Pearl Harbor before we knew what was happening. As Dad's eldest son, Frankie said to his dad, "What did you mean? God only knows what happened afterward. All people have free will!"

From what I was told by my dad, he said something like human beings continually make mistakes even with deadly intent, and with lies to boot and unknown levels of believable folklore. Sometimes, from what I found out, I only remember critically calamitous and disastrous life-killing things happen before anyone knew what happened. Dad said to Frankie, "You're sure a nosey rosy, son! You now get the point! I just meant we had a good time! Maybe someday I'll tell you the rest of the story about the front end of the war in Europe!"

What led to his potential problems included liquor, smoking, and body pain, and known internal physical health problems critically influenced his life about what happened as years went by especially with diabetes and his diseased pancreas. For most people, there are changes that showed both men and women are always for or against each other with ailments, as was my mother Jo, who took special care of her man, Benny. Mom knew that Dad was fascinated with cars and especially racers in his mind and his friends who were top notch on a well-known car racing team. A wise man like my dad knew himself to be foolish at times when he would be having fun. Fortunes and fun fool all.

How would a self-sufficient man want to cover up his ailments unless he would be accomplished by a steady mind of living in ways he wanted to be happy? Afterward in his mind, he was endowed with little thought of concern. Give any patriarch self-sufficient Father knew no one would predict what might happen at any time in his life. My dad lived with confidence that his life thrived with sound dispositions until his death.

Quite a few years later, I recalled after Fran was married but didn't know what to do, he called his father Frank, who told me from his memory by chance, being on the phone and that he loved being asked appealing with coming ad hominem, "Hey, Pop! How's it going today?"

Frank (On Phone) "Couldn't be better, unless I could sell at least three cars today! I already sold two!"

Fran said, "What are you up to? I've been picking fruits, and I got one for you! You want to buy lemons? I think I am one!" Fran began appealing to his dad about his individual passions and prejudices, awaiting for a response.

Frank sensed downheartedness in his last statement. Fran asked the question. "I want to know for myself, 'What's it all about?'"

His dad said, "You are not the first one to ask that question! I've asked it myself many times!" Frank then began to discuss his journey to convince Fran how to gain his desires without using a woman as a security blanket. He said, "Use your wits, son, when you go into a battle of minds. It takes wits and most times wisdom to solve problems."

Fran's problems stemmed from his business ups and downs as a car salesman, first, for his dad and later when he joined a new company in Kentucky. He said he had read about the great designer Joe Lencki, who built the 1938 Blue Crown Special especially for the Indianapolis 500 Race in 1941. But so far, within his pipe dream, he has not done anything about a plan to meet the son of Joe Lencki, who was a car designer also and working on a new car design. This thought must go through his dad's mind daily, but maybe Fran will get a new start in designing racing cars by himself because he has inherited talents for details and concentration from his grandfather and father.

The story of the 1938 Blue Crown Special involves some most colorful characters in annals of Indianapolis 500 history. His granddad pointed out that Lencki, the creator, was a bold foremost innovator of internal combustion engine developments and that he had learned a lot from him at the last race.

Frank remembered when his dad discussed things about Joe Lencki. Knowing what he knew, Frank told Fran later about Joe Lencki, that he had read that Joe had spent three years supervising and working with several legendary friends to build engines for American aircraft bombers starting with *Enola Gay* during the last part of World War II, readying it for dropping the atom bomb. Friends already knew that Joe was fascinated with engines since he was eight years old in 1911. He fell in love with the Indy 500 and, over the years, passed his memoir's bulk of information to his friends and his son.

From what I read and remembered later was that Joe built his first race car at age twenty and on advice given to him by his friend Charles Kettering, who had successfully run one of his first high-compression racing engines by adding tetraethyl lead to his fuel. At that same time, Lencki designed and built his own cylinder head, which incorporated recent advancements of hemispherical combustion chambers. There is a photograph of my friend driver Mauri Rose and Joe Lencki standing at the Indianapolis State Park in 1947.

Lencki first entered the Indy 500 in 1934, and in 1939, arrived with his innovative machine, dubbed its first time out as the Burd Piston Ring Special. Reflecting Lencki's background in aircraft engineering, he knew about its frame was of semi-monocoque construction, using sheet metal entirely bolted together without welding. The all-aluminum body was hand-formed by the Ringling Brothers and incorporated oil and fuel tanks by Frank Curtis. While the suspension used conventional Ford axles and springs, the Blue Crown Special was his first car's history to use disc brakes at the Indy 500, whose performance regularly astounded first-time drivers. As well, it was the car's engine that intrigued onlookers because, like its creator, it was one of a kind.

Fran's dad went on with the story because he knew Fran was interested in detailed drafting, the kind that was performed by the legendary Leo Gossen to

Lencki's specifications. The car was built at Fred Offenhauser's manufacturing plant. The 265-cubic-inch Lencki Double Overhead Cam Six car resembled the four-cylinder Offenhauser engine that was already well used at Indy 500.

Fran always let his mind wander in pursuit of a new car design; but without *the luck of the Irish,* he had only let the idea roll around in his mind as an Italian that has spaghetti and meatballs waiting for dinner before he does anything else. He was not able to solidify his car dream but did see his rough designs of critical improvements in new cars before the start of the new millennium.

Remember that no matter what you may have been told from memory by your grandfather, he never was put down or believed hearsay no matter how they told it when he was back in town. Fran now went back to work satisfied with his grandfather's all-star behavior. Frank went on about his dealership business a few years or so in the late 1970s. He felt good about his success as he was planning to redecorate his dealership; but with his concerns about his life's ailments, things changed critically with Frank and Betty's family's personal ailments and personalities behaviors.

The next thing that happened before the dealership was going to be redecorated, and later, he may be expecting to sell it. A meeting was called at the city hall with the mayor and specific police business at the time because they had located the hidden home on the edge of the city near Morris Creek. One of Tony's son, Johnny, led the pursuit with their special forces to break up and arrest drug dealers using both regular state troopers and federal marshals as part of the force. All I had to say was simply the FBI wanted to keep track with special investigators using the best police in Montgomery. They had the leadership and the resources to do it within the law so that it would leave drug dealers no way out but to be arrested and face criminal court proceedings. It did involve out-of-state deliveries, and they wanted perpetrators to be tried with offenses in a federal court.

That meeting was easy. Frank, later at the city jail, headed back to his mayor's office. When he appeared, some nighttime workers exited into offices, and others went outside to their cars with little conversation. Frank went into his office to relax. It went through his mind as he probably mentioned, *Why can't I solve all my problems that easy?* Then he thought, saying aloud, "I can't even solve my wife's and children's problems even when they were young, let alone now. And I am not getting any better."

Then the phone rang. Frank felt that he had a new problem rising because my day did not run smoothly two times in row. He remembered that the city was operating to ensure people are being protected, and it had started in the late '70s. Before that, he never had any problem that had grown worse before being solved. After that raid of drugs hidden in the house, Frank knew as mayor that he was going to be questioned many times in the next few days. Then the mission of gathering the drug dealers and distributors that were taken to other jails had happened. He sat down in the office to relax.

Three days later, he took advantage of it. He was ready to take a break and go to Charleston for a dinner. Then the phone rang. He knew something different was coming just by the way the phone rang. However, it was his mom asking him in her modest way, "Frank! What are you doing for lunch? Why don't you drop by and have lunch with me? We have not talked for a few days. Can you make it?"

At least he was seated at his desk, clearheaded and with a little whizzing because winds were blowing in bursts on this spring day. He answered her with a cool "Yes! See you around one o'clock. OK?"

Mom said, "Good!"

As Frank sat back reading daily papers put on his desk about the influx of undesirables in clubs near the racetrack, he thought about all the stories, especially when Uncle Tony on police duty walked in with a short greeting. "Frank! How's it going? I was talking with my son, and he gave me the news about the arrests."

Seeing Uncle Tony, Frank remembered one of his stories over the years. The one that came to his mind was regarding the Indy 500 Race venture, but he was open for a short one, and he said, "Did I ever tell you about your dad taking care of a rich woman for Mauri Rose?" The story was the one that his uncle Tony had already told him at least two times before. It was about his dad's woman friend that had asked Mauri Rose to ask his dad to look after her while he was busy getting ready for the race. What he had found out, much to his surprise, was that he added that they were easy around each other, but nothing happened. Tony laughed and said, "That's about all that happened!"

The new track was exciting, and the race was great. The new owner of the Indianapolis Speedway, Anton Hulman, had great vision for the event and rebuilt the overall racing facility beyond expectations. "One of these days, you should go the Indy 500 to get some ideas about racing cars." Then Tony said, "I gotta go get some lunch."

Frank said, "Uncle Tony, I'm going to have lunch with my mom." They both left and took different paths with a handshake. Frank said he walked to Mom's home, and Tony drove his police car.

After lunch, Frank said he thanked his mom for making his day.

Mom said, "I miss all of you as much as I miss my dad. I'm lonely, and I feel far away." I would imagine that they talked about Dad in particular; but as usual, I was never told anything about their conversations.

All I know was that Frank said his dad always wandered to his recliner and fell asleep for a short time, and from what he told me later over the phone, he dreamed of the 1946 Indy 500 trip and race. My dad said he dreamed about the whole 1946 Indy500 Speedway Race, as the story was told by Uncle Tony, who told him when they first came back from the race. The extensions of discourse were disclosed with each impressive event at the site with emphasis, so let it be whatever all of us remembered what we were told.

Each guy adopted their own way of vicariously living the excitement in their hearts if not totally bragging about the way they lived experiences riding in a new Caddy. This movement long after the war had been building cars and especially sports car for racing. Things had changed, and precursors to renewed inventions came about following the increase of students at major colleges across the country and elsewhere.

By the late '70s, major companies were experimenting with solar cars, and dominating professionals love the regular new cars more than the women they attract into sexual involvements on a regular basis with little effort; a variety of ways were dominated with money. Back then, women's interests had been placed in baseball but only for the stars and moneymakers. These women don't linger around ball players like they do race car drivers. The drivers are more like musical stars of the day, and that's saying more than anyone can top. They are now called "groupies" galore.

This appraisal includes players in professional football, basketball, tennis, soccer, and horse racing, who get the same caliber of women, and that is not a demeaning or castigatory description but one of significant recognitions of what it takes before looking down deep to be attracted to sport celebrities anytime. But nothing in these other sports compares or comes near touching the exhilaration produced in sports car racing enthusiasts. The attraction to ideas of racing and getting into major professional sports to win relates back to instinctive desires of men feeling their oats after competition. These vibrations of *amour* survive all the way up chains of life for both men and women. Work at home now includes home and housekeepers, garden keepers, factory workers, mechanics and craftsmen from way back, farmers, bankers, industrial and commercial builders, and railroad owners and operators. The many people who handled moving and transport companies using newly invented vehicles from the early '20s were cutting-edge rich-enough people.

They both would, after many times under different conditions, enjoy listening to old stories about the trip to Indy 500 in 1946 at that time because Dad had the humor and wit to flag listeners, and that included Mom, who listened with a peculiar demeanor using deliberate words but undisclosed, sensed, and mumbled discourse to maintain her position. Benny, full of excitement, continued without stopping or giving Jo credibility for her corrections about assumed smart word options. Dad was still the champ with his family even after his death. Benny always reminded Jo as they seated at the dinner table for the celebration that didn't pan out with happiness. The one most pressing on my mom's mind was, and remained, that she had more concern about his health, especially on Christmas Day in 1972 because of Dad's poor health.

Benny was always was so proudly pompous knowing he had practiced standing in his new wing-tipped shoes and with his brilliant white shirt and fully engaged with a necktie. One would think he was a millionaire because lots of times he looked like one. All he was ever doing was bragging about knowing Mauri Rose, one of the great race car drivers of the times past. He had nothing to say about the Caddy or about using the car as a family car because as soon as he bought it, he had to sell the car to continue his business, and overall, there was only a small amount of money achieved because he had only put an initial down payment. In his time, he continued to talk to the boys in his expressive way about the man he knew as Mauri. Then, vitally enthused, their dad continued mostly about excitements of the race itself as the scherzo that played music in his mind to the tune of recalling his sheer joy of the time that extended his feelings many years later even about times when they drove back home.

But without warning, Frank came by and stood to hear what the conversation was all about from his brother Richard. Frank smiled and nudged Richard, made a little smile, and then interrupted as he said to Frank, "Do you still hear Dad's voice in your mind? I sense it sometimes and dream it likewise, and I think, *Dad, are you hummin' the song 'Back Home Again' in Indiana . . . in your mind or mine?*"

"It's good that you stored a musical memory because it has been almost twenty-five years ago now that it is 1973. It brings you happiness to rejoice as one of your special times earlier in your business activities. I know that you know it was the first time that song was sung before the start of the race. James Melton did a great first performance. Dad was the one who told the story about special cars, and it opened my son Fran's desire to get involved with race cars when he grows up. It looks like a pipe dream to me."

Frank recalled why so little conversation was expended as he asked, "Dad! The story part about the Indy500 Race was caused by the men at the race in 1946, who mostly bragged when they returned because they won money and simply added whatever came to their minds in fancy expressions, having fun and tremendous praises for the race and their friends' winnings.

"Now, to me, it looks like my son Fran sees your dad's mind as a visionary ready to disperse the broad story of mechanics and drivers at the race to get inside of your mind to see how to invent new parts or designs of cars that make cars better when driving. The facts are that is exactly in the future, that is what various designers and craftsmen have done beginning in the new millennium adding different fuels and systems for engines and building driverless cars and sensors that do actions of safety unknown to drivers who are now trying to make his pipe dream come true."

I remembered everyone sat in named positions and marveled at setting pieces in Frank's refurbished dealership. Blushing, Jo, when she saw the celebration setup, was almost speechless. She looked as if she had for the first time seen a true cost of extravagance. The celebrators continued the eating, sounds of jawing and words of delight murmur and clink like musical notes of scale with few words and compliments loudly in a musical cadence like an exchanged in rote, singsong with slight attention to the sense. Especially the way the prime rib was being enjoyed, and the baked halibut was a surprise from the sea unheard of in West Virginia.

Tony, now involved in later days, said to Frank, "Benny usually had a lot on his mind with all the troubles in the world today and what was ailing him as he was getting older. The worst in the last ten years was especially his previous operation on his pancreas." The day had ended early for him, although he had a great time, and everyone was around for every word he would say. The next few days were during a recovery time, and he did it and went on to his next life's venture without a care in the world for the rest of the year.

Frank, looking back at national politics, recalled in the middle of 1972, Nixon was running for president for a second term, and he said, "I remembered when President Nixon was planning to end the Vietnam War." Frank had thought that troops were still living war disasters after the way they were treated when they returned home. This took from the country, and the blame was placed to the high-ups without resolve by those in power within states and cities.

Then a year or so later, after Nixon's Watergate ransacking burglary was conducted and after he had won the election with little effort, he was forced to resign because he lied about not knowing his burglars were part of the overall plan that he knew was going to happen.

Frank was always known as Benny Divita's son. He was also known as a successful city leader and owner of a major car dealership in Montgomery by everyone in town. Several relatives and friends are active in Frank's refurbished Montgomery Motors dealership. After the celebration, Frank aptly displayed new cars and some displays of specialty sports cars feted, and again with food and drink, and it was crowded with family members and friends and many locals so impressed with the areas, new sports car dealership, and the personality of the owner.

Frank, as the eldest son, must have embellished the past of his heritage into a vision of being on the same path as his father Frank, who was hell-bent on making his dream come true. However, he did not have the same kind of problems that his dad Benny had during his lifetime and just before he died.

After he understood the revelation that one might be easily suckered into a disloyalty mistake, he was specifically told by his father not to make mistakes. When Frank became a "big boy," his dad must have said to him, "Practice not making mistakes daily." Although in business, he confessed that he had managed some money mistakes, but with following his father's advice, he made much fewer major money mistakes. Frank always took the position to question others routinely so that he wouldn't be fooled by his friends and relatives and even some who may be enemies, at least in a business sense.

Frank was loyal to Betty all during their marriage for the past twenty-five or more years. What prompted this lack of clarity and backed allegations caused it to arise. After Betty was convinced by hearsay, she grabbed it as it tormented her personality of despair, if not depression with distrust having had a continued presence of mild depression at in her late teen age. She had threatened to leave immediately but then took on a more intense depression and a feeling of loneliness, and at that time, both Frank and Betty were compassionately still in love. The problem was the combined health problems had gathered tin their minds' dislikes. Their children were disturbed, if not disgraced by allegations of their father's actions. The feelings of his children led Frank wanting to part from his family by divorce. Betty had told me by phone that her desire was to stay in the marriage even if she had to live a life of unhappiness before she could gain an insight of their parting lives because it had been trustworthy all previous times. Now, with what she felt, and she thought of pending allegations, she might lose her mind. This unknown and possible coming aftermath ruined the family's well-being and ended personal familial associations for a long time. With time, it ameliorated the crisis caused by allegations without proof.

The coming years proved that he had no interest in other women at the time. The children could see that he had attached himself much later to Wanda. In those past few years, Wanda had been a friend to J. W. and later a friend of Frank, who was a partner in the automobile dealership after he had purchased the dealership. Wanda, who had divorced her husband sometime before, was still single at the time. Later, to a few people, the local knowledge was that she had spent time in some way or other with J. W. as a friend and later had hired Wanda's husband to work at his dealership. Frank had not been associated with Wanda except through J. W. until later times when she had a job in the city office when Frank was the mayor in his second term.

Frank's two sons, Jimmy and Fran, managed early to ignore him by leaving him out of their families' lives at the beginning. Even the three daughters, Beverley, Cheryl, and Janie, had divested their lives from his closeness after the divorce. Frank pleaded and want to maintain familial association and interests with his family because he felt that he had done nothing to cause the despair that plagued Betty. Frank told me that he had in his mind a desire that he needed a revamping of his life. He told me that having a drastic ailment with the disease hepatitis was driving him to make changes in his personal life. And to some extent, he was fully aware within the family that Betty did suffer from despair and some depression in her earlier life. Betty's treatment for depression had been carried out earlier in their marriage under doctor's care mostly related to postpartum depression. Betty's general personality was more reasonable and friendly while in the company of family and friends. No outsider knew more; even the immediate family, although aware of her mild depression, everyone always admired her, and everyone had good personal relationships with her in her home, as well when with others in her home, as well as in extended families' and in friends' homes.

Frank, even in his despair, showed his extended family that he had the ability to help them when they would ask. He, under all circumstances, maintained a cordiality of normalcy under the conditions of being separated because he had taken a pursuit to change his life's daily personal involvements with Betty on his own for his well-being. This approach as time passed may have caused a partial healing of feelings with the family's personal love, if only by a meager amount even in his later years.

After many years, Frank was convinced that he had been wronged during this age- and health-related period. Frank told me personally that he was not disloyal as was so opinionated by all. Frank even visited Ed and Pat's family in California, and when we talked with him, he told us he had married Wanda in Charleston, where they were living. Nothing else was related to me, but our association with Frank and Wanda was, with our distance and insight, more simply accomplished as we continued to visit all Divita families. He associated and participated in family activities with his children and his brothers and sister. He was helpful in letting family members know how to get loans of money for important personal things. The distance continued as time passed, but Frank continued his life with Wanda being his wife for the next almost thirty years.

The parting and changes were devastating and compelling to his sibling family's hidden complete story. All involved personally put their minds, bodies, and souls into mental action to show the pace that dispositions of family lives had changed completely from the beginning of doubt to near failure to stay together unless it would be critical happenings.

For the past nearly one hundred years, children from most of this extended family heritage accepted their heritage of *steerage* and *amour* from their moms and dads with leaders like Benny and Jo, Big Mommy, and even Big Poppy, when he was young and morally strong in his early years. All Divita family siblings followed their elders with teachings and tried to live by following the best path to "knowledge and experience." My mom and dad had significant influence on the families' children in nearby Montgomery. Our mom and dad connectively taught progeny of extended families and especially used compassion and love sensibly raising their children. The Divita family followed similar ways and raised their children, as did my brothers and sister, who also followed the ways of what I know and have observed in ways of teaching Italian *steerage* and *amour*. As most human beings would say, rational thinking is not just for Italians, even though the evolution in this story displays it, at least, morally; it is much more complicated.

With that ending dispensed, my memory takes me back to the New River Gorge, a wonderful impressive site in West Virginia when we, as the Divita family and families of Divita kids, camped in our young and golden days just getting big enough to be trusted when on our own. The whole group of boys and girls in the family loaded Dad's big red moving truck, the one that he, Big Poppy, and his brothers, Jimmy and Charlie, built in the yard at the *OverHome* years before.

Uncle Tony knew just the right place to fish for blue gill. We cousins loaded the truck with all the gear that we could get our hands on and food galore. We arrived late in the day while some daylight was enough to unload things that could be left outside. In the truck with some heavy covers used on the truck bed, we made beds for the night. Gone are those days forever. It was great fun, and different activities included fishing, swimming, and cooking by my dad, the chef Benjamin Franklin Divita, who can bake a cake with no help. The only thing was that it was put on a big rock and baked solid over the screened fire. When it was finished, it was like a rock. Dad threw it into the New River, which is above and east of the Kanawha River. He watched it sink as did the *Lusitania* during the First World War. The gang of cousins was running around and laughing and having fun! The whole camping time was reminisced many times, and we slept in the big red truck.

No more time was to be spent at the riverside like that ever again. Much later, camping and even parties were held in the mountains at the river when Frank was able to purchase a place along the Gauley River, which led into the New River, which then led into the Kanawha River, which headed onward close to one hundred miles across West Virginia into the Ohio River. The way my mom reported it was that Frank, who had many years of fun with his family, relatives, and friends, wanted to continue to stay in Montgomery, looking forward to seeing hills of the past and fun times. Benny and Jo's and Tony and Catherine's Divita boys roamed in mountains all the way to the top of the mountain where the Devil's Tea Table could be seen at or from our house across Kanawha River on top of Allegheny Mountain Range a couple of thousand feet below on Route 60 Highway.

Now we take a flashback to times when Grandfather Francesco was still living in the same *OverHome* in 1953, where he had built a complex of homes for his immediate family back in the early 1920s. For the most part, his dominating and demanding personal behavior had not improved with his age, maturity, or wisdom expectations. It got worse, and at sixty-five, he was certainly the same old aggressively dominating man mentally worn to threads but well-kept physically who continued being a miner and yet to be unbelievably retired.

Most of this reminiscing was told to us about Francesco continuously when something had happened. Big Poppy could threaten action with words, and he often dominated any member of his family. Even when his sons were still in their midthirties to forties, he faced different uproars. The sons had a fear of what he might do to comrades in mines or guys downtown in saloons. Francesco's trouble or troubles he had, even now, caused families to end up dragging his first son, Benny, into altercations. Benny always looked for a peaceable solution by hearing his troubles with whom members of the family and other people were involved. After Dad had heard both sides of the story or at least two-sided opinionated and exaggerated reasons made by perpetrators, he would give advice to stop any attempted fighting, and most of the time, it was dissolved.

Since Benny already knew goings-on of his father and the disdain expressed by neighbors and family members, he had a weighty question to ask his father. Benny said, as recalled from memory, wanting his declaration in Italian, which questions the title of this story, "Poppy! What's it all about?" Benny still and always called his father Poppy because it is a common Italian way to address the family gracefully with kindness no matter how much one's behavior might be diminished because of extraneous commitments at times that cause my grandfather Francesco to take a stand to argue the problem.

Careful associations with Big Poppy continued for many years. One important occasion had to do with Big Poppy wanting to get married in his later years. Francesco squeezed his fists like a warrior ready for conflict as Big Poppy told his son Benny with similar words, "I'm gonna marry my woman. Ah, Sally! All you wanta stop me. *È la mia vita!* (It's my life!) I want her!"

Francesco followed in an unusually sensitive way with a compliment, "La donna mi dà belle sesso." (The young woman being a sensuous sex partner.)

Benny responded using his instilled words, "You know that you're paying for sex by taking care of her and the baby in your home. I think she wants your money. Poppy, you're no young chicken. You are seventy-eight years old."

They were at Big Poppy's home, and both were talking in their bedroom just off to the right of the dining room. The dining room is on the right side of the kitchen and is farther away because of the noise and low-level talk emanating. Frank told me that he did see both the child and mother. She was seated in the kitchen. Benny fingered his son's attention, and the two tried to settle down Francesco, who was insisting that he's going to marry his sweetheart. Benny said in good Italian, "Facci sapere quando!" (Let us know when!)

Benny's son Frank was with his dad at the time because he was now working with his dad as a business partner in the taxi business to make sure they can get it going again. Frank and family had returned to Montgomery in the early 1950s when he left his teaching job, especially to help his dad recover his business and the business growth that came about and lasted for years.

Both got kissed by his infamous Italian father on both sides of the face, a pinch quinada, easily understood asa pinch on each cheek and seen with red cheeks, and then he hugged, first, Benny and then Frank.

Benny and Frank looked at the dining room table and the way the bit of pepperoni and cheese with teeth marks on bread and cheese were left on two dishes since he has been living alone for the last few years. They knew they interrupted his lunch to talk more seriously. More noticeable was how cluttered the kitchen sink was with dishes, pots, and pans; no housework was done like his grandmother Filippa always did. A bottle of cheap Merlot wine was on the table half filled and uncorked and a pint of Jim Beam whiskey was almost empty, lying on the flat side.

Without a word of conversation, Benny and his son turned to leave and go outside. Big Poppy was standing somewhat satisfied and yet standing with a pissed-off look on his face. Benny opened the car's front door. Poppy followed, and as they walked to the car, he shouted, "Si a mia tesoro!" (She's my treasure!)

Dad and Frankie entered the car, his son in the driver's side. He started the engine and took off in a trail of dust from the back road. Almost immediately, Frank waned to say something but was hesitant because the open issue would challenge his father before thinking. It was really none of his personal business and was especially his father's concern. Frankie, with his hands gesturing for approval to talk, motioned with a finger to lips to wait a minute. His dad finally got out his comment that changed what he expected completely. He said, "It is all finished. We must let him get married and let him see what happens. That's it!"

Benny recollected with a smile and said something like what one would expect, "When Poppy worked in various mines, he was always getting into arguments or nearly fighting mad at least once a week. This happened sometimes just for fun on his way home from the mine as he ran into friends and locals. It usually had something to do with politics, the union, or just the stupidity of our presidents, who always defended potential wars no matter how they were started." I don't remember how he got along while at the mine when I worked with him, but I do remember that he had very little to do with guys outside his group of a few Italians. The most revealed part of his recognizable life occurred when he was on his way home from railroad tracks near the main highway and Montgomery Road where the coal truck dropped miners in Smithers around the area at the B&O Railroad water tank as it filled coal carrying steam engines.

Then my dad Benny had to flashback to his father's home in earlier years. He revealed the source of character heritage and traits as a man who knew what he needed to do. Big Poppy was using his two sons, Benny and Tony, in the mine in the past. There were times they looked at each other and said almost simultaneously aloud, "We'll never forget that time in our lives as kids when we helped him in the mine. It looked like it could only get better, but it took a while."

Dad knew that Father Francesco displayed his womanizing openly and never considered it an imperfection but embellished it as an attribute to his manhood. And what's more important was no one would dare say that his heritage started with Frank's grandfather's way of life demonstrated all during his marriage. Dad had told Frank after many later interactions that his grandfather Francesco could get away with anything even if he had to use a megathreat of great bodily harm. From an outsider's view, his father Francesco had fearful respect from all he encountered during his lifetime. He demonstrated it many times. Sometime, stories were told after an event especially when it turned out to be nothing like the one with Mr. Cosentino.

One time was during his daily travel from the coal mine. I imagined their meeting and conversation after hearing many stories of situations that happened to even his neighbor Mr. Cosentino. On that day, Dad had said that his father had run into an old friend in the alley who greeted him in a witty way. Mr.

Cosentino, a longtime friend and neighbor next door, motioned to Big Poppy. "Uh, Francesco! You been away for a long time? I no see you since you lost case of beer playing casino in Al's Place. Where you been hidin'? In the mine!"

Big Poppy's wrath was in gear as he approached Dominick and punched him lightly in the stomach with a smile and a hug as a close friend. Francesco said, "Before you make fun, salute me first! Ha! Ha!" He laughed and grabbed Dominick's shoulder like he was just having fun with him.

Mr. Cosentino said with a greeting of enjoyment as the two came together, "Francesco, I'm OK! You got some time for a beer? You want to sit on the porch? We talk about old times!"

Francesco slowly said, "Hell, no! I don't share beer. I was fifteen minutes waiting for it! Goddammit, Sammy didn't know me! I tell, ah, his poppa. He'll bust his ass!" Then he said, "I gotta get home. My son Benny is waiting for me."

Benny, his son, the peacemaker by nature throughout his time, was standing by his car in front of the yard. Benny finally saw Poppy at the twisted gate at Mary's home, and he shouted, "Hey, Poppy, I'm here! I was in Charleston today and brought you some cheese and pepperoni from Cavalier's Italian Store in Smithers who had his choice cuts!" As a peacemaker, Benny had the position to use his talents to make sure any disruption that he saw was held to a minimum among family members and friends. He always used his personal influence, mediation, and careful demeanor and advice in most situations. Some adhered to his advice simply so that they would not lose a good connection.

Chapter XXIV

Amour Is Where You Find It in One's Mind . . . !

"Follow your love totis habenis," [with all one's might] *he
replied . . ., "The pleasure you have today you will not have tomorrow;
and if the affair stands as you say, I envy you more than I do the
King of England. Follow your star, I implore you, and do not use
one iota of your pleasure for anything in the world, for I believe, . . .
better to do and regret it than to regret not having done it."*
—The Man of the Renaissance, Ralph Roeder, The Viking
Press, 18 East 48th St. New York, 1933, p. 306

From what I was told, my brother Frank never pursued any newfound love after Betty and Frank were married. However, some close associates believed that he had made a final pursuit just before 1980s when he was asked to join a friend for dinner after working all day. The idea of going to a business meeting and then having dinner was an easy choice to make after a day's hard work in the same building.

However, just a month or so before that time, however, Frank had gone through a critical ailment. After that time, Frank was at odds with Betty's depressed behavior because they were doing well within the family and the business kept improving. As he told me, the critical ailment left him shy of being compassionate with her moderate depression. Frank also voiced interest about gaining relief from his ailment.

Betty was usually after him for minute things that were not previously pursued. Betty was more interested in checking his actions during various times when he was only involved with his work and free time activities. Betty did know how he came about the ailment, and she did not know how he had overcome his ailment because it was very serious and being cared by his doctor. Both Betty and Frank remained somewhat compassionate with each other but were slowing down faster than with aging while feeling despondent, if not sensing added depression foreboding both with disturbing states of mind.

After suffering some time, he had told me that he wanted a change in his life when he would get well. His emphasis was that he wanted to change his married life because he wanted to be on his own and do other things. Frank did not want to remain under all that he had gathered that bothered him grossly for the few years. In his mind at the time during his sickness, he realized that he wanted to be on his own and wanted to control his life on his own time.

What happened later was he had gone back to work running his Montgomery Motors dealership to carry on his business. A few days later, he did go to a business meeting in Kanawha Falls and was at dinner, and a friend demanded to join him for dinner, as was characterized earlier.

The very next day, Frank told his wife about their meeting while he was at his dinner table. Even his mother Josephine, within a few days, had heard the tumult of hearsay that had been getting dispersed by friends and family members who had seen some associations that seemed to occur during the dinner; but at odd times, a few of his associates said it looked like an affair. The hearsay that followed Frank had no way to refute that he had been with the woman, but he insisted that no way was it an amorous involvement. The many twists of disclosures pointed in his direction of cordiality, and eventually, with little concern when leaving, he had accepted her request to drop her off at her home because the friend she came with had left earlier and she had no car.

Frank felt that he had not done anything wrong. The next day, he had relayed to his employees that he wanted to know what people were telling others and asking about the night before. Disclosures were made later by Frank that he had delayed only a little time more so he could drive the woman to her home.

It turned into a judgment of disloyalty assumed by his wife Betty after so many comments were made about Frank. Some of the comments were at odds with various allegations. Frank's mother Josephine thought the right thing should have been that Frank should have explained being with her at dinner fully to his wife when he got home. If it were not believed, he should have left Betty alone so that she could rethink all that she had heard that next evening and the following day to sort hearsay from whoever had relayed it to Betty.

Frank's mother should be the only one who really knows his mind. His mother should have made sure and believed or made her business that what he had said was true. Then if it did, Betty should have considered whether she believed her mother-in-law Jo and, if so, forget the incident. On the other hand, she might have believed his frailty or then even continued living with him, as do many women. Other women do later pursue divorce proceedings. Soon after this onetime inferred affair sparked with current happenings, yet to be identified, one must find out if it were hearsay addressing infidelity or if significant credence was offered that it had happened.

Regardless of the standing, Betty had left the home in despair and disappeared to a friend's home for further advice because the story was told with a vengeance by whom she thought was a friend of Frank and Betty. Betty in her anxiety and distrust and somewhat with personal despair had caused dissension among the family already heading into adulthood. Some of Frank's children were at the dealership site working, and some were other team members working in the Firestone Store. God only knows the ongoing discussions of what everyone was saying about what their dad had done.

Frank and Betty had returned home. However, both were still arguing to try resolve his problem. Everyone knew that they were tied together by a Catholic promise solidly within the sacraments of the church that bound them as one, and they both felt it totally. The two former lovers had been gazing through the front door but not hearing their clamor of words except to make claims of a lack of belief in each other.

Here, we see love in various forms not only as young love but also as old renewed love that had grown into the form of possession, attraction, and sensual desires to do things together. After Betty had left the house to be on her own, Frank told his mother as straight as he could that nothing happened between him and the woman who may have had a crush on him; but later, she had spread lies around to hurt him personally because he was not interested in her. He asked his mother to stay on his side about the allegations because the story was a lie. Then he said, "I'm headin' back to the dealership to sell the business and try to remove the thoughts in my mind that will finally uncover the life that I wanted to live the rest of my life with Betty but lost my chance and resolve the rest of my life with Wanda."

END

DiVita Coat of Arms

Creating a family coat of arms carries with it a certain amount of bravado to claim a sense of innovation and creativity when the starting information is broad-scoped recorded information about the crest and coat of arms for Divita or DiVita taken from the existing genealogy files. However, it could be pursued by one having guts enough to revitalize the memory of the DiVita name during the planned first reunion in the new millennium, DiVita Reunion 2000, as a record that would evoke the remaining DiVita clan. The reunion was sponsored by siblings of the family of Benjamin Franklin Divita and Josephine Mary (Maruca) Divita to honor their forefathers and foremothers. Nevertheless, it also carries with it a pompous attitude that engulfs me since I wanted to deliver a coat of arms as a sign of sincerity to be a participant at the reunion.

This mind-set solidified in wood comes from my desire to use my knowledge of the family's origin and heritage based on my experiences, so with little else other than an impetus to carve it for the DiVita 2000 Reunion, which invited all the known DiVita families to make a first start impact on the continuation of the reunions up to this time. We know that many other DiVita families existed, and many may have direct ties to the current DiVitas as symbolized in the documented crest of the fluted eagle. To the best of my knowledge, however, it really started with our patriarchal grandfather, who was the last of the named DiVitas of his generation, Francesco, but all relations called him Big Poppy. Big Poppy was an extremely dominating immigrant from Italy (maybe per research originally from Palermo, Sicily) without papers of records but with names of his parents and siblings. His birthing records, to my knowledge, are unknown. My grandmother Philipina, mostly called Big Mommy of this time, was also Italian born with papers and records and was an immigrant to the United States of America with Francesco and several children. The children of record also are named on the papers, and as time proceeded, the remaining members of this incredible family were born in the USA. In my time, the most current generation is that of my grandparents and parents and my mother's parents, who were known on both sides to be Italian immigrants from the Calabria Province of Italy.

As stated, there is an existing crest for the Divita family as catalogued by one of the genealogy foundations, which describes the family's evolution and heritage and presents an artistic rendition of the mainstay symbol as a fluted eagle. This symbol was used in this design as the centerpiece but was amplified with an interpretation of the explained description and information known to me but artistically rendered by me. This rendering evolved in a pursuit of the DiVitas of times past and those currently defined by the modern-day families of DiVitas including the influences by the families and the distaffs so fatefully involved in the evolution of the families.

The modernization of the DiVita family coat of arms is much more extensive, and by design, it concentrates on the deeds taken from my general knowledge of the intimate family as opposed to the broad-scoped DiVitas across the globe. These known deeds have led me to the heritage expectation and my spiritual thrust taken personally as a general pursuit in life. The question is . . . where does the detailed heritage start? It starts with the knowledge of the family's history and heritage documented and portrayed through research and is continued as heritage of the living family based on knowledge expressed on this tablet of wood. In my mind, it is a watermark for the modern-day DiVita coat of arms.

In the detailed art, the design is influenced by my mother's personality and her heritage as well as the many matriarchal aunts. I gained from their heritage as is known scientifically through the study of theories of genetics and the evolution of human beings as expected from creationism by itself or augment with intelligent design and evolution from a source, or simply put, God. This assumption of inheritance includes the influence of my siblings' character and personalities on the design. This melding of minds is compatible because it is obvious that the distaff sides of the families of DiVitas were influenced throughout evolution of the coat of arms from the caveman era to modern days.

I had already obtained a few choice pieces of cut tree wood during the winter of 1999 and had them stored and treated it for cure. But when the idea became firm that the DiVita Reunion 2000 would occur, I began visualizing the design, and I selected a centerpiece section from the trunk area of my best piece.

The particular cut was near the trunk of a Monterey cypress tree whose origin of growth was in Santa Barbara, California, at the Shoreline Park overlooking the Pacific Ocean, which contains the Channel Islands about twenty miles offshore. The cut was part of one of the large trees that were blown down by a strong blustery wind during a "wintry" weather stormy night in 1999. After rescuing the log from the city truck already loading the cuttings and smaller logs that were destined for the green fill area or a firewood stack at the dump site, with some effort, I put three logs in the car. At home the next day, I put a drying solution of glycol on the log and stored it in a cover.

Much later, I cut about four inches thick piece from the vertical center from the log where a three-inch diameter limb had grown. I then drafted a starter design on paper so I could rough size a few of the major figures on the log on both sides for a comparative evaluation of figures. I continued creating the design concept on paper, placing the sketched fluted eagle as the centerpiece and adding the sword of honor insignia to be carved with the words "St. Vita," which means, per my research, that the origin of the family name De Vita—meaning, "from life"—has been reduced to DiVita, as Italians in Italy told me several times during a trip to Milano but after the coat of arms had been completed. The origin of the name and the researched crest revealed it as Divita. This misspelling reminded that Francesco's generation of Italian immigrants could have either accepted it in that form or written it himself when he arrived in the United States at Ellis Island. More likely, when the family was quickly ushered through the lines for inspection and approval to enter the country, it was deciphered by the immigration officer and "Americanized." That is how it was used from early times, but now, it has stepped through a rebirth to DiVita or even De Vita. So I put the "St. Vita" on as a reminder that the original evolution of the name may have had a basis because way back in times when babies were born, and if so as an orphan or a father unknown, they were given the name of a saint. This instance in my mind was likely the case in that there were no references to De Vita being any social class more than the common folk that dominated society rather than part of the minute aristocracy or royalty of Italy from the distant past. The two Italian words "De Vita," which was common in Italy whose translation means "of life", was from times predominant when census was poorly recorded. In any case, it will be the progeny that makes it worthy of the character so impressed on human beings. I offer continued affirmation of that, which produced the fluted eagle crest and an artistic expression of known attributes that support a modernization of the DiVita coat of arms as designed in this sculpture.

Continuing with the design as outlined, I sketched a background on the front and back sides of the wood and then on the widths or edges with grapes and vines that crossed over the top as a continuous pattern to meet the figures. The creative art was also sketched and then sculpted in detail; on the one side, the symbolic crest with added composition, the Divita name, and the slogan "Cose tutto il Italiana." (All things Italian.)

The other side shows the sculpted art as the influences of the family traditions taken from specific parts of Italy, Sicily, and Calabria as a collection of life's pursuits foremost in the minds of centuries of Italian families that created this heritage in four major areas of family commitments, which are *pace* (peace of mind and spirit), *mente* (passion for knowledge and intelligence), *opera* (work ethic and devotion to career), and *liberta* (fighters for liberty and freedom). These words in Italian are a practical collection of goals pursued and worked toward by the DiVitas that I have experienced in their lifetimes.

First Exhibition

My first exhibition of sculptures manifests realistic, figurative life-forms in motion. I visualize new compositions as one who writes music; the first cuts into the wood or stone are guides to the next cut, as the first notes on the staff suggest the next note. My sculptures are influenced by study of classical, modern, and contemporary art. Style with me is activated spontaneously with formulated thought and design to impose meaning and action in the composition. My fun occurs when I create sculptures of life-forms folding in new knowledge of evolution. My pursuit is to create new expressions of life in large sculptures.

For example, my *DNA Caduceus* (Australian tea tree) is a combination of mythology and modern-day symbolism used to create a contemporary version of the physician's symbol. I simulated biomedical ramifications of the four molecular bonds of the double helix tying to the body of Hermes Trismegistus, the Egyptian god of alchemy and magic, to express new biochemistry in the symbol.

Over the years, I studied fine art drawing, oil painting, and sculpture at several colleges in California. I also collaborated with my younger brother, Robert, a teaching artist. We produced a series of intaglios depicting mankind's search for life on other planets. These intaglios were displayed at Kennedy Space Center in Florida during the U.S. Bicentennial, and we jointly published it in the art journal *Leonardo* in 1978.

My recent juried showings include selection of my sculptures for SBAA and an oil painting, *The Impressionist Dr. Freud*, for the Faulkner Show, September 1996, and various sculptures displayed at Gallery 113.

I'm a true mountaineer, born in West Virginia and educated at West Virginia Institute of Technology, Drexel Institute of Technology, and UCLA. My family includes Patricia Kelly, my wife from Dublin, Ireland; and three children, Joanne, Edward Jr., and Catherine.

My career for the past thirty years was in nuclear engineering and space science. I worked for NASA's Jet Propulsion Laboratory in Pasadena on the teams that produced the successful Voyager and Galileo spacecraft missions to Jupiter, Saturn, and beyond. Just prior to leaving JPL, I worked on the Hubble Space Telescope. In 1984, I joined Santa Barbara Research Center to work on the development of infrared focal planes and advanced detectors for sensors for the Strategic Defense Initiative. I now savor my time, using it as an artist and as a radiation consultant, and I'm available for sculpture studies and commissions.

A complement of my sculptures of the past ten years is at Gallery 113:

--From Sticks and Stones--
December 29, 1996, through January 31, 1997.

Second Exhibition

Ed's second exhibition of sculptures continues realistic, figurative life-forms in motion and adds several abstract expressionistic forms. His carving style is activated spontaneously as he formulates the design and imposes motion and action in the composition. Quoting Ed, "My fun occurs when I create sculptures of life-forms folding in knowledge of science and evolution." One of his newer wood sculptures, *Ascending Spirit,* won first prize in three-dimensional media in the November 1997 *Un Ange Passe* juried show at the Reynolds Gallery at Westmont College.

Over the years, Ed studied fine art drawing, oil painting, and sculpture at several colleges in California and collaborated with his younger brother, Robert, a teaching artist, on a series of intaglios depicting mankind's search for life on other planets. These intaglios were displayed at Kennedy Space Center during the U.S. Bicentennial and published in the art journal *Leonardo* in 1978.

For sculptures and commissions, call ((805) 967-7384 or e-mail eddivita6@ aol.com.

ASCENDING SPIRIT
Gallery 113 - Sculpture on the Mezzanine
From Sticks and Stones II
June 29, 1998, through August 1, 1998

This *Ascending Spirit* was, at one time, a waning log of oak burl, which I salvaged. With the excitement of the coming *Un Ange Passe* (An Angel Passes) art show in 1997 at the Reynolds Gallery of Westmont College, I transcended this burl into an ascending spirit subconsciously as an abstract spiritual representation. I sensed that good spirits must be white or almost airy with a glow of white to be resurrected without revealing what the maker has forgiven. A look of a pearly white Carrara marble, quite fitting for an entry and eventually will return to its master earth as a carving, spiritually reinligneated.

LINKAGE OF THE SPECIES
(Australian tea tree)

This Family of Man expresses life from *Australopithecus robustus* and *africanus* to *Homo habilis, erectus,* and *sapiens* (Adam and Eve). It covers millions of years and billions of people all tied with the DNA chain at the cerebellum where it matters.

FORTY-NINERS HEADIN' TO PLACERVILLE
(Beached sycamore burl)

This single piece of sculpture expresses the fast gallop of two miners headin' down the Sierra Nevada mountains to the American river in Placerville in a fearless thrust and devil-may-care rush for *gold*. The rugged mountain terrain forces the muscular strains of the horses and the strenuous reining by the riders.

Fourth Exhibition

Ed's fourth exhibition of sculptures continues with realistic, figurative life-forms in motion and adds several abstract forms—impressionistic and expressionistic. His sculpting style is activated spontaneously as he formulates the design and imposes motion and action in the composition. His sculptures are influenced by study of classical, modern, and contemporary art.

Each piece is designed to combine meaning and action in the composition. Ed says, "My fun occurs when I create sculptures of life-forms folding in new knowledge of evolution. My pursuit is to create new expressions of life in large sculptures."

While a member of the Santa Barbara Art Association, California Carvers Guild, and Santa Barbara Sculptors Guild, one of his wood sculptures, *Ascending Spirit,* won first prize in three-dimensional media in the November 1997 *Un Ange Passe* (An Angel Passes) juried show at the Reynolds Gallery at Westmont

College in Santa Barbara, California. Another wood piece, *Forty-Niners Headin' to Placerville,* won runner-up Best in Show at the California Carvers Guild's Santa Maria's Artistry in Wood Annual Show in 1998.

Over the years, Ed studied fine art drawing, oil painting, and sculpture at several colleges in California. He also collaborated with his younger brother, Robert, a teaching artist, to produce a series of intaglios depicting mankind's search for life on the planets. These intaglios were displayed at Kennedy Space Center in Florida during the U.S. Bicentennial celebration and jointly published in the art journal *Leonardo* in 1978.

Ed's a true mountaineer, born in West Virginia, educated in physics at West Virginia University Institute of Technology, Drexel Institute of Technology, and UCLA.

His family includes wife Patricia Kelly, from Dublin, Ireland; children, Joanne, Edward Jr., and Catherine; and six grandchildren, Christopher, Ashton, Eddie, Alicen, Jackson, and Tessa.

His career for forty years was in nuclear engineering and space science: nine years at Martin Marietta and nineteen years at NASA's Jet Propulsion Laboratory in Pasadena working on the successful Mariner spacecraft to Mars, the Voyager and Galileo spacecraft missions to Jupiter, Saturn, and beyond, and the Hubble Space Telescope. In 1984, he joined Santa Barbara Research Center to work on infrared detectors for twelve years. Ed retired in 1995.

Ed enjoys his time now as an artist. For sculptures and commissions, call (919) 408-5050 or e-mail eddivita@sbcglobal.net.

Ed invites your attendance to view a complement of his sculptures at

A saga of an Italian family of emigrants in America during the early 1900s.

The family's historical living and memoir accountings and historical happenings of legendary events as visualized and extended from the thrust of the First Renaissance choosing "knowledge and experience" over "will of desire"!

Steerage and amour affaire d'amour (a love affair) and affaire de coeur (affair of heart) that demands the pursuit of happiness!

Carved sculpture of the Divita coat of arms.

Lightning Source UK Ltd.
Milton Keynes UK
UKHW010707240520
363742UK00004B/79/J